UNCONQUERED

by
Sieran Vale

Mead Hall
Press

Evanston, IL
www.meadhallpress.com

Unconquered
©2006 Sieran Vale

Mead Hall Press
848 Dodge Avenue
Evanston, Illinois 60202 U.S.A.
www.meadhallpress.com

Sieran Vale—1st ed.
ISBN 0-9764771-1-4
1. General—Fiction 2. Historical—Fiction 3. British History—Fiction
4. Norman Conquest—Fiction
I. Title

Cover art, content, typeography, and internal design by
S. Leigh Jenner

Printed in the United States of America by
Wave Graphics, Mattoon, Illinois

U*nconquered* is dedicated with great love to the memories of persons most dear to me who have recently traveled on: my kinsman Ronnie Sparzak (of Pittsburgh, Pennsylvania), my dear friends John Fisher (of Howell, Michigan) and Scott Nolan (of Chicago, Illinois), and to that of Kyle Edward Jones (of Sedalia, Colorado), a sensitive and intelligent young man who might, in another age, have lived beyond the brief span allotted him in this age bereft of brotherhood. I salute you all as Einherjar and, while sorely missed in the physical world, you fill the empty chamber of my heart with fond and stolid company. May we meet again!

Acknowledgements

The writing of *Unconquered* has been a labor of love, and I am grateful to all those who helped me breach the 900+ years between ourselves and those described with such affection in these pages. To my dearest friends Jennifer Goetz and Barbara Wittig, for honesty, editorial input, for loving and standing by me, and for feeling the importance of the work. To Janet Ladd and Mary Lou Griggs for early encouragement and seemingly endless hours of manuscript production. To Rob Zayia and Duane Trent who, like Edwin and Morcar, served as timeless and true brothers of the soul when I was in sore need of such. To Gary Allen and Kurt Chapman for love and support during years of late night writing and research. To the Vale family—my brothers, Jeffer, Mark, and Drew, and my sisters Beth, Katie, and Missy—for providing the perfect model of treasured kinship. To Danica, Ianthe, Amity, Bairie, and Leigha because my love for them transcends the ages and shines eternal. To Morcar and Edwin, for choosing me. And to the late Mr. Caley, who worked with me during my years at H. D. Ballantine and Stuart Occult Books on State Street in Chicago, and long ago showed me that, but for linear time, we are each of us a part of every age.

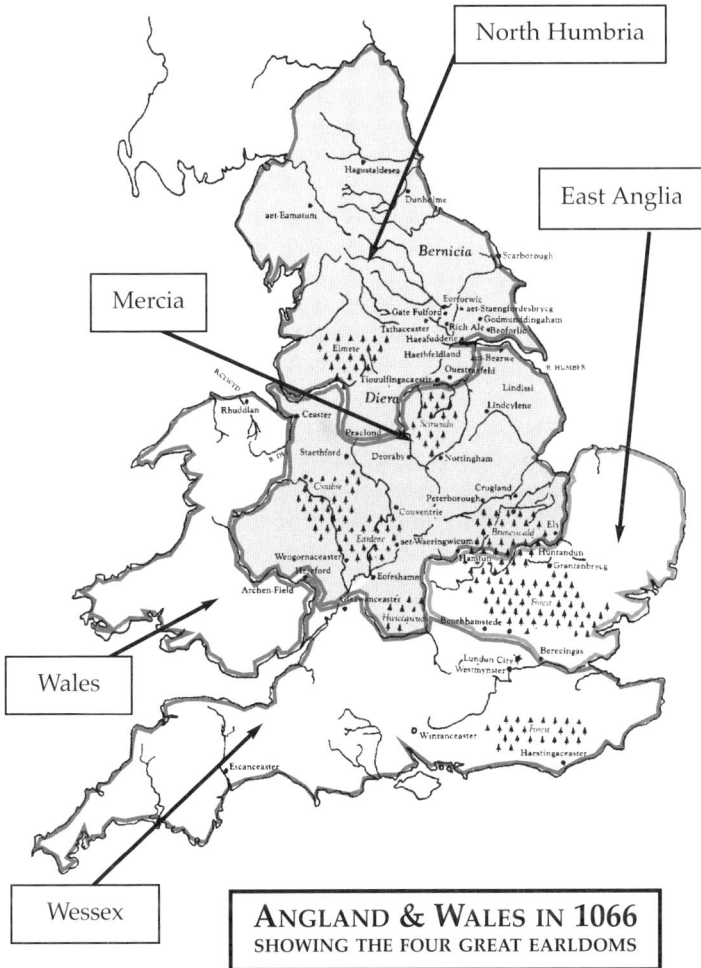

ENGLAND & WALES IN 1066

North Humbria

East Anglia

Mercia

Wales

Wessex

Hagustaldesea
Dunholme
aet-Eamotum
Bernicia   Scarborough
Eorforwic
Gate Fulford   aet-Staenfordesbryeg
Tathaceaster   Godmundingaham
Haeafuddene   Rich Ale   Segeforlid
Elmete   Haethfeldland   Bearwe
Tiouullingacaestir   Ouestrefeld
Diera   Lindissi
Rhuddlan   Lindeylene
Ceaster   Nirundi
Praeclond
Staethford   Deoraby   Nottingham
Coumbe   Crugland
Peterborough
Couuentre
Eandene   aet-Waeringwicum
Ely
Brunnesale
Wengornaceaster   Hamfih   Huntandun
Hereford   Grantanbryeg
Eofeshamm
Archen Field   Huscraeten   Baenhhamstede
Lundan City   Berecingas
Westmynster
Escanceaster
Suoc
Wintanceaster   Fercei
Harstingaceaster

ANGLE & WALES IN 1066
SHOWING THE FOUR GREAT EARLDOMS

0   50   100
IN MILES

Note that the grey area between Mercia and East Anglia represents hereditary lands held by the house of Leofric which were whittled from Mercia and given to Waltheof Siward's son by King Edward after the North Humbrian revolt in 1065. There was no hereditary or ancestral basis for the division into the spurious earldom of "Huntandon" and it was not recognized as one of the "great" earldoms.

UNCONQUERED

"The two brothers were respected, good men. They both were remarkably handsome, from a family of high birth and great influence; their vast estates gave them immense power, and they were well–loved by the people at large."

— Orderic Vitalis

CHAPTER ONE

. . . Disturbances of a serious nature arose between the English and the Normans . . . the relentless furies were let loose.

—Orderic Vitalis
Book IV, Chapter V

Autumn, 1072

Despite my will to stifle it, I let go a tortured scream as Hereward the Wake, his wild hair damp with the strength of his exertions, ripped the arrow out of my breast and worked it through my chain mail hauberk. Then I cursed under my breath, seething. Silence was our only hope, and we all knew it. Even the slightest noise seemed to echo in the huge, empty rooms of the monastery, and especially here in the cavernous church. Only the grace of God, and an intimate knowledge of the secret passageways through the stone walls, had kept our small band of rebels this long from harm. The king's men were everywhere; my outburst would not go unnoticed.

Hereward flashed a gleaming smile as if to comfort me, and tossed the bloody arrow hard against the floor. "No matter!" he whispered, grimacing. Then his tone sobered. "The second arrow need stay put. I scarce can get a grip on it." Gently as possible, he broke the shaft off, causing me a rush of pain that roared like the ocean. I began to laugh.

"Earl Morcar?" he put a hand to my brow as if checking for a sudden fever. I pushed him away, still giggling. He looked past me, worried, to Siward Bearn, but my cousin only shrugged helplessly. A tall and well-formed man, the Bearn looked extremely intimidating at that moment, inspecting the gory blade of his broadsword. His long, tangled, red hair had worked its way free of the helmet, and his stubbled cheek was smeared with blood. It was certain no Norman would be happy to face him.

It was Heard Ulf's son, my chief man, who finally brought me to my senses. Moving close, he locked a hard gaze into mine, his brown eyes lambent and earnest as ever. "In case there is no chance to say this later," he pronounced solemnly, "methinks you should know now that I consider you the best of men, and I have ever been proud to serve you."

There followed a swift embrace, and a moment of silence that lingered heavily until Hereward the Wake broke it.

"We are armed and ready to shed blood in the Lord's sacristy," he intoned with mock solemnity. "If we mean to murder King William's men right there on the altar, best we all delay dying until we are shriven!"

Here he winked at Brother Wulfget, one of the boldest-looking warriors amongst us. As if suddenly remembering a duty, the monk sheathed his sword, smiled sheepishly, and raised his right hand, issuing a hurried benediction. By now, we could clearly hear the stomping approach of the Normans. Well-attuned to the nuances of sound from our long months in the abandoned monastery, we could easily estimate their numbers. Despite the racket they raised, there were fewer than a dozen. If we fought well, we still had a chance.

The ferocious clamor stopped all at once; the jostling and clinking of metal told us the Normans were readying their arms in the dark corridor just outside the massive wooden doors. I held my breath.

"God's might!" Hereward cried low, signaling us into rough formation with a raised fist. "God smite!"

Scarce had we lined up on the altar steps when the huge double doors burst open. William the Bastard's men rushed us all at once, hollering and frenzied. My pain was forgotten in an instant as they lunged forward ferociously. Snarling, we reared at each other; the deafening echo of iron on iron filled the immense room. I know not where I found the power to wield my sword so deftly, but the first Norman to reach it was laid open, ear to ear. Then a cold feeling of horror surged through my veins as another stepped up in his place.

'Twas my own uncle, William Malet!

At first, I thought to turn and run, but he lifted his axe in earnest, pronouncing my name in a harsh whisper. "Morcar Ælfgar's son!" he exclaimed above the horrifying din of the skirmish. "Seems it has come to that moment I prayed would never arrive. God forgive my sin for doing it, but as King's man, I am forced to slay you as a rebel and a traitor."

Though I had relaxed my stance a little as he made this formal, ominous pronouncement, I swung quickly to action when he smashed his axe at me with all his might. I ducked, and he tumbled forward so heavily he almost lost his balance before spinning around to face me again.

"God forgive me, too, uncle!" I rasped in return, "but you have brought this on yourself!" I moved at him, jabbing, but with little power, as if only to fend him off. He laughed, raising his weapon again and bracing himself for the force of the blow he meant to deliver.

"You have proven me right, little Morcar!" he hissed as I reeled back, hearing the rush of his blade as it sliced past my ear. "Still air spews grave tempests! Once, when all dismissed the notion, I said you would make a fearsome warrior. And you have proven me right!"

I raised my sword to ward off death. His blade glanced off mine, coming down hard into my shoulder, splitting my chain mail hauberk. There was a sickening sound as he pulled his axe out of the tangle of flesh and iron. Enraged, I spun at him, knocking him against a wide stone pillar and slicing my blade into his upper arm with all my might. Screaming like a madman, he drew himself fast to his full height, forcing me backwards almost to the wall with repeated, vicious swings. As I raised my sword, he caught me in the side with near enough power to finish me. A painful, gurgling constriction rose in my throat; my blood gushed in his face as he fought to free his blade. Letting go a horrifying oath of avengement, I staggered forward, heaving my sword into his chest with all I had left of strength.

It should have ended him. He was bleeding so furiously that he could scarce keep his footing in the red pool that deepened around him. Nevertheless, he managed to hack me one time more, as if he knew not I had dealt him a death blow. I bit hard into my tongue as my hip crunched and the top of my leg burst open. His axe crashed to the floor. Suddenly, he stiffened, throwing his shoulders back and standing tense and erect. I drew back my weapon, ready to strike again. His mouth opened slightly, as if he had something to say, then relaxed all at once into a frozen, affectionate smile.

I stepped backward so his body would not hit me as it fell. As I looked down on his form, still twitching restlessly despite the wide-eyed stare of death, I suffered a torrent of emotion that entirely paralyzed me. The clamor around me reached a crescendo, then dimmed. I do not know how long I stood there gaping, but of a sudden men were pushing, prodding, pulling me, and then I was off my feet. They were talking hurriedly, heatedly, and I felt the rush of motion as I was carried away.

Then there was darkness, a panicked exchange of words, the sounds of a door closing and men moving away. I gasped for breath, smothering in my own anguish. Voices urged me to silence and suddenly something was in my mouth, which was already full of blood and spit. I struggled against suffocation for just an instant before I realized I could bite down on the thing, and so relieve the paroxysms of agony that shook my entire frame. Footsteps approached. They paused; seemed to hesitate; came forward again. Then a merciful unconsciousness seized me, and everything faded away.

*　　　　　*　　　　　*

I woke with a start, gagging and shaking. That thing was still in my mouth. My first tortured movement caused me to bite down instinctively; then, grabbing feverishly, I tried to remove it. 'Twas a hand—the hand of Heard Ulf's son! I mumbled a hoarse apology, and he stroked my brow, saying it was his ruined hand anyway, and he had felt no pain when I did it. Cradled against Siward Bearn, I became aware of the darkness and the cold stone floor. There was a wet, sickly-sweet stickiness everywhere, and my heart was pounding so hard and slow it seemed to tremble the very room.

The three of us were in the vestry, my kinsman told me low. The rest had made their way back to the safety of our hiding place in the walls. Soon as the Normans were preoccupied elsewhere, he said, our comrades would come for us.

"We scarce could drag you this far," he added, "much less hoist you through the secret door in the altar. We heard more men coming through the hallways, so Hereward the Wake closed us in here, and pushed a sopping body against the door before he fled, thinking to hide your trail of blood."

"We killed them all?" I managed to stammer.

"Aye."

"Our uncle?"

"Aye. He is dead, too, Morcar!" The Bearn's voice was uncharacteristically gentle. Both of our mothers were half-sisters to the bold warrior I had just murdered.

Could be Siward Bearn thought I did not remember killing William Malet, but I did. Even so, against all logic, a faint hope had grown that our uncle might have survived. It seemed a mystery, as I hovered between life and death, that I had fought to the finish with a man I had loved and respected since childhood. My own kinsman!

Thinking on it, I was swept by a strange and piercing fear. All that had just happened, I realized with dread, was now a part of me, and would be forever locked amongst my memories. In an eerie way, that realization unleashed a flood of recollection. Stiffening, I fought the tide of remembrances that threatened to wash over me. Often I had heard it said that, at the moment of death, a man's entire life recurs to him—a flash of fleeting memory. For that reason, I did not want to remember.

But I did....

CHAPTER TWO

Some of the men in power were . . . more
devoted to King Harold Harefoot, however
unjustly, than to the Aetheling—especially, it
is said, Earl Godwine. The earl, therefore
arrested Aelfred on his way to London . . .
and threw him into prison. At the same time
he dispersed some of his attendants, others he
put in fetters and afterwards blinded, some he
scalped and tortured, amputated their hands
and feet and heavily mutilated. . . . he put to
death six hundred of them at Guildford with
varied torments. Then, by order of Godwine
and others, Aelfred was conducted, heavily
chained, to the Isle of Ely; but as soon as the
ship touched land there, his eyes were most
barbarously plucked out while he was on
board, and in this state he was taken to the
monastery and handed over to the custody of
the monks. There he shortly afterwards died.

—Chronicle of Florence of Worcester

The things I remember most are of winter time. The first frosts seemed
to bring my father home to us. The spring and summer he spent poli-
ticking with my grandfather Leofric, the Earl of Mercia, keeping
council, moving from manor to manor, seeing after the affairs of the
earldom. The great press of hunting and wood-felling followed and
occupied him all the fall. Then he came home to Couventrie, where
most often we wintered, and stayed put through the Christ Mass and

year's end, and sometimes through the thaws.

Even now, when autumn finally gives way to the cold kiss of the north, and light snow swirls madly in blasting winds with the last of the withered leaves, my earliest memories of him come. They are vague remembrances of early descending darkness and of sitting at the fireside long into the smoke-filled night, hearing tales which are now a veritable part of me. My father's chief man, Cynewulf Cenwulf's son, was an excellent tale weaver. Many other of my father's guardsmen also had poetry as well as battle in their blood, and could make an epic of every scrape and skirmish they ever suffered. My father, though, had the greatest talent of all.

I can remember his proud, handsome face lit by the eerie glow of the roaring fire as he embarked on some woeful tale with every one of his men as intent as we were, rapt in the magic of his low, solemn voice. He had a way of creeping into a yarn so innocently that its full effect was upon you before you realized he had drawn you in. Of a winter's night, he delighted in nothing more than true tales of bloody deed.

Our family history was rife with such stories. Often Father told us of his cousins, Earl Eadwulf of Bernicia and Æthelgar Bearn of the Diera, who were cruelly slain along with many of their men by a usurper named Siward, who wrested away the lands they ruled between them. Siward the Usurper planned to reunite the two lands he had stolen, and reestablish the ancient kingdom of North Humbria. Some say his hope then was to battle King Edward for the whole of Angland, but this never came about, for the people of the north would not fight behind the Usurper, hating him for the murders of their rightful ealdormen. Without an army, the Usurper had no chance, so he pretended a great loyalty to the king instead. Edward, fooled by gifts of gold and bended knee, formally recognized him as the rightful Earl of the whole North Humbria, even though he knew the murderer had basely wronged the House of Leofric—*our house*—to claim it. Every time my father told the tale, we hissed at the end of it; when we grew older and more sure of ourselves, we cursed-low, muttered oaths like those of my father's men.

He shared sagas of the ancient Mercian kings, my forebears, and of the legendary Welsh wars which killed our kinsmen in every generation as far back as any man could remember. He waxed poetic on the bold exploits of Grandfather Leofric's famed brothers: Northman, Wulfric, and Eadwine the Welsh-Slayer, all dead in battle before I was born. Still, the fare which impressed me most was the accounting of horrible crimes accomplished by the bloody hands of our rival house, the family of Godwine. I well remember the first tale ever I heard of them, though I had scarce seen five years when my father told it.

It was winter, and we were keeping the Solstice, the birth of the sun. A few days hence we would celebrate the Christ Mass, the birth of the Son, as well. Most priests allowed the keeping of the ancient ways, so long as folk were careful to call their celebration the Twelve Days of Christ Mass rather than the Yuletide, as of old. "Yule" was said to be the oldest name of the pagan god Odin, though in the most ancient Norse, the word was pronounced Yu-We. Grandfather told us that on a long ago pilgrimage to Jerusalem, a Jewish priest there told him that the Israelites were certain the name of the Creator was Yah-Weh, and that was the same name by which Christians called him also. The Romans, we knew, worshiped one named Jove. which in the Latin tongue is spoken "Yo-Weh." All this, Grandfather Leofric told us, and the priests backed him in it, was proof that both pagans and well-churched folk worshiped an identical god, the All-Father and the Creator being one and the same.

In any case, it was a windy, bristling night, and strange tunes played through the high timber rafters of our great hall at Couventrie, where the household men were all gathered as usual after taking board. Some of them sat on the trestle benches which lined one side of the narrow, sturdy plank tables. Others sat, as we did, on the rush-strewn floor, close to the inviting heat of the fire. I recall sitting as near to my half-brother Burchard as I could get, as much for strength as for warmth. A tiny thing then, I was not overly bold and I admit it. I considered Burchard my great protector in those days; though nine years my elder, he never teased me for my shyness as my brother Edwin did.

The talk that night had centered much on King Edward, and my father asked us, seemingly out of nowhere, if we knew why the king had so many Norman men around him in his court. Certainly we knew they were there; Anglishmen were forever grumbling about it. Normans sat in the very highest places and because they did not know our laws or language there were often stinging miscarriages of justice under their auspices. As to why they were there, though, we did not know, so we all shook our heads.

"Did you know the king grew up in Normandy?" my father asked.

"But he speaks Anglish, does he not?" I asked, puzzled.

"Indeed, when he feels like it!"

Some of the men laughed then but, ignoring them, my father went on. "There was a time when Edward could not step foot in Angland, for fear of his life."

"But he is the king!" Burchard responded, no doubt trying as hard as I was to picture that possibility.

"But in those days he was not. He was only an ætheling. Know you what that means?"

He looked from one to the other of us with a questioning smile, and seeing that we did not know, Ælfgar went on. "'Ætheling' means a king's kinsman with candidature—a brother, son, nephew, or cousin with a claim to the throne. Edward was the younger son of King Æthelred the Counsel-less. His brother Ælfred was first ætheling, and he was second in line. His mother, Lady Emma—"

"There is a cursed woman for you!" cried one of his men, and the others laughed, even my father. Then he continued.

"The Lady Emma remarried, but instead of another Anglishman, she wed the Norseman, Canute, who took the crown of Angland by force after Æthelred's death. Canute had one evil son already, called Harold Harefoot, and Emma bore him another, named Harthacnut. She favored this rotten issue over her sons by her first husband, so Ælfred and Edward were exiled to Normandy at her command."

"By their own mother?" cried Edwin, caught in the tale.

"Aye. She had hated Æthelred, and so she hated her sons by him. And her other son, their half-brother, Harthacnut, hated them, too, craving the crown for himself as he did."

Ælfgar paused momentarily to crack some nuts, two at a time in his powerful hand. Except for the spitting of the fire and the whining of the wind, there was no sound in the whole great hall. My father settled himself back comfortably before he went on.

"Ælfred Ætheling was a blameless man, they say, and fair to look upon. I have met Normans in the king's court who spoke very highly of him. 'Tis said that he rode like a Norman, fought like a Cymrian, hunted like an Eirish, and thought like an Anglishman. This last and greatest of his virtues led him back here when he was a grown man, for no Anglishman can bear to think of his homeland without wanting to be there. So he came. He picked a bad time, though."

"Why, father?" we all wanted to know.

"King Canute had died, and his son by Emma, Harthacnut, was fighting for the crown against his own half-brother, Harold Harefoot. Whenever things are in such an uproar, 'tis a bad time for an unexpected face to be seen!"

Casually tossing nutshells into the fire, Cynewulf Cenwulf's son, the glint-eyed young Mercian warrior who was my father's firmest friend, picked up the thread of the tale.

"Godwine, the Earl of Wessex, was the man who came to greet him when he landed. Ælfred met with that Wessexman happily, and rode with his party all through the pretty Wey valley till they came to Guildford, where Godwine kept his chief house. The Earl of Wessex welcomed the ætheling there with a rich feast, clapped him on the back like a true friend, and bade him rest till the morrow. Ælfred was happy to do it, for he and his Norman retainers were very weary by then, and comfortable enough to want to stay there."

There was a long pause. I heard Edwin's impatient question. "Well?"

"Well what?" my father questioned back smiling, and we jeered until he continued, lowering his voice as if imparting a secret.

"Godwine had not room enough for all those men in his great, huge hall. Seems he had to portion them into smaller groups and send them out here and there through the town. And though he gave them every comfort, none of them slept well that night."

"But why is it that they should all sleep poorly just because they were quartered in different places?" Edwin sounded as puzzled as I was by this strange coincidence.

"Because it was a cold, damp night—the kind that puts a colored mist all around the moon and blots the starlight. Because the wind hollered mournfully in the rafters, louder than you hear it howling now. Because, unbeknownst to the ætheling, Godwine and his men were in the service of Harold Harefoot. Having led them hence, they knew where each and every one of the visitors slept. Godwine's men came upon them, all at a given signal in the dead of night, and ripped their scalps from their heads with well-honed blades and axed away their arms and legs, and bladed them in their innards till the croaking of death rattle drowned out all the wind-sound—"

"Father!" I was shaking, so horrified that only Burchard's strong grip kept me upright. "Is it true?"

"Of course it is, Morcar!" Edwin snapped, then wondered aloud whether they had murdered Ælfred Ætheling as well.

Ælfgar stretched and drew his heavy cloak tight around himself. "Nay! Godwine handed him over to the Harefoot's bloodthirsty men all right, just as he did all those who survived the massacre. Earl Godwine is an honorable man, though, and holds great respect for a man's station. So he told them 'This man is a prince; slay him not but wrap him tight in iron chains and sharpen your blades well before you put his eyes out!' and that, of course, is what they did."

Sick at the thought of it, I inched even closer to Burchard in the half-darkness, closing my eyes as if that might rid me of the picture of the man's face, swollen, bloody, and blinded. Then my father's chief man, Cynewulf, finished the tale in a matter-of-fact tone.

"Earl Godwine's men were efficient enough, but very crude and not at all careful. The handsome prince soon died of his atrocious wounding. 'Twas a thing truly mourned by all good Anglishmen. Not by Godwine, though! He was too busy being a loyal king's man to

Harold Harefoot, and when that king died a few years later, he made himself busy serving the Harefoot's enemy half-brother, Harthacnut. Then, of course, Harthacnut fell dead while feasting, and the good earl has been busy ever since being a loyal king's man to Edward, the brother of Ælfred Ætheling."

"How can it be, father," Burchard mused, "that Edward would have Godwine as his chief man after what the man did to his brother?"

Leaning close to us, as if to impart a great secret, Ælfgar spoke in a somber voice. "Is it not said that a tale with a moral serves for every man but the king?"

Indeed, that was the saying.

"Well, the moral of this tale—and the King has surely paid it little heed—is 'Never trust a man who kills your brother!'"

This elicited a dry but hearty laugh all around. For some reason, I have always remembered the adage, if only because it seemed like good advice.

From that night on, I never much cared for the Earl of Wessex. A powerfully built, yellow-haired man full of ambition and cunning, Godwine had attained such eminence in the role of King Edward's councilor that it could be said he ruled the country himself. Edward, despite an ungovernable temper, was a monkish man, and his priest-like manner permeated every aspect of his life so that his own spirituality numbed him to worldly politics. He was himself incapable of keeping the vastness of the Anglo-Saxon states united—for Mericians, North Humbrians, East Anglians, and Wessexmen seldom, if ever, agreed on anything. It was to Godwine that the king trusted for the wielding of force and firmness though there was ever a coldness between them. The Earl of the West Saxons, as the Mericians still called him after the old manner, was clever at gaining allegiances and keeping men with various interests united in purpose. He was very able, and Edward was shrewd enough to appreciate his influence. Whether or not Edward harbored misgivings about his under-king, I cannot say. It seems he could not have fostered him thusly if he did.

Grandfather Leofric, who knew Earl Godwine very well, declared him innocent of the charges; I lost no time in asking him after hearing that dreadful story, approaching him one morning when he came to the monastery where we studied. He admonished me.

"Do you not know that the man received a formal declaration of innocence from the king himself, and that it is therefore a sin to suppose him guilty?"

My grandfather was a strong, stately man with white hair and piercing blue eyes which belied his otherwise stern countenance. He had fought at the side of King Edmund Ironside in his youth and had been reckoned a great warrior. Now, though his broad, bountiful earldom stretched from the Eirish channel to the grey North Sea, more than a full quarter of the Anglish kingdom, he was mild-mannered, gentle and unassuming. He put his thumb under my chin, raising my eyes to his when he told me this, smiling. Even so, it bothered me to think that the king who had declared Godwine innocent was none other than Harold Harefoot—the one man who had most wanted to see his rival, the ætheling, dead. It distressed me even more that the king had not made the declaration of innocence until Godwine had gifted him with a stunning, gold-gilded, dragon-prowed battleship, manned by eighty magnificently armed warriors. Nevertheless, my grandfather was quick to remind me that King Edward had married Godwine's daughter Edythe. "If the king himself is willing to look past such a thing," he told me seriously as we walked, "then no other man has a right to continue the grudge."

Even so, I never quite trusted Godwine of Wessex, and if it is worth anything, it is plain that there somehow came to be wild and murderous blood in the hearts of his six, strapping warrior sons. All of them were a curious mixture of impulsiveness and calculating consideration, men of intriguing ends but ruthless means. I came to know them well—though much after this, for they were men of my father's age and paid no heed to me till I was grown. I swear by all that is holy, they were an enigmatic lot, courageous and one-minded in hatred, persuasive and two-faced in deception and, but for one, likable and pleasant. We raised swords against each other, and likewise raised cups in brotherhood. One became my sworn mortal enemy, and another my brother-in-law.

But my thoughts get ahead of me now, even as they did that fateful day….

CHAPTER THREE

Earl Siward and Earl Leofric and many people
with them from the north had come there to the
king, and Earl Godwine and his sons were informed
that the king and the men who were with him
would take action. . . .

—Anglo Saxon Chronicle,
Book "E" 1051

If ever I have come to know anything in this life, it is that I am a man of
Mercia. I am true Anglish. Long before the Danes established the
Danelaw, before a united Angland was born, when each of the four great
earldoms—Mercia, North Humbria, Wessex, and East Anglia—boasted a
leader like a king of its own, my people were native born on Mercian soil.

My grandfather was born of the ancient Mercian kings. First my
father and then my brother Edwin inherited the earldom of all Mercia
after him. I myself am the true Earl of the North Humbria, chosen by the
people there, but I have always counted myself a Mercian.

"Listen well, Morcar," my father once told me. "Wherever it is that
you go in life, carry Mercia with you, for Mercia is the essence of the
blood of our house, and our house is the very substance of Mercia." I have
lived in many places since—outlaw camps, castles, forests, and prisons—
but I never forgot his words; I carried my homeland with me always.

My first memories are all of Mercia, where I was born just before the
Christ Mass in my grandfather's great Stæthford Shire hall. In time I
came to know all of that magnificent earldom, but as a child it was the
pleasant sweeps of Nottingham and Lindcylene I knew best, and the
greenness of lovely Couventrie, where Father kept his manor mostwhiles.

I was named for Morcar, son of Arngrim, my mother's grandfather,
a man of Nottingham who was one of the chief thegns before the reign
of King Edward. This Morcar was an honored man, but he was unlucky.
During the great council held at the Ox Ford in 1015, he and his son-

in-the-law, Siferth, my mother's father, were lured into the chambers of an unscrupulous rival and basely done to death. Though this happened long before I was born, I have heard the story of those cruel murders since infancy. It is as famous in our family as the tale of my grandmother Godiva's ride through Couventrie, naked except for her hair.

Vague images occur to me from my earliest days: intangible, fleeting glimpses of people, places, and feelings gone but to haunt me. I recall a great sense of security and belonging which I have never since managed to recapture—except in dreams—and a great faith and trust in the will of God. This was no doubt inspired by my grandfather, a pious and goodly man famed through all the kingdom for the richness of his bounty to the glory of God. He was patron of the monks at Crugland and Thornie, and he financed the great monastery at Peterborough, a place of incredible splendor, with an altar frontal of solid gold encrusted with precious gems.

In that holy place I was educated with my brother Edwin, a year my elder. Our studies included Latin, Anglish, Welsh, French, Danish, and Gaelic. Grandfather was adamant about our catechism, which we studied daily after the mass. Grandmother Godiva herself taught us to sing, and we delighted from babyhood in chanting meaningless matins for her benefit. We loved her very much, my brothers and I, and even more so did our elder sister, Aldgyth. She was a clear-eyed, tall beauty of a girl with thick sweet-gold tresses the same color as Grandmother's, and the two of them were very close.

My mother, Ælfgiva, was of high Mercian and North Humbrian blood, and she had had a sad childhood. After her father's murder, she became step-daughter to King Edmund Ironside, who fell in love with her beautsome mother, Aldgyth, for whom my sister was named. Edmund himself died, most say was murdered, soon after, and Ælfgiva's twice-widowed mother fled to Normandy and wed a great landholder there. Ælfgiva thus had Norman half-brothers and was raised in the Norman way, which made her ever uneasy in her own homeland.

Ælfgiva was not affectionate. Though beautiful, she suffered from a cold heart and distant feelings—a lady who soured early to living, and from whom happinesses fled like larks from a whirlwind. So it is that my childhood memories of her are scarce. I can easily picture her, though, as I can most of my kith and kinsmen then, and they were very numerous. But, as I said before, it is my father's image which waxes strongest in my heart.

Ælfgar was a handsome, tempestuous, princely man with eyes of polished iron. There was no indecision in him. That which he loved, he loved deeply; what he hated, he hated violently and with passion.

Upright, but headstrong and so vehement that his temperament could not be crossed, he was all that I longed to be and all that I feared becoming.

People were wont to wonder where his wildness came from. Despite Grandmother Godiva's famous defiance of her husband—she heard him exclaim flippantly that he would lower the land-tax in Couventrie the day his wife rode naked through the town, so she did it—she was a docile lady, church-loving and moderate. Like my grandfather, she was bewildered by her son's driving restlessness. Ælfgar was their only child, not for want of trying, and both loved him, perhaps too well, because he was quick, bold, and fair to look upon. They denied him nothing and some say he grew prideful. Still, a good man, he was well loved by his people and especially by his men. They gladly accompanied him in his changing fortunes, choosing to follow him twice into exile and outlawry when he was wronged by the House of Godwine.

Ælfgar was a man born to be respected, but few could understand the passions which drove him. Assuredly, his parents did not. It was not their fault that they had but one son to Earl Godwine's six. They never rightly understood the threat this presented. Ælfgar did, though, and dealing with it as he was forced to do, it was his lot to see everyone he loved grow distant because of it. I never gave thought to this as a child, but now I have come to appreciate the fierce self-reliance which characterized his every mood. Indeed, I fancy that I have inherited it, and my brother Edwin with me. I have never looked into Edwin's melting eyes without seeing Ælfgar's impassioned vengeance there, and I myself have all my life shown the same ruthless resentment when injured or wronged.

As boys, Edwin and I wanted only to be like Ælfgar, and never more than the first time we watched him ride to war. We had seen him in arms before, but when I was nearing six, we saw him for the first time at the head of the great Mercian army and were awed. We knew that war was imminent, and the worst kind of all: civil war.

It came about because King Edward's Norman brother-in-the-law and his unruly men, rode into Dofras, the chief port of Wessex, and got into a fight with the townsfolk there. Seven Normans were slain and Edward commanded Earl Godwine to waste the entire town to avenge them. Godwine defied him. The folk of Wessex revered him for it but the king was rabid, remembering loudly then how his own brother Ælfred Ætheling had been murdered by that very man. Once named outlaw, Godwine challenged the king to battle. He was joined by his sons: Gyrth, Leofwine, Tostig, Harold—Earl of the East Anglia—and Sweyn, heir to Wessex, who then ruled a small earldom newly carved from lands the king had pared away from Mercia. When they marched on the king, the show of force took him by surprise. Edward called up the fyrd—the entire army of Angland—and, in doing so, summoned my father and grandfather to battle.

Ælfgar was loath to go. To answer the call meant fighting alongside Siward the Usurper, who had gained the North Humbria by killing our kinsmen, Eadwulf and Æthelgar—my father's cousins and best of friends. Grandfather argued they were bound to answer the king's call, though, and finally Ælfgar agreed.

We were at Kirton, my father's great Lindcylene Shire estate, that time of year. On the day that the men of Mercia rode to battle, my brothers and I watched them from the Lindissi Road. Ælfgar looked magnificent at the head of his impressively armed warriors. It occurs to me that this is my most treasured memory of him: a warrior, proud and straight in his gleaming hauberk, riding helmetless into the autumn breeze. Curiously, whenever I picture that man, and I often do, it is with his hair astream on some belligerent wind.

As it turned out, neither side cared to make battle against their own countrymen, especially not at harvest time. In the end, the armies did not clash, but King Edward commanded the rebels to appear in front of the Witena Gemot, the meeting of councilors, in Lundun City, with no more than twelve men between them. Godwine and his sons were too frightened to do it unless the king guaranteed their safety. An obstinate man, Edward refused. When they failed to appear, he named Sweyn Godwine's son, the heir to Wessex, a nithing.

News of all this began to filter through the shire long before my father and grandfather returned with their men. "What is a nithing?" I asked Burchard one morning as we walked in the orchards. He had seen fifteen years, and I thought he knew everything in the world.

"The worst kind of outlaw," he told me, "one who can never be forgiven." This answer only confused me more.

"Why should he call Sweyn a nithing, and no one else of that house?" I wondered.

"Well," my brother concluded, after much musing, "Sweyn has done worse things than any of the others."

"Like what?" asked Edwin, who was with us.

"Let Father tell you the tale," Burchard replied as we hurried into the brisk wind. "He tells it very well."

"*You* tell us!" I begged, and so he explained how Sweyn had murdered his own young cousin, Beorn, then mutilated and secretly buried him, and all because Beorn had sided with Harold against him in a dispute over some land. "He was outlawed after that, but the king finally forgave him. He did other things, too, much worse than that in the eyes of God."

"Worse than that!" We both wanted to know what.

"You are too young to understand," Burchard said severely, coming closer to condescension than ever before.

"Tell me anyway!" Edwin demanded, grabbing Burchard's mantle. Burchard batted him gruffly away with a broad grin.

"You are a bold brat, Edwin! When you are old enough, someone will tell you." He cuffed Edwin like he was a naughty puppy, and they wrestled a minute, leaving me to wonder what could possibly offend God more than murder. Only years later did we learn how Sweyn had abducted my father's pretty cousin, Eadgiva, from a nunnery, kept her till he was tired of her, then sent her back with child. That certainly did not occur to me that October morning as I stood in the whipping wind, wracking my brain for a sin worse than kin-killing.

I was still lost in morbid contemplation when Edwin let go a cry of surprised excitement, and broke out of Burchard's grip. From the rise where we stood at the orchard's edge, we could see across the newly scythed, golden hayfields to the beginnings of the uplands. There the manor-house nestled in a clearing carved out of the yellowing groves, its extremities encircled by wooden palings and high, stone walls. It was a lofty gabled building of wood and stone, much larger than the dozen or so out-buildings which surrounded it, and in the gilding sunlight it looked noble and fine, indeed.

We looked on a busy scene. It was nutting time, and great hampers of hazelnuts, walnuts, and chestnuts were everywhere, waiting to be milled or bagged and stored. A good many women were at the task of shelling; others were boiling the shells in large vats to make dyes for linen. It was past them we looked, though, to the huge, rough-hewn stabling barn outside of which, adding to the commotion, some twenty horses or more now stood, still richly laden with battle accouterments. Father was home with his household men, and I shrieked as loud as Edwin as I tore through the fields.

At many of our estates, the lodges where we slept and kept wardrobe were in separate buildings. Kirton, though, being especially rich and well-built, had four smaller halls opening off the main one, all under one roof and separated by timber doors. The finest of these lesser rooms was where we kept our quarter, and there my father was, with his chief men, Cynewulf and Ælfric White-Hair, working hard to remove his hauberk. It was a heavy, wide-sleeved dress of chained metal, split up the front and back so a man could sit a horse in it. Ælfgar's long hair, which he never twisted or braided as some of the other men did when they wore arms, had gotten caught in its interlocking links, and he roundly cursed and complained as they tried to free him.

Lost inside that heavy, uncomfortable garment, he could not see that Edwin and I were there or surely he would have bitten back some of those oaths. When at last they got it off him, by cutting some of his hair with a sharp blade, he let go a moan of relief, glad that its weight was gone. Stretching and turning, he caught sight of us and flushed a little for his rude indelicacies.

"A body should announce himself when he comes in at a doorway!" he said severely, looking at us, hands on his hips.

"Well, we did not think it much mattered, knowing Mother was not here!" Edwin replied brashly, cross at the disappointing welcome. My father chucked him under the chin, then bent to hug us both.

"Where is she gone?"

"She rode early on to the convent church at Stowe, to do embroideries," my brother answered, leaning down to finger the chain mail which the men had laid out on the floor.

"And she took Aldgyth with her," I added, knowing Father would want to know. Watching with great interest as Cynewulf unlaced the padded leathern hauberk he had on under the metal one, I asked why he wore two.

"If an axe pierced that mail shirt, making a gross wound and driving the links into it, the contusion would be unbearable. That is why."

"Has that ever happened to you, father?" I asked earnestly, but he laughed and his men with him.

"Praise God, no!" he exclaimed. "I am for the most part an unscarred man!"

"Do you always wear the two then?"

"Not always. A man is often tempted to go without the under-coat. You would do well to start praying right now that you never have need to go into battle on a sweltering day."

He was down to his linen tunic now, and to the braies he wore under it, tied around the waist and kept close to the leg with crossed garters from the ankle to the knee. He was sweaty and dirty from road dust and not washing.

"How long have you been in Gleawanceaster, father?" I asked him, pouting a little.

"Near a three week's stint."

"Did you not once take to bathing there?" Arms crossed in front of me, I demanded an answer. My father collapsed on the dressing-bench in violent laughter, both his men roaring and bellowing with him. I wrinkled my nose; it was obvious none of them had, and it vexed me.

As if to still his mirth enough to answer, Ælfgar bit his lip. "Even the king does not keep a bath in the field, my son!"

"You ought to get shaven, too!" Edwin added, inspecting the roughness of Ælfgar's neck and chin, and the three men laughed more. Then Ælfric White-Hair started rolling the metal hauberk, but my father stopped him.

"Let the underlings try it!" he suggested, and delighted we threw ourselves whole-heartedly into that work. Any little task which had to do with the keeping of arms was a pleasure to us, whether mending or polishing or preparing for storage. While we worked on it—for it was not easy to form the heavy coat into a compact, portable bundle—my father splashed with cold water and rubbed himself with wet sand and ash-soap before changing into a clean under-tunic. While he slipped a richly embroidered dalmatic over it, I was pleased to hear him order that a bath be set for him in the kitchen-house.

"And let the water be warm and every fire roaring! he commanded, "'Tis chill as a stolen bride out there!" Then, patting a little extra attar on his face and hair, he looked at us very matter-of-factly and said, "You had better hope they keep baths in the East Anglia."

"Why, father?" my brother questioned without looking up.

"Because the king has exiled the entire House of Godwine and named me earl there in Harold Godwine's son's stead."

We sat bolt upright, open-mouthed and incredulous. We were not too young to understand the import of this, though which surprised us more—the raising of my father or the outlawry of the king's favorites—I cannot say.

"Is it true, father?" Edwin whispered in wonder. Ælfgar could not hide a satisfied smile as he nodded.

Edwin was good at calculating. "Why, then, between you two, Grandfather Leofric and yourself will hold a third of the kingdom!" he announced, growing pink with pleasure.

"For a while, at least," my father answered, clasping a golden bracelet around his lower arm, and turning it so the garnet cross would show. "These Godwines are not so meek that they will not make a move for restoration."

"Will the king grant it, father?" I asked.

"Surely!" came his unhesitating answer. "When his rage passes, he will get the better of himself. Still, he has finally made a mark against them, and all Angland has waited a good long while to see him check their greed! And if, indeed, I am made to return the Anglia to Harold, it will not be for long. Edward says the House of Leofric shall have it when Harold takes over his father's earldom of Wessex. 'Tis his way of balancing things. He knows as well as any man that there are too many Godwine's sons!"

That was the truth of it—six, strong-armed, jealous sons, and not enough earldoms to pacify them. The king had already taken land from Mercia and put it in their greedy hands. Good that he had finally realized the mistake of that!

"You have said Harold will take his father's earldom," Edwin said casually. I knew what he was leading up to. "Sweyn is the eldest so by rights it should be his. Is't true he cannot come back because he is a nithing?"

"Indeed. He will never come back and his lands have reverted back to Mercia forever."

"Did the king name him nithing for kin-killing, Father?"

"For many sins."

"For sins worse than own-folk-murder?" my brother asked it carefully, pretending to be busy with the hauberk.

But my father did not answer. "When your mother comes," he told us, "she will be happy to know we will spend the Christ Mass in Lundun City, in the king's court."

"All of us, Father?" Edwin asked, looking at me out of the corner of his eye.

"Aye—the entire House of Leofric."

Slipping on his heavy, rich mantle and brooching it at the shoulder, he strode to the door and, turning there, added thoughtfully, "The king has always been blinded to all but his precious Wessexman. No doubt he will think we men of Mercia are very fair indeed, eh?"

With a nod, we watched him go. When the door closed behind him, we fell to speculating on this wildly exciting promise with such great anticipation and pleasure, that we ended up giggling and wrestling on the cold stone floor.

CHAPTER FOUR

The king held a meeting of his council and
proclaimed Godwine an outlaw, and all his host,
him and all his sons . . . Ælfgar, Earl Leofric's son,
was given the earldom which Harold had had.

—Anglo Saxon Chronicle,
Book "E" 1051

December, 1051
The weeks we spent in Lundun City, lodging in the king's great house
and keeping the Christ Mass season there, my mother seemed a different
person: talkative, sweet-tempered, and yielding. I recall that she combed
me herself every morning in the king's house, a thing she never did
before or after, and said that my locks were soft and fair.

"Pity is, though," I remember her saying in a low, mournful tone,
"this head will not keep its goldenness. You will be a brown-haired man,
my little Morcar."

"And Edwin, too?" I asked her, looking to where my brother sat
across the chamber in a stone window-seat. His hair was precisely the
same wheaten color mine was then, but she answered as if it were a
foolish question.

"Nay!" she cried, staring hard on him. "He will have his father's
glossy gilt hair, and his golden look, too, I fear."

She said it as if it were a distasteful thing. Often she confused me,
that beautsome, white-locked lady, and I never found much ease or
comfort in what she had to say.

Like her mother, whose loveliness had won the heart of King
Edmund Ironside, Ælfgiva was famed for her exceptional beauty. Her
name, Ælfgiva, means "gift of the elves" and well she might have been
an elven gift, so finely was she wrought. Small and delicately formed,
she possessed a beautifully transparent complexion and dreamy, radiant
grey eyes. Her hair was cloudly white; she seemed fragile and other-

worldly. It is said that Ælfgar, seeing her for the first time, vowed openly that he would have that inestimable treasure for his own and never wavered in his determination. Even so, despite her comeliness, she was a lady of cold and distant heart. She had early in life lost much that was dear to her and had not survived the pain of it whole and unscathed.

She was raised Norman. Her mother, the young widow first of Earl Siferth and then of King Edmund Ironside, wed Roger Malet, whose family had shown most courtesy to Edward and his brother, the unfortunate Ælfred Ætheling, when they were exiles in Normandy. Roger and she had two sons who bore Norman names, William and Durran. They proved staunch and true brothers to Ælfgiva and her elder sister, Æthelfryth, whom folk say died a death best forgotten. While yet young, Ælfgiva herself married a good man of Normandy but he, too, died untimelywise.

When Ælfgar first laid eyes on her, she was a grieving new widow with a toddling boy. Near a decade older than my father, she was not kindly disposed to him, for he was brash and impetuous and acted too boldly toward her. He was smitten with love and desire for her, though, and pressed his case with such impassioned fervor, that at last she agreed to wed with him on the condition that Ælfgar take her son Burchard as his son-in-the-law, making him his heir. This Ælfgar gladly agreed to do to win her, but he told us that once consecrated, she still did not come to his bed for many months.

She never held or hugged us as Grandmother Godiva did, and it was her way to speak cruelly of my father. She contended that he had never taken her but that he forced himself upon her, and that for nearly every time he used her, she had presented him with a child as token of his manhood. This is what we were to her, Aldgyth and Edwin and I, and we were bitterest of trophies apparently, for she would not love us overmuch. If her words were true, Ælfgar must have suffered agonies in that union, for he loved her with an earnest passion until the time she had drawn too far away to be reached.

Mayhap they might have had their moments of tenderness in spite of my mother's wanton bitterness. Ælfgar was an exceedingly fair man, and she cannot have been totally blind to his golden looks and pronounced devotion. Poisoned by sorrow and soured to life, love was like a curse to her, so often had Providence robbed her of her attachments. Nevertheless, I always felt it chief of her sorrows that she was almost entirely unable to show affection to us.

We had not been long in Lundun when we met William Malet, our avunculus, or mother's-brother. He was a king's man, highly favored and more popular with the Anglish than most of Edward's Normans, because he had the blood of Edmund Ironside's cwene in him and he dressed and spoke in Anglish fashion. Coming to our lodges, he embraced Ælfgiva and then Burchard before he cast my father a smile of greeting which seemed to hide some inner grimness. His holdings in the Lindcylene Shire included the great manor at Alkborough, but he had never visited the midlands since I was born.

"Pretty Aldgyth and Edwin you remember, I trow?" my mother asked him in a pleasant voice. "They are not such babes as when you looked upon them last."

William Malet nodded them a greeting without saying much. I could see that he was a very strong man, not as tall as my father but wide across the shoulders and neck. His look was manly and vigorous, his features decidedly like my mother's. His hair was sandy-colored, however, and his eyes had somewhat more color to them. He dressed in the way of all men-at-arms steeped in duty but not actual battle, with a light leathern hauberk instead of a dalmatic over his tunic and gartered kidskin breeches instead of linen braies under it. As I studied him, his gaze came to rest on me. I managed to flash a dim smile, though indeed there was something just the smallest bit frightening about him to me.

"This be your little Christ Mass token, then?" he asked without diverting his look. He said that because I was birthed three days before the feast of the Savior's coming. I did not know it then, but both my parents had done penance for my having been born in the Advent; it meant they had lain together during Lent.

"Aye," my mother replied bitterly, "another unlooked for precious thing from Ælfgar Leofric's son!" She said it in a way which caused me to burn red as summer sunset, and it irked me to see how those words made my father flush and quiver. My avunculus lowered himself to one knee and scrutinized me very carefully, no emotion in his look.

"He has not the look of a winter-babe," he said shortly, "Methinks he will make a fine and bold warrior!"

Tossing her head, my mother laughed sharply.. "Nay, brother! Shyness makes this one over-gentle for a change! He sinks in his own quietude."

"Be not so quick to judge of it, Ælfgiva! All storms are brewed from stillness; 'tis said that quiet air spews grave tempests!"

He looked then at Ælfgar who answered him with a small smile. A meaning passed between them, but I could not read it. They seemed to appreciate each other, these two men, yet some secret thing held them apart.

The next day my uncle came again. He gathered up Burchard, Edwin, and me, and with Grandfather and some other men we went to the open square near the old minster to watch a mad Eirishman bait a bear.

Now, occasionally when my grandfather's men killed a she-bear, they brought a cub back from the hunt and, if there was milk enough on the manor, they would keep it a few months and nurse and frolic with it. At that time in my life, those tiny, fuzzed play-things were all I knew of bears, so the sight of that shaggy, black creature, immense beyond all imagining, greatly impressed me. Bear baiting was a dangerous sport, and I gasped as the wild and frantic beast, chained to a solid oak tree, lunged with ferocity at his teasing tormentor. A nimble man, the red-bearded baiter taunted him to frenzy, swatting at the animal's snout with a carved wooden stick till he reared, a towering giant, on his huge hind legs. As the crushing forelegs smashed down, the worst was always expected, and rousing cheers sounded from the crowd each time the courageous acrobat escaped those killing claws unscathed. 'Twas a thrilling event, and I have held ever since a healthy respect for both bears and Eirishmen.

"What think you, Burchard," I remember William Malet asking when it was over, "that you would rather fight a bear such-like or a raving man—a Welshman or some other heathen?"

Burchard shook his head, laughing. "If it's all the same to you, avunculus, let Morcar take the bear and Edwin the wild-man, and I shall but stay upon my knees and pray for them!"

Everyone laughed at that except my grandfather. The Earl of Mercia was grown much older than the rest and could be he had seen enough sorrow come from blood and warring that he thought it not such a bad idea.

We did not go immediately back to the king's house. Though most had seen it all before, the Mercian men were eager to view the king's stabling barn and armory. Wider perhaps and longer, the great stone barn did not otherwise seem different from those at Kirton or Couventrie or King's Braumleigh, where my grandfather kept one of his chief houses. The great array of many-colored shields, both long ones and round, which decked the walls and rafters, interested me most of all; even to my childish eyes it was plain to see the king had many men more than my grandfather or father.

While the others made their inspection, I walked alone, looking from one painted shield to the other, trying to imagine what the men who had carried them into battle looked like. Some I recognized as having belonged to ancient men of fame—Ædward the Martyr, Ædwy the Fair, Monk Dunstan, and others long dead but in nowise forgotten.

I had worked myself well away from the rest of our party when I came across a boy sitting on the edge of a stone trough and staring intently at me. He was a dark-eyed child about my own age—tall, thin and stern-looking, with a regal, tellingly foreign air which somehow appealed to me. He wore his ebony hair in the Norman fashion, cut straight across the brow and hanging shorter at the back than at the ears. I approached him uncertainly and announced myself but the look in his eye told me immediately that he did not understand my Mercian dialect. I greeted him again in French, and he smiled. I had never made a friend before upon my own merits, being too shy to do more than cling shadow-like to my brothers. His reaction was very satisfying to me. I told him I was Morcar Ælfgar's son, of the House of Leofric, and asked his name.

"Fulke d'Aubermont. My father is equerry to the king," he said in a low and not particularly musical voice. Not knowing the word, I scrutinized him carefully for a clue. His rich mantle was ermine-lined. Under it he wore a dalmatic and under-tunic much like my own but cut longer, almost to the floor. His legs were covered in the same fitted hose that Norman men wore, something like braies in that they went all the way to the waist, but they were woven in such a manner that they clung to the leg and did not need strips and garters to shape them. His hose, dalmatic, and mantle were richly dyed. His silver brooch and rings were sizable and well made. An equerry is not a stable-hand, I thought.

"How long have you been in Lundun City, Fulke d'Aubermont?" I asked finally. He cast a curious frown.

"Always I have lived here," he retorted, as if surprised I would wonder. "I was born in this very house."

"Then how is it you are more comfortable with French than with Anglish?" I asked.

"I have never thought on it before," he replied, shrugging, and then we talked of other things.

We saw each other constantly the remainder of my stay. It was with no little pride that I introduced him to Edwin, who did not rightly understand the fascination my new-found friend held for me. My brother was of a livelier, keener temperament, and Fulke, like me, was quiet—a listener and perceiver, a planner without impulse. I cried when we parted company but we were destined to meet many times again and even my brother was to come one day to a realization of this perplexing Frenchman's true worth.

Another Norman was there that season, a far kinsman of King Edward's. It was no secret that the childless king was considering the man as his successor. He was William, the Duke of Normandy, renowned even in our land for his cunning and strength. Already he ranked with the greatest warriors of the age—men like the wild Welshman, Gruffydd of Llewellyn, and the terrifying Viking king of the North Wegians, Harald Hardraada. It was rumored that the king of France was as much a vassal to William as the other way around. All I remember of him with certainty is that he was the first man ever I saw who seemed greater to me than my father or grandfather.

I was not awed by the king. Introspective, white-haired and bent, Edward was monkish in dress and manner, and I could not comprehend then that he was the greatest man in the realm. Grandfather Leofric, vigorous and practical, entirely overshadowed him, and beside my flashing father, the king seemed a weak old man. The Norman duke, though, had power in his very gaze. His height and grandeur were so impressive that I thought him the most remarkable person ever I had looked upon. Dark-complected, with hair blue-black like the raven's wing, his look was direct and penetrating—his eyes a strange blend of serenity and ruthlessness. He was somewhat younger than my father, who had not seen thirty years then, and seemed to be of a similar temper. Those two enjoyed each other right well. In the brisk, snowy mornings they hunted and rode together. The long winter evenings they kept in the great hall, well-relaxed amongst their boisterous men, talking and gaming and keeping fair company. All else I remember of that first journey outside my homelands pales beside the recollection of the vibrantly majestic foreign duke. It was a strange feeling he gave me, a tender child, that our fates were somehow meant to touch upon each other.

Before our rich procession set off again for the midlands, my father was confirmed as Earl of the East Anglia, which had been held by Godwine's second son, Harold, before the Godwines' exile. The king restored to my grandfather's Mercian earldom all the lands he had previously granted to hot-blooded Sweyn, now called nithing with no chance for restoration. Then, of his own accord, King Edward put the ancient monastery of Peterborough, which had gone to Harold with the East Anglia, back under the protection of our house for all times. He promised my uncle, Abbot Leofric of Crugland and of Thornie, that he now would add the abbacy of Peterborough to his holdings. In truth, the new abbacy was his right.

So ended the most glorious experience of my early boyhood. Some years later, when my grandfather taught me to keep the Christ Mass eve, or Year's End, in fasting and meditation, sorting out the previous events of my life, it was with this marked occasion that I began tabulating my meaningful memories.

CHAPTER FIVE

harold's earldom was assigned to Leofric's son
Ælfgar, a man of great energy; he held it and ruled
it at that time with distinction.

—William of Malmesbury

February, 1052

Edwin threw a tantrum the morning we were to quit Mercia for our home in my father's new earldom. He did not want to part from Grandmother Godiva. Screaming and sobbing, he threw himself from one end of her chamber to the other, scratching his own face and neck till he drew blood, trembling violently. Burchard tried to still him but could not, and finally, in a kind of terror, my mother leant far out of the open casements and screamed for my father. It took Ælfgar a few minutes to make his way up from the courtyard, and in that time, Edwin, striking aimlessly and throwing anything he could lift, frightened us all to tears.

"For the saints!" my father roared, bursting in with his chief man, Cynewulf Cenwulf's son, momentarily stunned by the terrifying sound of my brother's ear-splitting shrieks. It took those two men all their cunning to corner Edwin and all their power to hold him down. Once pinned, Edwin slammed his head hard against the timber floor while my father, afraid to let go of him, shouted and cursed, trying to cushion the self-inflicted blows with his arm. Then, abruptly, Edwin stilled his dreadful screeching. His hoarse, tortured sobs gradually subsided, and my father lifted him in a crushing, loving embrace. When Edwin finally pulled away, sweating and flushed, I saw that he bled from the mouth and nose. For some reason, it inspired a deadly fear in me. 'Twas not the first tantrum that tempestuous creature had, and not the last—but it was the worst and, even now, recalling it makes me shudder.

"Thank God's tender mercy your grandfather did not witness that tumult," Grandmother was fond of saying for many years afterward. "It surely would have killed him!"

Father had a special affection for Edwin and always made excuses for his outbursts, as if they were to be expected in a child so comely and gamesome. It was a sore spot between my parents. Ælfgiva had no tenderness for the boy at all, and was not ashamed to let it be known. She called him "Ælfgar's issue" as if she herself had no part in bringing him forth.

Grandmother told Edwin, years later, that Ælfgiva would not have married Ælfgar but for his inheritance, the great earldom of Mercia, which she meant her beloved Burchard to have after him. Never had she thought to bear Ælfgar an heir, and when she did, she feared for her first-born son's position. In this she might have saved herself the sorrow. My father had sworn to William Malet, as part of his bride's-price, to take Burchard as his first-born son under law. To a man like my father, a sworn word was as God's breath.

When the immense train which carried our household finally set off for the East Anglia, Edwin rode proudly in the saddle with Ælfgar. They trotted back and forth constantly from one end of the party to the other. I was comfortable on the golden palfrey I shared with Burchard, but I would have given anything to ride even one furlong pressed against my handsome father that way.

We traveled very slowly. It was no small undertaking to transport my father's entire household from one domain to another. He carried in his service ninety household men—honorable, high-born friends and kin. The best paid and best armed of warriors, they served as his select-guard in battle, and were sworn with holy oaths to his allegiance. As the name implied, they became his actual household, for to attain the honored position of earl's man, they pledged to be by his side at all times. They slept in his hall or in lodges he provided for them. They ate, hunted, fought, and traveled with him, though most held vast estates of their own. Oft-times they carried their families with them, too. A goodly retinue of priests and skilled free-men added to that number made for a great and cumbersome party.

Working our way from one manor to the next, a night here and two nights there, it took several weeks to make our way from Couventrie to Grantanbrycg, where stood the manor my father had chosen for his seat. That journey, just like the ones to and from Lundun City, I remember as an endless round of sleeping, greeting, feasting, and tiresome riding, the monotony of which was relieved only by the gradual, subtle changes in the scenery as we came into the eastern fen-land.

All my life I had heard tales of the vast bogs and quagmires of the true fen country. Even so, I was unprepared for the misty, dream-like landscape we encountered as we rounded into Grantanbrycg where, far as the eye could see, there was nothing but the strange specter of green earth merged with black water. Those who knew the heart of the swamplands, where it stayed dark and still all the day, laughed at our awe. This, they told us, was only the outreaches, the floating fen—level, low plain drowned now by spring thaws. A man or horse could walk here if sure-footed, but the real depths could only be traveled by boat.

You might think the East Anglians, having been lorded by our rival house, might be restrained in their welcome to the new earl, but they were not. The ancient ties of Mercia and the Anglia were revered, and these folk were of the same Anglish and Danish blood. Unlike Mercians, they were not entirely clean-shaven, but wore smooth chins with their hair brushed behind their ears to reveal whiskers growing down their cheeks, meeting long, thin mustaches just below the mouth. It gave them a perpetually grim look and some of the men who swore to my father's household there frightened me. One such was the fen-man Æthelstan, whom my father elected as guardian to my brothers and myself. A gruff, hawk-eyed man, I early developed a wariness of him. He was neither cold nor unfriendly, but had a firm manner which could not be crossed, and was not above the inflicting of an occasional stinging reprimand. He even managed to keep Edwin in line.

Walking with him one morning from the timber church where we had heard the Mass, I asked why he wore mustaches. He snorted—his way of laughing. "Now you know, stripling," he explained, "apart from priests, the Mercians are alone of all Anglishmen in refusing to wear face hair."

I asked him why.

"'Tis their way of saying they are Mercian, I suppose," he answered thoughtfully. "When you see a man with shoulder length hair sporting a clean face, you know where his allegiance lies. An Anglian says it with a thin mustache, a Saxon with cropped hair and a thick one. A North Humbrian—"

I cut him off with a shudder. "I have seen North Humbrians!" I was picturing some of my kinsmen there who had hair that reached to their elbows and was reddened with dyes and tallow. They wore rings through their ears, and had pictures burned on their skin. They seemed to think themselves fine looking indeed.

"Well," said Æthelstan, "you surely cannot mistake one!"

I fast developed a fondness for the pretty manor house we took, though it was smaller than our halls in Nottingham and Lindcylene. One long, narrow room ran the length of each side of the great hall, and my father took one of these for his private quarter. His two closest men,

Cynewulf and Ælfric White-Hair, quartered there with him, while the others lodged in timber houses elsewhere within the high palings which surrounded the estate. My mother took the room opposite his, with Aldgyth. Burchard, Edwin, and I slept in a high, rush-strewn loft above the hall with Æthelstan and a handful of other household men. We used to watch the men below, delighting in their talk and bold jesting till sleep overtook us. Still young, we had to leave the hall with the women after the board was cleared. When my father let us stay for tale-telling or minstrelsy—always in winter when night came much the sooner—we felt a thrill of special privilege.

We were not to see winter in Grantanbrycg that year, though. As Ælfgar had predicted, the Godwines made their bid for restoration and were successful. The earl had gained the lasting respect of the men of Wessex by refusing to sack Dofras, and, in his absence, lawlessness was rampant where once his mighty sword had prevailed. The folk of the south petitioned the king for the return of their protector. Meanwhile, Godwine, never a man content to let things wend their slow way, raised a great navy and harried the Anglish coast. Some of his men were mercenaries raised by his second son Harold in Eireland, but many were soldiers of his own earldom, standing with the House of Godwine against king and council. They had come to think of him as a great champion of Anglish rights; their chief spokesman against the terrible plague of Normans the king had inflicted upon them. Finally, to retain his dignity and restore peace and order, the king buckled, returning the Godwines to power and favor as if the last year had just been a terrible mistake.

Lands and holdings restored, Earl Godwine hurried to grab the reins of authority from the fast-weakening hands of the king. He exiled the Norman archbishop of Cantwaraburg, replacing him with his own pawn of a church-man, Stigand. Humiliated by the failure of his one attempt to free himself from the Godwines, Edward settled back to watch them rise unhindered.

Handsome, unlucky Sweyn the Nithing died about this time. In exile, he went mad with repent for his young cousin's murder and made a pilgrimage to Jerusalem. Beset upon by robbers, plagued by disease, he finally became what the Eirish call "moon-burned" and educated priests call "lunacy" after the lunar cycles. He fell dead raving.

No sooner had we managed to resettle our household back in Mercia than the great earl himself, Godwine Wulfnoth's son, died catatonic after suffering a terrible seizure at the king's Easter table. 'Twas less than seven months after his hard-won reinstatement. His proud, handsome second son, fair-haired Harold, succeeded him as Earl of all Wessex. As Edward had promised, my father was named Earl of East

Anglia once more. For the third time in two years, he prepared to move his entire household from one earldom to another. With these three close-spaced moves between my grandfather's domain and the East Anglia began a period within our lives of intense, urgent journeying. The sweetness and security of our former life in Mercia was to be all but forgotten in the turbulence.

CHAPTER SIX

There was a council in Lundun, and Earl Ælfgar,
son of Earl Leofric, was outlawed without having
done anything to deserve his fate.

—Anglo Saxon Chronicle
Book "C" 1055

From the first moment I ever stepped foot in the eerie, cavernous, stone stillness of the monastery at Ely, it was a place which dreaded and haunted me. There was something nightmarish in the encroaching dampness. Those stark, shadowy cloisters began to figure prominently in my dreams, good and evil, and they have ever since.

Only a few miles outside Grantanbrycg proper, Ely is a broad, large island, itself divided into many smaller, boggy islands by the meandering marsh waters. On the least accessible of these stands the monastery. Surrounded on three sides by the deep fen and on the other by perilous and often deeply flooded wood, it seems like a walled island rising from the depths of the murky swamp. There are only two practical approaches to the monastery, and the stronghold's isolation seemed frightening to me. During the thaws or in seasons of heavy rainfall, it was completely unreachable.

Though boasting little beauty, the cold place was nevertheless awesomely majestic in an ancient, rough-hewn way. The priests were dedicated, well educated, and very much at home in the swamplands where they fished, hunted, and trapped eel for a livelihood. They were manly, kind, and friendly—but the place was still intolerable to me, so strong was the unnerving feeling that it bode me only ill and sorrow.

Ælfgar, however, was fascinated by its massive grandeur, strength and inaccessibility, and resolved to make it an object of special endowment if the East Anglia remained ours after his succession in Mercia. Not long after his second appointment, when we had resettled in Grantanbrycg, he brought us there. Actually, the monks brought us; they guarded the approaches very jealously and were resolved to keep their home well protected from the whims and warfare of the outside world. Even so, they welcomed the interest and intercession of their earl, my father, for he had allotted the place in his short tenure more benefactions than ever it had received from the House of Godwine.

It was Ælfgar's plan to have us educated at Ely, but after the glorious beauty of Couventrie it seemed so somber and depressing that we begged him not to leave us there. Our father was not a hard man, and he soon gave in to us.

So for a while, we took our learning in his lodges in the manor house, but it was not long before my uncle Leofric, son of Grandfather Leofric's elder sister, took over the abbacy of the great monastery at Peterborough, as King Edward had promised. He began immediately to enrich it with prizes from my grandfather and father, as if to make up for the neglect it had suffered in its years under Godwine rule. Soon, we went there to study under his auspices. Burchard, Edwin, and I felt much more at ease within those peaceful walls.

I had always loved and admired my Uncle Leofric, a tall, strong, brown-haired Mercian man. His mother died while he was a tot. His father, Ælfgeat, was cruelly slain by the treacherous Cymrians at the side of my grandfather's famed brother, Eadwine the Welsh-Slayer. So, as was the custom, my uncle went to live as a son to his avunculus, my grandfather. He was young then, pious and scholarly but valiant and forthright, too. Some thought the earl came to favor his namesake over his own son, for the younger Leofric was of a character perfectly matched to the elder, and Ælfgar was of a more tempestuous cut. Leofric and Godiva loved both boys right well, though, and my father and his cousin esteemed each other. There was never a hint of bad blood between them.

Though he had proven himself no mean warrior, my uncle eventually chose to be made a priest, which greatly pleased my grandfather, and he lived in the rich monastery Earl Leofric had built in Couventrie. While still a very young man, my uncle became the abbot there. Both King Edward and Cwene Edythe, Earl Godwine's daughter, admired and respected him, being greatly pleased with all his good works. Uncle Leofric held other abbacies, but he loved Peterborough more dearly, not only for its ancientness and holiness, but because it had belonged to us forever before the Godwine ascendancy.

The Peterborough monastery lay some thirty miles from my father's house. My father sent his men regularly to fetch us home to Grantan-brycg to be with him, and there was constant communication between the two places. One late winter's day, Edwin, Burchard, and I were visiting with my uncle in his private lodges when Ælfgar and his men arrived unexpectedly.

Savage Earl Siward the Usurper, who had killed Earl Eadwulf and Æthelgar Bearn and stolen the North Humbria from them, had recently died. His elder son was dead, and Waltheof, the younger, was not of an age to succeed him. Even if he had been, the North Humbrians might not have accepted him, knowing Siward's claim to have been false and murderous.

The one they wanted was Ælfgar, Earl of the East Anglia, and heir to all Mercia. In the bloody, feud-ridden land north of the river Humber, the House of Leofric was revered, and sure to be preferred over the claims of assassins, children, and malicious strangers. Too, my mother was the daughter of Morcar Arngrim's son, a most respected chief of the North Humbrians before his murder. He was beloved by his people there and called Earl of the Seven Boroughs, the Danelaw name for the true Earl of the North Humbria. What is more, my father was a man well loved—bold, courageous, pious, and easy to look upon.

But it was not to be. Fearing the power our house would then wield, Harold, the young Earl of Wessex and advisor to the king, prevailed upon Edward to give the choice North Humbria to his brother, Tostig. This the king did. Tostig being Edward's firm favorite, he ignored the desires of the people there, to whom the thought of being lorded by the House of Wessex was intolerable. Godwine and his men had supported the Danish invader Canute when he warred against King Edmund Ironside and, once Canute was king, had a hand in the assassination of many good men there because of it, mayhap even Ironside himself, 'twas rumored. Northerners did not forget that easily.

My father's virtues were many, but mildness was not one of them. His temper was implacable, and on the day of this unexpected visit, he stormed into Uncle Leofric's rooms in a quivering furor. "I spit on the Godwines!" He pushed past us as if we were invisible. Pacing, he vented his rage to my uncle who tried ineffectually to calm him, saying it was both useless and treasonous to argue against the king's decision.

"I care not at all about treason! Is it not treason to deny me a holding mine by moral right? This Tostig is a nothing—an ornament of the old man king. They think us blind fools, that know not what they mean to do!"

"What do they mean to do, brother?" my uncle asked. He considered Ælfgar his brother; their tie was that strong.

"They mean to usurp every earldom, to build their rotten house over our corpses. They mean to be poised to steal the crown when Edward dies. They mean to trample us!" My father was almost breathless with the counting of their aims, and his steely eyes narrowed with hatred.

"Let this one lie, Ælfgar!" Leofric carefully worded his reply, knowing it was never an easy task to calm my father's ire. "No south-erner has ever had a voice in the far north. The folk there will determine Tostig's unfitness; it is only a matter of time before they approach the king themselves. They will lay their discomfiture before him, and Edward will realize his error. It is only a matter of some small time—"

My father spun to face him. "Think what will happen to Mercia! They will surround it, encroach from all sides, and when my father is dead they will pluck it from us like some over-ripe apple! I spit on them! And if I lie down to this indignity, they will be determined to trample us more!"

"Becalm yourself!" my uncle cried sharply.

But Ælfgar pulled away, unbending. "The Humbria is full of my kinsmen; they will support me. In the council which means to do this dirty business, we will be heard!"

"To approach them in foolish rage will be your undoing!"

"No! The cursed Godwines will be my undoing!" Ælfgar strode roughly to the door, then turned to face my brothers and me, as if noticing us for the first time.

"Know you that the House of Leofric, from which you are sprung, is the greatest house in Angland!" he cried vehemently. "Our blood was the essence of Angland before ever the Godwines were heard of in this land. Your mother's mother was wife to King Edmund Ironside, and mayhap your mother—"

Here, my uncle cut him off with a strangled cry. Ælfgar looked from one to the other of us long and hard while my uncle begged him to let his temper cool. Father's anger, though, was such that Uncle Leofric's admonitions only fed it with more fire. When he left with his men for Lundun City, he did not even seek my uncle's blessing, his usual habit.

There was silence after his infuriated exit. I asked my uncle what had caused Ælfgar's awful anger.

The good Abbot Leofric answered that it was fear. "'Tis fear which taints his breast … and mayhap the same fear will be the thing that proves his undoing, after all."

*   *   *

Not long after, in the depths of a windy, whistling night, a priest came to the room where we slept and wakened Edwin and me, briskly commanding us to dress. I could hear a tremendous commotion in my uncle's lodges, and was immediately aware that something was dread-fully amiss. Once clothed, we hastened to my uncle's side. Some of my father's men were with him, afire with urgency. Catching Edwin's eye, I could see that he shared my terror. Soon, Burchard joined us, sleepy-eyed and confused, and then Uncle Leofric told us that my father had been ordered into exile.

I was stunned! My father was Earl of the East Anglia, and the only son and heir to the great Earl of all Mercia. It was not possible that he could have been outlawed! As we clamored for information, the men decked us in furs. 'Twas obvious that time was of the essence.

"These men will take you to the monastery at Crugland tonight, there to wait for your father and the rest of his people," Uncle Leofric told us. "His ships are being readied in the mouth of the Weolud. Tomorrow you will sail."

"Wherefore do we sail, uncle?" Burchard cried. He was a tall youth and thin, nearing manhood now, with mild eyes and an alert but gentle look.

"I cannot surely say—Eireland mayhap." Uncle Leofric touched our heads affectionately, then blessed us. In minutes, we were on our way, rushing through the howling night as if Death himself were at our heels. There was sadness in my uncle's solemn gaze as he watched us depart.

Frozen with fear and suspense, we waited at Crugland three days for Ælfgar to come. We did not know that the delays were natural ones, owing to the immensity of Ælfgar's project: gathering together goods and treasure with which to buy his safety in another land. Too, it was his objective to raise funds to hire an army, above and beyond his own many men—a time-consuming venture even for a man of his status. We had been told he would be there in a day, but three had passed with no word from him. In my terrorized state, it was easy enough to consider the most alarming reasons for it.

He finally arrived, to our vast relief, accompanied by my mother and sister and a train of considerable size. To a man, his household troops had elected to follow him into exile, no small indication of the regard in which he was held. We rode to the harbor where his fleet stood ready. It was an impressive sight: thirty ships fully outfitted and men enough from Mercia and the East Anglia to sail them all.

My father was like a different man on that voyage. Cold bitterness hardened his look and was never entirely to leave him. It was the quickened, apprehensive glance of the hunted, and it took in the truth of his precarious situation in a way which we were too young even to suspect.

We had been some days at sea, and had passed through the dangerous narrows between Wessex and Flanders unmolested. The channel was comparatively gentle after the booming, churning greyness of the dismal North Sea, but owing to the wretchedness of my spirits, I scarce noted the improvement. My father came that night, stealing round to waken us each in turn. With one arm around Aldgyth's shoulder and one arm around mine, he stood with us up top, and we watched the stars fade into sunrise. The brisk salt wind, whipping through our hair and mantles, found a curious, playful echo in the flapping sails. Gathering us to him, Ælfgar eyed us, from one to the other, in the lavender half-light of early sea-dawn. All around us were the vague outlines of the other ships; he pointed out for us the ship which held our mother and her maids. Then, looking past us into the wind, he spoke.

"Tomorrow, we will look upon Eireland," he announced without ceremony. "I feel a great need now to ask this—which of any of you doubts my honor?"

"Not I, father!" we chanted in startled unison. He gazed thoughtfully for a seemingly long time before he continued.

"In the event that God's Providence settles against me, I will want to know my house is in order." The words sounded ominous. He looked directly at Burchard as he went on. "My men, every one of them, have sworn to you after me. You have seen eighteen years now and are of an age to succeed me. Your blood is as the blood of the House of Leofric to the men of the Danelaw. They accept you and will be your men as they have been mine. You, in turn, must swear to protect your sister, my golden Aldgyth—"

Here he stopped, swallowing back a rush of emotion, and stroked my sister's hair gently. When he continued, his words came furiously and fast. Not once did he meet my eyes, or Edwin's, but kept his gaze leveled at Burchard. The two of them seemed suddenly like strangers to me, speaking some foreign tongue.

"I have a blood feud with these sons of Godwine now. They have broken honor with me. Tostig, who is no rightful heir to the North Humbria, swears against my blood, even to the next generation. And Harold, goodly Earl of Wessex, has lied against me in council."

"What was the lie, father?" I asked.

"Best you hear it from me than from other men, though 'tis something I swore to your mother and to her kin that I would never boast. Some folk claim your mother, Lady Ælfgiva, was not the child of Lady Aldgyth's first husband, Siferth, nor of her third husband, Roger Malet, but of her second."

"Her second?" It took a moment.

"King Edmund Ironside!" Burchard's voice shook.

There was a palpable silence, fraught with emotion. There were folk who thought we were grandsons of the great hero king—thought we were of royal blood!

"'Tis the thing believed in Normandy—that when your grandmother Aldgyth fled there after King Edmund's untimely death, or murder, she was with child and afraid to say so. King Canute had wrested away her twin sons by the Ironside and sent them off to be slain, though the better-hearted assassin put them into exile in Hungary instead. Grandmother Aldgyth never saw her sons again and was afraid the child she carried would be stolen, too. So she wed quickly, and when the babe was born, she gave it the name of King Edmund Ironside's own mother: Ælfgiva."

The four of us were stunned. "Is it true?" Burchard managed. My father shrugged.

"Most who could know for certain are dead. Your mother wants not to consider it; 'tis just another thing calculated to heap sorrows on her. Must be you know that, if true, there are a greedy and envious many who would hate and hunt you for it. William Malet believes secret is the better way to keep this. Just the hinting at it could cause great strife. Harold Godwine's son said in council that I believed it and had boasted of it; I should have nay-sayed him then, but my anger made me ask him why he feared that it might be true. They marked it as treason against me—and here we are!"

He exhaled heavily, and his shoulders slumped as if he had finally rid himself of some great weight. "Even so, 'tis best you know that some men think it of you. You will know how to answer them when they accuse you of base ambition!"

Burchard straightened. "So they have accused you of ambition, father—for us? Then I am sworn to fight with you now, to exonerate and avenge you."

His tight-lipped, determined stare made Burchard look different; he seemed a full-grown man of a sudden. I had no time to marvel on it, though, because my father's next words shocked me. "If you hear I am murdered or dead, see yourself and your brothers in safety to Normandy. Swear that you will champion them when they are of an age to assert their claims."

"I swear it!" Burchard stood firmly, inflexibility in his look. 'Twas true—he was much more a man now than a boy. He repeated himself, and Ælfgar smiled, then hugged him. It was a manly embrace, the sealing of a vow.

"They are not to step foot in Angland again until they have attained manhood, and then only with sworn men behind them. If I die, no place in the kingdom will be safe for them unless they are strong enough to fight for their station. These Godwines mean to have no rival earls. Your mother has kinsmen of high blood in Angland, and in Normandy—"

Burchard cut him off with an angry gesture. "William Malet, my mother's-brother, serves your enemy, Harold of Wessex!" The fiery voice was not like Burchard's at all.

My father gave a short laugh. "Nay! He serves King Edward, my son! He will ever serve the man who is king! He does not care that old Edward has become a pawn of the Godwines, because to him the king is the king and that is all there is to it. Even so, he has sworn to your mother that he will see to your safety and protection—and the rest of your house after. Edwin and Morcar are heirs behind you. Safe passage to Normandy is assured if I come to death in this venture."

Something in me panicked then. I scarce could imagine life if my father were dead—his handsome, indomitable brashness was the strength of my very life. Both Edwin and I tried to interrupt but he silenced us grimly. The morning sea mist settled cold against me and I shivered.

*   *   *

Like an ominous threat, the gravity of my father's words that night hung over me many a week, and so prevented the mystical beauty of Eireland from entirely captivating me at first. The initial glimpse of her was breathtaking enough, shining as she was through the filtered, sun-streaked dawn, like a precious green gem-stone rising from the depths of the churning ocean. By the time we disembarked, though, and after hurried councils and political bargaining, the precariousness of our situation was brought home to me again with disarming clarity. There was nothing in all my former life with which to compare the utter helplessness I felt now, a stranger in a land of foreign people and unfamiliar customs. I was not prepared for the primitiveness of the place.

My father had petitioned the Ard Ri, High King of all Eireland, for our safety, and he had granted it, quartering us in the camp of the mighty o'Briens, his own kinsmen, descended from the great warrior king, Brien Boru. These o'Briens were auburn-haired, green-eyed Gaels, stocky, strong, and broad of shoulder. They reminded me much of the North Humbrians of my own country, having long, wild hair, plaited at random, gold and silver rings through their ears, and designs burned on their skin. All of them were great warriors, but their fierceness was tempered by a habit of mind which set poetry at a level with battle-making, and attached as great an importance to music as to skill in arms.

To a boy as young as I, there was something frightening in their wildness, in their propensity to live almost entirely out of doors—and there was something inexplicably horrible about hearing them refer to my father as "the outlaw." My mother avoided them studiously, locking herself away with her own country-women in the small daub-and-wattle country house given over to her use. Because of Ælfgiva's excessive beauty, her obvious wealth and rank, and the distress of her situation, her coldness was forgiven her. She was held in a sort of reverential awe by even the highest born Eirish women. When she condescended to eat or walk with them, they considered it an honor, and gathered around her with gentle flatteries and pleasant words. My mother waxed more yielding then and would call us to her, petting and attending to us more often than was her wont. This did much to relieve us of the peculiar sense of abandonment we felt at Father's hands. Engrossed in the mean business of making alliances and recruiting mercenaries, he was seldom seen except at a distance.

In those first weeks he was constantly on the move. We saw him here and there, directing his household men, overseeing those newly sworn to him, talking, story-telling, and then, suddenly, making preparations to take to the sea again. He was sailing to Wales.

The Welsh were our hereditary enemies! As far back as any Mercian could remember there had been battle with the Cymrian hill people. It was primarily the Mercians who felt the sting of their murderous warfare, for Grandfather's earldom bordered the Cymrian states, and the definition of the borders is what always prompted the bloody disputes.

My uncle Leofric's father, the great warrior Ælfgeat, had died in battle against the Welsh, as had Grandfather's brother, Eadwine the Welsh-Slayer, and many other of our kinsmen. What business my father meant to have with Gruffydd, king of the Cymry, I could not imagine. Even so, Ælfgar sailed with a portion of his troops one mild May morn. We were not to see him or hear word of him for four long months.

CHAPTER SEVEN

Thereupon he went to Ireland, and added a force of
eighteen ships to his own household troops, and
sailed to Wales to King Gruffydd with that host;
and he took them under his protection.

—Anglo Saxon Chronicle,
Book "C," 1055

The chief of all the o'Briens in that place was Eamon, cousin to the Ard
Ri, and he had two sons, Eamon and Eoghan. After some time, they
began to lean towards friendship with us, particularly Eoghan, who was
the younger and only a year older than Edwin. At first, it was a comrade-
ship built upon competitiveness. The Eirish were constantly at games
and sports—hunting, birding, and riding—and it was inborn in them to
be ever proving themselves best at one thing or another. This eventually led to a mutual respect between us, Edwin and Eoghan being particularly well matched both in skills and temperament. It pleased the
o'Briens well, too, that my brother and I picked up easily on their
haunting, clear-toned Eirish airs. As the lilting, windy spring gave way
to cloudless summer days, we found ourselves more and more at their
sides. Whenever she could, Aldgyth joined us. It was her thirteenth
summer and she was fast becoming a rare and beautsome blossom.

One warm, whistling night, we sat all together in the eerie dark,
awaiting a long-promised rain storm. Burchard, who spent most of his
time with the men now, was with us. We had removed ourselves from
the main circle of activity with the wary permission of my father's man
Æthelstan, who forever watched over us like a brooding hawk. From a
grassy hillock above the camp, we watched folk below hurrying to and
fro, silhouetted against the orange glow of the huge fire. Occasionally,
voices carried to us on frenzied bursts of hollow wind. 'Twas a night
made for Eirish story-telling—for tales of warrior's spirits and the heads
of saints, the horror-laden revenges of dead chieftains, and the trem-

bling terror of the banshee. It was the night we met the Filidh.

They came up behind us out of the dark nowhere, so silent that one of them had cried a greeting before we knew they were there. The unsurpassed chillingness of that voice caused us to jump, but no cry escaped us, so fright-stricken were we at their sudden apparition. Even Burchard was speechless.

It was difficult at first to perceive their shapes. They bore on their shoulders great, heavy packs indiscernible from the shadowy darkness and wore long, sweeping dalmatics, embroidered with luminous silver threads. They were bearded, and their hair was exceedingly long. I stood dumb-struck in the howling black night, wondering at the ghostly ancientness of the six of them until, at last, one of them spoke again.

"Bear you no greeting to the Walking Wisdom, Filidh of the Tuatha?" he asked. I heard Eoghan's muffled cry of awe.

Uninvited, they sat down, but one of them reached out, tousling Edwin's flaxen hair. "Who are the Gall you have amongst you, sons of the o'Brien?" he asked.

"Mercians," Eamon answered, and his brother whispered to us as that to the Eirish, any foreigner was Gall: a strange one. Once the initial shock had subsided, the men seemed more intriguing than frightening. "Filidh of all the Tribes" they had called themselves in Gaelic. I wondered what strange title this was, and what meaning it held for my Eirish friends.

One of the strangers spoke. "So you wonder what word there is in Anglish to describe the Filidh, fair-haired one?"

Had he read my mind? I nodded.

"If I say to you I am of the Filidh, I tell you I am a poet knowing the secret of words, and a thaumaturge from whom no whispered knowledge is hidden. I tell you I am a worker of miraculous deeds, and a singer of indecipherable songs—historian, wizard, physician, and reader of inner thoughts." Over the distant lowing of thunder-rumble I heard my own hollow heartbeat. Instinctively, I moved closer to Edwin as the voice, fraught with wisdom, continued.

"If I say to you I am of the Filidh, I tell you I am the dreamer of dreams, the great Fragmentizer of Time, to whom present, past, and future are but smiles upon a single face."

Excited, Edwin leant forward. "Can you read my fate?"

"You have no fate. Fate is a word for fools."

"Can you tell me what will happen?"

"I can tell you there is one in this circle whose past has been longer than his future will be. And that he is not one of the Filidh."

"One of the Gall or one of us?" Eamon cried fearfully.

"That would be telling," came the answer.

Edwin began another question, but Aldgyth stilled him. "Seek for nothing that it will bode you ill to know!" she cried. "Besides, Grandfather would be greatly vexed to know you petitioned from fore-sayers!"

"Must be your grandfather is a wise man," another of the Filidh said knowingly. "The future is never less than a threat, never more than a promise." He had lowered his pack to the ground, and he searched inside until he found a little pouch of kidskin which he handed to Aldgyth.

"Will you accept this token, glass-eyed twice-cwene? For without saying the future, I can tell a portion of the possible, and I know it will not offend you. For you sit amongst the high-born, and are high-born yourself. And two, high-born with you, will hold more than your father holds now, but they will not hold it with less anguish, and you in turn will hold all that is theirs yourself—but 'twill be stolen from your very hands."

Clutching the pouch tightly, Aldgyth wore look of wonder. "You called me twice-cwene!" she exclaimed low.

"I called you truly."

"Mean you I will wed a great king?"

"That would be telling."

"What is in the bag then?"

"Leaves and seeds of knit-bone, reaped in the high mountains of Italy. You will need this to soothe the wounds of the two I spoke of before, for they, too, will be victims of robbers. Three times you will open this pouch—not for one person, not for three...."

In the brilliance of a lightning-flash, the faces around me flared into being, their somber, awe-struck gazes tempered each with a different essence: Edwin with boldness, Aldgyth with graciousness, Burchard with patient understanding. The Eirish I did not take note of in that split second, but the Filidh—their streaming hair, embroidered robes, and wizened faces frozen at that very instant in horrific splendor by the hauntingly garish light—were seared forever into my memory with crystalline precision.

Suddenly, Edwin broke the silence, his clear voice tinged with brashness and mild contempt. "'Tis easy to speak deeply when one speaks in useless riddles!"

Aghast, I nudged him with no little gentleness, but before he could react, one of the Filidh reached out and touched his long fingers lightly to my brother's chest, as if feeling for a heartbeat. I felt Edwin tremble as the wise one spoke in an awesome tone.

"All hail the boldness of the first-born son!"

Burchard and I exchanged a glance, wondering how the old man had known Burchard had no portion of our father's blood. We had not long to muse on it for he soon enough continued, in a milder but still disquieting voice.

"It happens that you will be a well-favored one, singular in beauty and filled inside with poetry. Men will glimpse this poetry in your gentleness and winning address, and even enemies will love you for it. But take care that it escapes you not, pouring out as rebelliousness or evaporating into darlingness. For when it flees your insides, you will miss it sorely enough to desire death. And you will be hard-pressed to hold on to it. Impassioned wildness—that will be your bane! Noble vehemence bespeaks your virtue—but beware! In eyes so intense, anger always brings the look of madness."

I do not suppose that Edwin, whose ashen look said he shared my own tremulous emotions, meant to make any answer to this mysteriously apt portraiture. At any rate, he had no chance, for the sky, so long overburdened with the imminent rain, now gave way to a swift, torrential downpour. Through the sound of it came the shoutings of my father's men, beckoning us with insistent urgency.

In the grip of what compulsion I know not, I leapt up and, without knowing why, I ran. I ran with all the force and might of my boyish being headlong down the wet, rolling hill as if answering a summons on which my life depended. Fists clenched and heart pounding with some unnamable sentiment, I threw myself into the storming darkness, overwhelmed by a feeling I could not hope to understand. It was not fear; more, it was a certain hollowness of foreboding which had come upon me, inspired by the way that stranger had put into words what should have remained unspoken, secret insights. I idolized Edwin then, and the strange one had spoken of things which had not yet unfolded. Somehow I truly knew they were impending. His words bode not well by me, either.

Too, I might have dreaded that the Filidh, one or the other, might have looked to me next, exacted from my manner the very essence of my fate, and put it into words. 'Twas a possibility from which I or any other boy of such keen and tumultuous sensitivity would surely have recoiled in panic.

Oblivious of all but my own heedless flight, it was an astounding sensation to feel myself suddenly lifted off my feet like a squirming, unwilling kitten. I found I was tight in the strong grip of my father's man, Æthelstan, who, realizing in an instant the depth of my agitation, demanded gruffly to know the whereabouts of Edwin and Burchard. When I assured him they were safe, he silently signaled the men alongside him to search up the hill for them. Soaking and bedraggled, he looked particularly fierce, but he was kind enough not to question me then or charge me with an explanation of my anxiety. Instead, he calmly carried me back to the noisy, smoky commotion of the hall. Shielding me from the alarmed exclamations of the others who crowded round us, he bade them leave us privately. They withdrew, staring curiously as we dried ourselves at the crackling fire.

Æthelstan was an ominous figure, a tall, square-shouldered warrior of some forty-five year's seasoning, brown of hair and eye. Largely mystified by my own irrational behavior, I could not quite decide what to tell him, but I knew that I was shaking and that however patiently he waited, I would sooner or later have to make an accounting.

For a long time he eyed me with a look of detached interest and sympathy and when it seemed I could stand the silence no longer, he unexpectedly spoke. "When your father came as earl to the East Anglia the first time, I liked the man for his boldness and I swore to him then. My word is true; that is why I followed him to Mercia when he lost the Anglia, and that is why I went back to the Anglia with him when it came his again."

He paused momentarily. His hawk eyes latched onto me in a discomfiting way which made me squirm. "Too," he resumed in his deep, steady voice, "that is why I followed him into exile, leaving all my lands and properties in the hands of lesser thegns and women. Earl Ælfgar is no mean fool; he knows the value of a word sworn in brotherhood. That is why he asked me, shipboard even before we came here, if he could trust me to protect his well-prized children. He petitioned me, of all men, because he knew that if he heard me answer yea, then his children—his heirs and underlings—would be safe until the outcome. That is the trust between an earl and his man. That is why, when an earl rides into battle with his select-guard round about him, he is secure. It is the knowing that their word sworn to him is of more import than life and of greater consequence than mean death itself."

I knew what he was leading up to, and I was truly abashed, groping for some excuse to hand him, when he continued, still staring at me as if to wring the truth of my predicament from out of my nervous looks.

"Now, I see that you have been threatened, stripling, but by whom or what I cannot say. As your protector, think you not I am in dire straits? Having given my word to my lord, your father, should I not know what it is that sends you dashing frenzied into the night, shaking like a new-born hare in a fox-den?"

Gazing steadfastly into the impressive sharpness of his eyes, I answered; the level coolness of my voice surprised me. "You truly have proven yourself well, Æthelstan, man of Grantanbrycg, and I would be the last to deny your duty—but I can tell you truly that no fear of harm is upon me."

"Fear of what then?"

"That I cannot rightly say," I answered miserably, looking away again. "I would that I could."

His voice softened. "Then you will tell me—someday," he said, placing a hand atop my head and turning me to face him. I was filled with a surprisingly comfortable sense of assurance when I saw his soothing smile. Delighted with his clemency, I accepted a handful of berries which he proffered. I might have been fooled into thinking him even gentle, but just then, Aldgyth and my brothers were escorted to the fireside. The moment he caught sight of their soaking, disheveled condition, his eyes once more became stern and unyielding, and his voice assumed its familiar harshness.

I was never again, however, entirely cowed by his grimness, and the day did finally come that I told him of the Filidh and all their dismaying words.

*   *   *

Among ourselves, we did not speak of the unnerving strangeness of that night, and the Eirish held their mystics in too great an esteem to make use of my embarrassment against me. Besides, within a very few days came long-awaited news which was to entirely alter our circumstances and overshadow everything else with its import.

It was a blossoming, fair, late-summer's afternoon. Edwin and I were off exploring on horseback when four riders galloped into view, Burchard at their head. We strained to understand the gist of his bellowed message. At the same instant, Edwin and I caught the phrase "ships from father" and took off like madmen, ignoring the curses and protests of the bewildered Æthelstan, who hovered nearby.

From the grassy crest overlooking the harbor, we saw the ships, one of them the the great, gilded dragon of the East Anglia, my father's personal transport. We made our way down the rolling hillside, following the stony course to the o'Brien's hall in the valley.

There, many men were gathered; some I recognized as my father's household men, others were dark, curiously garbed strangers whom we instinctively knew to be Cymrians. We caught snatches of conversation, but no word of my father. Tumbling from my mount and not bothering to tether or secure her, I dashed wildly into the hall, expecting at any moment to see my father's watchful, handsome face, and feel the grip of his strong hand.

But he was not there, and the sight of his chief man, Cynewulf Cenwulf's son, sitting at table between the elder Eamon and my grave-faced mother, entirely crushed my hope. The tall Mercian motioned us toward him and when we reached his side, he smiled, then spoke in a low voice. "Your father, Earl Ælfgar, bids me gather his children and their safe-guards, and their honored mother, and carry them to him where he now does his business with the king of the Cymry, Gruffydd, his sworn brother and protector."

Breathless, Edwin echoed my amazement. "What peace has he made with the Welsh king, that it amounts to brotherhood?"

Cynewulf began to make an answer but before scarce a word escaped him, my mother leapt to her feet and in a venomous tone answered Edwin herself. "He makes an ill-considered peace, I trow—casting his lady to pagans as a token, and trading his children away as blood-hostages! This is how highly your sacred father values the lot of us!"

With that, she gathered her skirts and stomped furiously away, leaving my father's normally unmovable man staring after her open-mouthed. Then burst in Æthelstan, who strode purposefully forward. Grasping each other's shoulders in the greeting that was the sign of their sworn camaraderie, Cynewulf and Æthelstan fell immediately into an animated analysis of their earl's predicament. Listening intently to their unguarded conversation, I learnt all that was relative to my father's situation.

"What bargain made he?" was Æthelstan's first question.

"Simple enough. For men in arms to stand in force behind him, he promises the lands west of the river Dee when he is named Earl of Mercia. Meanwhile, the greater part of the spoils, wherever in Angland they harry, goes to the Welsh."

"What think you?"

"Fair enough. Earl Ælfgar was surely wronged yet no man knows more than he how sorely he will need might behind him to force an apology and a restoration from the Godwine dogs. Those are rare lands he offers, but he buys with them the future security of his house. He means to make this brotherhood stand so that when Leofric dies the Godwines will not be able to strangle in on him from all sides the way they have planned it. When they make their move, 'twill be upon a Mercia united with Wales, and even with Tostig in the North Humbria they will be hard-pressed to break us then!"

Æthelstan gave a low whistle, and in the pensiveness of his look I could read the import of my father's dealings. "And this Welshman?" he asked, brows knit in consternation. "He means to honor this brother-hood indefinitely?"

Smiling slyly, Cynewulf had the look of one man impressed with another. "They have the same enemy," he said simply, and I remem-bered hearing how the Godwines—unlucky Sweyn, now dead, and

Harold, and Tostig—had wreaked havoc all through the Cymry on their blood campaigns.

"Gruffydd seems an honorable man," Cynewulf continued after a thoughtful silence. "He is forthright and much like Earl Ælfgar in his quickness and bold bearing, and I saw his true regard for my lord. A feeling like to kinship was genuine between them. You know well as any that Ælfgar has resolute fineness as a reader of men, despite his ungovernableness—and his foul taste in wives."

Suddenly remembering that Edwin and I were avidly listening, glint-eyed Cynewulf bit his lip in embarrassment and cast us an apologetic, if not repentant, look. As for me, I gave his words no heed. Such discourtesies where my mother was concerned were commonplace. Unlike Grandmother Godiva, for whom anyone in all of Mercia would have gladly laid down his life over an insult, Mother never had gained the love or favor due an earl's lady. The combination of her coldness, the bitterness of her tongue, and her unfeeling disregard for my father, had won her instead an unfavorable distinction, only mildly redeemed by her elegant dignity and the stateliness of her beauty, which did not dim with years.

"You needn't think you have shamed yourself!" Edwin was quick to reassure him. "Only tell us now what she meant by saying he had sworn us away as hostages!"

Now, recalling my mother's words, I was filled with dismay. There was no word more dreaded. It was not a dishonor to be named hostage; it was a mark of rank and distinction, and most hostages were treated with respect and accorded all the privileges of their station. Yet there was a dismal drawback: it was rare for such a bond-person ever to see family or homeland again. This cheerless aspect was uppermost in my mind as I heard Cynewulf confirm the dire pronouncement.

I will not waste detail on the journey to Wales for I scarce remember it. Seemed I was passively borne on the whims of circumstance in those days, and now was merely being carried away yet again. Saying fare-well to my Eirish friends was hard, but not particularly emotional. Most of the short voyage I slept, for as I related before, I am not and was not then a sea-loving creature. I do recall an odd mixture of dread, which centered upon my future prospects in the land of Cymry, and a burning anticipation to see my father, both permeated by a thrilling sense of danger and a peculiar sense of helpless resignation.

Elsewise, I remember little.

CHAPTER EIGHT

To Tostig, son of Earl Godwine, the king gave the
earldom which had previously been Earl Siward's.
Earl Ælfgar sought Gruffydd's protection in Wales.

Anglo Saxon Chronicle
Book "E" 1055

In the Cymry, we disembarked in the circlet of a deep bay with sloping
shores wooded by evergreens and shadowed by a promontory of dense
forest, whose mossy boughs overhung a scene of delightful wilderness.
Traveling for some time in the bold pink and purple brilliance of
autumnal sunset, we followed a road of sea-sand along which the line of
waves burst with a sound like thunder, casting up a mist of cold,
lavender luster. Turning inland and uphill, our party looked down upon
a narrow, circular vale suddenly disclosed in the midst of lofty hills, and
only accessible through a gate-like chasm in the rock wall of mountains
which had gradually surrounded us without our even knowing it. A
shower of declining sunlight illuminated a sprawling complex of primitive stone halls and battlements below, massive in proportion, of singularly simple architecture. This, said our Cymrian guides, was the quarter
of the Welsh warrior king, Gruffydd; I thought it inexpressibly grand. In
the last minutes before darkness, after a steep but easy descent, we
approached it, welcomed by a noisy throng of torch-bearing Welshmen.

The tremendous enclosed yard was well-lit by bonfires crossed by
spits loaded with sizzling meats, whose aromas hung tantalizingly in air
already heavy with smoke and mist. We saw many hundreds of warriors,
recognizable by their apparel as variously Eirish, Anglish, or Welsh. The
Cymrians who sailed with us had seemed curious to me in their full,
circular skirts of fringed doe and kidskin. Seeing this unusual costume in
such profusion, it no longer seemed strange now, but the Cymrians still
looked alien with their dark features and heavily bearded faces.

I walked as close to Burchard as I could possibly get; the great multitude of fierce-looking men frightened me. They pressed in upon us as we fought to make our way to the center of the immense, crowded court-yard, where stood the largest of the looming square buildings. As its massive oaken doors swung open, Cynewulf separated us from the rest of the party, so that only our family, with twenty or so of our retainers, entered into the comparatively quiet emptiness.

Inside, the hall hardly differed from the outer court. Stone walls enclosed a deeply rush-strewn floor, in the center of which blazed a magnificent fire. The room was only partially roofed and totally unfurnished. At one end was a raised wooden dais, behind which the walls were hung with skins and furs. In each corner of this platform blazed pitch torches, so that it was well-lit. At one end of it, a great quantity of furs were heaped in sad disarray, and from them Cynewulf pulled a number of thick ones and tossed them carelessly upon the floor. He offered my mother and sister such to sit upon. Lady Ælfgiva looked mortified, but being weary and seeing there was nowhere else to rest, she finally lowered herself miserably and sat, shivering with discomfort, eyes closed as if to blot out the distressing barrenness which surrounded her. I wasted no time but collapsed immediately, and my brothers followed suit. I could not remember ever being so tired.

I drifted in and out of sleep. At length there was a bustling and commotion as several men entered bearing an abundance of food. The richness of the proffered feast belied the primitiveness of the habitat: roasted meats of various description, savory venison and well-roasted boar, white kid-meat and veal served with plums and honeyed barley. Earthen bowls held fruits, nuts, and seeds of every order, and there were platters of soft cheeses wrapped in salt-soaked linen.

As we relaxed with the repast, all began to converse and speculate until only my mother was silent. Scrupulously avoiding her contemptuous looks, Cynewulf had just launched into an animated and brilliant description of Ælfgar's ever-growing war fleet when a sudden clamor erupted outside—a rumbling of triumphant shouts which increased to a thunderous roar, awesome to hear. The great doors swung open, revealing a handsome array of horsemen just dismounting. The exuberant host jostled into the hall, and I recognized many of my father's men amongst them, the soft colors of their Mercian garb standing out well against the earthy tones of the Cymrians' hides and leathers.

As the tumult rose to a deafening din, Ælfgar rode mounted through the doors, arm held high in salute. An imposingly comely figure, especially in arms, there was nevertheless something new and breathtaking in the strength of his look. He was bearded, and I had never seen him but clean-shaven before. His streaming hair was sunbleached, and he was so tanned and freckled by the sun that even by fire-light the difference was notice-able. But the thing which had changed most was the gleam of his iron blue eyes—there was an angry glint to them now which animated all his features. Spotting us, he gleamed a broad, victorious smile, but once he had dismounted, it was his men and the ecstatic Burchard whom he greeted first as was the custom, vigorously gripping their shoulders in manly welcome. Then he looked past to my mother, who had not risen from her position on the dais. She would not lift her sullen eyes to meet his searching ones so, at last, he turned to us. It was a joyful reunion indeed.

A second rider came in, his men heaving the doors into place behind him as if to keep out the din of the jubilant soldiers who clam-ored after. I stared in wonderment at the magnificence of the man's bearing. Dark and fire-eyed, he scrutinized us solemnly as he nimbly dismounted, his every movement a study in masculine power. As he moved to Ælfgar's side, I saw that they stood shoulder to shoulder and I knew at once what man this was. Gruffydd of Llewllyn lacked the patri-cian fineness of my father's aristocratic look, but his mien and manner were decidedly regal, and there was a lordliness about him unsettling in its forcefulness.

He strode to the dais, and with a sweeping gesture offered courtesy to my mother. He took her tiny hand and raised her to her feet. "My lord Ælfgar's lady!" he announced loudly. His voice was strong and pleasant, and he displayed her like a delicate treasure.

This respecting of women must have been the Cymrian way, for when he returned to us he greeted Aldgyth first, even before Burchard. He looked her up and down as if undecided whether to greet her as woman or child. Her pleasure was obvious when he called her "Lady," and when he took her hand, a rose blush lit her pale cheek. My father gazed on her with pride undisguised. The king then took Burchard's shoulders in greeting, and to our surprise, he greeted Edwin and then me in the same way, like men, speaking in low, earnest tones.

"You are well-come, sons of Ælfgar. Take table with me and my brother-lord, your father, for your company he has sorely missed. So well has he spoken of you, that I am anxious to earn your friendship!"

His Anglish was halting and formal, but his voice friendly and his smile intoxicating. Gazing into the scintillating darkness of his eyes, I knew I was his friend forever, and all I had ever heard of the ancient enmity between his land and ours was forgotten, wholly and totally.

So it was that Edwin and I went to sit, for the first time, with men at meal, feeling very proud and adult. We spoke of many things—of Mercia and Grandfather, of the East Anglia and Eireland, of the cursed Godwine's sons, and of a hundred other things relative to the turbulent wrath which had become my father's driving force.

My father looked very fine that night, flushed with an irresistible excitement which fired the enthusiasm of his whole company of men, just as the sight of him in arms, with his kingly blood-brother alongside, had roused the entire camp to furious impetuosity and hunger for revenge. There was something almost entrancing about his vehemence and glistening indignance when he spoke. Several times he caught me staring full upon him and he flashed a private smile. Now and again, he looked past me to my mother with an aspect full of some strange passion. She did not return his gaze.

As the night wore on, I began to drift in and out of a sleepy confusion, which embarrassed me, sitting as I was at the men's table. Once or twice I saw Edwin swallow back a threatening yawn, but he was not much better than I at disguising his blear-eyed drowsiness. It was strange to me that Burchard and Æthelstan and Cynewulf could seem so unaffected after journeying as far and hard as we had that day. I supposed it to be a reward that came with age, this indifference to fatigue, like face-hair and wine-tolerance. Even as I thought about it, I felt my head nodding, and before I could hope to halt it, a great, gaping yawn had escaped me. At its very zenith, I caught the Cymrian's eye straight upon me, twinkling with kind amusement.

"I feel that the hour grows unfortuitously late," I heard him say. He commanded his horse be brought to him, and there was a scrambling to do his bidding. Blushing red as berries, I had never before been so ashamed of my boyishness, and I think that was why I was so taken aback when I caught him winking at me! It was a gesture calculated to please, and it did the trick, putting me at an immediate comfort.

"This hall I have given over to my brother-lord, your father, for his use and for his household," Gruffydd told us as he stood to go. I was somewhat surprised.

"This is the largest of the halls, my lord! And why is it that you call for a mount when you mean to go only a short distance to another building?"

"Your father will tell you that it takes a great perverseness of nature to make Gruffydd, son of Llewellyn, sleep beneath a roof! And would I not be a fool to pick a hall within this stone yard to take up lodging in?"

Confused, I was at a loss to answer. "But is this complex not the quarter of the Cymrian king, yourself?"

"Indeed it is, little Mercian! But if I lived here, men would know where to find me, would they not? So you and your brothers here are now partakers of the greatest of my secrets: that I never am where men expect me to be."

As I pondered this piece of logic, Gruffydd took his leave, and the Cymrians who had been in the hall followed him swiftly and silently. As the doors swung closed, we heard them riding off into the night, far beyond the stone shelter of the battlements which surrounded us. I doubted I would I ever understand these enigmatic people, this fascinating king. Tired, I turned and watched Ælfgar lift Aldgyth from my mother's lap, kissing my sister's hair gently before he laid her in a quiet corner of the raised platform on a pile of furs, then covering her with more of the same.

Cynewulf, Ælfric White-Hair, and a dozen or so of my father's chief men remained inside that big empty hall but, out of deference, they took to far corners. Even in the greatest lodges at home, privacy was a rare thing, and only the mildest whisper could pass unheard. But there, at least, we were separated from each other by hangings, sometimes by true timber walls. Here, there was nothing between any of us but a willingness to ignore what we heard. So I was vexed and horrified to hear my parents exchange their first bitter words and furious whisperings. Always it was like this—my mother's hateful contempt gathering momentum until it became stinging cruelty; Ælfgar's untamed anger rising into passionate fury. Then breathing and sighing and shuddering, and we knew he was having his way with her. Pulling the furs as tight over my head as I could, I closed my mind to it and made myself sleep.

*　　　　*　　　　*

By cock's crow I was awake. I lay flat upon my back and took in the details of the immense room by dawn-light. Not far from me, Edwin slept a restless, tossing sleep, and beyond him Aldgyth's breath came even and regular. Already, Burchard knelt in morning prayer; it had always been his habit to rise in darkness as the priests did. My mother lay curled on her side; my father was gone. Some men were tending the fire, coaxing it back from smoldering ember. Through the roofless portion above it, the sky promised fair blueness and soft wind, all laden with mountain mistiness and bird-song.

Outside, all was in motion. I found my father finishing a break-fast of cold quail with the Welsh king, laughing and smiling within a circle of men. I would have to get used to seeing him tanned and bearded. The difference was pronounced by daylight, giving him a strange look, primitive and unkempt, much the way the Eirish had struck me. Meeting my searching gaze, Ælfgar flashed a broad, gleaming smile of welcome. "Smallest of my underlings," he grinned, "and first to come for provender!"

I blushed but took the bread and fruit he offered and ate hungrily of it. All the while I fed, I watched my father and the Welshman Gruffydd, delighting in their animated conversation. They were comfortable with each other and I could see in the ease of their conduct the signs of the soul-sensed kinship which Cynewulf had remarked upon. After a while, Gruffydd tousled my hair. "Gather up your brothers, little king's man, and we will take you to see your father's war fleet so you may remember his power and triumph!"

I sprang to my feet with no cajoling. Ælfgar winked as I took off. Before much longer, we were mounted, and in the middle of a mixed party of Welsh and Anglish, riding east into the golden shine of the sun. The wind-whipped wildness of the stony countryside delighted me, and the invigorating air was like a balm, healing the tender sense of help-lessness which had long assailed me. When we came to the wide, purple River Dee, not much of a ride east from the camp, Ælfgar pointed out the rolling fields and land mist across the ragged banks.

"There lies Mercia!" he called, and I strained to look. In truth, it looked no different than the Cymrian land, and very little resembled the reaches of the Staethford Shire, or Lindcylene, which were the Mercia I knew.

"These are the lands you pledge to King Gruffydd?" Burchard asked, drawing up alongside him, shielding his eyes from the sun which was higher now.

My father nodded aye. "The lands from there most all the way to Ceaster—a wide way of good ground."

I was puzzled. It was ordinary land—pretty, pale, fertile, flowered meadow and riff, but otherwise unremarkable. I did not want to consider that this was what so many of my kinsmen and Gruffydd's had perished over. I refused to accept that Grandfather Leofric's brother, Eadwine the Welsh-slayer, of whom I had heard only tales of boldness and daring, had died for a field. Or that Uncle Leofric's father, Ælfgeat Sword-Stopper, had murdered and been murdered for some miles of rolling grasslands. It was a fact of life I could not conceive of then.

"The coastal line, the inlets, the mouth of the river Dee, and the strength of the history—these are the things more precious than those pretty leas, little friend!" I turned to see the Welsh king staring full upon me, his face solemn and appreciative of my quiet reflection. I smiled to think that he could pick up on an unsaid feeling so quickly.

Turning along the river, we rode at a brisk pace, listening to Gruffydd's bold recounting of the border wars, embroidered by the stories my father remembered. Some of these we had heard many times, and others were new to us.

"All along this stretch between the Clwyd and the Dee, the disputes have been harsh," said Gruffydd, "But any Cymrian, or Mercian for that matter, will tell you that the battles here have been as boy's-play compared to those fought in the Archen-Field, along the Welsh border of the area you Anglish call the Hereford Shire."

My father bristled. The Hereford Shire was a sorry subject with our house, since King Edward had taken it from my grandfather to form an earldom for his Norman nephew Ralf, whom the Mercians had snidely named "the Timid." When Earl Ralf proved incapable of guarding the dangerous Archen-Field against Cymrian invasion, the king had it peopled with the fiercest fighters of the kingdom—contentious, highly-paid mercenaries who conducted constant raids into the Cymrian lands, even far beyond the contested territories. They were known for banditry and murderous cruelty to women and children. Being men of little or no conscience, they had become a despicable curse to the Welsh, and Gruffydd's hatred of the Hereford Shire men was very apparent.

"They say there is not a priest or a monk in all of Hereford that is not first and foremost a warrior."

My father agreed. "Except for their prelate, old and blind, they wear mustaches and arms like any West Saxon soldiers. They are fierce, too, every one a blood-letter!"

"We Welsh have much to avenge in the Archen-Field," Gruffydd of Llewellyn said solemnly, staring at Ælfgar as if to challenge him. My father took the cue.

"It would appease me well to revenge the robbery of Mercian lands!" he said firmly. A meaningful look passed between them.

By then we had ridden many hours, and the scenery as we approached the sea grew craggy and profoundly solitary. To our left loomed dark, woody hills, while the River Clwyd on our right outgrew its languid roll and became alive with the churning promise of ocean. The cool mistiness of the water and air combined to breathe a briskness into the wind-kissed atmosphere which affected a curious sense of anticipation. This was gratified as we mounted a stony promontory which dropped off suddenly in precipitous majesty, the edge of which overlooked a wide and picturesque bay. Gasping with amazement, my brothers and I looked directly down upon the war fleet my father had gathered, a huge force of many ships.

No one said anything for a long time, only gazed with untold emotion on the magnificent spectacle below, the visible confirmation of my father's power and the means of our liberation from exile. The force of men hurrying about their business below was as great as the army we had left behind in the Welsh king's quarter at Rhuddlan. Had they known their lords were above them they would have no doubt greeted them both with the same overwhelming enthusiasm we had witnessed the night before in the crowded camp. I looked at my father, and in the proud, bitter satisfaction of his grim smile I found, for the first time since we had taken to flight, a sense of hope and security. I drank of it thirstily, and was flooded with peace.

It was just a matter of time.

CHAPTER NINE

In this year Gruffydd and Ælfgar burnt to the
ground St. Æthelberht's cathedral and all the
borough of hereford. . ."

—Anglo Saxon Chronicle
Book "E" 1055

They ravaged in the Hereford Shire. After defeating Earl Ralf and his militia, they burned, plundered, and wasted the town to smoldering rubble. By the time Harold of Wessex gathered the king's army for an advance to the border, my father and Gruffydd had escaped into the mountains. All that remained of Hereford was the cathedral—blackened, stripped, and desolate.

Harold and Tostig tried to follow them into the Cymry to force submission. The Godwines knew not the Welsh way of nimbling through the foothills, though. After some weeks, bedraggled and decimated, they returned to King Edward with their proud tails between their legs and told him that it was unlikely they could hold out against this new and powerful alliance. Ælfgar, they decided, posed less a threat as an earl than as an enemy of Angland. King Edward sued for peace.

Harold met with my father at Billings Leigh and offered him restoration and the king's full pardon. He was careful to point out, though, that King Edward had decreed Ælfgar would himself carry the guilt for the murder of seven priests who were slain within the sanctuary. My father replied that he would come to terms only if Harold offered him a full apology before the council. Harold Godwine's son agreed to do it.

I heard all the details of the victory from Ælfgar himself. He and Gruffydd returned from Billings Leigh late one afternoon with the Welsh. Most of the Anglishmen had marched with the Eirish up the Clwyd, to sail the fleet to Ceaster and wait there for the division of the spoils. Both Ælfgar and the Welsh king were in wild and high spirits; I never remember seeing my father more exuberant, before or after. The two of them had broken away from the others, and came galloping back to the camp at break-neck speed. Before they were even close, we could sense the victorious outcome. Leaping, jumping, embracing each other, we celebrated the fact even before they dismounted. By eventide, the men were drunken with victory.

"By God, I thought Earl Ralf meant to laugh us all to death when I saw his army drawn up on that nob!" My father was in delirious humor, and his men and Gruffydd's were a cordial and appreciative audience, as we were. "I saw them all, balanced on those horses. and I thought, 'They mean either to bring us to amusement or make themselves a fast escape!' Did you believe they meant to charge us the way they did?"

Gruffydd roared with laughter. "Nay! Nay!" he bellowed, "and when they did—Eirish saint's heads! They tumbled off those mounts so fast I could not keep my eyes on them to aim an axe! Some going this way, some that, laying themselves out on the ground as if to save us the bother of chasing them!"

"Mean you they rode *mounted* into battle?" Burchard exclaimed. We had never heard of such a thing before.

"Every one of them!" my father, still laughing, told us. "From the first man to the last, they fought on horseback!"

"You flatter them, Mercian!" cried Gruffydd, "Not a one of them fought on horseback. Turning, running, fleeing—that they did on horseback. But fight, they surely did not!"

The men exploded with intoxicated hysteria, as if the absurdity of the memory were too much for them. When they had subsided somewhat, the Welsh king continued in a more serious vein. "That is why we were able to pick the arms and booty of over four hundred fallen in that place!"

Burchard gave a low whistle. It had been a full-fledged battle, no skirmish.

"Four hundred!" One of the Welshmen reaffirmed it, and added with obvious relish that none of our own forces had been more than scratched or scraped.

"None dead?" we questioned in obvious disbelief.

"Not a one!" my father answered, pounding his fist hard on the wall as he said it. "The crazy Norman made his army ride on horses!" He could not contain his mirth and we laughed at the ludicrous prospect right along with him.

"What makes a man so mad, father?" I wondered.

"They say that is the way of making war in Normandy—sitting mounted to fight."

"Well, Timid Ralf will be hard-pressed to get Anglishmen to want to try it again!" Cynewulf shouted, and we all laughed more.

The wild story-telling went on long that night. My father grew so drunken that Cynewulf and Æthelstan had to push him against a wall and hold him, to keep him from falling on his face. Never having seen him so deep in drink before, Edwin and I were fascinated. Even Burchard was merrier than it had ever been his wont to be. Gruffydd alone seemed to hold his own as midnight neared, and feeling the grip of sleep fast clutching me, I thought I should take advantage of a long, low lull in the commotion to approach him.

"How long think you it will be before those Mercian lands you showed us will belong to you?" I asked him shrewdly, leading up to my real question.

"Your father has given them to me already, little Morcar."

"But they are not his to give!" I protested.

"He says his father, Earl Leofric, will back him."

I frowned, and Gruffydd took my chin and raised my gaze to his questioningly. "I do not mean harm to say this," I told him earnestly, "but you killed Grandfather Leofric's brother, Eadwine the … the— Eadwine for whom my brother is named … and Grandfather is not very kindly disposed towards the Cymry now." I bit my tongue. I had almost said "Eadwine the Welsh-Slayer" and was very glad I had not.

"Nevertheless, he wants his son and kinsmen back, does he not?" Gruffydd's answer riled me more and, knowing it, he tweaked my hair gently. "What is it that bothers you little one? Do you not think I should have the land?"

"Oh, surely you should! Indeed, for the honor you have shown my father, you should have even more! Only—"

"Only what?"

"What if they make you wait until my father is the Earl of Mercia?"

Gruffydd studied me appreciatively. "I do not plan to take the lands until Mercia is his; that was our pledge. I only mean to see the council consent to it now, and your father swears he will stand by me until they have agreed upon it."

Faltering, I did not think I could ever force the question out, but at last it came. "Need we, my brothers and I, stay your hostages until the lands are yours?" I swallowed hard and faced him squarely.

"So that is it!" His puzzled look faded into a broad and amicable grin. "So this is what troubles my little man!"

I nodded; it had not left my thoughts the entire night.

"Let me tell you something," he said, leaning back against the stone wall and putting an arm around my shoulder. "When your father came to me, I thought 'What madness is it that this Mercian comes to me with such a bold design?' But until I came to know your father, I had never felt brotherhood with any man. We are the same, he and I, with a bold eye for the future instead of the past and—you will not understand this now—an ability to sense the salt-water before we drown at sea. What is more, we share an enemy, a house that means to overtake us both and feed on our desperation while growing fat on our powerless defense. Till now, both of us have watched them, knowing they have grown so hungry that 'tis only a matter of time before they consume us all together. Do you understand what I say?"

I nodded; I knew of which house he spoke—the Godwines.

"Together, your father and I are no longer helpless to fight them, no longer cornered and cowering. We may be devoured in the end of it all, but we will have seen them poisoned first. We will have starved them into feeding on themselves, and what feeds on itself is fast to fall."

I tried to comprehend all he was telling me. Smiling at my childish perplexity, the deep-eyed man finished.

"A man with honor can sense the security in a forthright word. I keep no hostages against your father's pledge." He tousled my hair in a friendly way. "You sleep now."

I did. It had grown much quieter by then, and I dreamt of my grandmother.

CHAPTER TEN

The sentence of outlawry against Earl Ælfgar was
revoked, and he was restored to all the possessions
of which he had been deprived.

—Anglo Saxon Chronicle
Book "C" 1055

You might think that because I bear a Danish name, the sea is in my
blood, but that is not the fact of it. There have been few ocean-voyages
in my life that set well with me. I trace that fact back to these early days
when it happened that every time we took to water it meant we were in
danger or distress. One journey only was an exception—this one, when,
fired with my father's victory, we sailed down the west of Angland and
up the river Temes to Lundun City. Even in the freezing bitterness of the
channel winds, I was warm with happiness, and glad to be in my homeland again with friends and kinfolk I had not seen in nine long months.

In heavy cloaks, we disembarked at my father's side. I was very
proud of him. In his rich furs he was fine to look upon and, I am happy
to say, he had scraped off his beard, leaving only long side-burns in the
East Anglian fashion. Some of his Mercian men had followed him in
growing hair down their cheeks, to show they would stand behind him
in whatever place he sat. Their loyalty was impressive in itself. They had
supported him to a man, and no one could remember so many following
their lord into exile before.

The king's house and the streets leading to it were packed. Thegns
had come from all over the kingdom for the Witena Gemot this Christ
Mass. Many others had come as well, to win a look at the savage outlaw
earl, son of the beloved Leofric and Godiva, and of someone far more
legendary: Gruffydd, wild king of all the Cymry, who came now to offer
peace to King Edward, and demand payment for it.

Even before we could greet our grandparents, our entire family had
to bow to King Edward before holy relics, and all our householders had
to voice allegiance before the Gemot and swear to bide by the king's

will. After Edward received his dues, he told my father they would council on the morrow. "By then, I will have received this Cymrian," he said, his voice solemn and impassive, "and if he means to be a true vassal unto Angland, we will reward his claim in due time. As for you, Ælfgar, son of Leofric, I have bestowed my peace on you. I am told you will do penance for priest-killing, such a sin as sorely grieves me and will mark ill against you all your life. You imagined yourself to be wronged but, even so, you acted foolishly. Still, despite your rashness, you brought an ancient enemy of our land to fealty. There are men who smell treason in this brothership between you, and say you would not scruple to use it against your own land. Others say you want only what you feel was robbed away. I would fain believe these above others, because I have always marked a boldness and honor in you. But time will tell, for after tomorrow's Gemot, Anglishmen will once more call you earl."

Dignified and self-assured, the king stopped there, expecting that his formal pronouncement had brought to an end the interview. He stood to leave, and his lady with him.

Now, Ælfgar was a bold man. Even those who hated him most would swear to his daring. Hands on his hips and eyes alight with defiance, he stepped directly in front of the royal pair, blocking their way. His voice was very civil, but gentle was not the tone of it.

"Not a man in Angland ever more will call me earl," he declared firmly, tossing his head, "until your man, Harold Godwine's son, Earl of Wessex, stands before this assembled Witena Gemot, and in a voice loud enough to be heard by all the land, proclaims me an apology!"

A shocked whisper traveled through the entire hall, and handsome Harold, in his earthen velvet cloak and robes of east-cloth, burned red with indignation. He said nothing; my father faced him, not budging out of the king's way. "Is that not one of the terms named at Billings Leigh, Wessexman?"

Harold Godwine's son paled. "'Tis one of the terms," he finally agreed. Then, swallowing hard and steeling himself as if for a fight, he spoke in a loud voice.

"Now I will take this very opportunity, Ælfgar Leofric's son, to ask pardon from you for any ill-considered charges which may have escaped me. In the future, you may be assured, I will be intent upon the word that passes unawares!"

Saying this, he spun his back on my father and strode purposefully away. When he was half way out of the room, he stopped and looked back over his shoulder. "And worry not that I will hesitate to repeat these words in official council, Mercian!" he added with a mock courtesy before he stomped away.

"It did not occur to me!" my father laughed after him. Then, turning with a calculated, disarming smile which he aimed first on Tostig Godwine's son and then on the king, he shrugged. "It would not occur to me to doubt the sworn word of an honest man—not even one whose solemn oath had proven false!"

With a gesture of courtesy to the king's lady, Ælfgar motioned us to his side and then took his leave. As the astonished crowd parted to let us pass, we left Tostig, along with his brothers Gyrth and Leofwine, staring open-mouthed after us. As for the king, I could not imagine the look on his face, and I did not turn back to see it.

*   *   *

Flat on my back on a bearskin, I took it all in—rich woods, chiseled stone, marble window fittings, and carven timber doors. The king's house was the finest I had ever seen. In this room alone, I counted six heavy hangings of the finest Anglish embroidery and no fewer than two dozen lanterns! Every bench, chair, and stool was padded with leather, and there were rich rugs and furs scattered in profusion over the ornamented wooden flooring. Some of this opulence I recalled from our other Lundun visit, but it was even more of a delight after the rough-hewn crudeness of the Welsh camp at Rhuddlan.

Behind me sat Grandmother Godiva, singing softly while she did stitches with Aldgyth. Her delicate voice filled me with warmth. I was very comfortable despite the fact that I had been fasting all day. It was the eve of Christ Mass, the year's end, and Edwin and I were preparing to keep that solemn occasion in the men's way, for the first time.

On the second day of council, my father had been restored as Earl of the East Anglia, and all his holdings and lands, there and in Mercia, had been sworn back to him. The very next day, the councilors had heard him petition on Gruffydd's behalf. They agreed to allow Ælfgar to cede the lands between the Clwyd and the Dee to the Welsh king, when they were his own to give, provided Gruffydd of Llewellyn remained a true and faithful under-vassal to Edward until that time. The magnificent Welshman, with his powerful men behind him, left a lasting impression on all the folk of the realm, but I cannot honestly say they received him warmly. As for Gruffydd, he wasted no time in making his escape from the strangeness of Lundun City; within hours of seeing his demands assented to by the nod of the Gemot, he had sailed, and all his party with him, in the two stunning eagle-prowed war-ships which were the pledge-gift of my father.

Our family had personal cause for rejoicing, too. After an inauspicious first meeting, during which each vented his anger, resentment, and outrage, my father and grandfather had been reconciled. Grandfather Leofric, cutting short his tender greeting to us when Ælfgar entered the room, had led Father to another chamber without even giving Ælfgar time to greet his mother. After the heavy door closed behind them, they argued. The voices had been muffled but the tones unmistakable; Grandmother Godiva could not distract any of us from the welling misery we felt as words and phrases of their heated confrontation assailed us. Grandfather Leofric could never condone sacking, burning, or priest killing, he said. He would be hard-pressed to forgive the traitorous alliance his son had made with his kin-killer and enemy of enemies. Ælfgar, being a tempestuous, passionate man, might have forever alienated him had he expressed himself with the fury and vehemence which were his usual wont, but he pressed his case carefully, uttering all the bitterness, hurt, and anguish he had felt at the injustice done him.

"What recourse had I but to fight my way back?" I heard him ask. "From what quarter was my aid to come? Would you have me believe that you, a king's man, would have risen against Edward and all his advisors on my behalf, even if you had believed my oath of innocence?"

"I never doubted your innocence, my son! Well I know the hatred that waxes betwixt you and the sons of Godwine."

"Aye! By my standing heir to you, there is one earldom they cannot have. That is what the 'hatred' is!"

"No, Ælfgar! The enmity between Wessex and Mercia is an old one, one which should be forgotten."

"The old enmities I have forgotten, father—I swear it! There is a new cause for hatred, though, and you know it. Think on it! Fifteen years ago, you and Godwine were equal in power; if there was unbalance 'twas in your favor because of the ancientness of our line. Only—" and here my father's voice grew rife with bitterness and he faltered. "Only in one thing Godwine surpassed you. Lady Gytha bore him six sons, father! Your lady bore you but one—and so tip the scales of justice in the generation which follows yours!"

I will long remember the look of agony that settled on my grandmother's gentle face as we listened that very moment. We all knew that Ælfgar's argument rang true.

After a long pause, I heard Grandfather answer. "Even if the Godwine's sons carve an earldom out of Angland for each of the five that live, you know they can never claim Mercia!"

I think I heard my father spit. "Nor could they ever claim the North Humbria!" he cried, "But they did! And besides, 'tis not just the earldom of Mercia they seek—they want the crown. The whole kingdom! You know it is true. King Edward will die. There will be no heir. That will be their opportunity. I would oppose them, and they know it. How well they would like to be rid of me in some bloodless way before then—outlawry or exile! How easy for them that way to have a son of Godwine at the head of every earldom when they force the decision—and therefore no opposition anywhere in the land!"

"Earl Ralf is Edward's nephew. He would oppose them. He might even be named as successor."

"Pah! Do you think Timid Ralf will outlive Harold? Or Tostig? Besides, Anglishfolk will not have him as king, for he is Norman."

Grandfather's voice was cold. "Ralf is a good Christian man. You treated him shamefully, harrying in his domain."

"Where would you have had me do it?"

"I would have had you search another way. Whether the charges were right or wrong, just or unjust, there are better ways to come to vindication."

"Name me one."

"Negotiations—"

"Think harder, father!"

"I never doubted your honor, my son. I knew with what false oaths they betrayed and cornered you. Many a time I have regretted your temper, but never your honor, Ælfgar. I had hoped you could avenge it without shaming yourself, but I would not have you think I disbelieved you!"

"Father!"

There was a silence, a long silence, and I knew they had made their peace. When the door opened, my father's face was flushed and, though he looked somewhat less prideful than I was used to seeing him, he seemed happy. They both did.

So things had been made right between them, and now, two days later, father and son fasted and prayed together in the king's chapel while I lay in our rooms before a good, crackling fire, listening to my grandmother sing, thinking of them and wondering, for some strange, inexplicable reason, whether I would ever see my friend Gruffydd again.

It grieved me that I had not had a chance to say him a fare-well. Except to watch him bow to the king, I had not seen him at all since we departed the Cymry. He had sailed on a different ship and once in Lundun the king's men busied him with things that were not the concern of boys. Having grown fond of him, I had not expected our parting to be so abrupt.

"Do you know what Gruffydd told me just before we left?" Edwin asked suddenly. He was sitting well across the room from me, with his back against a leathern bench. He had been so quiet that I had almost forgotten he was in the room, but it did not astonish me that he had spoken on the very subject that I was weighing in my mind, for that was a common thing with us. I made no answer and he continued, unbidden.

"He said, 'Some folk walk through life, trailing long tendrils of fate behind them, all waiting to intertwine.'"

"A strange thing to say," I mused. "What meant he?"

Aldgyth answered me, saying, "He meant we should meet again, don't you think?"

"That is what I thought," my brother agreed, "but I could not say for sure that he meant us. He might have meant Father."

"Well, I for one shall certainly see him again!" exclaimed my sister, tossing her head.

Edwin turned on her. "Don't be foolish! You cannot predict a thing like that!"

"Indeed I can."

"What a body wishes for and what comes to pass are two distinct things!" Edwin was adamant. "No one can see ahead!"

"The Filidh did!" I protested feebly.

Edwin laughed. "How can you talk such madness, Morcar? Not a thing they said has come to pass, and you cannot know that it will!"

"Well, I *feel* that it will."

My sister defended me. "He is surely right, Edwin. A person can feel that something will happen. I feel we will meet again with Gruffydd. I know it!"

"We shall see, shan't we?" Edwin scowled, and I noticed that Grandmother looked at him curiously.

"What do you think?" I asked grandmother. "Can the future be read?"

Her answer came softly. "If it is something that is written, I believe it is there for the reading."

I did not understand and I said so. "Some things exist which are possibilities only, but which might not come to be," she explained. "By changing ourselves or our feelings, we might avert them. Other things are meant to be and they cannot be changed. These are the matters which might be read, but they are also the matters men most fear reading!"

"Well, I should hope there is very precious little about me that has been written!" Edwin teased. "I suppose it has been written, though, that I should terribly much crave some provender in the next hour or so. I am famished!"

"And far we have departed from the purpose of your year's end fasting," admonished Grandmother, standing suddenly as if to put an end to a talk which had disturbed her. I noticed how very small she was; already Aldgyth stood taller. She bent to kindle a pitch-stick in the fire and then used it to light the lanterns. It was fast growing dark, and I knew they would call us soon for vespers. No sooner had the thought crossed my mind than Burchard was at the door.

Like my father and grandfather, he wore courtly dress in the king's house, a green gown of finer cloth than usual, which hung to the floor instead of stopping at the knees. I thought it curious that while father looked flashing and princely in such garb, Burchard looked more like a priest. Perhaps it was his manner. Studious and watchful, he reminded me of Uncle Leofric, his face always impassively solemn and his gaze carefully lowered in a monkish way. I loved him. He was gentle, never condescending, and he perfectly understood my shyness and forgave it. Grandfather Leofric was very proud of him and all his accomplishments. The Earl of Mercia had never contested the fact that Burchard, who was not his true flesh-and-blood, stood as my father's heir. Undoubtedly, he saw more of himself in this Danelaw grandson than he did either in Edwin, who had more the temperament of Ælfgar, or me, who had not much of a temperament at all. They were very, very close.

"Have you eaten anything?" Burchard asked as we moved quietly down the long, drafty corridor that led to the nave of the king's chapel. Edwin and I shook our heads, very proud of having kept a full fast.

"That is good, because you will find that Year's End is a very solemn night, and it will be meaningful for you if you keep it in the prescribed manner. For you, Morcar," he added, "it should have special meaning more. Having been born three days before the Christ Mass, 'tis a true year's end for you, is it not?" He smiled gently, but I groaned. I did not like to be reminded of my birthday. Ælfgiva never failed to remind me that she and my father had done penance for my having been born in the Advent and oft-times when she spoke of it she wept, saying it had not been her fault.

"More than a year's end, even!" Edwin cried, nudging me playfully. "'Tis a decade's end for him, Burchard!" That was true; I was seeing out my tenth year.

We heard the beautiful, droning harmonies of the priests as we approached the chapel, and Burchard raised a finger to his lips to signal silence. As the doors swung open, the rich tones enveloped us, and I was filled with a glorious sense of well-being and peace. It was my fervent prayer that the feeling would last; the uneasiness and agitation of the last year had been burdensome. I prayed on that desire all through the service, devoutly and piously, though my thoughts wandered occasionally to the chancel, where the king and the very highest men of the realm, my father and grandfather amongst them, knelt at the altar-rail in their devotions. Even from behind, I knew them, every one.

There was Harold, Earl of Wessex, tall and athletically built, golden hair curling to his nape. Next to him, his brother Tostig knelt, the king's darling, taller yet and broader of shoulder, dressed more finely than any of the others, sporting bracelets and belts of precious metals. Although he had been Earl of the North Humbria near a year now, he still wore his brown hair in the manner of the West Saxons like his brother. Earl Ralf, though not tall, was a square-shouldered, solidly built man; even from the back he looked defiantly Norman in a French tunic and mantle and Flemish green hose. His dark hair was cropped close and his sleeves were long and loose. Anext him was Grandfather, every bit the Mercian, more than sixty years now but strong and hale and manly in his court clothes of subtly colored linen. By far the fairest of them all, my father knelt, stoic and strong in a slender, more patrician way. His long, flaxen hair was streaked and darkened by winter, and encircled by a small silver band—the courtly fillet that marked the Mercian nobleman.

Then there was the king—the mysterious, enigmatic Edward— poised in the middle of them like a contemplative figure from a painting or tapestry. Though not much older than Grandfather, his hair had been white for many years, and his complexion nearly matched it. He looked delicate yet he was not a frail man. He looked saintly yet men said he had a terrible temper. He had accused Earl Godwine of his brother's murder yet he married the man's daughter and made the man's sons his favorites. He surrounded himself with the Normans whom all Anglish-men despised yet he himself was loved and revered. There was much in the wide world that I could not comprehend.

With reverential awe we watched each of these great men humble himself before the altar, coming one at a time to bow low at the feet of the bishops, to be blessed by them and take the sacrament. By the time the mass drew to an end, the room was thick with the scent of precious incense which, mingling with the glorious tones of holy song, created an impression that has lingered long in my memory. 'Twas a hint of other-world sanctity and purity of purpose—a feeling that there was no such thing in all the world as enmity or hatred.

Afterwards, some stayed and some went with the king to his chamber, but all the men of our house retired to a small, stark room, a confessional just off the main chapel, alive with the glittering of many lighted candles. Except for a huge carven crucifix and the wooden benches upon which we sat, the room was cold and bare, though the sweet perfume of the incense lingered still. Those men whom I respected most in all the world were gathered in that little chamber; 'twas a thrill beyond telling to be with them. I sat between Burchard and Grandmother's brother, Turold, an old man now. Across from me, my father sat—Edwin at his one side, his chief man, Cynewulf, at the other. Alone and apart from us sat William Malet, my avunculus. Though he kept vigil with King Edward most years, he had elected to be with us, his kinfolk, this time, in part because our visits to the south-lands were so rare.

My grandfather, the great Earl Leofric of Mercia, staunch and silver-haired, was the center of our attention. In a rich, deep voice he read for us the scriptural accounting of the first coming, and it seemed as if I had never heard that familiar tale before. When he ended it, we crossed ourselves and knelt, then prayed silently our acts of contrition and supplication. When Grandfather seated himself, we all followed and there was a long, reverential, reverberating silence before he spoke.

"He who would exercise what is best in himself, and eliminate what is worst, has need to see clearly what be those worths and errors. There is simple wisdom."

I did not entirely understand his meaning, but I said nothing and in a little while he went on.

"So it is that on the last night of the year, a man sits in the highest state of earthly sanctity, having fasted and prayed in contrite spirit, having confessed and been shriven, having balanced the indulgences of any penances in which he was negligent. In this character of holiness, he reviews the events of his past life, both in cause and effect. Then God, in his tender mercy, shows him the meaning of these things as he is deemed worthy to understand them, until a man comes to see the pattern of his mortal life and understand the Father's purpose for him. For nothing ever befalls a man for naught; all things spring from God's reasons."

I pondered this, and though the formal words confused me, the import somehow sank deep into my breast.

"When a man keeps the year's end in proper meditation, each incident of the passing year will come back to him in vivid remembrance, and those things which hold a key to what he is and what he might be will remain forever with him. Never will his memory fail him in the recalling of those instances. Good or evil, they are his forever to carry. That is how it is meant to be. And on this night, each year for a man's entire lifetime, the same occurrences and thoughts and actions will come to him—only tempered more with understanding and wisdom with each year that passes. Here is how we build the image we carry with us to the next life—the image by which we are recognized by our Lord and creator."

Without even meaning to, I lifted my eyes, as if to assure myself the words were having the same effect on the others that they were on me. I found myself flooded suddenly with a throbbing sense of peace and rapture. It surprised me more than anything when I looked at my father and discovered that his eyes were on me, staring in a strangely sorrowful way, the inestimable depths of them lambent with nameless emotion. I felt a piercing stab of love for him then, and for a moment I think I understood something in him that no one else had ever fathomed.

"Sons of my son, Edwin and Morcar, since you make this accounting for the first time, you must go back in your minds to what was first truly meaningful for you." My grandfather's voice was no more than a whisper but it filled the entire room. "Starting there, you must make a distinction between those tendencies which are noble and excellent and those which are ruinous. When the bells chime the mid-of-night, announcing the feast of the Coming and the New Year, you must make firm resolution to put aside your inclinations to evil. You must resolve to be aware of them all the next year and to avoid them and to punish yourself for any heed you give unto them. For only thusly can a man become free of them and stand in righteousness. In a year's time of faithful attendance, you can do that. Yet let it not surprise you if each Year's End you find a new inclination to dispose of, for that is the way with mortal men. Ever there is a new temptation, or a recurring one, so care must be exercised in the eliminating of them, lest they build up and bury a man."

After that he said nothing more, but knelt down on the cold flagged floor, resting his chin in his folded hands. Burchard followed him and after some while Cynewulf Cenwulf's son and William Malet did, too. I did not want to lower myself until my father did. I could see that it was hard for him. The events of the last year must have shaken him to the soul. He was penancing for priest-killing, for blood-letting and church-plunder, plus whatever private sins he had accrued. Sometimes I watched him dress while we heard the morning low mass in his chambers. He oft-times wore a harsh-woven wool shirt—the scratching, abrading kind that meant contrition for immoral deeds.

Even as I thought on this, I was startled by Ælfgar's touch on my shoulder, and looking up I could see the shine in his eyes of welling tears. He had Edwin by the hand and wordlessly raised me to my feet. Then we walked in silence to the foot of the great wooden crucifix. We knelt before it, the three of us. I leant on my father, and my brother did also. He supported us both.

I settled on that other Christ Mass we had spent in Lundun City as a fitting place to begin my account. It was a vivid memory and a pleasant one, and from that time forward I could easily follow the course of my spiritual and emotional growth. By the time the bells chimed in the New Year, I had captured the essence of my childish self and the discoveries I made that night of my spirit and being have lasted me, just as Grandfather promised, all of my life.

CHAPTER ELEVEN

From the Jutes came the people of Kent. . . . From
the Old Saxons came the East Saxons (Essexmen)
and South Saxons (Sussexmen) and West Saxons
(Wessexmen). From Angle land . . . came the East
Anglians, Middle Anglians, Mercians and all the
North humbrians.

—Anglo Saxon Chronicle,
Book "E" 449

"Put a mantle on you, Edwin," my father said, striding into the chamber
where my brother and I pored over a fine-made gammon board. "Make
it a warm one; the sun will be sinking 'ere we make our return."

Edwin was already on his feet and half-wrapped in his furs before he
asked where they were going.

"I mean to ride out and inspect the foundations of the king's new
minster, the new Peter Church he is building in the place of the old
one." They were almost to the door when Cynewulf, brooching his own
mantle, tossed me mine.

"You come, too, Morcar!" he nodded to me, after darting a quick
glance my father's way. Ælfgar stopped abruptly and turned back to face
me, flushing uncomfortably, like a man who has unintentionally
insulted another.

"Aye, you come too, Morcar!" he said off-handedly, and Cynewulf
winked at me. I broke into a grin of pleasure. My father had been
arguing, harshly and miserably, with my mother in the next chamber for
the better part of an hour. It was his wont to turn his back on her after
confrontations and ride off somewhere. He usually took Edwin with
him. The hollow emptiness which always assailed me when he did had
already begun its gnawing when his chief man flashed me that spur-of-
the-moment invitation. I was very grateful to him.

Cynewulf Cenwulf's son was one of my favorite people in the world, a comely, good-natured, high-born Mercian of an age with my father. They had been best of friends from boyhood on, and the handsome, brown-eyed guardsman was as close to us as a man could be without being actual kin. I always felt he had a special liking for me. He took time to smooth me when I was ruffled or downcast, and once when we were hawking he let me throw his prize peregrine, which thing he told me no other person had ever been allowed to do. The man was excellent with birds, and his brother Cynric was my father's falconer, though he too might have been a guardsman had he not lost two full fingers of his right hand when he was very young.

As we mounted, I looked in vain for Fulke d'Aubermont. In the weeks we had been here, I had only seen him a few times. Once, we had managed a whole day of gaming together—the day the king took all the noblemen out to hunt harts for the Christ Mass feast. He was precisely as I remembered him, stern and impassive, but he had learnt more Anglish since last I had seen him. He had not seemed inclined to do so before; our language was not highly prized by the Normans.

Looking west over the city walls, we had seen the great stone shell of the king's new minster, but its beauty and grandeur could scarce be imagined at that distance. It was only as we drew near that we were full-struck by its majesty. We had never seen another building similar: it was shaped like a cross. "Cruciform," my father called it.

"'Tis the way they build churches in Normandy," he explained, as we gazed in wonder. "All of it will be hewn of stone but the high reaches of the towers." Bending back as far as I could, I was not able to see the tops of them.

Cavernous and stark, the lofty, unfinished interior was hauntingly hollow. It did not seem possible that a thing made by the hands of men could be so immense. When we spoke, in our normal tones, the sound of our voices echoed endlessly.

The season being cold, the workmen had abandoned it a spell, and it might have been the desolation of the place that made it seem so awesome. We did not speak much on the way back, both because the biting air worked hard to still us and because we had each been inspired to lofty thoughts.

When we arrived back at the king's house, kitcheners were working fast to lay board in the gigantic hall. A few men were already seated, laughing and conversing, or drinking watered wines. When my father saw Burchard with my grandfather and some other Mercian men, he joined them, leaving Cynewulf to guide my brother and me to the trough at hall-back, where we could wash our hands after riding. We were near to it when Tostig Godwine's son, a long-limbed, muscular man, rose from his seat and moved directly into our way, as if he meant to greet us. There was a smile playing across his wind-tanned face, but I did not think it was a particularly friendly one.

"I bear you greetings, Cynewulf Cenwulf's son," Tostig said lightly, his tone almost mocking. "How be it you are saddled with the care of children this night?"

My father's man eyed him with a cold smile of his own. "'Tis a responsibility and a pleasure I have taken upon myself with no bidding, my lord Earl."

"By God! You are an unmarried man!" exclaimed the Wessexman in a forcedly pleasant voice, still grinning. "They are not your bastards, I hope?"

"Nay, my lord," replied Cynewulf, unflinching. "You know right well whose sons these be, though I can see it wounds you to think on it when he has three and you have none!"

Tostig bristled, but in a fleet second resumed his mask of sardonic courtesy. "Comely youths!" he exclaimed, taking a lock of my hair in an affectionate way, but tweaking it hard enough to hurt. "Handsome childlings—and yet, in a way, vulnerable looking, think you not?"

He reached to yank Edwin's hair the way he had mine, but my brother boldly reached up and grasped the tall man's wrist, stopping it in mid-air, glaring all the while. The earl threw his head back and laughed, greatly amused. "Word is that Ælfgar thinks these scions have inherited something of worth from their mother's line," he whispered harshly to Cynewulf. "Let us hope it is not her madness, eh, Mercian?" Then he sauntered back to his seat with a prideful look.

Anticipating our puzzled questions, Cynewulf put a hand firmly on our shoulders and led us to the trough. From his look, I knew we would get no answers.

That night, Edwin and I talked long into the small hours on the floor of my father's chamber. Our stay in Lundun City was drawing to an end. Father and Grandfather had ordered the packing of the train this evening. We had carried nearly everything we owned into exile with us, but much of that had been dispatched to Grantanbrycg immediately upon our arrival from the Cymry. A good detachment of our household men had been sworn to protect our riches; by now they would be well settled in my father's house, awaiting our return.

"The men here think not well of us, Morcar," Edwin whispered in a mournful voice. We always spoke low though there was no real need to; we were always quite alone in the chamber till late when the men quit hall.

"Mean you Earl Tostig?" I asked, knowing he did.

"Aye, and all his house. 'Tis just as father always said. They hate us for no reason but for who we are." He turned on his back and put his hands behind his head. "They even hate you and me, and we have done nothing to them."

"Cynewulf says 'tis their Saxon blood. Saxons have ever boasted an inborn meanness, he says, and they have always held a hatred for true Anglish."

"That is naught but ancient history, Morcar ..." Edwin yawned loudly. "Mayhap centuries ago 'twould count as a reason, but Grandfather claims those old enmities are of no account now, though 'tis plain they think Wessexmen are somehow better than Mercians."

I mulled this a moment. "Father says they want to take Mercia, so all Angland will be theirs. He says they hate us because we stand in their way."

"What think you, Morcar—that Mercians would bend to usurpers like the West Saxon Godwines?" I heard him spit in the darkness.

"They somehow took the North Humbria," I mumbled haltingly. He spit again, so I thought to change the subject.

"What meant the man by remarking about our inheriting madness from our mother?"

"Poisonous jest is all." Edwin's tone, though firm, was not convincing and I was suddenly reminded of how our mother's words oft-times confused me.

"Think you she is somewhat—bewildered?" I asked, picking the word carefully but still hardly daring to say it.

His answer came coldly. "I am not the right person to ask for comforting thoughts on that lady, Morcar. I can think of little to say that honors her."

"But ever have you thought she—"

He cut me off. "I think she is a mean-spirited shrew. There it is! Pleases you that you made me voice it?"

"Nay, brother." I shrugged him an apology. I could not help thinking how beautsome she was; even past forty years now she possessed a clear-eyed, girlish loveliness. My brother interrupted my reflections.

"How is it you would let that Wessexman pull on your hair that way, Morcar, insulting you like that?"

I burned scarlet in the dark but made no answer.

"Best you begin to put a bolder face on, else you will be early marked as a mild and flinching man. You show no fear with beasts or birds, so 'tis no lack of courage, I trow."

I mumbled something that was not exactly an answer.

"Gentleness is good only if it does not drown out every other virtue. Father means to see you an earl some day—"

I silenced him by pulling coverlets over my head. After some time, his regular breathing told me he had drifted into sleep. Too many thoughts crowded my mind to allow it. I wondered where this earldom was to come from that I was supposed to hold. I thought of the Wessexmen's strange pronouncement, and Cynewulf's grim-looked reaction to it. I remembered, too, how it had angered me when Tostig yanked my locks. It had not occurred to me to fight him, though, and it had, in fact, shocked me when my brother did.

I was still tossing when Ælfgar and Cynewulf came in from hall, in good spirits. They spoke softly, thinking we both slept, as they undid their knife belts and ornaments, then slipped out of their costly dalmatics and fine under-tunics. When they were abed, they talked a few minutes more and Cynewulf told my father about the meeting with the North Humbrian earl. When he mentioned how Edwin had stilled the towering man's hand, my father chuckled with undisguised pride. "He is a treasure unto me, that one!" is what he said.

"I took care to remind the Wessexman of all your treasures," Cynewulf said, yawning, "and it ired him well to think he had none, of that I am sure."

They discussed it a while longer, but my father's man never repeated Earl Tostig's strange comment. Seemed he was scrupulous in avoiding it, and realizing I would hear nothing more of use from them, I tumbled finally into sleep.

CHAPTER TWELVE

Their relations were of high birth, and very numerous.

—Orderic Vitalis,
Book IV

Midsummer 1056

The first summer after we resettled in Grantanbrycg, Aldgyth turned fourteen years, marrying age. As was the custom, my father held a great celebration to which he invited all our kith and kinsmen that he might decide whether or not there were any fitting candidates amongst them. This formality was more an excuse for feasting than anything else, for Father was not nearly ready to part with his pretty first-born yet, and he let it be known. Even so, cousins came from all over the north and midlands; many we had not seen in a long while. In addition, any who thought he knew of a likely prospect was invited to bring the same along, which further swelled the number. We had a full fortnight of jollity and merriment.

Most high-born of our kin were my mother's North Humbrian connections. Brihtric and Maldon were brothers almost of an age with Edwin and me, great-nephews of the unfortunate Morcar of the Seven Boroughs, for whom I was named. These good-natured kinsmen were great favorites of ours, and we always grasped gladly at any chance to pass time with them, which occasions were not as frequent as you might think, as they lived far north in Eorforwic.

My cousins Ealdread and Siward, sons of Æthelgar Bearn, murdered by the other Siward—called the Usurper—came from Tathaceaster. Siward Bearn was a strong, grey-eyed man, taller than most. He was almost Burchard's age, even and staunch of feature, bearded and long-locked in the North Humbrian way. In ancient times, when the North Humbria was a kingdom unto itself, the Bearns had been mighty rulers, and the title passed from father to first-born son. Ever since the long-ago uniting of all Angland under a single king, the Bearns held no authority, but the title was one of the most ancient and noble in the land. Siward Æthelgar's son was a true Bearn of the Diera, first-born of first-borns from beyond the time of King Ælfred the Great, generations back, and was a powerful, respected, and wealthy land-owner. His brother Ealdread was a quiet man. He was already hand-fast to Lady Gweneth, the handsome daughter of the Warden of Bereuuic, but he came anyway and we were glad to see him.

Siward and Ealdread brought their sister Briana with them. She was four years older than Aldgyth and still unwed, which puzzled me for she was very beautiful. Mayhap she and her brothers waxed too proud to make a match; with her comeliness and blood-ties she surely could not have lacked for suitors.

One who had vied for her, we knew, was our cousin Gospatrick Maldred's son. He came all ornamented in heavy metals, else no one would have noticed him, I trow. Despite his long, undyed locks and big earrings, everything about his look was nondescript. There seemed to be no special color to his eyes or hair and nothing about his high-boned face commanded attention, unless it were the pallor of his complexion.

Another of our kinsmen was flashing Oswulf, son of the Usurper's other victim, Earl Eadwulf of the Bernicia. Handsome he was and of a good age, only a year older than Aldgyth, but he was headstrong and haughty and tried too hard to force his affections on her. He brought his best friend with him, a noble Bernician kinsman of his named Cospatric Arkill's son, and to Oswulf's chagrin, Aldgyth had warmed to that youth immediately. The two flirted openly and seemed very happy together, which made Oswulf sulky and cross.

Lady Godiva's Mercian kin were too numerous to count. Among them were Æric and Ælfmaer, grandsons of her brother, Turold. They were a comical two, twins who looked scarce alike and were laughingly called Flax-Head and Apple-Cheek. They were always steeped in mischief of one kind or another and Edwin and I ever waxed rambunctious in their company, as did Brihtric and Maldon. During gatherings, we were still jestingly referred to as the devil's half dozen, a title coined by Grandfather Leofric when we were all tots.

Our entire estate was crowded with the company who came, and every possible building had been turned into lodgings. Many of the visitors had been there a week or more, when one kinsman came who was entirely unexpected—my avunculus, William Malet. He brought a candidate with him: the son of King Edward's equerry, my friend Fulke d'Aubermont. He did it more to please me than Aldgyth, but all told, the Norman might have been a rewarding match for her. His prospects were high and his father held land both in Angland and in Normandy. Still, he was but twelve years old, Edwin's age, and like most of the others had come more for the fun and frolic than to pursue any serious intent.

My father many times half-jestingly had hinted that he thought his man Cynewulf would be best of any match for the girl, but Cynewulf, having watched on Aldgyth from the very cradle, felt not much inclined to look on her as a wifely possibility. He would answer Ælfgar's insinuations courteously, but always with an excuse. "She is a creature made not for earl's men, Ælfgar Leofric's son," he would say politely, "but for alliances with kings and princes." This was excellent gallantry, but all of us knew she was not likely to wed so highly. She could not be considered a great heiress with three healthy brothers holding a lien on her father's properties. Nevertheless, William Malet, sitting at table in the hall with us one fore-noon, was quick to point out that King Edward had married Earl Godwine's daughter Edythe, and she with a great many more strapping brothers besides.

"So think you I should save her for the man who takes the crown when Edward makes his passing?" Ælfgar asked, looking straight at him, as if daring him to name that man. My avunculus shook his head.

"Nay," he answered firmly, "William of Normandy has a wife already, and children besides!" Then I saw my father glance to Cynewulf with a musing, thoughtful look.

That very eve, Midsummer's Night, the sabbat feast of Litha, we held a festival in the bushy, flat valley land that bordered the Grantanbrycg manor. My father and his men had worked several days piling the wood for the great bonfires that we lit late in the twilight. Ælfric White-Hair directed the lugging of large vats of honey-mead into convenient positions, and provided troughs and buckets of ale for the common-folk on the other side of the fields.

Canopies were pitched, with couches, chairs, and bolsters beneath for guests to make themselves comfortable. A few sat all the evening watching the gay activity, but for the most part everyone was in constant motion. As was usual, the night started with a dance. The ladies, with wreaths of flowers around their unbound hair, held hands, dancing in a lively circle, while all the men and boys did the same in a larger ring around them. Edwin loved this sort of play and forced me with him into the dancing. I was quite shy, but once the drone of the bag-pipe began and the whirling and twirling commenced, it proved an agreeable sport.

Afterwards, we played at tossing with a pig's bladder, inflated into a good sized ball. I tired of it before too long, as many of the younger folk did, eventually leaving the game to the men, who played with a great deal more energy and daring. I went to my father's canopy to join my mother, who sat there with William Malet and a handful of other guests. Aldgyth was with them. She complimented me on my dancing, saying I had a light step which would avail me well when I began my courting. I laughed sheepishly. She was looking very grown up and, as everyone took great care to pay her special compliments, was in glowing spirits. "Think you I jest in this, Morcar?" she asked with twinkling eyes. "For if you do, I will put my wreath upon your head!"

I laughed and refused it. When a maiden put her flowers round a gentleman's hair, she promised him the honor of holding and twirling her in the last dance. That being the only one wherein the dancers paired off, it was a singular honor. I feared I would have done a grave disservice to many a hopeful fellow of better age and interest.

Sitting on a low, padded stool, I let Mother play absently with my hair while she talked to her brother. It had grown late, and the huge fires had smoldered into ember. The men took turns jumping the length and breadth of the glowing piles, each embarking on their broad leaps with a long running start. Great sport to watch, I thought, but in thin leather shoes there was a certain challenge to it, and the long-limbed vaulters, like my father or cousin Siward, seemed to have a definite advantage.

When the men tired of contesting each other, they gathered round the mead-buckets, laughing and talking. Then the low music of the bagpipe began again, and they scattered in gay spirits, those with garlands to seek the ladies who had bestowed them, and those without to make compliments and courtesies till they received one. A sizable crowd had gathered around my sister. I listened with fascination to their flirtatious, teasing words. Aldgyth merrily heard each of her would-be suitors in turn before making a choice; it surprised me that she answered and jested with such womanly ease.

On Midsummer's Night, even the wedded women, who usually hid their hair under circular veils, wore it unbound. My father had always been fond of Ælfgiva's snowy tresses. Uncoiled, they reached her knees, exceptionally thick and lovely. In high and happy spirits tonight, he fondled her pretty locks, cajoling and pleading with her to dance.

"'Tis strange to see so fair a lady still wears her wreath of baby's breath!" he said in a soft voice, holding her head gently between his hands.

"And 'tis strange to see so fair a man wears none!" the lady replied, Her voice was cold, and my father grew angry.

"I bid you dance with me, Lady Ælfgiva!" he cried imperiously, pulling her to her feet. Soon as she was in his arms, she began to weep. I looked away, mortified. Bad enough they argued and made their senseless insults in private, but in a goodly crowd it seemed shameful.

Covering her face, my mother sobbed like a babe. Ælfgar shook her till her hair flew and his whisper was hoarse with emotion. "By God, woman!" he growled, forcing her to look at him, "Whatever ails you, smite it out lest it drive us both to madness!"

She pushed him away with clenched fists and fell back into her carven arm-chair, a swollen pout on her tear-stained face. Ælfgar turned to her again, but Aldgyth, to avoid any further unpleasantness, reached to him from behind, spinning him round to face her, then placed her garland of cornflower blues on his golden hair. He smiled slightly, and casting one last icy look over his shoulder, let her lead him away.

They did not get far, though. My kinsman Siward Bearn stepped up just as the dancing began and though I could not hear what passed between them, I soon enough saw he had traded his sister Briana to my father for the prize he sought most, and he led pretty Aldgyth into the flow of the music with a satisfied smile. They made a handsome pair, both tall and well-formed. Siward Bearn was not comely in the strictest sense of the word, but there was a pleasant winningness about his smile, a nobleness to his cut, and his wide-set grey eyes were handsome and alert. He dressed as well as any earl, though he wore earrings and too much jewelry, and his long, copper-dyed North Humbrian hair gave him a roguish look. He was obviously smitten with my sister, and since I liked and admired the man, I was happy to see she let him slip an arm around her waist half-way through the dance.

Soon, Fulke and Edwin came and sat anext me. I was glad they had missed the shadows which passed between my parents that night. Looking for Burchard while the two of them talked, I finally spotted him with a pretty cousin of ours, a great-niece of Grandmother Godiva's. He had gained his wreath early in the evening, every lady of marrying age being anxious to attract the future Earl of Mercia. In a few years, I thought, they would hunger after Edwin in the same way. Not only would he be heir to the East Anglian earldom, but an exceptionally fine-looking man as well. Just thinking of that brought to mind my father; I did not have to strain my eyes to find him. Both his hands tight around the waist of his pretty young niece, he danced, smiling and distracted, as near to our canopy as he could get and in my mother's full view. It stung me like nettle that he would purposely try to fire Lady Ælfgiva further that way. They would fight and argue the whole night long now with the house full of company.

When the long tune ended, folk straggled back to the house, the crowd dissipating into a confusion of couples and clusters of high-spirited folk whose muffled and indistinct voices carried on the mild night breeze. We made good-nights to Æric and Ælfmaer as their

mother headed them off, then to Brihtric and Maldon. The devil's half
dozen were being forcibly separated this evening for we had kept folk
awake long into the night before with our silly chattering.

With Fulke and Edwin, I trailed along behind Burchard, who was
conversing merrily with Siward Bearn in a little circle of their friends.
They were teasing one another about the ladies—gentle, courteous jests,
unlike the bolder sort which passed amongst the wedded men. Seemed
to me that with youths of courting age there was only one topic of
interest and I did not find much fascination in it. It just happened that
when they fell into a silent pause for a moment, Edwin and I, at precisely
the same moment, broke into song. 'Twas an uncanny thing between us,
like the fathoming of one another's minds, that we had been wont to do
since babyhood. It always startled folk who were unused to it. When we
burst into our simultaneous harmony, the little party ahead of us stopped
dead and turned round to look at us, laughing gaily.

"They do it often," Burchard explained. "In the night, just before
they fall to sleep, suddenly they sing like that, four phrases or five, and
then they fall silent again."

"Never much seemed to me they were of a single mind," mused
Siward Bearn, walking backwards and looking from one to the other of
us in the moonlight. "Methinks 'tis a sign they will be inseparable, even
as men."

"No such thing there is as inseparable, cousin," Burchard said
solemnly. "Not in this mortal life, anyway."

"Know you that you are a priest-talker, brother?" Edwin asked him
with a frown, and the others laughed. Burchard pretended to cuff him,
then slipped one arm around Edwin's shoulder and one around mine,
and we walked happily. I was proud to have such fair brothers.

When we finally came to the manor house, I was exhausted. My
brothers and I had graduated from our sleeping quarters in the open loft
and now shared my father's chamber, which had been spuriously divided
by woven hangings into two. My mother and sister still kept the
narrower room on the other side of the great hall. Occasionally, Ælfgar,
without a word to anyone, would stride purposefully after his woman
and Aldgyth would meekly scurry in to take a pallet with us, but otherwise we followed a regular habit with no change.

That night, though, Ælfgiva brought Aldgyth with her to our
quarter. Pacing nervously, she bade Edwin lay her pallet in the furthest
corner, and arrange her sheets and pillows. He grew very flushed with
anger. "Think you I am a page or chamber servant?" he began, but
Burchard silenced him with a stern gaze and gestured him off to do it,
which he did, grumbling and complaining. I exchanged a worried glance

with Aldgyth when my mother suddenly asked Burchard to hide her, for she was afraid Ælfgar meant to find and harm her.

Burchard held her protectively and tried to comfort her with tender words. "Nay, mother!" he said patiently. "You must know your man is a good one!"

She threw his hands off her and faced him with glaring eyes. "How say you such? Even now he plans to be done with you."

Burchard placed a finger gently on her lips. "'Tis a mistaken dream you have, mother! You have naught to fear but the thing that makes you harbor such an evil thought."

As Burchard extinguished the pitch torches, a melancholy silence settled over everything. I finished undressing in the dark, bothering not to fold or roll my clothes, or even to say my prayers. Before she went to sleep, Ælfgiva warned us to waken her when Ælfgar came. 'Twas something she need not have worried about. He did not come back that night, nor did he sleep in chambers with us for several nights afterward.

                    *   *   *

Whatever estate we occupied, the mews were the private domain of Cynric Cenwulf's son. His brother Cynewulf and my father were the only men allowed to frequent the place and even they realized that within the confines of those draftless, wide-timber walls, the word of the chief falconer was law. "The man knows as much about birds," Ælfgar used to laugh, "as monks do about cooking fish, and always has!" This was true; Cynric's hens set the standard all over the kingdom.

A handsome man, nearing thirty and five years then, he had early on lost two full fingers to his calling, and later the tips of two others. He was fond of bragging about it. "I can count on one hand the number of times a bird has bested me!" he would say, holding up that oddly mangled right hand. It never failed to shock folk, ladies especially. Like Cynewulf, he was very fond of women. Once he had been married, but his lady, a great favorite of mine, died in childbirth, and the babe followed soon after, even though my mother found a woman to suckle it and helped keep it right well.

Not long after the Midsummer, when all our guests had taken leave except my avunculus and Fulke d'Aubermont, my father decided that Edwin should have a bird of his own. He chose him an Iceland peregrine, one of the sleekest and swiftest treasures, as a twelfth-year gift. My brother's birthday was not until the first of September, Byzantine New Year, but Cynric insisted that he begin working with the creature immediately if he hoped even to show it briefly on his wrist by that time. So Edwin was given the honored privilege of entering the mews with Ælfgar once or twice a day, to practice hooding and unhooding the bird, and to our intense pleasure, Fulke and I were allowed to accompany them.

"A peregrine is a man's bird," Cynric told us severely as we looked on the stunning creature. "When you work with one of these, no longer are you toying. Because she is smaller than you, do not underestimate her capabilities. She is strong and sure as any other wild animal, and just as wroth to be captured and used. You must be the one to bend and break her, else she will never be truly your own."

Till then, we had only birded with house-hawks, docile things, already well-trained by the falconer and with no mind to rebel. The house-hawks were so dispirited that they could be handed from one to another, some so gentle that you could hold them with no glove. They were good for learning the rules of the field, or gaining arm strength, but they were merely a base imitation of true hunters. Despite the work and care demanded in the raising and training, every boy looked forward to his own bird with immense anticipation.

Edwin was good with her. He had practiced hooding and unhooding on other birds and had a deft, sure touch. He captured her in the cowl before she could decide to fight. Cynric looked pleased; he had argued Father's wisdom in giving Edwin such a valuable bird at his young age.

"Remember you not I was just that age when my father let me choose from the brace of Viking birds that came to Lindcylene?" Ælfgar had asked him, scowling.

"Remember you not it ate my hand?" Cynric answered.

"Aye. But even so we trained it well, did we not? We did no injustice to the prize of it, did we?" They laughed, and Cynric added that he thought Edwin had as much of a bird-gift as his father had, else he would not have consented to it. My brother glowed with undisguised pride, and Ælfgar did, too.

A hawk on the wrist was a sure sign of gentle birth, and the mark of a man's prowess; a peregrine who would perch stock-still on a wrist, even in crowded company, was a living announcement of a man's patience, strength, and ability. Watching Edwin, I figured that by the Christ Mass, he would have his hunter sitting hooded on his wrist the entire length of a high Mass, if the priests would let him bring it in the church. Some clerics were opposed to the practice of admitting lower creatures in a sacred place. Nevertheless, 'twas becoming a fashion; I had seen more than a few in the minsters of Lundun City, and here in the East Anglia it had gained somewhat of a forbearance. This was largely because my uncle, Abbot Leofric, was fond of wearing one, and everyone knew it was hard to find a man holier than that one.

My father and the two sons of Cenwulf took as much pride and pleasure in the bird as Edwin did. The challenge of working one to perfection was a delight to them, and in truth, it really pleased me to see Ælfgar engrossed in something to his liking. He had been in very low spirits much of the time since his restoration, and like a child, when depression was on him, he behaved badly, quarreling with his woman and drinking to stupor. The strain between my parents was pronounced and obvious; they fought constantly and on many a night, Ælfgar slept in the hall, or in a storehouse, or elsewhere. That way, he managed to avoid his lady for days at a time. Ælfgiva accused him of womanizing, but in truth, what rubbed her was merely the fact that he had abandoned his gentle and pacific attitude towards her lashing cruelties. Till that summer, I think he truly believed his love might have conquered her. Now, it was as if he had given up any hope of happiness in the union. They both were worse for it.

Other pressures were on him, too. Word came that Gruffydd had raided in the Hereford Shire again; my father claimed to be expecting it. A new bishop had been named there: Harold Godwine's son's chaplain, a worldly man named Leofgar who wore mustaches and was better known as a warrior than as a priest. He had conducted raids into the Cymry and directed his murderous strikes at helpless families and home-steads. Baited and fierce, Gruffydd had made his move in return. The shire-reeve, many of the best men, and even the bishop himself had been slain in the Cymrian attack. The king, needless to say, was outraged; and so my father was also when he discovered Edward had summoned all his earls together to council about it, but had not called him. What fired him especially was that Grandfather had answered the call, and had gone along with the council in deciding that Gruffydd, by his rampage and ravings, had forfeited his right to the lands Ælfgar had pledged him.

That last news came to us as we were riding back to Grantanbrycg from the northeast, where my father had been called to settle the claim of some peasants who charged the gentry there with destroying their crop by riding drunkenly through the rye-fields. Cursing and swearing, Ælfgar determined immediately to ride to Gleawanceaster and confront the king's advisors. William Malet was the one who prevailed on him most not to do it, reminding him how ill it served him to be seen in unreasonable temper. "You know they will mark it against you," he said. "You, of all men, ought to know that a word against a king's decision says to them only that you are a traitor or madman, and you will find no support either way."

"Aye." My father's voice was bitter. "Only think you not there is something dishonorable in my own father making no defense of my pledge? He at least understands I am neither."

"You know he bears the Welshman no love. He thinks perhaps you swore the lands away out of desperation and here he sees a way to save you from compromising Angland without despoiling the honor of your word."

My father spat with annoyance. "You know that is not the truth of it, else they would have called me to council."

"Then think on this, Ælfgar Leofric's son." My uncle's stern voice was unyielding. "That sometimes it matters more to serve your king than your family. An earl is, after all, a king's man, is he not? In that, your father knows and values his position. 'Tis something you give not the impression of understanding, and 'tis what turns many a man against you."

My father's eyes narrowed as he turned a cold gaze full upon the other. "You have always prided yourself on this unflinching loyalty! Well I have noted it is an esteemed thing amongst all the king's favorites to be so sworn to further his schemes—because they find great advantage to themselves therein!"

"Brother, mind your words—" William Malet began, but Ælfgar talked right past him.

"Here you look on a man who gains nothing from such groveling play, because the very same ones who design the king's decisions in their own behalf do so at my expense." He paused for a moment, then added, "At my undoing, even!"

"Never has it occurred to you that you have made your own self unloved of the king and his men with this self-serving attitude of yours?" My uncle's tone was harsh and I felt a leap of unease at the turn their converse was taking. Riding directly alongside my father, I could sense his defiance rising; he was quick to argue these days, and I did not want to see these two part as unfriends. Looking about, I sought for something with which to distract him. The other men, except for Cynewulf Cenwulf's son, had fallen back to allow the brothers-in-law to speak freely. Edwin and Fulke were now far ahead, frolicking with my uncle's huge Danish dogs. When Ælfgar had been still a long time, he suddenly threw his shoulders back and said lowly, almost under his breath, "Ever have you judged me harshly, wife's-brother, for knowing what it is I need and want."

"Nay," came the other's answer, "only for your taking of things, against all council and advice!"

"The matter of a woman is somewhat of a different thing than that of survival," my father glowered darkly, sitting erect in his silver-studded saddle, mouth set in a grim smile. "Well you know there are men about the king who would gladly see me dead and my sons disinherited. They have made no secret of their intent."

"Perhaps you fear them more than you need to."

My father spit again, but his voice was stiffly courteous. "I am a man who takes no chances where life and honor are concerned. If I misjudge their intentions, that will be proven to me in time, will it not? In the mean time, I choose to protect myself. No man can grudge me that."

William Malet eyed him curiously. "Take care in your dealings—" he began. My father silenced him with a look.

"Aye," he replied, staring hard into the other's eyes. "I know what side you would be forced to take if they instigated the king to declare against me."

"No man wants to raise a sword against a kinsman," my avunculus answered levelly, "but in the end, the king's peace must prevail at any price."

"Only remember that they are her sons, too!" exclaimed Ælfgar, with a quick, impassive glance my way. My uncle winced, ever so slightly.

"'Tis not something I am likely to forget, Ælfgar Leofric's son," he said very quietly. Then they both fell silent till Cynewulf turned the talk to other things.

When all was decided, my father determined to bide his anger, and made no move to confront the council. Some days later, when William Malet took his leave, Ælfgar was careful to tell him, in no uncertain terms, that the pact that stood between him and Gruffydd had been made with his own breath, and only his own breath could serve to break it. "I tell you this because I know you will share it," he said solemnly, with a careful and deliberate look, "and therefore will not all the land be amazed when I keep my word to the Welshman."

My uncle made no answer, only shook his head with despair before he rode off. He knew how harshly our house was plagued by the ambition of the Godwines. He realized they had played us false and understood that there lay my father's quarrel, and not with the king. He might even have felt Ælfgar was not entirely wrong in his forebodings. Nevertheless, he still trusted Providence to right things, something Ælfgar had given up on long since.

"What hope is there for a man who cannot find one other soul to stand by him in his own land?" my father asked Cynewulf miserably as they watched the king's man gallop away. "What hope for a man who has to find brothers amongst his enemies because his father and kinsmen all think he misreads the men who mean to deal him baseness?"

Cynewulf only shrugged, and then they returned to their birding.

CHAPTER THIRTEEN

The praiseworthy Earl Leofric, son of Leofwine, a
man of illustrious memory, died in a good old age in
his own vill called Bromleigh, on the second of the
Kalends of September (31st August) and was
honorably buried at Couventrie; which monastery,
among other good deeds of his life, he and his wife,
the noble Lady Godiva, a servant of God and a
devout lover of St. Mary the Ever Virgin, built from
the very foundation out of their own means, and
had sufficiently endowed it with lands, and so
enriched it with various ornaments, that in no
monastery in Angland could there be found so great
an abundance of gold and silver, gems and precious
stones, as at that time was contained therein.
As long as he lived, the wisdom of this earl was
of great benefit to the kings and all the people
of Angland.

—Simeon of Durham, 1057

Autumn, 1057
At summer's end, soon after Edwin turned twelve, we traveled back to
the monastery at Peterborough for our learning. We were very wroth
with Father; he had promised us a visit to the grandparents at
Couventrie but now he was so painfully fallen out with Earl Leofric that
he would not let us go. My uncle, the abbot, took this bad blood
between father and son very hard. He bade us pray that it would rapidly
dissolve away, but it did not. We kept the Christ Mass at Grantanbrycg
without them, and Ælfgar turned away a party of Grandfather's men
who came to claim us for our usual Eastertide visit.

Just before Edwin's thirteenth birthday, news came that Grandfather was deathly ill. Burchard announced his intention of going thither with Uncle Leofric, saying he would take my father's blessing or go without, it mattered not much to him, because he loved Grandfather dearly and could not bear to think of him dying unless his kinsmen were there to lighten it. Then Father relented and said we would all go.

Grandfather Leofric lay at Couventrie, in the manor house he had held and lived in so many years. Grandmother Godiva met us there, hollow-cheeked and wan, her shoulders wrenched by sorrow. She asked my father why he had bothered to come at all, saying it was his cold indifference which had smote the old man. My uncle took her in his arms, and she cried and begged forgiveness for saying it, reaching to stroke my father's cheek as if he were a little boy. The three of them went up to see the dying earl, leaving us in the great hall with a cold supper of fowl and bread.

In a while, Grandmother came back alone, and after hugging and kissing each one, she sat watching us eat. She asked many questions, as if to keep her mind busy. She wondered why mother had not come, and we explained how it had been with that lady of late; she had grown withdrawn and sullen, praying and fasting so much that the priests feared for her health and commanded her not to do it more.

Grandmother commented on how pretty Aldgyth was grown, how tall I was, how manly and husky Edwin's voice had become. Her face was crossed by a network of tiny wrinkles I had never noticed before. Her eyes were dimmed and faded, her golden hair besprinkled with silver. I had not seen her for a whole year and half again another.

We did not see Grandfather that day or the next, though Father and Uncle Leofric were with him every minute. Late on the third day, however, he sent for us, and Grandmother led us into his dimly-lit chamber. Though it was a warm day, a huge fire blazed in the hearth, and several steaming pots hung over it, spewing forth a scented mist of healing herbs. Grandmother told us to stand anext his bed but warned us not to tire him. When I looked upon the old Earl of the Mercians, I scarce recognized him, he was so changed and withered.

First thing he said was that Edwin looked so very much like his son, that he had almost mistaken him for Ælfgar. "Such a thing as a confusion of time comes upon a man when he is old and dying," he whispered hoarsely, looking from one to the other of us, "so that it is easy to misplace a span of twenty years or so, and mistake one person for another."

We all smiled, and Aldgyth patted his hand, telling him he was silly to suppose death was near. He shook his head and said that was one visitor no man had trouble recognizing.

He had great trouble speaking. For much of the visit he just touched us, stroking our arms or hands or brows, a happy, contented smile playing over his haggard, thought-worn face. Now and again he would stare off, as if watching something being played out a great distance away, far beyond the thick timber walls of his house. After a long time of silence between us, Aldgyth indicated with a nod that perhaps it would be best if we left him to his rest, but when we began to move away, he begged us to remain longer and so we did. Seems he was happy just to have us near. We might have stayed till he fell to sleeping, but Grandmother came to the door and motioned us away.

"I should like to have the children with me one at a time," Earl Leofric told her softly. "I would like to have a word with each alone."

"Tomorrow!" she answered. As we filed out, I cast back one short glance. She was resting her tiny frame against his, her head upon his heaving chest, and he hugged her to him stroking her bounden hair. It was the last I ever saw him in the world, and the picture was not unpleasant, for he looked strong and bold again, holding his woman that way.

At dawn, we wakened to the commotion of the laying-out, and the somber sound of a priest's chanting in the death-chamber. We dressed hurriedly, as if a pressure were on us to be ready for something. Then, not knowing what to do with ourselves, we tarried in the room, sorrowful, silent, and bewildered. With Edwin, I undid all the pallets and folded them flat against the wall, while Aldgyth sorted and rolled the linens, piling them with the raw wool stuffed pillows atop a high garderobe. Then we sat wordlessly, waiting.

After a while my uncle came for us, his thin lips twisted into a smile which belied the woeful emotion of his eyes. Leaning against the door, he told us how things had gone, assuring us the earl had died peacefully, tight in his son's warm embrace. Ælfgar was gone now, and no one knew where. He had run from his father's room within minutes of the passing, flying into the black night, no saddle on his mount and not so much as a mantle to ward off the nightly chill. From the open casement, I looked down upon two men hard working to fashion a trestle for my grandfather's bier.

Late in the day, the abbot brought us in to pray before they carried the coffin to the monastery. Now it stood in the middle of the room, draped over with sheets and linens of purest, bleached white, surrounded by planks full of lighted candles. In my heart I was glad not to have to look upon the body. I well remembered the strange, glassy eyes of Cynric's dead babe, half hid by its clammy lids. Mother had made us kiss its cold and dewy cheek; I dreamt of that sometimes.

Mourners had gathered in the corpse-chamber. Some knelt, some sat, some paced back and forth. In the shadows, on a bench with his back pressed hard against the wall, was my father. There was something disturbing about the look of him. I had never before seen him weep, and the blank-eyed, prideful arrogance of his gaze was strangely at odds with the childish vulnerability of his tear-stained sorrow. I went to his side while the others genuflected at the coffin and hovered near Grandmother. Father did not acknowledge me, but I felt that somehow my presence brought him comfort.

After a while, someone came and sat anext me—a broad-boned, stoic-eyed boy of fifteen or sixteen years, with tonsured, rusty-colored hair. This was Wulfget, the ward my grandfather had sponsored at Peterborough after the boy's parents passed away. Edwin and I had grown fond of his friendship; the months we spent at the monastery were always happier for his company. Father and Grandfather had spotted his capability and promise when Wulfget was still young, and had provided him an education which few but the very high-born would have expected.

Now, leaning close to me, he whispered, "I am truly sorry for you, Master Morcar!" I answered earnestly that I was sorry for him, too. Wulfget had loved Grandfather right well; the men of our house stood in stead of kinsmen to him.

Uncle Leofric rose and went to the head of the bier. He read the litany, and all in the chamber chanted after him, crossing themselves on his words and striking their breasts as they replied with their pleas for mercy. It was a long and uncomfortable service and my knees began to ache against the cold stone floor. I could not keep my eyes or thoughts from wandering and I felt guilty about it. Of a sudden, I wondered why my father and I sat in the back of the room when all the rest of the family were gathered close to the flickering, glittering tapers which surrounded the corpse-bed. Then, with a pang, I realized that Ælfgar was not kneeling.

My uncle blessed the coffin and everyone rose as one. Grandmother stood with Burchard and Grandfather's chief man, Elfhelm, at the arched door which led to the great hall, where the grave-ale was laid. As folk filed past they hugged her, kissed her or offered condolences in some way. Uncle Leofric extinguished the tapers, lest the warmth of them bring on the breath of decay before the funeral. A few of Grandfather's men came over to talk with Father but he was sullen and would not speak. When everyone had left, the two of us still sat there. I moved close and leant against him.

Thusly we stayed awhile before Cynewulf and Ælfric White-Hair came in to claim Father. "Know you not you are sorely missed in the next room?" Cynewulf asked him frowningly. My father shrugged but made no answer. His man grew angry.

"'Tis an unbearable selfishness that keeps you from your grieving mother's side," he hissed. "Best you go in there where you should be and help shoulder some of her sorrow!"

Ælfgar's voice cracked. "Think you I could trust myself to drink my father's grave-ale? Would I not chance wreaking dishonor on him in death as I oft had done him in life?"

The other men exchanged a puzzled look. "Methinks you need not torment yourself now by dwelling on things long past," said Ælfric consolingly. "He died thinking he had reconciled them with you."

"Nay!" my father exclaimed hotly. "With his very last words he named me blameful."

"'Tis not the way I heard it—" Cynewulf began but my father stopped him with a violent gesture.

"Take your leave now, Earl's Man! I am in a temper such that I would gladly fight you for my solitude."

Cynewulf bit back a reply, then invited me to leave with him. Ælfgar still held me loosely, so I shook my head and the two men left us. Soon after, Uncle Leofric came and drew up a stool to face us in the gloomy chamber.

"Tell me what it is that lies so heavy on you, brother."

My father glanced at him in a belligerent way. "Think you not I am entitled to a portion of grief?"

"I think 'twould take more than that to keep a man from praying for his father's repose, or to separate him from the kin-table at the grave-ale."

"The prayers of a traitor and priest-killer could not buy him much indulgence, could they? And I think that in life he boasted little of my sonship, so grievous were my faults to him!"

Abbot Leofric stared open-mouthed. "How can you talk in such way, Ælfgar Leofric's son? The man loved you better than any father ever loved a son! You know as much. Never a wild misdeed you made but that he forgave it; never a fault that he would not forget."

"But one!"

"Name it."

"That I was not alike to him." A sob rose in his throat, but he choked it down. "Every choice I made wounded him because of it; not a day since I came to manhood but that I pierced him through with what I had become."

Springing to his feet, my uncle made the sign of the cross over him. Then my father stood, and the two men embraced, weeping both with a sound that rent my very soul. When they pulled apart, my father wiped his face with the sleeve of his fine-woven tunic and forced an abject smile.

"I tried to be what he wanted. God knows I did!"

"Aye. That He does, brother," my uncle answered. "Yet forget not that it was He in His infinite wisdom who decreed what it was you would be; He who created you fully formed in spirit to be as no other man. He also determined how it would be that you differed from the man He made your father, in order to fulfill His own purposes. Think you how Earl Leofric told us on the eve of every Christ Mass, year after year: that nothing ever befalls a man for naught, but that all things spring from God's reasons."

Groaning, Ælfgar pulled away from him. "I would not come to him his last Christ Mass!" He walked to the middle of the room and crossed himself.

The abbot smiled darkly. "Then mayhap you gained more by not coming! Always you have been a man who learns best from the hardest lessons."

I stood and traced my way to my father's side where he knelt now beside the shadowy bier. As if it had just occurred to him, my uncle spoke softly, with a sort of wonder.

"Only one son in all the world ever was everything his father wanted him to be, and he was cursed and bruised and reviled and scorned of men. For God so loved the world, that he gave his only begotten son...."

Then I was weeping, and my father was holding me close.

*   *   *

A fortnight after Grandfather was buried in the great monastery he had built at Couventrie, the king called the Gemot to confirm my father as Earl of all Mercia. Despite his former assurances, he took the East Anglia from our house again, dividing it into smaller holdings for Godwine's younger sons, Gyrth and Leofwine. Luckily, Ælfgar had not been at Gleawanceaster to personally hear the pronouncement. Might be they would have cut him down in blood had he exhibited there the rage he showed when he learnt of it at Grantanbrycg.

Cynewulf, Æthelstan, Ælfric, Uncle Leofric—everyone begged my father not to set his household up at Ceaster. 'Twould bode him only ill, they said, to be seen setting camp right across the river from the hated Welshman.

"I smell trouble of the worst kind in this," the abbot of Peterborough told him severely. "Just the fact that you mean to keep your land-pledge to the Cymrian king is enough to fire them. If you move your home anext him, you know they will be forced to act against you!"

But Ælfgar would not be moved from his determination. The thing he had feared so long had come to pass. He sat alone in a whittled down Mercia—the only earldom not a Godwine holding—surrounded by his enemies. One brief stretch of the northwestern boundary they did not hold, and that was the land he meant to share with his Welsh blood brother.

The rolling, frost-covered reaches shone moon-like silver as we wended our way through the midlands to take a new home once more. Winter had come early, and in the interest of expediency, Father quartered the bulk of the household at Scrobbesbyrig till the thaws, carrying to Ceaster only his family, his priests, and his men-at-arms. There was a great deal of grumbling about it. The guardsmen were not happy about the prospect of being separated from their women and children through the Christ Mass, but none of them felt strongly enough about it to petition their earl for special consideration. Because we had no working household of our own with us, we moved into a manor already staffed and running. 'Twas my father's right as Earl of Mercia to claim any estate he wanted, and he chose the great house in Ceaster which belonged to our kinsman Siward Bearn, who had expanses of land there, in the aet-Waeringwicum and in Deoraby besides his awesome holdings in the Diera. The place was occupied now by his brother, Ealdread, who had fled the North Humbria near a year earlier, his quarrel with the new earl, Tostig Godwine's son, having become irreconcilable.

We had not been settled a full week when my father sent a party to require a council of Gruffydd. "Tell him I will come to whatever place he names, with hostages and pledge-gifts if he so desires it. If the evil talk has come to him of the Gemot's decision to retain the Dee-lands, stress to him that I bide not by it, that my word stands as sworn."

Days later, when their swift ship reappeared in the mouth of the Dee, we were amazed to see another vessel with it—the beautiful eagle-prowed war-ship Ælfgar had given the Welsh king to seal their blood-pact. Gruffydd had come to us.

My father decked himself in splendor that day, in his finest tunic with belts, armlets and necklaces of precious metals. He wore a blue-dyed mantle lined with black wolf fur and bossed in silver and garnet. His hair was banded round with a fillet of gold. He bade my mother and sister dress in seemly fashion. Æthelstan, after helping array Edwin, turned himself to the task of dressing me. I wore braies now, having seen my twelfth year, gartered in dyed suede, with suede shoes to match. Over that was the finest of my woven tunics, bleached white with green and blue stitching at the wrist. My dalmatic was richly embroidered with fruits and leaves; gold keys and a silver knife-sheath hung from my girdle. Ælfgar was doing honor to the Welshman by dressing us as if to meet the noblest and most powerful of kings.

He set the hall in the same magnificent manner. The venison had been slaughtered a month hence, so salt meat was all he could offer on short notice, but he bargained with kinsman Ealdread for the game of the dove-cote to supplement it. The cider was fresh, there were great quantities of ale and mead, and nuts, seeds, and dried fruits were plentiful.

It was not a common thing to sit men on both sides of a table in the continental way, but my father arranged to do it, putting Gruffydd and the ten chief of his men on the one side. He sat himself and his family on the other, along with Cynewulf, Ealdread, Ælfric White-Hair, Æthelstan, and Cynric. The fact that my sister and mother mingled with the men at table was a sign of the highest honor for our guests.

The Cymrian king may not have understood the intricacies of our welcoming customs but the splendor of the proffered display was surely not lost on him. Nor was the genuineness of Earl Ælfgar's greeting, which Gruffydd returned in kind. My father stood impulsively when the Welshman entered the hall, and there was only a moment's hesitation before the two strode purposefully together, eyes alight with emotion.

"Seems you look thinner and not so hale as when we last met!" Gruffydd smiled as they walked to the table together.

"Aye." My father nodded ruefully. "'Twas summer then, and I felt more of wind and open country and less of hall-smoke and hurt and sorrow!"

Edwin and I exchanged a surprised glance when we heard this. We had taken our leave of Gruffydd two years ago in the Advent. Must be Ælfgar had seen him furtively since then.

The king made his greetings first to the women, as was the Cymrian way. Naught of him had changed, which pleased me. The handsome, weathered face was still framed in its unruly, thickly curling mass of dark hair and beard. Those fiery, strange eyes, the color of ripened black cherries, remained endlessly deep and unfathomable. The smile I remembered so well was just as indomitable; he flashed it as he took my hands and made salutations. I grinned back. When he was seated, we all burst at once into pleasant talk while the rest of the men filed into the hall.

"How is it all your underlings have grown so?" the Welshman asked with genuine wonder. "Now there is not much of childishness left even in the youngest two, and the first two are well-nigh whole grown man and woman!"

Aldgyth blushed and Burchard glowed with pride. My father looked from one to the other with a thoughtful look. "What you say is true," he mused, as if it had only just occurred to him. "Now that nothing separates my holdings from yours, we must make certain that not so much time passes between our meetings." He leant across the table and took his friend's hands in a hard and manly grip. "From this very day, brother," he said in a low voice, "the lands I pledged to you are Welsh lands and it is to me as if there is no border between us. Come you into my Mercia for safety or succor or pleasure whenever the want is upon you, and you will be welcomed as a lord of the land."

Gruffydd swallowed hard, meeting the other man's gaze with one of unabashed emotion. "You have well-proven your brotherhood, Ælfgar Leofric's son," he said pensively, "and against all the reproaches of your countrymen and kinsmen, you have held true to your sworn word. For this I give you thanks. And more, I give you all the Cymry for shelter or sanctuary, or home and hearth, whatsoever you may desire of it. Yet I little see how you can stand alone against all your land in keeping that promise you made unto me—"

My father cut him off, lifting a mead-horn, rimmed round in silver. "Methinks I stand not alone, brother," he said firmly, and Gruffydd's ruddy features lit in a grin of pleasure.

"Nay, 'tis certain you do not!" he cried, raising his own horn. Then they drank together.

I said little during that long meal, being absorbed in the fascinating converse of the two well-matched men. I had not given much thought to Gruffydd in the last year or so; now I realized how sorely I had missed him. Now and again, I caught his eye upon me and when I did, he smiled or winked with cordiality. His attitude was much like that of an uncle or cousin or well-deemed kithsman. His manner towards my mother was one of deference and concern; even she seemed to warm in his company.

One thing was certain. Whenever the Welshman's gaze met Aldgyth's, it gave me to know my sister was a child no longer. When the women were taking their leave, I saw that he watched Aldgyth's every movement until she disappeared through the timber archway. I could not help feeling embarrassed when I saw him lick his underlip in a brooding way and then bite hard into it, as if to suppress some unwanted thought. This time, when he shifted and found my gaze on him, a flush rose under his sun-brown skin, and he grinned carelessly, as if in apology.

Later, so late that we had to be wakened to greet him, my cousin Siward Æthelgar's son, Bearn of the Diera, arrived with a party of his men, all splendidly arrayed in the North Humbrian style. They had ridden long and hard from Tathaceaster. My father greeted the younger man with particular fondness, asking after his sister and his household in a most intimate way, so that we knew he had visited there also without having said aught to any of us about it. Gruffydd and his men had long since taken to bed, in the stone monk's house, which was the finest of the many out-buildings on the estate. Apparently, my copper-haired cousin had expected to travel with Earl Ælfgar into the Cymry; his surprise was obvious when his brother Ealdread told him Gruffydd was already there, visiting in his house.

"Think you not this is a great boldness?"the Bearn asked Ælfgar guardedly, as we sat in the chill, near-empty hall drinking hot mead. Ælfgar shrugged his shoulders; Cynewulf was the one who answered.

"It matters not where we do the meeting," he said. "They will construe it as treason whether here or there."

"Nay. Methinks 'tis a boldness greater on Anglish soil," my cousin answered, looking over his cup as he sipped.

My father's eyes narrowed. "'Tis on Mercian soil we meet, kinsman!" he said. There was a finality in his tone which gave me shivers. I looked to Burchard for an explanation but he signaled me to silence. Edwin and I had more or less tagged along because we had wakened with the other men in the chamber. Now my brother let me know that the business had naught to do with us. Suddenly, it plagued me that so much secrecy was about. I realized instinctively that Ælfgar had conspired to bring these like-minded men together, but for what purpose I could not say.

We rode for mass on the morrow to the timber-church in the hinter-lands which Ealdread and Siward's father had built to the memory of his dead wife, my mother's sister, who had died violently by her own hand. It was a lonely place but well made and serviceable, with one tall wood tower and a great bell cast of iron, brought from the Nor Way many years hence. It was a small party that rode there: my brothers and sister and I, Siward Bearn, Ealdread and his lady, Gweneth, my mother and her ladies. Six of Siward's men-at-arms followed us and six of my father's, but they rode some ways behind us and stayed in the back of the drafty church the length of the hurried service. My mother, fair in white furs, looked very small standing between Burchard and Siward Bearn, who was one of the tallest men I knew. She was very fond of her sister's son. Even with his long, dyed North Humbrian tresses and studded ears, he was an imposing sight. She would gladly have had him wed with Aldgyth, even at the cost of buying off the ban of consanguinity which would be very expensive because of their close kinship. The only match in all of Angland that could have been higher for her would have been an earl, and seeing that every earl but my father was a son of Godwine, 'twas not likely that she would so wed.

When the service was over, the men brought our horses to the church door. As Siward Bearn lifted Aldgyth to her saddle, I heard him question her in a half-mocking voice. "What answer mean you to make to our cousin Oswulf when he comes hither to seek your hand, lady Aldgyth?" His voice was jesting but he looked right into her ocean eyes to ask it.

She tossed her head, giving a small laugh. "I have heard naught from fair Oswulf," she answered lightly, "nor my father has, that I have learnt!"

"Nevertheless, his intent is to have you, and he makes no secret of it." Siward's look was impish and his voice over-mournful. Edwin drew his horse close, a look of contempt and unwonted fierceness lighting his features.

"Tell Oswulf Eadwulf's son he cannot have her till the day he fights Ælfgar's sons who mean to stand in the way of his intentions!"

Siward Bearn, Ealdread, and Burchard all burst out laughing at once. Cousin Oswulf was not a great favorite of ours though he was stunning to see. Aldgyth waited till the merriment subsided, then leant over and lightly tweaked at Siward's red locks, whipped and tangled now by the bitter wind.

"I will make him this answer," she said with a merry twinkle, "that my heart belongs wholly, totally to another."

My kinsman's look grew suddenly sharp and his grey eyes shone seriously. "'Tis the same answer you would make to me, I trow?" he asked in a woeful half-whisper.

"Aye, cousin," she answered somberly, touching his rough cheek for just an instant and looking as if it pained her to say it. Then she nudged her white palfrey to a pert trot, trying to catch up with Ælfgiva and Gweneth and the rest of the ladies, far ahead. Siward Bearn gazed after her, crestfallen.

"You would do well to ask her again," Burchard said, trying hard to lift my cousin's spirits, "only do it by firelight or under a black sky studded with star-shine!"

My cousin shook his head. "Nay," he said heavily, forcing a smile. "You know we would be hard-pressed to get a dispensation...." His voice trailed off morosely and no more was said about it, but we all knew she had hurt him.

*   *   *

Towards twilight, it began to snow. Edwin and I, teeth chattering with discomfort, made our way back to the hall. Despite the bitter cold, we had spent most of the day outside, the hall being too noisome and crowded with men, and the smoke too intense from cooking for all of them. We had explored some of the many out-buildings—the high-lofted monk's house and the byre and the stabling barn—and then amused ourselves by throwing stones through the mirror-like surfaces of frozen-over puddles. Now, we sat huddled as close as we could get to the huge hearth fire, warming ourselves.

We had not seen Burchard, Ealdread, or Siward Bearn since we returned from the Mass. My father, behind closed doors with Gruffydd, had called them immediately into council, and they had not yet emerged from the boxed room that opened off the raised dais where the high table stood. Of all his men, Ælfgar had taken only Cynewulf and Ælfric White-Hair in there. Gruffydd brought but one, the warrior Carr—his cousin and the chief of his men. Whatever it was they were pacting amongst themselves, they meant to keep it secret.

"Get you up, knaves, and dressed for table!" Æthelstan, a cross look in his hawk-like eyes, eyed us as we sat feeling forlorn and forgotten anext the blazing fire. Edwin lifted a red-cheeked face to make his answer, but his usual defiant tone had given way to one of half-hearted resignation.

"Methinks we are well-arrayed enough to sup with this crowd," he said wearily, making no protest as Æthelstan unwrapped his mantle to inspect his garb. My brother was still in his Mass-dress and the fen-man found little fault with it, though Edwin's braies and leather shoes were, in fact, soaked. I thought my own dress was well enough in order, but Æthelstan scowled in disappointment as he inspected me.

"Put on you a necklace or some accoutrements, Master Morcar!" he commanded with a grimace. "You sit tonight with high-born men. Get you presentable! Comb those tresses, and do not come back unless they are bound 'round with a fillet!"

Æthelstan's voice seemed to follow me through the hall as I made my way out. I turned around to nod my assent, purposely exaggerating a look of long-suffering patience, and headed to claim some article of adornment with which to grace myself. Having passed my mother and Aldgyth in the hall, I expected our room to be empty. So it was that I was very surprised, when my eyes adjusted to the gloom, to find Burchard within, laid out on an unmade pallet, flat on his back. He gave a start at my entrance, but as the heavy door fell shut behind me, he whispered a listless greeting. I could barely make him out in the light of the single spitting pine torch sconced to the stone wall.

"What is it ails you, brother?" I asked. "All this time I took you to be with Father and the others."

"Nay, Morcar. I came away to keep vespers."

I looked at him curiously. "Keep you all the hours?"

"Aye, unless worldly affairs keep me from them." Burchard had lain his mantle over him for warmth and it fell to the floor as he sat up. Retrieving it, I asked what he prayed for.

"For Mother and Father mostly," he said low, pinning the cloak at his shoulder with the fine sapphire-set brooch he had gotten from Grandfather. "For Mother with her fiercesome dreams and Father in his harsh wool shirts." He shuddered. "What is it you are here for? Have they not taken to table?"

"Soon enough they mean to," I told him, rummaging through one of my chests for a heavy gold neck-chain that I liked, hung with two pendants—a gold sun and a silver moon. "Father and the others have not yet quit their talk."

I struggled a minute with the necklace, then Burchard leant over, lifted the tangled hair from my nape, and adjusted it.

"How is it your hair is such a mess as this?" he asked, tugging at it playfully. "You ought to know by now that a fillet will keep it from snarling like that."

I nodded mournfully.

"And when last did you have it washed?" he wondered aloud, parting into it with his fingers. I had to think.

"Before we came to Ceaster," I mumbled low. He spun me around to see his look of disapprobation.

"Morcar, only three things there are besides jewels and precious metals that set us apart from the peasants and lower of men!" He paused there and drew in a deep breath, trying hard to keep a look of severity in his mild brown eyes. "We sleep in shifts or night-shirts," he said, holding up a finger as if to count it, "and never in our day-clothes."

I nodded my silent assent. He held up a second finger.

"We wash with water, all over, as frequently as we find a need— once daily at least. A man of gentle birth is not to smell unless he is in arms at battle!"

I agreed with him again. Then he held up the third finger, drawing his brows together into an accusing glare. "We keep our hair fresh and free of living things by having it washed and rinsed with herbed or flow-ered water. When the sweet smell is gone, 'tis time to have it scrubbed again, else you may find it harboring things that ruin your sleep and are ill-marked against you!"

I shuddered, thinking how father, who always fed beggars and pilgrims and traveling priests in the kitchens or cook-houses of our manors, would order all the floors and benches swept with rush when they took their leave, and the gleanings tossed into the fire. Any scullion of his found harboring living things fast became a stable boy or field hand.

"This is your twelfth year. From now on you will be reckoned more as a man, and folk will look for these things in you," Burchard continued, watching me bind the newly-smooth hair with a simple silver fillet. "Why do you suppose Father is so loved by his people? 'Tis the graces of his person! An earl need not have more than that and a balance of boldness and piety to have the liege of all his folk."

"Seems not likely that I will ever be aught but an earl's son or brother, Burchard," I commented soberly.

"What think you they have been about in that closed room all day?" he asked in a voice suddenly hardened. He took the torch from off the wall and dunked it in a bucket to extinguish it as he answered his own question. "They are scrounging earldoms for the sons of Ælfgar! Whichever comes vacant first will go to Edwin, either Mercia or the North Humbria. The other is for you."

I stopped dead in the darkness, stunned and confused. "Mercia is your sworn right, and always has been!"

"'Tis my will to take the cloth. I know I would be robbing God if I did other." He sat down heavily on the pallet and I made my way over to sit anext him. His strong shoulders were bent as with a great weight.

"Does any man know of this, brother?" I put my hand on his, thinking to give him strength.

"Aye. Father and I have talked of it long since, and Grandfather and Uncle Leofric. We took it to Bishop Aldred when we were in Lundun City last. He says that to put the earldom aside will take a special dispensation from the Pope, but he sees no reason that it will not be granted."

My head was spinning, my mind full of questions. "What thinks Father of this?" I thought how proud he had been with Burchard at his side ever since my brother had come to manhood.

Burchard paused a long time before he answered. "He thinks it best to hide it from Mother till it can be hid no longer."

I felt a sudden chill. This was something that surely would break her, she had longed so hard to see her first-born sit in the earl's high-chair with Mercia at his feet. It oft-times seemed it was the one thing she lived for. Without even meaning to, I let go a breathless sigh of despair, and Burchard put his arm around my shoulder.

"I have not done well to burden you with this, Morcar, but the news lies so heavy on me and there is not another I could think to share it with."

"Edwin?" I asked.

"Edwin has too light a tongue! One thing only Father required of me: that this remain secret till he has another heir of an age to succeed him. It works on him like poison that the sons of Godwine would see him slain and take Mercia if he had no son old enough to keep it in tow."

"'Tis not improbable," I said in a melancholy way, though I knew

Burchard felt differently, the way Grandfather had, that the quarrel could never grow as stringent as that.

"So this is no easy charge I have put on you," he went on, ignoring my doleful comment. "I made oath to Father on relics that knowledge of this would come to no man who could use it against him."

"He made you swear?" I asked, incredulous.

"Nay." He swallowed hard. "I found myself doing it all of my own accord, because—just because he took it so ill when first I told him."

"He has come to accept it now, I trow?"

"Oh, aye. Even he is somewhat prideful of it. He thinks to see me groomed to hold all our house's church-land—abbot of the four great Mercian monasteries like Uncle Leofric. You know there is no one in all the world he holds in higher regard than that one, and Uncle Leofric has stood firm behind me in this since ever I first approached him."

While we sat talking, a tremendous shout of salute went up in the hall, and a great buzz of merriment and commotion, which gave us to know that Ælfgar and his high-honored guests had finally come to table. I pulled myself to my feet; Burchard did the same. "Glad I am you have spoken on this with me, brother," I told him with love and earnestness. We lent each other a brotherly embrace before making our way into the jostling busyness of the hall.

CHAPTER FOURTEEN

Tostig was advanced by King Edward after
Siward's death to the earldom of North humbria
. . . his habitual fierceness roused the North
humbrians to revolt.

—William of Malmesbury

January 1058
Three days later, the time came for Gruffydd to take his leave. Soon afterwards, Cynewulf summoned Edwin and me to a chamber where father sat waiting. Cynewulf took his leave and closed the door behind him, leaving the three of us alone in the dimness there. A bitter wind, roaring in from the north, had beaten away the lingering snow-showers during the night. Now it howled with early morning ferocity, forcing its way through the canvas which screened the narrow window slits and rustling noisily among the rushes which were strewn thickly over the stone floor for warmth. Despite thick woolen robes and a mantle of northern fox fur, Ælfgar was shivering when we found him, apparently not finding much comfort in the steaming cup of mead on the table before him. He gestured us to sit and his smile was grim. Though he had accepted neither sacrament nor break-fast, 'twas plain he had partaken of spirits some while already, an unusual thing for him at that hour. He had counciled with the Welsh king far into the night, Siward Bearn and his men having left on the yester-noon. I could tell by my father's eyes that he had not slept.

"Tell me the man-price named by law for one of gentle birth," he commanded, looking from my brother to me as we seated ourselves opposite him. The drink put a boyish flush to his pale, hollow face. He never looked weathered as some men his age did; he was nearing thirty and six. Not understanding him, we made no answer, so he asked it again.

"King's man or earl's man?" Edwin's brilliant eyes narrowed over a puzzled frown.

"Earl's son." My father's voice was thick.

"First-born or one born after?" I asked. Ælfgar, elbows on the table, bit at his thumb-nails with his hands clasped tightly together. In the greyness, the golden ring of the Earl of the Mercians gleamed, almost as if it had a light of its own. It was a massive, handsome prize. While I watched it glitter, Edwin gasped and sprang to his feet.

"Must be this is some powerful bargain you have struck, father," he cried accusingly in a shrill voice, dissonant with anger, "that you must seal it by standing us hostage to your pledge. Ever I have wondered when this day would come!"

Never as quick as my brother to pick up on Ælfgar's feelings, it took a moment for his meaning to strike me. Turning a look of open-mouthed shock and bewilderment on my father, I cringed to hear his low whispered reply.

"Well you know I swore you both away three years ago," he said, looking past us. "Then the Welshman chose not to claim his due. Things have grown more crucial since. Now other men than the two of us have great stake in this; they mean to see our alliance sealed with more than an arm-clasp. It is their right to demand it for they involve themselves in deadly business! Think you this does not lie heavy on me?"

Edwin pounded his fist on the table and turned his back, stomping a few paces away with ferocious vehemence.

Rubbing his brow as if to stifle a pain, my father continued, his voice tremulous with emotion. "All night I have weighed on this. God knows I am forced to make my promise good. Three princes for a childling of mine was the bargain, and Gruffydd is now gone yonder to his war-ship to bring me the sons of his cousin Carr."

Stopping abruptly, he drew a sharp breath, swallowing hard to keep his feelings from showing. "I thought it best to tell you this before he returned to claim you." Trembling somewhat, he finished off his mead, now grown cold, in a single mighty gulp. With a despairing sigh, Edwin sat down.

"Which of us do you mean to send away?"

"The choice is his," Ælfgar replied tonelessly, settling back in his heavy chair. "The heir to Mercia he promised he would not take." He flinched, and I recalled with a pang all Burchard had told me of the secret circumstances of which Gruffydd knew nothing. For an instant it seemed I felt the weight of my father's unbearable sorrow. Then, I realized suddenly that Ælfgar surely must have been praying that the Welshman would choose me rather than Edwin. Shaking, I crossed my arms in front of me and put my head down on them.

A thousand thoughts assailed me. Life had not been unpleasant in the

Cymry, despite the primitive way of life. Gruffydd had been kind and generous—a mentor and friend. With my privileges assured and his friendship, it might be bearable. I would have frequent access to Mercia, at least until the king and his advisors came to full warfare against the Welsh and Mercian alliance. I shuddered. It would only be days before the king's men learnt something had transpired at Ceaster, important enough to require the bonding of an earl's son to seal it. They would not hesitate. If the Anglish fyrd took the Welsh border, if my father or Gruffydd was killed, then I was open prey to any warrior who might seek to buy King Edward's peace with my person. I had to shake the thoughts away....

Later, when we sat to table in our richest attire, I could not speak the entire length of the meal. Seated between Edwin and Aldgyth, I found my gaze drawn to the broad-shouldered Cymrian king, so inexplicably distinguished in a plain brown dalmatic. Except for his earrings and a choker of cast silver, he bore no ornaments, yet no man could doubt that he was a king. He wore the look of it.

As the board was being cleared, Gruffydd stood. Raising a gold-rimmed horn high in the air, he addressed my father with lofty words of honor and friendship, the genuineness of his meaning making itself felt through his stilted and formal Anglish. Ælfgar stood, managing to look proud and imperious despite the well-aled warmth of his blazing eyes. When they drank together, a tremendous cheer resounded.

Across the board and some places down to the left of me, three brothers sat. They were the sons of Gruffydd's kinsman, Carr. The youngest appeared a scant year or so older than Edwin. The other two, who might have been twins, seemed to have seventeen or eighteen years to them. I scrutinized the trio carefully, taking in the richness of their garb. Over their leather tunics they wore dalmatics of yellow kidskin and fur-lined mantles, brooched with copper-cased gems. Like their father, their thick black hair curled in massy ringlets, giving them a look of unaffected wildness. Each hung his neck with three or more necklaces, and their ears were studded. For some reason, watching them I grew uneasy despite myself. When the youngest one turned and inadvertently met my eye, I looked quickly away. I felt he appraised me with somewhat of a wonder that it should take the three of them to equal the worth of one of us.

When Ælfgar and Gruffydd stood again, the entire hall grew still; the crackling fire, the wind in the high rafters were the only sound.

Then the Welshman spoke. "I pray all here to be my witness," he said, dark eyes flashing defiantly, "that the words I have sworn unto Ælfgar the Mercian be true words: that my fate is joined with his, and the fate of his people with that of mine. That an insult laid upon him is as one lain on me; that his vengeance is my own! My word is pledged to protect alongside him the rights of his house against any who would despoil him by word or arms. Even to the making of battle, I am sworn to stand by him."

The holler of enthusiasm which greeted his words seemed to rock the very foundations of the huge hall. Before it could subside, the king of the Cymry lifted both his hands high over his head, fists clenched, a picture of commanding power and majesty. The effect was immediate; silence settled in the space of a breath and every warrior in the room turned eyes of unguarded respect upon him. He stood that way a moment longer, then turned to the three dark-headed sons of Carr, motioning them to stand. When they had come to his side, he spoke again for all to hear.

"On the lives of these dear to me I bind my promise. Three sons of a kinsman whose worth is well known, are what I offer. 'Tis long since that we reckoned between us, Earl Ælfgar, what the price of this sealing would be."

My father stepped back as if to appraise the three young men who approached him. Their manners were lordly. They appeared unconcerned, even proud, to have been chosen. One by one, they took Ælfgar's shoulders in salute. Impassive, motionless, he accepted their allegiance. Then he spoke. His voice was firm and resolute, betraying none of the fever of emotion which must have been upon him.

"There is naught you have pledged to me, Gruffydd, son of Llewellyn, that I do not pledge also unto you—favor and protection and men to stand behind you. Lands, goods, and gold I use to make fast my word to you, and I know that such is our brotherhood that you would trust these things alone, and my honor, to bind my pledges. Nevertheless, custom demands a trust-price, and one was named between us near to three years hence, when first I came to you. To appease those men who have joined my endeavor, you have this day met that price which was agreed upon. Now, I also am prepared—"

But here he stopped abruptly, floundering for words. For just a moment, his fine features wrenched into a mask of utter helplessness. Every muscle tightened, and he staggered slightly, then caught himself. Forcing once more his look of icy unconcern, he turned and put both of his hands on the Welsh king's shoulders, gazing levelly into his eyes.

"Choose then, brother," he said formally, clenching and unclenching his fists. "Choose that which is sworn unto you."

Gruffydd turned slowly towards us. The instant seemed an eternity. The entire room, pregnant with expectation, seemed suspended in an eerie, smoky silence. Heart pounding madly, I neither blinked nor breathed as he came toward us, his mouth tightened into an emotion-less frown.

"'Tis the maiden I will require, Ælfgar Leofric's son!"

My father's jaw dropped in unabashed shock and confusion. My mother, passing the back of her hand over her brow, gave a shrill cry. I glanced from one to the other as the hall erupted into a thunder of whispers and Aldgyth sprang to her feet, open-mouthed. Her skin flushed apple red. Her blue-green eyes glittered like light on water.

"Pray you will not play with us in such-like manner!" She cried, stifling a sob; tears welled over her dark lashes. Gruffydd studied her appreciatively with a gentle smile.

"'Tis the maiden I will require," he repeated, walking slowly back to where my father still stood speechless, "and I mean to take her as no hostage, but as Cwene of the Cymry."

Jumping to his feet with an audible gasp, Burchard flew to Aldgyth's side, for she had grown visibly weak at the sound of the words. Standing behind her, he held her shoulders tightly, looking past her to the Welshman who seemed totally delighted with the uproar he had caused amongst all the men, Welsh and Mercian, in the crowded hall.

"Make you no answer to my demand, Earl Ælfgar?" Gruffydd asked cunningly, turning to face my sister. My father stood mute, as if lost for words, considering the proposition. Trembling and unsteady, he avoided Aldgyth's troubled gaze.

Burchard broke the uncomfortable silence. "Under Christian law, no man can force her into wedlock, neither father nor king. The right is hers to refuse him."

"She comes as hostage if not as wife," spoke Gruffydd bluntly. Turning, he eyed my father squarely. "Methinks you cannot help but see the advantage to yourself that lies herein, Mercian, wroth as you are to part with son's blood!"

"Aye!" exclaimed the other, unflinching. "But it will seem the greater treason, I fear."

Gruffydd laughed, unmockingly, without artifice. "Now that the Godwines hold all the lands but Mercia, think you they will consider degrees of treason with you, brother? Nay! The fox is slain that eats a small hen every bit as soon as that which steals a large one!"

Shrugging with confusion, my father spun full around, turning his back to the Welshman in an effort to conceal his thoughts. Exchanging one hurried, nervous glance, Cynewulf Cenwulf's son and Ælfric White-Hair leapt to his side, huddling with him in whispered confer-ence. They gestured vehemently but kept their voices so low that naught could be heard of their whispered arguments. Gruffydd stood with his hands on his hips, lips pursed into a confident, knowing smile. His eyes were on Aldgyth, but he turned them full upon Ælfgar when that man pulled away from his advisors and approached him.

"My sworn word was that you should have choice of my childlings, it is true," he said, iron eyes flashing. "Never have I deigned to break my word with any man, enemy or friend. Seeing you have set your mind upon this, I am bound to defer to your decision. The child is yours. As to the manner in which you carry her home—"

He paused then, and drawing a long, deep breath, cast Aldgyth a tense, miserable look which she returned with a fleeting flicker of a smile. He looked away. "As to how you shall carry her, in that she must make her desire known to you in my hearing."

Aldgyth's face was pale and drawn with the weight of the moment but when she spoke, her voice was calm and even. "My Lord Gruffydd," she said, locking her gaze boldly into his, "still my father calls me 'child' though 'tis a year or more gone since I reached marrying age. Mayhap you also mistake me for a bewildered babe and believe I would not hesitate in choosing between hostage and king's lady."

She stopped a few feet in front of him, fingering the golden cross laced round her slender throat. "Yet a choice of such import I cannot here and now make," she continued, "unless you will answer for me one telling question."

Gruffydd tried to hide a smile of amusement, biting his lip as he bade her ask it. She paused a moment, as if to summon courage. "Is it as a woman you desire me, Son of Llewellyn, or as a traded trophy?"

Amazed at her forwardness, the Welshman had a hard time voicing his answer. His wide-eyed, vulnerable astonishment was almost comical. Blushing like a callow youth, he stammered. "Surely Lady Aldgyth must know that my feelings are—" He faltered, helpless, then caught himself. "Surely my lady knows it is her womanliness which compels me to make such uncourteous suit for her."

Her stern look grew suddenly gentle and meek. Smiling, she reached her hands to his shoulders, just as the sons of Carr had made allegiance to my father.

"Then surely my Lord Gruffydd knows," she retorted in a voice loud enough to be heard by all, "I would be proud to be made wife unto him."

*   *   *

Gruffydd and Aldgyth had no wedding; there was neither time nor need for it. Gruffydd was anxious to return to his homeland, and the bride-price was already settled. Nevertheless, the Welshman postponed his voyage near a full week to allow Aldgyth to pack her wardrobe, gather what she could of an accompaniment, and make her fare-wells. On the very last day, the hand-fasting was performed, so my sister had one day of her bride-ale celebration in Mercia. Then she left, starry-eyed and radiant, bringing only a single priest and four ladies with her. She meant, she said, as Cwene to become Cymrian in her mien and manner, and she needed no great number of Anglish to help her attain it.

We rode out to watch the couple set sail. From a low rise, we followed the glinting, gilded, eagle-prowed ship till it disappeared in a swirl of snow and sea mist. Then we reined our mounts around and made for home at a brisk pace, silent but satisfied, watching our horses' indignant breath cloud the chill late-day air.

It was a love match, there could be no question. No one had expected it, Gruffydd least of all, but as one day followed another till the hand-fasting, it became an obvious certainty. Aldgyth could not hide her feeling; her eyes spoke it, fairly bursting with reverence for him. And Gruffydd came soon enough to resemble an awkward, love-struck country-boy, gazing off into unseen distances at the very thought of her, and prating of nothing but her quality and charm. When the bride-ale was begun and the priest joined their hands, not a one of us could stifle a smile of joy. Even my mother was caught up in the contagion, her early objections having melted once the finality of the decision had been realized.

Somehow, in all the bustle of preparation, we hadn't thought of fare-wells. Towards the end of the feasting, as she was preparing to take her leave, Aldgyth drew us aside, Edwin and Burchard and I, and reminded us of a certain long-ago day which all of us had almost forgotten.

"Recall you the Eirish fore-sayer?" she asked us earnestly. "Truly I think that ever since he called me 'glass-eyed twice cwene' I knew this day would come!"

I shivered, remembering the awesome Filidh. Looking past us with a dreamy, thoughtful smile, Aldgyth went on. "The first night we were in the Cymry, when he rode mounted into the hall and kissed my hand and called me lady, I told myself that surely my king would be like that! My fate was bound to his. Methinks I knew it even then, though I never dared to think on it. Methinks I knew it even then...."

"You said so!" I cried, excited at the recollection. "You insisted to us, when we were in Lundun City, that you were meant to meet with him again! 'Tis certainly a wonder!"

"The wonder is that such a bold and honored man should choose a skinny girl-child like Aldgyth!" Edwin teased.

"Brat!" she cried, pretending to strike him. Then, of a sudden the four of us were embracing at once, laughing like tickled babes and feeling very close. That was as near as we came to a parting word.

It did not take long for the news of the marriage to spread, and the first murmurs of disapproval soon reached us. The king made no statement so, for the most part, we were left to imagine what things were being whispered in the tight little circle which surrounded him in Wessex. Of one thing we were certain: the sons of Godwine would never let it lie.

*   *   *

The winter, damp and thick and grey, passed all at once into spring, as it was wont to do in the west. That portion of my father's household which had quartered the season in Scrobbesbyrig came to us soon as the booming winds had carried off the snow and frost, moving with haste before the hardened ground could give way to mud. The confusion which ensued with their arrival was overwhelming and soon, out of deference, Ealdread Æthelgar's son moved his own household east into the Peaclond. Like many another seemingly innocuous and unrelated happening that year, this was something well planned; the move established him in a central spot half-way between Tathaceaster, where his brother Siward Bearn kept his manor, and Ceaster, where sat Earl Ælfgar now. Expecting the worst, my father had decided it was vital to remain well-linked with those sworn to him.

Through the chaos of this exchange of households, Edwin and I amused ourselves by exploring the countryside in the company of our new and intriguing friends, the strange, silent, doe-eyed sons of Carr. Not a one of them spoke overmuch, and this was widely misread as haughtiness and held against them. The elder two, Daffydd and Ywen, looked like twins, both roughly handsome in a decidedly foreign way. Wide of chest and narrow of hip, neither was tall but no strength was lacking in their finely muscled form. Daffydd was in fact a year older than the other, being nearly eighteen years. He had an annoying habit of twisting his forefinger into his hair, where the thickly curling black ringlets rolled over his forehead. On the backs of his hands and arms shone dull white patches of thick scar. He had fallen into a cooking fire as a toddler, which accident nearly cost him his life.

Where Daffydd was stern, Ywen was surly and quicker to voice his thoughts, usually in a biting under-breath. He was born on an unlucky day, the other two hastily assured us whenever he vented a bitter word, as if this fact excused him. Ywen never made a move to defend his sarcastic commentary. If a man took issue with him, he merely shrugged and backed away. In fact, he shrank so wholly from any kind of physical confrontation that it took us several years to realize how bold and skillful he was in arms.

Hwell, the youngest, was the most likable. He was a year older than Edwin, and a head shorter than me, with lively, darting eyes and a peculiar ability to handle animals as if he spoke their language or read their minds. More finely featured, he was boyishly fair without the thick beard of his brothers. A strong, curved nose and full, firm mouth gave him a comeliness which the others seemed to have outgrown.

Cast aside in the confusion of the times just as we were, they seemed glad for the excuse to escape with us, hunting and birding. In these arts they were well-skilled, though it took them some time to attain an ease on horseback, being accustomed to the husky, nimble-footed Welsh mountain ponies.

By the time the dun-colored mists of March gave way to April's brilliance, they had relaxed into the pattern of Anglish life. Their first taste of it could not have been impressive. My father struggled against everyone's dampened spirits to establish discipline over the turmoil and disorder of the huge manor. All through Lent, the men speculated on what the king and his councilors would accomplish during the Easter Gemot. The Imbolc Sabbat and the Feast of the Resurrection, always celebrated same as the pagan feast of Easter on the first Sunday after the first full moon following the vernal equinox, came and went. Still no whisper traveled through the midlands.

"Must be Edward has determined not to trouble the land with this," Cynewulf said one fair morning, sitting to break-fast with us in my father's chamber.

"Else we would have heard of it by now, I trow," Burchard added in his quiet voice. My father shook his head.

"Nay," he said, stabbing his knife into a thick piece of barley bread as if it were some living thing. "If he shrinks from moving against us, you know we can count on his friends to decide him otherwise. Every one of the Godwines will be eager to meet us; they have not the old king's prudence!'"

"Could be they will gain it, though, when they see the strength of our numbers!" Cynewulf retorted with a laugh.

Burchard rubbed his chin thoughtfully. "They will be hard-pressed to call up the Anglish fyrd in spring-time," he said, working the piece of oaten cake he held into crumbs, then distractedly watching them drop. "Few Anglishmen pant for battle when their fields need ploughing and sowing. Methinks the sons of Godwine dare not call the fyrd to arms, for fear the whole country will give refusal!"

"'Tis a certainty they will not want to embarrass themselves!" Stretching his lean frame, Cynewulf yawned and scratched his neck. "Pray you they underestimate our strength and come to face us each with his household troops alone."

Edwin began pacing, hands clasped behind him. "Methinks there are enough earl's men in Wessex and the North Humbria to wage a hard battle without ever the fyrd's being called."

My father agreed. "But there are not enough in Wessex alone to wreak a victory against us," he added. "Earl Tostig is at Gleawanceaster with the king, but his household troops are in Eorforwic. Siward Bearn sits near them with as many men or more, ready to bar the way of those loyal to Tostig. Harold would not have Tostig's strength behind him."

"By God!" I exclaimed easily, then blushed red at Burchard's admonishing look.

Amused at my reaction, Cynewulf laughed, then grew serious. "To hear Siward Bearn tell it, mayhap no more than two hundred are loyal to Tostig!" he said. "The rest have declared secretly for the House of Leofric."

"Their cursed accusations and writs of outlawry will hold little weight when we ride with a full half of the kingdom behind our standard," laughed my father. Then, signalling to Cynewulf, he made his way out, tousling my hair absently as he strode past.

CHAPTER FIFTEEN

ÆElfgar, Earl of the Mercians, was a second time
outlawed . . . but by the help of Gruffydd, king of
the Welsh . . . he quickly recovered his earldom
by force.

—Simeon of Durham, 1058

April, 1058
I was riding with Edwin and the sons of Carr in the long-grassed lea
beyond the palings of the estate when Tostig Godwine's son himself
came to the Ceaster manor with twelve well-armed guardsmen. Seeing
the glint of their hauberks against the pink-tinged sky, we waited on the
hillside till they passed on the road beneath us. They rode at an easy
pace, laughing amongst themselves and talking low while their well-
decked stallions snuffed the saltiness of the unfamiliar west-sea air. Then
we galloped off straight-away to warn of their approach, short-cutting
down the slopes at break-wind speed.

The women had quit my father's hall by then; the men were in
merry but quiet mood. At the high table, Ælfgar was deep in converse
with Æthelstan the Fen-man and Ælfric White-Hair, and two other
Mercian men of his, Eadsige and Ordwulf. Cynewulf and Cynric sat at
the end of the board, gaming with a rook set that had been my grandfather's, carved of amber. They all startled when we burst in, exhausted
and agitated. By the time Edwin coughed out the news, every man there
had strapped on knife and sword, but my father commanded them to sit
again and hold tight to temper. Then he sent kitcheners out to make a
respectable welcome, and bid Æthelstan dunk and comb us, and sit us
to the table. The three Welshmen, uneasy at the prospect of meeting
face-on for the first time with their blood enemy, took their place alongside us.

Before long, Tostig made his proud entrance, a mantle of fine
mouse-grey moreen thrown casually over his broad shoulders. His

brown, neatly oiled hair was center parted, and tucked behind his wind-burned ears. The drooping, longish mustaches gave a grim look to his handsome, square-jawed face. He wore an icy smile as he made his way to us. 'Twas easy enough to see why King Edward placed great store in such an imposing, majestic man. Even so, 'twas plain he was one who got what he wanted through strength, cunning, and cruelty.

My father stood as the tall Wessexman stepped up on the dais, and for a moment the two eyed each other silently, almost rudely, from opposite sides of the narrow plank table. Then Ælfgar told the Earl of the North Humbria that he was well-come, and asked whether it was barley mead or wine or ale that he craved. The other put his hands on his hips, laughing slightly and shaking his head.

"Nay, Mercian!" he said in a voice low and nasal, "I am not one of those who journey hither to consort with you! What words I carry are from King Edward himself. Best I give them to you and take a hasty leave. It seems that those who tarry here are not spoken well of in the south-lands, though they are spoken of often. Near as often as you, and these days your name is bandied about there quite frequently."

"That I can well believe," Ælfgar replied in a cold voice, raising a cup and sipping it. "And in no wise do I doubt you are eager to tell me what things are whispered."

"One thing they say is that high-born Welshmen sit at your table as if they were your very kin!" Tostig stared directly at the sons of Carr as he said it, eyes steeped in venom. Then he pursed his lips. "Till now no man knew it was a certainty, though it fit so well with something else that is rumored of you, Ælfgar Leofric's son: that you have married your daughter to a king. What say you of this?"

"I say 'tis true enough!" my father grinned, looking smug and boyish. "Surely you understand the pride a man takes in wedding a fair child to a great king, your father having secured your fortunes by doing the self-same thing!'

Tostig stiffened but managed to hold on to his well-bred smile. He reached into a pouch strapped round his waist, drawing forth a piece of stiff parchment folded in quarters. "Who will be the one to read this?" he asked, looking up.

My father laughed. "Think you there is need to read it?"

"Aye," the other replied levelly, "I have things to say that men would think unseemly spoken to an earl. Best all here assembled should hear that the king calls you outlaw, so they will know you are fit to hear them!" He handed the writ to Ælfgar, who passed it to his chief man without even glancing at it. Cynewulf stood and after looking it over, read loudly in a flat, toneless voice.

"Upon the twenty-third day of the month of April in this, the Lord's year one thousand and fifty-eight, King Edward declares that the peace previously granted by him to Ælfgar his Earl now is withdrawn. And he informs all that it be his will that a writ of outlawry be upon that man and that every house he holds, and all his lands and everything lawfully pertaining to them, shall be made forfeit to the hands of his eldest son and heir."

He spoke some other things, but I did not pay much attention. I was watching Tostig finger the hilt of his fine broad sword. It was all of gold, the handle of it, and made to look like a long-necked bird with teeth, gnawing upon its own clawed foot. Its eyes were flashing rubies. I wondered at its richness. Father's sword-hilt was not cast in any design, save it were a vine of bronze and one of gold intertwined, and it was a strain upon the imagination to see even that.

Cynewulf sat down again. A low murmur ran through the hall; Edwin whispered to me but I could not catch his words. Tostig, with a satisfied sneer, moved closer and, grasping the table edge, said something only my father could hear. It made Ælfgar burn with fury. He lunged at the Wessexman with vicious rage. Tostig nimbly stepped aside, grateful no doubt for the table which kept his enemy from him but pretending to be unconcerned. Cynewulf, Ordwulf, and Ælfric White-Hair sprang to their feet, forcibly holding Ælfgar back though it took all their power to do so. Finally, Cynewulf grabbed my father's hair with such violence that the silver fillet which bound it flew to the floor. Yanking his lord's head back in a strangle hold, he whispered hoarsely, "Think you what the penalty might be for an outlaw who puts harm upon an earl! Restrain yourself lest he goad you to it!"

Ælfgar relaxed. I shivered, hearing Tostig Godwine's son's vile laughter. Had my father laid hand on him, it would have warranted summary execution. The king's men would have been justified in murdering Ælfgar on the spot!

The hall was in total confusion. My father raised his hands for silence. When the noise died down somewhat, he turned back to the Wessexman who still stood on the dais.

"If you be man enough, Tostig Godwine's son," he said loudly, "voice again the threats you just made against me and my house—only voice them loud enough for my sworn men to hear, and my sons. Let them know what unseemly hate and gross vengefulness you bear me so they can wonder how you pass yourself off as honorable to the king and all his court!"

Tostig shook his head, giving a careless sneer. "You are in no position to intimidate me, Mercian. 'Tis my right to say unto you whatever

I will. I have come hither with a dozen king's men as my witness to hand you King Edward's decision and carry back to him a report of your conduct in return."

Then he turned to the men behind him, who stood somewhat nervously, arms drawn as if they feared the outlawed earl might wreak vengeance by ordering them slain then and there. They knew they were badly outnumbered in that great hall full of men and apparently they had little faith if any in Ælfgar's honor. "What think you?" Tostig asked them slyly. "That he acts somewhat like to a madman?"

My father growled, knowing the other had the upper hand. After that, it was not long till Tostig took his leave. As he mounted his tall brown horse in the courtyard under a fast-darkening purple sky, Ælfgar reminded him of one thing. "A great many men feel they have been wronged in this," he said simply. "Be certain to tell the king."

According to the writ, my father had six days before the king's price was on his head, making him open game. Nevertheless, early the next morn we took ship for the Cymry, not bothering to take much of our household with us. Riches and goods and wealth were not all the outlaw Ælfgar left behind him; he left the greater part of his best sworn men and his Danelaw first-born, Burchard Ælfgar's son, to serve as Earl of Mercia in his stead.

*   *   *

Sometimes when Edwin suffered nightmares, he cried out in his sleep or murmured in a dread, hollow voice. The priests had taught us it was an ill policy to force a man in night-terror awake: the fright would be apt to hover round him, they said, waiting to descend in waking life. All knew how Grandfather's chief man, Cenwulf Centwine's son, father to Cynewulf and Cynric, had been roused from a terrifying dream of a she-wolf, and a year later had been thrown to his death when his horse reared at one which crossed his path.

We had been four months in the Cymry when a terror came on my brother one stifling, windless night. That very day, Gruffydd had returned with news of my father's stunning victory, a quick and splendid triumph. One look at Ælfgar with the Cymrians lined behind him to the west, and at Burchard with the men of Mercia lined to the north, and King Edward had been impressed with an immediate desire for peace.

'Tis strange, being so ecstatically happy, that he would suffer such a terrible nightmare, but he did. His thrashing and terrified screaming woke Aldgyth and her husband. They leapt up, lifting and shaking my brother till he came to his senses.

Edwin was furious that they had dared to stir him from the evil slumber. Stumbling in a half-sleep, he threw himself at his brother-in-the-law, cursing and hollering, taking into account neither the other's size nor strength. He flailed, bit, kicked, and struck blindly till Gruffydd flung him over his shoulder, carried him out into the moonlight and there chastised him for his fury, using a supple larch branch.

When I made my way out after them, my shift was stuck to me with cold sweat, and I could hear my brother's sobbing and protesting that now he would be haunted in life by the grotesque specter, and it was all his sister's fault.

But my sister was heavy with child and later, when she came out to join us, she swore she had felt Edwin's dream entering the mind of her unborn babe. 'Twas not an uncommon thing, we knew. Our own cousin Oswulf, while yet in the womb, had suffered a nightmare his father had while laying at the side of his wife's round belly and it had tainted his destiny. After making Aldgyth comfortable again, the Welshman asked us to walk with him down the pebbly road which followed the wending way of the narrow river.

The camp was pressed between the feet of tall, black mountains and decked with clusters of fir, yew, hawthorne, and gnarled oak which looked stern and wild under the shadow of night. The river itself, though, was a silver coil of glittering reflected moonshine.

"Here is something it would hurt not at all to dream about!" Gruffydd started in a gentle way, trying to bring some comfort to Edwin who was still cross. Neither of us made an answer so he added, "Yet 'tis said that to dream of a river is to dream of your entire life."

"I dreamt we were looking on heads," my brother spoke out woefully, as if someone had asked. "Heads of men we know."

The Welshman threw a pebble in the water and we heard it splash. "Maybe it is that you are worried about your father," he said in a low voice, "though even now he is negotiating a restoration with your king."

Edwin shrugged, apparently unconvinced. "This victory was firm enough," he whined. "Methinks I have no fear on his account."

Settling comfortably back against a mossy boulder, Gruffydd put his hands behind his head. "I am not a superstitious man," he said, "but when I was young like you, I put great store by dreams and such-like. I remember one howling night, I dreamt that my brother began to have sons by his woman. One after another they came forth, wrapped in hides and wearing thongs with silver charms around their necks. When I told of it, everyone marveled that they came forth thusly arrayed, supposing it to mean they would be great warriors. Seven came in all, strong and healthy—never a better omen! My brother feasted me for the telling of the dream and 'twas boasted of in our family for a good long time."

Here he paused, musing, and we listened to a dog braying disconsolately far in the distance. "Nevertheless," he continued after a bit, leaning back and closing his eyes, "when a year had passed, my brother was dead by the knife of a common thief, and neither had he any sons or even any childlings at all." Gruffydd drew a heavy breath and let it go again, slowly.

We considered this a while. Then Edwin said it was not the same with all dreams; some were truly meant to happen, he said, others were but tales and pictures. "But a nightmare is a different thing. Uncle Leofric says they are given by a Power. And to be roused from one—" he shivered, taking a handful of white pebbles and tossing them far. "To be roused from one ensures it shall come to pass!"

"This I have never heard before," answered Gruffydd thoughtfully. "It seems such a thing would be common to all men and not just to Anglish. Yet methinks I have been pulled from many a noxious dream that has never come to pass!"

He said it without teasing, but Edwin bristled. "'Tis not to say it will not happen," he whispered sharply.

"Nor to say it will." The Welshman gave Edwin a momentary, manly embrace like a father might do a son. My brother tossed him a wan smile as he pulled away.

Later, when we had returned to the white stone-built hall, and Gruffydd had climbed back beside his cwene—he apologized for it, saying she had tamed him into sleeping indoors—Edwin and I sat in the darkness, whispering. He was afraid to sleep and I knew it. I spoke of different things that were unimportant, glad to distract him. I wanted him not to dwell on the memory of it, for fear he would share more of the details, none of which I wanted to hear. After a while, though, he mentioned the grisly horror of it once more, asking if I supposed the men in the dream would truly be beheaded or if they would die in some other, more reasonable fashion.

Shuddering, I told him it was not something I could determine, but that it seemed not to matter for 'twas an ill omen either way. Then fearfully, against my will, I asked him if one of the heads he had seen had been Father's.

"Nay," he replied in a mournful tone, "but I knew his was there. 'Twas as if I looked to find it but could not. Burchard's, too. I told myself, 'Amongst all these heads, his must be!' but I could see naught of it." Then his voice grew low and dreadful. "Morcar, I saw my own!"

My heart felt like a hide thong snapping. "Methinks you could not have looked upon your own," I argued feebly.

He shook his head vehemently. "I found one, a man's head, and a voice within me said, 'You look upon yourself, Mercian!'"

Here my brother let go a long, labored, shaking breath and fell back, limp, on the straw bed.

"Tell me there were no others!" I mumbled.

"There were.'

"Was I one?"

"Nay, Morcar. But others. Men we know."

He did not say more and I was glad of it. Before he would consent to sleep, he begged me to make the sign of the cross over him. I did it several times, then lay beside him. I pretended to slumber, thinking it might ease him, but I did not sleep till dawn. After that night, we did not mention the dream again between us till a good number of years had passed.

CHAPTER SIXTEEN

Eadwulf became earl . . . but in the third year after
. . . he was put to death by Siward, who then
himself held the earldom of the whole province of
the North humbria.

—Simeon of Durham

May 1059

I never liked my kinsman Oswulf. It was not just that he was brash and haughty and over-proud of his comely looks, but he had no love for God. Grandmother Godiva always said it was because of what happened to his father, Eadwulf, Earl of the Bernicia, who was my mother's cousin. Now it is true that Eadwulf was more than harshly slain when the usurper Siward stole the North Humbria, both the Diera of which Æthelgar Bearn was earl, and the Bernicia which was Eadwulf's earldom. But seeing as Oswulf was a babe in arms then, I do not understand that it could make him what he was in this life: a cynic and a scoffer and a man with no respect for Providence.

He was flashingly handsome, but Oswulf Eadwulf's son was a liar. He pretended to a great outward show of piety whenever he was with people who might admire that. With those of us who knew him best, though, he never missed a chance to boast of his own unconcern with matters spiritual and eternal, or to dismiss his sins as harmless. He claimed there were no laws of God, only laws of men disguised as such.

Nevertheless, folk were fooled by his pretenses, and he was a respected man throughout Mercia and the North Humbria. This may have been as much for his noble connections and his father's memory as anything else, but there could be no doubt that he had a large and loyal following who wished to see him Earl of the Bernicia, as his father had been.

Soon after my father's second restoration, Oswulf, his friend Cospatric Arkill's son, and a great party to the Kirton manor in the Lindcylene Shire. Oswulf was to be wed with Briana of the Diera, and it was a well hailed occasion of great rejoicing. It was the sort of match that inspired the imaginings of men. The bride was the sister of Siward Æthelgar's son, Bearn of the Diera, and Oswulf held hereditary right to the Bernicia, so folk saw in that uniting another joining of the ancient earldoms. It seemed romantic, too, to those who remembered how Æthelgar Bearn, the bride's father, and the groom's father, Earl Eadwulf, had died together at the hands of the Usurper when the two were still very young men.

I could not understand, though, why Lady Briana consented to wed with him. A pretty, flaxen-haired thing, she did not seem the kind to be blinded to the man's faults by his excessive fairness. She was three years older than Oswulf, who was not yet eighteen years then, but the difference might have been twenty if you estimated it from her manner. She did not smile once in the three days of that bride-ale.

Though it was the custom to have the wedding, or betrothal, some months before the bride-ale and hand-fasting, Oswulf and Briana held theirs the very day before. I was too naive to discern whether there was unkind speculation about it or not, but any scandalous talk was proven wrong. Several years and all vestiges of affection between them were to pass before the lady ever showed signs of a childling.

As the best man, my father had to guarantee to the priests that Oswulf was honorable in his pledge to keep the bride in a manner befitting to her, had to swear to champion her rights if Oswulf died, and to support her till he could wed her off again or make a permanent provision. Siward Bearn named his sister's bride's-price. He was then about twenty years old and very impressive in stature. "You are my kinsman, Oswulf Eadwulf's son," he said in a powerful voice, "and so I seek from you neither silver nor gold nor precious things, but a promise for this lady's well-fare. I need your oath not ever to put her by, to honor your heirs by her over any others, and to refrain from lying with her on any day the church declares it is unlawful."

When he said this last, he looked straight at his sister, who sat blushing between my mother and grandmother, with her ladies standing behind her. Oswulf gave his word.

Then, Uncle Leofric called Briana to him and asked if she thought her price was fair. She said it was. "Then, will you take this man when the time comes and will you let him take you?" he asked, looking hard upon her. She blushed and nodded without raising her head.

"It will be so then, according to the teachings of the law. You will keep your chastity for the space of three days and nights after your bride-ale," he told them both, "though you may lay side by side. On the third day, after taking the Eucharist together in the Mass, you may come one unto the other in wed-lock, and thereafter forevermore according to the word as it is set down." Then he anointed them with water and chrism, and blessed them and joined their hands.

The next day's being the bride-ale, the men had to keep separate company from the women on its eve. We sat at table in the great hall and took no meat, only eel and fish and water-fowl. Oswulf was fasting from foods but drinking quite freely, and he kept complaining that there was no way for a man to lay himself at the side of a woman for three nights and still keep his chastity.

"Well, you had better mind your sacred pledges," my father told him coldly, "or you will be wearing a wool shirt for the next year or so."

"And that is an uncomfortable penance," Uncle Leofric rejoined, adding, "Just ask Earl Ælfgar, who can well tell you how hard a man suffers in one!"

The explosive laughter of the men drowned any attempt at conversation for some full minutes. As for me, I was hard-pressed to understand how they could find such hilarity in it. Here at Kirton, we had separate quarters, but in many of our manors and estates I slept in the same lodges as my parents, and it was an undeniable fact that Ælfgar did, indeed, wear a wool shirt, and all too often. Oft it rubbed his breast and back so raw he needed priests to salve him.

While I mused on this, Oswulf spoke up again. His voice was harsh and arrogant, for he was a man who grew icy instead of warm with ale. "A man would be an ass," he declared flatly, staring straight into my uncle's eyes with a defiant look, "to do penance for bedding a woman. 'Tis quite unlike pillage and murder, is it not? It seems not to hurt anyone over-much, and mostwhiles I think it does both parties much good."

Without waiting for my uncle to answer, Siward Bearn leapt up, so flushed with anger that Cospatric and Burchard and Daffydd had to hold him back. He was well-weighted with drink himself. It had not taken me long to see that drunkenness was apparently the custom of the bride-ale eve, but 'twas strange to see kinsmen at each other's throats.

Whatever darkness had passed between Oswulf and his bride's brother was soon forgotten, though, and the happy mood restored. From then on, the men grew merrier and the jests bolder, until almost unfit to hear. Seated together, the devil's half dozen—Edwin and myself, with our kinsmen Æric, Ælfmaer, Brihtric, and Maldon—took it all in with relish. Soon as we gained the gumption to make a few jests loud enough to be heard beyond our own table, though, Burchard made his way over and herded the lot of us out of the hall.

"I know you will want to ride with the wedding party and throw alms tomorrow," he said severely, "and you will all need some rest to do it."

*   *   *

All the men rode out at the golden break of dawn on the day of the hand-fasting, splendidly dressed and wearing wreaths of aconitum, starflower, and valley-lily in their hair. It was the custom for the bridegroom and the best man to give alms and grant special privileges on that day. The road to old Saint Mary's, which we had elected to travel, was lined with people, young and old and rich and poor, in need of special favor, gathered into crowds of varying sizes. When a great number milled around a single man, waving and gesturing frantically, you could be sure it was an especially important, or at the very least interesting, claim. The fact that the best man was the Earl of Mercia made for an exceptional number of hopeful cases.

Most of the folk assembled called for my father by name; he was a popular man and known to be very generous. But when we had come nearly six miles from Kirton, a single man threw himself suddenly into the middle of the narrow street, landing in a miserable heap, hollering over and over for Oswulf Eadwulf's son in a powerful voice. When we drew near him, we could clearly see that he had but one leg.

Oswulf was less than his usual pleasant self that pretty morning, having made himself so merry on his bride-ale eve that he had not entirely recovered. Nevertheless, he bade us stop for the man, though indeed we had but little choice, and he himself dismounted to hear the beggar's story. Fascinated and morbidly curious, Edwin and I both reined in close, staring down with condescending sympathy and listening intently to his tale.

He was probably not much older than my father, but life had obviously been unkind to him. He was wizened, with glassy, moist eyes deep set in a gaunt and weathered face. His hair, thin and greying, was worn long in the North Humbrian fashion, and there were scars in his earlobes where once he had worn studs or hoops. He stared hard on cousin Oswulf, eyes darting as he looked up at him. At first I thought it was the excessive fineness of my kinsman's dress and accouterments that drew his gaze; then I heard him say musingly, "Very, very alike to him you are, Oswulf Eadwulf's son, and almost of the age he was when last I saw him." His accent was thickly northern, Bernician through and through.

Dropping to one knee, Oswulf scrutinized him carefully, then asked in a halting way, "Of whom do you speak, man?"

The other looked surprised. "Of your father, of course: Eadwulf, Earl of the Bernicia!" So saying, he crossed himself quickly though his entire weight was resting on one elbow, and he had to balance himself painfully to do it. "Does not the name Thored Gyric's son mean a thing to you?"

Oswulf thought a moment, then shook his head, his fine features drawn into a pensive frown.

"You were but a new-born babe," the man said sadly. "I suppose there was none left to tell you when you were old enough to hear of it. I am that man, Thored Gyric's son, and once Earl Eadwulf had no truer carl!"

Then my father, too, dismounted, moving close to the stranger and gazing at him with a kind of wonder, as if trying to remember something just out of his mind's reach.

"Are you that same one who carried Lady Ecfryth and the babe to Tathaceaster?" he asked. When the man nodded happily, Ælfgar looked up at Cynewulf and whispered low, "By God!"

Oswulf was on his knees now, speechless, staring in a helpless, boyish way. Without waiting for them to be asked, Thored Gyric's son began answering his questions.

"The day your father was betrayed and murdered along with Æthelgar Bearn, I fought at his side," he said mournfully, latching his eyes into my cousin's. "I was one of two dozen who accompanied them to King Harthacnut's very hall, and one of only a few who escaped. Soon as we were seated, Siward the Usurper emerged from behind a curtain, with his best men in battle gear. I took the axe of none other than that cursed man in my thigh just before he smote your father's life-breath with it. Then he murdered Æthelgar Bearn. Knowing he was dying, Eadwulf grabbed my hair and pulled me to him; we were best of friends and not much older than you are now. He bade me ride to Dunholme and gather up his wife and child and see them safe to Tathaceaster for fear mad Siward would bring them to harm. He could not see I had taken a gross wounding, else he would not have put that task upon me, I know. On Lammas Day that year, we learnt that evil Siward had been given both the Diera and the Bernicia by Harthacnut—the entire North Humbria. 'Twas the very day they took my leg off, though I remembered not much of that till later. It had grown feverish on the long and frantic ride, and it made as if to suck me in and kill me with its grossness."

The man fell back a little, then deftly caught himself working his body into a sitting position. He spread a pitiful, threadbare mantle patched with wadmal over his lap, as if to hide his deformity. Then he went on, looking from Oswulf to my father and back again. Both of them were engrossed, sitting now cross-legged in the dusty street like a pair of children.

"I grew a bitter man, knowing I was useless," Thored Gyric's son's voice grew somber as he went on. "The very next year, crazed young Harthacnut dropped dead at his feasting table; a fitting end that gave me joy. Then Edward was made king, but he was such a Norman at heart

that he cared little for our Anglish quarrels or for arranging any avengement. He allowed Siward to remain earl over all the land north of the
Humber. We had no one old enough to put in his place anyway, and no
force left with which to wreak revenge.

Poor Lady Ecfryth … your mother was such a gentle soul. She could
not bear the horror of this life afterwards. Oft she had told me how she
had lain beside Eadwulf when he dreamt of his death and hers—"

Springing to his feet, Oswulf cried out in a pained hoarse voice.
"Speak naught of that evil night, earl's man!" he exclaimed. "His nightmare came to me even as she carried me within her. Still it haunts me!"
Normally he was a man who well-hid his sensitivities, but now my
cousin was shaking with emotion, eyes wide and nostrils flaring like a
stag with a death arrow buried deep.

Thored Gyric's son shook his head sadly, shoulders slumping under
the weight of his memories. "So it was she knew her own end was
approaching, and in truth she welcomed it; but she feared for the babe,
and even for Æthelgar Bearn's little ones. He was her kinsman and had
died with her husband. It made her feel a responsibility, especially since
Lady Æthelfryth already had put a silver blade to her own throat."

At that, a murmur ran through the entire wedding party. The evil
death of my mother's sister had not been openly remarked upon or even
hinted at in many a year. Some of the younger men flushed red and were
indignant that such a seeming stranger as this should voice that shame
so openly. Ælfgar raised a hand to still them. "We are all kinsmen here,"
he said, "and we have all heard the story, I trow."

The one-legged man looked disdainfully at the shocked faces of the
rich and highborn, as if wondering how men could find disgrace in the
misery of a soul long dead. Spittle had gathered in the corners of his
mouth and he drew it in with a strange twist of the lips. "What I say is
true," he insisted listlessly. "Lady Ecfryth feared for those other children
as much as for you, her own man-child. Siward Bearn was but a tender
tot then; Ealdread and the little maid younger yet, and both sickly. The
good Lady Godiva agreed to take them, all four and found a kinswoman
to suckle the infant Oswulf. One day, gentle, pretty Ecfryth came to me
and gave me bracelets and gold-ware, 'for your kind and loving service,'
she told me. I wanted not to take them but she cried and said she had
no need to wear them in the ground. Next day, she was dead.

"I have lived all these years, and my woman with me, by selling off
the trinkets your mother closed into my hand that day and the things
that were mine: my arms and accouterments and such-like. So it is I
have not suffered as foul as some, though 'tis not the life I was born to,
I can tell you that. I fell quickly out of high circles after Lady Ecfryth

died; cotters, coopers, and tanners are the men I break bread with now. Always I have scrounged for news of you, though, Oswulf Eadwulf's son. Any word that filtered down I grasped on eagerly. I was pleased ever and anon when King Edward granted you all the wealth that had been your father's 'ere his murder. True, what joiced me most was to picture old Earl Siward's rage when the king's men took it from his coffers!"

Here, Thored threw his head back and laughed uproariously, a laugh so hearty it seemed impossible to have emanated from a form so thin and grizzled. When he finished, he turned a somber, appreciative gaze on my father.

"That was your doing, I trow, Ælfgar Leofric's son? I heard you petitioned those arrears from the king when you were high in his favor, when he gave you the East Anglia." He paused, frowning. "Eight years ago, is it? You might think that for a man like me, one day is much like another and time an endless commodity. But nay, 'tis not so! Methinks it scurries far too fast away. But it was a bold and good thing you did for your nephew, and 'twas not unnoticed by caring men. Earl Eadwulf always spoke high and well of you; he was a tempest and said you were the same."

Oswulf had grown pale through all this talk; his hands shook as he threw away his flower-wreath and brushed his ashy-colored hair back from his sweating brow.

"You have not much of a Bernician look to you!" Thored Gyric's son said thoughtfully, inspecting my cousin's beardless face.

Though Siward Bearn and his siblings had returned to Tathaceaster while yet childred, Oswulf had stayed in Mercia until he was nearly grown. Still, in his heart, he was a North Humbrian through and through.

"It may be I appear as a Mercian," I heard Oswulf say now, "but I am my father's son. I swear to you by all that is holy, the Bernicia will be mine one day again. I will be earl there—I swear it!" The glitter of hardness had returned to his flashing eyes all at once.

The look of him seemed to startle the other man; he scrutinized him carefully with squinted eyes. Then he said in a low voice, "God knows I speak no treason to tell you there are men there that would support you in it—many men!"

Out of the corner of my eye, I saw my father exchange a glance with Siward Bearn. "How know you this to be true, Gyric's son?" he asked.

"Neighbors talk!" the man said with a thin-lipped smile. "After the Usurper died, I made my home again in the Bernicia. Eadwulf still is loved there, and always will be, I trow. Folk bear no respect for the Saxon who oversees it now, forsooth! This Tostig Godwine's son is worse than a scoundrel; a nithing with the king's blessing is what he is. Besides, for nearly twenty years now they would have us believe the Bernicia was but some pock-marked corner of the Humberland. Mayhap the outsiders will believe this deception, but I can tell you any man born north of the Tyne knows the difference well enough!"

Oswulf had walked away and stood now a few feet off, leaning against a wide, twisted tree as if he had grown weak and needed to support himself. In truth, he looked ill, whether an after-effect of the last night's carousing or as a result of all he had just heard, I could not tell. He closed his eyes a little while, but the party grew restless to make their return so, after a time, he called out in a weary, lifeless voice to Thored Gyric's son.

"How is it you have come here, earl's man? What prize or privilege seek you from me?"

"There is naught I would have from you, Eadwulf's son," the man replied earnestly. "Rather, I have brought you something!" He fished awkwardly through a pocket-pouch and finally pulled out something small enough to hide in his hand. Somewhat shakily, Oswulf strode to him, and when he was anext him, reached down and took the thing, looked at it once, then clasped it tight in his own white-knuckled fist.

"'Twas hers," the poor man said with a slight smile. "Lady Ecfryth's. My lord Eadwulf had it cast for her the very day you were born. She gave it to me that long-ago day I spoke of and told me to see that it came to you when you were a man. She never suspected we would be so long parted, you and I. Oft-times I have felt the weight of having it when I knew it should be yours, but hard-pressed I was to find you or in anywise reach you. Ne'er could I have entrusted it to another. You can understand that, I trow?"

My cousin stifled a choking sound and nodded, turning away from us. "How came you here, man?"

"When I heard you were to be wedded, I knew it was my due. In all respect, though, I can tell you I hoped hard you would be wed at Tathaceaster. 'Twould not have been so burdensome a walk for me."

Oswulf spun to face him, eyes afire. "What say you? That you walked this way from the Bernicia?"

"Aye, sire. From Hagustaldesea."

All of us murmured at that, but Oswulf, trembling mightily, walked back and grabbed his horse's leathern reins from the hands of Siward Bearn. "Help him to this mount!" he commanded hoarsely. When we stared in astonishment and made no move to lift the man, he cried it out again, "Mount him!"

Then someone tried to pull him up, but Thored Gyric's son protested, his face a mask of shock. Siward Bearn and a few others of our kinsmen dismounted, casting frowns of worry and perplexion amongst themselves as they moved to Oswulf's side.

"The horse wears a fortune in bridal-trappings—" one of them started, reaching for my cousin's shoulder.

"I said mount him on the horse, by God!" Oswulf's voice grew angry. My father tried to calm him.

"A fine animal perhaps is not the wisest gift, kinsman," Ælfgar whispered. "Such a man would be hard-pressed to feed and board the thing."

Shaking, Oswulf unbrooched his fine mantle and threw it down. Then he tore off his rich necklaces and bracelets and threw them down on top of it. "Buy land to board it on with these!" my cousin cried shrilly.

Voices rose in protest again, Thored Gyric's son's amongst them. My cousin stomped some few paces away, then slammed his clenched fist into the trunk of a tree with all his might. When he turned again, his eyes burned furiously. His face was flushed, and he looked for all the world like a child in tantrum, fighting back tears. Teeth gleaming, he snarled. "The man shall have the horse!"

So saying, he moved quickly to where we all sat or stood staring. Jumping lithely onto the back of the grey that Siward Bearn had been sitting, he reined her back, cast one long, unreadable look at the broken body of his father's carl, then spurred the animal into a thunderous gallop.

*   *   *

On the third day of the bride-ale, the bride and groom quarreled openly at the high table. Everyone murmured at this, shaking their heads and saying 'twas most inauspicious.

Oswulf had been morose from the first because Thored Gyric's son, who had finally been prevailed upon to accept the horse, had sent us back with all the bridal trappings of rich serge and silver. He said it was beyond his conscience to accept them, and my cousin grew so sullen upon hearing of it that the hand-fasting was put off a full quarter of the day to give him time to regain his temper.

Then, after Uncle Leofric had blessed the couple and fixed their hands fast and firm forever, Briana took the bridal wreath from off her unbound golden hair and tossed it over her shoulder. It separated in the air, and some said this was an ill omen. Even so, the unwedded women leapt eagerly forward, trying to claim blossoms from it to pin into their locks for love-luck.

The next morning, my father and Oswulf exchanged mean words after the Mass, all because Ælfgar said aloud that a gentle man did not go to his bridal-chamber so dumbfounded with drink that he frightened his lady. My cousin arrogantly answered that he had never heard of a man denied the right to drink his own bride-ale and that it was his privilege as bridegroom to go to his woman any way he pleased. "I trust you know 'tis rumored that you have not always been the gentlest of husbands yourself," Oswulf declared then, challenging him with a bitter stare, "but what one lady despises another may take for manliness, think you not?"

My father flushed with anger and said he would be glad to teach him about manliness, but some other time. "I fear me I would break you very badly if I tried to do it now," he said, "and 'twould be a shame to put misfortune on you in the midst of the festivities."

Oswulf made no reply to that, but proudly tossed his head and strode away, haughty and insolent. Ælfgar stared after him, and when he had gone, said coldly to the men gathered round that it was a pity his nephew had not been chastised more often in his childhood. "Now it will need be done to him in manhood," he added, "and methinks it will be likely to kill or maim him."

Later that same day, though, when Edwin and I sat with Father and Uncle Leofric 'neath the tall sycamore at the far end of the courtyard, Oswulf came out to us, arm in arm with Burchard. I wondered how much of this sudden mildness was my brother's doing, for the bridegroom was very amicable, chatting and jesting as we drank barley-beer together. After praising Ælfgar for the richness of the feasting fare, he spoke a little of his love for Lady Godiva and recalled for us some things from his earlier years. Looking at his fair, fresh, boyish face, 'twas hard to imagine he could engross himself so entirely in the furious rages for which he was known, or display such wanton and ferocious spitefulness. His was a look of patrician innocence. When he took his leave, smiling and gay, Burchard went with him, arm draped over his shoulder in brotherly fashion. One looked as gentle and undefiled as the other.

That night in the hall there was nothing but merriment and good spirits. Perhaps that is why everyone was so shocked and dismayed on the morrow, when Oswulf and his bride broke into their violent argument. They flew shamelessly to their feet in front of all assembled, jeering each other with cruelty and cutting words. No one knew exactly what inspired the tumult; it began soon as they sat to table for the first meal. Uncle Leofric and Burchard and Daffydd Carr's son finally managed to cajole Oswulf away. I would have followed them out to the courtyard gate, but Grandmother Godiva stopped me with a commanding whisper. When Lady Briana made her way out, still shaking with anger, I stared after her curiously. I had never heard a woman use such wicked words— not even my mother, who never bothered much to hold her own tongue.

If ever there was a man who could bring out another's hidden malevolence, though, 'twould have to be Oswulf Eadwulf's son. I felt sorry for the golden-haired lady.

Ælfgar, who had passed out dizzy in his drink somewhere the night before, slept so late into the day that he was not there to witness the dispute. Cynewulf finally managed to find him in one of the out-buildings and led him, rumpled and staggering, into the hall, but not before things had calmed down to their usual tenor. Everyone was relieved that he had missed it. His men said that certainly he would have made a fight over the disgrace young Oswulf brought into his house and that would have made matters much the worse. As it was, Burchard, with his gentle way of smoothing things, was eventually able to lead our cousin back to his seat at the high table, where he sat silent and subdued till we took to the fields in the noon-time for a hare-chase.

Edwin and I wakened before dawn the next morning because we heard father and Burchard moving and dressing in the dark. As best man, it was Ælfgar's duty to oversee the loading and mounting of the pack-saddles and all the other details that needed to be attended to before the bridal train could depart. Without hearing the Mass or breaking fast, we all went down together to the stabling barn.

We found that some of the grooms and hands were already about their tasks. Every one of our guests—even Oswulf, who had not much of an appreciation for things domestic—had marveled at how precisely and efficiently my father's estate was ordered. Here at Kirton, it was true, things went ever smoothly. This manor and the ones at Nottingham and Sempringaham we counted chief of all our houses, and it had been a pleasure to return to them after the steadfast confusion and turmoil of the Ceaster manor which we had handed back to Siward Bearn's brother, Ealdread Æthelgar's son after the restoration. King Edward had decreed my father was not to live breast to breast with the Welshman anymore, though they could keep a communication. Ælfgar and Gruffydd had decided between them that Ceaster should be constantly occupied by someone who could bring them together swiftly in case of crisis, and that man was Ealdread. He had not even left there for his sister's bride-ale.

Most of the gear had been stowed by cock-crow when Siward Bearn, Oswulf, and Cospatric Arkill's son came and met us. My father took them over to see the Welsh cart ponies which Daffydd Carr's son had brought back from the Cymry for breeding and training. Then he led them to a stall where stood one of the brawniest, strongest of his stallions, snorting and snuffing. The handsome blue-black beast had been decked out just that morning in the bridal trappings, and wore brass

French bells braided into his mane and tail.

The steed was fine and costly, and my father already had presented Oswulf with a set of silver drinking cups, twelve in all, which once had belonged to Grandfather Leofric. So, at first, none of us understood Ælfgar's intent; he had to explain very carefully that the mount was a bride-ale gift to replace the one Oswulf had so generously given away. For a moment, the look of pleasure and amazement and appreciation which settled over my cousin's fair features gave him a look of surpassing gentleness and peace; then he swallowed it back as if his own emotions frightened him. 'Twas a gift he could never have expected.

CHAPTER SEVENTEEN

Ely is an island. . . . seven miles long and as many
broad . . . surrounded by water.

—Chronicle of hugh Candidus

Autumn, 1060
Wulfget, the boy who had been Grandfather Leofric's ward, received
Holy Orders from my uncle in the last year Edwin and I took our
learning at Peterborough. The morning of the occasion, which was just
after the feast of St. Martin, my father arrived from the Lindcylene Shire
with Burchard and Cynewulf and a score of men-at-arms. From the high,
square window of the chapter house, my brother and I watched them
dismounting and though we begged to go to them, the monks would not
allow it.

"Those men have barely the time to shake the road-dust off their
garments and seat themselves in the chapel," one dour-eyed sacristan
told us admonishingly, "so your gossip and news-changing will have to
wait till later."

Edwin tossed him an impertinent reply, which was his way, but I just
bit the inside of my cheek impatiently. We had not seen anyone from
home since the thaws, nearly eight months before. The uncommonly
long separation had seemed like an age, and now I worried that my
anxiety would distract me from the sacred rites.

That was something I need not have feared. As the monks lifted
their voices in rich intonation, I was drawn fully into the majestic
feeling of the service. The simple, compassionate quality of these men's
lives found a perfect counterpart in the strangely haunting, resonant
melodies they made. It never failed to thrill me. *Justorum animæ in mano
Dei sunt.* The souls of righteous men are in God's hands. *Non tanqet illos
tormentum malitiæ.* The torment of wickedness does not touch them.

All too soon, the ceremony came to an end. Wulfget turned to face
us and we fell to our knees to accept his first blessing. I noticed immediately that his look had changed. I had oft-times seen him with his

tonsured hair, in priestly dress of ash-grey wadmal, but till that very moment I had not seen more than a likable friend, a play-fellow and confidant. Now there stood before me Brother Wulfget, a man of God endowed with powers beyond the grasp of worldly minds: the power to forgive, to absolve, to consecrate; to take that which is earthly and frail and mortal and translate it into something eternal and perfect. The power to reveal God's wisdom to man, and to tender man's imperfect love to God. The power to heal and make whole. To understand. I shivered at the transformation. When I looked at Burchard, I was not surprised to see his eyes were dimmed with tears; feeling the force of his emotion, I offered a prayer for him.

Grandfather Leofric had provided well for Wulfget's endowment, gifting the monastery with the income from one of the manors he held in Scrobbesbyrig. My father added to this a gold-gift of indescribable beauty: a relic case formed in the shape of a fish surrounded by loaves. It contained hairs of St. Ælfheah, which my grandfather had purchased at considerable price while still a very young man. Everyone seemed quite astonished at the richness of this offering, for our family was not bound to give more than Grandfather had named. Still, my father said he felt it was a privilege to so honor my uncle's house, and in my heart of hearts, I was glad he had done it. Wulfget had never known any family, which seemed both strange and depressing to me. No doubt it had lifted his spirit somewhat on this most glorious of days to know he was so well-considered.

Afterwards, we sat to a sumptuous supper in the huge refectory and heard all the news of home. I do not remember that Father ever before spoke to us as men, but that day he did. Edwin had turned sixteen years by then, the age for taking to arms, and I was nearing fifteen. We drank our mead unwatered and had begun to wear flowered attars, though the monks pretended to disapprove of it heartily.

Burchard was sitting next to me and asked if I remembered our kinsman, Gospatrick Maldred's son, whom I had not seen in several years. His mother had been Earl Eadwulf's cousin and his father was a Mercian nephew by marriage of Grandmother's, but beyond that I could recall only that he had stayed in North Humbria and sworn himself to Tostig Godwine's son when that man became earl there. This had put bad blood between him and my father, and most of the rest of our kinsmen as well. Nevertheless, the young man had ridden down to Kirton during the summer, attempting to make peace. Burchard had taken a liking to him, he told me, and had been disappointed that Ælfgar received him coldly and gave him little hope of reconciliation. I listened with attention to all this, but like my father, I rather doubted the North Humbrian's motives. We all laughed a little when Ælfgar, who sat across the table, said Burchard was so tolerant that if he were a deer, he would gladly make friends with an arrow.

"'Tis always wise to keep a distance from a thing which has no feelings," Ælfgar added guardedly. "I fear me the result of coming too close is harder on the deer than on the other."

The talk turned from one thing to another but one topic seemed to hold a special interest. Word had filtered down from the North Humbria that Cynesige, archbishop of the great city of Eorforwic, was dying. The man most likely to succeed him, it seemed, was Bishop Aldred, who had been a great friend to Grandfather Leofric. He was a scholarly, well-traveled, unprejudiced man, and though no house could possibly claim to have his strict allegiance, we all realized it could do us naught but good to have him seated in ecclesiastical power in the north. He was fond of Uncle Leofric, and held a high opinion of my father. In fact, he had been the one who worked diligently between Earl Ælfgar and King Edward on the two occasions of my father's disfavor and had ultimately arranged the terms of both reconciliations, even managing to get the king to take Gruffydd of Llewellyn back into partial trust. He sat now as Bishop of the troubled Hereford Shire; there had been no unpleasantness on the Welsh border since his election. The truth was that we could hope for nothing more favorable than to have him in Eorforwic, and the men of our house speculated on it with glowing enthusiasm, until they had entirely exhausted the subject.

"What news hear you of Aldgyth and baby Nesta?" Edwin asked when the meal was nearly over.

My father flashed a smile. "The little girl is quite healthy," he said, "but there is no news of a boy-child yet."

Nesta would be about two years old now, I figured, and it pained me that I had never seen her. We had ridden to Ceaster late in the last summer in hopes of meeting with all three, but in the end, Gruffydd had come across the river without wife or babe. Aldgyth could not be cajoled into traveling through the mountains with the little one. She was very well settled at Rhuddlan and bade us all come there instead. One thing after another had happened to delay it, and finally, Ælfgar and Burchard had gone there with a small party while Edwin and I were at the monastery. "Aldgyth blooms like a wild lily on a creek bank," Burchard said with a merry twinkle, "but you would never recognize her!" We wondered why and he told us simply that she had become a true cwene of the Cymry.

Later, when we sat with my uncle in his private lodges, just my father and my brothers and I—and Cynewulf Cenwulf's son, who dozed—I asked about Ælfgiva. I had hesitated to do so before, for fear my father would say some unseemly thing in front of the monks of Peterborough; he had not much of a sense of deference. Now when I asked, though, he only shrugged and sank carelessly back into the heavy, high-backed chair. "The woman holds some evil spirit in her," he muttered wearily. "I swear it is true."

Burchard coughed a little, as if the phrase bothered him. "She wanted father not to come for this—" he began, then stopped himself as if he knew it was useless.

"How badly?" Edwin asked off-handedly.

"How badly what?" Burchard did not catch his meaning.

"How badly did she want him not to come?" Edwin's voice was cool. "How soundly did she curse him; how often did she force herself to tears?"

Uncle Leofric chastised him then, saying he would not have such talk in his house as it went against the commandments. "You are well nigh unto manhood, Edwin Ælfgar's son, and ought to know better."

"I know the woman, Uncle, and I know her ways."

My uncle's voice grew stern. "Still yourself! Ever has it occurred to you that the lady might have a reason to be distressed over it?"

Just then a shadow passed over my father's face, and shaking as with anger, he came suddenly to his feet. "Best we would talk of other things," he declared hotly. "God knows it suits me ill to speak of her!"

I was sorry I had asked. We all sat in glum silence for a little while and the dark mood eventually passed. Then Ælfgar said musingly that he was minded to visit the monastery at Ely again, and my uncle said he would take us there on the morrow, if he thought he could trust us not to harangue each other in front of the monks there. We laughed so heartily at his drollness that we wakened Cynewulf, who had made himself too comfortable on the floor near the low-burning hearth. He asked us what it was we chuckled over, and we were hard-pressed to tell him.

So it was that just after matins and lauds, we traveled out into the sun-streaked mistiness of the fen-way, taking a party of twelve in three long-nosed eel boats. Into the marshy forest, past oxen and cattle grazing knee-deep in green water, we floated noiselessly till at length the towering, titan clouds were hidden entirely from our view by the mossy overhang of the deeps. When the cavernous stone-built place loomed large before us, I felt the familiar welling of dread and discomfort that came when I saw it. I had no reason to sense evil and foreboding in a place hallowed of God, but I did, always had, and the feelings were the more disturbing because I could not explain them.

Sometimes I thought it was the story of Ælfred Ætheling that had soured me to Ely, for it was at that place the man had died of his atrocious woundings after his eyes were gouged out. Other times I thought it was because the place was entirely surrounded by the fen—not just bordered on one side like Peterborough, but rising like a cold, slate island from the very depths of it. The fen did not suit me. The eerie, echoing, splashing stillness of it encroached on my senses like nightmare, from all sides at once. Even the smell of it, dank and musty and never-new, was discomfiting. The marshlands, it seemed to me, were but a wound-hole in the bowels of warm mother Earth. That men, and holy men of wisdom no less, could seek to live within the confines of it, was something beyond my understanding.

The monks were surprised but pleased to discover the Abbot of Peterborough had come to them, bringing the great Earl of Mercia with him. Gyrth Godwine's son was the Earl of the East Anglia now, and the monasteries of the fen-land had fallen somewhat into obscurity again, ignored and deprived of all but the most basic pledge-gifts. The men of Ely had not forgotten the favor my father had shown their house during his brief sojourn as earl there. They made him a warm if unostentatious welcome and showed us immediately to the alms-house. 'Twas not that we were seeking alms, indeed, but that was the traditional place to await an interview with the abbot, and here, where we were relative strangers, we submitted to formalities we had long ago dispensed with in my uncle's house.

I can tell you that I fast grew impatient with waiting there. It seemed I had never sat in so grim a place before; even the pleasant, low chatter of the other men did not put me at ease, such a sense of disquiet had taken hold. Edwin asked if anything ailed me and I grew disturbed and defensive. Many years ago, when we had first come to the Anglia, I had told him somewhat of my fear of the place and now I thought he meant to tease me for it so I ignored him and his fine features clouded with concern. Telling him I was quite well, I strode away, stepping through the tall door-way into the drafty, dark corridor. It looked endless, and my own breath seemed to echo menacingly. I rejoined my kinsmen after a very few minutes of isolation, moving to the far end of the room to inspect a heavy, faded tapestry. It was one of three which covered great sections of the otherwise bare stone walls, draping from ceiling to floor and looking as if they were woven as much out of dust as worsted. I was inspecting and fingering it gingerly when it suddenly moved. As I pulled instinctively away, the ripple of motion traveled to the end of the hanging, from whence suddenly emanated a broad-built, stolid man in monk's garb, clutching a threadbare blanket.

It was the Abbot of Ely, and I knew him at once, having met him several times before. Nevertheless, his unexpected apparition had taken me aback, and my shock must have been apparent. He laughed heartily as he greeted me, not tauntingly but with true amusement.

I made myself as comfortable as I could on a low, wooden bench while he beamed a genuine welcome to the other men, particularly my father. The two had not met since the time Ælfgar held the East Anglia; they had grown a firm friendship then. With surprise and true humility, the abbot accepted the gold-gift my father pressed upon him. Then they talked amiably for a while. Edwin came and sat anext me, and we listened silently as they conversed. For the most part, father shared the same tidings he had brought to Peterborough. Ely was particularly isolated and the men there were obviously eager for news. After a time, though, the abbot pushed himself away from the table where they sat and came over, apologizing for the start he had given me earlier.

"Near four centuries ago, when first this place was built, they put passageways through the stone of it so that men might hide within from the enemies of God, or conceal therein the things of worth should misfortune fall upon the place." He walked over to the hanging and we followed. Pulling it back with a great deal of effort, for it was exceptionally ancient and heavy, he pointed to a narrow door hewn into the stone of the wall. "Here you find doors where no man knows a door is, and stairs where stairs cannot be."

My father and Burchard had come over by then, curious as we were. The abbot gestured to my brother, that he might take a lantern from off the corner board, which he did. We all followed the abbot into the close, dark passageway. When the tapestry fell back in place behind us, swirling dust for a moment in the already thick air, I felt a sudden sickening surge of panic. My senses told me I was in a tomb; my heart beat hard. Blindly, though, I followed. The monk took the light from Burchard and held it high.

"See you this corridor?" he asked us. "One way it leads to the church—to the sanctuary. 'Tis built between the walls." He swung the lantern in the other direction and it flickered eerily as he began walking. Close behind him, we listened intently to his words. "When you come around the bend yonder, you find drafts of fresh air and some light if it be daytime or bright moonlight. There this hall runs between the kitchen and the sick-house, and no level of building sits atop it. Shafts go through the ceiling, like smoke vents, and let in the air and a hint of the light."

Just then, we rounded a corner. The passage grew wider here and all was lit with a strange silver-blue glow, a fractional remnant of the sunlight which filtered in from the outside world, seemingly a lifetime away. Carved into the floor, alongside the walls, were troughs of water. The abbot pointed them out to us.

"Two hundred years ago, when the heathen host invaded the land, they burned and demolished much of this place, all but the stone foundation. 'Tis said a good number of men stayed alive, hidden within these walls. When St. Æthelwold came in the year of grace 963 and restored the monasteries—this house and your uncle's amongst them—he found many of the most precious relics hidden here, in this passageway."

We had come to a steep stone stairway carved out of the ancient rock itself. Slowly and carefully we ascended; there was not much room for a foothold. After a dozen steps, we stood before what seemed to be a wide, low timber door. It took the brawny monk all the pressure he could exert to force it open. When we bent down and went through, we found ourselves in one of the nursing cubicles of the sick-room. The door was, in fact, the wooden skirt of a sturdy doctoring table which stood against the wall, cleverly disguising the chiseled doorway. It was dim in the partitioned chamber, yet after the darkness below the light seemed almost dazzling.

From the sick-room, the abbot led us through a corridor to the spacious, wide cloister, past the kitchen and the huge refectory. All the while, Burchard and Edwin discussed the age-old network of secret rooms and passages, asking first one question and then another on their use and past history. I was myself conspicuously silent; in truth, the stifling, dank closeness had entirely unnerved me, and I had to work hard that it would not show. I did not begin to feel better till we came out into open sunlight and made our way across the courtyard, back to the alms-house where my uncle and the other men were waiting. We had gone the entire length of the monastery under ground.

Later, gliding through the stillness back to Peterborough, I listened half-heartedly to some tales Uncle Leofric told of the fen. It had amazed him when first he came there, he said, to discover how easily the priests traversed the swamps from the East Anglia to the North Humbria, just as if the sunken causeways were well-marked streets. "Now, in this short time, even I know where every boat is hidden from here to there—where every hut and secret refuge is, and the access to every monastery. The exile or outlaw who is unjustly wronged knows there is no better sanctuary than what he can find with us."

My father looked at him darkly. "Mayhap I should have sought my shelter here, say you, brother?"

Abbot Leofric shrugged. "Many another man has hidden himself safe away till his name is cleared. If he stands in the right, that usually comes to pass."

"Usually but not always," my father scowled, looking away and trailing his hand in the smooth water.

"I do not say you chose wrongly. All has come to pass for the good, at length. You are a king's man again and back in favor." My uncle waited a while before he added solemnly, "Had it been I, Brother, methinks I would have crouched low awhile in some place like Ely till the king regained his senses. I doubt I would have sprung so swift to arms."

Ælfgar raised his handsome face, giving a short laugh. "Had it been you? Nay, never have you had need to strike out at a thing—never in all your life, Leofric Alfgeat's son! Nor ever will you, I trow!"

"Ælfgar—"

"Yet even so," my father continued, considering him carefully with narrowed eyes. "Even so, I am hard-pressed to picture you crouching."

Leaning forward, my uncle smote him ever so gently on the shoulder, fist clenched. They smiled at each other. Then my father drew a deep breath. First he glanced at Burchard, in the boat alongside ours, then to his own right-hand side, where Edwin sat, and then at me, opposite him anext my uncle.

"See how my two youngest childlings sneak into manhood?" he asked softly. Edwin and I exchanged a glance. He went on. "Now they are finished learning all the gentle things. When I take them home to Lindcylene they will put on hauberks and practice raising battle-axes and ruling estates. Two or three seasons hence they will be whole-grown men, and I will be welcoming my fortieth year. Seems this not a strange thing?"

Uncle Leofric pursed his lips in mock thoughtfulness. "What is stranger, perhaps, is that a man with your temperament should ever live to see forty! I scarce can believe it will happen—" He tried to say it lightly but the tone was forced. Suddenly, he reached and took my father's hand, clenching it tight in his own. "If ever distress is upon you, brother, remember my house is yours!"

My father shrugged. "You know how it stands with me."

"Here in the Anglia, I am privy to much that the Godwines say and do." My uncle's voice was adamant, and he lowered it. "They will never let you flee that way again; it sits too ill with them. Either they will block your way or hunt you thither. Surely you must know it yourself!"

Ælfgar pulled his hand away, and throwing his shoulders back, sat straight and stiff. "Mercia is ours and they know now I have the strength to hold it. Also have I an heir to succeed me, so the earldom would not even fall theirs for the trouble. Methinks they will let me be."

The Abbot of Peterborough looked grim. "They say you have designs on the North Humbria," he said accusingly. My father flushed a little; he and his cohorts still kept it a well-hidden secret. Stroking his chin, he looked away and said nothing, so my uncle went on. "Ever since

Oswulf Eadwulf's son moved his household to the Bernicia, they think you are planning to take Tostig's earldom."

Still Ælfgar said naught.

"They will bait you!" Uncle Leofric declared in a harsh voice. "I swear that they will corner you, and you will not be able to withstand the temptation to—"

My father cut him off with an abrupt gesture. "Even if they do," he said miserably, "do you not suppose they would come for me at Peterborough, knowing what we are to each other? And think you there is guile enough in you to keep me hid from them?" He laughed and looked away.

My uncle sat quiet, as if feeling shame for himself. Finally, he spoke. "Go to Ely, then," he whispered low.

Ælfgar's face twisted with a strange half-smile. His voice sounded gentle, resigned. "Nay," he said, "I think I will not need avail myself of it." There was a long and somber pause. "'Tis good to know it is there for my sons, though!" he added after a while.

A silence settled over everything. I plunged my hand into the water, chill now with approaching eventide. My fingers sliced a purple wake into the smooth, silver surface and the embroidered hem of my sleeve grew soaked and heavy.

I would never go there. The place was hateful to me: stark, foreboding, nightmarish. My mind was well made up. I would never go there again unless it was Death himself that forced me.

CHAPTER EIGHTEEN

Mighty the Mercian . . .
hard was his hand—play. . . .

—Early Mercian Poet

Summer 1061

"Keep it straight above your head—there! Lean back not too far with it; it juts your chest out like an invitation to your enemies and ruins what you have of balance."

Looking particularly gruff and demanding, Æthelstan the Fen-man took the heavy axe out of Edwin's hands and, bracing his legs wide and firm apart, lifted it high to illustrate his lesson. Scowling, my brother grabbed it back, walked a few paces away and raised the weapon once more. From where I sat, panting and exhausted in the shade of a twining old oak, I could see the sweat that drenched his hair and brow and glistened on his muscled arms below the capped sleeves of his leathern hauberk. With a ferocious cry, he slammed one of the shining double axe-blades into the spongy grey trunk of the long-dead tree we used for practice. When he let go, the carven handle quivered momentarily from the force of the strike, making an almost musical sound in the still air.

After wiping his face, my brother strode towards me, yanking ungently at the laces which held the hauberk to him. He almost had it off when Æthelstan's low, nasal voice stopped him. "'Twas a child's throw, Edwin Ælfgar's son!" he called accusingly. "Surely it did not give you pride!"

"Virgin curse you, fen-man!" Edwin hissed low, under his breath. Then he turned to face the man, hands on his hips, eyes glaring. "Well?" he asked, bracing for the other's rebuke. I smiled inwardly, having just tasted of it myself.

"The horror of the battle-axe is in the swiftness of the sideways slice," Æthelstan's tone was reverential, as if he imparted some poetry of pure philosophy to us. "If you waste your power chopping up and down, the fleet second it takes you to regain your might could—"

My brother bristled. "Five months with a war-axe in my sweaty hands and you think I have not learnt to deal a blow?"

Æthelstan snorted. "Methinks you have better exercised yourself to receive one! A heathen would have cloven you head to neck had he chanced on you swinging that way!"

Dipping a ladle of water from an earthen pail, Edwin swished it around in his mouth, then spit it out. "By God, Anglian! I have half a mind to smite you!"

The man laughed uproariously, as if the thought were comical. "'Tis true that you look pretty in arms, Ælfgar's son," he said, squinting his eyes against the sun, "but not frightening, so your babish threats are as a tickle to one like me!" Still chuckling, he strode back to the shady stream bank and sat to drink with Ælfric White-Hair and his two young sons, Sihtric and Siferth, who were waiting there.

My brother watched after him a few seconds, then threw his hauberk off and dropped down into the grass next to me. "I swear to you," he said crossly, "the man probably criticized his mother's tit!" He peeled off his sleeveless under-tunic, stuck to him with perspiration, then fell back in the grass bare-chested with his hands behind his head. Unlacing my own hauberk, I spoke morosely.

"You heard what he told me, I trow? That a slender man like me was better suited to swing a sword?"

"Pah! The man likes to act like a bug beneath the skin, that is all!" He turned his head slightly and appraised me. "Methinks you are not much leaner than father, and no man would dare to say he should not wield an axe!"

I let myself be content with that. 'Twas true that none of the men of our house were bull-necks, yet they were fine fighters, every one. Even Edwin was gracile raher than hefty, and it was plain to see he could move a heavy Danish axe as well as any other man, despite Æthelstan's barbed censuring. Even so, I had already made the decision that I would be a man who relied chiefly on the sword. It seemed to me there was more of an art to handling it, and an axe ached me in the chest and shoulders for a good long time after I worked with one.

A little way off, I could hear Ælfric's underlings playing at battle, banging things with heavy limbs which served as axes, then accosting each other with mock swords. They issued occasional fierce cries, in imitation of the ancient Mercian war-cry, just as Edwin and I used to do when, fired by watching Burchard practice, we retired to some clearing to play the same games. Then it seemed we would never be the ones holding the true iron; such glory was a thing to be dreamt of and looked forward to with longing. Now, sticky and tired, my only hope was that grim-faced Æthelstan would find it in his heart to dismiss us for the day. It was past high summer, and the days were waning, but the heat had not diminished in a month's time.

Still listening to the raucous play, I heard someone approaching from the other direction. I glanced at Edwin, who was half-asleep in the velvety grass and seemingly unconcerned about his nakedness. A man old enough to sport chest hair was never to be seen unshirted unless bathing or doing penance, and we both knew it. I tossed him his sopping tunic. It jarred him and he bolted up, groaning, just as father and Cynewulf Cenwulf's son came into sight.

They had been gone seven days to the aet-Waeringwicum and I feared they would expect some demonstration of the skills we had accrued since last they watched us practice. When the two of them looked on us, though, they broke into unrestrained laughter so genuine that I felt myself flush with embarrassment. Then, to make matters worse, Ælfric and Æthelstan, hearing the commotion, came over to where we were and joined in the hilarity which waxed entirely at our expense. Edwin's ire was rising, I could tell, and my own temper was not far behind his, when suddenly my father grew sober and gruffly commanded Ælfric's striplings to run to the manor-house and fetch us clean tunics and braies. They complained, as boys of ten or so years are wont to do, but finally set off, fast as the wilting heat would allow.

My father turned a thoughtful eye on us, soon as they were gone and fell to talking with his men about our possibilities. Cynewulf told us 'twas no shame to feel fatigue and faintness after straining in arms; rather, he said, any man who had ever left a mark of his boldness on the battlefield was one who gave all his strength like that in preparation. "We laughed only because the picture was such a one as we remember ourselves," he said with a grin, wiping his own forehead with his sleeve. "Earl Ælfgar and I poured many an ounce of sweat in such pursuits."

Ælfric White-Hair, their friend then as now, nodded his head in agreement. "Aye," he said to my brother and me, but loud enough for all to hear, "and in pursuits of another nature as well."

We both smiled, finding not as much merriment in such jests as the others did, but proud that Ælfgar's guards had begun to talk to us like men.

Æthelstan suggested at long last that we cool and clean ourselves, and we gave out a groan of relief which caused another round of laughter. The habit being to bathe out of doors in all but the coldest weather, we made gratefully for the stream where we stripped and plunged ourselves into the refreshing water. By the time we were relaxed into better humor, the sons of White-Hair had returned, bearing fresh garments. We dried ourselves with the tunics before slipping into them. Edwin feigned anger because the boys had forgotten garters and threatened playfully to send them back for some. Finally, we bound our braies to our lower legs with rumpled ones salvaged from the dirty outfits. All the while, Edwin moaned and groaned about shabbiness, to the great amusement of the youngsters. They idolized him, as most of the children in my father's household did, because he played freely with them—rolling, gaming, and acting as wild as any untamed brat. Oft-times it seemed that he clung desperately to his boyishness, fast slipping away now. He suffered none of the agony of awkwardness that I did, though, as manhood overtook me; he just slid gracefully from one state to the other as if the golden fairness of his babyhood had been naught but a promise of the greater manly beauty to follow.

Back in the small circle of men which lounged beneath the shady trees, my father was boasting of Burchard's accomplishments. My brother had been gone nearly four months now on his long-awaited pilgrimage to Rome. Accompanied by our long-estranged cousin, Gospatrick Maldred's son, with whom he had made peace and friendship, he had joined a rich procession of nobles—the highest ranking pilgrims of the realm—who left together from the king's court. It seemed that Ælfgar spoke of him incessantly, waxing eloquent on his strength and gallantry and skill in arms.

It rubbed me strangely to hear this talk, knowing as I did that Burchard would return only to put aside forever the glories of warriorhood and contest. Often I wondered if my father had yet accepted the inevitability of it, but there was no one with whom I could discuss it in order to appease my hot curiosity. As far as I knew, not another man there knew of Burchard's decision. I supposed my father had shared it with Cynewulf at least; there were no secrets between an earl and his chief man, particularly when they stood in such closeness as those two did. I might have taken all my questions to Cynewulf—indeed, I oft was tempted—but I felt strongly that to do it would be to betray my brother, who had sworn himself to keep it secret and bade me to do likewise.

Edwin had not an inkling, of that I am certain. Sometimes I felt small but gripping pangs of guilt about it, particularly when he bragged to the sons of my father's men about Burchard's stunning prospects, or intimated slyly that his brother might marry this lady or that according to her wealth or beauty. It weighed on me then, as it ever did when I kept a thing, no matter how slight, inside me and away from him. I felt the nagging bother then as we sat down. Edwin joined into the converse, telling how the heir to Mercia had ridden to join the line of pilgrims in Lundun City, looking so fierce that even Tostig Godwine's son paid him homage.

"It well surprised the Earl of North Humbria to discover that the heir to the House of Leofric was to travel cross half the world in the same train as himself!" he said, letting Æthelstan comb him as he talked. "He flinched a bit at the sight of him, too, I can tell you— thinking no doubt 'twas good there were priests and holy men enough in the party to keep him from incurring the blood anger of such a bold one as Burchard!"

In a while, my father asked suddenly and unexpectedly of his men whether they thought Edwin had attained his full height. My brother blushed a little as they all turned to appraise him where he sat cross-legged in the cropped grass.

"His fingers be long and lean," Ælfric White-Hair said, squinting. "That speaks he will be taller than most."

"Aye! Yet already he is taller than most, methinks. He stands nearly at a head with Earl Ælfgar." Æthelstan nodded thoughtfully all the while he spoke. Having stood guardian to us for so long, he took a particular pride in everything concerning us, as if he might even have been responsible for our form and coloring.

Ælfgar leant back against a tree trunk, hands behind his head. "It has occurred to me to put him in a mail coat now," he said easily. Then, with a glance my way, he added, "Morcar as well."

There was astonished silence before Edwin and I broke into excited babbling. Mail was an expensive proposition and it would be foolish to fit a youth still growing. Burchard had passed eighteen years before he graduated from a leathern hauberk, Ælfric White-Hair reminded my father, but Cynewulf cut him off, grinning. "Must be Ælfgar cannot bear to ride out without a flashing son in arms beside him, so well he is accustomed to it. 'Tis a healthy enough conceit, so let him be prideful of these two if such be his wish!"

We all laughed and Cynewulf added that it would do all the other earls of the realm well to be reminded that the Earl of Mercia had three strong scions, for not one of the sons of Godwine had yet borne himself an heir.

"Harold of Wessex has sons—" Æthelstan began seriously.

My father laughed. "Aye, but they are bastards! They will never sit mounted anext their father while King Edward lives!" He chuckled, then grew somber. "In truth, what think you?" he asked Cynewulf Cenwulf's son. "Must be all their fast-growth is done by now. Can there be harm in giving such to them early?"

Cynewulf's eyes sparkled mischievously, but his tanned, handsome face looked properly pensive. "First you gave them birds too early and against all advice. Next, you sat them on stallions at the age most brats move from ponies to palfreys. Too, it seems to me you began shaving them when there was naught but down beneath their noses."

Here he paused, stroking his chin as if deep in thought. "Now I fear that if I say nay to this idea of yours, it may come to you to lead them round to maiden's chambers instead, to start them into other such education—"

There was a great bellow of laughter from all assembled, but Ælfric White-Hair threw his hands up in mock amazement. "Mean you they have worn hair on their chests and bellies a full year and he has not done so yet?" he cried, and there was more merriment. Then Æthelstan replied that he had robed and disrobed the two of us, on and off for many a year and had not seen a wool shirt, so he supposed those endeavors, at least, were being reserved for their proper time. All the while they jested, I worked vigorously to keep myself from blushing. I had learnt the hard way that my father's household men thrived on our discomfiture; the slightest show of embarrassment would release another great barrage of boldnesses, with our callowness as their central theme.

In the end, though, it was decided that we should have our hauberks of chain mail after all. Ælfgar sent immediately for the armorers at Scrobbesbyrig to fit us and begin working on the project. No doubt his desire was that we should ride alongside him as men when we traveled to Lundun City at Eastertide, to be seen as warriors, capable of protecting their portion, when he announced that his oldest son had renounced the earldom. Needless to say, we were both ecstatic over his unexpected decision, but as we lay abed late that night discussing it, I realized somewhat guiltily that I was the one who far more certainly understood his motives.

CHAPTER NINETEEN

The cuckoo stirs with
plaintive call,
The herald of summer,
with mournful song,
Foretelling the sorrow
that stabs the heart.
—Early North humbrian Poet

Spring 1062

As the hot summer gave way to rough winds and fast-falling twilight, we moved our household south from the Lindcylene Shire, as was our wont to do most years. We spent late autumn in the aet-Waeringwicum, where Siward Bearn had invited us to hunt boar, which were plentiful in the forest-lands round his estates. From there we went to Weogornaceaster.

Of all our manors, the great one at Weogornaceaster was my least favorite. It stood in the very shadow of the Eardene, and all men know those woodlands are touched by dark magick. The shadowy downs and heath all around it were best avoided after sundown, folk there had oft warned us, for the forest was sullen and belligerent and made no attempt to contain its own wayward evil.

My father had recounted oft enough how in one year, the place had spewn forth not only devastating earthquake but wild-fire as well, which had stripped the earth bare from there to the Peaclond. So great a mortality of men, cattle, and sheep occurred then, that the stench of death hovered over the entire Eardene, long into frozen winter. A man had to pass many miles around the cursed place, he told us, and even then found it hard going if he covered not his mouth and nose with a wool-cloth bunting.

As it happened, we kept the Christ Mass there. My father had meant to move the household on to Couventrie, where Grandmother

Godiva was, but the freeze came so harsh and swift that his men feared 'twould be awful folly to bring their wives and children even that short distance. As the winter wore on, it occurred to Ælfgar that perhaps it was not an entirely unlucky thing that the weather had kept us there. The manor was only a small way up the river Afene from Gleawan-ceaster, where King Edward held his Easter Gemot. With our household quartered so near, it would be easy for us to make a strong and impressive showing there. This is surely what Father wanted to do at that council, where he was to show his two younger sons for the first time as men in arms. It seemed somewhat propitious that we were so conveniently based.

I was seeing in my sixteenth year that season and so proud of my imminent manhood that I did not indulge my fearful fantasies of the place as I had been used to do in my boyhood. I could not know then how soon the ill-fated place was to vomit its evil miseries on us.

It was at Weogornaceaster that the sons of Carr finally adopted Anglish dress, putting aside hides and leathers in favor of subtly dyed linens and wool. They even shaved their beards away, mustaches, cheek-hair, and all, so that the look of them was entirely different, and not at all unpleasant. It was surprising to see how close they resembled Anglish once they disposed of the outward signs of their Welshness. Nevertheless, a man could tell immediately from whence they hailed as soon as one of them opened his mouth to speak. Their Mercian dialect was close to perfect, but they insisted on talking their own musical tongue, if they ever could be cajoled into any converse at all.

They had become Burchard's men; my father had sworn them to him the second time we fled for protection to the Cymry, leaving my brother to stand guardian of Mercia till the restoration. They grew so fond of each other, Burchard and these three, that they became near inseparable. When my brother began his pilgrimage, they were forced to remain behind. My father could not risk the harm which might befall them in hazardous travel through foreign lands. As hostages, they were under his strict protection and such journeys were fraught with perils of the most threatening kind. So they stayed, and in that time, Edwin and I grew closer to them than ever we had opportunity to do before.

'Twas an association not always regarded with the greatest tolerance by our elders. The Welshmen were occasionally disposed to lusty drinking, as well as wenching of the sort most despised by our nobility—with hired women. They knew just which scullion maid would exchange a night for a brass boss or ring, which peasant girl gave most for a riband or chunk of salt. Being princes deprived of princedoms, they had all the means, attraction, and appeal of the very high-born, but none of the responsibilities. Pulsing as they did in the very strongest prime of their manhood, they now and again gave in to these idle pursuits. Burchard was old enough and strong enough to withstand them and, indeed, even hold them in tow, so father had no worries on his account. Edwin and I, though, being green and untried, tended to see their misbehavior as a sort of compellingly romantic boldness. In our fidgety impatience to prove ourselves men, we fell occasionally to reveling with them during that long, depressing winter. Not that we womanized in any but the most harmless ways, fondling and kissing; our upbringing had been too pious to allow of more. More, we were still so shy and boyish in that regard that the mere contemplation of real contact terrified us, though we would never admit it. Our nights of dissipation consisted mainly of over-partaking of strong spirits, jesting boldly, bragging loudly, and in general, making asses of ourselves till we lost consciousness or incurred my father's wrath so coldly that he had us thrown in the loft to sleep it off. Then came morning's bleary-eyed discomfort and the embarrassment of confession and penance, and we would manage to hold our own against temptation for another fortnight or so.

Early one morning in March, Edwin and I rode out with the Welshmen along the trodden track which led across the rolling meadows and into the wood. We carried bow and arrow against the possibility of rousing ptarmigan but had no serious intent of hunting. Our wont was more to enjoy the unseasonable warmth. The ground was spongy and moist with spring, and the heath scattered with small clouds of white mist, so heavy a man scarce could see his way through them.

We had ridden out of sight of the manor, into a sparse copse at the foot of the forest, when Ywen Carr's son enticed my brother and me into doing the unthinkable. He had carried with him several skins of potent honey-mead and we let ourselves drink it, full well knowing it was Lent. Without dismounting, we drained the stuff to the last drop, passing it from man to man as we traveled. This sport grew increasingly more precarious and caused us more and more merriment as we progressed in our silliness. In very short time, we were sodden: singing merrily and taking an unusual number of branches in the face.

I know not what caused us to meander into the Eardene; surely it was not a thing we consciously agreed upon. We had gone but a little way in when we stopped of a sudden, all at once, and grew curiously silent, as if noticing our surroundings for the first time. Without a word, we began to turn our horses, each taking for granted that not a soul of us wished to be in such a place as that. There was a sudden sound of scampering and a flurry of wings as we made our move, and I let go a loud gasp of surprise as my stallion shied after taking some creature too near to the nose.

Then, above the customary noises of a forest trail, another sound came—low at first, then waxing unmistakable. 'Twas a woman's voice in song! It seemed to come from no great distance, but echoed eerily through the leafless wood, deceiving ear as to direction. I wanted no part of it, but Edwin grew stiff and straight in his silver saddle, cocking his head, looking for all the world like a fox with his ears perked for grouse. In seconds, he had reined his mount off the path and, not to be intimidated by his boldness, the rest of us made ourselves follow him.

We went but a few paces before we came to a slight ridge, heavily wooded, which overlooked a small marshy clearing. At the far end of this bare dale stood a miserable hut, made of a few logs stuffed with bracken and heather. Before it, her back to us, a woman knelt, doing something which seemed to require a great deal of her strength. She was all the while singing, and not unpleasantly, in a thin, tense voice. We stared in silence as she worked; even from a distance we saw that her shift was only a filthy tatter.

I could not tell what she was doing; 'twas impossible to discern from there. Casting me a frown of concern, Edwin kneed his horse forward, moving some lengths ahead of us, straining to peer through the trees. Then, with incredible suddenness, the air all around was rent by the sound of his voice, as he let go a horrified oath.

"Mother of Christ!" he cried. "Know you not that to eat of horse meat is a sin?"

He lunged forward in a ferocious gallop and without a second thought I spurred my stallion to follow. The Welshmen must have done the same, for we seemed to arrive at the same split-second, all five of us pulling to a jarring, jolting halt directly anext the woman. Soon as she saw us, she threw herself writhing and groveling on the ground, begging for mercy and crying that the horse had been found there dead many weeks since, and that they ne'er would have cut from it had they not truly thought the thing was abandoned.

The next moments have congealed in my memory as a mass of gross and indistinct terror: the sudden, unsubtle stench; the sight of the wretched, scabby animal; the slow realization of what the woman was doing. Then, even before I could straighten it out in my mind, another figure crashed through the stiff and woody underbrush, brandishing a great stick and spewing a downpour of crude oaths and curses. Stopping in his tracks when he saw who we were, this same man threw himself face down on the sopping turf, as if waiting for the death blow which would end his miseries.

Trembling mightily, my brother dismounted, staring at the awful scene. Holding his horse, he moved closer to the woman and, as he approached, she rose to her knees. I was horrified to see she held a knife—the one she had been using to hack away the animal's flesh. I cried out, but when Edwin was near her, he held his hand out; she offered no resistance, but handed it to him. Then he backed away, still shaking, and in a tremulous voice repeated his question. "Know you not that to eat of horsemeat is a sin?"

Her face, already swollen with fright, grew even more distorted as she began to sob again, saying there had been naught to eat in more days than she could remember. "To find meat, my lord! Seemed 'twas sent by God himself, we thought, in his tender mercy. Elsewise, surely we should have starved to death. No living things yet are in bloom or blossom on the land, nor even can we find more of rotten winter-nuts or dead roots; we are not used to living in the wilds."

"How came you here?" my brother demanded low.

The woman clasped and unclasped her small, thin hands. "My husband is disowned, run away from the North Humbria where Tostig Godwine's son has robbed us of our hearth and fields and put an unfair price on us for some unnamed treachery of which we are blameless. Mayhap it was our backing of Earl Ælfgar in his claim."

Even as she spoke, her man raised his head. "I swear to you all, my lords," he stammered in a strained, rasping voice. "We wanted only to eat a share to stave our hunger. All the night we have held at bay the black wolves who smelled of it and came to claim it for their own."

That is when I reined my horse around and broke away, hot with sweat and sickness, forcing my animal to sprint through the brush and timber. I know not how many minutes I clung to his neck, but soon as I was away from them, I slid down with a power not my own, and was violently ill.

When I had regained somewhat of my strength, I led the animal a short while, not daring to sit him for my weakness. The mixture of the strong drink and the horror had worked to produce a clenching pain both in my head and my gut, and my legs were so weak I scarce could guide them. Still, in a short time, I began to fear myself that I would lose my way in the dense trees, for I had not yet found my way to the path. Gritting my teeth against the dizziness, I lifted myself once more to the saddle, and gave my mount his free rein, hoping he would take himself back to the other horses, as stallions are wont to do. In a very little while, I was approaching the clearing again, but I would not go closer than the base of the wooded ridge.

"What be the penalty upon runaways in this shire?" the wretched man was asking. When no one made a reply, he added in a fearful tone,

"In Godmunddingaham, from whence we are fled, the earl's price is upon our head and we might bring you some reward if you think to spare us." I saw him raise a feeble look to my brother—a sad, expectant grimace.

Without answering, Edwin remounted and tossed the dull blade back to the woman, who came to her feet in amazement.

"Mean you not to have us accounted for, sire?" she cried, her voice quivering with emotion.

By way of answer, my brother tossed his head admonishingly. "You would do well to cook your meat before you eat of it!"

The woman started once more to weep, and the man hung his head, shamefully and helplessly, explaining in a humble voice that they feared to light a fire as the smoke might be seen. Edwin paused a moment, then reached impulsively behind him, loosening his bow and quiver-bag of arrows. Moving his horse closer to the astounded man, he handed them down. His strong voice was gentle and compassionate as he spoke. "Catch you some fresher game then, man!" he commanded gently with a wan smile. "Lest you contaminate yourself and your woman!"

He turned his proud horse away. The Welshmen followed. They had come half the way to me when the man called out, catching back a sob. "What lord be you, sire?" he cried.

My brother answered without looking back. "I am Edwin."

"Edwin the earl's son, of the House of Leofric?"

"Aye. I am Edwin Ælfgar's son."

Then the man fell to his knees, almost as if in prayer, speaking with undisguised reverence. "By the virgin, God bless you and all your house, my lord!"

My brother raised an arm as if to acknowledge a genuine salute. When he drew near to me, I pulled my horse around and paced anext him as we moved slowly out of the forest.

We spoke not at all amongst ourselves about what had passed, but late in the day I found Edwin in our chamber, morose because he had not been holding bread or cheese or food-stuffs to give to the starving couple.

"Think you we should make our way back there and leave them clothes and provender?" he asked me very seriously.

"Nay!" I shook my head with such violence that my hair flew. "You did for them all you could, brother, and 'twas more than they could have expected from any man!"

Whether he took comfort in that or not, I cannot say. To my great relief, he did not suggest it again. I had no desire to go back into the cursed Eardene. I was uncomfortable enough on the grounds of the great manor, which to me had always seemed tainted by its mere proximity to the evil wood. Since boyhood, I had felt an unluckiness in that house; older now and more sensible, I tried to dismiss it but could not. The happening in the forest had done little to lighten my dislike of the place. I worked hard to erase the memory of it, but to no avail. The picture of those pitiful creatures, and the shame of my reaction to them, remained to haunt me, lasting even through the far greater misfortunes which befell us in that grim place soon after.

*   *   *

Ælfgiva had been waning in mind and spirit ever since Burchard took his leave of us. She was given to senseless weeping alternating with periods of violent rage, and was grown so thin with her constant fasting that, as before, the priests forbade her do it more. She had no need of penancing, they said, for she had grown heedless and childlike and so could not be held accountable for her distemper. Still, she deemed herself sinful and full of shame, and her outbursts were always followed by long days of self-inflicted miseries which only worked to weaken her further.

Father made us visit with her every day: sit and pay courtesies and talk of this thing and that, in the hope it would comfort her. Sometimes we met her in the garden or chapel, but most often it was to her chamber we retired. More and more of her hours were spent there of late, though she still brought herself daily to the hall for the great meal.

Our time with her was never comfortable, and Edwin especially despised it. She had come to treat him unmercifully, constantly accusing him of gross crimes of thought and deed, for the idea obsessed her that he had conspired to have her first-born removed from his inheritance. After Burchard left on his pilgrimage, the months became incalculably long to her and fraught with suspicion. In her worst periods of mind-lessness, she charged my innocent brother with falseness, treachery— even murder. All this Edwin bore with stoic and unflinching patience, but he no longer let her handle him physically, and shrank from her touch as if it were poison.

Sometimes incoherent, sometimes stony still, sometimes sharp and evil-tongued, we never knew what to expect of her. On the morning after our experience in the Eardene, Edwin and I met with her in her room after the mass, and were surprised to find her calm and pleasant. She smiled as she bade us come in and chatted agreeably as she did her stitching. 'Twas a piece of embroidery which had occupied her many years: lions, stags, and flowers, all the emblems of Mercia entwined in a design which she worked in bright-dyed threads on a length of fine-woven wool. "Think you not this will make a fine court dress?" she asked us holding it up. We agreed that it would.

Still her exceptional beauty belied her age. She was near to fifty seasons now, but a man would never guess it. Her hair had always been snowy white so she suffered no change of greyness. Her hands, her cheek, her unlined brow, all retained their softness. Her tiny figure seemed girlish, and there was a childish innocence, almost too childish, in her tourmaline eyes. Now, she knit her brows and spoke in a worried tone. "I hoped my Burchard would wear this one day," she said, "when he was Earl of Mercia...." Her voice trailed off and she shook her head sadly. "'Tis not to be, I trow!"

My brother and I exchanged a look. With Burchard's return and the king's Easter Gemot looming very near, Ælfgar had that very morning drawn us aside and explained the purpose of the pilgrimage: Burchard's decision to take the cloth and all the import that it had for us. Edwin had been astounded; I had feigned surprise. Now we wondered how it was the lady had come to know of it, for father had not mentioned telling her.

She looked up suddenly, before either of us said anything. "I should give it you, my golden Edwin," she said softly, staring at him in a strange way. "You are such a fair child, and never have I made aught for you with my own hands!"

I flinched a little, remembering how she had oft-times sewn handsome pieces for Burchard, Aldgyth, and myself when we were youngsters, often giving them to us in front of Edwin. "He is not to have treasures and such-like," she would admonish in his hearing. "He is too like his father, and pretty things will make him cruel!"

Perhaps 'twas guilt for those times that plagued her today. She asked if he would be pleased to take it.

"'Twould be senseless to gift it away now, mother," he answered tonelessly. "You have promised it to Burchard these many years, and he will be glad to have it."

At his words, she dropped her needle and pressed fingertips to her temples. "I fear me I will see him nevermore," she moaned, looking from one to the other of us. "Methinks I have been many days deceived to think he lives!"

Edwin paled and grew rigid, expecting her more usual behavior, but sensing things were different with her this time, I put my arms around her slender shoulders and tried to soothe her. "By all the saints, I swear this is naught but an imagining of yours, mother! Burchard has made a holy pilgrimage; he has taken special blessings and even now returns to us! Well you know how Father is confident he will have his first-born by his side at the king's Easter Gemot!"

"Say you it is so?" she besought hopefully, and I nodded, saying I swore to it. Then she turned to Edwin a look far gentler than was her wont, questioning him as well. "Is it God's truth, Edwin, that things are well with him?" He joined me in reassuring her. Relaxing visibly, she held her arms out to the two of us. When I bent to her, she hugged me affectionately, which thing she had not done long since. Standing back, just out of her reach, Edwin watched expressionlessly as we embraced.

*   *   *

It was late in the cloudy noon a few days later that we learnt Burchard was dead. We were sitting in the hall at Weogornaceaster, taking our great meal, when a king's herald was announced. The doors swung open to admit five visitors, and we saw immediately that the man at their head was Harold Godwine's son, Earl of Wessex.

He let his armiger take his mantle away; it had drizzled most of the morning so the thing was sopped and muddy. Beneath it he wore a dun-colored dalmatic of smooth broadcloth, made handsome with silver embroidery and belts of precious metal. His straw-colored hair was soaking wet, matted and unkempt, and he ran his fingers through it furiously, trying to make himself presentable as he approached our table. His set, hard mouth wore a faint smile which seemed to flicker uncertainly under eyes full of reserved sympathy. I did not know the man well, but had met with him occasionally in the king's house. So different was this look from his normally unreadable gaze, that a dread sensation gripped me soon as I saw him.

Ælfgar stood, and the two greeted each other formally. Harold seated himself opposite us, sharing a table with my father for the first time in a full dozen years. There was a long and awkward silence; then Ælfgar ordered mead for his guest. My mother, who was not always careful to perform her lady's duties, brought it herself, serving it in a richly carved horn banded round in gold.

The earl delivered his message while she yet stood near the table, speaking quickly and with genuine regret. The pilgrims had returned from Rome after great hardships, he said, bearing news that Burchard had succumbed to fever and rested now neath the stone floor of the great cathedral church at Rheims.

Ælfgiva uttered a single, heart-rending cry and fell to the floor in a dead faint. My father, stunned and shaking, translated his own anguish into fury. "God smite you that you would tell such in front of the woman!" he cried, coming to his full height, and smashing his clenched fist on the table as the words exploded from his lips.

Harold Godwine's son was dismayed but seemed to instinctively understand the other man's grief, so he made no issue of the curse. He bent himself to my mother's aid and later, when Ælfgar's calm and confidence were restored, the two men walked out together for a while in the courtyard. When they parted company at twilight, they were less unfriendly than ever they had been before. Still, my father stared after the small party as they made their leave, with a look of bitterness which spoke more of suspicion than trust.

After that news, my mother did naught for many days but stare tragically and uncomprehendingly, twisting hair round her fingers and moving her lips in noiseless speech. She let herself be led about and cared for but gave no heed to comfort. The sorrow swept through our entire household, and even the boldest of men lamented openly. I am not ashamed to say that I wept; methinks there would be no honor in me if I did not. I loved that brother and have all my life carried for him a reverence which few others have ever earned.

In the very midst of our grief, Ælfgar selected a guard to accompany us to the Easter gathering at Gleawanceaster. We made our way there, a proud, handsome, and somberly dignified party. We found the city swarming with men; all of the great earls, and many high-born thegns and noblemen had come, bringing large numbers of their armed household men.

On the first day the Witena Gemot assembled, Burchard was eulogized and Edwin was presented as the heir to Mercia. A buzz of appraisal filled the hall as he made his way in, splendidly decked in costly court dress and looking particularly patrician and manly. My father had not frequented the Gemot since his successive fallings out with the king, coming only now and then to perform short ministrations dealing with matters exclusive to Mercia or our kinsmen and their vested interests. Edwin and I had been seldom seen there, Burchard having been the one who accompanied him always. Now, in the wake of the fast-spreading news of our house's great loss, our appearance seemed to have exactly the effect Ælfgar had hoped for. The men of Angland were somewhat surprised to realize that the House of Leofric now boasted two other blooded scions, both come capably to manhood.

My father was more subdued than men were used to seeing him, but he busied himself greatly with the council that season, sitting all the sessions, debating and witnessing charters. Could be the distraction of it was a blessing; no man ever felt a loss more keenly. From the first day, men came to us singly and in groups to make condolences or say favorable things of Burchard. The king took us aside in his private chambers to say his regrets, and even the other earls, all sons of Godwine, shared kind words, finding naught to criticize of his memory. One only of them made no attempt to approach us. Tostig Godwine's son had avoided us scrupulously all through the counciling, even though he knew we were asking amongst the returned pilgrims for news of Burchard's last days.

On the second night of the Easter feasting which followed the dismissal of the Gemot, we decided to retire early. We were none of us in celebrating mood this season, and our plan was to leave on the dawn of the morrow. Cynewulf Cenwulf's son, who shared our chamber with us, carried a pot of ale, and the four of us made our way out of the jostling festivity of the king's great hall.

We had gone a way down the wide, dim-lit corridor when, of a sudden, three figures stepped menacingly out of the gloom. We stopped dead, recognizing them even in the sputtering light of the tar torches as men sworn to Tostig, the Earl of the North Humbria. They stood still, making no move to come nearer, and all the while held their right arms high as if to assure us they carried no weapons. Even so, in a single motion, Cynewulf had deposited the ale and drawn his sword; treachery, even in the king's house, being no unheard of thing. My father put both hands round the hilt of his sword, and my brother and I followed suit. Before we had need to move further, one of the men spoke.

He was a tall, elegant figure, a half-Dane whom we knew to be called Gamel Orm's son, one of Tostig Godwine's son's select guardsmen, a follower of the Northern way who was known to worship Odin alongside the Christ. "This be naught of a perfidy, Earl Ælfgar!" he declared, and to prove it, unbuckled his leathern swordbelt, studded with silver heads, and tossed it to us. It was empty.

"What business have you with us?" my father demanded gruffly, unsheathing his sword all the way and motioning them closer with it.

"Truly, I fear to speak it here, my lord," the man said. "Let us move into this chamber—"

"If we are to speak, *we* will name the place!" Cynewulf snapped, probably suspecting as I did the possibility of an ambush. My mother's father and grandfather, Siferth and Morcar, had died that way in a king's house, and Oswulf's grandfather, Earl Uhtred, as well. But if my father had qualms, his voice did not belie them when he told the man to name his companions.

"On the left is Eswig Broad-Brace," he replied, "and the other is Ulf Dolfin's son."

My father stared, appraising them in the dimness. "Are you son of the Dolfin who holds lands in Tiouulfingacaestir?" he asked sharply, and the man nodded. Ælfgar and Cynewulf exchanged a glance. All three were high-ranking earl's men.

Then Edwin handed over the empty scabbard, and we led them back the way which we had come. Taking torches, we pushed open the door of the deserted buttery and made our way in. Cynewulf kept watch at the door, still nervous, but my father made himself comfortable, sitting on the edge of a cutting table in the very center of the room. Catching a deep breath, he crossed his arms on his chest and looked from one to the other of the men expectantly. Finally, Gamel Orm's son cleared his throat.

"We are three men of the twelve Earl Tostig carried with him to Rome." After that, he paused as if not knowing what next to say.

Ulf Dolfin's son stepped forward then. He was a large man and fair, but with skin marked harshly by scrofula. "Best you would know your son died no lingering death," he said in a half-whisper. "He waxed healthy one day and was a dead man the next."

My father stiffened. "What mean you?" he asked. I felt my heart pulsing and closed my eyes for a moment. The man's voice seemed to come from far away when he made his answer.

"'Twas at Rheims this tragedy occurred. The night Burchard Ælfgar's son died, he gamed and drank with the earl and his man Gospatrick Maldred's son—the same Gospatrick who is kinsman to you but gave over the love of your house to serve Tostig when that man came north. Not a house-carl in the north has not heard that man's dour mutterings about your haughty dismissal of him. Long has he sworn against your blood."

"Aye," my father muttered bitterly, "only not so deep as I have sworn against his." I remembered with a wrenching pang how Burchard had defended Gospatrick the summer Ælfgar refused to receive him at Kirton.

Gamel Orm's son clenched and unclenched his fists. "Those three dined alone together and the next day Earl Tostig bade us tell the arch-bishop and the other men that Burchard had many days complained of cramping and pain."

"'Tis God's truth, we will not be party to him any longer!" Ulf Dolfin's son spat. "The man has a madness, yet also has he an eagle eye. The fact does not escape him that you have held secret councils with your kinsmen Siward Bearn and Oswulf Eadwulf's son—and with Gruffydd, the Welshman."

The man called Broad-Brace, who had not spoken till now, broke in suddenly, his voice deep and cheerless. "Earl Tostig asked me whether I thought 'twas rebellion against him that was brewing in your meetings. I was honest; I told him aye. Then he bade me tell him who I thought would take his place: Siward Bearn or one of your sons. I told him I knew Siward Bearn well enough to know the man had no great craving for power. Then he laughed and asked me what would happen if Earl

Ælfgar had no sons to rule the North Humbria should he manage to wrest it away."

Groaning as with pain, my father came to his feet and paced back and forth. Edwin and I moved closer together, instinctively feeling each other's depth of hurt and sorrow.

"Long have I been a blind man," Ulf Dolfin's son said after a little while, "and I have treated other men's sins too lightly. Methinks, in the north, Earl Tostig is seen by many for what he is now. Any man who still stands by him does naught but condone his murdering cruelty and other men know it. We could not condone it more."

Ælfgar nodded a wordless thanks. Then the man continued, slowly and firmly. "It occurs to us there may be many more good men in the north, who only lack a means of cutting themselves away from the man." Gamel Orm's son came close to my father, looking him in the eye. "Good men who would not oppose you if you made a bid for the Humbria."

"By God, though!" cried Eswig Broad-Brace. If you have the means and the strength to overthrow him, be swift to do it! The man waxes evil in his madness. Your son is not the first one he has so brutally mistreated, nor will be the last, I trow."

We tarried a short while longer with them, wondering amongst ourselves how the king could have so blinded himself to the faults of his favorite that he would hear no man's complaint against him. The three were eager to make their leave, though, and fearful that their betrayal would be discovered and marked against them. At length, we parted, and they made their way back to the earl they now plotted against. All they had spoken of weighed heavy on us, and I cried myself to sleep that night at the thought of my murdered brother.

CHAPTER TWENTY

Who bears it, knows
    what a bitter companion,
Shoulder to shoulder,
    sorrow can be.

    —Early North humbrian Poet

Autumn 1062

Five months had passed. High summer had been kind, and now the cobalt sky shone its timeless smile over golden fields rich with rye and barley, over thick flocks of plump, frisking lambs and thriving goats. The meadows of the Weogornaceaster Shire shone with a shadowy green and purple prettiness, much unlike the silvery, mellow beauty of Lindcylene, but still inspiring. From the great Eardene forest emanated the ceaseless song of cricket and cicada, lending a new mysteriousness to its gaunt, grim greenness.

Edwin turned eighteen. We celebrated by riding through the shire in a huge party, decked all in asphodel, corn-flowers, and brown-petalled lilies, passing alms. Our cousins Ælfric Flax-Head and apple-cheeked Ælfmaer, eighteen themselves now, spent a week with us in celebration. We had not seen them since we took our leave of the Lindcylene Shire the summer past and they had somehow snuck well into manhood during that time. Father gifted Edwin with Grandfather Leofric's illuminated psalter, bound in tooled hide with a hasp of solid gold. Mother gave him her embroidery, sewn now into a gorgeous robe collared with fox fur dyed black, laying it over him in his sleep as if she could not bear to see his look when he took it.

That fall, while we cut and hauled timber with our householders, Siward Bearn raised secret armies, gaining the allegiances of men in Tathaceaster and in the aet-Waeringwicum. Word came that Bernicians were flocking unabashed to the standard of our kinsman, Oswulf Eadwulf's son, hoping to see him earl there as his father had been. In Ceaster, Ealdread Æthelgar's son hosted the Welsh king and a contingent of his warriors. They decided to move through the Cymry, cross the river Saefern at Scrobbesbyrig, and travel through the forests to Weogornaceaster, where we waited for them. Earl Tostig still lingered with the king in the area of Gleawanceaster; we meant to surprise them with rebellion while they enjoyed their yearly stag-hunt together.

Our first awareness of trouble came when we learnt that Oswulf Eadwulf's son and his entire household had been banished from the North Humbria. My over-bold cousin had made a fight with Copsige Sword-Stinger, Tostig Godwine's son's chief man and deputy of the Bernicia. Oswulf's presence there had always been a bane to Tostig, who readily grabbed this excuse to be rid of him. We were hard-pressed to tell whether they seriously suspected him of plotting or whether they had just been rubbed sore by his lack of endearing charms. Regardless, it was not a lucky omen for us. His removal robbed us of a great deal of strength we had in the north, and upon which we heavily counted. What is more, it shook our confidence, and we began to wonder how closely they were watching us, and what they knew of our aims.

Mad as a hornet, Oswulf had scarce settled himself at Ceaster, wreaking oaths of avengement, when worse news came. On a clear, warm day in late September, William Malet arrived at our Weogornaceaster manor with three other riders. They had sidetracked themselves from a party of king's men who were traveling north to pay head-bounty to the hill-wolf hunters in the aet-Eomontum, where the beasts still ranged wild. He made at first as if the purpose of his visit was to pay courtesies to his sister; word had reached him that Lady Ælfgiva had been abed many weeks with a lingering illness of mood. Later, though, when he sat in the hall with us, taking meat and drink before his leave, he dropped us a piece of information which he must surely have known we had not heard.

"Must be you wax uneasy, brother," he said darkly, looking over the edge of his cup into my father's eyes, "knowing King Edward has put his price on the head of Gruffydd of Llewellyn."

Our astonishment was visible at once and my uncle pretended to apologize for himself, as if he had accidentally let go a great secret. "Even now," he said, scrutinizing all our faces for a reaction, "Earl Tostig and Earl Harold are mounting a great force against him—many of their own best men and more than a hundred of the king's. 'Tis said the Welshman is grown so brazen that he has crossed the front-tier and even now wanders on Anglish soil. But you would know naught of that, I trow?"

He spoke accusingly. Ælfgar did not answer. Edwin asked how it was that such an expedition could be in the works, with our house knowing nothing about it. "'Tis a boldness for the king and his advisors to make such a decision without calling every earl to council!" he exclaimed sullenly.

William Malet pursed his lips. "Seems they feel they have a great need for swiftness and secrecy," he said in an off-hand way. "I must trust that you will all be discreet about the mention of it."

There was no mistaking his meaning. He was bending the king's confidence to give us warning. Tostig, far from being blissfully ignorant of our plans, was raising a strong army against us with the aid of his brother earls and the king. Long after my uncle took his leave, we sat at that table with the chief of our men, trying to come to a decision.

As it happened, things were to be decided for us, and very quickly. Early on the morrow, even before the dawn, we were brought awake by a furious pounding of hooves in the courtyard, and the commotion that ensued as the guardsmen who slept in our hall took hold of three well armed and unannounced night visitors. In robes flung carelessly over night-shifts, we went to meet with them where they sat anext the hearth fire, having easily and unprotestingly surrendered to my father's men, who now surrounded them.

We found them sweating and dirty, their eyes, nostrils and mouths full of dust from the forcefulness of their ride. The one who spoke wore long hair in the North Humbrian fashion, though undyed, a blonde beard just starting, and a well-wrought image of Yggdrasil worn on a silver chain round his neck. He identified himself as Gamel-Beorn, son of the Gamel Orm's son who had come to us at Gleawanceaster to tell us of Burchard's fate. My father sent for warm mead, and we sat with them. The others were Osbeorn Dolfin's son and his nephew, Heard Ulf's son, a strongly built, brown-haired man about my own age. One was brother and the other son to Ulf Dolfin's son, the leader of the North Humbrian earl's men who had approached us in the king's house.

Gamel-Beorn had a shrill, unpleasant voice, but 'twas obvious he was high-born and well-bred. He spoke quickly and nervously, as if he liked not the task and wanted to be done with it, but he was careful to use all courtesies. Now and again his eyes wandered toward me or Edwin, and he seemed to regard us with an absorbing interest, almost giving the impression he had heard tales about us and wanted to confirm them. It occurred to me that whatever knowledge he had gleaned of us would have been spoken in the household of Tostig Godwine's son. I wished desperately I was dressed and armed, like he was, instead of shivering in a thin shift and loose bed-robe.

Gruffydd and his men had been seen crossing the river Temes, moving from the Cynibre woods into the Eardene. The word had reached Earl Tostig. "He will be riding out this very dawn, with a great force of men, hoping to surprise the Welshman in the woodlands at nightfall," said the North Humbrian earnestly in his whiny voice. "From here, you could find your way to Gruffydd a most-day quicker, and give him warning and time enough to flee."

"What think you of our facing him?" my father asked quickly. The other shook his head.

"Twould be foolsome risk. He rides with a king's army, in the hundreds, well-armed and sniffing for blood." He reached into a small pouch that hung round his waist with his knife-girt, took a pinch of salt and crumbled it into his mead—a Danish habit. I looked at him curiously. He pretended not to see me and went on, after taking a sip. "Mayhap if there were time for you to muster what you have of men in the aet-Waeringwicum and the Peaclond—but, there is no time!"

My father settled back glumly, biting his underlip, rubbing his unshaven cheek. Edwin clasped his hands together, leaning forward and asking low, "What chance then?"

Before an answer could be made, Gamel-Beorn mentioned that two days hence, Ulf Dolfin's son had been sent with a party of men to Eorforwic, the capital city of the North Humbria, to warn Tostig's retainers there to be armed and ready to confront Siward Bearn's forces from Tathaceaster. "He is not certain that the Bearn has an army, but he suspects as much. You know Tostig keeps over three hundred retainers at Eorforwic, fierce fighters all, since he is away so much of the time." He paused a minute, then added quickly that every one of those men was loyal to the earl. "We know as much, having tried in one way or another to petition support for you amongst them."

There was a long and gloomy silence. Things had fallen apart. More than anything, we had counted on the element of surprise—on being able to catch Tostig unaware at his court-play in the south-lands, while Siward Bearn caught his army off-guard in the north. This, coupled with the blow of Oswulf's sudden removal from his strategic seat in the Bernicia, brought a sudden end to any hopes we had of accomplishing our coup now—maybe for a long time, depending on how long it would take Earl Tostig to relax into carelessness again. There was only one thing to do: disband, sit back, play innocent. And wait.

First and foremost, Gruffydd, camped now in the Eardene with no suspicion of trouble, must be warned. It was this matter we were beginning to discuss when Gamel-Beorn, suddenly grown very somber, stood and walked a few paces away from the table. We were all staring at him expectantly when he turned round to face us, wearing a grim smile.

"All this news is sour enough, I trow," he said, coming close again, "but worse there is to come. I have not yet touched upon that word my father bade me carry."

Ælfgar stood, too. "Name it."

"Earl Tostig carries a king's writ against you."

My father threw his head back and laughed loudly. "By God! Another turn at outlawry and exile!"

The North Humbrian shook his head. "'Tis a writ of execution he carries this time, my lord."

There was a moment of stunnedness. "What right—" I began furiously, then caught my words back, unable to speak. My father sat down slowly, suddenly pale.

"What of my family?" he asked quietly, voice shaking.

"Total king's peace—your sons not to be harmed in any way and your oldest, Edwin, to hold all Mercia after you."

My brother oathed, slamming his cup down on the table.

"For my men?" my father also asked.

"King's peace," the answer came. Then Gamel-Beorn Gamel's son whispered, "I am sorry, my lord."

Ælfgar stiffened, then laughed quietly. "'Tis not a great matter," he said. "I will but sleep a year in the Cymry while our forces wax stronger here. I have fought my way home twice before; no doubt I can do the same again."

"You have every chance if you are swift," said the tall, brown-haired man named Heard, who had been silent till then. "Tostig Godwine's son knows as much. That is why he plotted to take you unawares. Naught but a dozen men know of this writ; by God's grace, my father, Ulf Dolfin's son, was one!"

We thanked the three riders with all the emotion we could muster out of our shock and let them be on their way. After they had gone, we sat a while in the hall, trying to gather our wits. After a few useless minutes, my father sprang into sudden action. He quickly selected ten of his men and ordered them to make ready for flight. He sent others out to deck the horses in harness and arms. Then, without a single word more, he turned his back and made his way purposefully to our chamber. Speechless with bewildered emotion, Edwin and I followed him there, then sat miserably on the edges of our cots and watched him ready himself. He said naught to us but dressed quickly, bothering neither to be combed nor shaven. I stood to help him lace his leathern hauberk, while Edwin climbed into the garderobe, reappearing with my father's finest coat of mail. At that instant, Cynewulf Cenwulf's son burst in, furious that he had not been chosen to ride with his earl. My brother and I sat mute while the two men argued about it.

My father's man protested violently that the two of them had never been separated from boyhood on, and that 'twas not a healthy time to start a new policy. Ælfgar replied calmly that, as chief man, Cynewulf's duty was to perform the most important task.

"Then let me fight anext you and defend your blood—"

"Defend my blood?" Now my father's voice was as loud and harsh as the other's. "For God's sake, man! I ask you to hold my sons … my woman! Call you that something other than defending my blood?"

They stood facing each other eye to eye in total, deafening silence. Then they embraced, long and hard, with all the force of their brotherhood. After that, Ælfgar sent his man to oversee other of the preparations, and we realized that he wanted a time alone with us.

Even so, for a long time he said nothing, only paced the length of the narrow chamber back and forth, stopping finally at the far end. There, he stood leaning against the wall, hands behind him, lost in thought.

It was Edwin he called to him first, and my brother flew to his side with an eagerness. They talked so low that I could not make words out of the murmur of their voices, but I watched them all the while, impressed more than ever with how alike they were. Equal in height now, and of the same lean and muscular frame, they had the same way of walking, of standing, of moving. Edwin's hair was of a slightly darker hue, his expressions perhaps more youthfully vehement; they differed in not much more than that. My father pressed something into the unwilling hand of his first-born son; then they hugged, taking each other's shoulders and drawing close.

When it was my turn to stand there near him, my father gazed a seemingly long time into my eyes before he spoke. Then he said with a wan smile, "Always you have been the one who carries most your mother's blood, Morcar—more than Aldgyth even, for she is her grandmother's girl."

I nodded numbly. It was not what I had hoped to hear, and my face must have belied my disappointment because he laughed a little. "'Tis not a thing that seems to sit well with you now, methinks," he said softly, "but I recall when she was yet fair of mind. 'Twas the way with her to seem so gentle that it fooled a man; underneath was she a sea of strength and persistence, and deeper than could be imagined! So it is with you, I trow—not a man will know what boils in there till the day he faces you!"

"You have loved her well, father." I said, choking on words and not knowing what else to say. He took my shoulders.

"Aye. And I have loved you well also, my son." He scrutinized my face carefully, then asked low, "Know you how it fares with some midsummer blossoms? How they stand tall and true in sunshine but are broken by the rain?"

I nodded, watching for his meaning.

"Well, oft-times I have thought that you are not that way, nor ever will be. Seems to me the strength is in the blooming weed and not the dazzling flower, because the roots grow deeper and clutch onto everything, taking life from soil, or sand, or water—even rock if it comes to that. There is where you differ finally from the lady—even from your brother. 'Tis the same with folks as with weeds and flowers: some break in rain or wither when the soil is not to their liking. Others grow all the same."

I could not help looking at him curiously. He flushed a little as if wondering whether he had said the right thing. Then, at exactly the same time, we smiled together. "Think you I am a madman?" he asked, his smile turning to a broad, boyish grin. "Methinks what I meant to say is that when we are done with this business, I will come back and plant you in the North Humbria, and we will grow as fine and weedy an earl as they have ever had there before!"

We laughed and hugged. Edwin joined us, and then we unrolled the metal hauberk and decked father in his arms.

A short time later, after a hurried Mass and sacrament, we rode out with him through the meadows to the woodland. Ælfric White-Hair, Daffydd Carr's son, and all the other men he had chosen to go with him looked fair under the sparkling kiss of the early morning sun, but none as fair as Ælfgar Leofric's son. He broke away from them all and, hair streaming and arm raised in salute, he urged his fiery white steed towards the forest at a fast and furious clip which the others were wroth to follow for all the weight of their arms.

At the very foot of the wood, his horse suddenly reared. Though it made a bold and handsome picture, I could not help feeling that the animal pawed the air in proud resistance to the powerful, unseen spirits of the cursed Eardene.

*   *   *

My father said not a word to Ælfgiva about his leaving. He feared it would spark her to distemper, so he kissed her in her sleep and told us in a low voice that it did not matter, for 'twould probably take her a fort-night to realize he was gone. In fact, it was but two days before she asked me about him, coming to the garden where I sat distracting myself.

It was flowering time. The blossoms to be used for scenting wash-waters and making attars had been picked earlier, in bud or new bloom, and now it was the last of the crop being harvested: larger, milder blos-soms for distilling into flavorings and remedies. The gentle ladies always enjoyed the pleasant task of picking flowers by the hamperful and strip-ping them of petals—near as much as the gentle men enjoyed sitting nearby and watching them. Edwin and I had discovered that the daughters of some of my father's men were developing into creatures definitely worth viewing. Though there were only a scant handful staying at Weogornaceaster who were yet of an age we could enjoy, we were careful nevertheless not to miss any opportunity of chatting and playing with them, such occasions being rare.

So we sat on the low stone wall that bordered the garden, with Ywen and Hwell Carr's sons. None of my father's men had sons of an age with us; most earl's men were too busy rising through the ranks of the household troops to bother with wedding and breeding till later. Even then, soon as their sons came anywhere near to age, thirteen or fourteen even, they were sent to the estates owned by their fathers, to learn how to manage them. So it was that my brother and I and the Welshmen had the undivided attentions of any young ladies who stayed, and all the compliments and flirtations and attentions did much to relieve us of the anxiety we had felt since Ælfgar took his leave.

Soon as I saw my mother coming across the courtyard towards the flower-field, I knew she was in a raging mood. There was a way she had of moving when violence was upon her that gave it away: a constant, pert tossing of her head and a bold stride entirely at variance with her fragile form. As she drew closer, I could see the pale, sparkling glitter of her eyes, a look that accompanied only her vilest tempers. I sprang to my feet. Following my gaze, Edwin did, too.

"By God! The shrike descends!" he whispered low to me, without even a hint of humor. Then he jumped up and strode hard away, not even looking back when she called him by name.

He feared her when she was like that, and all knew it—except Lady Ælfgiva. I walked a little in her direction, and she came to an abrupt stop as I blocked her way from him. She trembled with anger as he disappeared finally into the still-house without acknowledging her shrill commands to stay. Knowing everyone was watching and listening, while studiously pretending not to, I led my mother back towards the house some distance, pulling her firmly by the arm.

"The man's issue waxes rotten as he does!" she cried when I finally let her go. "Sneaking from house to house doing detestable things and frightened to answer for them!"

I gave a weary laugh, trying to make light of it. "Methinks Edwin will not be about any detestable business in the still-house, mother, with the place full of old women boiling flowers!"

"There is naught but shame in him!" she hissed. "How is it otherwise that he has not kept his bed for two nights? He makes himself a plague of sin unto some gentle maid in my employ!"

I took her shoulders, making her look into my eyes. This always seemed to calm her. "I share a chamber with him, lady, and I swear to you he has kept his nights there with me!"

"Think you I know not how he night-wanders?" she glowered darkly. "Even he has tried to take my bed!"

I shook her hard, almost hard enough to hurt her. Next to kin-killing, this was the most evil charge she made against him and she did it often. "You are mistaken, mother," I growled roughly. "'Twas only some dream of yours—"

"But nay!" She was crying now, and rubbing her eyes like a child. "He came to me and kissed my cheek and brow and touched me, and now he is shamed to face me." She went limp all at once. I lowered her to the grass, then sat beside her. It occurred to me suddenly that she spoke of Ælfgar, who had visited her chamber while she slept, just before he took his leave.

I arranged my thoughts carefully before I spoke again, all the while stroking her hair while she sobbed with her head in my lap.

"It was Father who came and kissed you, lady," I said gently, "to make a fare-well. He has been gone these two days since, and so has not kept his bed."

Her voice was but a muffled murmur. "Edwin Ælfgar's son is so very like him."

"Aye. He is like him enough."

I was puzzling on it now, how she had oft-times confused these two in her speech and in her mind.

"I would not have borne that bold thing in me," she lamented in a hoarse whisper, lifting her head, looking wild.

"He is your son!" I answered, turning my gaze.

"Nay. He is Earl Ælfgar's son!" she declared firmly.

"Methinks you know well enough he is your son as well," I softly reminded her. "Grandmother Godiva has told us oft how you were delivered of him on a wolf-skin coverlet in her kitchen-house." I watched her closely. She pulled little tufts of grass, held them in her hand, let them blow away. Presently she looked at me, and a smile came to her.

"Aldgyth was a girl-child, quiet and good and very happy. I almost forgave your father for forcing me for, in truth, I delighted in that tiny maid. You, Morcar, you were one who was wont to sleep upon my breast and kiss with me." Her voice trailed off. When she began again it had grown fiery. "Edwin would have naught of me. Even when he was a babe he did not love me! 'Twas as if he knew I had taken away from him his title and his holdings, so that my Burchard might be avenged for all he had lost. Neither would Edwin nurse upon me nor take comfort from my arms—and all because his father begot him roughly."

I put a finger on her lips. "So you have said it was with all of us, mother: that father was ungentle, that you thought not to bend to him but he demanded it."

She looked confused; I raised her face to mine. "Ever have you thought on this, mother?" I asked her solemnly. "That if I had been the first born and Edwin the one born after, naught of your love would have come to me, and he would have been the one now holding and embracing you?" I lifted her to her feet.

Trembling, she paled a moment as if the thought gave her great pain. Then she pulled away from me just enough that I felt it, and turned her head. "He would not let me hold him when he was a babe. He knew I oft-times wished him dead. 'Tis why he tries to force attention on me now, I trow—"

"Woman! You are bewildered!"

"'Tis why he came to me some nights ago. He needed to tell his love for me, Morcar—do not tell him I but pretended to sleep!"

"Father it was that came to you!" I let go a hard breath of deep despair. "It was Father took his leave of you then."

Tossing me a questioning look, as if she had just heard of it, she wrinkled her brow, then smiled a distant smile. "Still the man runs from me, whenever he gets not his way. Spoiled brat that he is—long it has been that any bed would do him. I should never have let myself wed with such a boy as that. Such a child he was! But I told me he would grow up and be as my other man had been. Burchard's father was a good man, Morcar—no hot blooded games in him; no toying."

She stopped suddenly, biting back a memory. Never had she spoken to me of her other husband, or to any of us that I knew. Now she began to tremble. I reached to steady her.

"Burchard's father was a good man," she repeated, holding tight onto my hand. "I lived with him in Normandy till he came here. Your father has told you that, I trow?"

I shook my head; she seemed surprised.

"We came to Angland with Ælfred Ætheling," she said simply.

At first, it did not register. Then, slowly, a sense of horror crept over me. The story my father used to tell in the smoke-filled hall! The first tale ever I heard of the House of Godwine! The horrid recounting of how the earl and his men had fallen on Ælfred Ætheling and his Norman protectors, blinding the prince till he died of the wounding—mutilating, murdering, massacring his followers.

"Was his fate with the Ætheling?" I asked her, working to suppress a sharp, sickening terror.

She nodded. "Earl Godwine himself and his son Tostig were amongst the men who broke into the hall where we slept," she answered stiffly. "They axed my Robert as he lay helpless in the bed beside me and hacked away his scalp. 'Twas the most trembling of horrors, Morcar! But I clung to him even then. Methinks I hoped to die with him. They laid hands on me, though—pulled me from the bed and sported with me, making as if to force me to wear on my head the mass they had sliced from my husband's. After that—"

She paused just long enough for me to realize the gruesome picture. I was shaking so that I hardly could keep my feet. She turned to me a stony look of earnest. "After that, they were not kind to me, Morcar!"

Assailed by sickening dizziness, I tried to console her but couldn't. She looked at me as if with wonderment.

"I scarce can believe your father has kept this secret from you all these years," she said, shaking her head. "My brother named as part of my bride's-price that Burchard never was to know this awful thing. Mayhap Earl Ælfgar feared that he would learn of it from his brothers and so did not tell you ... " she broke off, stifling a sob, then cried out miserably, "Oh, God! Sometimes I fear me I have sad misjudged him!" The agony of that thought was so real to her that I could not help but fold her in my arms.

We stood that way a long time and it seemed to calm her. When I loosed my grip, she stepped back, looking lost, small and helpless. "Even so," she added in a strange half-whisper, "'tis a pity the boy is so much like his father! It kindles me with wrath, the way he flees from me in shame always. Sometimes, I pray he will make peace with me; yet I fear him. He would give to me embraces that flush me with fear."

Her voice trailed off. She walked a few steps, then stopped and turned to me again.

"I do not like this place!" she declared, casting a look all around. "The air weighs heavy and I sleep not well at night. Truly we must bring our house back to the Lindcylene Shire, soon as Burchard comes."

As I watched her move away, I felt naught but an utter helplessness.

*   *   *

Whether it was the noise that woke me, or the light of the torches, or the cold kiss of iron at my throat, I will never know. Mayhap I became aware of them all at once. All I remember with certainty was the fearful sensation of flying from sleep to consciousness in the frenzy of a split second and feeling the glare of many hateful eyes.

Then I was taken, half pulled and half carried, from the pallet. The smack of the cold air on me as I stumbled still hot from the bed-covers, wet through with the sweat of deep sleep, was strong as the sting a man feels diving into a deep river on a hot day. No doubt about it; it cleared my head of everything—sleep and fear and surprise—all at once, leaving only the shivering wrath of my outrage. Someone crossed my arms behind me and, clenching them in an iron grip, steered me out of the chamber into the great hall.

The glint of metal was everywhere. It seemed I never before had seen so many armed warriors assembled. Pushing me forward through this sea of men, my captors brought me to the dais, forcing me to sit on one of the benches there while still holding me in that merciless, vise-like grasp. Edwin was already tangled in another man's stranglehold. In a few seconds, Cynewulf Cenwulf's son was thrust forward and seated roughly anext us, then Ywen and Hwell Carr's sons. They had emptied the earl's private chamber.

I recognized Tostig Godwine's son's guttural Saxon voice even before I saw him. He shouted a command, ordering the men to search every chamber, every out-building, even every tree. "In the king's name, bring me Ælfgar, son of Leofric, who does treason to the king and state of Angland!"

Immediately the bulk of the men took their leave, moving to the rattle and clang of iron. As the huge timber doors swung open, we caught a glimpse of our retainers, who had been sleeping in the hall. They stood huddled in a miserable, defiant group, along with the priests and free-men who had been dragged in from elsewhere on the manor, kept in tow by drawn swords. Soon as the earl approached us, our captors loosened their holds. For me, relief was instantaneous and the rush of blood back to my arms was so distracting that I almost missed Tostig's low-voiced question.

"Think you 'tis wise to hide and cover for a traitor with the king's price upon him?" No one made an answer so he asked us where my father was.

Edwin was the one who answered, glaring. "Must be you know it is hunting season!"

Tostig laughed loud. "Aye! And best you believe we mean to do some hunting!" A few of his men snickered dryly. Inspired, he added something about beating his prey out of the underbrush, which made them laugh more. My mouth went dry of a sudden.

Two of his men came back, and said there were naught but women in the other chamber. The earl said to bring them. Then he paced back and forth a bit, trying to seem casual. "Where be the third of these?" he glowered, staring at the Welshmen, and I told him Daffydd had gone hunting with my father. Roaring, he crashed his fist down on the table with a force that moved the heavy trestle several inches. "Play not false with me, little Mercian!" he shouted. "I have a mind to strangle you in your lies!"

His sun-browned features seemed to merge with the flickering darkness; only the flash of his white teeth as he snarled left an impression. I was hoping to God he would remind himself that the writ proclaimed no harm to be done unto the outlaw's sons.

In a few minutes, his men returned with my mother and two of her ladies. That is when I began to feel true fear: when I saw the look on Lady Ælfgiva's face. It took but one glance at Tostig Godwine's son to bring her to frenzied tears. He was cruel enough to laugh at her discomfort. "Save your weeping till we lay hands on the man, lady!" he said coldly, moving close and looking down on her. "Methinks there will be great sorrow to sob over then!"

Soon as he said it, Cynewulf pushed away from the table, drawing himself to his full height. He had slept in his day-clothes and hauberk; the fear of trouble had not fled him once since Ælfgar took his leave. Now, even unarmed, he was impressive. As he lunged, Tostig involuntarily moved back, hand on his sword. "Already you have brought enough grief unto this house by your murdering treachery!" my father's man exclaimed harshly. "Best you would not threaten more unless you are prepared to pay for it."

For a moment, the Earl of the North Humbria looked at him with surprise, then he threw his head back and laughed deeply. "Think you that you are in a position to reward me for my crimes, Mercian? I have king's men here enough to slaughter away this entire household in a twinkling!"

From half-way across the room, I could see my mother trembling where she stood. Edwin saw her, too. He had heard the story from me by now and he waxed furious. I watched him fight his own temper briefly before he flew to his feet.

"Your threats are idle, Wessexman!" he growled in a hoarse voice, sounding much like my father. "All the country knows your writ forbids even so much as the touching of a finger upon this family, so I fear me you will greatly dishonor yourself in front of many witnesses if you begin to dwell on slaughter!"

Those words threw Tostig Godwine's son into a rage. It had not occurred to him that we might have known about the writ of execution; now he realized with certainty that Ælfgar had made his escape. He quivered, at a momentary loss for words. Then he drew his sword and laid the flat edge of it hard against Edwin's cheek, turning my brother's hot gaze away with it. "'Tis but a matter of some short time before you feel the horror of death at my hands, Edwin Ælfgar's son! Be you prepared for it. I will put it on you harshly and suddenly and with no mercy!"

I stiffened. "The way you put it upon my other brother, I trow?" I asked with cold voice. Tostig yanked his sword away and spun to face me. He hesitated a long time, as if wondering whether the joy of saying the words would be worth the admission of guilt. Then his hatred got the better of him and he forced a mad, spiteful grin.

"Nay, Ælfgar's son!" he cried, shaking his head. "His fate will be far the worse. I could not bloody my hands with the other one; your own kinsman Gospatrick helped to feed him the burning poison. But I will not need worry me about leaving marks on this one's body. This bold-mouthed brat I will hack down in blood!"

Two of Tostig's men moved close, as if to still their chieftain, but he pushed them away. With an evil lunge, he grabbed my mother suddenly by the waist, pulling her close, shaking her like a lifeless pelt. "Tell me where he hides, woman! Else I will do to you here what God may not forgive me—and well you know I am able to do it!" She tried to pull away, but he wrestled her, violently ripping her shift and bruising her shoulders. Speechless, helpless, hopeless, we watched, held in place by the poised swords of the earl's men.

Letting go a tremendous oath which echoed round the hall, Cynewulf Cenwulf's son pushed away the two armed men on either side of him, taking a mean slice in the upper arm from one of them as he sent both flying. He crashed his strong body into Tostig Godwine's son, tearing him away from the lady and forcing the man's head far back in a painful stranglehold. Three of the earl's guardsmen were at Tostig's side in an instant, brandishing swords and axes. Bold Cynewulf let go a terrifying scream of agony as the first blade bit into his shoulders. The second, through his side, felled him. The third, a broad Danish axe, split through the left side of his chest. Must be it finished him, but he writhed and gasped on the ground till Tostig Godwine's son made his way over and kicked him in the head with great enough force to still him.

After that, no one moved. A hollow, eerie silence pulsated through the room, unbroken till my mother began shrieking. There was blood in her beautiful hair. Her shift, torn open to the waist, was soaked with it. She fell to her knees—clutching, hugging, trying to lift and hold Cynewulf's crushed and broken body. Tostig finally signaled his men to sheath their weapons. The instant they let us go, Edwin and I were at the lady's side, trying to pry her away from the warm and sopping corpse.

If anyone spoke during this, the words did not impress me. I moved as if by some unknown power—locked in a spell of horror and fear and over-whelming sorrow. I remember seeing the Wessexman, hands on his hips, impassively watching the scene of infinite terror and confusion being played out on the floor before him. His own outer tunic was naught but a dripping, gross scarlet stain—even his metal hauberk showed the gore. I found myself wondering for some ungodly reason what a man did to clean it. Æthelstan never told us that. He never told us blood spurts wide under the crush of an axe, despoiling everything around. He never told us.

After a while, strange noises began to intrude on the heavy breathing blanket of nightmare which so entirely encompassed me: the sound of a cock's crowing … the clatter of armed men's mounting … shouts and hollers growing distant. That in truth, is how I realized the men were gone, though even now, I scarce can believe the Earl of the North Humbria could have made a quiet leave without dealing more threats and curses. Mayhap he could see that it was useless to taunt us more; we were lost to any emotion by then: unseeing, unfeeling, unnerved.

The priests told us 'twould be best to bury Cynewulf quick, he was so badly mangled, but we could not stand the thought of putting him with the spirits of the evil Eardene. We swathed him well and carried him in a solemn procession to Nottingham. Grandmother Godiva begged us to have him interred in the monastery at Couventrie where prayers for his soul could be sung from the chantry day and night. We put him beneath the grass of the green lea though, knowing he would have appreciated it more. 'Twas where he and Ælfgar had played and hawked and ridden together as boys.

It took me near a seven-night to finally mourn the man, my shock was that deep. But I never have thought of him since without a pang of grief and sorrow. The handsome, brown-eyed guardsman had a love and care for me at a time when I most needed it, and I have scarce a child-hood memory that does not include him.

*   *   *

Off and on again when we were young, Ælfgar had settled in the small but comfortable manor at Nottingham—most usually in the autumn because he liked to hunt the Scirwudu. We had not kept house there in many years, though. My father had quite outgrown the place by the time he became Earl of Mercia and carried the number of retainers required by that position. I had always liked it. The stone and timber manor-house itself stood well off the wide Roman track-way, nestled between the boggy hollows and the pretty, peaceful wood. All my memories of it were pleasant, because we stayed there in times before we ever were touched by trouble—in days when words like outlaw and blood-feud and vengeance had no meaning except in tales and legends.

Surely 'twas a strange choice for us that year. We were traveling constantly between Ceaster, where we hoped to hear word from father, and Couventrie, where we had left Lady Ælfgiva in the care of our grandmother. My mother had not spoken a word since the night Cynewulf Cenwulf's son died.

Scrobbesbyrig would have been the wiser choice, but our main objective had been to get away from the ill-fated air of Weogornaceaster and we were drawn somehow to Nottingham. It was, after all, in the very heart of Mercia, and we could not be approached from any direction without knowing of it well in advance. I know not exactly what it was we feared, but we were heavy-hearted and most exceedingly cautious. Neither Edwin nor I ever rode out, even a trifling distance, without a large guard of men, heavily armed against the possibility of danger. In our hall, a night-long watch was kept.

'Twas a strange, dim, depressing time for us as we went about the ordering of a household entirely upon our own for the first time. I grew quiet and intense, withdrawing into private, troubled thought. Edwin's fast-mounting tension took another form. He became hot-headed and quick to anger, sharp-tongued and wild-eyed in his rage. No one dared to cross him, even in matters of small importance—the amount of mead to be doled at great meal, for instance, or the choice of meat to be served on Advent Sundays. In part, his distemper was due to overwork and lack of sleep; he was in constant motion every day and undertook at least one healthy journey a week, even in the worst of weather.

Those of us closest to him bore the brunt. He entirely alienated Ywen Carr's son for a period of near a month, and I often waxed so furious with him that I could not make myself sleep at night. Yet there was no denying the strength of the strain which gripped him, and he oft-times tried to word apologies for his outbursts. One night as we lay abed in the chamber-loft we shared with the Welshmen, he spoke aloud, hours after I thought he had fallen into slumber. "Methinks I cannot sleep, Morcar," he declared dolefully, "knowing you are fuming there and passing sore judgments on me."

I was still a little stiff with hurt and anger; he had taken issue with me over the choice of men I made to ride with me to Couventrie. I made him no answer and in a little while he spoke again, saying he well enough knew I was awake so it would do me no good to ignore him. I replied that I cared not to hear his boldnesses long into the night; I had taken enough from him all the day long.

"'Tis truth, I am a fiend, brother!" he exclaimed in a tone of earnest shame. "Never has it been in me to bite back the mood I feel, though.

You know as much!"

I told him that indeed, I did know it.

"And hard words are the least of my sins right now!" he whispered. "I have felt a want to kill. The urge on me for avengement is stronger even than my fear of God, I trow!"

"Aye, I have felt of it, too," I replied miserably. "Daily I count what we have suffered at their hands."

"Methinks I would do well to send to Peterborough for Brother Wulfget," he said decisively. "Seems 'twould do me good to have a confessor of my own now, since my self cannot attain to any peace."

There would be no harm in it, I agreed. Could be our old friend's presence might serve to lighten our mood and maybe inspire us both to a better disposition. I told Edwin to send a small party to the monastery on the morrow. They could bring the good brother as far as Liccidfeld, and I would meet with him there on my return from Couventrie.

Oft-times it is assumed that priestly men are somber and obsessed with their other-worldliness, but not so with Wulfget. He had a subtle warmth and humor which made its way into every word he said, every thought he imparted. If ever a man had been slated by the Creator for the role of confessor, it was this gentle, brilliant soul. His advice was simple and compelling; he had a way of putting a man back into good heart in the midst of his miseries of guilt. Like Uncle Leofric, his grasp and understanding of humanity was so strong that he never showed aversion to another's sins; one could confess to him unashamed, and the lessons of his shriving tended to linger in the heart a full long time.

As it happened, he could not have come to us at a more propitious time. He was in our house but a scant week when I turned seventeen. Six days later, the third day of Christ Mass, news came of a great slaughter in the Cymry. Harold Godwine's son had marched forces from Gleawanceaster to Rhuddlan and met his brother Tostig's huge army there. All we knew for sure was that king Gruffydd had made an escape by sea. Of the outlaw Earl of the Mercians, there was no word.

We were plunged into a whirlpool of fear and anxiety. Another four days passed and a proclamation came from King Edward. His Christ Mass Gemot had confirmed Edwin Ælfgar's son as Earl of all Mercia. Ælfgar Leofric's son, who had been earl before, had done treason to the king and state and people of Angland, and so his death was not to be mourned. He was not to buried on Anglish soil.

It is strange to say that no agony of grief came upon us then, but that is the truth of it. Locked in a strange, cold calmness of mind, we went about our business, clenched desperately to routine, living each in a silent, deadened world. Edwin and I particularly avoided each other, A single, private moment together, a single meaningful look between us would have broken us then, and we knew it.

Three or four days we went on thusly. Then one grey and violet twilight, I made my way out of the smoky hall into the frosted fields beyond the byre. I fell on my knees in the frozen grass there and cried—cried till I could not cry more. By then, the coldness of the air and ground almost surpassed the iciness of my heart; every breath was painful. I lay down on my back, staring at the wintry heavens—hurting and aching and wondering. Brother Wulfget found me there and bade me return to the hall, but I would not move.

"'Tis as if you say your own life is of no value to you, brother," he said carefully, kneeling anext me. I told him that was so; so hateful I was of this world of sorrow that 'twould be a relief to be done with it.

"See how it is that God chastises men with life?" he asked me gently, putting a warm hand on my brow. "It is living that is his sternness. Death is but his fond embrace."

No words could have helped me more.

I made my way back in and found Edwin in our chamber, silent, staring blankly at the flickering tallow tapers. "Methinks I knew I would never see the man again," he said quietly, without even looking at me as I sat myself near to him. "Even I said it inside me when I watched him ride into the Eardene, 'I will never see him more!'"

He reached under his dalmatic and pulled out a golden chain which he lifted over his head. I bit my lip when I saw what hung from it. It was my father's ring: the ring of the Earls of Mercia, countless generations old. Wordlessly, my brother unloosed it and placed it on his finger. Then he laid down his head and sobbed till his body wrenched and wracked.

That was the thing I had seen Ælfgar press into his unwilling hand. Edwin was the third man I knew to wear it.

We gave ourselves entirely over to our long-suppressed sorrow that night and for many nights after. Perhaps it is that in such evil circumstances, memory has a trick of turning fond and pretty, as if to comfort a soul in distress. I cannot say, but I know that we found naught to remember of him but what was bold and honorable and good. The love and humor of his gentle moods occurred to us, and the fiery, indomitable courage of his vehement ones. We spoke of his manliness, his comeliness and his iron-eyed determination. Despite Edward's decree, he was mourned all over Mercia and remembered as a just and generous earl. He was a fine man, my father. He lived thirty-nine years.

CHAPTER TWENTY-ONE

Truly the world's glory droops and withers like
the flowers of grass, and is spent and scattered
like smoke.

—Orderic Vitalis,
Book IV, Chapter XIV

Just after Twelfth-night, Uncle Leofric came to Couventrie, and
anointed Edwin, at the king's bidding, naming him Earl of all Mercia. It
was with no little emotion that I gazed on my brother all that long
service. He had chosen to wear mourning robes of plain black worsted,
and their simple elegance perfectly suited his flashing, manly beauty.
Slowly, almost imperceptibly, he had shed his boyishness, and his
coming of age had brought new intensity and determination to the aristocratic fineness of his features. Now I shivered to see how like Ælfgar
he was; the grave gleam of his eye only half hid the impassioned bitterness there. Every gesture, every expression, every movement cried to me
memories of my murdered father.

Looking about that crowded room at the solemn faces of the thegns
and high-born men of Mercia, I knew they saw in him what I did, and
that because of it they would be loyal men and true to my brother. The
king had denied them the right to mourn their earl. "Weep not for
treason's crushing!" had been his spiteful decree, but he could not keep
them from honoring the image of Ælfgar they found in his son. I could
picture the bent-shouldered Edward shaking with rage when he learnt
Edwin had worn black for his anointing.

Our twin cousins from the Lindcylene Shire, Æric and Ælfmaer,
swore to Edwin after the service, and apart from the sons of Carr, were
the first he accepted as his own guardsmen. They were wealthy men and
well-armed, and all my father's householders, who used to laugh at their
antics and make jests about their silliness, welcomed them now with
respect and brotherhood. They sat at the head table with us during
repast, and Æric raised a horn to Edwin with words finer than many a

bard might have strung together. Not a one in the hall was unmoved.

The occasion was accompanied by none of the usual feasting and gamery. The new earl would not allow it, and the men understood. One by one, those who had served Ælfgar came to him, privately in sealed chambers, and as was their right made their decision known to him, whether they wished to be retained as earl's men or not. Almost all chose to swear fealty, and those who begged release from their duties did so not out of an unwillingness to serve Edwin, but because they had grown older in Ælfgar's service and had no longer the stamina and stoutness which the household troops demanded of a man. Æthelstan the Fen-man was such a one as this.

Despite the fact that the man had seen more than fifty years now, my brother was wroth to let him go. It was the good man's desire, though, and he had righteously earned his leave. Edwin gifted him for his service with the income of two manors, one in Deoraby and one in the aet-Waeringwicum, but it was to his own house in the low-lands of the East Anglia that he wished to retire.

Full late in the bleak coldness of the night, Æthelstan met us in the chamber which Grandmother Godiva had given over to our use while we stayed at Couventrie. Despite the lateness of the hour, we waited for Uncle Leofric to join us also. Edwin had sent for them both. He had not been sleeping well since Father's death; it was at night that he chose to vent his grief and anger and he was entirely unable to cope with his own moodiness alone.

Yawning, I pulled my woolen robe tight around me and sat as close to the crackling fire as I dared, watching the new earl pace distractedly in the half-lit dimness. His ill-humor, which had lifted a little with Brother Wulfget's coming, had returned in force. In these last days, he had become distant and quarrelsome, especially with me. In my own grievous distress, I could not offer him the patience and comfort I knew he craved.

Now, addressing the weary, sleep-eyed Æthelstan, Edwin's voice was unusually cold. "It truly vexes me to think of a man of my father's living under the hand of a Godwine earl."

"The East Anglia is my home, my lord," answered Æthelstan sleepily. "I have lived all but the last ten years of my life in that place. My lands, my home, and my kinsmen are there, but Gyrth Godwine's son will never claim my allegiance."

"And I say it will appear you offer it willingly, running to take up board in his cursed domain."

"By God's holy book! You know I have been over-burdened with hatred for that house! God keep me from them!" cried the exasperated fen-man, hurt and angered. I spat, annoyed with my brother's unfeelingness for the man who had served us so well. Then I gathered my wits and tried to be reassuring.

"Gyrth at least is the most harmless of the lot," I said, looking to Edwin for concurrence which was not forthcoming. "He is only a sort of tongue-biting follower who takes what is tossed him and bothers not to reach for more. He lacks the gall which made the old earl what he was, the stuff which makes Tostig the king's eyes and ears and makes Harold his conscience."

Without actually saying anything, Edwin snarled from across the room in a manner which quickly silenced me. Sullenly, I turned back to the fire, content to let an embarrassed silence envelope everything. We were still unspeaking when my uncle entered.

"The kingdom is rife with rumors," he declared, sizing up our discomfort. Having already experienced Edwin's trying touchiness, he knew that only a complete change of subject would bring reason back to him. "They say the king means to finance Tostig and Harold in another expedition against Gruffydd. And the word is that if the new Earl of Mercia intends to aid the Welsh, the earldom will be snatched away from this house forever."

"Making every earldom a Godwine holding!" Edwin shook with rage. "And so they wait to pounce like wolves on the traitor-earl's son, praying and petitioning that he will make one move false enough to be construed as treason, so they can have what they want without further bloodying their spotless hands! Holy Jesus!"

"Take not his name in vain with me!" my uncle bristled. Then he added more gently, "But I see you have a perfect understanding of their motives."

"Then pray for me, that I will have the strength not to go to Gruffydd's aid when he sore needs me because, by God, no one else shall have Mercia!"

"Gruffydd had the victory over Harold's Wessexmen before; he may escape them again. He is not a tender babe, you know."

Edwin collapsed in a wretched heap anext me, shivering with both fury and cold. I ached for his misery because, indeed, it was the same as mine.

Uncle Leofric continued, as if it were best to have it all out at once. "'Tis said that the king means to give the Ox Ford Shire to East Anglia, and shave off from Mercia several of the out-lying shires."

Edwin groaned, but made no answer.

"And, of course, he has reclaimed Hereford. He would like to have the whole Cymrian border, to keep you and the Welshman apart, but he will not risk open confrontation with the Mercians. To a man they are firm behind you, bitter and resentful, so he takes only what Harold says he can under the guise of a prior claim!"

"Council me, uncle! Because I swear to you I can make no sense of this and I am helpless … even more helpless than my father before me!"

I cringed at the desperation in my brother's voice, feeling it myself. I saw Æthelstan touch his shoulder as if to offer comfort, and he said with confident surety, "There is only one thing you can do, my lord, and that is—to do nothing! You know, the king greatly loved your Grandfather Leofric for his piety and honor. Your one great hope is to make him think that Leofric's blood is stronger in you than Ælfgar's. If you mean to continue your father's quarrel—and I do not say you should not in some way avenge his foul death—then you must hide your intention and bide your time. This most of all, for you are young, my lord, and time is on your side truly. The king is old and he is a true blood-king, which thing no Godwine's son can ever be. If you stay in Edward's favor, then, with Mercia behind you, you can spring your quarrel on the Godwines when he is gone, and they will have no crown with which to make you look the traitor."

"What he says is true," my uncle agreed. "You must play the good subject, the king's man, and make no move that will mark ill against you in his eyes. If he believes truly that you are of Leofric's cut, he will not tolerate even his favorites to toy with you. Then Mercia will retain some voice in things, and folk will listen. And they will be listening still when the good Earl of Mercia screams against the injustice of a Godwine usurpation … if such a thing then comes to pass."

"*If?!!*" I fairly spat the word.

"It still is thought that Edward has promised the crown to his cousin, Duke William of Normandy. From what we have seen and heard of him, he is not the sort who will let it go so gently."

Remembering the powerful gaze of the dark-eyed duke, I was forced to agree, but it did not still my mistrust of the House of Godwine.

"Also 'twas thought that the Wessexmen would never lay touch on the North Humbria," I found myself saying bitterly, "and Providence proved that what men think means little."

With fond reproval, my uncle smiled at me. "The Humbria may play itself out of Tostig's hands yet," he said. "Ælfgar is not forgotten there. King's favorite or not, Tostig becomes more and more despised—and the northerners have always had ways of dealing with those who are a curse unto them. If God sees fit, there will be great changes. For now, though, 'tis not to our advantage to take risks."

We tossed words for a while longer, till sleep nearly overtook me

right there on the floor. Then I begged Edwin to let us have our beds for
a few hours, and he grudgingly let the others go. I was near to slumber
even by the time I climbed onto my wool-stuffed pallet, but I noticed he
did not sleep. He sat himself anext the fire and read from the illuminated psalter which Father had given him.

Early on the morrow, my uncle and his party departed for
Peterborough, and Edwin made the decision to move our household to
the great manor at Kirton in the Lindcylene Shire. For eight days afterward, we were feverish in our preparations, for 'twas a long journey for
that chill time of year. We had overstayed ourselves at Couventrie,
though, which was not a large estate, and my brother was anxious to be
about his earl's duties.

I am sorry to say that our leave-taking was not altogether pleasant.
We left our mother there no better than we found her. As for Grandmother Godiva, gentle soul, we waxed angry with her because she had
so unquestioningly accepted the king's declaration of treason on Ælfgar.
She sorrowed and mourned for her precious son, but never forgave him
for the indiscretions she considered he had committed.

Æthelstan had decided to winter at Couventrie and make his way
to the fen country in the spring. On the morning of our leaving, I made
a special visit to him in the loft-house where he slept. There we sat in
the thick, warm rushes, eating oaten cakes and remembering things
together. We had many memories to share and talked long of Cynewulf
and of father, of Wales and of Eireland. I apologized to him for Edwin.
'Twas my brother's way of letting him know he loved him and was wroth
to let him go, I said, that he would quarrel with him in such a way as he
had done.

The fen-man grinned as I said it. "Edwin Ælfgar's son and I have
long had an understanding between us," he said, face crinkling in a
broad smile. "We never have used gentle words to tell our affection—
not since he was a tousle-headed brat! If he had no sharp outburst for
me, then would I worry. Just as he has all his life fretted when he found
no word of reproval in my mouth."

I laughed at that, knowing it was true, for it had always been the
way with those two. Yet I know my brother never appreciated a man
more; he spoke all his life afterward of Æthelstan the Fen-man with the
greatest of reverence.

As for me, I amazed the man that morn by telling him about the
Filidh and all their awesome predictions about Edwin and Aldgyth.
"They told us that there was one in the circle whose past already was
longer than his future would be," I told him mournfully and in the
manner of a great confidence. "I knew not then that it was Burchard

they spoke of, but I know it now."

The man shook his head slowly and scrutinized me. "Oft I have wondered, Morcar Ælfgar's son," he said with earnesty, "what it was that trembled and shook you so that rainy day. Even then, I knew you were not a one to quake at trifles."

I wondered how it was that he could say such a thing, for I had always seen myself as timid.

We embraced when it was time for me to go. I was not to see the man again for many long years, and then 'twould be under circumstances neither of us could have hoped to imagine that cold day in Couventrie.

CHAPTER TWENTY-TWO

Earl Harold marched from Glewanceaster to
Rhuddlan, the seat of Gruffydd, and burnt his
residence, his ships and all their sails, and put him
to flight. . . . Meanwhile, Tostig marched against
them . . . and overran the country.

—Anglo Saxon Chronicle
Book "D" 1063

Spring 1063
Ælfgar had taken ten men with him when he fled into the Cymry, and
we had given them all up for dead. This was a great sorrow to us, for
Daffydd Carr's son was amongst them, and Ælfric White-Hair and other
of our friends and kinsmen. Even though Tostig and Harold had finally
withdrawn their troops from Wales, we knew from Uncle Leofric that
they were planning another invasion for the summer. We worried and
wondered constantly about Gruffydd and even more about Aldgyth and
her little daughter, Nesta. A half year with no news at all was an
exceeding long time.

But Tostig, gloating over his successful crushing of the attempted
over-throw, began to wreak havoc and punishment on any of the men
in the North Humbria whom he suspected of plotting against him. First
to feel his fury was Siward Bearn. He was banished from the earldom and
his vast lands there were confiscated, including the rich, hereditary
estate in Tathaceaster where he had lived nearly all his life.

Never a more bitter man than that one was when he moved his
huge household down into the aet-Waeringwicum. He side-tracked from
his party to visit us at Kirton, and he was full of hatred and plans for
vengeance. "Earl Tostig acts the wounded statesman and forces us out,"
he said bitterly, "yet I wonder how long 'twill take him to resent the fact
that we all sit together in Mercia now, Oswulf and Ealdred and I. How
long before he complains to the king that we are here to plot with Earl

Edwin and conspire with Morcar the outlaw's son?" We spoke little about it, but we wondered, too.

Siward Bearn was but three days gone from us, when my brother and I were summoned to Ceaster. It was our kinsman Oswulf Eadwulf's son who came to claim us, with a small party of his rowdy Bernician men. We had not seen the man in a while, and scarce could believe the change in him. No more a Mercian in dress and fashion, he wore his ashy-colored locks past his shoulders in the manner of the North Humbrians, though undyed like the other Bernicians. He had a beard now which gave a somewhat menacing look to his boyish face. Golden hoops hung from his ears; he was decorated with pictures burnt about the neck and wrists. For a full long time after he dismounted, we stood and stared at him. He laughed at our amazement.

"Best you would be thinking about changing the look of yourself, too, cousin," he told me in a low voice, when we were alone. "Talk is that a good many men plan to see you Earl of the North Humbria soon. 'Give us another Morcar!' is the word most often whispered."

I did my best to ignore such speculation. It had been fifty years since the murder of my great-grandfather, Morcar of the Seven Boroughs, and there could be few alive who remembered him. He had not been old when he met the sword, scarce thirty-five years, and his son-in-the-law Siferth, my mother's father, had been but one score and four then, a child-earl, really. Both must have been bold men and true for their reputations to have lived so long and well; I could not help but worry that folk might ultimately determine that I had nothing alike to the man but his name. He had been a great warrior; I was entirely untried and felt it as a great lack in myself.

That aside, though, Oswulf's message was of an urgent nature. Some men had come to Ealdread Æthelgar's son at Ceaster, he said, and they bore news of particular interest which they would not impart till Edwin and I were there. One of the men was Daffydd Carr's son; the other was Gruffydd of Llewellyn! We ordered mounts harnessed and set out immediately with Æric, Ælfmaer, and a dozen other guardsmen. We only allowed Oswulf and his men the briefest respite of food and drink before we put them on the road again; my cousin was tired and not well pleased.

Spring rain had stretched the fen far into the midlands that year, and even the Roman trackways were sodden and deep with yellow mud. The journey seemed painfully slow, wracked as we were with excitement. Though we rode late into the mid of the first night, against all cousin Oswulf's insolent complaints, we did not gallop into the court-yard of the Ceaster manor till dusk of the second night after. Still, our resoluteness had brought us more than a hundred miles in two-and-a-half days of riding—forty-five miles on the last day alone which, considering the conditions, was extraordinary.

Ealdread sent immediately for Gruffydd, who was keeping well-hid. In the huge hall, where we shed our damp mantles, the Welshman greeted Edwin and me like sons, embracing us both at once. He looked tired, restless; his dark eyes had the same hunted look I remembered so well from my father's. The massy profusion of dark curls seemed wilder and his gaze a bit more solemn. Otherwise, he was as unchanged as ever.

A very few minutes later, Daffydd Carr's son made his way in. We greeted him affectionately after he embraced with his ecstatic brothers. 'Twas something beyond what we ever expected, to see that man again. We sat all together at the high table, where we were joined by Ealdread and Oswulf and Edwin's men. Despite the lateness of the hour, Ealdread's wife Gweneth and Oswulf's wife Briana came to oversee our serving. Cold fowl and warm drink were put out for us and we hungrily indulged while we talked.

Gruffydd gave us immediately to know we would have to wait for that which we sought most—the details of Ælfgar's fate. He started instead with other news, handing us each a lock of Aldgyth's pretty, sweet-gold hair. "The precious woman does well," he told us with a smile. "She carries another child in her womb now."

This news delighted us, but we both picked out the note of concern in his voice. "What is it worries you, brother-in-the-law?" Edwin asked him earnestly. Gruffydd shrugged.

"I have had to hide her," he said, pursing his handsome features into a frown. "Things go not well in the Cymry. The sons of Godwine have offered triple the king's price to any Welshman who will bring them my head. 'Tis much to worry about in a country like mine, where famine runs rampant and loyalty is such a recent innovation."

I looked at Edwin, not liking what I heard.

Daffydd Carr's son picked up the thread of the Welsh king's thought, running his fire-scarred hands through his massy black ringlets. "Could be there are desperate men who would use her to get to him," he said decisively. "He has had to move her to the far interior camps. And he misses her."

"Aye. That I do," the Welshman said miserably. "'Tis a thing you will understand when you grow used to having a woman next to you."

Oswulf Eadwulf's son laughed loudly, and let his gaze rest over-boldly on his woman, who blushed crimson and hurried out of the hall. Watching her go, I thought about it—the peace it would bring a man to know someone warm and wifely was always waiting. It was a concept just beginning to appeal to me, and I felt a strong sympathy for Gruffydd, who seemed to love my pretty sister so well. Edwin broke into my little reverie, asking the king if he knew that another expedition was about to be launched into the Cymry. Gruffydd said he did and was doing his best to prepare for it.

"Must be you know that we are on the run now, though," he said in a low tone. "The great camp at Rhuddlan is waste; they took care of that during the Christ Mass raid." The thought made me sad; 'twas a place I once called home.

"What think you of my coming with Mercian troops?" Edwin asked him suddenly. "What think you of our following them over the front tier and blocking their escape?"

Gruffydd shook his head. "Nay, Edwin Ælfgar's son," he firmly said. "Time is come that you must see to your own house now. Our chance to win is to fight like Welshmen, nimble and quick and wild. Yet, in the event that I cannot evade them, the only peace I can have is to know that you sit in Mercia still and that my woman has a place to run to; that my children can claim the honor of an avunculus who is not a hunted man."

"'Tis a strange way you talk, brother!" I exclaimed. We had never called him brother before; he had been Ælfgar's brother, not ours. But now it seemed like a natural thing, though I could read in his look that he wondered how we had come so fast to manhood, these two he had known as children.

"Nay," he told me after a little pause. "Methinks it is not so strange for a man to think about such things—not when he has children. Even your own father looked ahead to this time, when it might happen that we could see 'twas no avail to hold out longer against our enemies. I promised him I never would keep the two of you to a brotherhood that might mean your fighting a battle which could not be won."

"Speak no more!" my brother commanded hoarsely, coming to his feet. "It bodes naught but ill to talk in suchwise! I will not listen."

Gruffydd stared at him long and hard, and his face broke suddenly into a wide grin. "By God, you are like to him, Edwin!" he said, shaking his head. "Methinks you could not be anything more alike to him than you are!"

"Pain me not with such evil speech," my brother cried defiantly. "We have avengement now to think of, along with everything else!"

Gruffydd looked at him levelly and his tone hardened. "I am a man who has seen more years, more blood, more fire than ever you have realized, brother's son! This I tell you: that you will do your best to make your revenge from where you sit, right here in Mercia. An internal revenge they cannot expect from you, and they will not know how to deal with it. But if you move after me into the Cymry, you will be playing into their hands. 'Tis what they want you to do. 'Tis what they want the king and the people of the land to see you do."

"It is not as hopeless as you try to make it seem—" Edwin began, but Gruffydd silenced him.

"If you come to the Cymry, you destroy everything Ælfgar and I put into action by making this brotherhood of ours."

"I do not understand you."

"You will!" Gruffydd slapped him on the back, then took his hands, both of them. "This is a thing already settled, Earl Edwin!" he said softly with a smile. "It is a thing Ælfgar and I decided between ourselves and swore to. If I took you away from your earldom, even for a day of battle, I fear me I would do dishonor to the memory of man I revere."

Edwin turned his back and spoke sharply. "You know not the strength of the army they are raising, brother! You know not the force of their will!"

Gruffydd laughed loud. "Think you so, Mercian? Remember I was dealing with these same men, fox-eyed Harold and shrew-hearted Tostig while yet you sucked mother's milk and cried for cradling! I know their ways of gaming well enough."

My brother slammed his fists together, shaking, and the Welshman's voice grew gentler. "Your brother Morcar can tell you something mayhap you do not know," he said, looking directly into my eyes. "Remember you, Morcar, how we talked late one night in my hall at Rhuddlan? I told you then what the purpose was of the pact between your father and myself—not to kill these men in blood but to make ourselves so poisonous to them that they feared to feed on us … to make your house and mine such a thorny meal that they were forced to devour each other instead. Remember that?"

I nodded, looking at his somber gaze. "What feeds upon itself is fast to fall," I murmured low, and he nodded back.

"You two are but youngsters," he whispered firmly, "though you will hate to hear it said. You have tasted death and hatred and itch like the devil for avengement. You think right now there is no revenge but blood and gore in all the wide world."

Edwin turned, looking at him curiously. He went on.

"I tell you now that you will put an avengement on them far more evil than any you thought possible. You will sit back in honor and favor, growing strong and worthy in the eyes of other men, while they devour themselves with their own dishonor. They will do it, too! And they will vomit each other up in the process, the sons of that house, all the while growing weaker for the disgusting taste of themselves."

My brother and I exchanged a glance. Edwin shrugged.

"That was the purpose of our brotherhood," the king added. "We have accomplished what we set out to do. We did not fail each other, he and I. Even this we could foresee."

"It seems not right to me, brother!" exclaimed Edwin miserably.

"It will sit better when the men of your country hold the two of you in a high esteem, where you can get a good view of the Godwine's tumble!"

My brother laughed shortly, shaking his head. "'Tis not the way I see it unfolding," he said. "I cannot see what we have gained."

"You have all Mercia in your possession. You have a chance to keep it by holding yourself here, or a chance to lose it. Earl Ælfgar lived and died that you might have it; do you avenge him by giving it up?"

We both shook our heads.

"'Twas one of three things he spent his life's blood on: the keeping of Mercia, the taking back of the North Humbria, and the restoring of your house to honor. All are possibilities if you can still your hand till the tree bears fruit. Then you pluck them, all three. They grew too high for him and he knew it; but also did he know they would be within your reach. He chose to let them grow there for his sons. Think you 'twould be wise to lift an axe now and chop the tree just to spite it for being taller than he was?"

We shook our heads again.

"Then let your axes lie," he said firmly. "You will have more opportunities to swing them in this life than you can even imagine right now. Stay here and be good king's men while Harold and Tostig do their business. Jump into it and they will gnaw on you. Stay clear and they will be forced to gnaw themselves. Understand me?"

I am not entirely certain that we did, but once more we nodded. Then Edwin said, "I swear you are naught but a perplexion to me! Talking always in poems and riddles!"

"Must be he has priest blood," Oswulf said casually, and the laugh that followed ended all our quarreling about how best to be brothers. It irked us to admit that Gruffydd was right, but we knew he was. He had not said a thing that Uncle Leofric had not told us beforehand. Both were men we trusted, men who were worldly wise and honorable. Neither of us liked the feeling, though, of being powerless to help a man we loved. It had happened to us too many times before.

We talked till late in the night—all but Oswulf Eadwulf's son who soon fell asleep at the table after his five days in the saddle. As we readied to retire, Gruffydd drew us aside and asked for private converse. Eagerly, we followed him out to the lofted monk's-house where he slept. When we were there, we sat around the low-burning central hearth and shared an ale-horn with him, just Edwin and I.

"Know you any word of how he died?" the Welsh king asked us when we were settled. We told him no, and he grimaced.

"After Ælfgar and his guard met with me in the Eardene, we made for the camp at Rhuddlan with all speed. We knew the king's army would move to the border, but we never expected them to follow us into the Cymry in that cold time of year. Your father and his men were less than a dozen. I had not many more to winter with me, though a good many waited at my beckon. Between us all, we kept but one hall of the camp open in the snow. The one called the King's Quarter."

Leaning over, Gruffydd filled our cups again before he went on. "'Twas surprise that the man Tostig meant to lay upon us and he did it well. Must be he snuck all through the valleys, for we had no thought that he had pursued us thither. One night, some hours before the dawn, I was wakened where I lay in the stone lair I keep high in the hills. 'Twas the sounds of slaughter that wakened me."

Here he paused and drank greedily of the warm ale. I was thinking back over many years, to the confusion it had caused me to discover that he never slept in his own hall. The greatest of his secrets, he had told me: "that I never am where men expect me to be." I had thought it exceedingly strange then; now I understood it.

"Tostig brought no more than thirty men with him, but they came in quiet, laying a deadly massacre on those men as they slept."

Edwin paled, rising slowly to his feet. "Mean you to say they murdered them in their beds?"

"Horribly."

Now I was standing, too. "All of them?" I asked, looking past him as if I could see through the stone walls into the night beyond.

"Of all your father's men, only Daffydd Carr's son was left alive," the king told us mournfully, "and that only because he sleeps like a Cymrian, away from bed and fire."

"My father?" Edwin asked it coldly, implying a need to know all.

"Tostig did not let him die fast."

"For God's sake, tell the story, man!" I cried, sounding hoarse and furious despite a welling of tears. Gruffydd signaled us both to sit down again and we did, cross-legged in the rushes anext him. Edwin put his face in his hands, resting his elbows on his knees, but I stared straight into the Welshman's bitter eyes.

"A few men made their way out of the camp and came to me. I had but sixteen all together, counting those and myself and the ones who guarded me. We mounted fast, and stampeded every spare pony down the mountain with us. All the way, we bellowed and screamed harsh battle cries and shouts of vengeance. 'Twas an instant rout; must be the Wessexman thought I had all my army with me. They were long gone 'ere we reached the hill bottom and made our way into the camp. Twenty men—dead or dying." He made a small choking noise. "A handful of women were in the camp, and some children. All slain. I had sent for Aldgyth, so she could see her father; another day and she would have been there, too."

Edwin whispered a coarse oath and lifted his tear-stained face. "Tell me what the bastard did unto him!" he commanded, looking at the other. Gruffydd cleared his throat.

"He was half in life, half in death when I found him: pierced through and laid open. Yet he spoke."

The Welshman sprang nimbly to his feet and walked across the room. He came back with my father's sword. At the sight of it, against all my powers of resistance, I began to weep, sobbing openly like a babe.

"Morcar is to have the sword," Gruffydd whispered in a soft, sad voice. I looked at him quizzically, afraid to touch the gleaming weapon but taking it at last in a weak, unsteady grip. Scarce could I believe it had come to me, and when my gaze met Edwin's, I shrugged miserably as if in apology.

He glanced away, asking the Welshman in a low voice if that was all. Gruffydd shook his head. "Also said he this: that his other two sons were to have his other weapons—the axe to the warrior and the knife to the priest."

"Must be he thought Burchard still lived," Edwin said bitterly, and Gruffydd agreed that a great madness of pain and agony came on the man at the end. He handed my brother a silver knife, girthed in its case of gold-bossed leather.

"God knows you will be wroth to hear this, Edwin Ælfgar's son," the king said dismally, "but the axe was not to be found there. Must be the Wessexman stole it away with him when he made his escape."

My brother cursed the entire House of Godwine, slamming his fist over and over on the rush-strewn floor. Then he threw the knife at me, saying I might as well keep that, too, as it was not meant for him. Those words hurt me more than they should have, knowing as I did how Edwin had loved and idolized my father and how sore it must have pained him to be robbed of this legacy.

Yet my heart, grown bitter with wretched death and sorrow, was telling me even then that I was the one who was robbed. I had naught but the sword of a dead man. Edwin, the favorite, was the one who had claimed his love and attention and admiration and fondness, and that while the man still lived and breathed. I made a quick sign of the cross upon myself to still the demon of jealousy. Long had I known it was there, but I despised myself for letting it surface now when my brother waxed so miserable.

"What else said he?" I demanded, just to change my thoughts to something else.

"Naught but madnesses," said Gruffydd, turning away.

"Name them, though!" Edwin's tone was brusque, petulant. The Welshman shrugged.

"The man was dying and in the worst of ways; he said many things. He said things that made no sense—"

"Think you not it is important to us?" I pleaded, wanting desperately to know and not even understanding why.

"Aye, Morcar Ælfgar's son! I think it is. But you should also know that I sat and clasped him like a babe while all there was of him drained out on the earthen floor. I gave not much heed to his murmurs and babbles, thinking only to still and comfort him." The bold king of the Cymry spoke in a shaking, disconsolate voice. I was surprised to see there were tears in his eyes, too. A sudden, throbbing sense of shame came on me as I realized I had given no heed to this man's feelings. In my own grief, it had not occurred to me what the appalling murder must have done to him. Ælfgar had been his brother in the fullest sense of the word. Gruffydd of Llewellyn, who had never bent to arms or threats or curses, had near been broken by my father's death.

Edwin must have shared my abrupt sense of guilt. We rose, the both of us, at the same time and went to the man. He put an arm on Edwin's shoulder and an arm on mine, letting us apologize without words. Never were three men tied closer than we were that moment by our pulsing grief. There was a long silence before the Welshman spoke again.

"God knows it was a long and drawn out dying," he said, "and if I had to witness it again, methinks I would myself slay him out of it. Death thoughts most always are a man's most noble ones, they say, but scarce they seem to sound so to others. So dazed I was with what was happening that I caught but little of his ravings. I swear 'tis the truth! Yet I remember that he cried out over and over again for forgiveness— because he had not been like his father. Because he never was what that man wanted him to be—"

"What you say is true," my brother spat, pulling away. "The man spoke madnesses!" He walked across the room, put an arm against the wall and buried his head into it. In a little while I heard him sobbing. It reminded me of the long ago day when Ælfgar had cried the same way— the day of my grandfather's grave-ale.

"I hope you buried him well," I whispered.

"Indeed," the king said, "we put him near the purple river Dee, in the lands he gave me when first we made our brotherhood—lands that will be never rightly Anglish, never rightly Welsh. All his men we put around him, and I faced him east, towards Mercia."

Not for many months would I see that grave in the wind-swept grass-lands, but I could picture it then. "You did right, brother," I whispered, nodding numbly, "for the man in truth loved Mercia!"

"Wherever it is that you go in this life," Ælfgar once told me, "carry Mercia with you. For Mercia is the essence of the blood of our house, and the blood of our house is the very substance of Mercia."

And so it has seemed to me, ever since.

CHAPTER TWENTY-THREE

Gruffydd, the head and shield and defender of
the Cymrians, fell through the treachery of his
own people: the man who had been hitherto
invincible was now left in the glens of desolation,
after having taken immense spoils and after
innumerable victories.

—Brut y Tywysogian

August, 1063
Less than half a year later, Gruffydd was dead also.

Harold and Tostig had stormed through the Cymry, laying waste to everything they passed. Not a single Welsh male was spared their murderous fury, regardless of youth or age. Nor left they in their wake any dwellings or fields or beasts or implements. In three months, from May to August, they reduced the entire borderland to a starving, smoldering ruin.

Still, they were not able to capture the king on their own. Unable to fight with what was left him, Gruffydd fled here and there, never staying a full day in the same place. So he managed to elude them. Mad with their vengeance and eager to be home, the brother earls raised the price on Gruffydd's head. They promised any Welshman who would bring it to them five times what Edward was offering the Anglish. They were wise enough to know, after all their weeks in the Cymry, that they themselves would never be able to corner the Welshman in his own wild domain. With the land in ashes all around, the game and fowl driven away, starving Cymrians began to consider the offer.

When Gruffydd had joined my sister in Gwennydd, where she had given birth to their son, some of her attendants betrayed him, striking off his head while he slept, and rushing it to Earl Harold wrapped in a kidskin blanket. Then Harold offered the kingship to Gruffydd's own brothers, Bleddyn and Rhiwallon, in exchange for hostages against their word of loyalty to Angland. One of the hostages he demanded was Cwene Aldgyth. Along with her two children, she was turned over to Harold Godwine's son at Porthiscoed.

With all the humility of their breed, the brother earls marched victoriously back to Angland and paraded the spoils of war through Lundun City. Harold Godwine's son rode tall in the saddle, holding my sister and her new-born babe in front of him—Cwene and Prince of the defeated Cymrians. Tostig carried the golden eagle-prow of the ship my father had given to Gruffydd as his pledge-gift. Carried high on a pole before them both was the bloody, lifeless head of Gruffydd of Llewellyn, King of all the Cymry—first man to dream of a united Wales and a peace with Mercia. So die all such dreamers.

Edwin and I watched that gross procession from the steps of the king's West Minster, where we sat with saintly Edward, who ogled the head with light-hearted satisfaction. With us were the two other earls of the land, Gyrth and Leofwine Godwine's sons, bursting with undisguised pride and exhilaration. We acted the way we were expected to act, stoic and noncommittal, which pleased the old king well. He had warmed to Edwin immediately, as most men did, growing almost fond of him when he decided the new Earl of Mercia had no intention of involving himself in the problems of the Welsh.

While we were careful to pretend unconcern with Gruffydd's sad fate, we took every opportunity to plead vehemently on Aldgyth's behalf. She was very young, we argued, and her marriage had been arranged between Ælfgar and the Welshman. The thought of her living the rest of her life as a hostage in the king's court was near intolerable to us. We begged to bring her home to Mercia. We discussed it with King Edward at his high table during the great victory celebration which followed the triumphal entry of his two chief men. He promised to consider it, but later Earl Harold sat anext us and he was adamant in his refusals. She was, after all, well-loved by the Welsh and they would never, never attempt to weave intrigues at her expense. Besides, Gruffydd's son might be considered by some of the bolder Cymrians a rightful king. He was just an infant now, but he would grow up. Harold smiled politely and spoke to us almost as equals, but we were well impressed with the unspoken fact that my sister and her children were being held against our interests, as well against the possibility of the sons of Ælfgar embroiling themselves in avengement or plots.

The man was bold enough to apologize to us for our father's death. He held himself to the official story which was spread about the kingdom: that Ælfgar died during an ambush he made on Earl Tostig. Harold looked us right in the eye as he made his condolences. It took me a great concentration of will not to spit upon him.

His brother Tostig, of course, gave us not a word and came nowhere near us. Every now and then, though, I caught him smirking at my brother in an evil, leering way. The man's purpose no doubt was to catch his eye and remind him of the mean threats which had been dealt the night he broke into our hall. If Edwin was in any way concerned, he hid it well beneath a dignified manner and an impassive smile.

Our avunculus, the king's man William Malet, was most impressed with our behavior through the long ordeal of feasting congratulations to the men who had murdered most everyone dearest to us. He told us so. He was one who believed firmly that loyalty to king and peace must always come before personal quarrels, else disaster could be the only outcome. He himself had no reason to love the king's favorite, Tostig. He held the man responsible for his own sister's sad state. My mother sat at Couventrie still, like a statue it was said, till she waxed suddenly violent, shrieking and tearing at herself. No one had heard a meaningful word from her lips since that awful night in the manor at Weogornaceaster. No one expected to, ever again.

We had been arranging with our avunculus for some time to have Lady Ælfgiva sent home to his paternal estates at Graville Sainte Honorine, near Le Havre in Normandy. She had relations there who could see to her care, for the duties involved in keeping her clean and safe were far too much now for Grandmother Godiva. He had resolved to take her across the channel himself, in a summer hence. No better thing could be done for her, he thought, than to take her away from this land, which had never shown her kindness. Her life here had begun with sorrow and blood and anguish and had come full circle back to it. The lady did not even realize yet that Ælfgar was dead and buried. She mistook Edwin for him every time we visited her, and caused him much misery with alternate caresses and affronts, which she always addressed to that man who had loved her so much.

'Twas only because of William Malet's intercession with the king that Edwin and I were allowed to visit with Aldgyth before we left. This we appreciated, though the meeting was short and formal, conducted in the king's chamber with a full host of men gathered round us. At least we were able to see for ourselves that she was healthy and in bloom despite her excruciating ordeal. Pretty little Nesta, who was her image save for the tousle of raven curls, greeted us gravely, calling us both "'avunculus" and laying kisses on our cheeks. The babe, I was glad to see, had the same rich, curly black hair and in every way resembled his bold father. It was easy to see the comfort this gave to sweet Aldgyth. She had named him Gruffydd after the man she loved.

We made her swear to us that she was well treated, and she gave oath that she was, both at the time of her capture and now—lonely, she declared, but handled with respect. From time to time while she spoke, I studied her. She was dressed in a striking gown of embroidered kidskin and deer hide and wore her long sweet-gold hair rolled round her head in pretty silver nets. The Cymrian styles were most flattering to her, for she was tall and slender and carried them well. She was naught but twenty years old, I thought with a pang, and Providence had been so merciless. The Wessexmen had stuck the pole with her husband's head upon it in the courtyard of the king's house. It could easily be seen from her casements.

King Edward, of the white hair and transparent skin, did a surprising thing as we made our fare-wells to our sister. He admonished his favorites, saying it had always been the way for hostages to be treated according to their station and so he could see no reason why Edwin and I could not visit Aldgyth at our will, anywhere in the king's house. If we cared to, he said, from this day on we could see her in the hall or in her rooms or in the gardens. She was not to be restricted like a common prisoner. This seemed to take the Wessexmen somewhat by surprise but they had to assent to it, and did so readily. All the things Uncle Leofric had predicted would happen if we played the part of good king's men, were coming to pass. Sensing our willingness to bend, the king himself was going out of his way to conciliate us and show his fairness.

One other thing he did fairly shocked us. Wales was subdued now, he said, and there was no reason fair young Edwin should suffer for Ælfgar's treasonous alliance. He decreed that the vale of Clwyd, all the lands west of the river Dee which my father had sworn away, were now reverted back to Mercia and given to the control of Earl Edwin. My brother and I exchanged a glance upon hearing those words. Without knowing it, he had rescinded his own order that Ælfgar was not to be buried on Anglish soil. For that was where he lay, and now it was part of Mercia again. Earl Harold waxed petulant at this unexpected ordinance. We well knew that it was his aim to hold the entire Welsh border himself; surely he did not deem it fit that we should have it now for we had, he claimed, in no way proved an unwillingness to commerce with the Cymrians. To our great satisfaction, the king moved not at all to the man's lusty arguments. Thus, our father's grave, and the graves of our kith and kinsmen, came into our holding.

Leaving Lundun City with some of the king's favor bestowed upon us, Edwin and I returned with our men to the Lindcylene Shire. It happened that we were keeping separate households then. His grief made him short-tempered and mine made me over-sensitive so there was no way we could live with each other in constant, close contact. His bold-mouthed arguing wore me too far down, though I well enough understood it was but an effect of his over-whelming anxiety and unhappiness. I took my own manor at Sempringaham, and from that day on our friendship throve. It was a pretty holding that had been mine since childhood, and was less than an hour's ride from Kirton. Edwin and I could see each other near daily and go about the business of the earldom together, but make an escape whenever we wanted or needed to do it.

In the company of the three Welshmen, now the chief men of the Earl of Mercia along with Æric and Ælfmaer, and a hand-chosen guard of others, my brother and I were in constant motion all the rest of that year and well into the spring of the next. We visited at Couventrie and Peterborough, hunted in the Peaclond with Siward Bearn, and kept the Christ Mass Gemot in Lundun City where we met daily for a fortnight with Aldgyth and her babes. We settled a grave winter-war land dispute near Ouestraefeld and kept the Easter Gemot at Gleawanceaster. In between, we made two visits to Ceaster. On the first, we crossed the Dee into the wind-swept grasslands where Ælfgar kept his rest. Brother Wulfget hallowed the place for us, so at long last my father got his Christian burial. On the second visit, the conversation settled entirely on the many unfortunate mistakes Earl Tostig had foisted upon the unwilling North Humbrians. The general consensus was that the men there were fast growing eager for a change of rule. It did not go unnoted that I had attained my manhood; I turned eighteen during the Advent.

Oswulf Eadwulf's son brought his woman and a handful of his Bernicians to make a visit at Kirton just after Ascension Day. Despite the fact that he was usually of a good and easy humor, the man was a makebate through and through. He had been with my brother several days when the two of them nearly came to blood over my kinsman's treatment of one of the women in Edwin's household, the wife of one of his men. Deep in his mead, handsome Oswulf had tricked her out to the byre-house and thrown himself forcefully upon her. She attempted to escape by biting him so harshly on the neck that it left a scar forever, so he drew a dagger and threatened her before he had his way.

When she made her way back to the hall, Edwin and I, with Æric, Ælfmaer, and Brother Wulfget behind us, stormed outside where we found Oswulf lolling in the courtyard, bleeding from the mouth and neck and barely able to keep his feet for his dissoluteness. Never too drunk to fight, though, Oswulf Eadwulf's son pulled his sword, and he and Edwin nearly bit into each other with iron. Brother Wulfget threw himself between them and held them apart—he was not a frail man—until he talked sense into both. Eventually, he managed to make them bring the quarrel inside, after which the woman's husband settled upon a gold grant and two horses as the price of his lady's honor.

All this had taken long enough that I decided to keep the night there with my men. I settled them in the hall, where Oswulf had long since fallen asleep at table, and made my way to my brother's chamber. From the room anext his, though, I heard a violent sobbing and when I knocked upon the timber door, I discovered Oswulf's wife in there, lying on the cold floor, weeping. Never felt I such a surge of pity as for that pretty thing, lost to mortification and unhappiness for her husband's evil ways. I lifted her up and tried to comfort her, but Lady Briana ended up burying her face in the front of my dalmatic and crying more.

There was naught that I could do but stand and hold her, which seemed eventually to have an effect. She pulled away after a little while and dabbed at her eyes with the sleeve of her tunic. Under her married-woman's veil, her face looked very young and vulnerable, though I knew she was older than Oswulf. When she had regained her composure somewhat, she tossed me a wan and half-hearted smile.

"You are a good man to be so understanding of my distress, Morcar Ælfgar's son," she said, turning away from me. "Truly your gentleness gives me comfort." She held the door open for me. I flushed with discomfiture then, because I realized she had wanted to keep her humiliation to herself.

In the next chamber, Edwin was wide awake, on his back, staring at the ceiling. I knew he must have heard her misery, too, but had not bothered to go to her. I asked him why.

"The woman frightens me, brother," is what he answered in a cold voice. "She is an unhappy soul, and you would do best to keep yourself clear of her."

I was astonished that he could say something as heartless as that, and I told him so. He only turned over and put himself to slumber.

Later in the night, though, I thought about it and it came to me that there was indeed a certain danger in comforting a lady like that—and especially in a dark and closed chamber as I had done. She had a hot-headed husband and he was fast with a sword.

*   *   *

Oswulf took his leave a few days later, in a surprisingly good mood. That man always was a hard one for me to figure; when he was in decent temper he was most especially likable, but otherwise could scarce be tolerated. I know my brother breathed a sigh of relief to see him go, but both of us were glad he left in a placid state. He was one you did not like to see unsettled, just for fear of what he might do.

Oswulf's party traveled not back to Ceaster immediately, but struck out for Lundun City to visit with Aldgyth. Having been robbed by Tostig of his permanent home-stead in Dunholme, our kinsman had become obsessed with travel and visiting. I suspected he did not get on well with his brother-in-the-law at Ceaster for long periods of time. Ealdread Æthelgar's son was an exceedingly mild man, but Oswulf was the type who could rub anyone raw. Could be I am wrong in this, though. Mayhap Lady Briana was adamant about seeing my sister, for the two of them were best of friends. Also, 'twas no secret that Oswulf's man, Cospatric Arkill's son, had an eye for Aldgyth, and that ever since they had both come of age. He asked about her unceasingly, and his marked attention never sat ill with us. Both Edwin and I liked and admired him, for he was not of the rough and debauched cut of most of Oswulf's retainers. He was a well-come man anywhere, and there were precious few others in my kinsman's service who were.

The summer passed us with no grief and saw Edwin rise to a great popularity with the Mercian people. He was fair and just, good to the poor, and showed himself amongst them constantly—a thing which has forever been to the liking of the common-folk. I rode always at his side, as his chief of men, and their zealous admiration of him never ceased to amaze me. Speculation waxed high all over the earldom about his marriage. He was nearing twenty years so people thought it must be imminent. It seemed that every woman in the country considered herself a candidate. Sometimes it embarrassed me, the boldness they exhibited with him.

Just after Midsummer, my avunculus, William Malet, left with a fleet of three well-laid ships, for his lands in Le Havre. He took his sister, our unfortunate mother, with him. We tried to make a fare-well to her at Couventrie, but she was completely uncomprehending. In their party was Harold Godwine's son. A strange choice for a companion, we thought, though we knew he was friendly with William Malet. Besides, 'twas rumored all over the kingdom that he bore a message from King Edward to William, the fire-eyed Duke of Normandy. What the message was, men could only guess, but there was a great deal of discontent about it. The Anglish surely were not ready to accept the idea of a Norman monarch, remembering all too well the problems that prevailed when Edward kept his foreign favorites in all the high offices. Whether he truly meant to offer the kingship to the duke or not, I cannot say. To me, the question was only one of lesser evils: the alternative was probably the king's darling, Tostig Godwine's son. Men were saying, though, that Earl Harold was himself making a strong bid. If there were any reason for the crown to go to the House of Godwine, the tie through Cwene

Edythe being the supposed link, then they insisted the right should go to the eldest son, by virtue of inheritance as opposed to personal preference. It was even being talked that Harold and Tostig were beginning to dispute between themselves over this all-important issue. My only intent was to watch them devour themselves, as Gruffydd had predicted they would. As to the outcome of the battle for the throne, I could not hope to foretell it.

Edwin and I had both by now accepted that a North Humbrian rising in favor of our house, was inevitable. We were eager for it, but understood it was imperative to wait for the right moment before making any move. 'Twas by plunging in too fast two years ago that our house had come to such disaster. The trick was to have patience, to bide our time and let things play into our hands.

As the hunting season came, this began to happen. The North Humbrians were growing more and more distraught with the unfair rule of their Saxon earl. He had outlawed many more men from the earldom by then, in the same way he chased away Siward Bearn and his brother and Oswulf. Men despised the way he grew richer by confiscating property in this way—Siward Bearn's estate in Tathaceaster alone was larger than any holding Tostig had before in Wessex. He was relentless in his pursuit of criminals. This might have been to his credit, for thievery and murder grew less in the wild north than ever they had been, but he made no distinction between real crimes and imagined ones. Men who in any way held a blood claim to the Humbria, for instance, were immediately suspect and usually dealt with harshly as traitors or rebels. It took naught but the barest suspicion of plotting or intrigue to condemn a man. outlawing and confiscation of property in time gave way to harsher sentences.

One day in the late summer, two North Humbrians came to me at Sempringaham and asked to be sworn to my service. They were Gamel-Beorn and Heard Ulf's son: the same who had come to us at Weogornaceaster with Heard's uncle, Osbeorn Dolfin's son, to warn my father of Tostig's writ of execution.

It was nothing surreptitious this time. They came in broad daylight, having ridden hard and long with pack horses and a great portion of their personal possessions in tow. I greeted them warmly but quizzically, and sent for my brother.

Even before Edwin arrived, I had heard their woeful tale. They had resolved to come to me five days earlier. On the morning of that day, their fathers, Gamel Orm's son and Ulf Dolfin's son, broke fast with Earl Tostig in his private chamber at Eorforwic.

Two-and-a-half years had passed since those two had way-laid us with Eswig Broad-Brace in the corridor of the king's house and told us of Burchard's murder, the first of our many sorrows. I was hard-pressed to picture them as the men spoke, for I had seen them only in passing since then, and we were always careful to give no sign of recognition or friendship. Thusly it had to be when they were in the close service of Tostig Godwine's son, else he would have suspected surely the part they played in Ælfgar's escape from that mad-man's writ. All our careful pretense had not been enough, though.

On the morning in question, they had relaxed in the earl's chamber, in his peace, totally unsuspecting. Six other guardsmen kept table with them, eating barley bread and dove breast, talking casually of the day's affairs as they had many times before. At a signal from the earl, two of them, Amund and Ravens-Worth, reached under their bench and drew forth battle-axes, with which they hacked the two men to death, then and there. Earl Tostig, confident of the support and loyalty of the other men, put his hands on his hips and laughed aloud afterwards. "So have we put our judgment upon those who would betray their lord!" he told them.

Though he pretended, or believed, that his guardsmen had backed him in this crime, in truth the onlookers were frightened and disgusted by this gross deed. One was Osbeorn Dolfin's son, who had watched the murders of his own brother and his best friend in stunned horror, then taken on the sad duty of reporting those men's deaths to their horrified sons.

"I beg you, Morcar Ælfgar's son," Heard Ulf's son said, placing his hands on my shoulders in the manner of an earl's man, "put me beside you and I will spare not an ounce of breath or blood to win you victory over that tyrant." Gamel-Beorn begged the same boon. Neither asked more than that they be allowed the privilege of personally executing Amund and Ravens-Worth when we triumphed in Eorforwic.

I thought of the sworn brotherhood of the household troops. That two guardsmen could turn on two others, with whom they had lived and ridden and gamed and slept and kept company for years, was an abomination of brutality. I readily agreed to it. Gamel-Beorn, Heard Ulf's son, and I stood silent together a long time in the bright autumn sunlight which filtered through the narrow window, listening to the far off ring of axes in the deep woods. We had all come to manhood since last we met. We had been hardened by death and treachery and we had all lost fathers to the same evil enemy.

Those two were the first of my own sworn guardsmen, and they prided themselves on the fact. Two days later, Osbeorn Dolfin's son arrived, having stalled to reclaim from Tostig his dead brother's coffers. He pledged himself my man as well. With him were my North

Humbrian cousins, Brihtric and Maldon, the great-nephews of Earl Morcar of the Seven Boroughs. From that day onward, I never rode out without these five men, until the time came for the Christ Mass Gemot. I could not risk being seen in Lundun City with a following of my own, however small, and especially not a following of disenchanted northerners. When we rode to council, I traveled as one of Edwin's men. We were fast growing proficient at showing the faces men expected of us. It was becoming a talent.

At that Gemot, King Edward allowed Edwin's chief men, the three sons of Carr, to sit in his hall for a time. He had decided they were no longer figureheads of Ælfgar's traitorous alliance, but members of a conquered race serving fealty to a high-born Anglishman. The king had grown very comfortable with my brother and had a wish to placate him as far as possible. Also, it visibly impressed him that the foreigners had adopted Anglish look and fashion. Harold, newly returned from Normandy, and Tostig, spiteful and silent as ever, watched the king bestow these small favors on our house with considerable suspicion in their smoldering eyes.

Something happened at the Christ Mass Gemot which was of serious consequence to us, but we did not realize the implications of it till several months later when Oswulf made us another visit in the company of Siward Bearn. Cospatric Arkill's son, Oswulf's closest man, had been murdered in the king's house on the fourth day of Christ Mass. 'Twas a great and sad scandal, for the Bernician nobleman was young and comely and because his death, by mutilation and beheading, was particularly grisly. I had known him since childhood; he was one of the few men in Oswulf's household who brought a smattering of dignity to my cousin's life-style.

Apart from the fact that Cospatric was one of the men outlawed from the North Humbria with Oswulf, it was not known that there was any particular enmity between him and the Godwine's sons. When the rumor began to fly that Tostig was in some way responsible for the unfortunate guardsman's cruel fate, it was generally disregarded, and laughed at by some, who said even the over-bold Wessexman was not brave enough to murder a foe in the king's house and leave the body in the self-same spot it dropped. I was one to ascribe to that, knowing first hand how devious, guileful and cunning the treacherous earl could be. He was far too ambitious to leave evidence of his crimes in full view of the king.

Oswulf surprised us when he said Cospatric had been seriously courting with Aldgyth. We all knew he had first become enchanted with her many years ago, during the Midsummer's feasting my father held in her honor when she came of marrying age. During Oswulf's last visit to us, Cospatric had become impressed by our constant talk of her sad plight in Lundun, her widowhood and captivity. Seeing her again, he had been hard smitten. He resolved to make a suit for her, and if she proved favorable to it, he meant to approach Edwin on her account and his, with the possible view of wedding her to himself.

We had noted throughout the festivities that the handsome man paid her marked attentions and that she seemed to reciprocate, smiling and laughing and looking altogether happier than she had in a long while. Nevertheless, it shocked us greatly to discover this news, for we had known naught of the seriousness of the affair.

Oswulf claimed that Tostig learnt of the blossoming attachment from his sister Edythe, the king's lady. She had made a great pretense of friendship and concern for my sister and had gained somewhat of her confidence. My cousin said Cospatric had come to him after the Year's End fasting and told him Cwene Edythe had rebuked him in private, asking what treason it was that made him seek to unite the House of Leofric with the claims of the old Bernician house, against her brother Tostig's interests. Cospatric denied seeking any political advantage in the match and protested that his thought was for the lady alone. Then, Oswulf told us, Lady Edythe made a polite apology to him saying, "'Tis no secret that the sons of the traitor-earl Ælfgar have designs on my brother's land. Could be they would use any means to cut themselves a foothold there, even the wedding of their sister to a member of the ancient house." This she said because Cospatric was a distant kinsman to Oswulf, even though he was scant relation to us.

Cospatric Arkill's son had not thought much about it because the lady had seemed so friendly. Even so, the words had been sitting heavy ever since on Oswulf's breast, and he was convinced that the sweet lady Edythe had ordered the slaying of his best friend, in her brother's behalf. In time, this came to be an accepted fact throughout the land, but when first he broached it with us, we were near incredulous.

We discussed it this way and that amongst ourselves. With all our kinsmen and sworn supporters, our talks were assuming the aspect of councils. We all knew Oswulf was hot for revenge on Tostig and we feared he might not be able to hold himself from rash action. It took all our combined strength to prevail upon him to sit tight, to wait till we had entirely consolidated our strength before we broke the peace. In the end, he gave in to us, but we could plainly see ourselves accelerating towards rebellion; things could never hold as they were for another year.

Already some decisions had been made. Barring some other unforeseen and favorable opportunity, we meant to launch things as originally planned, while Tostig kept the hunting season in Wessex with the king. If nothing else, there would be a greater element of surprise in this; Tostig, having thwarted us once in the same attempt would be slow to believe we would try it a second time. It had long since been agreed that once the Humbria was ours, we would divide it once more into the old states of the Bernicia and the Diera. Oswulf, as Earl of the Bernicia, and Siward, as Bearn of the Diera, would be under-lords to me, the Earl of North Humbria. This was the only sure way of keeping such a vast holding united—something that Tostig, for all his well-hailed political acumen, had entirely failed to realize.

At precisely the most opportune moment, Oswulf would ride to the Bernicia. We had no fear that the men there would fail to flock to him. Siward Bearn already had large armies secretly in his pledge, and we knew the men of Mercia would be glad to follow Edwin when he rose in my behalf. Bleddyn and Rhiwallon, the two brothers of Gruffydd who lorded the Cymry now, had expressed an interest in reviving the alliance between Wales and Mercia—secretly, of course. They had intimated they would come to our aid under Edwin's banner, soon as he called for them.

Upon a given signal, these factions would spur to motion. Oswulf and his Bernicians would descend on Eorforwic from the north at the same time Siward Bearn and I approached from the southwest. Tostig kept over three hundred highly-trained house-carls in his capital city, but even amongst these, his personal retainers, there were many we could count on. Once the city was subdued and any necessary executions carried out, the Bearn and I would make for the Wessex border with the largest portion of the forces to confront the king's army and sue for terms.

We were not sure yet where we would mass. With an army that size there was sure to be a certain amount of plunder and looting, and we were all in agreement with Edwin's determination that no Mercian shire should be subjected to it. Most of us favored the areas of North Hamtun and Huntandun; those lands had been long ago robbed from Mercia and given to the House of Godwine. Earl Gyrth lorded them now, but nearly every estate within the boundaries of those two shires were owned either by Tostig or his chief man, Copsige Sword-Stinger. Edwin, who would ride all through Mercia and call his subjects to arms after recruiting the Welsh sympathizers along the border, would remain mobile. His army would be by far the largest and strongest, and he would keep the whole force in readiness to face any unforeseen hazard. Eventually, he would meet with us where we waited for the king to council. When Edward and his advisors finally faced us, they would must needs be intimidated by our size and strength.

By the time we broke our little gathering that spring and returned each to hearth and home, I found I was looking forward to the autumn with a great deal of anticipation. Things looked very, very promising.

                    *   *   *

Our avunculus, William Malet, was the lord of the great Alkborough manor in the Lindcylene Shire. Whenever he came to inspect his properties, he took advantage of his proximity to meet with us. He invited us there on Martyr's Mass day, and Edwin and I ate with him alone in a private chamber. We were able to talk freely, a thing which we always enjoyed and had little opportunity of doing. He had come north bearing very welcome news. Harold Godwine's son had decided to release his hostage hold on our sister.

"I would swear the man was smitten with her!" my uncle exclaimed. I could not help laughing. Edwin, smiling, poured honey mead from an earthen pitcher.

"Let him be!" he said casually. "As long as it is his concubine and his bastard sons who feel of his discontent, and not pretty Aldgyth."

"'Twould not be the worst match!" said the king's man with genuineness. I laughed again. Next to the house of Cerdic, the king's house, our house was the oldest and most honored. In Grandfather Leofric's time, our wedding into the upstart House of Godwine—who were half Saxon and half Dane and held not an ounce of Anglish blood in their veins—would have been considered an unseemly and rude degradation. Not the same scandal, perhaps, as Godwine's daughter marrying the king himself, but surely a reason for pause. Now the balance of power and favoritism had so shifted that we, of the line of Mercian and North Humbrian kings, were expected to feel it an honor to be accepted by, or in Aldgyth's case, sought after by, the Godwines.

After we had been quiet a little while, Edwin spoke softly, shaking his head. "You amaze me, uncle! After all the man has done unto us!"

"Here is where you are most like your unfortunate father, Edwin Ælfgar's son," said William Malet, drawing his tanned, leathery face into a dismal smile. "So obsessed you are with pitting one house against another, that all men lose their personal merits in your sight. To you, each one of those brothers is like the next."

I shook my head. "Nay, uncle! Tostig is by far the worst of the lot, but the rest of them stand behind all his stinking sins!"

"How say you?" he asked severely. I shrugged, so he went on. "If your pretty brother there robbed churches and put violence upon maidens, would it be your damnation also? And would it weigh upon you to hear people say that all the men of the House of Leofric robbed churches and raped women?"

I raised my hands to him, as if in defense. "Never would you see me condone such sin or pretend that it did not happen; not even for him."

"Would you believe a man who came to you and told you that your brother did those things?"

"Nay—"

"And yet, think you that you know his conscience? Think you there are not inner things of him that you do not know?"

I looked at Edwin, wondering, but I only said, "You make it all too simple. It goes much deeper between those two, I am sure of it."

Our avunculus gave a wan smile and looked from one to the other of us. "I have reason to believe Earl Harold knew naught of what occurred in your hall one night at Weogornaceaster, for instance."

Edwin stiffened and asked why he said so. "Because he told me," was William Malet's answer, "while we were ship-bound to LeHavre, with your mother in tow."

"You can see beyond that, I hope?" my brother cried, clenching his fists. "By the saints! The man's house wants the kingship; is he not apt to engage in such games as that?"

My uncle shook his head. "Nay. I myself told the man of Cynewulf Cenwulf's son's base murder and what it did to Lady Ælfgiva. I do not pretend to know all the workings of men, but methinks I know true astoundment when I see it! He had come to me in the first place to confess that he feared the lady was in that state because he himself had delivered the news of Burchard's death within her hearing."

"And you think he knew naught of the other?" Edwin's voice was cold.

William Malet crossed his arms, looking firm. "I know as much!" he said emphatically. "What happened that night, Tostig never told him. He claimed the Mercian had thrown himself on him in the dark, fully-clothed and armed … that his men had defended him against the man."

I groaned and looked at my brother. Edwin had a frozen, far away stare—a look I had seen often these last years. When he spoke, his voice was like ice. "Did you tell the man that my father was murdered in his bed? 'Twould be a great astonishment he would show at that, I trow!"

I was remembering how Harold had made condolences to me, looking straight into my eyes. I nodded, looking defiant. My uncle looked at us both quizzically. "Would you have me broach that with him?" he asked, "and give him cause to think you suffered discontent and thoughts of avengement?"

Edwin threw back his head, laughing loudly. "Tell me he does not suspect we mean to take an avengement! By God—they watch us like hawks and murder our friends and kinsmen on the suspicion of a whisper passing between us!"

William Malet stood suddenly. "Are you planning a revenge?" he asked, looking through us both at the same time. I felt myself flush, but my brother looked at him boldly. "What have you heard of it, uncle, in the king's busy court?"

"Until this very moment, sister's-son, I suspected naught but that the proud House of Leofric had finally determined itself to serve the crown instead of itself!" My uncle's voice was hoarse with half-suppressed disdain and anger. He scrutinized Edwin with a look I had often seen him toss my father—a most unhappy look.

My brother spoke coolly. "Perhaps it is that we serve the crown by looking to see that no pretenders wear it. "

He was silenced by a sharp wave of the hand. "Best you would speak no more to me of your aims and ambitions, then, Earl Edwin," my uncle declared in a harsh tone. "I would rather not be party to it. I bring you news that one of your rivals has spoken out against his brother's misdeeds, and you condemn the man for it!"

I looked at him curiously. "What mean you? That he has spoken out against what Tostig did?"

"Twice."

"How came this bold defense of us?" The bitter sarcasm in Edwin's voice made William Malet flinch. He answered levelly, though.

"Very near to Le Havre, we were blown off course. You have heard the story, I trow." We nodded. It had traveled all over the kingdom that Guy de Ponthieu, a vassal under-lord to Duke William, had claimed Earl Harold his hostage and the Duke of Normandy had paid his ransom. The grasping and rapacious Count Guy had freed my mother and uncle at once, knowing they had Norman connections and fearing the wrath of Duke William. Harold, though—what a prize! He made out well on the earl's misfortune, and without breaking any laws.

My uncle went on. "Duke William and Earl Harold waxed friendly from the start and felt a full appreciation, each of the other. One night Harold confided to William that Edward favored Tostig to succeed him."

I was incredulous. "Say you the king did not send the man there to offer William the crown?" I asked. My uncle laughed.

"Nay! That strange rumor has reached this far, I see! Never have I understood how men could think Harold Godwine's son would have done it, even if the king had commanded him! You know what the Godwine stand is on foreigners. Or was."

"What mean you?" Edwin was interested now, leaning forward with a look of determined concentration.

"Those of us that Count Guy released were the ones who carried to

William the news of Harold's capture. I had your mother with me. Naturally, the sight of his country-woman in a condition like that filled the duke with considerable curiosity. Later, Harold was the one who told him the whole story, in front of his court."

"Methinks I do not understand—" I began.

"He told Duke William how his brother had accosted her, and killed your father's man with a broad-axe. He even recalled the horrors she had witnessed during the crushing of the Ætheling, so many years ago and blamed his brother for that, also. He claimed Earl Tostig was with the men who taunted her that night in Guildford. That is the truth of it, too. Ælfgar told me years ago she had told him the same."

I caught my breath. Then Edwin and I exchanged a long, troubled look. My brother cleared his throat. "Earl Harold, it seems, will do anything to assure that he gets the crown instead of his brother! Even he accuses him now of all these things which have never bothered him over the years till he realized Tostig would get the kingship instead of him."

"You are wrong, Edwin Ælfgar's son!" William Malet's voice was firm. "He never knew how it was with his brother till he heard it from my lips. The next day, Duke William ordered an exorcism on lady Ælfgiva, but 'twas of no avail. The cleric said she was beyond an earthly cure. Harold cursed his brother when he heard that, and cried out against him. I took that opportunity to tell him about Burchard."

"What?" In unison, and we stammered several questions about the man's reaction to such an accusation.

"It troubled him greatly," came the answer. "He asked how we could have known such a thing, and I swore to him that Tostig had boasted of it. Also, I told him that Ulf Dolfin's son and Gamel Orm's son would swear to it, if 'twas his desire. He trembled mightily, like a man deep in illness, when he heard my words. Next day, he swore an oath to Duke William: that he would support the Norman's claim to the crown if Edward meant to name Tostig his successor."

We were stunned; this was too much to believe!

"What mean you, uncle," Edwin finally managed to ask, "that he said he would stand by him, or swore that he would?"

"As I told you, Ælfgar's son, he swore an oath to the man, hands on holy relics. I watched him myself." Our avunculus settled back, watching our faces for a reaction. What he read, I cannot say, but Edwin voiced my own thought.

"We shall wait and see," he said, raising his eyes carefully to William Malet's. "I cannot help but think the man would rather be brother to a king than sworn vassal to one. We will watch him very carefully, and see what he does."

"One thing he has done already, Edwin," my uncle said, musingly. "He has released your sister and ordered her sent home to the midlands in a rich party of king's men, borne in a stately litter. Here is an indication, I think."

"Nevertheless, we shall see!" my brother declared in his usual, unrelenting tone. Then he raised a cup, and our avunculus took the salute, but without a hint of a smile.

CHAPTER TWENTY-FOUR

Vengeance is better than
bootless mourning.

—Early North humbrian Poet

September, 1065

Not many days after my uncle took his leave, Edwin received a king's
writ confirming Aldgyth's release. Three weeks later she still had not
come. Worried for her, we dispatched a party of messengers to determine
the cause of her delay. In summertime, we were far too busy with the
affairs of the earldom to go to Lundun ourselves.

The messengers returned a few days later. Aldgyth, it seems, had
refused to remove herself. The king's advisors, Harold and Tostig,
expected her to leave little Gruffydd there. That boy was just a babe, less
than two years old, and she could not be made to part with him. After
we talked about it, we sent Brother Wulfget to Peterborough to see our
uncle. Abbot Leofric, who was well loved by the king and admired even
by the Godwines, agreed to intercede on her behalf.

Surely his arguments would have been adamant: that 'twas unnatural to part so young a child from his mother, that no true interests could
be served by such a course of action. However assertively he spoke,
though, King Edward and his men would not be moved. Aldgyth and
Nesta might take their leave in freedom but the child Gruffydd would
live a hostage in the royal court. It was with great bitterness that my
sister finally left. Even then, she came not to the Lindcylene Shire, but
had herself brought to our cousin's house at Ceaster. Word came that she
had arrived there on the Nativity of Mary, a week to the day after
Edwin's twenty-first birthday. Could be she only craved the company of
her fondest friend, Lady Briana, but from early on my brother and I
feared she might have had another purpose in going there. Our men
assured us she was quite unsettled and it occurred to us she might have
developed some wild scheme to reclaim the child, moving herself close

as possible to the Cymry and Gruffydd's two brothers, Bleddyn and Rhiwallon, with whom she had never lost secret contact. I resolved to go there immediately and, indeed, it fit in well with the rest of our plans that I should do so. We had aimed to meet at Ceaster near the start of the hunting-time.

I found Siward Bearn had already come and resumed the rule of the house. Besides the guardsmen he carried, the place was already crowded with Ealdread's household and Oswulf's.

Men were everywhere, sleeping in every available out-building; still-houses and stables and byres, even the kitchen and buttery bulged with them. He had put Aldgyth, with her daughter and Welsh waiting ladies, in the tall, lofted monk's house, a handsome building, very old and warm. This was to become laughingly known during those busy weeks as the harpy-house, for he eventually quartered all the women there, removing them from the main building to make room for the high-born men who gathered. The day I arrived with my men, the last of them—Ealdread's lady, Gweneth, and Lady Briana and their maids—moved themselves there. Oswulf took it with bad grace. He had till that very day slept in the same chamber with his woman, an intimacy which the men of our house thought unseemly. He complained he was wroth to sleep in a room full of graceless men, because ladies made gentler pillows, but soon as he began to be teased for his lack of boldness and inability to live in war-camp conditions, he stopped his grumbling. He was leaving for the Bernicia in a few days anyway, so it was no long and drawn-out hardship.

With more men arriving every day, we soon saw that it would be advisable to set a camp. Down on the grassy yellow Dee banks, we oversaw the pitching of tents and building of palings, to contain the fast-massing pack horses and war steeds. There scarce were enough trees there to tie the stallions separately, so horse fights became a common disturbance, adding to the confusion. Spirits were high amongst the men, though, so there was not much quarreling or drinking. Most of them were land-holding men, or house-carls, or guardsmen, and all with a grievance they wanted desperately to see come right. Siward Bearn himself moved into the camp after a few days, inspiring a discipline and order so striking that these scores of warriors might have been mistaken by any for king's men.

The fourth day I was there, Cousin Oswulf left with a party of twenty. He meant to raise an army, and he looked bold and compelling enough to claim the allegiance of any Bernician who looked at him. We had no fears for his success; in the far north, his claim was so favored that men took no pains to hide it. They had refused to accept the usurper Siward who murdered their fair and forthright Earl Eadwulf, and

they staunchly defended the claim of Eadwulf's son over that of Tostig.
All the rest of the North Humbria might bow under the Godwine yoke,
they cried, but not the Bernicia! No one would do for them but
Eadwulf's son, so when Oswulf rode down to lay siege to Eorforwic, we
knew his force would be formidable. Among those at his side were
Gamel-Beorn and Heard Ulf's son, gifted with the power and privilege
to execute the two gross murderers, Amund and Ravens-Worth.

A few hours after Oswulf took his leave, I walked out in the fields
with Aldgyth and Lady Briana. Pretty, dark-haired little Nesta was with
us, too. Sometimes I carried her, other times I walked her by the hand,
leading her here and there to show her things while the two ladies
chatted and shared. I did not listen to much of their woman-talk, but I
found myself watching them almost constantly. They were both very fair
and, despite the look they had of being kinswomen, almost complete
opposites of each other.

Oswulf's woman was the smaller and though she was five years
older, she looked the younger of the two, despite her married-woman's
veil. I think it was the light in her eye; unlike Aldgyth's, her look was
still unsullied by death and tragedy. Her cheeks bloomed with perfect
health. Could be she reddened them, but she did it gently if so. Her dress
was soft wool-stuff, dyed saffron and embroidered in green and black—
happy colors, I thought, and very fitting. She smiled a lot and moved her
hands with much expression as she talked in a gay and musical tone.
There was a look of girlishness to her, and that was something Aldgyth
had entirely lost.

Not that my sister's beauty had faded, for she was radiantly lovely:
pale and translucent and perfect of feature. She dressed herself entirely
in the Cymrian way, in soft tan hides and brown and beige leather, the
only real color to her dress being a short kidskin over-tunic of woad-dyed
blue. On a chain round her slender throat she wore Gruffydd's golden
ring. I wondered if she knew how often her fingers wandered there, to
touch it momentarily in a graceful, unconscious way. She reddened her
lips and cheeks with berry juice and though this fashion looked unflat-
tering on many other women, it gave a startling prettiness to her solemn
face. Her gold hair was gathered in nets over her ears. I was glad she did
not hide it away as any Anglish widow would have done. I liked the look
of a woman's tresses. In that, I suppose I was like my father, who often
hungered just to see and touch my mother's cloudly locks.

"Pray, what makes you look on us so boldly, Morcar Ælfgar's son?"

Lady Briana's voice held just the slightest hint of impatience and
rebuff. Feeling a burning blush come over me, I turned away quickly,
hoisting Nesta to my shoulders where she giggled with delight.

"Do not be hard on him, cousin," I heard my sister say, "the men of our house are always quick to favor with an admiring glance."

"Aye," the other answered softly, "there is no harm in a gentle look, I trow." I knew she was thinking of Oswulf's craving eye when she said it, but it nevertheless discomfited me to hear them laugh low afterwards.

The very next day, Edwin came with Brother Wulfget and the Welshmen with forty of his guardsmen in tow. One look at his drawn and sleepless face convinced me he bore the worst of tidings. Without dismounting, Edwin asked where we could go to talk alone. I ordered a mount put in harness, and then we rode towards the camp on the river, at a slow and easy pace. All his men but the sons of Carr fell far behind us out of deference. As Edwin's chief men, it was accepted that the sons of Carr were privy to our private talk; as with my men Heard and Gamel-Beorn, I scarce noted they were there.

"Gruffydd, son of Gruffydd, is dead," is the first thing my brother told me when we had ridden a little way. "'Twas said by the king's herald that he died of some quick fever."

"By God's blood!" I cried, not meaning to curse. "What think you, brother?"

"Truly I know not, Morcar," he answered miserably. "Could be they had him purposefully slain, but methinks 'tis just as likely a babe like that could die for the want of a mother!"

"Here is another great evil done to us!" I exclaimed, hot with anger. "I cannot help but think it is!"

"Aye, either way it is a throbbing injustice. I fear me for the lady." Edwin's voice trailed off and he looked away, then added, "How is it with her now, brother? Think you she can bear the weight of this?"

I did not have to think long. "She would best not hear of it till after we have made our move. There is no telling what she might take it upon herself to do, I swear it!"

"So I have thought," he said, nodding sadly. "We would do best to hide this thing between ourselves as long as possible—but then, we need discover a way of telling her, and explaining why we kept it."

"What of Brother Wulfget?" I asked. "He has that gentle manner. Could be he knows a way to tell her."

Edwin shook his head. "Nay, he thinks she should be made aware of it right away. 'Tis her mother's right, he says. He will never take it upon himself to tell, unless I bid him do it, but he will ne'er defend our motive to her afterwards. I fear me she will be wroth."

"Aye."

We rode the rest of the way in silence and our gloomy greeting to Siward Bearn gave him to know immediately that something was amiss.

After showing Edwin the camp, he saddled and rode back with us. We told him on the way; his strong shoulders bent with sorrow over it. The man was still most especially fond of my sister and could not bear that such suffering and misery should be hers. I could almost hear him thinking how different, how very much more secure and happy she might have been, if she had but warmed to his embrace.

But the Bearn was of the mind also that to keep it from her would be a sin upon us, and said she would never forgive us if she found we had held her from knowing for any length of time. He made a suggestion, though, which served to lighten our mood somewhat. His sister Briana, he said, should be the one to tell her. She would know just what to say.

The three of us went to seek that lady, soon as we reached the manor house. We found her finally in the kitchen-house, overseeing some of the cooking, and we led her out to the garden. We all sat there, on the cold, stone garden benches, a miserable circle of souls. The lady came to tears at the news of it; Aldgyth had talked unceasingly since she came of her darling boy, of her hopes and fears for that tiny creature— one of the only real things she had left of her dead, beloved Welsh king. Briana did not want to be the one to tell her. Edwin and I plead vehemently, and at last she gave in. Then we tried between us all to think of the words which would break it to her most gently of all.

It was while we spoke low and argued softly, in this distressed and somber state, that Aldgyth came upon us. We grew so suddenly, solemnly still at her approach that she covered her mouth and gasped as with pain. Looking from one to the other of us, she began to tremble. We did not have to say a single word to her. She read the dire news in our faces.

Day after next, early on the morrow, Edwin left for the Cymry. We knew that the news of the child's death would inspire more Cymrian sympathizers to our cause. The son of King Gruffydd had been an emblem of hope to them: the symbol of a fine, fleeting moment when the enmity and bloodshed of generations had shrunk to nothing under the embrace of a sworn brotherhood. For two years that hope had lived beyond the deaths of the bold warrior-brothers, Ælfgar and Gruffydd: the hope of a united Welsh and Mercian midlands, strong enough to withstand the ravenous hunger of the Godwines.

*   *   *

The days seemed slow to pass. Aldgyth, not to be comforted, kept to her own in a misery so overwhelming that it robbed her of all interest in life. I tried to keep her company but her gloom began to affect my attitude towards all the other projects which weighed so greatly on me then. I am sorry to say I began to avoid her. Oftentimes, though, I would go of a morning and claim little Nesta from her nursemaids, making it my private duty to distract the child from her mother's grief. When it came time to send her back, I kissed her and sent her with the ladies because I could not hazard seeing Aldgyth. I had tried well enough to lift her, but the heaviness of her sorrow was too great for me to bear.

Ceaster felt a sea-wind but it was mild, breeze more than bluster. Though well into autumn, it felt more like mid-summer, warm and dry. Folk said the Dee had never been so low for that time of year and all were preparing for a harsh, long, snow-laden winter in consequence. Throughout the weald, axes rang in staccato disunion; firewood, nuts, roots, anything which could be put to use against the possibility of snow-boundedness was being gathered with a frenzy.

Craving the luxury of solitude, it became my habit to ride out alone when I could. I liked to follow the course of the river as it curved and sparkled through the fields of the Ceaster manor, teasing over knolls of fern and rock till it separated round a pleasant strip of moss-ground. There, under sheltering tufts of foliage, I would dismount and sit, lost to this thought or that, until the urge was on me to leave again. One gentle noon on my way there, I met Lady Briana coming from the timber church beyond it with her ladies. When she saw me, she signaled them to go on, then reined around and rode with me a while.

"Do you like this land here, Morcar?" she asked me. Looking to the green and grey shoulders of the overhanging steeps and the brilliant sun, crossed by hurtling clouds in the ever-restless sky, I was forced to admit I did.

"Always I have loved it, too," she said, adding mournfully, "What Oswulf finds to hunger after in the shadowy Bernicia I know not."

"'Tis his homeland," I said. "Do you not miss the Diera?"

"Not as much as you might think. Ceaster satisfies me."

"Aye. Aldgyth seems to like it, too."

She looked at me knowingly. "Because she can look across the river Dee there into the Cymry, and dream of her man."

"She loved Gruffydd very much," I admitted, stepping my horse aside to let her pass when the stone road grew suddenly narrow. When it widened again I caught up to her side.

"I think it wonderful for a wife to crave her husband so!" she said after a long pause. There was a wistful gentleness to her tone that, somehow, did not match her eye-light. "Gruffydd must have been good to her."

I did not make an answer. We had come to the staunch, stone bridge which led over to my well-prized thinking spot. It was a low, borderless span, and I dismounted to walk her horse across, handing her my long rein so that my animal could follow in tow. It was a brilliant day, and the gurgling waters glittered in prismatic colors. The fair greenness of the bank did not suffer a single shadow. I took in the beauty without speaking or looking at my cousin's wife, and just contemplated silently as if I were alone.

"You are a very shy man, sir," she said at length. "I do not understand it because it does not seem to be a thing which runs in your house!"

I was blushing and glad she was talking to the back of my head. "I do not always find it comfortable to talk, lady."

"Fie! You show no ill-ease with men, Morcar! Methinks you have an abashment of ladies. Can it be?" Her voice was teasing. Though I knew she meant no harm, it irked me, I know not why. "Have you never courted?" she asked me suddenly.

"Lady!" I turned a look of cold disapproval on her, and she shrugged in an impish way as if to beg apology.

"I did not mean to be bold," she said, holding out her hand so that I would help her down. "I have seen your heavy mood of late, though, and only thought to lighten it."

Setting her gently on the ground, I was forced to smile. "Do what you can for my sister, then. It is she who sore needs lifting." Not far down the stream, a wild red stag stood, meaning to drink, but when I pointed him to her, he was alerted and bounded away.

"Is this where you come every day when you disappear?" she asked while I put our horses to a tree.

"I knew not anyone missed me when I left." I answered and then we walked awhile, without saying much, listening to the stream water and frog songs.

We reached the flowered, mossy lawn where I usually sat. "A beautsome corner, surely!" she cried in delight. "Let us sit a moment, Morcar, and enjoy it!"

I put down my mantle and she lowered herself, looking pleased. Soon as she had settled herself, she reached up deftly and undid her heavy, circular veil, letting her hair show. It was plaited and wrapped around her head now in the wedded woman's way, still the same pretty, golden color I remembered. Standing not far away, my hands behind me and my back against a wide, handsome oak, I found myself studying the woman. Her fair face and form had changed little since her bride-ale but until this time at Ceaster I had never noticed the boldness of her gaze, which Edwin had remarked upon disparagingly in the past. He told me she had several times contrived to put herself unnervingly near to him when no others were about. That had long made me want to avoid her but, truth was, there was something appealing to me in her brazenness, and it stirred rather than shamed me.

"You may sit if you please!" she said, looking up suddenly. I turned hastily away, hoping she had not caught me staring, and shook my head.

"I am comfortable enough," I said.

She laughed pleasantly. "Well, surely you rob me of my comfort— standing there like that!" she patted the mantle opposite her. "Come here and sit!"

Feeling sheepish, I moved closer. As I seated myself, she looked at me with a frown. "What is it about me that displeases you, Morcar?"

"There is nothing, lady!" I moved my hand softly over the top of the mellow grass and picked a handful in a clenched fist. She tossed me a queer half-smile.

"I am glad to hear you say that. Sometimes I have felt you wished to be elsewhere than by me."

"It is only my manner," I confessed humbly, looking away. "I am sorry for it."

"Do not be sorry!" She reached over and touched my cheek, making me face her. "I fear I have embarrassed you, sir, and that is one thing I would I had not done. You are such a man as deserves never to be wounded."

The touch of her hand had sent a shudder through my whole body. Not wanting her to sense my confusion, I pulled myself awkwardly to my feet and turned away, fearing my burning flush must have been visible. She was indeed a fine looking one. In her soft dress of dyed blue linen, with her hair shining in the gold sunlight, the nearness of her almost lost me my composure, and I was ashamed to let her know it.

"Perhaps 'tis time we went back now." I told her in a low voice.

Behind me, her voice was wretched. "Pray tell me what it is I have done to offend you!"

She stood, and I felt her hand momentarily on my shoulder, but I said nothing. She turned; there was a rustling as she gathered up my mantle. When she approached with it, I faced her and our eyes met. She reached up and around me, placing it over my shoulders, drawing the ends as if to brooch it for me. I suddenly felt very weak, and her voice seemed to come from far away as she spoke, "Very often I do this for Oswulf. It is his pleasure that I dress him and lay on his accouterments."

I managed to keep my voice level. "Indeed, my lady?"

"Aye," she whispered, "and undress him too."

She pulled at my mantle until I was pressed full against her, my eyes entrapped by the daring invitation of her hot gaze. I thought to push her away, but only momentarily. Arms locked tightly around her, my hands took on a will of their own, kneading her body to mine with desperate force.

"Think you this is a great wrong I do, Morcar Ælfgar's son?" she asked in a whisper. When I began to nod to it she put her hand forcefully behind my neck to still me and drew my mouth hard to hers.

"God forgive me then," she breathed, cupping herself harder against me. "I know not how I can crave you so fiercely!"

*   *   *

Later, I lay there outstretched in the grass with my back to her, lost in curious memories. It was because I wore only my linen under-tunic, and that open to the waist; I had not lain in the sun bare-legged and unclothed like that since I was a boy and I had forgotten the invigorating freedom of the feeling. Now it brought back half-remembered pictures of younger days and all the emotions attendant to them. I savored those remembrances for, in truth, I could not bear to think or speak of what had just happened and I was glad to fill my mind with something else.

It dismayed me to think how little control I had, that I had fallen so easily to the ground with her, and it trembled me in my soul to realize how well I had enjoyed it. Spent now and drained, I could think of one thing only: the agony of making confession. It filled me with such icy dread that I did not want to look at her. When she reached around me, slipping her pretty pale arm through mine to stroke my chest softly, my voice was exasperated and not as gentle as it should have been. "Are you not afraid?" I asked her. "Does this thing not frighten you?"

Pushing me forcibly down on my back so that I looked up into her face, she held my head between her hands, fingers wrapped tight in my hair. "It does not frighten me enough to make me sorry it happened," she breathed, leaning close. The wind was not quite as sparing now. Some of her hair had come loose and it framed her pale, fine face with gilded light. She had wrapped my mantle around her, but it scarce hid her perfect breasts, glistening with the dewy sweat of our exertions. The perfection of her look made me shudder again. Without even meaning to, I drew her down, caressing her lips to my chest and holding her tight to me while I tried to make some sense of the situation.

"This will be the end of it," I said at long last, with all the finality I could muster. "Do not put yourself in my way again while I am here, Lady Briana."

"Morcar—"

"Do not do it!"

"It is for you to decide, then...." she murmured disconsolately.

When she pulled herself away, I let go of her quickly and turned my back again, not to let myself be tempted into watching her dress. She took a long time and I could feel her eyes upon me during much of it, but as to what she was thinking, I had no way of knowing.

Later, we rode back at a slow pace over the hill-crests, wrapped in glum silence until she broke it. "Oswulf has not been an altogether fair man to me," she said, her tone surprisingly plaintive. "Must be you know as much."

It vexed me strangely to hear his name. I said nothing, so she went on. "He is a golden man to look upon, but he lacks a gentleness."

"He is your wedded man!" I cried. "And he is my kinsman!"

"Then you realize his flashing temper, I trow, and can think what a hard man he is to bend to. Mayhap you can even imagine how he ill-uses me, taking me at his own pleasure with no thought to my feeling ever. From the beginning that has been his way!"

I cannot say why, but it wounded me to think about her marriage-bed. "Perhaps you should have denied him your hand," I said coolly. Her laugh was not gracious.

"Did you think he was my choice?" she cried. Her voice was so strained that I looked at her and saw she was choking back tears. "Even then I was not so foolish that I would have taken such a brazen tempest of a man, despite his comely look! It was Siward who forced that match! 'Tis my own brother I have to thank for it!"

Moving my horse to hers in such a way that she was forced to stop, I stared hard at her without saying anything for a moment. Then, afraid of my own feelings, I commanded her not to tell me more.

"What secret can I have worse than the one I share with you already, Morcar?" she asked in a mildly mocking way. "Oswulf Eadwulf's son claimed me before we ever were betrothed. He claimed me against my will on the dirt floor of a timber church and when Siward found us there, he contracted me to him, as if to punish me for what I could not have prevented! He knew it would only cause me misery, and that Oswulf could in nowise be tamed. My brother told me himself that he almost murdered Oswulf the night before our bride-ale. I would to God he had done so!"

Her voice trailed off listlessly. Suddenly remembering the frenzied hate that had passed between my two kinsmen on that night, I shivered, feeling no satisfaction at learning the cause of it after all these years. I do not know what she read in my gaze, but when she raised her eyes to me again, Briana was flushing red with shame.

"Thus it is you hate me so, Morcar!" she cried. "You have been blameless till now and may be you could sense I was a woman ruined and sin-ridden even from the time you were a boy! I have touched you now and, against all my hopes, that touch brings you only anger and sorrow. You do well to despise me for it. Only pity me, in that I was so misused I thought I never could desire a man—until you."

She paused, staring into my eyes, her green ones brimming with tears. Then she cried out in a dismal, strangled voice, "I had fooled myself to think you wanted me too! God's mercy!"

Cracking her crop, she took off at a fast clip, but not before I had full well felt her misery. I stood there, staring after her until she was gone. She was wrong. I had ached for her.

CHAPTER TWENTY-FIVE

> The North humbrian thegns entered Eorforwic
> with two hundred soldiers to revenge the execrable
> murder of the noble North humbrian thegn
> Gospatrick, who was treacherously killed by order
> of Queen Edythe at the king's court on the fourth
> night of Christ Mass, for the sake of her brother
> Tostig; and also the murder of the thegns Gamel,
> the son of Orm, and Ulf the son of Dolfin, whom
> earl Tostig had perfideously caused to be
> assassinated in his own chamber at Eorforwic. . . .
> They therefore on the day of their arrival, first
> seized his Danish house-carls, Amund and Ravens-
> Worth . . . and put them to death . . . and the next
> day slew more than two hundred of his liege-men.
>
> — Florence of Worcester

A week went by, and I was the most miserable of men. The harder I forced myself not to think of Briana, the more I longed to see her. Yet when we did pass, I burned with a shame so intense I felt I must have been marked in the eyes of men as well as in God's, and it hurt me the more to think she felt the same shame, maybe even stronger. I wanted desperately to go to her and say I did not mark any of it against her, that it had been the fault of my own base weakness. But I knew that to exchange even a word with her would be my undoing.

When I was ready to make my confession I rode to the country church at Fearndun, taking only four men with me. I was glad to see that the priest there was a worldly one. He wore a knife girth and had not shaved his pate. I did not ask his name, nor he mine. I felt he knew me surely, though I came hooded and dressed in common grey moreen, just as I felt he knew the lady I spoke of even though I did not name her.

"Have you forsaken her?" he asked me severely, and I reassured him emphatically that I had. After he made a penance to me—a three days full fast every week for a season—I gave a gold offering for his church. It was a well-made armlet, rich with amethyst, which had been my father's. Fingering it gently, he said, "This bespeaks that you are a high-born man, sir, and I would give you warning: to all men whose ears might hear of this, you must bear the dishonor. That is a thing men of noble birth sometimes forget to do, so conscious are they of their station."

"I am the one to blame," I admitted woefully.

"And will you be willing, my lord, to stand by that on the day this kinsman of yours discovers you have lingered with his woman?"

Drawing in a long, slow breath, I nodded numbly. It was something I did not want to think about, considering Oswulf's violent temperament. The priest put an arm around my shoulder reassuringly. "You are yet a young man," he said, "but you have been fully formed some years now, and I see easily by your manner you have never had a sin like this to confess before. Perhaps you would do well to wed before long."

I cut him off with a shrug. "There is no one I can consider now. Things are too confused with me."

His eyes narrowed. "You do not feel bounden to this wedded woman, do you?"

I shook my head.

"Because if you did, then it would increase your sin. You would be wise to look on this lady as little as possible."

"Aye. That I have already commanded myself."

"Good!" He slapped me on the back in a friendly fashion and then gave his blessing. All the while I rode away, I felt him staring after me and it was not an easy thing to take.

That very night, Siward Bearn made his return, coming to me in the herb yard where I walked with Aldgyth and Nesta in the deep blueness of eventide before darkness. Once the sun set, the air no longer hinted of mid-summer the way it did during the noon. It was October surely, and I held Nesta tight under my fur-lined mantle as my sister gathered the last of the second borage and the browned and brittle healing herbs best gathered not in sunlight but in descending darkness. Her huge basket was half-full when I heard my cousin's powerful voice ring out.

"Morcar Ælfgar's son!"

With a kiss, I put Nesta to the ground and strode to meet him. We took each other's shoulders just as we had always done, but it seemed a strange thing to me that I had lain with his sister and he did not know it. I was glad the dimness hid any flush of guilt I might have had, but perhaps I need not have worried, my voice came so casually and level.

"How stand things with us, cousin?"

His voice was prideful. "We have a certain victory, Morcar! You would be hard-pressed to picture the number of men who have rallied to Oswulf in Dunholme—a good force, mean and vengeful! We are assured of many of the North Humbrian thegns and even some of the house-carls. If we move fast, we will be done with this by November. Tostig still lingers at court with the king, unaware of what is brewing. Your brother has begun the gathering of the Mercian carls and the Cymrians. If the Welshmen are swift, we could be in Eorforwic in a week's time."

Heartened by his broad, beaming grin, I asked how sure he was the king and his southerners would submit to our demands. "He cannot exile over half the land!" was his exultant answer and we clapped each other on the back. Then my sister, who had not said anything till now, walked over to us with her big basket, her free hand guiding her daughter's steps through the near-darkness.

"I will hold you personally responsible, Siward Bearn," she said dourly, "if either of my brothers come to harm in this bold escapade!"

When I hissed her to silence she began to weep, so I gathered her to me as best as I could. "You are over-burdened!" I told her. "You know not what senseless things you say. This is the moment we have waited for since Father first was wronged!"

"You speak to one who sees clearly that Power and Death are brothers!" she snapped, pulling back as if our presence pained her. Taking Nesta, she stomped away. I stared morosely after her.

"Let not her words weight you, cousin! This is scarce even a contest, the outcome is so assured!" Putting his arm around my shoulder, the Bearn headed me back to the hall where most of my best men and his now were seated. We proceeded to get wholly, entirely drunken, and I can tell you it did my heart good, so tensed and high-strung I was.

Everyone knows I am not an extroverted man, but that night I waxed worse than merry, drunken to rowdiness on quantities of ale and greater quantities of emotion. I was twice hoisted out into the cold night air by Siward Bearn, by no means sober himself, in order to prolong my consciousness. By mid-of-night, though, I had mellowed to a foolish stupor, though I was still hot-headed enough to argue when I could force meaningful words out.

By then, some of the men were unconscious, stretched out on the floor or curled over on the hard benches. I never had an appreciation for sleeping drunken in hall. It was something my father had despised though some of our kinsmen, like Oswulf, made a habit of it. The first time my head dropped forcefully onto my arms, which were crossed on the table in front of me, I resolved to go to the privacy of my lodges. After a few false attempts, I gained my feet. There was a rush of hot blood to my head which almost sent me reeling as I staggered to keep my balance on the fast-spinning floor. Siward Bearn, who had not yet retired, caught me in my discomfiture and, taking me by the elbow, led me out into the biting night. There I stood shivering and pulling my mantle tight about myself while he paced, waiting for me to stop my distracted singing. I know not what made me feel so merry, but suddenly I broke into peals of laughter.

"Do you know, cousin," I gasped when I had caught my breath, "it would be good sport if Edwin were here with us this night. I should like to see him!"

"More than he would like to see you in your condition, no doubt," Siward grumbled. The chill air quickly chased a little of the fog from my head and I felt defensive.

"What mean you, complaining about my state when yours is not much the better? Do you think I am blind, cousin, that I do not notice the mead in your brain?" I tried to spit but was so unsteady that I almost lost my balance. Turning casually, Siward placed placed one powerful hand flat against my chest, pinning me to the wall. I started laughing again, and it sounded almost like a maiden's giggle.

"I think you are jangled, that is all," he said with a piercing look. Seeing I was steady, he let go and leant back again. "I can well enough read the pity and fear you feel for your sister and, I trow, taking shield and helm for the first time must not lie easy on you."

"I suffer no war-horrors, Siward Bearn!"

He answered nothing for a long time. I shivered mightily, hearing the chatter of my own teeth. Then he said, "Know you what your brother told me, just before he took his leave? That murder and blood-letting, even in long-awaited avengement, will be a harder and more scaring thing than else he has done ever before."

I spun round in indignation, holding onto the wall for dear life. "Why is it you think Edwin so much bolder a man than I, cousin?"

"I have never said so, Morcar."

"Nay. You have not, but you have thought it! That he is a daring man and I am a mild one."

"Pah! You are too drunken tonight to be a reader of men's minds, Morcar Ælfgar's son." His voice sounded irritated. "Best you would lay your body down and sleep this night's work away. And suffer yourself to be clear-headed when we ride to Eorforwic! Whether we come to arms with them or not, it would be well for you to know who you are when we get there!" Saying this, he put both his hands on me and steered me off towards the lodging house where I quartered. I heard him walk back to the hall after he had watched me some time. Clenched with an almost unbearable dizziness, I was glad I had not fallen on my face in front of him.

Halfway there, a boy approached me, his eyes heavy-lidded. "Someone has given me a message from your sister," he yawned, "and I feared I might not get it to you, for I was told to deliver it only when you had come from hall and in nowise to go in to you there. Then I grew very sleepy for she did not say how long you might take table." He yawned.

"This is not my usual habit," I tried to apologize. Even on those simple words I stumbled. I asked for the message.

"She says come to her side, no matter how late tonight. She fain would speak to you of something, and 'tis a weighty thing. Do not mind the hour, she says, she will not sleep till you come."

Remembering her state when I left her in the twilight, I felt a surge of anxiety. I thanked the boy, promised him pay, and went to her.

Siward had been wise to Aldgyth's need for solitude and had assigned her a private cell in the lodge that had been the monks' house. It was a loft room, neither large nor small, with an indoor stair which was narrow and steep and hard for me to maneuver in the darkness. Reaching the top, I leant hard against the wall to catch my breath. I found her door with some difficulty. Pushing it open, I almost tumbled in on my face before catching myself and, suffering that swift rush of blood to my brain, I was forced to steady myself against the first thing I could latch onto: a solid timber beam in the center of the room. The fire was well stoked and through the fire-hole above it streamed dusty beams of the moon's whitish light. I felt very odd; the dizziness had become pulsating and the room spun with uncheckable force. Hearing the door close behind me, I turned slowly, still supporting myself.

"I have a great need to talk to you this night, Morcar."

It was not my sister, but Briana! Groaning, I turned my back to her and crumpled against the timber beam, letting it support my hapless weight.

"You do not have to look at me; only let me speak!"

"Speak then!" I tried to focus my eyes.

"You men pretend there is nothing to fear," she began haltingly, "but well I know that in less than a week's time you will ride to Eorforwic, possibly to battle."

"It is true."

"Then I will hear from your own lips, before you go, that you forgive me." She stepped forward and then I could see her clearly. Her long golden hair was unbound and it outlined her lush figure in the dimness.

"I have not my wits about me tonight, lady." I faltered, forcing myself to look away.

"Then say what I want to hear and I promise I will go!"

"What is it that you really want to hear?"

I lifted mantle, brooch and all, over my head in a single, swift motion. All seemed like a dream. I knew exactly what I was doing but could not stop myself. Stepping closer, I put my arm around her waist and drew her close to me, trembling as much from emotion now as drink. I do not know that she ever answered my question but, when she began unlacing her dress, I knew with certainty I was a lost man.

*   *   *

Aldgyth woke me, and harshly, too. "Was it you she met here last night, brother?" she cried, shaking my shoulders hard. "Was it *you?*"

Stiff and heavy with head pain, I moaned and crossed my arms over my head feebly. Though afraid she would strike me, it took a few minutes to find enough voice to reprimand her.

"By God, woman!" I croaked harshly, "if you value your unbruised skin, unhand me!"

She dropped me back suddenly, and I groaned as my head hit the straw-covered floor. "You are hell-bound, Morcar; truly I fear it!"

"Nay," I said, knowing I was being deceitful, "if every man who overtook of mead in the mid-night went to hell, heaven would be full of craving women!"

She looked at me hopefully and questioned in a gentler tone, "What is it you are doing here, Morcar?"

"I came last night to see how you fared after your tantrum," I lied, amazed at how easy it was. "You did not tell me you would be out."

She eyed me suspiciously and I hoped I was not flushing. "What hour came you here, brother?"

"Lady!" I near shouted with pretended exasperation. "Until a scant minute ago I did not even know I was here at all! Now what is it that ails you?"

With painful effort, I pulled myself up, trying not to whine. Except for my mantle I was fully dressed, though everything was well-loosened and my beltings were on the floor. Bending to pick them up, I groaned again, and she said impassively, "You will need to drink of hare-water today, I fear." Whenever a hare was stewn, the water was saved in flagons for an ale-pain remedy. I shot her a cold look.

"I should not like you to go the way of the untamed North Humbrians," she somberly declared, staring down at her own hands. "Even if you are to be earl there."

Walking over, I took her shoulders and looked down into her face. Much of the liveliness had fled her eyes, but her beauty had in no way dimmed. I touched her hand to the fillet that still bound my hair. "Can you not tell I will ever be a Mercian?" I smiled. "Does not my look bespeak it?"

"For now." she answered dolefully. "But it will not be long before your tresses are reddened and hang to your waist, your chest and arms burned with pictures, and face hair—"

I laughed uproariously, even though it hurt. "There is a thought!"

"Siward Bearn says so. He says the men there will be holden to you when you go their way. He says you will want to do it!"

I laughed again and pinched her cheek. "Even so, what means it? I look at you, with cherry juice on your lips and cheeks, wearing kidskins instead of worsteds, your hair in plaited coils. It does not make you less the Mercian girl I grew up with."

She smiled softly and turned away from me. I was dipping my face in a bucket of cold water when I heard her speak. "The men of Eorforwic have risen and sent for you."

"What?" I thought I had not heard her correctly.

"Kinsman Oswulf could not contain his wild-men, it seems. They went to Eorforwic and held a council. They have slain over two hundred of Tostig's retainers and all the men of the Diera have joined with them to send for you."

Shaking, I wiped my brow with my sleeve. "Where is Siward Bearn?"

"At the Dee banks where all the soldiers are gathered—"

I did not hear the rest; I was already on my way down the narrow stair.

CHAPTER TWENTY-SIX

... The North humbrians united to outlaw Tostig,
their earl. They slew all his retainers whom they
could catch ... They sent for Morcar, son of Earl
AElfgar, and chose him to be their earl. he
marched south with all the men of the shire,
together with men from the shires of Nottingham,
Deoraby, and Lindcylene, and occupied North
hamtun, where he was joined by his brother
Edwin and men from his earldom with whom were
many Welshmen.

— Anglo Saxon Chronicle
Book "E" 1065

In the yard, I jumped bareback onto the first horse I found, and made my
way through the meadow to the reedless, rocky bank, then followed it
till I could hear their commotion and, finally, glimpse their numbers.
Siward Bearn I spotted at once. He was standing with his brother
Ealdread, who must have brought the news, a ways off from the main
body of men. I rode directly to them and dismounted, letting the horse
run free. Ealdread looked weary, worn; he had ridden hard.

"Well?" I asked him, impatience putting a note of demand in my
voice.

"We have no need to ride to Eorforwic ourselves to claim the
allegiances," he said solemnly. "That is assured. To a man, the folk there
are behind your standard. It seems that any who resisted were slain."

Oswulf Eadwulf's son is mad!" I spat, watching the great force of
men mounting their arms.

"You would be hard-pressed to tell who had the worse madness,
cousin: he or the men behind him. Once gathered, he could not hold
them still, so wild they were for avengement."

"We had need be swift," added Siward Bearn, "if we are to be gathered in force by the time news reaches Tostig and the king at Brytford."

"Where is Edwin now?"

"Straight south, on the Welsh border," Ealdread told me. "He should have a good army of Cymrians by now, eager as they are to back him."

I thought about it long and hard. "Get a message to him. Bid him meet us at North Hamtun. 'Tis a central spot between the king and the Northlands, and should we come to battle there, our own lands, Mercia and the North Humbria, will be spared. Call him to North Hamtun."

A glance passed between them. "You cannot mean North Hamtun, Morcar," Siward Bearn said with a twisted, puzzled smile. "Edwin is south of Billings Leigh now, and to meet with you at North Hamtun, he would have to leave behind the men of Nottingham, Deoraby, and Lindcylene. He never could move north fast enough to collect them all and still make North Hamtun in a reasonable time!"

"I will call the men of those shires!" I declared firmly. Both stared at me open-mouthed as if I had taken leave of my senses.

"Those are men who answer Edwin's call," Ealdread said after a little while. "They are sworn to the Earl of Mercia!"

I threw my shoulders back and narrowed my eyes. "They are men sworn to the House of Leofric, and you know it!" I said, wondering where my confidence came from. "Methinks they would answer the call of Morcar Ælfgar's son."

Siward Bearn eyed his brother. "What think you?"

Shrugging, Ealdread looked past us to the droning busyness of the men. "I think that if they answered Morcar's call, we would have the greater half of Angland fused under one banner. "

"Plus the Welsh," I added meaningfully.

"Plus the Welsh," he repeated. Suddenly Siward Bearn broke into a great, gleaming grin.

"By God! That is as like to one earldom as two could be," he agreed, "that each would answer the call of the other's earl!"

There was no hiding his excitement and, suddenly, Ealdread and I were caught up in it, too. Within a quarter hour we had dispatched the message, and another to Oswulf as well. Siward rode back to my lodge with me, where I washed well and let him lace a leathern under-coat over my clean, linen tunic. He twisted my hair and tied it before he slipped the heavy metal hauberk over my head. Once it was on me and adjusted, I let my locks down again, remembering how impressive my father always had looked, riding into the wind with his hair free. After strapping on two knife-belts, I reached for my sword and unsheathed it. While Siward buckled the girth to me, I handled the weapon, inspecting its glinting silver heaviness. "ÆLFGAR" was engraved along the well-honed blade, for it was the one that had been my father's. When I took up the North Humbria, I thought, I would have a sword-minter add the letters to make it read "ÆLFGAR'S SON" and engrave it with my own name on the other side. It was a fine piece of work. When my kinsman had finished with me, I sheathed it and took his shoulders.

"Already you are my best man, Siward Bearn," I told him, staring straight into the deep grey boldness of his eyes, "but no doubt you will take more pleasure in it when you can call yourself an earl's man."

"I take pleasure enough in reclaiming what was taken from me, holdings and homelands," he answered, "and in seeing you claim what should never have gone to the murdering usurper, Tostig!"

We walked together to the stabling barn. I was surprised to see the mount he had chosen for me: a tall, red stallion decked flashingly in the North Humbrian way, rich plates of linked silver at his throat and flanks, his mane and tail braided with beads and gold-cloth strappings. He was skirted in embossed leathers riveted with silver and the sight was enough to blind a man. I looked questioningly at my cousin.

"It would do well for them to see something North Humbrian about you," he shrugged, "and you have not time to grow a beard!"

Laughing, I mounted. A stabler handed up my helmet, hooking it to the saddle-side by its mail lining. Then he lifted the shield girth up to me, and I hung it over the back of my shoulder. He attached the shield twice, once there and again at the horse's breeching. After he had done the same for Siward Bearn, we rode out.

The men who had been gathered on the banks, mounted now and splendid in their arms, rode to meet us and we paraded all through Ceaster before striking out on the Water Gate Street. No finer sight ever was than that of a shining army, and we were well-cheered and greeted both in the city and on the folk-ways. Messengers went ahead of us with my call to arms, and in town after town the Mercian men joined with us. By the end of the five days' march, when North Hamtun was close before us, we were a formidable array.

*   *   *

I remember thinking, when Edwin marched his army into the environs of North Hamtun from the southwest, how incredibly fine he looked and how immense and impressive was his huge force. As I pondered with awe the effect of it, Siward Bearn reined in close to me.

"They almost look as proud and fearsome as we do, cousin!" he cried. When my brother's line joined mine, the host stretched both sides of us as far as the eye could see.

Harold Godwine's son came later the same day, with his brothers Gyrth and Leofwine, and as many men as they had raised hastily between them. They drew up facing us, a quarter mile away. There was a long wait before they rode forward to meet with us, arms held high in salute. I could tell Harold was shaken. All his hopes that the House of Leofric had died with my father were gone.

"Speaking as King Edward's mouth, I say lay down your arms," he bellowed as he approached, "cease your ravages, and if you have some matter against a king's chosen earl, bring it forward in assembly for lawful discussion!" As he spoke his formal words he scrutinized us and it was plain he had already sized up the hopelessness of his position.

"There is nothing to discuss, Wessexman!" Siward Bearn called out, answering for me in the manner of an earl's man. "We have made our decision and it is a final one. Now all we need to know is whether the king accepts our bidding or whether we need confront him to force it."

"You have no say in the naming of earls, Bearn of Diera!" Harold's voice was cold. "Your family has held no recognized authority in a long century of generations."

"Aye, has held no hearth or homestead even, since your evil brother came to power!"

The Earl of Wessex tossed a cool smile. "If that be your grievance, voice it to the Gemot!"

"Our grievance be a far greater one than that." It was my brother who answered him, drawing boldly close and staring hard into his eyes. "Well you know it, too, Earl Harold. Yet it is not the private complaint of our house that draws men from half of Angland here. Your brother is a robber of life and land, a man who is hardly even seen north of the Humber but who rules that land senselessly through the cruelty of his fawning friends. All these men you see came to us with an election and we have upheld it. Now we ask you to take that election to the king and discover for us whether he means to recognize it. Tell him my brother is the Earl of the North Humbria. Tell him it is a thing already decided."

A great cheer went up which echoed through the field, grew to a thunder and drowned any attempt at conversation. All through it, Harold stared past Edwin, right into my eyes. I felt my defiance rising.

"What think you, Morcar Ælfgar's son," he asked finally when the tumult had subsided, "that you will be able to enforce yourself over these Northerners? It seems my brother could not do it. He is a hardened warrior and well-seasoned man while you are but—"

"A child, Wessexman?" I spoke the word harshly myself before he could say it. By the way he looked at me, I knew he deemed me callow. "It is not surfeit of years that makes a man a rightsome ruler, Godwine's son."

He made a handsome warrior, blonde, wide-shouldered, and of the age Father would have been now. He was less Saxon-looking than his brothers, his mother's Dane-blood showing in his aristocratic cut. Now he watched me impassively, and glanced down the length of our line.

"How is it that your kinsman Oswulf son of Eadwulf has not marched hither with you?" he asked sarcastically, brows knit over a tight frown. "What arrangement have you made with him—that you council while he does your murdering?"

Edwin threw his head back in laughter. "Oswulf Eadwulf's son will be here soon enough. By God! I have never seen a Wessexman anxious to meet with him before! In that you hold a distinction, king's man! But of our arrangement, one thing only have we pledged: that he will fight behind us, and that my brother will make him his under-lord, Earl of the Bernicia. That is not an unfair thing, is it?"

"Nor is it a fair thing, Earl Edwin, that he would massacre two hundred of an earl's best men!"

"Speak not about fairness, Harold of Wessex!" I cried impulsively. "It is a subject best not touched upon between your house and ours!"

His look hardened. "This is what you bid me tell the king, then? That you have determined to rebel and that you will not come to any terms but battle if he does not accede?"

"Nay! One demand more," my brother declared firmly, "and that be the banishment of Tostig Godwine's son from the kingdom, for gross crimes and murder!"

"Pah!" Harold tossed his brothers a smug and knowing smile.

The youngest brother, long-nosed Gyrth, spoke somberly. "Take caution that you confuse not justice and execution with crime and murder, as you have excused your own crime and murder in Eorforwic as justice and execution!"

Edwin pulled himself to his full height, eyes glinting with bitterness. "Describe to your brother the difference in meanings when you go back to him," he said angrily. "Then let him swear to you on the relics under which name my father's death might be captioned!"

"That is the charge you wish to level then?" Harold asked, glancing back and forth from my brother to me.

"Nay. On that murder at least he covered himself well!" cried Siward Bearn, grey eyes flashing. "We lay to him the murders of Gamel, son of Orm, and Ulf Dolfin's son, slain in Tostig's own lodges, while under his pledge of safety. High-born men, these, and their deaths can be attested."

"Pray you have your facts right, North Humbrian!" hissed the Earl of Wessex.

"There lies not our worry," Edwin insisted. With a gesture to the great crowd of men behind him, he added, "It would do you well to ride swift with this message, though, and return swifter with your proclamation. Here sit half the fighting men of all Angland, in war-mood. No one knows better than you, I am certain, the hazards of quartering such a force, or of keeping them satisfied in idleness."

"Can it be you follow not your father in his love of blood and plunder?" asked Harold in mock surprise. "So nearly you are like him in everything else, Earl Edwin—the look and sound of you even."

Edwin threw him a furious glance, "Aye! I am more alike to him than you can know, Wessexman, and my brother with me. Toy with us more and it will be your undoing!"

He might have said more but I silenced him with an outstretched arm and turned a hard gaze on Harold. "Now you know our terms, king's man, and out of mercy to this pretty shire be quick to bring them to the king. We are not so hard that we will not listen to his answer, but tell him this: that he wastes precious time if he sends you back with any proposal which suggests even the remotest possibility of your brother's reinstatement. To that we will not yield. If he agrees to our demands, he will count North Humbrians amongst the finest and truest of his subjects. He will see what loyal men they can be, lorded gently and well by a ruler of their own choice." I paused.

"Fair words, Morcar Ælfgar's son," said Harold, glaring.

"Yet I am not finished," I told him, letting my voice grow louder and more insistent, "for I need you must tell him also that if he attempts to force Tostig back upon us, then we will deal with him as an enemy."

Saying this, I reined my horse around, heading back to the main line of men from which we had separated ourselves, my right arm raised high over my head, fist clenched in determination. The sight of that started another roar of salute and it fired me so that I broke my horse into a trot and rode back and forth in front of them, spurring them into powerful crescendo. I realized suddenly that what they were shouting was my name, "Morcar! Morcar!" over and over, as if it were a battle cry, and I flushed with pleasure and excitement. By the time I drew up alongside my brother again, Harold and his party were half-way cross the field to their own contingent, the sound of my name still ringing through the vale.

*   *   *

We camped that night as we had before, ready to spring to arms, and even more alert because Harold left his army behind him. In the distance, we could see their blazing bonfires, while the light of the hundreds of ours put a red glow in the air all around us. It was fast growing chill now, and the night wind was shrill and whipping. The day's confrontation had given us all to suppose we were assured of blood-less victory, so spirits were high. That night, I kept company with my brother and Siward Bearn and Ealdred. The moon was large. All the while we talked, my eyes wandered off towards it, as if it had some special power to attract me.

A week had passed since we had left Ceaster and in all that time the great press of activity had kept me from dwelling on what had occurred in my drunkenness. The great increase in sin I had made by not forsaking Briana hung over me like a weight but I had not felt of its crushing yet. I numbed myself to it. I had to, it frighted me so. We had been called to move with such haste that there was no time to hear the Mass, and I had actually been relieved. It would have embarrassed me not to take Eucharist. Uncle Leofric always told me sin would sear my conscience, and it must indeed have done so, that I could ride willingly off to uncertainty in such a spiritual state. I had not even kept one day's full fast in the eight days since my confession, but had managed to heap sins of looseness and drunkenness atop the unresolved one. I shivered now, and it was not from cold.

I had refused to make a fare-well to her, though she had come out with my sister and the other ladies to the manor-gate. Armed and mounted, I had bent to Aldgyth's kiss but would not suffer myself to turn Briana's way. I turned back as I rode, though, and saw her small frame, bent as with sorrow, making a meek retreat. A pang shot through me. It was not the stabbing shame I had felt the first time, just a vague, intan-gible regret—and another surge of longing for her. I was hardening. God save me! I would confess, and soon. It would be easier now. I would be moving back to my own household and distance would work its cure. Surely I was strong enough to put her aside, I told myself, and would never have tumbled with her last time had it not been for the drink. Unbidden, details of that night rose to assail me. Still staring at the luminescent moon, I found myself wondering if I had managed to please her in my mindlessness. In truth, I could remember little of it.

"Cousin!" It was Siward Bearn. "If it intrigues you so, share what you are thinking!"

Pulling my gaze from the heavens to his inquisitive face, I felt myself burn scarlet with a heat more intense than the crackling fire. Not Siward Bearn! Of all people in the world, he was the one I should most like not to know of it.

*   *   *

Late in the noon of the next day, Oswulf came. His gleaming eyes had an odd look to them, half glinting and half glazed; my brother called it battle fever. Leaving all his men but four with the North Humbrians who were spread out along the river, he came to where we were camped to take some provender with us. Like an earl's man he greeted me, grasping my shoulders, and though I had thought it would be a hard thing to look him in the eye, it was not. He was one man to whom I did not feel guilty about lying.

"How is it that this country-side is yet only little scarred?" he asked me accusingly, sitting at the fire. There was greed in his voice, and I shot him a look of poison.

Before I could make an answer, Edwin stood and spoke firmly. "Best you would not set your heart on any treasure from this district, cousin!"

Oswulf's features lit in mirth and he threw his head back and laughed. "It is not treasure I crave, Edwin Ælfgar's son—only women! I think to take me some, at least, and give you mighty thanks for reserving them for me!" He had been helped off with his hauberk and, after rolling it, put it down like a pillow and leant back on it, hands behind his head.

"Keep yourself clean!" I said harshly. "In a fortnight's time you will be home to your lady, will you not?"

"A fortnight is a long time, cousin," he answered, "and besides, seems my lady oft yields too easily. I long again for a rough and meaningful fight."

Siward Bearn had risen and walked away, and I made as if to follow him, kicking as if by accident into Oswulf's ribs as I passed by and then apologizing for it.

"He is going to bring dishonor on us," Siward mused when we had gone a little way. "I can see it in his eyes."

"Surely he had his fill of rape and plunder in Eorforwic, to hear the Wessexman tell!"

"Nay. His army did no burning there and had little time for women or drink, fast as they were forced to settle and march to meet us. Seems as if Oswulf has waited all his twenty-four years for a chance to let his turbulence run free like this. He is a violent man by nature, you know as much."

Glumly, I was forced to agree.

The next fore-noon, Oswulf came to us mounted and armed, a stunning sight. He rode proudly through the whole camp, stirring the assembled men to realize his intent, then brought himself to the very brink of the spot where my brother and I sat with our guards. Jumping to his feet, Edwin, with an ice in his eye, commanded him to dismount. "Sit with us a spell, Oswulf Eadwulf's son, and your fire."

"Nay, cousin!" Oswulf's voice was cold and willful. "I have held my

Bernicians still long as I can or care to. Yet, I invite you to sport with us!"

Edwin spat full upon him, and my kinsman reared his horse back, burning with indignation. The fire-light in his eyes was strong. "Make not of this a quarrel between us, sons of Ælfgar! I have sworn my armies to you but they insist on the normal privileges of war. 'Tis only fair, and you cannot deny it, else you will be hard-pressed to hold them."

Reining his horse, he was about to ride off through the crowd that had gathered round us but, stopping, he threw Edwin an arrogant glance of contempt. "'Tis spoken all over the kingdom you are a manly man, Edwin. I trow this is not deception?"

Quivering with rage my brother leapt at him, but his Welshmen helped me hold him back.

My cousin took about a hundred men with him. That first night saw no sign of fire, but nearing to dawn, there was much commotion as more men, mostly from the North Humbrian contingents, saddled and armed themselves. As the day wore on, pillars of smoke were spotted here and there. Edwin sat mounted all day, riding through the camp to urge men to keep their place. Siward Bearn and his brother and I did the same. By nightfall, the town had been torched, though, and then there was no holding on to them. A full quarter came and went at will. Huddled morosely around our fire, fully armed and wrapped in furs against an exceeding brisk night, we were assailed by the boisterous sounds of ravaging which carried on the wind, and the noisome unrest of the camp itself. Daffydd, Ywen, and Hwell spoke softly amongst themselves in Welsh. Ealdread honed his sword with sand-rock. Siward Bearn lay flat, staring at the stars, and Edwin, for some ungodly reason, sang country tunes, staring blankly into the fire.

"It wears on me!" I cried suddenly, jumping to my feet, startling them all as I did so. I called out for a horse.

"Seems it is not the best-made night for riding out alone," my brother told me mournfully.

"Come with me, then," I said, and he agreed to do it. We pledged to our men we would not ride far so they would have no need to fear our safety. Once we had stepped our mounts carefully through the men, we took to breathless, wild racing. Starting at the river bank we galloped a great circle back to it, knowing it was dangerous to ride thusly in a dark, uneven field. It was something we needed to do. The very instant we pulled to a halt, we began laughing together.

"Brother—" I started when we had quieted and he looked at me questioningly. I meant at that moment to tell him about Briana, about what had passed between us, but found I could not. He waited in silence and all that while I wondered if he had ever had a woman. It never

occurred to me before that we could have kept such a thing secret from
each other.

"Well?" he asked, after some time.

"'Tis nothing."

After that we rode slowly until the sharp air began to gnaw at us.
Then we headed back, our eyes riveted to the flashing orange glow and
billowing smoke of the eastern sky.

"North Hamtun is where the holdings of Copsige Sword-Stinger
are," Edwin said suddenly. "That is why he tramples there with such a
vengeance! His men say he was raged even to madness when he did not
find that man in Eorforwic.

"What exactly is his blood feud with the man?"

"What is a blood feud ever?" he replid. "Oswulf is a man who craves
power and he knows the Bernicia is rightfully his. Tostig gave it to the
Sword-Stinger, so it is Copsige that Oswulf swears against. Besides," he
added darkly, "'tis said there is a matter of a woman between them."

I groaned. "That I can believe!" I cried, as if it pained me. Edwin
laughed.

When we reentered the encampment, it was full late. Men sprawled
on the ground in sleep while fires smoldered to ember. With any who
recognized us and came to make greeting, Edwin tossed words with
good-humored mildness, as if each nameless face were a friend dear to
him. The men of Mercia idolized him, there could be no mistaking it.
None of their ranks had been made thinner by men running to plunder.

Edwin's select-guard and the warriors who hoped to serve as mine
when I made my choices had closed a great, tight circle around the
clearing in the center of the camp where my brother and I quartered
with the Bearn and our other chief men. We dismounted at that line and
gave our horses over to willing men for rubbing and care. It took us a
long time to walk those last twenty yards or so, for all the men knew us
and as we strode forward, it was in and out of men's conversations we
went, always with a greeting or word of encouragement. Our bonfire had
been kept stoked against the chill. Siward Bearn, his long form
outstretched, slept near it, face down, head cradled in the pillow of his
crossed arms; near him, Ealdread snored under a heavy fur mantle. The
Welshmen slept further back, seemingly immune to the breeze.

I judged it was near to the mid-of-night, but sleep was nowhere close
to claiming me. I sat down heavily, arms around my knees. Watching
Edwin unlace his leathern hauberk, I was struck again by how much he
resembled my father. Even Harold Godwine's son had remarked on it.
Darker of hair and eye but with features and manner near identical, he
stretched and moved in just the same way, and in the firelight he could

have passed for him. I still missed Ælfgar with a panging ache and thinking of him made me wonder if I hated Tostig Godwine's son as much as Oswulf hated Copsige—wondered if I would rush to slay him, given the chance.

Settling down on a pile of furs, my brother pulled his mantle tight and lay on his side, facing me. "It irks me, brother, to think that Gospatrick is a kinsman of ours! Even more than Tostig, he is the man I think I would kill if I had a means to." His voice was very sleepy.

"It seems to me that always when you are groggy or hazed you read my thoughts best, Edwin," I smiled, inching closer to the warmth. "That Gospatrick could choose to side with Tostig is a grievance, but I doubt he murdered Burchard. That to me still seems Tostig's idle boast. What think you?"

"I do not think—not on those things. Not any more." Sometimes a cold vehemence came into Edwin's voice and that, too, was just like father's. I could tell by his breathing that he was fast slipping into sleep. When I asked my next question he answered with an impatient groan. After that, I did not hear from him more.

I settled back, stiff in my leathern hauberk, resting my head against my metal one. The grass was cold and dew-soaked. I contemplated lying on a pile of furs the way Edwin did, but noticed none of the Northerners slept that way. The truth of it was, field life was distressing to me. I was not entirely at ease sleeping under the sky and would have preferred a timber floor to open ground, and the eye-biting smoke of a hall to the nipping wind. I wondered if other men around me were as uncomfortable as I was and, if so, why they looked so peaceful and easy laid out in sleep.

Far down the river, a series of shouts broke out. I strained to understand the fracas, but it was quelled almost immediately. In the distance, shouts and shrieks erupted now and again and, as I listened, I grew aware of the sound of a horse's hooves, not far, and the stirring and jostling of men letting someone pass. There were few men the select-guard would have let through like that. I knew it had to be Oswulf.

I could barely see him when he came in at the clearing but I rose to meet him straight-away, that he might not waken the others. Weak from fatigue or drink or the combination, he could hardly sit his mount. He trembled and held himself in the saddle an exceeding strange way.

"I have no quarrel with your brother or with you, Morcar Ælfgar's son," he said in a thick voice when I was close enough to hear him. "Help me down, cousin, I bring you a peace offering!"

He nearly toppled off and then I could see he was not alone. A woman rode pressed tight to him under his mantle, a frightened thing with no head-dress and no shoes. The instant he loosened his grip on her, she slid forward, clinging desperately to the horse's neck. Putting my arms around Oswulf's waist, I pulled him down, trying to stand him up but he was so far beyond balance it was hopeless. Holding the reins so the animal would not bolt, I laid Oswulf out on the grass, not even gently, then reached up to aid the lady. She struggled, slid from my grasp and fell to her knees, face in hands, sobbing. Putting my hand under her chin, I lifted her eyes to mine. She was a miserable, tiny, fragile thing no more than fourteen years old, shuddering through and through as with fever. Unbrooching my mantle, I put it around her shoulders and brought her gently to her feet.

"See to it Edwin gets his turn, cousin!" Oswulf Eadwulf's son grunted as I led her past him to the fire. Then he groaned and lapsed into senselessness.

Where it hurts a man most, that is where I kicked him.

CHAPTER TWENTY-SEVEN

There came Earl Harold to meet them, and they charged him with a mission to King Edward, to request that they might have Morcar as their earl. This the king granted.

—Anglo Saxon Chronicle
Book "E" 1065

October 27 – 28, 1065

Reports came to us in the morning that the destruction had now spread beyond the North Hamtun Shire into the surroundings of Huntandun. To the northeast, we could see cropfields in flame. Every manor, from where we stood to the edge of the fen-land, had been wasted. All we could do now was hope that Harold would come soon with an answer to our demands.

When Oswulf had not stirred by twilight, Siward Bearn went to check and found him cold and dim-breathed. Priests were called, and they looked him well over, even taking off his hauberk and tunic. Except for human bites on his wrists and neck, he was unwounded. Then they checked his head for cracks or bruises and listened with their ears on his chest. He was not injured, they told us, but stunned. He stayed that way well into the night. Long after we had sent his peace-offering girl off to Peterborough for succoring, he finally came to consciousness. It took him a good hour to remember where he was and why he came there. He did not seem to recall his ravages of the night before and was surprised to find himself so bruised, aching, haze-headed, and sick. As for me, I enjoyed seeing him weak for once, and it was, in truth, a blessing, for it kept him in the camp where we could quell his furies.

By the second day he was civil. When I asked if he planned on confessing, he tossed his ashen-streaked locks back and laughed with a passion. "You need sins of your own, Morcar, that you will not need to worry about mine!"

"What? Think you I am sinless?" I asked, but I could not look in his eye to say it.

Musing thoughtfully, he looked away as if his words were hard to utter. "If ever there comes a quarrel between us, Ælfgar's son, I did not mean to put it there. Methinks there is a demon in my brain."

"Aye!" I agreed whole-heartedly. "I have felt of it, cousin!"

"It makes me a hard man to read. Think you, Morcar, you can read me?"

"Nay. You perplex me."

"That is why I am a stranger to every man. No man, even a favored cousin, can read me!" For a moment it seemed the idea pained him, but he soon broke into a gleaming, broad grin. "Surely you did not, kinsman! I did not bring that girl-prize to tempt or wound you, but to say that so akin we are that I would gladly share a woman with you."

I drew away so fast I startled him. Despite my realizing he could not have known, his words shook me so that even hearing his genuine laughter did not calm my spirits. I slept that night with a gnawing discomfort.

The white milk fog of morning was so chill I could see the messenger's breath as he reported Harold Godwine's son's return. Learning of the wild harrying of the shire, the Earl of Wessex had ridden all night. While the men decked our horses, we helped each other into arms. Like Edwin, I let a priest do a shaving on me; Siward Bearn and Oswulf found much mirth in that, teasing me for my Mercian ways.

Minutes later, we waited solemnly while Harold, accompanied only by his brothers Gyrth and Leofwine, crossed the field slowly beneath the royal standard. We had chosen not to ride out to meet them so that Oswulf, the Bearn, and our select-guard could hear what passed between us. Harold was tight-lipped and grim as he approached. "Seems you are a man well-loved in this kingdom, Morcar Ælfgar's son," he said with somewhat less than his usual degree of sarcasm.

"Perhaps less popular in the North Hamtun Shire than elsewhere, now!" added Leofwine coldly.

Harold stilled him with a weary gesture. "Long and hard have we councilled at the Ox Ford," he said, "and I can tell you the king has been well-minded to chastise your insolence with the edge of a sword. Even so, though no man alive now can be blamed for them, the long-ago murders of Earl Eadwulf, Æthelgar Bearn, Earl Uhtred, and your forebears, Sigeferth and Morcar, were base and unfair, and have made men in the north predisposed to right those wrongs by raising your bloodline once more to power there. The king sees the support strong behind you and agrees that such an insurrection would be a hard one to put down, as well you have calculated, especially as the winter approaches. So it is that, speaking as King's mouth, I call you Morcar, Earl of the North Humbria."

The resounding bellow that rose at the sound of those words cannot be described. It carried through the lines like the noise of a storm at sea, gathering momentum until it shook the dale. As the din subsided, Edwin stepped his horse to the Earl of Wessex, "Declare unto the king from us we see it no humiliation to him to yield to demands so squarely backed as ours," he said. His look bespoke satisfied victory but not surprise. "His was the wisest recourse surely. All the kingdom will agree he has done right."

Harold's voice was harsh. "It is not right or wrong we speak of in this matter, Edwin Ælfgar's son, but peace or war. It is not in my heart, at least, to watch Wessex and the East Anglia make battle on Mercia and the north-lands."

"Nor in ours, surely!" I cried emphatically. "With armed force we have demanded release from an intolerable injustice. We have sought only to right a grievous wrong done on the North and felt sorely there. Surely you have marked we made no move for a separate kingship nor stirred our men's imaginations to that! Always it has been our desire to remain faithful subjects and so we bade you tell the king such!"

"I told him all your words, Mercian! It seems I should call you North Humbrian now," he added with a rueful smile. "But, in truth, you always will be Mercian, will you not? Only with more lands to sit upon!"

I glared at him, unable to help myself. "I will be more of a North Humbrian than ever your brother was, I trow! I will make my home there, as folk of my mother's blood did for generations and which thing Tostig has never done!"

"Dare you stray too far from your brother?" asked Gyrth Godwine's son of me, with a daring tone. "So like-minded are you in your treason it would be wise for you to perch close!"

"I am minded to still you!" Edwin hissed, glaring full upon him. "Only blood-letting I will not do when king's men all sit together under a royal banner. Our quarrel never has been with you, Earl Gyrth, though it might have been when you took the Anglia after it was promised to our house."

"After your father broke the lastingness of that pledge by his dealings with Cymrian traitors!" shouted Leofwine, fired in his brother's behalf—and his own, for he had taken a part of that earldom, as well.

"Never made we a quarrel of that," my brother went on, as if he had not heard, "nor of a thousand other wrongs. I trust you know well enough what they were. In this matter, though, our hand was forced. By his crimes and misdeeds, your brother Tostig himself forced it, until the men of two great earldoms all hungered for avengement on him. Only then did it come to this." Gesturing across the fading grasslands of the smoke-rimmed dale, he brought their eyes to the signs of the harrying and waste that surrounded us.

Harold gazed impassively around, then said, "These lands you have sorely mistreated, and the king decrees you will not have them, sons of Ælfgar."

"These were Mercian lands before—" I began.

"It makes no matter. He has given you the north at your bidding, but these two shires which you have ruined will go to another; he will not suffer you to have them."

As we talked, we had ridden slowly further afield with Harold, out of our men's hearing, but now I noticed he was looking past me to where Oswulf stood anext Siward Bearn in the line of guardsmen. I hoped he would not call him over; I was afraid my cousin's temper would bring us dishonor. "If you mean to heap rebuke on Oswulf Eadwulf's son," I told him honestly, "best lower your tone, or trust to Providence!"

Harold's eyes narrowed; he spoke in a whisper. "Here is the king's way of warning you to choose carefully your earl's men, Morcar Ælfgar's son: he gives these shires to Waltheof, son of the man who murdered your kinsman Oswulf's father!"

"Waltheof Siward's son has no claim!" Edwin's voice momentarily betrayed his bitterness. "These were Mercian lands till your father borrowed them to gift upon your worthless nithing brother, now dead and condemned."

Harold looked like he meant to answer harshly but thought the better of it. "Waltheof does have a claim," he said smugly, ignoring the remark about Sweyn, "the claim of king's gift. He has stayed loyal to the king and not supported your adventure here. King Edward thusly thinks to reward him. I let you be the one to break this news to Oswulf, though. Mayhap you are not as grieved as other men by his foul temper."

At the same moment, Edwin and I made a noise of disgust. It had not suprised us that Waltheof had denied us his support; could be he had hoped the king would gift him with the entire North Humbria, against all odds. Harold looked from one to the other of us with a look fast hardening. "If as you say you are loyal men of the king, then you would not want to argue King Edward's right to make land gifts, would you?"

"Nay!" said Edwin in sudden lighter tone. "If 'tis what it takes to pacify the king, let Waltheof keep the holdings stolen from my grandfather. Could be he has not the sins of his murdering father and will do right by them."

"Such as they are," said Harold darkly, "now that you have finished with them!"

"Aye. Such as they are," I repeated, looking past him to the blackened waste.

Then Harold reined his horse sideways, cutting us off from his own brothers' view. His rugged face looked sincere as he sat, outlined by his yellow hair against the clouded sky. "I trow you will mark I have not councilled harshly against you. You have said things fair and well-considered and those things have I taken to heart. Where truth was in your argument, I stressed it as such to the king. Though it grieved him, he has come to see Tostig's faults."

Narrowing my eyes, I eyed him suspiciously. "Well we know Tostig has ever been his favorite," I said. "Did King Edward agree to put him into exile?"

"He did—though it near broke his old heart. Witnesses swore to what you told me, that my brother murdered Ulf and Gamel. And after questioning his guard, we knew there was no doubt—" here he broke off suddenly and started to turn away. Edwin reached a hand forcefully onto his gilded bridle to stop him.

"What else is it you would say to us, Wessexman?"

There was a long pause while Harold collected his thoughts, drew in a deep breath, then let it out slowly. "Never was there great love between your father and myself, you know that surely. But ..." here he stopped again. I saw that he clenched his reins in tight fists, knuckles whitened with effort. When he spoke again, his words were hurried and he looked away from us. "But I would have you know that when Tostig marched into the Cymry to lay execution on Earl Ælfgar, I was not at his side."

Stunned, I looked at my brother. "Can it be he has told the truth about that night?" Edwin asked in a strangled tone. "Before the king and you?"

"Not only told but boasted it," came the rueful answer, "Even now, Tostig is shipbound for Flanders, a man robbed of might and treasure; robbed of all his brothers' affection, and even the king's."

Like myself, Siward Bearn, Ealdread, and Oswulf—who had moved close again at that moment as if by instinct—were obviously shaken by these words of long-awaited vindication. Edwin, pale with emotion, backed suddenly away and rode aimlessly into the field. I called after him. Soon as I did so, his Welshmen broke the line and rode his way, all three with looks of consternation. He turned and halted them with a gesture, signaling them back to their places. Then, in a voice forceful, loud and vehement, he shouted, "Let it be told to every man who has marched hither. Tostig, son of Godwine, has suffered his banishment! Let it be told!"

The word rumbled through the line. Harold turned away, wordlessly, and stepped his handsome horse back across the field. His brothers joined him. He sat high and tall, king's man that he was, cutting a proud figure. But he knew....

CHAPTER TWENTY-EIGHT

The North humbrians . . . maintained that, being
born and bred as free men, they could not brook
harsh treatment. . . . 'If you wish to keep us as
subjects,' they said, 'set Morcar the son of Ælfgar
over us; you will learn by that experience how
pleasantly we will obey when managed by one who
treats us fairly.' hearing this, harold . . . recalled
his forces and . . . firmly established Morcar as earl.

—William of Malmesbury

"I knew by the look of him he had long sensed his brother's guilt," I said firmly, fingering the carved bone chessman and holding it up to the fire-light to inspect the detailed fineness of it.

"You speak like a babe, cousin!" Tossing me a disdainful smile, Oswulf inched closer to the blazing hearth. "Harold said that which he knew you wanted to hear because your house sits over half of Angland suddenly and he cannot afford to have you unfriendly to his claims. He told you himself the old king is ill-worn and fast slipping since Tostig's leveling! He means to be the favorite himself now—to claim the crown when Edward passes. 'Twas useless for him to side with a man whose fate was sealed anyway, so he seized the chance to buy you with his brother's ruin. Be not fooled!"

I scrutinized him pensively, not sure what to think. There had been a genuineness to Harold's manner and I respected it, knowing how reluctant I would have been to believe such ills of my own brother. Even so, I was anxious not to misplace my trust, and Oswulf's arguments were sound.

It was more than a fortnight since we had marched our men out of the ruins of North Hamtun and Huntandun. Here in the Lindcylene Shire, we had sent most of the North Humbrians on ahead and now we waited for our households to come from Ceaster and meet with us at Edwin's vast estate in Kirton. All those who liked to foretell weather by

river-sign and sky-omen had been proven right so far: the blasting bitterness of the early December air promised the hardest winter in years.
Even now, lying on thick furs in my brother's chamber, I felt the chill,
more pronounced because I was on my third day of a full fast and not
much enjoying it. Edwin and I had detoured through Peterborough on
our homeward trek to visit my uncle there and take his blessing.

Where I had gotten the courage to confess to him, I cannot say. His
voice sounded strained as he upheld the other priest's penance for me,
adding to it severe admonitions which truly cut me hard. I wept while I
spoke to him. It was good to know I was clean again, though I wore a
wool shirt now and would have to wear it through the summer.

"Of you, in particular, this was not to be expected, Morcar!" Abbot
Leofric told me severely. "Let your repentance be lasting, that you do
not live and die with the self-same sin, as many men do!"

I assured him I was done with it and took my penance gladly. Being
cleansed made it somewhat easier for me to be in Oswulf's constant
company. I had waxed uneasy in his presence ever since the strange
remark about sharing a woman with me. Now he seemed almost agreeable. After his furious tantrum over the election of Waltheof Siward's
son had subsided, my cousin had lapsed into an unusual state of level
temper. He was glad, I suppose, that Siward the Usurper's son was given
only the tiny mock-earldom of Huntandon, instead of the Bernicia or
even the whole of North Humbria.

More than ever, though, I continued to despise him when he over-
drank. Then his violent rantings waxed unbearable: grossly detailed
plans for taking revenge against the men he hated most—Waltheof was
one, and Copsige Sword-Stinger another. I could not see how a man,
especially my own kinsman, could delight so in the prospect of murder
and mutilation. Perhaps he had handed away enough of it that it did not
bother him any more. The tales that came back to us of his dealings in
North Hamtun, the amount of blood-letting and carnage he had put
himself to there, were sickening. It was always a relief to me when he
finally slipped from ferociousness to stupor; his pain when he came out
of it made him put off drinking, and we would be assured of his good
humor for a while.

Clear-headed, though, he often shared impressive insights. I puzzled
over his last words an exceeding long time while I watched Siward
Bearn play at chess with my brother. Could be there was truth in what
he said, but it still seemed to me that the look in Harold's eye that
morning had spoken of more than ambition. It was the look of a man
who had been cheated by his own willingness to trust. Still, I already
had decided not to say more. The trick in handling my cousin, I had

found, was not to labor a point. Once fired, it was hard to douse him.

It was Edwin who broke the long silence, pushing away from his game and lowering himself to the fur-strewn floor. "'Tis a bitter season for moving households," he declared with a genuine shiver. "Aldgyth and the other ladies will come to us half frozen, I trow."

"Mine always is half frozen!" Oswulf replied with a short laugh. Both Siward Bearn and I shot him a hard look and for once it silenced him. Ywen Carr's son, who had been quiet till now, spoke up from his shadowy corner, a mean remark in Welsh concerning Oswulf's rudeness. I smiled inwardly, thinking how wroth my cousin would have been had he heard it, but he did not. He was listening intently to an invitation from his brother-in-law.

"Bold as the north air waxes," Siward Bearn was saying, "I fear you will not make the Bernicia until the thaws—not with your household in tow, anyway. Dunholme is a trying distance away and though you would like to be there, mayhap you should plan to winter-quarter with us at Eorforwic."

He looked at me, hoping I would second his offer. The Bearn, for the first time in years, was feeling a modicum of friendship towards his kinsman and was hoping to seal it. Also, I knew he was genuinely worried for his sister's health and safety. Even so, I ignored him, hoping the conversation would take a more comforting turn. I would not risk having Lady Briana there in my daily presence.

"How long does it take to put those hoops through an ear?" I asked suddenly, knowing it would please and distract him. He broke into one of his beaming, broad grins.

"'Tis not a long process, cousin, but a man should be well-aled before he lets himself be led into it."

"Let us start then. I am thirsting, anyway!"

Every one of them stared at me, astonished.

"Madness, Morcar!" My brother spat, but Siward Bearn was elated, I could tell. Jumping to my feet, I went to the doorway that led into the main hall and ordered some men sitting at the fire there to send for honey-mead.

When I returned, Oswulf suddenly sat upright and cast me an approving look. His eyes danced but he spoke solemnly, "You can start your drinking in here, cousin, but your North Humbrian men will feel sore cheated if they do not get to watch you take your studs!"

Siward Bearn nodded an agreement. "In the North, 'tis a ceremony, always shared," he said firmly. "A man gains a true respect for another when he helps him to go through it."

For a moment, I wavered. "It is truly painful, then?"

"Nay, the first stab only," Oswulf answered. I began to regret my rashness.

"You are not the man to tell him about it, Oswulf Eadwulf's son!" Siward Bearn laughed, hands on his hips. "You would not remember the initial stab even, so grossly were you stupored!" Looking back at me, he added, "Some half-day later he wakened on the high table in the great hall, with rings in both his ears and scabs on his arms and shoulders—mad as the very devil and screaming for avengement!"

"What mean you … scabs?" I asked, feeling very weak. Suddenly, I suspected the answer; the sight of the blue and purple burn-scars winding like bracelets around Oswulf's wrists had brought it to me.

Nodding his head so emphatically that his red locks flew, Siward Bearn spoke insistently. "You must do it all at once, Morcar, pictures and piercings! It is the only way."

I groaned. "I have no need of pictures on me, kinsman. Stretch out my ears and let me grow my hair; that is enough! Indeed, there is no need of the pictures!" Without realizing it, I had begun backing away. Siward put an arm around my shoulder and gazed at me levelly.

"You are Earl of the North Humbrians," he said, "and that is need enough." Dropping his mantle, he opened the neck of his dalmatic and began unlacing the tunic underneath. When it was loosened, he pulled it down far enough to reveal an intricate pattern of burnings, like a chain of small stars and flowers, which stretched straight across his collar bone in a double row from shoulder to shoulder. Even the normally impassive Welshmen drew near to eye it, obviously impressed. Edwin shot me a glance of frantic sympathy.

Oswulf touched the middle of my chest at a point only slightly above my breast. "A goodly star, right here!" he said, as if it were a thing already decided. "You want it to be where it will show through an open shift, so a woman can finger it and marvel on it while you try to convince her!"

"Osbeorn Dolfin's son will do it," Siward Bearn added, naming one of the first North Humbrians I had chosen for a guardsman. "He has a monk's touch, and is forever whittling new designs in green birch twigs." Then he sent for him.

I felt a nauseous but happily, at that very moment, some kitcheners came bearing pails of mead and strap-hung horn goblets. I took the largest of these quickly and, dipping it full to the brim, commenced immediately upon quelling my fears. "I hope you will drink with me, brother!" I said to Edwin, pleading for his support in this wild undertaking.

With a short sigh of resignation, he dipped his horn, too, and holding it high above his head, whispered purposefully, "To Morcar

Ælfgar's son, Earl of the North Humbria!" He drank it down without coming up for air, then saluted me again in exactly the same way. The third time he did it, his grin was big enough to catch a hare.

The other six of us were soon gaining on him. After a while, we became vaguely aware of the rumbling commotion of men coming into the great hall, and soon Gamel-Beorn Gamel's son, entered to fetch us all to table. Seeing what was afoot, he stayed. In a very short time, those few of us in the earl's chamber were making three times the noise of all the men in the adjoining room. I am sorry to say I was singing again—my crazy mindless songs, a thing I cannot seem to resist doing when my brain is overcome.

After board was cleared, we burst into that hall where three dozen guardsmen, newly sworn to me, and as many of Edwin's men or more, sat waiting for us. We were not the picture of stateliness and bearing one would expect from two of the greatest earls of the realm and their closest men.

Osbeorn Dolfin's son, brother to the murdered Ulf Dolfin's son and uncle to my man, Heard Ulf's son, entered with a pile of scrawny sticks and a bucket of water. A great murmur went up amongst the North Humbrians, who realized suddenly what was about to happen. They all gathered closer around the head table where we sat, while Edwin's Mercian men buzzed with amusement.

Somewhat confused, I watched the brawny, gold-haired guardsman climb onto our table, seating himself cross-legged at the head of it. Someone handed up the bucket and he placed it anext himself, along with a strange, narrow-bladed knife, which glinted cold as ice.

I had taken so much drink after a three-days fast that, by the time Siward Bearn pulled me to my feet and unbrooched my mantle, I had quite forgotten what the blade was supposed to mean. When he unbelted my rich, embroidered dalmatic and pulled it over my head, leaving me shivering in under-tunic and braies, I felt the nudge of panic. But it was not till they had dragged me onto the table and put me on my knees in front of Osbeorn, arms held firmly behind me, that I began to piece it all together. Then I pulled my arms free of Daffydd Carr's son's good grip, and reached for one more hornful—an act which caused a roar of merriment amongst all my new men. They must have chosen Daffydd to hold on to me because he is broader and far more powerful; in his tight grasp, I felt no blood below my elbows.

Without warning, Osbeorn took my head, turned it sideways, and plunged it into the bucket full of icy water. The shock caused my brain to reel with a frenzy. Then he lifted me out of it and pushed my head hard into his lap. There came a sudden feeling of burning warmth on my cheek and neck which contrasted strangely with the numbness of my face. As both men eased their grab on me, I raised my hand that way, and brought it to my view red and dripping with blood.

Blank and wordless with perplexion, I had no time to contemplate the mystery of it before the entire process was repeated on the other side. This time, the sensations were strong enough to bring me to the very brink of senselessness, but I remember raising my head to the sound of hearty cheers and hollers, then looking at my brother Edwin's mindless grin I laughed hysterically. The instant they freed me this time, I reached out for another helping of pain-cure—though I must admit I felt no pain. I just sat there in the middle of the narrow table, wondering what next to expect, still aware of the strange, liquid warmth on my face.

While I tried to pull my thoughts together, a man came forward with a pan of burning hot embers. which I thought exceeding strange. I watched enthralled, drinking all the while, as Osbeorn heaped little piles of powdery stuff on a small, thick plank someone had put on the table for him. I saw that some of the piles were crushed leaves or berries, but for most, he scraped charring off little sticks of burnt wood. Then he added water to the piles, drop by drop, keeping each mixture separate as he mixed it into a thick paste.

My head spun with such fervor that I hardly could focus my eyes on this activity, and I was almost unaware of my cousins, Siward Bearn and Oswulf Eadwulf's son, climbing up onto the table. Both of them were talking to me, I knew as much, but I only nodded numbly to whatever they were saying. Then they were lifting off my under-tunic and I heard Oswulf's astonished exclamation, even through my dazedness.

"A wool shirt!" he cried. "By God, you are ever an amazement to me, cousin!" Suddenly, I felt very vulnerable. I could not think why the entire hall roared with laughter.

Before I had much time to muse on it, I was on my back. Siward Bearn had put my head in his lap and crossed my arms over my face, but at the insistence of Oswulf and the other men, he sat me up and offered me another taste of mead. I tried to refuse it, but so intent was he that I gave in, practically gagging, so full I was of the stuff.

Next, he lifted a steaming hot rag, soaked in some kind of many-herbed soup. After forcing my head down again, he held it on my nose and mouth. Then followed the most curious sensation: a weightless, floating confusion almost intolerably sweet. The noise of the room dimmed near to nothingness, then waxed and waned with a strange, musical, droning hum which seemed to inspire pictures all around me, of the most vivid and unusual hues.

Through it all, I was aware of a pricking, teasing sensation, not entirely comfortable and yet by no means painful. Then, of a sudden, a powerful terror was upon me, inspired by the smell of burning hair and flesh. I began to struggle. Then Siward Bearn crossed my own arms harder over my face, leaning his weight over them to still me. It seemed I would surely suffocate, and feeling entirely helpless, I resigned myself to my fate.

Seemingly a lifetime later, I opened my eyes to find I was free. A good half-dozen men surrounded me, looking down with an odd combination of merriment and concern. After some amount of searching, I recognized my brother amongst them.

"Did I sleep?" I asked him, amazed that I could talk.

"For an instant, perhaps," he said with that sparkling grin of his, and it put me at an ease. Looking past him, I could see that Osbeorn Dolfin's son was only now gathering up his strange condiments. When he caught my eye on him, he flashed a grin of approval. "Well done, Lord Morcar! Not a cry nor a groan, and I have made of you an art-piece!"

I did not know exactly what he meant, but I smiled a tipsy smile back at him, asking how he did it.

"Bunting into your skin with the smoldering ends of green-sticks, then rubbing dye-pastes into the circle-burns."

He said it so matter-of-factly that the meaning did not come clear to me right away. When it did, I threw a panicked, apprehensive glance to my own bare chest, and I was sorry I did. Oozing, swollen, red, raw— it looked like anything but an art-piece! With Edwin's help, I pulled myself awkwardly to the edge of the table and lowered myself, sitting down on the bench with a moan that was less of pain than of self reproach. My brother laughed when he heard it, merry in his mead. Feeling my own spirits flagging somewhat, I thought I had better refresh them. As I reached for a cup, I found Siward Bearn holding one up to me, a look of undisguised admiration and unguarded contentment in his grey eyes.

All I remember of the rest of that night is that I sang some more, and I slept flat on my back in Edwin's chamber. My chest had taken to pulsing, and neither ear would bear the weight of my head.

*   *   *

"I do not understand this!" Aldgyth exclaimed, her reddened lips gathered into a sour frown. I fingered my ears. It was three days later and the size of them had gone down considerably though the soreness had remained constant. Osbeorn Dolfin's son had cut a neat little cross into each with his glinting, thin blade, then studded them with gold posts nearly as big around as my little finger. Now, sitting in the great hall, my sister had come over from the ladies' table to eye them disdainfully.

"What think you of this, Edwin?" she asked in an exasperated tone.

"I think I am glad to be the Earl of the Mercians," he replied, his eyes twinkling. "It requires of me only a pretty golden fillet worn round my hair."

"You should be shamed that you let him do it!" she snapped, tossing her head.

"Lady, the man enters on his twentieth year. You would be wise to see that he decrees his own actions now!" It was my cousin, making a move in my defense, but Aldgyth spun on him with decisive anger.

"You still yourself, Oswulf Eadwulf's son!" she cried.

He threw his hands up in mock defense while he flashed a daring smile her way.

"I am not so blind that I do not see your hand in this!" she added, reaching out and yanking at his tangled, ash-colored locks. He had done a surprising thing. He had let himself be shaven, and though he always was a comely man, with a clean face he was stunningly handsome. He was on his feet and over the trestle bench in one lithe movement, moving himself so close to her that she backed away. Hands on his hips, he leant down and whispered something in her ear—something that made her burn with fury. Throwing his head back, he laughed wildly as she turned and hastened away.

Edwin was beside him in a second, eyes narrowed in indignation. "Take care you be not bold with that lady, cousin!" There was no mistaking his tone, and Oswulf tossed him an innocent smile.

"Trust me, Edwin Ælfgar's son! I have my own lady here to be bold with tonight."

"Then mind your manners," my brother told him curtly as the both of them sat back down.

"That I will try to do if it means avoiding hotness with you," Oswulf said agreeably, but he added in a low, mournful tone. "I was born without resistance to fair ladies with fire and fight in them." He reached out for a mead-cup, and Siward Bearn glared at him.

"There is not the way for you to build some!" he said, but Oswulf drank it anyway.

The hall was full that night; the wives and pages and priests and children of all my household men and Oswulf's having arrived late in the noon with Siward Bearn's brother Ealdread at their head. Edwin was not stinting in his welcome; every table was well laid with repast, and he had promised to give the hall over to sleep the wedded men. They had not seen their women in six-week's time.

I looked around at the crowded merriness, still somewhat awed by the fact that this great multitude of men were sworn to but one purpose: to serve my brother and me. I had chosen a hundred and a half men for my household troops, the same number Edwin held in his service. Some of them were Mercians I had known a long while, or kinsmen like Siward Bearn, but most were North Humbrians I had chosen either on reputation or recommendation or on the willingness I sensed in them to serve me.

In addition, Oswulf, my under-earl, had a guard of nearly one hundred, mostly Bernicians and fiercely loyal to him. Many had already followed his example by shaving their faces, so despite their identical hair and garb, it was easy to tell them from the rest of the North Humbrians now. This was, I knew, my cousin's way of telling all Angland that the Bernicia was a land apart—true to the Earl of the North Humbria and sworn to his call but separate and independent of the Diera, as in old times. Oswulf had waited all his life to have it that way, thinking it the best way, I suppose, of avenging the foul murder of the father he had never known. He was in his glory now, there was no denying it, and it must have contributed a great deal to the happy humor he had exhibited of late.

As my eyes swept the length and breadth of the immense room, I spotted Briana at my sister's table, deep in converse with her. There was no longing in me for her any more, not even a stirring of it, but I still hoped she would be able to forgive me for my ill use of her. Being wedded to Oswulf, surely she understood about drunkenness. In one thing that shameful episode had served a purpose. She had told me it was my gentleness which fired her, and though I never did rightly remember how it went that night, I knew certainly I gave her no reason to respect that in me any more. I actually hoped I had left her with a distaste for me; it would make it easier all around. With Oswulf Eadwulf's son my under-earl, we would probably be thrown together time and again for years to come. It would be best if she and I could meet right now at the same conclusion about the whole, regrettable affair.

Feeling a nudge, I turned to look into my brother's pensive eyes. "Here is a thought, brother," he said, as if having carefully weighed it. "Mayhap we could send our men elsewhere and let Aldgyth take a pallet in the room with us tonight. Might be our last fair chance to be alone together for a long while!"

I was thrilled at the prospect of having time with the two of them before I took up house in Eorforwic. The pace of things had kept us from sharing any private moments of late. Feeling light of heart, I stepped into the swirling night and made my way to the weaving lodge where I knew she was quartered. Set back some way from the kitchen-hall, it was a tall, lofted, daub-and-wattle house we had always liked as children for its many rooms, small and drafty, all leading one into another with door-less arches. The loft wrapped three walls around, accessible only by ladders, and the rooms up there, hung thick with furs and skins and yardage, had no windows. Whenever Yuletide guests had came to Kirton, the looms were shoved aside and the house given over to hostelry as it was now. In summer, though, the loft was uncomfortable and was only used for drying and storing herbs. The childhood memory of the aromatic perfumes of these still haunted me, for it was usually the summer months we had spent at Kirton. Even now, pushing open the heavy framed timber door, I missed the familiar fragrances just enough to make the place seem strange to me when I smelled hearth smoke and straw instead.

The first person I saw in there was Briana.

She was standing not far inside the doorway, in her long woolen cloak with white fur all about the shoulders of it. Turning, she seemed surprised to see me. She put a finger to her lips and spoke in a pleasant, low voice, "You have come into a house of sleeping children! It is good to see you, Morcar—nay, now I should call you Earl Morcar, methinks."

"And good to see you, Lady Briana," I replied. Reading from her look that more was expected, I smiled. "Everything has turned out just as your brother promised it would."

"Aye," she whispered, looking straight in my eyes. "Only tell me this, for I have such need to know! Am I lady to two earls now, Morcar Ælfgar's son?"

Unflinching, my smile came easy, and I shook my head. "Nay, lady. It cannot be. You must surely know that!"

"Indeed. You are right, of course." Her voice was small and miserable and she looked away. "Oswulf has come home, and you must hand me over to him."

"'Twas not a seemly thing we did. You know as much."

"You regret it then?"

"Nay. I regret that I brought hurt and misery on you by my weakness, that is all." I had wanted to say that a long time and was glad it had at last come out. "I was mindless—"

"It was not your fault, Morcar. You gave me warning." She stopped a minute and turned slowly back to face me. "The first time, you know, I thought it was a sad misjudgment, but when it happened again then I believed it was a thing meant to be. Have you not considered that?"

Like a brother, I put my hands on her shoulders. My voice was gentle. "It was not meant to be, lady. It is a thing which cannot be. Both of us know it is so."

For a long time, she said nothing, only searched my face as if she might have missed some secret sign. Finally, she nodded with a wan smile. I released her, and we stood in the dimness looking at each other awhile. Strangely, the moment seemed neither awkward nor uncomfortable. I asked whether she had confessed.

"Aye, but I have need to confess again, for truly, I have only forsaken you this very minute, Morcar."

The meekness of her voice made me feel stronger. "Do you think," I asked her solemnly, "that we can pretend well enough that it never happened?"

She nodded her assent as Aldgyth started down the ladder. "You are good and gentle, Earl Morcar," she added in a whisper too soft for my sister's hearing, "and you will ever be special to me."

I smiled, then reached Aldgyth my hand, telling her our plan. It seemed to please her. When we headed out into the blasting air, I put one arm around each of them, drawing both to me as if to warm and protect them. The innocence of it felt good to me, and when we deposited Briana at the door to her husband's chamber, I felt no qualms and no regret.

Later that night, snuggled under a warm pile of furs before the hearth while the December wind cried loud miseries in the high rafters, I listened as my sister described for us her life as cwene of the Cymry. I was not as talkative as I should have been. The scabbing of my chest was cracking and falling away now and itched so intensely I could scarce forbear tearing at it. Aldgyth had not learnt about that part of my adornment yet, and I did not want her to suspect until it was prettier to see.

"'Tis time you should be thinking of marriage again," Edwin was saying to her. "It is not deemful for a lady of your birth and beauty to be without a wedded man."

"Nay. You know that cannot be, Edwin." A soft and lilting voice usually, hers was melancholy now and pain-ridden. "I would not dare give myself to any man I could not love as much—and there is no such man!"

"Not every wedding is a love match, Aldgyth!" Edwin told her, gently chiding. "Folk marry for different reasons."

"Would you have me marry for your own power, brother?"

"Nay. Not for power but for security, for peace of mind. For Nesta."

"Better for her I would have stayed in the Cymry!"

"Not so!" I interjected, thinking how lost she would have been there without Gruffydd. "Here you have kin!"

"There also I had kin."

"Of a sort, perhaps," I admitted, "but you did well to come back home."

"Methinks I had but little choice," she said listlessly, "carried away, like a spoil of bitter war. In one brother's hand the head of Gruffydd, and in the other one's hand his babe and widow."

"The sons of Godwine—did they honor you in every way?" My brother's voice was terse, but she quickly reassured him.

"Earl Harold himself served as private guard to me, and he constantly stilled his brother's evil tongue against our house—for my benefit alone I am sure. Yet his eyes on me seemed very forward."

"You must know you are a lovely creature, Aldgyth," Edwin mentioned carefully. "Your beauty will fire many a man more than Harold Godwine's son, I daresay!"

Her laugh was hollow. "You need not tease with me, brother! I have grown thin and empty—lusterless—and well I know it. I do not think I ever will be what I was."

I studied her in the firelight. True, she was thin, but it did not detract from her beauty. Her delicate face reflected our mother's fineness of feature, and her eyes danced with a depth of brilliant feeling. They were strange eyes, ever-changing like the inconstant sea, cloudy and grey, or shallow green, or glass-blue. Any man would be proud to have her, I thought—very proud.

Unexpectedly, Edwin rose from his spot on the floor and began pacing. From under my pile of furry warmth, I wondered how he could walk in braies and an untied under-tunic without shivering. Not once in the whole night had he nestled himself under coverings the way Aldgyth and I did. He must have felt my eyes on him, because he tossed me a sheepish smile as he reached for his mantle of heavy Eirish worsted. When he wrapped it carelessly around him as if to ward off a momentary chill, I knew he had fathomed my thoughts again, something which always amused me. I had read somewhat of his just then, too, and knew something weighed so heavy on him that he was uncertain whether or not to tell it. Finally, he drew in a deep breath and looked full on my sister.

"I would have you know," he said, laboring to keep his voice level, "that the Earl of Wessex came to me at North Hamtun and asked if I thought a time ever would come that you might consider a pledging from him."

Aldgyth gasped, and I sat bolt upright. "Why said you nothing of this before, brother?" I demanded.

"Because I knew not how to take it till I had questioned Aldgyth, that is why. I was not sure how to read him."

Clutching the heavy gold chain which held Gruffydd's ring around her throat, my sister let go a sobbing sound she had worked hard to suppress. "Do not let me believe you would condone this, Edwin!" she pled in a wounded whisper. "Do not let me think you could consider it!"

Sitting down suddenly on a low, wooden wall bench, as if his strength had failed him, Edwin only shrugged. "Never would I force such an issue, lady. Surely you know that."

"What said you to him, then?" she narrowed her eyes accusingly.

"That if such a time were to come, he would hear from us." He paused a long time before he added hesitantly, "Methinks there is a longing in him to make amends."

I spat into the fire and pounded my fist on the flagged floor. "That is not how some men read it!" I cried hoarsely. "Some men see right through this sudden sympathy he bears our house; this sudden craving to right things he claims he had no hand in. Oswulf Eadwulf's son says—"

"Holy Mother of God! What store ever have you put in what Oswulf Eadwulf's son says?" Edwin leapt to his feet again, eyes ablaze. "If Harold meant to buy us, seems he would have started with a lower bid than that of putting half of Angland into our hands at his own brother's expense! If the time has come to put an end to this blood-shadow which has hung over us from the cradle, think you there could be a better way than to wed the lines?"

"By God, brother, they are our enemies! Always they have been our enemies!"

He brought his voice down low and hard. "When you call yourself Ælfgar's son, remember that he had the wisdom to know when it was time to end a feud, and the courage to make a brother of an enemy!"

Aldgyth sobbed then. I reached over and stroked her gilded hair softly, trying to offer her a strength I did not really feel inside me. I remembered Harold's eyes when he talked that morning—forthright eyes. I had sensed his honesty in my heart. Why I would not admit to it now was something I could not explain. Edwin sat down again, elbows on his knees, passing his fingers unconsciously through his thick hair, the look of him bitter and disappointed.

When my sister's voice came again, it scarce seemed her own, "I will ponder on it," she said emotionlessly.

"I said I would not force it, Lady Aldgyth!" My brother's tone was sharp. "If it does your pride dishonor to think on it, then do not!"

"Best you would think somewhat about dishonor yourself!" I cried hotly. "The man murdered her husband! True, he was innocent of our father's blood, I trow, but in the other matter he has sought to claim no such blamelessness."

With a startled cry, Aldgyth reached, took my chin, and turned my face to hers in the fire-light. "Say again what you just said, Morcar. Tell me you would swear to it on relics!"

"Say what, lady?"

"That Harold Godwine's son is innocent of our father's blood! Think you that is true?"

I looked at her levelly and my voice was earnest, because I knew it was the truth. "I have no doubt of it, Aldgyth. That murder was the cause of the disgust between those brothers, and the reason Harold took our part against Tostig's in counciling the king. I have no question."

For a long time, she stared into the crackling fire, then she asked softly, "Believe you this also, Edwin?"

He bristled, scowling. "Give me honor enough to suppose I would not have mentioned any of this if I did not!"

Rising to her knees, she reached over to him, delivering a playful, gentle strike to the side of his head. "Always you have been a brat, Edwin," she said teasingly, "with a temper too bold to hold inside you!"

Slowly a smile came to him, the handsome, gleaming grin that was his alone. Standing, he pulled her to her feet and hugged her tight, mouthing some mild, whispered word.

"I will consider it, brother," she answered him. "In truth, I really will."

*   *   *

Hours later, when both of them had long been asleep, I lay flat on my back, victim of my own churning thoughts. In the next chamber, Oswulf Eadwulf's son, well-aled and tempestuous, was claiming his lady, or trying to, and the violence between them ached me with a passion. Surely it was the hand of Providence that Siward Bearn had not slept in there with us that night, or there would have had a murdering, I am sure of it.

My sore breast, pulsing and throbbing, gave me no respite and kept me from the only thing that might have brought me peace: sleep. Try as I might, I could not distract myself, and it near killed me to hear her with her man.

Thank God we had made our decision between us today, and everything had been said and sealed! Against all my will, I felt myself fired towards her again; never could I have broken with her so cleanly feeling as I did now. She would have sensed it in me, and all my protests would have been useless. Now it was finished between us, and by all that is holy, I meant to keep it that way. The one thing she must never know or even suspect was that I might have felt a hunger for her after those words had passed between us.

I knew what I had to do, and it took all my effort. Throwing off the furry pile of warmth, I made my way to Edwin's side, dropping a log on the smoldering fire as I passed. Quietly, gently, I shook him till he came to his senses, moaning and murmuring.

"I need words with you, brother!" I whispered so as not to waken Aldgyth.

"You are mad!" he choked, but he sat up right away, rubbing the sleep from his eyes like a child might do. "What is it ails you, Morcar?"

I lowered myself anext him, a heavy fur pulled tight around my shoulders. Inhaling deeply, I thought it best to tell him all of it at once, but did not know where to start. I sat there dumbly a small while till I gathered my wits enough to say, "I must ask you to favor me with a small lie!"

He looked at me curiously. Swallowing hard, I continued, trying to disguise my turmoil. "Siward Bearn bids me quarter Oswulf and his household for the winter when we come to Eorforwic." I had to stop and think ahead.

"You know how hard it would be to take his party all the way north in this bitter season—and dangerous." Edwin was yawning, with no idea what I was going to tell him.

"Aye," I answered miserably. "Only … *all* his party cannot stay with me."

"Go to sleep. You are over-taxed!"

Reaching out, I grabbed his arm, and my voice was fervent. "Hear me out, brother. This weighs heavy on me!"

"What is it then?"

"Devise a way to keep Lady Briana here. Say she is ill, say she needs succoring, or that Aldgyth cannot bear to part with her, Say anything! Only make him leave her here!"

As if the disquiet in the next room had just occurred to him, Edwin stared at the wall. "What is he about now?" he asked, groaning. Then, as if answering his own question, he added, "We have no say over that lady, Morcar."

"She cannot live in my household."

"I know not what you mean!"

"I am meant not to look on her more. It is part of my penance."

"Say you this in truth?" he asked incredulously. "Have you sinned with her?"

Anguished, I managed a miserable nod. "I am sworn away from her now, brother, but—I swear to you—I cannot bear to listen to this! It stabs me even where I knew not I had feelings!" My voice cracked with desperation, and I did not dare look at him. It was a long time before he said anything.

"No one knows of this, I trow?"

"You do, and Uncle Leofric, and the priest near Ceaster. None else. You well can tell I would die if the Bearn were to discover it. Or Oswulf."

"By God, you would die sure enough then!" Edwin exclaimed without a smile. Then he stood and paced like a caged cat. Under my fur I shivered. Wrapping my arms around myself, I rocked back and forth, wondering what he thought of me now. In the next room, Oswulf finally stilled himself but the low sound of Briana's sobbing filled me with a wretched despair. Then, of a sudden, my sister's voice came through the darkness; the sound of it caused a whirlpool of emotion in the pit of my stomach.

"I should be the one to ask Oswulf Eadwulf's son to leave her," she said listlessly. "He would not refuse me."

"Aldgyth!" I cried it with horror, everything in me aching. "I would have had you never to know!"

"'Tis no matter, Morcar," she said, "I have known longer than you think, but it will comfort you perhaps that I read it more from her look than yours."

"Nay, lady! It comforts me little!" I exclaimed miserably. Never had shame been more overwhelming! I put my face in my hands. "It grieved me to lie to you that morning," I told her with forlorn apology. "It will not happen more."

Rising softly, she moved and stood behind me, kneading my shoulders in a gentle fashion, touching her forgiveness to me instead of saying it. Edwin, now on a bench near the wall, said nothing more about it.

All the next day I spent in making preparations for the move to Eorforwic. Those things shipped from Ceaster stood ready in the outer houses, but I had need to choose what would go with me from Kirton. It was not an easy task. I knew little of what waited for me in my new home. The banished Tostig, arriving with the king's guard to claim his goods, had probably stripped the place. I heard he had even taken the bath with him, for fear he would not find one in Flanders. I made a mental note to order one hewn for me. From the stable, I chose a dozen of the Welsh cart-ponies so carefully bred and trained by Daffydd Carr's son. I had grown very fond of the red stallion Siward Bearn had given me at Ceaster, and each of my men had a fine mount of his own, so I took only six other steeds and a prize palfrey for Osbeorn Dolfin's son's lady; the man had been good in tending my ears and chest and would accept no gift of thanks from me himself.

I had ordered my entire wardrobe packed, and Edwin divided with me those things that had been our father's. Of the many fine dalmatics, I chose freely. Ælfgar had been an extravagant man, and the handsomest works of the best weavers and tailors and seamstresses lay rolled in his richly carved wooden chests. I took two sets of precious court dress, one a firm fabric with bosses of silver and garnet, the other a fine

cloth of gold tissue, rich with bullion, woven through with random fila-
ments of rare silk, dyed crimson. That robe had been my grandfather's
before him, and at first I was reluctant to take it. It was exceeding rich,
though it showed much of age and stain and wear. Leofric had received
it from the hand of the hero king, Edmund Ironside himself. When
young, they were friends who fought off the invading Danes together.

"It is a prize which belongs to Mercia," I said firmly, but my brother
smiled and shook his head.

"'Twould do well to impress the North Humbrians with how close
these two domains are now," he told me, "and they will be proud to share
in the treasures of your homeland."

I felt no such hesitation in taking furs and cloaks and mantles.
Despite the fact that I was a winter-born babe, summer blood flowed in
my veins, and I was the first to admit it. One mantle in particular, double
thick, of red squirrel and white wolf fur, I put aside to wear on the biting
journey. It had come to my father as part of his pledge-gift from Gruffydd,
and a proud thing it was. armlets, beltings, bracelets and other ornaments
we divided evenly, though they were far more a pleasure to Edwin than
to me. Like Ælfgar, he doted on a flashing and comely look, and apparently the Mercian people loved to see that in him.

When it came time to take table, I was fatigued and disinterested,
but managed to dress well and have myself combed. Leaving as I was on
the morrow, I did not know how long it would be before I sat to meal in
Lindcylene again, so I decided to break my fast for that night. A man
cannot find strength to travel with naught but liquid in his system is
what I told myself, though I admitted with some remorse that I broke
these fasts far more often than I kept them. Before year's end, I would
have to make an adjustment in my gold-gifts to cover the balance of my
indulgences.

The night did not start well, because Oswulf Eadwulf's son sat
himself anext me in an ill-humor as always after a night of stupefaction.
Of all men in the world, he was the one I least wanted to see just then,
and I was helplessly forced to converse with him. All the while he said
his mean-spirited things, Edwin and I exchanges grimaces. I scanned the
hall for my sister, trying to discern whether she meant to approach
Oswulf tonight or not.

"This is the very house I was wedded in, cousin!" is what Oswulf was
telling me against all my will to ignore him. "Six years past now; you
remember it, I trow? You were a pup then, but you recall it, do you not?"

I forced myself to smile as I nodded. He was holding a chunk of dry
white cheese and carving little bite-sized pieces off, one at a time, eating
them as he talked. He continually offered them to me, and I kept

refusing, my eyes distractedly following the glint of his silver dagger as he did it. That was easier than looking into his eyes.

"A man like you," he continued, "who is not hand-fast to any woman might think that one grows stale in that much time, and is a dull thing to slam to bed."

I flinched.

"Mine, though, fights me just like a maiden. I swear it, cousin! Sometimes I know not whether she does it out of liking or hate, that is how well she plays it. Certain she knows it fires me, though. That is one thing she is well able to do." He was staring across the room at her with those daring eyes of his, and suddenly the fear gripped me that he would not consent to leave her behind. I do not know what made me do it; I poured him a great cup of strong brown ale.

"Drink with me, Earl Oswulf!" I commanded him. In an hour's time he was roaring. Not the best course of action, I knew, but it distracted him and stopped his discourteous talk.

As the board was cleared and the women began to take their leave, I was relieved to see my sister make her way over. Flashing a look first to me and Edwin, I saw her lower her lashes with an uncharacteristic coyness as she approached our merry cousin. You could read in his look that he was pleased she had sought him out, but it sickened me to see the way his eyes lingered on her. I saw my brother grow taut with defensiveness, even before one word passed between the two.

"Cousin Oswulf, I crave a moment with you," she told him from across the table. He signaled her forward, standing to meet her and making no attempt to hide his eagerness.

"What is it that weighs on you, lady?" he asked, wiping his knife on the hem of his tunic before he sheathed it.

"Something worries me, and you are the only man who can set it right," she said decisively, staring boldly into the sparkle of his eye— an answer perfectly calculated to please him. Laughing appreciatively, he leant casually against a wide timber and said she had come to the right place.

"Not a man there is better able to relieve a lady's distress! 'Tis my best talent!" He was trying to charm her with his audacity, so little did he know her.

She lowered her lashes and continued. "It has been a hard time for me, Oswulf, homeless and husbandless."

My cousin shot a quick glance at Edwin, who was exerting all his effort in pretending not to listen. "What is it you require of me, lady?"

She pouted prettily. "Indeed, I hesitate to ask, such a great favor it would be."

He tried to edge her into the shadows along the wall, more sheltered from my brother's sight and mine, and she let herself be led. Then I could barely hear them. I hoped she would not misjudge the amount she could afford to fire him. Before I knew it, she was leading him out of the great hall, into one of the smaller ones. Instinctively both Edwin and I rose, but when my brother began striding after them, hand on hilt, I stopped him with a touch to the shoulder.

"Give her a moment," I said, trying to convince him. "She seems to have it carefully planned."

They reappeared. With a look of ecstatic satisfaction, she led him by the hand to our table, announcing loud enough for Siward Bearn and the rest of our chief men to hear, "Cousin Oswulf has agreed to let Lady Briana stay with me till the thaws! You are good to help me, kinsman, in my sore need." Reaching up, she kissed his cheek in a warm and sisterly way. He came closer to blushing than ever I suspected he could. She had entirely outmaneuvered him. Before he had time to think it over, I handed him a cup.

CHAPTER TWENTY-NINE

King Edward of holy memory died at London on 5
January . . . and was buried in the new minster
which he had founded . . . and had dedicated only
the week before. . . . There, on the day of the
funeral, whilst the crowds watched the last rites of
their beloved king with streaming eyes, Harold had
himself consecrated by Archbishop Stigand alone
. . . without the common consent of the other
bishops, earls, and nobles, and so by stealth stole the
glory of the crown.

—Orderic Vitalis, Book III

The Gate Fulford was a wide, natural street formed of level grassland,
bordered on one side by the river Ouse, on the other by a deep beck,
beyond which the fields descended swift into marshes. The ground of it
was trampled hard as flagging stone; for centuries it had served as the
official access to the great city of Eorforwic. That is the way we entered
my new capital. I rode with Oswulf on my right, Siward Bearn on my
left, all our guardsmen, and a full hundred and a half of the best North
Humbrian warriors in the rear. Summoned by couriers, they had armed
themselves in splendor and ridden out to meet us, that our entrance
might be stunning and auspicious.

It was. Jubilant crowds flanked both sides of the streets from the
foot of the city wall to the mighty minster, where the bells pealed an
unceasing, splendid welcome to our magnificent party. The archbishop
Aldred was not there to meet us for he was in Lundun, attending the
Witena Gemot which would confirm and sustain my election.
Apparently, that was a formality indulged in for the benefit of the
southerners. Here there was no need for it—no question but that I was
the chosen and favored Earl of the North Humbria and that I claimed
the unswerving allegiance of my subjects. One by one they came into

the minster to do me homage, scores upon scores of thegns and merchants and high-born freemen and priests and stewards and men-at-arms. It brought to me a flash of vanity, for with Oswulf, Earl of the Bernicia, on one side, and Siward Æthelgar's son, Bearn of the Diera, on the other, the folk of Eorforwic were being treated to a rare picture of incomparable fairness.

After a solemn high mass, I took my house. A great, stone-built hall, it stood on a ridge off the High Street, past the bustle and jostle of the crowded market areas, and in view of the ancient, crumbling war-walls of Roman times. Strong, square, unornamented, it stood near as tall and wide as the king's Lundun lodging, and with its stone out-buildings and stables and courtyards, it was like a small, walled city in itself. The great hall was thrice the size of the one at Kirton, all of stone with fires built into the walls at each end. My lodges alone were three chambers, with closets, shuttered windows, and a lavatory.

Straightaway, I began to guide and order my household but it took me all through the Yuletide to get settled in and to people the vast estate with retainers of my own choosing. I had brought my chief steward with me from Mercia. He was Edmund Half-Dane, who had directed the manor at Sempringaham, both in my time and in my father's. A loyal man of some fifty years' seasoning, with hair the color of iron and a mind like a Rome-schooled cleric, I knew I could trust him over any other to put my domestic affairs into fruitful harmony. He did not disappoint me. Comfort and order were quickly restored. The running of the place eased into a goodly routine within a matter of days, it seemed, and life began to take on a regularity upon which I soon became reliant. Eorforwic did not seem such a cold place then, when it came alive with house-life.

On the chillest, cuttingest night I could remember, I kept the year's end in my chamber with Siward Bearn, Heard Ulf's son, Gamel-Beorn, and Osbeorn Dolfin's son. Oswulf was invited, but elected to spend the night with a woman he had discovered eyeing him in the kitchen-house; three weeks without a wife, or a likely substitute, had been hard on him.

Since that first year's end I had kept with my father and grandfather in Lundun, so many years ago, I had never had had so much to reflect on in the hours of that sacred night. The immensity of power so suddenly thrust upon me, the realizations I had made concerning the frailties of my inner will, my first bitter entwinings with true temptation and the crushing weight of hatred and vengeance felt towards other men—those were the thoughts which assailed me through my prayers that night. Seems it was the first Christ Mass eve of my manhood, and attended by all the piercing ironies of peace and turmoil that have been mine since.

It was not long after that, some few days past Twelfth Night, that we rode long into the north-east to take a black bear in his winter den. Oswulf Eadwulf's son, who engaged himself in much winter hunting with his men to pass the time, had discovered its whereabouts from the men of Aldby, and came to me all fired with reports of its monstrous size and fierceness. Choosing twenty men by lots for the honor of accompanying us, I rode out with Oswulf and Siward Bearn, all wrapped in furs and woolens, and armed to the hilt.

"'Tis a beast which has terrorized all the forest and weald-land from here to the aet-Staengfordesbrycg!" Oswulf told us gleefully as we rode. His cheekbones were burnt red by the biting wind, for this north air did not disagree with him, and he spent hours out in it daily. "Brace you for a great battle when he learns what we mean to do with him!"

"Best you would not give him much teasing time to build his temper," Siward Bearn told him severely, "if he is huge and ferocious as men say!"

Shooting him a look almost scornful, Oswulf Eadwulf's son spurred his horse past us and called back over his shoulder, "When is the last time you fought with something, cousin, and meant it?"

The lair was a wide-mouthed hill cave, open at two ends. We hacked gorse-bushes, brambles, and woody shrubs out of the snow and piled them at one mouth, lighting them with pitch and tinder till they gave their wetness up in smoke. Armed with rocks, limbs, swords, and lances, Osbeorn Dolfin's son and a few other men went in from the other way to stir the animal into wakefulness, prodding and pelting him till the thunder of his roar convinced us he had realized his danger. Soon as those men tumbled out of there, we formed a tight, thrusting half-circle of swords and axes all around the open end of the cavern. In a few minutes the staggering giant emerged, twelve feet tall or more, rabid with fury. Confused by our shouts and hollers, blinded by the smoke and the silver flash of our swords, he lunged forward, initiating the attack with fearsome ferocity. Swiping aimlessly with his powerful claws, he landed first one rocking blow then another on our upthrust round-shields, screaming with madness when the first blade met him. It was a solid slice to the thigh thrown by Heard Ulf's son with his mighty two-handed battle-axe. As the creature's blood spurted steaming into the snow, he let go a bellow which echoed round the hills louder than our own taunting shouts.

Jumping round to reach for that which had wounded him, he took another stabbing blow just above the first, then felt Oswulf's Danish sword three times in quick succession high on his ribs. Infuriated, he threw his full weight forward with such violence that it broke a hole in our circle, but those men who had leapt back regained their composure quickly, coming at him with stab after stab, until one landed a sword near enough to his belly that he reeled, then fell on all fours. Immediately, I crashed the edge of my blade into his thick neck with such intensity that it took me half my strength to pull it out again. That decided the fate of the roaring beast and blows fell upon him one after another until the white snow all around him was melted in the streaming red heat of his life's blood. Gasping, breathless, every muscle aching from the effort, we stood wordlessly a short while looking at him, his awesome thews and sinews stilled forever. Then we cleaned our weapons in the snow.

After disemboweling him, we roped the carcass securely onto long wooden skis, bloodying ourselves well in the process. Even dead, beaten and ruined as he was, there was a breathtaking impressiveness about the shape and size of him.

"There is a fine trophy for a man to linger on with his lady some chill winter night!" Oswulf told me with a wink. I gifted him with the skin of it, which pleased him right well, and told Osbeorn Dolfin's son that he could have the belly fur to make play-creatures for his daughters.

Famished and fatigued, we rode the High Street through Gate Helmesleigh, coming into the courtyard of the Eorforwic hall just as the purpleness of twilight waxed victorious over the last gleam of day. I had barely dismounted when Edmund Half-Dane ran to us cloakless from the hall, a grim look on his lined and weathered face.

"Couriers from Lundun City," he said shortly. I turned with him and, seeing that he shivered, quickened my step, signaling my cousins to follow.

"Must be they carry the writ of my confirmation!" I told them as we walked. The Half-Dane shook his head.

"Seems 'tis news of a different import, my lord," he said soberly. His tone perplexed me and I shot a worried glance to Siward Bearn, who only shrugged. Reluctant to let the visitors see us in our unkempt wildness, we came in at the storehouse door, stealthing round the hall to my lodges. I washed there and had myself combed and laid out in better looking dress, and when Siward Bearn and Oswulf had done the same, we went to greet the Lundunmen, looking fair in fine embroidered woolens and glinting precious metals. There were four of them and they rose to salute us, their faces drawn and mirthless. Forcing a smile, I gestured them to sit at my high-table.

"I see your board already has been spread," I said, "but for the sake of fellowship, sit here and quench your thirst with us, and tell me what business brings you hither in such season as this."

"'Tis bitter business, Earl Morcar," said the one who seemed to be chief of them, a burly, thick-necked Saxon.

"First dispatched we were of all heralds, to bring word here before men rode to the other parts of the kingdom," added another, "so that it should not seem to you that the men of the North are neglected, or last to know what brews in the land. This news you shall hear at the same time it is proclaimed in Wessex, and in Mercia, and the East Anglia."

"Here is a change in policy!" I exclaimed, tossing a glance of surprise to both my kinsmen. I could not imagine that the king bore me any love enough to change his long-standing attitude of unconcern. Not after what I had wrought on his darling Tostig! "Seems Edward has never much worried before beyond the borders of his own seat."

"King Edward is dead."

Stunned to silence, I rose to my feet as the messenger continued slowly and impassively, "He died peacefully in the grace of God and was buried in his newly hallowed minster on Twelfth Night, the feast of the Epiphany."

I crossed myself.

"On the same day," his voice was low now, "was crowned Harold, son of Godwine."

"Holy rood!" Siward Bearn was on his feet now, too. "They have dared to name a king without even calling the earls to council!"

"Say you that the Wessexman put the crown on the very day the old king was buried?" Biting his lip in bemused arrogance, Oswulf played his goblet back and forth, drumming it with his fingers. "Whatever you feel about his claim, you must admit he is strong and skilled in self serving!"

Oswulf pushed himself away from the table, spitting on the floor as he strode away. The Wessexman watched him go with faintly disguised disgust.

"Seems he would be a hard man to council with," said the one who had spoken first, turning his eyes back to me. "I pray you will be more open in your judgments, Lord Morcar, and hear the reasonings I am told to share with you."

Narrowing my eyes, I stared at him questioningly, his command to continue. He swallowed a long draught.

"Two claims there are on this kingdom from without our own land," he said carefully, watching for my reaction. "I trust all here know that Harald Hardraada, Viking king of the North Wegians, feels he has a claim of promise from Canute, who was King of Angland before Edward's time."

"A narrow claim!" I answered, finishing my cup and signaling for more.

"Even the smallest of claims gains credence with a strong sword behind it. Surely you are a man who understands that, my lord." He looked at me accusingly, and I bristled but said nothing. He was red-faced and hard-looking. He was Godwine kin, I knew, and he talked with a high-born manner. I glanced at Siward Bearn as I waited for the man to go on; my kinsman's face betrayed no emotion.

"The other hand which feels for the crown is that of William, Duke of Normandy," he said at length, "also a claim of promise, and he is one who shares a blood-tie with Edward, though a scarce one. What think you of these two candidates?"

I was hungry and tired, not having eaten anything since before the hunting. The smell of roasting meats came at me like a physical assault. "Well I can appreciate your arguments," I told him wearily, "but mayhap it would be best if we were to discuss instead the claims of Harold Godwine's son."

"Claims of necessity, my lord earl. Must be you can read the need to be swift with a decision."

"And who was it sat in on this decision?" asked Siward Bearn, a glint of scarce-suppressed anger in his grey eyes. "Methinks it is not the work of any lawful council."

"Aye, and you are right, Bearn of Diera," said the other levelly. "'Twould be a long and tedious thing to beg council in this freezing season. A month, two months, with no king on the throne would surely fire the imaginations of our foreign claimants, would it not? Best they think we have a solidly chosen king from the outset, with all the men of the land behind him willing to fight any opposers."

I had to agree. "There is a certain wisdom in it," I said thoughtfully as pages carved joints and slices at the table's end and heaped them into bowls and trenchers. Our guests had already eaten, and I found no embarrassment in feeding in front of them. I was too hungry to be bothered by formalities, so I signalled him to continue while I ate.

"King Harold begs you to understand his need for haste. It is his particular concern that you and your brother feel not affronted by his decisive action."

"Why is that?" I asked it looking directly at him. He shifted uncomfortably and looked at his fellows.

"There is more to it than you might suppose, Earl Morcar," he said at length. "He means to see an end to what once existed between your house and his, and to see a unity between all the earldoms that never before could be because of it. He bade me give you assurance that the rights and claims of Mercia and the North Humbria will weigh as heavy with him as those of the south. He means to accord you every right and privilege of a king's man, and to seek your council in all matters. That is why he bids us request that you will receive him here the first week of the thaws."

Now I stared at him open-mouthed. No Anglish king had journeyed north of the Humber in living memory. "The man already wears the crown," I finally managed to say, pushing away my plate, near untouched, "and it seems he has felt no need to hear my assent to it, nor that of my kinsmen. So what purpose is it that brings him hither?"

"He means to take your allegiance while looking in your eye, I trow," the Saxon said, not a hint of sarcasm. It was an honest answer, and I appreciated it, turning a studied gaze to Siward Bearn while I pondered the thought. While we looked at each other, the courier added one thing more.

"King Harold sends another petition unto you, and the same words he has sent to Mercia as well, that his two earls may consider on them from now until he comes to speak with you. This message he bids us deliver in the same words with which he formulated it."

"Say it then!" I commanded, looking at him curiously.

"King Harold says that if it is in you to see past that which both you and he know to be true, then mark that it is his desire, fond and sincere, to be made wedded with your sister, the lady Aldgyth."

I rose from my seat, trembling. "We control not the lady's hand nor heart!" I hissed low. There was a sudden hush in the immense hall as my people strained to hear a word of the news that inspired such obvious emotion in me. The messenger went on as if I had not interrupted.

"And he bids us make it known to you, that it is not only a hand-fasting for political advantage, either to you or him. Having seen the lady, his is a suit of the heart now, as well. Take care to approach her, if and when you see fit, in a way that will cause her as little hurt and harm as possible, but press fervently. He told me not to quit your side until I was sure you understood how strongly he felt."

Staring blankly ahead, I retook my seat, making no move to acknowledge his words. It seemed a long time later that Siward Bearn nudged me gently. "My lord? Make you an answer?"

"Aye," I nodded numbly, turning to the brawny, yellow-haired man who had done most of the talking. "What are you called, king's man?"

"I am Esgar, chamberlain to the king."

"'Tis no ordinary herald he sends me."

"Nay, my lord. He takes particular care to impress you with the import of his thoughts."

"You have done well by him, Esgar—a fair speaker."

The man bowed his head humbly, scanning my face while he did it.

"The words are all his, my lord."

"What think you?" I asked, leaning closer to him, narrowing my eyes. "Am I what you expected to find me?" I could see he thought it an odd question, and he mulled it over a minute before he replied.

"I knew your father," he said simply. "I find you ... milder. Milder than I expected you to be."

I grinned, wishing suddenly I had greeted him decked in the bear's blood after all. He could not read my thoughts, though, and thinking I liked his answer he smiled back at me. "My lord Harold claims you are a forthright man," he added, "so I did not come disposed to dislike you."

It pleased me that Harold had considered me thusly to a man with whom he had no reason to pretend. Standing with sudden certainty, I raised my hands. Siward Bearn pounded the table with his fist, to turn all the attention in the hall to me. Soon as every eye was forward, I spoke loud and levelly in a voice that was devoid of all my multitudes of feelings.

"King Edward is dead. May his soul rest in peace."

The sound of the silence was deafening. I raised a cup.

"Long live Harold, King of all Angland!"

CHAPTER THIRTY

Edwin and Morcar . . . had taken over the earldom
of the North humbrians and managed to keep it at
peace with a defence force which they shared.

—William of Malmesbury

Spring 1066

Harold Godwine's son did not come the first week of the thaws, but
Edwin did. His hair had grown darker as it was prone to do in winter, but
he was flashing as ever when he rode in with his three Welshmen and
two dozen of his guardsmen, ahead of the larger party that brought my
sister north for her bride-ale.

"Saint Olaf's mercy!" he exclaimed with wonder, when first he
looked on me. "Seems you have spent the season in strange pursuits!"
He fingered my hair, much longer now and dyed the russet color of
leaves in late autumn. I laughed at his amazement and showed him my
wrists, circled by thin chains of interlocking blue and purple stars.

"They are fine to look on now!" I smiled, "But I was so dazed that
I scarce wakened for two days after Osbeorn Dolfin's son burned them
on me!"

"In one thing, though, I see you are still a Mercian!" Edwin touched
my chin, smooth and clean-shaven. I had to smile sheepishly. Face hair
was the one thing I could not abide. Somehow, it seemed more pagan to
me than earrings, dyes, plaited locks, or burnt pictures. I had long held
the memory of the way my father had looked during his outlawry in the
Cymry: savage, untamed, and fearful. It was a look to which I could not
reconcile myself.

Walking in the courtyard, rife with mud caused by spring coming
all at once, we took turns talking of the things that had passed with us
since last we were together. My brother had a new man rising fast to
favor, a thegn from the Lindcylene Shire named Hereward who had
come to him out of exile in Flanders. I would meet him soon as he came
with the wedding party. Edwin was sure I would be impressed. He bore

me news about this man and that, but what interested me chiefly was what he knew of Aldgyth, now grown resigned to the match she had agreed to make.

"She is hard to fathom!" he told me with a dark smile. "Seems she one minute looks to it with a certain fondness, but the next rages at her own folly in accepting him. Surely there is no order to her mood!"

"Aye. That is the way with people soon to be wedded," I said miserably. "Siward Bearn has been courting seriously with a Danish woman and suddenly there is no reading the man any more. I scarce can get him to share a thought with me at table, so dream-eyed he is watching her move. And all night I have to listen to him count her virtues."

My brother stopped dead in his tracks, bent double with mirth, "You sound like a jealous maiden, brother!" he cried, gritting his teeth against his own merriment. "What is it you fear—that some lady's soft body will steal away all the affections of your chief man?"

He laughed more, and I flushed with annoyance, resenting my own feelings. Could be it was true that I harbored an envy. In these last months, my cousin had become what Edwin himself was to me once, and I had come to rely on him for council and companionship. Since he had grown love-blind, I had been spending my time more with Oswulf Eadwulf's son, and though we had come to a certain understanding of each other, I could not feel as a brother to a man like that. He had grown somewhat more temperate, it seemed, yet his capacity for sin still staggered and disturbed me.

So it was, I made Edwin's jest no answer. Sensing he had grasped a raw nerve, he let go quickly, leaping away to romp for a few minutes with the two wiry wolfhounds that had followed us afield. Watching him play like that, I was struck by the lordliness of him suddenly, pronounced enough to show through his frolic. Even at foolery, he boasted a commanding aristocratic look. It occurred to me that he was a man who never had to prove himself the way I always felt need to do. Returning from his playful sojourn flushed and smiling, he spoke seriously. "If I calculate rightly, Morcar, Cousin Siward waxes on twenty and seven years! Best you encourage this suit of his, lest he miss an opportunity long overdue."

Smiling, I put an arm around his shoulder and we walked back. Soon after, word came that Grandmother Godiva's train had been spotted, and we rode out happily together to greet her.

Next day, rain fell gently and steadily all morning, washing the world with the clean smell of spring. I wakened early but stayed long abed listening to it. I had dreamt of Briana—dreams best not remembered—and now was remorsefully reminded that I had not worn that scratching wool shirt more than a handful of days in the five months since it became my penance. Maybe if I did, those dreams would not come to torture me the way they did, so realistic and taunting.

After the mass, Edwin and I broke fast with Grandmother before I sent for Edmund Half-Dane to give me an accounting of the lavish preparations being made for the bride-ale feast soon to come. He offered to ride with me around the manor that I might make a check, which thing I was anxious to do and Edwin with me. It was years since there had been a royal visit in the north, much less a king's wedding, and all of the Diera was in a frenzy of anticipation. Goods and finery, ales, meads, and foodstuffs of every description arrived daily from all over the earldom. The many storehouses were near bursting with sumptuous fill. Mounted, we inspected the slaughter barns where the meat animals were quartered: a full six dozen of the finest fat lambs to be found, three months' calves of the best form, and handsome kids, well fattened on barley and wheat-grass. We needed to be ample with our meats. A spring-time wedding meant little in the way of fresh-grown things to proffer, though nuts, root foods, and dried fruits and grains were in abundance, every thegn and free-man north of the Humber having contributed his due. By the time the game and fowl were gathered, it would be a rare spread indeed, and easily as fine as any ever laid in Wessex. Of that, after our guided tour, I was confident. It had taken us an entire day to glance from one thing to another.

"What think you?" I asked Edwin later as we readied ourselves for table, "That he will be a good husband to her?"

Shrugging carelessly, he put on his armlets. "'Tis a thing to be hoped for, I suppose; yet she has well decided already it can never be a love match."

"Then feel you no pity that she has forced herself to take him?"

He looked at me incredulously. "She has had her romance, brother! Whether she wedded rich or poor now would make no difference to her, I trow. So best it be a match that brings a benefit."

There was a hardness in his tone and it surprised me. "She deserves not to be unhappy," I said, low but firmly, looking at him.

"She has only to give in to him a little and he will be fair to her. I am determined to trust the man, Morcar. I prayed and considered on it long, long whiles before I approached her with it. Now the suit is made and we must content ourselves that we have done rightly, by her, and by him. It is that simple."

I do not know why it bothered me. Reading my thoughts, he added with a soft laugh, "*She* is the one who said yes to it, brother!"

That comforted me some, but later, in the hall, one thought kept returning to me. It was commonly known that Harold Godwine's son kept a mistress, Edith Swan's-Neck. He had near-grown sons by her and had never foresworn her in twenty years, not even to please the pious old king. It rankled me. Since both the bride's brothers were allowed to name a bride's-price, I decided to demand a total rejection of the woman as mine. That might help to settle things. Still, I hoped it would not put a quarrel between the Wessexman and me. That was no way to start out a brotherhood.

I mused on these thoughts all through meal. After board had been cleared and the hall emptied somewhat, I thought to bring it up with Edwin. He was grinning and jesting in a circle of men, though, and because it was something best kept close between us, I decided to bide my time.

Oswulf Eadwulf's son had not taken food with us, and the women had been gone from hall near an hour when he finally came. He was in one of his maddening states of disarray, well-aled and tempestuous. Six of his Bernicians were with him in the same rowdy state. They made us no greeting but gathered themselves at one end of the hall, before the large hearth, boisterous and unrestrained. Whenever he was in that condition, I made a point of not involving myself with him, knowing too well the risk in doing so. Tonight, though, I found myself watching him carefully, struck by the strength and heedless defiance that characterized his every movement. 'Twas a pity such a fair creature should let all his power go to waste in ale-rages and the beguiling of women. There was no holding the man back from his own turmoil; it had always been that way.

While I gazed at my cousin, lost in these reflections, the great outer door which led to the courtyard opened inward and there was Siward Bearn, his coppery hair and the gold border of his blue mantle glinting in the fire-light. Not having seen him all evening, I stood to make a greeting, expecting him to come to the high table in his usual way, but he did not. The man stood immobile, his tall frame outlined against the night-blackness which waited beyond the door. Then with a sudden, tense lunge—as if he had lost the power or will to hold himself back— he strode with quivering intent to the bench where his brother-in-the-law sat heedless of him. Once there, the Bearn locked fingers into Oswulf's long, tousled locks, pulling him harshly to his feet.

"You are a dead man, Oswulf Eadwulf's son!" he cried, his voice fraught with measureless rage. As soon as he said it, every man in the hall rose, shocked into a dreading silence. With a clench of fear, I realized Oswulf's hand was on his knife. He unsheathed it at the same instant he wrenched himself free, turning to face his attacker with a look on his bloodless face so full of impassioned, reckless fury that it made me shudder. Snarling, he bared his gleaming teeth like an untamed thing, and as he threw himself growling and frothing at Siward Bearn, I felt my fist smash forcefully hard onto the wooden table and heard myself shouting.

"Hold the man!" I hollered. Osbeorn Dolfin's son leapt over men and benches, and with Gamel-Beorn's help captured the cursing Oswulf in a choking stranglehold. Once they held him helpless, Siward Bearn, shaking with infuriated madness, drew and raised his sword. Somehow, in the very same instant I realized what he meant to do, I reached his side, and putting all my strength against his arm, managed to stay him, yanking his hair at the same time to make him face me.

"By God, cousin! Here is not the time for blood!"

"Never again will he put himself against a woman in my claim!" he hissed, his voice so icy it stung. As Oswulf worked himself free, Siward Bearn let go his sword with such force that it flew several feet before crashing with fearful, echoing clatter onto the stone floor. Then, his knife was in his hand and in one swift streak of motion, the two men came together with violent force, slashing and howling in enragement. Soon as I heard Oswulf Eadwulf's son's agonized scream and saw him fall back, I threw myself on Siward Bearn, slamming him down with all my weight. Then, lost in a kind of madness myself, I pounded the back of his head harshly on the stone floor till the fight was out of him.

Gasping for breath, I rose to see Heard Ulf's son and my brother wrestling Oswulf, who was still strong and spitting mad, though his dalmatic showed a fast-spreading scarlet stain at the left shoulder. Grabbing a bucket, quarter-full of bubbling mead, I doused him with it. He let go a choking groan of agony and anger, then fell back breathless and frustrated, his steely eyes still glinting with wrath.

For a moment I knew not what to do, looking from one to the other as my wits slowly came back to me along with the voices of the men in the hall who, till now, had only watched in dumbstruck horror. I felt naught of a pity for Oswulf, but now that the stunnedness was wearing off him, I could tell he was hurt, though it was only the quivering curl of his lip that spoke it. Not even when Edwin pulled him to his feet would he allow himself a cry or groan. I told some men to take him to the priests in the kitchen-house, and then I helped Siward Bearn up from the floor. As Edwin and I left the hall with him, disappearing into my lodges, the place erupted in a thunder of excited speculation and converse. There had not been feuding to draw blood in my hall since I had come as earl.

For a long time, Siward Bearn did not want to talk about it, so we just sat morosely on benches in the dim-lit chamber, saying nothing. After a while, a man brought my cousin's sword to the door and offered us a bucket of mead. Grateful for it, I drew off three horns full, and started quickly on mine. Edwin followed me but Siward leant forward and purposefully poured his into the blazing fire. We all three watched as it sizzled and steamed.

"Suppose not that I will thank you for not letting me murder him," Siward Bearn said finally, and his strong voice was cracked and strained.

"'Twas not thanks I had in mind when I stayed you," I answered dourly. "Only that a bride-ale and a grave-ale in the space of a fortnight might be too much for me to bear."

Managing a grim smile, the Bearn rubbed the back of his head. I was sorry I had handled him so cruelly and I apologized. He let go a dry and joyless laugh. "Think naught of it, Earl Morcar. Holding tempers seems not to be an easy thing this night." Edwin dipped another horn and held it out. This time my cousin sipped it.

Biting the inside of my cheek, I watched him drink, wondering whether to question him or wait. While I still considered on it, he suddenly burst out in a hollow whisper, "The man brought her to the storehouse, and he put himself against her there."

Edwin looked from me to him. "Your woman?" he asked.

"Aye!" I had never heard such a miserable tone. "'Twas my lady Gythrun. He put his hand on her mouth and half-ways stripped her. Then he forced her to the wall with his men looking on and he—"

I was on my feet, hand on my own sword hilt, and it surprised me to realize it. "Did he damage her?" I almost gagged on the question.

"Nay. He touched her boldly and frighted her well, saying he had taken many a maiden with more will to fight than she had. He kissed her hard—" He broke off, swallowing. I spit into the fire.

"Drunken talk—the man's best talent!" Edwin cried angrily.

"Not just talk, cousin!" Siward Bearn's voice was rigid with hate. "Edmund Half-Dane heard her begging and led three men in, swords drawn, else Oswulf would have done with her what he promised!" He slammed his clenched fist down on the wooden bench. "I have reason to know the man acts every bit as meanly as he speaks. You must know she would not have been the first maid he forced to do his bidding!"

I had to look away, feeling guilty for knowing the secret that plagued his private thought. I wondered suddenly how many times since his sister's bride-ale the urge had come on him to murder her husband. I remembered so clearly the look on Burchard's face as he held the Bearn back that night. No less vividly did I recall the prideful scorn in Oswulf's glittering eyes. I felt a burning pang for Briana.

It was Edwin who broke the long and somber silence. "Someone should go and see how he fares," he said low, and then he added with a level look at my wretched cousin, "you must know we cannot have blood spurting between us with the king due to arrive here. Whatever the truth of it is, a picture of feud-ridden kinship he will not have! It puts a brand of weakness on us!"

Siward nodded numbly, then rubbed his head through his thick, copper hair again. "Make the man avoid me," he whispered listlessly, "and I will swallow back my venom!"

"Here I see my own fault in this," Edwin added, with an accusing glance my way. "Oswulf Eadwulf's son is a man who must never be held separate from his woman else he over-steams himself."

I tried to silence him with a look. It was not something well calculated to make Siward Bearn take comfort, though my brother had no way of knowing it.

"Let me be the one to go to him," I said firmly, helping myself to a last draught of mead. "Might be I can bring him to understanding." Just as I reached the door, my cousin laid a command on me.

"Do not tell him I am sorry!" he croaked defiantly. I nodded to it.

Things were unusually quiet in the kitchen-house, the priests having sent everyone away, even Beornwald Strong-Leg, Oswulf's chief man. I found my kinsman in the back, where one of the fires was now partitioned off for a nursing chamber. He stared coldly as I entered and sat myself down opposite him, but made no move to acknowledge me. He was sitting on the edge of a cot, as still as a stone statue, his undertunic pulled off the sore shoulder which was wrapped in steaming rags. All the vehement sparkle was gone from his eyes now; he looked drained, weary, and blankly impassive. From the pile of red-soaked linens on the floor beside him, I could tell he had bled freely.

"Cousin," I said lightly, hoping a jest would relieve him, "I hope that be all the bad blood you had in you, wrapped in those poultices there!" His nostrils flared, but he made no answer. I leant forward earnestly and looked him in the eye. "It grieves me that it came to this. Tell me how it is with you." Still, he would not talk.

"The blade glanced off the shoulder joint and went deep through his arm into the breast there. " One of the priests lifted the linen up to show me; the wounds were not pretty. "It will not finally harm or cripple him, but he will be well reminded of this night for many weeks!"

I thanked him, and when the priest had left us alone, I turned back to my cousin, determined to break his arrogant stillness. "The man meant to kill you," I said in a hoarse whisper. "Know you that, Oswulf Eadwulf's son?"

He did not even flinch.

"Next time you put hot arms around what is not yours, he will finish you, I am sure of it!" I knew I was toying with my cousin's tender temperament, but he sat mute, no sign that my words held meaning for him. I grew irritated. "Seems you will play right into his hands, too," I added, tossing my head in a careless way, "because you drink yourself too stupid even to fight like a worthy man!"

Out of the corner of my eye, I could see the color rising in his pale cheek, while his lower lip trembled out of its steadfast pout. I turned the full harshness of my gaze on him, bending very close to taunt him.

"In truth, cousin, I think sometimes all you have of manliness is that panting way you look at women!"

For an instant the fire came back into his eye he quivered as he uttered me a hissing reply. "What makes you think I will hear from you what I would not take from any other man, Morcar Ælfgar's son? Suppose you I know not it is because I am helpless that you dare me this way?" A pang must have pierced through him because he shot his hand to his wounded shoulder abruptly; a noise came to his throat, but no cry escaped him. Then he relaxed again into his same emotionless daze, looking past me with unreadable eyes.

"Siward Bearn is not the man for you to torture with your sullen sinfulness," I told him decidedly. I could tell Oswulf wanted to spit, but he held himself back so as not to give me the pleasure of seeing him heated over it. "He would as soon visit death upon you as—"

With sudden, unanticipated force, he grabbed the front of my dalmatic, flying to his feet and pulling me with him. The icy furor of his look was perfectly matched to the cutting cruelty of his savage tone. "Tell Siward Bearn that the lady came to me!"

I wrestled his hand off me. "You are a liar, cousin."

"Nay. Tell him that it was the lady who sought me out."

Now I was the one who shook with rage. "Came to you, I trow, in the same manner that Lady Briana came to you in her father's timber church?"

He paled suddenly and trembled so violently I feared he would lose consciousness. I was forced to reach out and steady him. He looked at me with an expression of wonder so exceedingly strange it made me shudder. The windings bandaged round his shoulder grew suddenly blood-sopped, and he sat down heavily, exhaling a breathless moan. I noticed all at once that his hair was tangled and matted with sweat, and his brow dripped with it. There was a uncharacteristic note of resignation in his whisper.

"Tell the Bearn I was mindless and knew not the lady was claimed."

"He is not slow-witted enough to believe it."

"Then just tell him I was mindless."

Clenching both his fists till the knuckles showed white, he bit it back till he almost choked on it, then let go a piercing cry of anguish. For some reason, it satisfied me right well to hear it.

*   *   *

Never in my life did I surprise myself the way I did when the bride's train arrived at my hall in Eorforwic. Late in the damp, green-skied day, they rode through the Gate Fulford. Though there was no ceremonial welcome or pomp or pageantry, cheering crowds flanked the way to ogle the rich procession and catch a glimpse of the legendary Lady Aldgyth, widowed of one king and bespoken of another.

Tired, chilled, and muddy, my sister's party unhorsed in the courtyard. While Edmund Half-Dane governed the confusion of unpacking and directed people into lodges and guest-rooms, Edwin led Aldgyth and her ladies into one of my chambers, bouncing the delighted Nesta on his shoulders all the way. Oswulf, in a bad state of disrepair, had kept sullenly to his bed in the kitchen-house since his leveling of the night before last. Despite meads, herbs, and strong barms to ease his discomfort, he suffered much. It gave me a certain, unlooked-for satisfaction to know he would not be greeting Lady Briana in his usual fashion.

When most of the guests were settled, Siward Bearn came to me in the hall, obviously worried. I stepped outside to walk with him while the board was being set. "It lays a heavy thing on me to tell my sister that I have drawn her man's blood," he said, looking past me into the descending twilight. "I think not I could tell her that I fought him over a woman. 'Twould be a thing to wound her, surely!"

I said I scarce believed it would surprise her. "Must be she knows his ways by now, cousin."

Discomfort twitched across his face. "Aye, she suspects it, no doubt. Yet it is not a gentle thing to have to speak to her on it, and it would not astonish me to find she was wroth about my temper." He stopped dead and grabbed my shoulders. "You be the one to tell her, Earl Morcar!" he besought me. "Surely you can discuss such tender subjects with her more easily than I."

I could not help it. I threw my head back and laughed. I know he thought me mad.

I finally found her in the chamber Oswulf had used till his indisposition. Soon as her lady announced me at the door, Briana sent her attendants away and bade me enter, eyeing me curiously. I could not help staring at her, either. She was dressed in fair-woven light blue stuff embroidered over with birds and flowers. Her veil was off, and her long braids gartered round with ribands of blue-dyed muslin.

"What is it that brings you here, Lord Morcar? Must be it is an important thing." She was wringing her hands nervously, unaware that she did so.

"I bear you some news, and I am sorry to say 'tis not pleasant." I leant back against the door as it closed behind me, trying to sound casual. She turned her back.

"Waste not words to make it easy. What has he done?"

"My lady?"

"Oswulf Eadwulf's son! What dishonor has he wrought you?" She faced me again, tossing a plait behind her shoulder as she did so. "You do come to speak of him, do you not?"

I nodded, breathed deeply and recited the entire story. "Your brother truly hesitates to face you," I told her at the end of it. "He thinks he has shamed himself in your eyes."

Joylessly she laughed, looking past me. "The shame is that the wound was not a mortal one, else I would have thanked him for it!"

"Best you would not talk in suchwise, lady!" I said severely, but I felt a rising swell of pity. She brought her eyes to mine, flashing and defiant.

"You are a good and gentle person, Earl Morcar, but I am not that way! Well I know that hatred is a sin, yet it bothers me not to hate him. Seems it does not worry me to sin when there is a reason for sinning!" Her eyes narrowed and the set of her soft mouth momentarily hardened. "We have talked of this before, have we not? This thing wherein we differ, you and I?"

"Aye, we have talked of it," I said softly, "yet methinks we do not differ in it so greatly as you say. More alike we are, perhaps, than either of us knows."

"Nay, sir!" she answered with a reproachful tone. "Either you say I am gentle and virtuous or you say you are hard and sinful." She broke off suddenly and walked slowly away till she stood by the hearth. Then she turned, gazing into my eyes from across the dim chamber. She looked fragile; her shoulders seemed to bear some great weight.

That is when I surprised myself. Looking at her, I decided once and for all that she would be mine: wholly, totally, irrevocably mine. Not for a stolen hour or day or night; I would make her mine forever. I would devise a way.

"Do not look on me so strangely, Morcar!" The tremble of her voice made me suddenly wild with longing.

I felt I could not possibly stay another minute without dishonoring us both, yet with no effort I crossed the room and faced her, a strange feeling of unfamiliar strength playing through me. "Let me take you to the kitchen-house," I said quietly and firmly. "Let you and I make a visit with him. Seems he has somewhat of a respect for me, and together we can talk away the bad blood he feels toward your brother, you and I. 'Twould be easier on you that way, I trow, than going there alone."

She stood motionless, pale and slim and fair, looking past me with her sea-green eyes.

"Let me be something to you," I whispered in a little, seeing she would make no response. "Let me be a brother, a friend. Or is it you will not have me if I cannot be—that?"

Trembling, she raised both her hands to her brow, pressing as if a pain were there. "What is this that you offer to put on me, Earl Morcar? That I should stand in the kitchen-house with two men who have bedded me—one whom I hate and one…." Moaning, she broke off, then brought her hands down and looked at me glaringly. "Are you such a boy that you cannot see what it would do to me?"

Burning with some unnamable heat, I turned my back on her. "Nay, lady, boy I am not!" It bothered me that she had said it; I had all but forgotten the eight years that waxed between our ages.

She laughed mockingly. "Yet you speak like a gamesome youth, Morcar! Like a boy grown tired of a toy but still responsible for the care of it."

I heard the suffering in her voice and spun to face her, backing away while fighting the urge to enfold her. "Sore false it would be to suppose I had grown tired of my toy, lady." I tried to sound harsh but my voice shook. "More likely it would be to say the toy was wrested from me."

There was a long silence.

"'Twas after all a stolen toy," I added mournfully.

Another stark silence, then she walked to the bench and picked up her cloak. "I will look in on the man," she said shortly, "but you will not go with me, Morcar Ælfgar's son!"

I took her shoulders roughly as she tried to pass and made her look at me. "Think you not it would have been as great a torture for me, Briana?"

Softly, she touched my cheek. "Nay," she whispered, "I think it could not be!"

Gently, I pushed her away, weak from the perfume of her hair. "I will not come to you ever more if seeing me or speaking with me wounds you," I said as she laid her cloak over her shoulders. "Never was it my intent to harm you. 'Tis my own selfishness, really, that I cannot come clean away from you, lady, but long to be near you, even knowing you cannot be mine!"

Catching her breath, she looked away. "Sometimes I think that to look on you is naught but sorrow for me, Morcar. Yet I have missed you sorely these months, even knowing the pact we made between us. Sometimes it seems that I, too, have longed just to change a word with you, or sit near you, or touch your hand in innocence."

"Then can it not be that way for us?" I cried in desperation. "Seems we realize strongly enough what we must deny each other. If we are faithful in that, can we not be—" I stopped myself miserably, at a loss for words.

"Brother and sister?" she questioned with a short, wretched laugh. Then, flushing, she spoke low. "I have dreamt of you, Morcar!"

"And I also of you, lady!" I said it before I could stop myself then burned with a strange discomfort as she looked at me wonderingly. My voice grew suddenly calm and comforting. "There is no reason we cannot pass each other without base feelings. Let us have just a fondness between us, so that we can talk to each other when the need is upon us. Seems I do need sometimes to talk to you, woman, and I feel you have the need to speak to me. We can stand together now even in a closed chamber like this, alone, and I feel no shade of that guilt any more. Can you not do it?"

"Guilt never was the feeling that plagued me when I stood by you, Morcar. 'Twas a harder one than that."

"Be free of it, then, so I do not have to fear grieving you whenever I share a thought or word with you! Give me your leave to come to you sometimes. I will not abuse it! Only, when I feel a need to offer you strength or comfort, like tonight, do not deny me that opportunity. It aches me because I feel there is none else who can give it to you."

There were tears in her eyes but not tears of sadness. She brushed them away, forcing a smile. "Good you are to me, Morcar. In some ways, truly better than a brother!"

I knew how she meant it and I shook my head. "Siward Bearn is an exceeding good man," I said in a deliberate way. "He cares for you more than you know. Consider not for a moment that he does not see Oswulf for what he is. It sore has wounded him that he forced you to wed the man. I read that in his eyes every time he speaks your name!"

"Has he never told you that he did not believe my word against Oswulf's that day in the church?"

"Lady, never has he breathed mention of that day—not to me, or to any man, I trow. 'Tis a penance he carries all by himself!" She seemed surprised at that but said nothing. After awhile, seeing she meant to say no more, I entreated her earnestly. "Time it is you forgave Siward Bearn those grave mistakes of his, lady. He was not the first man to be fooled by Oswulf Eadwulf's son."

She nodded numbly, casting me a sad smile.

"'Twould not have happened had he known what he knows now about the man," I went on as we walked to the outer door. "Even now, with all he has set himself to, Oswulf claims the respect of many men who will not believe the truth of him."

"'Tis that mock look of innocence he wears," she answered bitterly. "Even would he fool me with it, if he could. Many is the time he has put sin against me while making me feel the guilty one." A violent tremor traversed her entire body.

There was little I could do in the crowded corridor to comfort her so I just stared straight ahead as if I had not seen. Some men swung the heavy door open for us and we stepped into the night. The noise from the great hall, crammed with the company newly arrived from Mercia, was like the roar of a river, constant and indecipherable.

"I can find my way to the kitchen-house," she said firmly, when we had gone a little way. "A good many men await you in your hall, Earl Morcar. You ought to go to them."

Promising to find and send her chamber-ladies to her, I let her go. Watching her walk into the blackness with the spring wind playing through her dress and mantle, I felt a strange surge of happiness. It seemed I was watching my own woman. I had made her mine in some secret, unspoken way which brought no guilt or shame to either of us.

Siward Bearn was not to be found immediately in the boisterous hall. Leaning in the doorway, I watched my brother for a few minutes at the high table, surrounded by an admiring circle of his men and mine. What it was he described to them I could not discern, but their interest was unbounded and his fair features well-lit with the enthusiasm of telling it. Daffydd Carr's son sat on his one side, and on the other a large, comely, square-shouldered stranger with piercing eyes and a strong-set, grim look. It had to be Hereward, the thegn of Lindcylene Edwin had spoken of. I scrutinized him carefully for some sign of what his great appeal might have been.

The man appeared to be some thirty-five years of age, or more if one took into account the masses of silver that streaked his brown-gold hair. His dress spoke of no great estate. There was no glint of precious metals at his arm or neck, and his dalmatic was a simple worsted with no embroidery or decoration. His look of sizable strength was impressive enough, but I could not see much more to commend him. When the circle of men burst suddenly into merry laughter, I heard his voice, deep and strong, above all the others. He turned suddenly in the midst of it, catching my curious eye full upon him. With a hard and unreadable look, he examined me just as carefully, making no attempt to divert his gaze but locking his gaunt stare into mine until I almost felt it. I was the one who broke out from it, forcing a smile as I approached the table. The man stood instinctively when Edwin called a greeting to me, and I could see he stood near as tall as Siward Bearn, and brawnier besides.

"My brother, Morcar Ælfgar's son, of Leofric, of Leofwine." Edwin was introducing me in the formal way which meant he set great store by this man. Suddenly, the stranger's proud look gave way to a friendly smile and he held his hand up in a sort of salute.

"Hereward," he said simply, "whom men call 'the Wake.'" He waited till I took my seat, then followed me, still looking me over.

"Find you a thing in me, Hereward the Wake, which bears such solemn inspecting?" I did not mean to sound bristling and arrogant, but his constant gaze disturbed me somewhat.

His laugh was deep. "Nay, my lord. Only was I thinking what fair men these sons of Ælfgar are. Even that wildness of a North Humbrian look on you can not disguise it!"

I looked from his face to my brother's. Edwin obviously delighted in such playful banter, but I was not quite sure how to take it. I had never convinced myself that I was handsome. I had been told that I had deep and winning eyes and that my smile, which in truth is crooked, was a pleasing one and true, but had never considered that any thought me fair in the way of my brother or my father. You might think it would please me to hear it, but it disturbed me more.

"Think you that I jest on this, Earl Morcar? I meant no affront." Hereward's sharp eyes were earnest but I looked away with only the slightest of smiles.

Edwin's eyes narrowed and he leant close. "Spoke you with your man's sister? He told me he had sent you to her."

Feeling suddenly uncomfortable, I made no answer but signaled for a cup of mead and downed it all at once. Then I turned back to the man Hereward, asking in a flat tone, "What is the part of Lindcylene that you come from, Mercian?"

"The bulk of my lands surround Sempringaham," he answered curtly, as if the subject sat not well with him.

"'Tis curious," I mused, taking another cup. "I hold a house in Sempringaham, and your name is not a familiar one to me. Seems strange I could have missed it."

"Nay, 'tis not strange at all, my lord." His was a stabbing, icy look. "Already I had quit those lands of my own accord while still you sucked at your mother's breast."

I felt he had said it just to raise my ire, but I could not be sure.

"What is your father called then?" I asked.

"That it would give you little help to know," the man answered, his hands grasping the table-edge. "I do not bear my father's name."

I felt some surprise that he had said it so matter-of-factly. "Are you bastard or have you dishonored it?" I asked coolly, staring levelly into his eyes and wondering why I felt so coldly towards him. "What might a goodly thegn and earl's man do to be denied his father's name?"

Stiffening, a tremor ran through him. I could see my words had ill-pleased him. "Not unlike many another unknowing man, you have read things wrong, Earl Morcar," he replied gravely. "I am the one who chose not to bear the name of one who had dishonored me."

I cannot say why I laughed so rudely. Edwin shot me a look of shadowed surprise, then turned apologetically to his friend. "I hope you will forgive my brother's humor tonight. He is not usually so sullen."

"Nay. Seems not," said the other, giving me a hard look. "Looks to me that his more usual way is quiet and close, and not so sure of himself as he pretends to be just now."

I burned indignantly, but the realization was swift to hit me that I was being unreasonable. I felt myself relax into a grin. "Prize you yourself as a reader of men, Hereward the Wake?" I asked him in a milder tone. "What you say of me is true. It takes much urging to make me quick and bold."

"Not so much as you think, my lord," he retorted evenly. "You are quick to think one man compares you to another and bold to answer an imaginary insult."

I frowned at his insight. "Well, I pray you will indulge my moodiness. My brother well knows and can tell you I suffer often from my own visions of myself." I turned away quickly after because I thought it strange I had shared so private a thought with one I had not yet made up my mind to like.

As if reading my mind, Edwin flashed a knowing grin. "He draws you out, brother! You will come to appreciate it!"

I smiled and, seeing the board was about to be cleared, helped myself to a huge chunk of roast fowl, now grown cold. I tore at it greedily. "Where be Siward Bearn?" I asked with my mouth full.

"Somewhere in the shadows with his lady," was Edwin's reply. "He ought to surface soon."

I scanned the room but did not see him.

"Word is," Edwin continued, "that the king's party has come as far as Elmete. May be, tomorrow we will be looking on the royal bridegroom."

I cut him off, putting my hand on his arm. "If Siward Bearn comes, tell him I have drawn a bath in my chamber." I stood to go, and Edwin followed me.

"Best you tell me if things are not well with you, Morcar," Edwin said with concern, even worry, in his voice.

"Nay," I reassured him, "I am in a confusion of spirits, that is all, and wanting some quiet time to sort things."

He nodded, but I felt his gaze till I left the hall. I went into my private lodges, barred the door, then stood wordlessly for a long time in the middle of the room, feeling both empty and full to overflowing—a curious sensation. Then I ordered my bath prepared while I undressed myself.

At one end of the chamber was a closet which could be curtained off for a dressing room. It had its own separate hearth-place and, when the hangings were drawn, was quite warm and comfortable. That is where I kept the bath. Actually, I had the despised Tostig Godwine's son to thank for the arrangement. Accustomed to the friendlier climate of Wessex, he had built the bath in such fashion to help ward off the Eorforwic chill. In fact, he had gained somewhat of a renown for his innovation, a luxury above any I had known in Mercia where the baths were naught but huge pails, kept in the kitchen-houses and offering little of comfort or privacy.

Usually, I prefer the invigoration of cold bathing, but tonight I craved relaxation, so I ordered the water well heated. There was a considerable amount of grumbling. My people were growing tired of bath duty lately. Edwin had availed himself of the pleasure several times since he had been here, and Aldgyth had quit the room only an hour or so ago after a long and luxurious stay which had required several rewarmings.

While the water was being readied, I had my hair washed. It was well past my shoulders now. As I had never been diligent about combing, it was usually so snarled and tangled that I had no patience for doing it myself. Kneeling on a leathern bench, I bent over a silver basin while an attendant doused, scrubbed, then rinsed me with flowered rain-water. The redness was fast fading, he told me, suggesting I refresh it for the bride-ale. Earl Edwin, he added, had earlier spent several hours soaking his locks in hard cider, ash, and chamomile to inspire a lighter golden glint. I was amused to hear it and wondered if Aldgyth, so wroth that I tampered with mine, knew that our brother was also wont to alter the handiwork God had done on his glossy tresses.

By the time they finished shaving me, the bath was ready. They wanted to sit by the door in case I needed more hot water or aid in washing, but I dismissed them entirely. Seems to me a man would have to be helpless in the worst sort of way to want others helping in his bath, though my married men assured me I would feel differently when the cloth was in the hand of an adoring woman.

While I steeped myself, I studied my look in a rich, silver-bordered glass. It was near big enough to see all my face at once and finely wrought so the image was pleasingly true. Carefully, I scrutinized. My eyes, no doubt, were my best feature, watchful and full of impassioned feeling. They lacked the animated brilliance of my brother's and that dash of wildness his had, but they were deep, clear, and gleaming. Long and thin, my face missed a certain symmetry, but it was nicely carved and the streaming, russet-hued hair set it off nicely. There was good color in the cheek. My mouth was too soft to be truly handsome, and the upper lip protruded in a way which spoke of tremulous over-sensitivity. My weakest feature, I knew, and yet not entirely unpleasant, my teeth being white and straight. My neck was surely too long, but my chest hair started just at the throat and saved it from looking maidenish. Tilting the glass ever so slightly, I admired the dusky blue and purple star at my breast-bone, a manly and striking adornment I had grown proud to wear.

By the time I finished my critical inspection, the water had grown cold and I shivered as I patted myself dry and rubbed my arms, chest and shoulders to a glowing sheen with borage attar. Then I slipped on a fine-woven shift, floor length and long-sleeved and open to the waist.

I had a strange hunger for red meat that night. It was Lenten time and I had taken naught but fowl, eel, and fish for some weeks but it was curious that such a longing would come on me of a sudden the way it did. I knew we would interrupt the season's fasting for the king's bride-ale and wondered what harm it would do to order some veal slain and roasted on the morrow to welcome him. 'Twould be a thing easily forgiven under the circumstances, and it did not seem to me that Harold was such a godly man that he would hold it against me. archbishop Aldred would be with us, though, and he might take it ill, so best I should wait for his formal decree of dispensation. All the while I said my evening prayer, the desire teased me, another embodiment of the strange turn my mood had taken since my talk with Briana. I almost felt I had no control over myself anymore.

I put me to bed while men's voices yet carried loud from the hall. Sleepless, I listened a long time, listless and devoid of emotion. When Edwin came in to take his pallet, I put an arm over my face and pretended to slumber, avoiding conversation. Long after his breathing became slow and regular; long after I heard Siward Bearn and the Welshmen take their beds in the adjoining chamber; long after hushed silence settled over all my house, I tossed and turned, unable to focus my still-wakeful mind.

I do not know that it was a conscious decision. Seems it could not have been because I was out of my own chamber and walking down the chill corridor before I realized where it was I took myself—else this is how my inner self has chosen to excuse it. I cannot say. Never before or since did such a confusion of emotions churn within me. I went to her room. Pushing the door, I let myself in, then barred it behind me. Standing anext her cot, I studied her in the light of the dying hearth-fire, until I thought the pounding of my own heart would waken her. I touched her soft, unbounden hair, her brow, and finally her cheek. When I felt her quiver, I turned the furs back and wordlessly laid myself beside her in the narrow bed. Her reaction was instantaneous. Whispering my name, she drew my face to the hollow of her throat.

*   *   *

I slept late into the day. The night had been complete. Every time I drifted into rest, she found a way to rouse me and we were still whispering together when the house began to come alive under the sullen stare of dawn. Her ladies came to the barred door and she sent them away. We giggled about it, then slept pillowed against each other like children.

Edwin came after the noon. He was insistent, pounding and kicking at the door. Briana begged him to leave but he answered he would beat the walls down first, and threatened to enlist Siward Bearn's aid in accomplishing it. She slipped a mantle on and made a half-hearted attempt to bind her hair before she let him in, but I was forced to greet him in my night-shift, not having thought to bring anything else with me and not daring to put on anything of Oswulf's. As soon as she unbarred the latch, he pushed himself in, heaving the timber back in place behind him. He was furious.

"How long think you this thing can be hid," he asked me, eyes ablaze, "when you leave your own bed empty for all to see and drag your sinning out the length of an entire day?"

I shrugged, and he went on in a harsher tone than before. "Thank you your merciful God that this lady's husband is out tossing with wound-fever! I do not want to be sitting alongside either of you when he discovers what you are about. God help you! If you cannot feel shame, feel fear then!"

Raging, he threw the pillows and furs off the pallet, then sat down on the edge of it. Flushed and shaking, Briana withdrew to the furthest corner, but in the tiny chamber she could not get away from his hard and accusing look.

"What is it you would have us do, brother?" I asked him finally, resenting the way he stared on her so roughly. "'Tis my own house, and I have no need to beg pardon of you!"

Right away, I knew I should not have said it. He sprang to his feet in trembling distemper, coming dangerously close to me before he stopped himself. "Put on you a mask of decency at least for your sister's bride-ale!" he whispered hoarsely. "God curse you if your dishonor is cast about while the king is here!"

Briana threw herself suddenly between us. "This is my doing, Earl Edwin!" she cried, pushing him away from me. "Blame not your brother; 'tis truly my fault!"

My brother fell back wearily into a heavy oaken chair. "That is the truth of it, I trow!" he said, looking at her in a hateful way. I was so angered that I let go a mighty oath in her hearing.

"Brother, if you mean to make this your business, consider well how you conduct yourself, else you will sore feel the pain of dealing with me!" I cried, my voice easily as fierce as his had ever been. I must have been glaring like a savage. His jaw dropped in utter amazement, and I blushed as I realized how ludicrous I must have looked, standing there in only a rumpled linen shift, dealing threats.

All of a sudden, we were both hysterical with laughter; I heard Briana sigh with relief as we grabbed each other's shoulders and wrestled in our foolish mirth. The boyishness lasted only a moment before we grew solemn again, but the tenseness had lifted a little, and my brother's voice sounded more resigned, if still apprehensive.

"I know not how you can find peace, involved in this—" breaking off, he searched for a word, "—involved in this dalliance," he finished finally.

"'Tis no dalliance between us, Edwin " I addressed it to him but gazed straight into Briana's eyes as the words escaped me. "This is my woman."

"Nay," he answered without emotion. "You know that is not the case of it." Briana and I looked away from each other miserably. "Do whatever it is you have to do," he added, forcing an apathetic smile, "but take care to cover your tracks. By the cross, I pray this of you!"

"Think you anyone knows?" Briana asked him with a darting glance. "Does my brother?"

"To me, seems any pigeon brain should be able to tell it!" he declared hotly. "But I trust not." Stretching, he stood to go, commanding me with a cool look to do the same. He had almost turned away when Briana caught him by the sleeve, bringing his gaze back to rest on her. Her voice was low, but tinged with earnesty.

"I should like to know that you do not think basely of us, Earl Edwin. I should like to think I can trust you." Her eyes narrowed just a bit, taking on a harder look.

"My brother knows well enough he can trust me, lady!" was his toneless reply.

She touched a hand to his cheek, as if in thanks. I felt the smallest clench of jealousy as their eyes met. 'Twas easy enough to see she thought him a fair man and his eyes grazed her in a forward way which I knew he would never have allowed himself if he did not think her already steeped in dishonor.

All the other of my chambers were deserted that time of day and we met no one in the narrow corridor. Back in my private lodges, the door closed behind us, my brother reached a hand to my shoulder.

"I want you to know," he said, eyes intent on mine, "that what sickens me is not your coupling with the woman. It is the knowing she can bring you nothing but misery—biting, wretched misery. Truly, I fear it."

I grit my teeth against the hurt of his words. "I love her, brother."

"She cannot make you a happy man."

"Surely, it is not a misery I feel with her!"

"Nay," he said in a somber voice, looking away. "When you are with her you feel well enough. 'Tis when you are parted you will feel the pain and taint of it." He reached over suddenly and pressed hard against my burnt-on star. "Does it hurt?" he asked with a piercing look.

"Not now, it does not. Why ask you?"

"Because—and I swear this is true, Morcar!—sometimes I think you crave torment!" He did not smile; his voice was level. "Sometimes I think anguish is your meat."

I said nothing. He unrolled a dalmatic he had taken from one of my chests and tossed it to me. Pulling it on, I heard him add morosely, "That oft was said about father, you know."

I stiffened. "You are the one like father; not I."

"Think you so?" he asked with a wonder and it sounded genuine. "Always I thought you more nearly resembled him, brother, in the important things."

"Well, you were wrong," I said shortly, tightening my belt with a hard tug. "From the time we were babes 'twas your likeness to him folk talked of. He marveled on it himself, even."

"I speak of things other than the shape of a smile—" he began reproachfully, but I cut him off.

"Bother me not to hear it!" I snapped in a knife-edged whisper. It seemed to surprise him; he stepped back with a puzzled look. I had no way of explaining how sore it rubbed me. The light of Ælfgar's eye, the turn of his temper, his power and willfulness: all these things were my brother's inheritance, and I had known it too long to doubt of it now. Neither the man's look nor his strength had come to me. Sometimes, I fancied it was my mother's madness I had more than anything—that and my quietude and indecision, and I knew not where I came by those.

Edwin left after a while. He told everyone I had kept my bed all day with head-pain, and I told him best he would say I suffered it still for I had no inclination to take table or make converse. After he had gone, I put myself down, fully dressed, on my cot. I did a lot of thinking and, towards darkness, I fell asleep. When I woke later, there were furs thrown over me and all the household was still. Things went from bad to worse then. I drifted in and out of fiendish dreams and wakened myself four times in night-sweats.

CHAPTER THIRTY-ONE

The earls Edwin and Morcar, sons of Ælfgar, the
foremost of the Anglish earls, were attached by the
strictest ties to harold, and employed all their efforts
to support his cause, he having married their sister
Aldgyth, who had been the cwene of Gruffydd.

> —Orderic Vitalis
> Book 3, Chapter XI

April 1066

I will never forget how he looked—King Harold, son of Godwine—
when I named his bride's-price. He was arrayed splendidly in dyed
moreen, the very truest shade of summer-skies, topped with a mantle of
white ermine. Against the sun-burnished yellow of his hair, the stunning
golden circlet, crown of the Anglish kings, gleamed brilliantly,
reflecting the light of hundreds of tapers. The Eorforwic minster had
been filled with them. Not a single one was cheap tallow; all were of the
finest bees-wax, imported from France.

Everything about him made an impression. Folk were already beginning to call him Harold the Fair. He was bull-chested like a Saxon and
long-legged like a Dane and flashing as any king had ever been. A man
who looked so fine must have been well aware of it. Perhaps that
accounted for some of the pridefulness in his gaze, or the easy, solicitous,
almost condescending smile which played over his handsome features so
attractively. Never before had I seen a man so sure of himself.

When the Archbishop Aldred bade us name the price, we looked at
each other, Edwin and I. I was the one who voiced it, telling him plainly
and firmly that we demanded a complete renunciation of the woman
called Edith Swan's-Neck, mother of his bastard sons, and this to be
made upon holy relics. Harold looked from one to the other of us, his
face totally impassive except for the deep blue eyes which smoldered
with indignation.

"I see no cause to keep the woman," he said at length, coolly, "but it must stand that any properties she holds now by me will remain hers, and be legacy to the underlings."

"Fair said, King Harold," my brother answered in the same well-modulated tone, "but you are not to visit the concubine, or her issue, long as you are wed to this lady."

Harold looked across the room to where my sister sat with her ladies. She was clothed in a stunning gown of sunny eastern cloth, and wore emeralds at her throat along with Gruffydd's ring. She was astoundingly beautiful and Harold stared at her a long time before his gaze returned to us. "Think you this is a high price you ask of me, sons of Ælfgar?" he asked with a trace of a cold smile. "If so, best you know it sits not heavy on me at all to agree to it."

"'Tis decided then," Edwin exclaimed with a satisfied glance my way. He held out both his hands to seal the bargain. Harold took them and their eyes locked together for a moment. More was named to the price—gold-gifts and manor-taxes—and then Archbishop Aldred, a stately, broad, silver-haired man, called my sister forward. She meekly agreed that the price was fair. The pair were anointed with chrism. Then we left the minster and made our way in a huge procession through the cheering throng, smiling and waving till we came at last to my house. There, the women went to the chapel to help my sister keep her fast, and the men retired to the great hall to keep Harold company in his.

Edwin sat at the king's right and did most of the speaking with our new brother-in-law. I was between Gyrth Godwine's son, not much of a talker, and Siward Bearn, who was partaking copiously of the fine mead and urging me to do the same. Oswulf was conspicuously absent. Brother Wulfget had lanced and packed the man's shoulder again that morning causing him to lapse again into fever, made worse by drunkenness and lack of food. We gave strict orders to keep him in the kitchen-house and even posted a guard there.

Someone else was missing, and much to Edwin's dismay. His man Hereward had refused to sit to table with Harold Godwine's son. No matter that the man was king; he had been responsible for an uncomfortable exile the Wake had suffered over a matter of small consequence. The Mercian was obviously not a forgiving man and he was adamant in his refusal to drink to the new king's health. Edwin had laughed at him, reminding him that we ourselves had undergone exile twice under the heavy hand of Harold's family, but Hereward the Wake was not to be moved. He kept to chambers and out-buildings the entire length of the king's visit. Sometimes Brother Wulfget or Uncle Leofric or even Edwin himself snuck away to keep him company, and he seemed altogether satisfied with his lot. As for me, I cannot particularly say I missed him all those days. Something about the man grated me, though I could not finger it. He was too unlike other men.

I feared the night was off to an inauspicious start because of the coolness which waxed between us in the minster. Harold was all smiles and courtesies, though, as if he had either forgotten the unpleasantness or truly meant to ignore it. I had to respect him for that; we had caught him off his guard in a rather compromising way.

Next day began the bride-ale. The weather's being sullen, we spent the morning gaming in the great hall, listening to Eirish harpists and drummers while we picked from delicacies and subtleties splendidly laid out everywhere upon the tables. For the ladies' amusement, we held sham fights in the middle of the hall and played many rounds of hoodman blind in gay, mixed company. By noon, the sun had reappeared so a large party walked through the cobbled courtyards and streets, anywhere the mud did not prevent it. Meanwhile, scullions worked feverishly to lay the lavish feasting tables. The rich banquet was unsurpassed. Even Harold, used to the finery of the royal court, was amazed at it.

We were fast growing comfortable with our new brother-in-the-law. I had early noticed that his polished and perfect mannerisms did not quite conceal a casual openness and earnest desire to please. He acted almost as if he wore the golden crown upon his head by necessity and not choice, and so expected no special deference because of it. He was my father's age yet there was no condescension in his address to us and, if anything, he seemed to revere my sister. He had a gentle, soothing way of speaking to her and would ignore everything around him to catch a phrase of her talk, no matter how seemingly unimportant. As for Aldgyth, she looked in no-wise unhappy, as I had half expected she might. Lady Briana sat anext her, in a gown of fine woven seafoam-green, and they whispered much together, looking altogether pleased with the turn things were taking.

On the second night of the bride-ale, the eve of the hand-fasting, Harold did something entirely unexpected. 'Twas the night for the exchanging of gifts. Harold had named Edwin his best man, though it was unusual to choose a brother of either contracting party, particularly the bride's. He did it out of deference to us, knowing that if anything were to happen to him, we would want the say in the lady's affairs to revert back to our house. My brother had chosen a rare and extraordinary gift for the couple: a small, richly carved aumbry, or relic-chest, inlaid with gold, silver and many-colored gems. It was near as precious as the one in the Eorforwic Minster, but of a much lesser height, standing only to a man's elbow. There was a sudden hush as the thing was carried in, and it was followed by cries and claps of appreciation. Later, Grandmother Godiva was to tell us it was the finest treasure ever she had seen presented at a bride-ale, and surely one fit for a king and his cwene.

Harold, obviously moved, stood and faced my brother, both hands on Edwin's shoulders in brotherly fashion. He said he apologized because his gift would probably seem nowhere near as fine as that one and he hoped we would not be insulted or take offense. Then his men carried in a long, narrow box of carven cherry-wood, finely done. They set it on the table before the Earl of Mercia, and everyone craned and strained to see what it might hold. My own curiosity was so strong that I stood behind my brother, peering over his shoulder as he undid the golden hasp.

Edwin stiffened when he saw what lay inside. He spun round to face me, a look of indecipherable emotion shadowing his face. It was our father's gleaming battle-axe, shined and honed to perfection. Alongside it was a golden chain and cross that Ælfgar had been wont to wear for many years. As if suddenly grown weak, my brother fell back to his place on the bench, staring wordlessly at the king.

"Tostig carried them both like trophies," Harold explained in a low voice. "I made him give them to me 'ere he fled for Flanders."

"You could not have made me a finer present than this one, brother!" Edwin whispered. For a moment, I feared he might come to tears, but he lifted a horn instead, and the two men drank together as was the custom.

Next morning, when the wedding party rode out to throw alms and hear petitions, Edwin wore the flashing weapon, hanging it round the neck of his proud grey stallion in a sling of gold-chain and silver. I wore the cross.

After the hand-fasting, we settled quickly into the third and last night of the feasting, always the richest, most boisterous and unrestrained. Edwin left the king's high table for a while to sit with Uncle Leofric and Grandmother Godiva and other high-born Mercians. This action of his was well-received by his people, so I followed suit, sitting myself amidst the noble North Humbrians, squeezed between Gamel-Beorn and Osbeorn Dolfin's son. I think that was my first mistake of the evening for, by the saints, those men could drink! Even before the first courses of provender were picked and finished, I was waxing well into excess merriment, even singing a little, which always means trouble for me.

After three days and nights of revelry and feasting, nearly every man in the place was in the same state of mind so there was no reason to feel shame. Some had drunk themselves to unconsciousness two nights in a row, so I might even have applauded myself for my temperance. The king himself was loose-tongued and starry-eyed; something fiendish kept reminding me that this was the night he finally got to bed his lady and that might have contributed a good deal to his happy spirits. His brothers, Gyrth and Leofwine, had grown raucous on the very first night and had never truly settled down since. The same held true for Siward Bearn. In true North Humbrian fashion he was thoroughly enjoying the accumulated effects of the finest, most potent ales and meads in the land. Edwin was inordinately happy, laughing at everything and moving in a peculiarly dizzy and light-headed way. With everyone it was the same.

So I wondered why it was that I felt guilty for giving way to drunkenness, except that I had long known that mindlessness only bode me ill. Four years had passed since Edwin and I had drunk ourselves silly with the Welshmen and wandered into the Eardene, but I had never forgotten the horror and sickness of that day. And the night I had lost reality in the monk's-house at Ceaster—that had been the true start of my sins and woes. 'Twas too late now, I told myself, drinking more, but I resolved this would be the last time I gave in to such frivolity. There was no need to make myself suffer, as my brother said I was wont to do.

The hall was so crowded and noisy that bonfires had been set outside and the partying had spilled over into the courtyard and meadows. In truth, despite the dampness of the air and the slight chill, 'twas much more comfortable under the sky than in the smoky, over-loud hall. I found myself seeking the respite of the night air more and more as time wore on. I was heading out for the fourth or fifth time when Lady Briana joined me, sidling up beside me with a soft greeting. Full well knowing it was the wrong thing to do, I clutched her feverishly, drawing her mouth to mine and kissing her then and there. She laughed a little and pulled away from me, casting a worried glance all around. We were in the shadows, though, and unobserved, so she let me slip an arm around her and we walked a way, not saying anything.

"The storehouse or the byre?" she asked suddenly in a breathless tone. I stopped dead, amazed at her boldness.

"Lady!" I stammered, staring at her. "You have a madness! This place is over-run with people!"

"Aye," she said, stroking my cheek, "but any who would come to the storehouse would surely be about their own private business, think you not?"

I trembled as that familiar feeling, that surge of combined strength and weakness, fast overtook me. "I know not, lady! Methinks we would be taking unreasonable risk."

"In the field, then!" she breathed, putting her arms around my neck and bringing her body as close to mine as possible. Feeling a sudden fear as my control slipped away, I pushed her back harshly.

"I think not, lady!" I said coldly, shaking my head.

"Do not pretend with me, Morcar!" she snapped, taking me firmly by the hand and leading me further into the meadow, towards a tall tree. I know I could have resisted her, but I did not. "Surely you know well as I do that Oswulf will be moving me off to the Bernicia in a few days. What chance will we have then?" Her husky voice was logical and convincing if not entirely passion-steeped. When we came to the tree, I grabbed her shoulders suddenly and made her face me.

"Know you what a great discomfort this will be?" I asked her roughly. "Methinks 'tis unseemly for an earl and a fine lady to roll in the grass!"

In the wan moonlight, I could barely see her smile. "Do you not remember, my Morcar?" she asked softly, undoing my belt. "The first time you took me 'twas in the grass!"

I shuddered at her touch. "I think I had almost forgotten it," I whispered in her ear.

She leant back against the wide tree, arching her back. "Then I must make you remember, sir!" she cried, and gave a little gasp as I moved my cold hands up inside the wide sleeves of her tunic to her warm and waiting body.

For a little while, the noise of the rowdy celebration seemed very far away.

                    *   *   *

For fear of discovery, we did not undress ourselves. Afterwards, when we realized how rumpled and disheveled our finery was, we laughed hysterically. The warmth of the spirits and the heat of my woman had put me in a playful, affectionate mood—a dangerous mood, for I was grown heedless and over-bold in my drunkenness and did not even know it.

We did our best to straighten one another, teasing all the while and laughing and embracing. When she brooched my mantle into place, I drew her under it and wrapped her close to me. When we walked, she held up most of my weight. Whenever I staggered, she clenched me hard around the waist and whispered silly words of reproval. We had grown so loose and gamesome that we did not see the two men sitting in the shadowy meadow till we were near on top of them. Even when they stood up suddenly, staring at us in shock, it took me a moment to recognize the chief men of two earls: Edwin's man Hereward and mine, Siward Bearn. I felt a painful surge in the pit of my stomach and tried to stand straight.

Siward Bearn was the one who spoke first, spewing harsh words at his sister. "Best you would make yourself gone from here, woman!" he hissed. "Else you will feel my enragement!"

"You suppose too much, brother!" she cried feebly but even as she said it the man's eyes were hard upon me. He was every bit as drunk as I was, I could tell at a glance, and trembling with anger. Never a figure looked more ominous to me than he did then, his tall frame silhouetted in the moonlight, his long, coppery locks spiked by the April breeze. I shivered as he stepped closer.

Suddenly, Hereward the Wake was between us, a hand on my chest and one on my cousin's, as if to keep us apart. "There is no quarrel here," he said with certainty, "until this thing can be spoken out between you—not till the morrow!"

Even so, the instant the man stepped back, freeing us, Siward Bearn lunged at me, and I was helpless against the force of the powerful blow he struck to my jaw. "Methinks I despise the way you repay love and loyalty, cousin!" I heard him say as I went sprawling in a wild rush of pain. I lay there, groaning and swallowing blood. Then Briana stooped to cradle my head, sobbing. I was so stunned that it took me some time to realize that Hereward had wrestled the Bearn into a savage strangle-hold and held him there helpless.

"By the relics, man," he was saying, "it rests now between the four of us and not a single man more need know—unless you drag it before the whole party by your mindless fury!"

Siward Bearn gave a hoarse, choking cry as the other man released him. After a silence, my cousin spoke in an iron voice. "I will avenge your sick misuse of her, kinsman! God knows you will pay for your night of drunken romping!"

Then my head fell back as Briana flew to her feet with a shrill, sullen laugh. "You are the same fool you ever were, brother!" she cried bitterly. "The one who sore misused me, you rewarded with my hand and dowry! You could not make him love me, though, nor I him!"

Siward called her a witch, and she laughed again. "'Twill be a shameful thing for you, brother, I am sure, to know I have been Earl Morcar's woman for many months now!"

I heard more than saw the slap he delivered, almost knocking her to the ground. Spitting out a mouthful of my own blood, I forced myself to stand.

"You will not harm her, cousin!" I threatened, head spinning. "She is blameless in this!"

The Bearn laughed wretchedly. "I know better than that! But, 'tis true you are the one who should suffer the reprisals, Morcar Ælfgar's son, because you advantaged yourself of her—" he broke off suddenly and turned his back, but I heard him add low, "—and lied to all around you!"

I wiped my face with my sleeve, abject with misery. "Methinks 'twas not something I could easily boast of, Siward Æthelgar's son!"

He groaned, running fingers through his hair as if his head were paining him. "You are the last of all men I expected to deal me deceit, kinsman. From the very first of all this, I thought we had a brotherhood between us."

"For the sake of it then, try to understand!" my voice seemed a pitiful whine. I felt like a little child begging for subtleties.

"I understand well enough, Earl Morcar!" He turned back to face me, hands on his hips. Briana came to my side then, defiantly wrapping her arms about my waist in a tight and familiar embrace. My cousin quivered with anger, then took the back of her neck roughly in his powerful hand and yanked her away. Without thinking, I reached for her and he slammed his fist down on my arm so hard that it sent me flying again.

"She is not in your claim," I heard him declare in an icy voice as I hit the grass. "Best you would realize that right now, else it will fare ill with you!" Grabbing her, he stomped off into the darkness. She had to run to keep pace with his long-legged stride.

Hereward pulled me to my feet. Numb, I let him lead me.

"How many share your chamber tonight?" he asked calmly, as if nothing had happened apart from the norm.

I could not think; then I remembered. "I have given it over to Aldgyth and Harold tonight."

"Have you another room which can be barred?"

"Aye. Edwin and I mean to share the small one tonight, near the storeroom." I had never been that dizzy before.

Suddenly, the man stopped and began to fumble with the brooch that held my mantle. Surprised, I drew away from him, flustered and tense. He laughed heartily. "You are wearing a mantle of white ermine, my lord," he explained with a merry grin, "and you are bleeding from the mouth and nose."

I let him remove it. He spit on the sleeve of his tunic and wiped my face with it. "Best you would hang your head when we pass people," he said, eyeing me critically. That was no problem; I scarce could lift it anyway. We went in through the storehouse and when we came to the chamber, he chased away the men who were in there sharing horns and talking. First thing I did was throw myself into a miserable heap on the floor. I did not want to talk about it, and especially not with this man.

He brought over a bucket. "Dunk your face," he commanded I let go a moan but, afraid he would do it for me, sat up quickly and splashed myself. The coldness only magnified the pain in my jaw and cheek. I discovered I had bitten a large chunk out of my tongue. The man tossed me a rag and told me gruffly to scrub the blood off better than that—just as if he were my guardian. I shot him a mean look.

"'Tis strange to see a dyed-red North Humbrian without a beard," he said musingly as I glared. "You ought to let it grow to its own hue. What is it, that browning-gold of Edwin's?"

I shook my head. "'Tis a sad-mouse brown," I said, wondering why I was answering him.

"Well, you ought to let it grow back!" he exclaimed. "The only thing that saves the shaven Bernicians from looking womanly is the fact that they do not dye those long, long locks of theirs."

I glowered. "What mean you to say, Mercian? That I look womanly or that it would be good to make myself look like a man of Oswulf's?"

He flinched a little. "You mistake me, my lord," he said low, turning away. I flushed with shame and laid back down again. "You would do well to change those tainted clothes, too," he added in a less imperative tone. "Should I send someone for clean ones?"

I nodded miserably, and he left for a while, closing the door gently behind him.

It seems I stayed there a long time alone, lost in depressing reflections. My cousin's hurt and anger had been genuine and he was not a man who loved or hated by halves. My fear was not that he would make good any blood threats or drunken warnings; more, I feared he would forswear me now, and I had come to count heavily on his council and his friendship. Closing my eyes, I rubbed my throbbing jaw and wondered whether it was still whole. Edwin had been right; the lady did not bring me happiness.

When Hereward returned, he latched the door again, then tossed some clean garb on the floor beside me. "I can stay here with you a while or not, Earl Morcar," he said emotionlessly, "whichever you think best."

I rolled over and made myself sit. "Must be you think Edwin is a very different man than I, is't so, Mercian?" I looked him in the eye, pouting sullenly.

"In some ways different," he replied casually, helping me to my feet. "In some ways, much alike. By the saints, I swear he needs a woman, though. I think he envies you yours."

"What mean you?" Eyes narrowed, I spoke iron-toned.

"Do not forget she has lived a season in his house, Earl Morcar, and all that while I watched him looking on her."

"Speak carefully!" I warned him, trembling with anger. He laughed in a good natured way.

"He did naught but look, my lord! He hard resents the woman for the way she has bewitched you."

"Those are his words?"

"Aye."

"By God! What does he do? Speak of it openly as if it were the weather?" I was truly furious with my brother for sharing this secret with a virtual stranger. Hereward shook his head, showing an earnest smile.

"Nay. He tossed hard words with her one night, and I asked him about it, that is all. Methinks I am the only man in all the world he has ever told. In truth, it shames him." The man broke off quickly, probably afraid of offending me again. He waited a while, then added, "Earl Edwin has not the temper to entangle himself in something as complicated as your affair. He would drive himself to ruin with all his raging. Besides, he likes so well to be master that he could never be happy with a woman as bold as that."

I could not help it; I swung at him. He stepped back and looked at me curiously. "Why is it you take offense at everything, my lord? Surely the woman is bold! Any man could tell you as much. Her own husband says it even, and methinks he is a man who likes to be master, too!"

I was storming inside. Everything, every little thing the man said rubbed me. I sat down heavily on a bench, put my elbows on my knees, and buried my face in my hands. Hereward the Wake sat down, too, on the floor in front of me. "You are wrong if you think I am saying one kind of man is better than another," he said solemnly. "'Tis just that some are masterful with women while others like to be managed by them, just as some prefer muslin shirts and some choose linen."

"You irk me, Mercian!" I mumbled, but he caught it and laughed.

"I only speak the truth, sir!" he said merrily. "'Tis the truth that bothers you. You would be surprised how many men do not like to think upon it. There was no insult in what I said. You will find that some of the boldest—men who will bend to none other—need to be led around by a strong woman else they cannot be happy." He leant forward in the manner of a confessor, his voice lowered to a whisper. "Look you at King Harold," he said. "Your sister will rule him entirely, and he will revel in it. 'Tis said that his other woman, the Swan's-Neck, was a perfect shrew."

Suddenly, I was laughing. "You are mad!" I told him, slipping out of my dalmatic and unlacing my tunic. All the while, I was thinking about it, though, and remembering how Gruffydd loved to boast that Aldgyth had tamed him.

Seeing that I had relaxed somewhat, Hereward bent down and gathered up my garb, unrolling and uncreasing each piece as he handed it to me. "I, for one," he said emphatically, "will always prefer a forward woman. I married the first one who ever pulled me to the ground with her. She was Flemish and spoke not a word of Anglish!"

I shot him a quizzical look. He shrugged and nodded. "'Tis the truth, my lord!" His face creased into an easy smile. "Think you I would let a prize like that get away?"

I shook my head, laughing a little. "You are a strange man, Hereward the Wake."

"Aye. Not as strange as some, though," he replied very seriously, helping me buckle on my girts and belts.

"Where is your lady now?" I asked, holding out the two necklaces for him to fasten. He lifted my hair up and did them deftly. He had much more the touch of an earl's man than Siward Bearn; but then, Edwin was always more particular in his dress than I and would have demanded it of him.

"I left her in Flanders, in the court at Ghent. Now I am glad of it, too. The woman would have been in the straw with your pretty brother in a twinkling."

I looked at him with shock. He had not said it in a rude way, just as a matter of course. I was still cloudy with drink, I thought. Perhaps I had misunderstood him. No man would speak of his wedded woman in such a way. He must have felt my eyes hard upon him; he sat down on the bench and returned my stare.

"I would never begrudge him the woman, my lord," he said defensively, "but that she would do him no good. He is the sort who needs them meek and submissive. Earl Edwin would never warm to one unless he could entirely have his way with her—bend her completely to his bidding and use his own hardness to subdue her."

I was so amazed by now that I backed up to the wall and leant against it for support. "How is it you can speak openly of such things?" I asked him suspiciously. He looked at me with wonder and shrugged.

"I thought 'twas what we were talking about, my lord!" He was searching through all his pouches for a comb but was obviously not carrying one. I walked over and handed him mine. He stood and began to comb me. "I meant no boldness," he added in an apologetic tone. "When one man lives anext another, he begins to notice things about him. Never have I admired a friend more than I do your brother. Yet, in some ways, any man can see he needs correcting."

I turned right around and confronted him. "What ways?"

"The man needs a wedded wife, that is all." He repositioned me and combed some more. "I have never yet met your mother, my lord, but I have heard enough about her from him to know one thing with certainty: she has frighted him away from women."

An hour ago, I would have taken umbrage at the remark; now I let it pass. "She acted very harshly to him," I admitted.

"'Tis why he needs a type unlike her. And best you should realize that when he finally finds one, he most likely will be harsh to her in turn."

"By the Cross, man!" I exclaimed nervously. "What do you do? Stay up sleepless all night and think on these things?"

He laughed. "Nay, Earl Morcar! That has just this moment occurred to me! You will see I am right in it, though."

I shook my head, trying to make some sense of him. In a little while I was telling him about my mother—long-buried memories that I never expected would come to converse. It surprised me, but I could not seem to stop myself. What is worse, before we left that chamber to rejoin the commotion in the hall, I had told him things about Briana! I even shared my fear that Siward Bearn would loose himself from me because of what I felt for her.

"'Tis an exceeding strange thing, my lord," he mused, just as we were going, "but do you know what it was that the Bearn was telling me, sitting out there half-drunken in the darkness?"

I said no.

"He was describing how sore he had longed for your sister all these years."

I gazed at Hereward curiously. He did not seem to notice I was staring at him. *"He draws you out, brother! You will come to appreciate it!"* is what Edwin had told me. Leave it to the Wake to pull those words out of Siward Bearn.

*   *   *

If Oswulf had been wearing a metal hauberk when Siward Bearn revenged his woman, his stabbing through the shoulder would have been but a skin wound. Men have been known to take great crashes of axes to the back or swords to the stomach and come away with naught but ugly scars provided they are wrapped in iron. Even a leathern under-hauberk would have saved him a great deal of agony and disfigurement. The fact was, though, that the Bearn had wounded him when he wore no protection, and the mean slice was deep, wide, and gross. It had early grown tainted so the priests had opened and packed it several times, making it deeper and worse. My cousin had lost much of the power in his left arm because of it, despite the fact that he had moved and worked the limb studiously almost from the first day.

I had almost forgotten the man in all the bustle and busyness of the bride-ale and so did not wholly realize the extent of his misery. But on the second morning after I fell out with my chief man, King Harold called a council and he specifically asked that Earl Oswulf attend along with the other highest men of the realm. The king was taking his leave on the morrow and he wanted our homage.

Oswulf did not look well; he was thin, pale, and listless and his eyes and hair seemed faded. He clenched and unclenched the fist of his sore arm constantly, unconsciously, staring off in a distracted way. To my great relief, there was no fight in him; he accepted everything I said as a matter of course and wordlessly allowed the priests to ready him. After washing his long hair, which had been stiff with sweat, and bathing him, they decked him in fine robes. The left sleeve of his tunic and dalmatic hung empty. The wounded limb was too swollen and rigid to be maneuvered.

Even so, he looked near as fair as ever by the time they finished with him. I led him into a chamber where the others were already assembled. King Harold rose and greeted him in smiling, friendly fashion, calling him his earl and brother. Then he waited for Oswulf to kneel, but my cousin appeared not to understand what was expected of him. I realized the man was too weak and helpless to cause any real trouble but it irked me that he might bring unpleasantness to the house when our dealings with the king had proceeded this far without any. Gazing into Oswulf's eyes forcefully for a moment, I moved forward myself and knelt in front of Harold, voicing my allegiance. My cousin made no attempt to follow my example. When I stood, he followed me silently to the table and sat down, looking off past everyone and everything as if entirely unaware of the embarrassed silence which had ensued.

After a minute or so, flashing Gyrth, Earl of the East Anglia, rose purposefully, then knelt to his brother. His words were pronounced carefully. A bit too loud and ostentatious, I thought, yet his pride in his brother was obvious and genuine. Soon as he had finished, Leofwine, who looked like a taller, thinner Tostig, did the same.

Then Edwin knelt, the highest man in the realm save for the king himself, and told his brother-in-the-law that he never had need to fear the loyalty and support of the midlands. He said it was like a balm to him, knowing that the old enmity between Mercia and Wessex had been dissolved by the union of their houses. Harold took my brother's shoulders, lifted him to his feet, and embraced him. Then Siward Bearn bent his tall, powerful frame before the king, and lastly so did Waltheof Siward's son, new Earl of Huntandun and the North Hamtun, lands Mercia had lost through the razing of them during the insurrection against Tostig.

When everyone had returned to the bench, I caught Siward Bearn's eye a moment but there was nothing to be read there. I had not changed a word with him since our rough parting in the lea, and he had kept

Briana hidden well away from me.

After a while, when Oswulf made no move to rise, the king came to the head of the small table, staring expectantly at the Earl of the Bernicia. My cousin looked sullen but when he finally spoke, his tone was quite mild. He looked directly at Harold and announced casually that he had suffered much at the hands of Tostig Godwine's son, and would be a liar if he swore himself now, before he had a chance to cool. Harold bit his lip, anger rising. He asked levelly if Oswulf Eadwulf's son was in accordance with the earls of the land.

"You will find I am ever in accord with men who treat me fairly, my lord," my cousin replied wanly. "I do not bend myself easily, though. I am not as pliant as some."

Harold Godwine's son could have swelled the issue with rightful ire but to his credit he chose to placate the Bernician by apologizing for the banished Tostig's faults and improprieties. "You will find I am of a different cut, son of Eadwulf," he said, running fingers through his straw-colored hair. "I will give you time to make that determination. Even so, know you that I will expect your presence, if not during the summer, then by the Christ Mass Gemot at the latest. It sits not well with me to have no oath of loyalty from one of the chief men of the realm, an earl by hereditary right. Yet, as you are liege-man to Earl Morcar, who is himself sworn fully to me, I will concede this time to you. Mayhap when you are fully recovered, you will come to higher sense about this, for 'tis a matter of gravest importance."

His eyes lingered a while on Oswulf's useless arm, but he asked no questions about it. My cousin still looked sick and feverish, and the king had considerately agreed to let this account for his untoward obstinacy.

The question of our trustworthiness hung heavy with Harold Godwine's son. 'Twas no secret Tostig meant to invade the north in an attempt to regain his earldom. Rumor was that he had joined forces with Harald Hardraada, the Viking King of the North Wegians, who felt he had a claim to the Anglish throne because his predecessor and King Edward's had once drunkenly agreed that whichever of the two survived longer should have the other's kingdom. Apparently, the deposed Tostig had first offered the services of his men and mercenaries to the Duke of Normandy, not knowing the Norman had been inspired to hate him by the tales of William Malet and Earl Harold, and the sad plight of our mother. Tostig had promised to fight for Duke William in return for the lands north of the Humber when the kingdom was won. Ignominiously expelled from the duchy of Normandy, he had sailed north and allied himself to the ruthless North Wegian king and his famous Vikings—no doubt offering the same rate of exchange.

Harold must have inwardly known that we would defend our home-lands with blood and fury but he had to be certain. He could not trust to fate that the Anglish fyrd would be able to come north to fight off the invaders. William of Normandy had declared open war on him, too, and was known to be readying a large fleet to attack the southern coast.

King Harold swore forever after that he had only promised to support the Norman's cause if and when Edward named Tostig his successor. He said he could not have foreseen then that his brother would deliver himself into exile with his crimes and misdeeds the way he did, else he would have made no commitment at all. He never denied swearing on relics but he insisted that his oath had not been to support William's claim, only to support William's claim above Tostig's. He declared his pledge to back the Norman had no validity since Tostig was not named to the kingship.

The Duke of Normandy saw it differently. So did another man who had been there when the handsome Saxon put his hand upon the reli-quary: our avunculus, William Malet. He protested at Harold's corona-tion that the king was beholden to the Norman duke. A tremendous argument ensued after the ceremony and my uncle, once friend and protector of Earl Harold, had taken ship across the channel to inform William of what he considered to be Harold's great perfidy. Closest of our kin, our own avunculus had not drunk Aldgyth's bride-ale.

Perhaps Harold swore to more than he realized or perhaps my uncle only thought he did. In Angland, no one could be sure. The rumor even gained credence that Harold, indebted to the Norman for his ransoming from Count Guy and dependent upon him for a means of returning to Angland, had sworn under duress. One version held that William had hidden the relics and Harold did not know he had made a holy oath! Harold himself laughed at this story. The agreement had been pledged openly in a crowded hall, he said. Only later, William had changed the terms of it to his own advantage. Some believed one way and some another but, in the end, most of our countrymen agreed that a strong Anglishman with no claim was preferable to a strong foreigner with a slight one. Even so, no one, and least of all Harold himself, expected the crown to rest easily on that golden head.

In order to be free to deal with the Norman's forces, Harold had to be convinced that the earls of the north and midlands stood firmly behind him. The reason was this: he knew the people of the north and midlands stood firmly behind their earls. Especially in the North Humbria where the triumvirate of power—Siward Bearn, Oswulf Eadwulf's son, and myself—was the result of a popular uprising and elec-tion, and the House of Godwine was passionately despised, he wanted to be assured that when the people followed the men they had chosen, those men in turn would be following him.

This private councilling took the place of the Easter Gemot for us that year. With such an imminent threat of invasion not a one of us felt free to travel south. We made use of what time we had with the king and the southern earls to plan the action we would take if and when the worst of our expectations came to pass. Afterwards, we met in the great hall with the rest of the thegns and high-born men. The men of the North, who had for so long been neglected by the king and ignored by the rest of their countrymen, put great stock in this occasion. They called it the first Eorforwic Gemot, and spoke eagerly of greater unity in the land, long divided both emotionally and geographically. Harold swore then to come north at least once a year, bringing his popular cwene with him. The cheering brought on by that promise of his echoed through the hall for several long minutes.

The king's bride-ale train would travel in great state through Mercia, the lady's homeland, before returning to Lundun City. Harold, quick to note and appreciate the great enthusiasm which the people of the midlands showed for their comely, dashing earl, had asked Edwin to ride in the party with the highest of his guard, including the once-hated Welshmen, from Lindcylene to Couventrie. Nearly everyone who had come north for the royal marriage left with that huge, splendid party early on the morrow of the day after our meetings, including Lady Godiva, with whom we had a tearful parting. Many of the Bernicians and North Humbrians had already taken their leave, so when that train glittered its way out of the Eorforwic Shire, my house and grounds which had been so thoroughly over-crowded for so long, seemed suddenly still and empty.

CHAPTER THIRTY-TWO

At that time, throughout all England, a portent
such as men had never seen before was seen in the
heavens. . . .

—Anglo Saxon Chronicle
Book "C," 1066

April 24-30, 1066
One warm, clear evening a full fortnight later, Heard Ulf's son burst into
my chamber and bade me come out to the courtyard to look at the sky.

Things had gone very well since the king took his leave. Edmund
Half-Dane had eased my entire household back into happy and produc-
tive order. Oswulf Eadwulf's son had recovered nearly whole in strength
and temper, and left for the Bernicia in high spirits. Lady Briana and I
had come to another understanding by then: this one final and absolute
and not at all unpleasant. Having brought misery to another and shame
to ourselves by our rashness this time, we had been truly ready for repentance. I had confessed, this time to Brother Wulfget, who could not hide
his shock, and been shriven. The lady and I managed a furtive but
unemotional fare-well, like a good-bye between a fond brother and sister.

Best of all, though, the day Oswulf and his woman took leave with
their party, Siward Bearn returned unobtrusively to his duties as my
chief man, setting his pallet nonchalantly in my chamber that night as
if naught had passed between us. He was less talkative than before, but
that lasted only a few days. He did not mention the cause of our quarrel,
not even once. I had to suppose that Hereward the Wake and Brother
Wulfget had between them forced him into a reconciliation. They had
tended him constantly since that night and were always in his company.
Those two left for Kirton with the remainder of Edwin's party, though,
having said not a word to me about it. I would not hazard asking the
Bearn, either. I was happy enough just to have the friendship restored.
A few days later, I served as his best man when he was made hand-fast
to Gythrun Olavsdätter.

Uncle Leofric warned me once about becoming drunken with power and pridefulness. As ale inspired a happiness and freedom which were entirely false, he said, so would conceit inspire a sense of security when none was in truth to be had. Perhaps that is what I was given over to that windy, fragrant spring; surely I had cause enough for satisfaction. I was one of the highest men of the realm now, Earl of the North Humbria and brother-in-the-law to the king. Our house sat over half the kingdom and everything my father had fought and died for had come to pass. As if to absolve herself of all the wrongs she had done us, Providence seemed suddenly to smile with special favor, and the warmth it inspired in me was, indeed, similar to the tingling comfort of intoxication. I have never been a self-assured man or one who is over-confident, but I carried no doubts or fears with me that season.

Not until the night Heard Ulf's son pulled me out to the courtyard to look at the sky.

Suspended in the eerie clearness of the heavens was a long-haired star, the most awesome of heaven's portents, drawing behind it a vast, streaming wake of glare. I crossed myself, awed that it had the power to inspire such a strange sense of foreboding in me.

It kindled in the darkness all that night—a long, sleepless night that saw many men craning their necks in the courtyard, engaging in hushed converse fraught with speculation, long hours after they would usually have been abed. It disappeared with the dawn, but dusky twilight brought it back. Seven nights it burned the heavens. Seven long nights. Then, by the grace of God, it went away.

The promise of it stayed, though. Every man who looked upon the thing tried to fathom its message. 'Twas a grave-light, many whispered, or a war-beacon. Seven nights had it burned; within that many months, the wise-folk said, all the horrors that it heralded would be upon the land. So it had always been with hairy stars. They told warning of one thing only: tragedy.

Near a century before, one had blazed at the accession of handsome Edward, most unfortunate of the six successive boy-kings. Uncle Leofric once let us read about it in the great chronicle kept year by year in the monastery at Peterborough. Most Anglishmen knew the story: how the star had three nights lit the sky and the priests read it to mean three years of famine, earthquake, blood, and battle. But none foresaw that the unlucky young king would be murdered three years to the very week later—stabbed in the back by his own step-mother then dragged eight miles hanging in agony from the stirrup of his wild stallion. The past was proof that comets most often portended the death of a king or the fall of a kingdom. Or both.

My knowing that helped assuage an irrational fear that plagued me: that the beacon had been loosed specifically to terrorize me for my personal sins. Like many another, I fast brought myself to the confessional and made good all my penances. Logic told me, though, that if the star had indeed been tossed by the angry hand of God, it must have been for a sin of some far more awful consequence. Almost against my will, I found myself wondering what it was that Harold had sworn to William of Normandy and whether 'twas true, as the Normans hotly declared, that the Anglish king was a breaker of holy oaths.

CHAPTER THIRTY-THREE

Tostig sailed with a fleet of sixty ships . . . to the
humber and despoiled everything near the mouth of
the river with piratical raids; but by Edwin and
Morcar, two brothers who used their power as one,
he was vigorously driven out of the province.

—William of Malmesbury

May 1066

My great house at Eorforwic was but a full day's ride from Edwin's at
Kirton, if the weather was fair and the party fast, free of women and
baggage. In addition, I quartered horses at Hæafuddene and my brother
kept them on the Axeholme ridge, so that in times of emergency we
could quicken our time by employing boats on the Trent and the Ouse,
weather willing. Our communication was constant and well ordered
and we had truly become what Ealdread Æthelgar's son had once
predicted we would: as close to being one earldom as two could hope to
be. The people of Mercia and North Humbria identified themselves
with the interests of the House of Leofric every bit as much as with
either of us personally. Just as the men of Edwin's earldom had answered
my call to arms, we knew my people would happily march to the aid of
Mercia. Both the Mercians and the North Humbrians found great security in the confederacy which gave either earldom a double strength in
times of need.

We were soon forced to press this alliance into use. Less than a fortnight after the omen disappeared from the sky, word came that Tostig
had finally returned to the kingdom. He had harried meanly along the
southern coast with forty ships full of mercenaries raised in Flanders and
Scot Land. At Sandwic, his man Copsige Sword-Stinger met him with
a fleet of seventeen ships hired in the Orkneys. We knew that the worst
of Tostig's hell-bent revenge was reserved for us, and 'twas only a matter
of some short time before he would sail north to deal it.

Within days, I had assembled my army, and I knew Edwin had his great Mercian force in readiness, too. Beyond that, we were helpless to take any action; we did not know whether he meant to invade the Humbria at once or plunder first in Mercia for armaments and supplies. In the end, he chose the latter, pulling the bulk of his fleet into the mouth of the Humber and unleashing an orgy of pillage in the northern Lindcylene Shire. The very day he disembarked there, my army was mounted and on the march. Ywen Carr's son had come immediately with the summons, traversing much of the distance by swift river boat.

Such consolidation must never have occurred to the Wessexman. Apparently expecting to face only those Mercians quartered in Lindcylene, he had meandered his men far inland, burning everything that could not be carried. Moving at a furious pace east along the river bank, my North Humbrians under Gamel-Beorn's lead were able to cut the invaders off from their ships. Meanwhile, the sight of the red and gold standard at the head of my forces to the west, and my brother's blue and gold gonfalon leading a massive contingent from the south, threw the former earl's unruly, plunder-drunk army into a terrible confusion. Even as we began to dismount and make ready for battle, a goodly number of them fled far afield, ignoring the curses, threats and commands of their leaders. From the broad, sloping ridge, we watched almost with amusement as our unwanted guests tried hurriedly to organize an offensive. Except for a small guard of former North Humbrian guardsmen, the great warrior-earl Tostig had naught but pirates with which to fight us; he had counted too dearly on our inexperience and disorganization.

As my select-guard formed their tight circle of defense around me, I heard the voice of Hereward the Wake ring out over the lea. Speaking as chief man of the Earl of Mercia, he bade the intruders to lay down their arms or prepare themselves for imminent slaughter. Tostig's man, Copsige Sword-Stinger, voiced loud his master's reply, saying boldly it was their plan rather to lay down Earl Edwin and deal him what had long been promised in the way of gory death. Then he addressed himself to me, bellowing with mock gleefulness how it pleased them to see that Morcar Ælfgar's son, pretender to the North Humbria, had presented himself in arms.

"'Twill be naught but a satisfaction to us, child earl," he bellowed, "to plant your bowels here in Mercia where they belong. To stomp your bloody remains into this cursed soil!"

I glanced at the Bearn while these vile words were said. My cousin was quivering with rage, just as I was, and watching me expectantly. Unsure of what to do, I gave the slightest shrug of my shoulders, causing

Siward suddenly to raise his Danish axe high and let go a terrifying shriek. Instantaneously, all noise was drowned in an ear-splitting thunder of hundreds of voices. "God's might!" is what they cried—the battle cry of the North Humbria. As it rent the air, the entire force heaved forward with a speed and ferocity seemingly impossible for the great weight of our arms, driven by the lowing fierceness of "God's might … God's might!" chanted over and over—yelled and screamed and howled—until it was transformed with fury and vengeance to "God smite! God smite!" There was a jolting crunch as iron crashed into iron.

But it was less a battle than a rout. Tostig's marauders fought bravely but all the while we were driving them backwards, like sheep, towards the river and the wall of ferocious Mercians who rushed to meet them there. They broke and ran in panic. Their confusion and despair were so great that we did not even bother to keep a defense against them. I broke free of my circle of guardsmen and led them after me, blood boiling in the exhilaration of easy victory. Like wild dogs after wounded game, we chased them, hacking from behind as they fled, then trampling over them. They bounded east, to the grey mouth of the Humber, where a handful of their ships were moored and guarded. Those of them strong enough, plunged waist-high into the churning waters and waded to their vessels while others ran aimlessly south, unopposed. They were thoroughly beaten, and we were too breathless to follow.

At the very last moment, Tostig Godwine's son, with his well-armed select guard, turned and tried to rush my brother's circle. I was two furlongs up the bank with my line, all of us panting and gasping and worn, but I screamed them into tight formation again and surged towards the desperate skirmish. I had never seen a warrior who looked bolder, stronger, or more skilled than Edwin did at that moment. Heaving his axe ferociously, he cut down three of Tostig's retainers before turning to the banished earl himself. That is when Copsige Sword-Stinger and the other men took forceful hold of the mad Wessexman and pulled him from the fray, dragging him still fighting to his boat. In total silence we watched them depart. Then, with a great shout of victory, our men ran to plunder the field.

The closest of my guard crowded round me: Siward Bearn, Heard Ulf's son, Osbeorn Dolfin's son and Gamel-Beorn. One after another, we saluted each other. Then Edwin made his way over with Hereward and the Welshmen and a few other Mercians. My brother and I embraced, then laughed with relief and exultation. We were near hysterical by the time our horses came. We mounted and bounded off in high and happy spirits to inspect the spoils of war.

When the Wessexman fled, he had only enough retainers left to man twelve ships. The rest of them, harbored down-river in aet-Bearwe, came into our possession, forty-seven in all. One was the proud, gilded beauty my father had given to Gruffydd of Llewellyn as part of his pledge-gift. The golden beak, an eagle head of the finest Danish work-manship, had been sawed off and replaced with a dragon-head of Wessex, golden but of far inferior artistry: a glaring, hollow-eyed thing which seemed to foam with madness. That was the only thing I asked for of all the spoils. Somehow, it reminded me of Tostig himself, and of how he had reduced himself to nothing by his own dishonor, just as the great king of the Cymry once assured us he would.

Later that day, after dispatching news of our victory to King Harold, we sat to a feast at Kirton, riotous with triumph. Though they did not seem of much importance during those hours of celebration, two facts still shadowed our spirits. Tostig himself had escaped unscathed, madder and more vengeful than ever. Worse yet, there had not been a single North Wegian ship in the lot. If 'twas true as rumored, that he had joined himself to the cause of Harald Hardraada, then we knew he had not tapped his resources there and would be back—with more ships and fierce Viking warriors instead of untrained mercenaries.

At the high table in the great hall of Kirton, that very day, we began to formulate another plan of defense, sounder, stronger and more strategic. We were convinced the man would never return to face us again in undisciplined field warfare. Next time, he would go for a city: take it, subdue and fortify it, make it headquarters for his further attacks. We were certain he would choose Eorforwic, the northern city he knew best. Some men set wagers on which approach to the capital would see the confrontation: the Gate Fulford or the Gate Helmesleigh.

Edwin was merrier that night than ever I remembered seeing him. Late in the night, he stood and gathered his wits enough to thank my North Humbrians for their support, promising them Mercian aid in any venture demanding it. I found myself standing, too. When the two of us embraced and raised cups together, a cheer went up which rocked the hall. Ever thereafter, our men half-laughingly referred to 'the earldom of Mercia and North Humbria' as if it were a single domain. Siward Bearn, deep in his cups, even suggested to Edwin the possibility of burning his chest and wrists in the North Humbrian fashion, since I had remained clean-shaven like a Mercian. My brother emphatically refused to involve himself in such unpleasantness, saying he preferred to live and die an unscarred man.

"'Tis a noble ambition, surely," my cousin replied seriously, "insofar as a man can control it." For some reason, we all laughed as if there was humor in that sobering thought.

Early on the morrow, we went out to oversee the burying of the dead. Of the common-folk of Lindissi, two score and a dozen were found, most of them murdered in the Wessexman's pillaging rather than in battle. Four of my North Humbrians were killed, and six of the Mercian carls. My brother and I paid a gold-gift to every family that lost a man, rich or poor the same price.

We found the remains of a full hundred and a quarter of the invaders. We were sorry to learn afterwards that a good number of them had been abducted from the southern ports and forced to bear arms, a fact which might have accounted for the reluctance to fight which had broken Tostig's line. Knowing this, my brother ordered every man a Christian burial, and had each one wrapped in wadmal that had been plundered to nakedness.

Hwell Carr's son found amongst the booty a dagger, girt, and shield which had belonged to his father. The Welshmen had not heard a word of him since Gruffydd died, and knew not whether he was alive or dead. Sadly they agreed such evidence as those well-prized treasures of his pointed to an unfavorable fate. These had probably been plundered from him during the invasion by Harold and Tostig which followed my father's murder at Rhuddlan. Edwin gave the brothers leave to travel into the Cymry to seek for news, but they protested 'twould be a hopeless task in that wild land, so thoroughly wasted and subdued by the house which now ruled Angland.

That afternoon I dismissed the North Humbrians and sent them home. A day later, I followed with my select-guard and we resettled into our life at Eorforwic with a greater sense of security than we had felt since first I came there. We knew it would be months before Tostig could reassert himself with any power and it was pleasant to be finally free of his threat, if only temporarily. Our spirits were eased, the weather was mild and pretty and there was nothing which truly disturbed me all that balmy summer.

Until I rode to the Bernicia to council with Oswulf Eadwulf's son.

*   *   *

Oswulf's ancient stone house was a striking picture in the rose and molten-gold sunset of late summer. 'Twas planted in the heather-clad undulations of the rugged, up-lying country, opulent with glorious color and detail. Naked crags, rolling lawns, and fern-clad slopes all contributed to a beauty so breathtaking that my little party and I rode slowly and carefully, just to be sated with the sight of it. Later, when I sat at the high table with my cousin, I tried to tell him how that mystical loveliness had delighted me, but I could not find the words.

The Earl of the Bernicia was looking his lean and handsome best after a summer in the saddle, "keeping down the foxes" as he put it. Courteous and quiet, he smiled frequently but in a distracted, impassive way. I wondered if the responsibilities of a house and earldom had begun to mellow him.

He was anxious for news, and I told him everything I knew of King Harold's efforts to fortify the south against the expected Norman invasion. The king had been at Sandwic since May, I reported, gathering and assembling troops. I told him, too, that I had mobilized a good number of the North Humbrian carls again and Edwin had his in readiness; we were fast growing more apprehensive about Tostig's return, now that the autumn was drawing nigh. "'Tis a goodly part of the reason I have traced my way here to you, cousin," I told him solemnly. "We expect you know you must be ready to march your Bernicians to us, soon as the need arises. Rumor is that a great fleet of hundreds is building in the Nor Way. With Harald Hardraada's Vikings behind him, the Wessexman is not likely to be driven so fast away."

Oswulf bit his lip and leveled a gaze at me. "I have thought much on this already," he said, lifting a cup. "You know I will be behind you if they come to the Humbria; my troops are enough in order to come immediately to your summons. Yours only, though."

I stared at him, puzzled. "What mean you?" I asked.

"That if they make their battle again in Mercia, I will not march my army there." His voice grew suddenly hard and cold. "I think 'twould be wise to keep my allegiance to the Bernicia—and to you in the North Humbria, if need be." He looked away. I opened my mouth to make a surprised reply, but he spoke again himself, changing the subject to news more personal, asking how it fared with Siward Bearn, whom I had left behind to manage affairs at Eorforwic.

"He missed you at his bride-ale," was my reply. "It would have pleased him had you come."

"Nay!" My cousin shook his head. "He still begrudges me on account of the woman. He would not have wanted to be made hand-fast to her, with my looking on them all the while."

He said it humbly, and I gave a short laugh. "Feel you shame for what you did, kinsman?" I asked low, scrutinizing his sun-tanned face for a reaction. His eyes turned icy but he said nothing. I asked how well he had healed.

"Of what he did to me, naught is left but a shining scar at the shoulder and one upon my breast." He moved his hand there unconsciously and kneaded it. His arms and wrists were heavy with gold, fine bracelets and armlets of great richness. Wealth and power agreed with him, I thought; he looked very fair. It was while I was considering his mien and manner, that his woman came into the hall with a huge silver ewer to do her lady's duties at the high table. Our eyes met for just a single, unreadable instant before my gaze was drawn to the rounded swell of her belly.

She was with child!

I felt a rush of inner heat, but my words came easily as I turned back to my kinsman with a smile. "How is it you have kept this secret from us, Oswulf Eadwulf's son?" There was neither shake nor tremble in my tone, though I know not how it happened that way.

That familiar, boyish pout settled over his features as he glanced at her coldly. "Aye, she carries a brat," he muttered, then lifted his cup and drained it all at once.

I held my own cup up in salute, then took a sip. "Perhaps 'tis a boy-child and heir she will bear you, cousin!" I forced a merry tone.

Oswulf tossed his head and swallowed back his spite. "She is more than half way to the birthing of it," he growled, staring hard into my eyes. "Does that tell you anything?"

I made no answer, for Briana had turned suddenly and come close, speaking me a proper greeting while refilling our cups. She did not linger, only did the same for each man at the table and then took her leave, placing the ewer before her lord as was the custom. Oswulf fast finished his cup again and poured another. There was an uneasy silence between us, filled by the sounds of our men talking of other things. Then I casually mentioned that I hoped the Bearn and his lady would have the same pride to boast of soon; all I could think to do was pretend I knew not what my cousin had meant. He was drinking hard of a sudden and his voice was thickening.

"Methinks indeed there is something unnatural about Earl Edwin … about a man waiting so long to seek venery with his own claimed woman," he said meanly. I watched him drink another one, waxing indignant at his implication and truly bristling when he added that he thought it counted against Edwin's manliness, too, that he had not yet chosen himself a mate. "Your father had one before his eighteenth year," he said firmly, as if it proved a point. I remembered that Oswulf was but seventeen when he wed and I grew hot with anger. Even so, I kept my voice level.

"What difference makes it, cousin," I asked him coolly, "to marry right out of boyhood if your woman bears you no babe till you have seen twenty and five full years anyway?"

I bit my tongue even as I said it, full well knowing I could not afford to rile the man. He was already half sodden, though, and fortunately seemed not to realize my coarse implication. I felt a welling of relief when he moved the talk to other things, but it irked me when he made a point of reminding me that I waxed onto twenty-one years myself and had ought to think of my reputation, too. He was hopeless in his fits of drunken obstinacy; but then, I had known as much for years and it would be foolish to let him goad me into bad blood now with his mindless prattle. Saying I was worn and weary from my long ride, I pushed myself away from the table.

Beornwald Beornwulf's son, a brawny, dark-haired warrior whom men called Strong-Leg, had been Oswulf's chief man since Cospatric Arkill's son's murdering at the king's court that grim Yuletide past. Like many another of the far Northerners, he was burnt with rune-signs and wore amulets of Odin and Tyr alongside his Christian charms. With a faint smile, he beckoned, then led me to the earl's chamber, which my cousin had offered to share. The house was stone-built in the old Norse way, with a narrow, windowless corridor behind the dais which ended at two massive timber doors. One led to the lord's room and one to the lady's. Beornwald Strong-Leg pushed open the appropriate one and my eyes adjusted to the dusky light. I could see that it was comfortably furnished in comparison to the hall, which was quite spartan. Too small to be drafty, it must have been cozy in winter with its good-sized corner hearth and walls hung with tapestries, but now it held the summer air close. Besides a pallet, there were a table, bench, two chairs, and several chests crammed into the existing space, leaving not much room for extra pallets. I looked at Beornwald quizzically and he gestured me to take the cot. "Earl Oswulf never sleeps in here but on the floor," he told me. "He thrashes too much to keep his bed."

"'Twas not his way when he was a boy," I told him, remembering the many years my orphaned cousin had lived with Grandmother Godiva.

"Aye," replied the bull-necked man in a surly way, "but then he had not yet learnt to steep himself in mead, I trow." He asked which man was serving as my chief in the Bearn's absence so that he could send him in to me. I answered firmly that I would put my own self to bed. He took his leave, tossing me a strange look.

Despite my unfeigned weariness, slumber long eluded me. The import of what was happening in my life hammered away, causing an anguish like physical pain in my depths. 'Twas my child Briana carried, no doubt of it. I had known it the instant our eyes met. There was no way to keep my balance now! My heart flew with happiness at the same time it thrashed in guilt and despair. Oswulf was obviously well assured the thing was not his doing; he near had said as much. Yet he had received me gladly and without scorn, so it was certain he misplaced the blame. Tossing and turning, I tried to sort it out. With a pang, I recalled how sorely wounded he had lain when she came to Eorforwic. Surely he had not touched her in all that time. No wonder he was so positive it could not be his own! Before that, she had been three months away from him, at Edwin's estate in Kirton. A dizzying rush of apprehension came over me, strong as a wave of sickness at sea. What was it he had said at the table? " ... *if they make their battle again in Mercia, I will not march my army there.*"

He held my brother to account for it!

We had deceived him well, the lady and I. Flat on my back, I crossed my arms over my face. This is what it had led to, our sin and weakness: an impossibly hopeless situation, about to explode misery over all our lives. I had to confess to the man now; he blamed Edwin. Must be he had fixed the idea firmly into his brain, too, and was already foaming for revenge. That was the way with Oswulf Eadwulf's son. He doted on avengement like no other man. He was mad with it.

For seemingly endless hours I planned the way I would approach him and the words I would use to explain it. Yet all the while, a voice deep within worked hard to convince me that 'twould be better to say naught and let things take their course. Best I would wait, the demon whispered—wait till the child was born, lest he harm the lady in his rage and cause tragedy. Wait at least till all the threatened warfare was done with, because the men of Eorforwic would be hard-pressed to hold out against the Vikings without Bernician aid. Bide your time, is what my darker side seemed to command me. The gist of it was that I did not think I could steel myself to face the man just now, and mayhap if I delayed, Briana and I could scheme some logical explanation to give him. There must be some lie somewhere that could exculpate my brother without implicating me. I felt a flush of shame soon as the thought entered my mind and I feverishly crossed myself. So hardened to sin had I become that falsehood and untruth now seemed my only salvation.

Somehow, despite the great weight of my turmoil, I managed at length to drift into sleep. I was barely aware of some commotion my cousin made when he struggled into the room, arguing sullenly with his chief man. Aside from that, not a thing disturbed me the rest of the night.

I wakened later than was my wont, a little confused by the unfamiliar surroundings. Stretching, I caught sight of Oswulf's inert, seemingly lifeless body sprawled upon a wolf-skin coverlet tossed carelessly on the cold floor. Except for his mantle, he was fully dressed; the sloven had not even managed to undo his beltings and slip out of his costly dalmatic. Looking at him, I felt a surge of disdain. Except the patrician fineness of his look and the wealth of precious metals and jewels with which he decked himself, there was nothing noble about the man. In fact, he was a disgusting creature: profligate, dissolute and sinful. He deserved his lot, I thought meanly: a woman who cheated him and a child without his own blood. He ne'er had used his charm or spirit to earn himself more.

All the while I dressed, my gaze was drawn to his wretched, senseless form. The sight of him was like a remedy, balming away all the guilt which had plagued me, soothing my conscience to complacency. I owed him nothing. Not a thought, not a word—surely not a contrition! The scapegrace had driven Briana to the torture which entangled her life now. And mine. His ceaseless evil had urged her into my protection. The man had no affection—not the slightest comprehension of love and, beyond his own selfish urge for satisfaction, no feeling.

If he remained blind to what was between the woman and me, all the better. Given time, I knew I could devise a way of convincing Oswulf of my brother's innocence. If I was forced to reveal the truth, I would do it. By the blood of the saints, I would fight him for her if need be! Looking on him, laid out in his stupor, it occurred to me how easy 'twould be to win if I was careful in choosing my moment.

Quickly, I crossed myself again. I knew not what was coming over me. The sight of that swollen belly had made me drunk with uncontrollable determination. I would find a way of working things out, and it would not have to come to kin-killing to settle it. Besides, with sobering logic returning to me suddenly, I remembered that even in wild headiness Oswulf Eadwulf's son was a merciless fighter. Best we find another way. I bent down and shook him; he howled loud, as if I had hurt him, before he came to his senses.

I stayed two days more before the coarseness and lack of discipline in that household began to gall me. I watched constantly for a chance to talk with Briana, but none happened. We both realized the need for extreme caution so, though it pained us, we avoided each other except for occasional, brief glances. These casual looks spoke much, however; we had grown very well attuned, one to the other.

I thought of her all the way home—of how all our resolve had came to naught. Our firm avowals to keep impersonal distance between us counted for nothing now. We had made them less out of conviction than fear of putting misery and mistrust into those around us the way we had with Siward Bearn. Neither of us had truly felt a willingness to part. But nay, I told myself, if God wanted us to deny each other, He never would have let this thing happen. For now, the seed of our love had taken a tangible, physical form and we were inextricably knotted to each other forever, the lady and I, by the issue of our conjoined hearts.

Thus far had I strayed from all I had been taught of virtue. I was entirely at peace with these thoughts.

The ride back was leisurely and pleasant; the prettiness of the season put us in high spirits. We returned to sobering news, though. The very day we rode into Eorforwic, messengers came breathless from Scarbyrig, high on the east coast. The Vikings had landed and burnt the pretty town to the ground. I sent immediately to Edwin, to Ealdread Æthelgar's son, and to Oswulf for more aid, at the same time dispatching news of it to the king. Meanwhile, Siward Bearn took a party north to determine the strength of the foe. The messengers who had brought the information told tales of huge war-ships stretched far as the eye could see in any direction. We thought surely they exaggerated, but the Bearn returned with doleful confirmation: nearly three hundred proud vessels, including one hundred and twelve longships, each bearing forty or or more warriors. Our best schooled monks pored over the counts; we would be facing close to ten thousand men!

They had already begun to mass into the mouth of the Humber when Edwin came, the first to arrive. Already, many hundreds of his Mercians were camped in expectation along the river from Rich-Ale to the Gate Fulford. Now he carried with him all his household troops, the number of his guard having swelled to more than two hundred since we became brothers-in-the-law to the king, and a hastily raised but large force of Mercians and Welsh. These joined my guardsmen and Siward Bearn's—we held two hundred each—and the two thousand arms-bearing men we had culled from all over the Humbria. Soon after, a great contingent of monks arrived from Peterborough, led by my Uncle Leofric. All told, we had three thousand fighters assembled, every one of them fierce and expectant.

During the next two days, Waltheof Siward's son joined us with five hundred, and another thousand streamed in from the Bernicia as we solidified a strategic defense. We were determined to mass my North Humbrians across the hard trod way of the Gate Fulford itself. It was a narrow approach, a furlong and a half across of firm ground which fell off quickly to the river Ouse on one side and steeply into deep marsh on the other. Here, we could block the only massive approach they could make—from the south. Elsewise than the road itself, they needed to wade through boggy marsh, thigh to waist deep with dangerous footing. Either way, they had to ford a deep beck and a number of flooded ditches, and tromp a small hillock to reach us. Edwin and his highly trained Mercians would line the riverbank so the invaders could do naught but charge forward uphill or be pushed harshly into the swamp, and would be hard pressed to do either.

When word reached us that Tostig and the Viking king had disembarked and were marching towards the city. Edwin, Siward, and I met at the minster and we each took the five closest of our men into the chancel with us. I was surprised to see Brother Wulfget at my brother's side there, in addition to Hereward and the Welshmen. He had insisted on fighting beside Earl Edwin. Like Uncle Leofric, he was well-skilled in arms and it seemed he would make a ferocious warrior. I could not help noticing that he wore the knife Ælfgar had bequeathed on his deathbed, a gift from Edwin.

Siward Bearn knelt on my right and anext him, Osbeorn Dolfin's son, Gamel-Beorn, Heard Ulf's son, and Ealdread Æthelgar's son. My prayers that day were that they would survive the contest, and that I would live to see my child.

We confessed and took a benediction. Afterwards, we rode to the Gate Fulford, where the men from Rich-Ale and further upriver had fallen back to make ready for the attack. Late that night, every priest in the line, more than two hundred and a half, said a simultaneous Mass, and our thousands of warriors took the sacrament, bedecked in arms. I did not want to take it myself. I was still penancing but had outright refused to renounce my sin. Uncle Leofric lifted my chin, though, as I knelt before him. He looked hard into my eyes, then administered the bread.

CHAPTER THIRTY-FOUR

> . . . King Harald from Norway came unexpectedly
> north unto the Tyne with a great pirate host; it
> was anything but small for it numbered about 300
> ships or more, and Earl Tostig joined him. . . . Earl
> Edwin and Earl Morcar had gathered as great a
> force as they could from their earldom, and fought
> that host and made great slaughter of them.
>
> —Anglo Saxon Chronicle
> Book "C" 1066

Wednesday, September 20, 1066

Three massive armies, we lined our defense in the darkness. My North Humbrians stood the center—two and a half thousand determined warriors lined behind the gold and scarlet bars of my banner. To our right, Edwin's blue and gold gonfalon marked the head of a hundred score Mercian house-carls, fighters of the finest quality, the closest and hardest loved of our kith and kin amongst them. To our left, Waltheof Siward's son, Earl of North Hamtun, had lined near a thousand good fighters, hastily raised and with great difficulty, for his shire bordered Wessex, and many of the best fighters he had recently been set to lord over had answered the call of the Anglish fyrd, the king's army, sent by King Harold against the possibility of an invasion in the south by Normandy. As I have said before, I never much cared for Waltheof Siward's son, but it impressed me that he had so aligned his interests with our house that he chose to fight at my side rather than the king's. But then, the king had encouraged it; none knew better than he the strength and savagery of Tostig Godwine's son.

As the sun rose, we became aware of the massiveness of the invading host. They were drawn up, facing us, no more than a single, heated lunge away—a blazing wall of red and black, yellow and blue shields. Near the sharp rise which dropped to the river-bank of the green river Ouse, I saw the contingent of Harald Hardraada, killer-king of the North Wegians, hero of Sicily and Africa. I felt a cold thrill; he was one I had never expected to look upon. I had heard many tales of his valor from my father, from Gruffydd, from Æthelstan the Fen-man and from bold Cynewulf Cenwulf's son. The Viking was already a legend when I was born. His banner was the black raven, Land-Ravager. It had never been unfurled in battle but that Harald Hardraada, called the Ruthless, had been victorious.

His house-carls he called Sword-takers, just as the Danes did, and they were sworn followers to the death. They were rabid in warfare, in large part, it was said, because on the brink of battle they chewed and swallowed mushrooms that worked a madness in their brains, making them not only physically stronger, but sure that they were being directed by higher powers housed in Æsgard, as their heaven was called. I wondered how Edwin, whose flank would have to face and take the brunt of them, felt as he gazed on them now. We could not see the Mercians where they were lined along the banks, nor could we see Waltheof's forces along the deep beck, but we knew that the invaders were even now staring full upon our combined armies, and could see that we were formidable in size and strength.

For a while, great host gazed upon great host in the haunting morning stillness of the beautiful Eorforwic Shire; now and again, that silence was rent by a rash of harsh threats and mean taunts slung loud, as each army tried to terrify the other with curses and descriptions of bloody death. Then, all at once, an iron voice rang out, cold and terrifying. It was Tostig, son of Godwine, drawn up with his wild mercenary force opposite me.

"You will resign to me, Morcar child-earl, this earldom which is not yours by right. Submit to me now, else this very day I shall see you beg in your own blood, as Ælfgar of Mercia did before you."

I did not wait for Siward Bearn to speak as earl's man; I answered myself, shaking with rage. "It pleases you to call me child, Wessexman, but I am old enough to know my father no more begged mercy than did you slay him in fair combat, as you so haughtily boast! There is naught but shame in putting slaughter on a man in his bed!"

I heard his hideous laugh. "The shame is that we had to kill the pretty Welsh thing he lay upon!"

I was so furious that without thought or hesitation I put up a fierce North Humbrian battle howl. My guard, who obviously approved, picked it up instantly, lunging forward with me in determined, ferocious attack. In that instant, I felt the earth tremble as the two mighty armies heaved headlong into each other with bloody savagery. I will never forget the nightmarish sound of iron on iron, flesh on flesh, as we met head on.

It took but minutes for the war-cries to become indistinguishable from the death cries. Already, as my wild North Humbrians pushed their way into the enemy wing, we were stepping over corpses and the mangled masses of the dying. Tostig and his men were taken in surprise by the violence of our attack as we cut our way through them with murderous rage. Many of his mixed force, having nowhere else to go, crawled into the marshes to escape us, and drowned there in water made red with blood. Many of our Anglish died that way also, but in the first hours, it appeared we had them in retreat, so harshly had we beaten them back. We kept our line firm, and they could scarce advance a row at a time in the narrow thoroughfare.

My memories of that day are a mass of indistinct horrors: the heat, the screams, the smell of blood and sweat. But I remember with crystalline precision the moment that I realized the callous hand of Fate had turned against us. It was well into the noon. We had forced ourselves so far into the enemy's line that Harald the Ruthless feared we might surround his force and cut them off from their ships.

The noise of the battlefield was no longer a rushing roar. Though hundreds still fought, they had breath only for that, so the war-cries and curses now were fewer. Even the moans, screams, pleas, and delirious rantings of the wounded seemed muffled with resignation and despair. On the wind came the constant chanting of the last rites, carried from Edwin's line where the monks of Peterborough and Couventrie prayed as they wielded sword and axe. Suddenly, above the drone of their voices rose the fierce blast of a horn and a tumultuous wild shouting in the Norse king's army. He had unfurled the banner Land-Ravager and ordered his troops into suicidal, berserk fury. As we hammered through the weaker, straggling flank on the marsh, Harald's vicious Sword-takers literally hacked down the Mercian wing along the river. The sound of that slaughter was more horrible than anything I can describe. Those of Tostig's mercenaries whom we had left alive followed the Wessexman and the remnants of his guard, rushing across the field in the grip of a demented blood-fury, forcing the Mercians backward and east into the fen, already glutted with the bodies of the dead and dying. Then came the terrible instant I recall so well: the hollow, chilling sound of the ancient Mercian battle-call rose agonizingly over the Norsemen's ravings. Instinctively, I knew that Tostig and the Viking king had reached Edwin's shield circle.

Blinded by fear and fury, I forced a way through the defensive screen of my select-guard, broke away, and headed to my brother's side, hearing the pounding of my own heart over the furious protests of my men, who waxed aghast that I ran unprotected. Almost immediately, they overtook and surrounded me again. With a morbid shriek I surged them left, cutting through the stunned Norsemen with horrible rage and emotion. The greater part of our forces followed us cross field.

Now I could make out the faces of Edwin's guardsmen. They were ferocious fighters, those high-bred Mercian thegns. The House of Leofric had lorded them for generations, and they were eagerly dedicated to my brother's defense. The flash of their iron and the gore which covered them said as much. Now they gathered about their earl a slashing, slicing, thrusting wall of swords and shields and axes. Throwing off my helmet so they might know me, I worked my way into their circle—a last, desperate attempt to hold our ground. Still, the Norsemen hacked in their rabid fury. So intense was the fray, that I could not see Edwin, though by now I had forced my way to the inner wall of his guard. Even there, the action was thick and constant as, time and again, battered soldiers broke through the line, bleeding and crazed, with only the vicious furor of their madness keeping them alive.

The attack was so frantic that we were driven back and there was tremendous slaughter in the Anglish host. Along the riverbank, the Vikings had pushed themselves through the Mercians and found firm footing behind the chokehold we had set on the Gate road. We were surrounded on three sides now, though the bulk of our fighting men had no way of knowing it. I had no doubt then that the battle was lost. In the midst of the horror and carnage, I prayed with all the strength of my impious heart that God would spare the glorious city of Eorforwic, and the lovely shire. It was fervent pleading for, by all that is holy, I had come to love my earldom.

At length, a great, choking cry of anguish went up, and Edwin's name was shouted over and over throughout the guard, sure notification that his enemies had finally reached him. I sweated, fought, killed for a sight of him, but he was lost in the misery and madness. Before I could spot him the cry resounded—he was down! Although my own circle held firm, many Anglish panicked and ran in terror through the fen, into the midst of which we had worked ourselves deeply, trodding upon the bodies of the fallen. When I realized the last remnants of the bold monks of Peterborough, worn and wasted, had finally taken flight, I knew the battle was over.

Then my only thought was to reach Eorforwic and somehow defend the city. As late afternoon sunlight filtered hazy streaks through the autumnal clouds, we fought our way in retreat back across the Gate Fulford to the Ouse, where we broke and fled upward along the river. Less than a third of us, the flower of all the north and midlands, remained alive. Even so, in the horror of our desperate flight, many of that remaining number—shocked, bloody and beaten—drowned in the cold waters.

Numb and vulnerable, I found myself once more surrounded by my guard, but the invaders made little attempt to battle us as we fled. They were war-weary and greatly broken also. They had not the strength to jeer us as we ran.

Only those of us strong enough to run the distance survived the day. So deadly was the fray at the last, none glimpsing it believed any could survive. Good fighting men who had witnessed the frantic removal of my brother from the field carried the tale to Eorforwic that 'twas I who was hauled away thusly. For long months after, I was forced to confront the rumor that I had perished on that God-forsaken field. And for much of the time that came after, in truth, I wish I had.

CHAPTER THIRTY-FIVE

*. . . But a great number of the Anglish were either
slain or drowned or driven in flight, and the Nor
Wegians had possession of the place of slaughter.*

—Anglo Saxon Chronicle
Book "C," 1066

We reached Eorforwic in purple twilight, but there was to be no respite for us there. The invaders, we knew, were too weakened to follow us this night but they would be at the city walls at dawn, refreshed and reinforced. We had only until then to determine a course of action, and all the city was a mass confusion of grief and agony. The extent of our losses and the hopelessness of our situation were becoming clear as the bloody rabble of the vanquished straggled in. Stripped of all hope for defense, the good people of Eorforwic looked to me, their earl, for resolution. Council was called immediately, even before I could wash the battle from me. In the distance, we could hear the raucous chant of the Norsemen: "Land-eyda … Land-eyda … " They saluted the Land-Ravager as they mercilessly plundered our Anglish dead.

Intoxicated with despair and indecision, we tried to make sense of our circumstances. The archbishop, the thegns, and all the chief men argued with vigor and emotion, some in favor of defending the walls until King Harold could come with the Anglish fyrd—six days or more, if he could pull them away from the southlands at all. Others, better assessing our worth and thinking to preserve the great ancient city, called for immediate submission. archbishop Aldred threw his lot in with the latter; an immediate surrender, he said, coupled with a plea for mercy and a welcome of goods and hostages might cause the invaders to accept Eorforwic as their own fortress. Then they would be loath to allow their men to waste it. After much effort, this plan gained credence, but before we could be resolved, we needed indication of the enemy's intent. At length it was agreed that we would petition on the morrow for a truce—two days in which to retrieve our dead and two in which to allow the citizens, except for men of soldiering age, to remove themselves unmolested. The way in which they received our requests would give us clue to their motives, and would give us time to regroup ourselves if siege was imminent.

Whatever the city's fate might be, I was not to be a part of it. My retainers were adamant in their demand that I take to flight. My presence would not affect the outcome, they argued, and Tostig Godwine's son suffered a vindictive madness which surely would require my summary execution. They urged me to gain as much distance as possible before the Wessexman knew I had fled. There was nowhere north of the Humber that he would not seek me. No one said as much but the implication was clear: 'twas likely I was the last of the House of Leofric now, and my person must be preserved.

Coming to the mid-of-night, I began to feel the ravages of the day unrelentingly, both physically and emotionally. Sore and badly bruised, I had not yet had a chance to assess the losses of my carls, but I knew them to be great. Many amongst them were kith or kin. Despite the turbulence of the incessant debating, my mind constantly wandered to thoughts of those men of my guard whose fate had been to die in defense of me and the North Humbria. My cousin Maldon had been hacked to pieces before my eyes, and his brother, Brihtric, had taken a ferocious wounding trying to save him. My steward, Edmund Half-Dane, too, had fallen, and I saw plainly when it happened that there would be little left of him to claim and bury. As the hours wore on, and more casualties were realized, I wondered how long I could delay my grief. When I met a party of priests bearing the viciously mangled body of Ealdread Æthelgar's son, Siward Bearn's genial and good-hearted brother, I could control myself no longer. I wept openly in front of many men.

Though aching with hunger, I could not force down bread. I swallowed great draughts of water and ale but it did little to fill my emptiness. I battled the weariness that threatened to overtake me as the arguments wore on and every minute brought news of more death and tragedy. Despite constant application, I felt myself drifting into incoherence. Nevertheless, I flew to my feet, bruises and wretched fatigue forgotten, when I saw Ywen Carr's son, with my cousin Æric and three other of Edwin's guard behind him, forcing his way through the noisy, disheveled throng. The man strode purposefully forward and gripped my shoulders, his dark eyes flashing. In a hollow and weary voice he announced loudly, "My lord Edwin, Earl of all Mercia, lives!"

The message quickly worked its way through the suddenly hushed hall. Before I could make any answer, an exultant cheer went up. Even before it subsided, Ywen and the others had steered me firmly out into the windy night, Siward Bearn, Heard Ulf's son, and Gamel-Beorn close in tow.

Ywen led us silently to the ancient, crumbling war-wall of Roman times, near the city-center now. There Uncle Leofric stood waiting. The abbot of Peterborough was a grim sight, wet, filthy, and well-bloodied from his attendance on wounded men. His monkish robe, or what was left of it, was tucked up, revealing sword-girt and leather breeches. I hastened to him. He did not wait for me to ask the news.

"In that final onslaught, Tostig met him," he began.

I trembled. "Is he truly alive?"

"Aye, but 'twas agony he took from the Wessexman's blade. He was stunned to the ground and it met flesh again and again before his guardsmen trampled over him to push Tostig and his man Copsige back. Those two had made it their personal business to hack him. Once they were beaten away, my men escaped with Edwin into the fen." Uncle Leofric's tall figure sagged as with a great weight. He gestured to the five weary, bedraggled, and bloody guardsmen. "Only these men here and mayhap fifty more remain of his guard."

I shivered. Of more than two hundred good men! I glanced at Ywen. Reading the concern writ in my eyes, he hurriedly assured me both his brothers lived, but Æric shook his head sadly when I questioned him. His twin—clever, happy Ælfmaer, the one of the "devil's dozen" once fondly called Apple Cheek—had perished.

In the dark, Uncle Leofric put a comforting hand on our kinsman's shoulder as he continued his tale, telling how they had carried Edwin to boats the priests had hidden deep in the fen. My brother was so crazed with pain that they feared he would drown both himself and the men who carried him, but at last he went senseless. My uncle, realizing the massive extent of the wounding and seeing that the invaders surely had the day, resolved to take him through the marsh to Peterborough. He selected four monks, Brother Wulfget amongst them, who knew all the wet-lands and dispatched them, along with Hereward and Ywen's brothers, garbed in monkish dress. Uncle Leofric bade the men stop at Lindcylene if it appeared my brother could bear no more. I prayed they would not have to do so. 'Twas surely the first place mad Tostig would seek for either of us.

Peterborough by the high road could be near a three day's trip with a wounded man, but traveling the fen and rowing in shifts, the party might reach Lindcylene in a day, and the monastery in less than two. If Edwin held out that long, my uncle was hopeful he could be nursed to recovery.

"They had to carry him in his hauberk, though," he said gravely, "for fear he would lose too much blood when they pulled it from him." Then, he took me by the arm and drew me near so that even the men with us could not hear and prevailed on me to follow my brother to Peterborough. "You are a dead man here," he told me solemnly, "and the House of Leofric can bear no more loss."

Those words, and the realization of Edwin's condition, filled me with trembling dread. He pulled me to him, just as my father might have done. That embrace strengthened me greatly. He made the sign of the cross over me when I finally pulled away, and in a low voice he bade me choose one from amongst my guard to accompany me. Unhesitatingly, I chose Siward Bearn.

We went back to the minster to inform archbishop Aldred of the decision. I washed there and straightened myself as best I could. Before we left, I took the archbishop's blessing and confessed to him. I am not ashamed to say that the sin I confessed to was vengeance. Like my father, I counted it chief of all my faults.

*   *   *

In truth, I remember little of that flight through the dreary fen. Exhausted, I collapsed into a miserable, aching heap at the bottom of my uncle's eel boat, and there drifted in and out of sleep the full day. No one disturbed me for a turn at the rowing, and late in the night I wakened to find they had disembarked at Lindcylene, leaving Siward Bearn and Ywen Carr's son to guard my slumber. Both were sound a-sleeping, though, and I pitied them; they were so battle-worn. I am not a man entirely at ease in the fen but after the terrifying din of battle there was something tranquilizing in the eerie, moonlit solitude. On my back in the enchanted silence, I let my sorrow come at last.

It seemed an age passed before my uncle returned with the other men, bringing warm bread, honey mead, and news of Edwin. Yes, a company of the Peterborough monks had rested there. One of their number was gravely injured, the priests had told some of the towns-folk, and they had come to press for calendula, arnica, and leopard's bane to relieve his wounding. No one seemed to know exactly what the man's condition was, but one man remembered hearing that he bled from the head and had gone into cold shivers from his over-bleeding. Two of the priests from Stowe had gone to the boat in the marsh where the man lay, but had traveled on to Peterborough with the party. That was all we could learn, and though 'twas not particularly encouraging, it hinted that Edwin was alive.

We resumed the journey as we choked down food and drink. The second leg was more difficult; in a half dozen places we were forced to wade and carry the boats. Walking in the mire was peculiarly unpleasant. The bottom ooze was deep and slippery so that our footing was precarious at best. The repeated exposure to cold water and then to wind filled my muscles with a clammy ache which was to last me many days. In addition to this external discomfort, my sore body was beginning to admit its bruised condition. There was little of comfort for me in that hard-bottomed boat.

But I was not the only one to suffer. The strain was clearly marked in the weary features of my companions. Most especially was my uncle's discomfort obvious to me. His face, which had always seemed ruddy and rugged, was pale and drawn with pain. He was nearing fifty now and had not suffered the indignities of battle for many years. His breathing became labored as the trip wore on, and his grip grew weaker. Still, he made no complaint and constantly engaged himself in encouraging the rest of us, keeping our attention with tales of his many adventures in the fen-land from Peterborough to Ely.

I began to drift in and out of broken, restless dreams until it became hard for me to distinguish what I dreamt from what was actually being said. I remember Siward Bearn talking low and telling the men in the boat which glided alongside ours that the men of the Diera would never let the invaders raze their ancient jewel of a city. "They are cunning men," I heard him muse, "and they would pretend to join the Vikings and fight against the Anglish rather than let that happen." There was a long, somber pause before he added vehemently, "But they will never accept Tostig as their earl, or choose any other man over Morcar."

The rest of the journey passed like a strange, dark dream. When at last we reached the massive stone walls of the monastery, I was sleeping. I startled and cried out when Uncle Leofric shook me awake because my dream was of battle.

I wanted to run directly to my brother but that was not to be. Despite their head start of eleven hours, the other party had arrived scarce an hour before us. One monk shared all the information he could, saying Brother Wulfget and Hereward were with Edwin now, while the priests dressed his wounds and swathed and stitched him. I would be naught but a nuisance if I went there; things were too critical. Everyone bade me eat, bathe, and be patient, and swore they would call me if it appeared my injured brother was losing his hold. Silent and dismal, I let myself be led to a small stone cell. Someone brought me water and linen and food. Before touching any of it, I fell to my knees beside the hard, blanketed pallet and begged God in his infinite mercy to spare me any more wounding sorrows or harsh, unwelcome death. Truly, I thought I could not take more of it, I felt that broken.

Afterwards, I went to seek the men who had carried my brother, craving more word of him. I found the three sons of Carr before a blazing fire in the cavernous kitchen. Daffydd and Hwell leapt to embrace me. My dark-haired friends were less stoic than usual. If there was one thing in all the world they understood, 'twas brotherly ties. The depth of their compassion alone was enough to tell me how sore it fared with Edwin.

While we nibbled on cold fowl and sipped mead, Ywen and I listened while the other two related the horrors of their long, tedious journey, made much worse than ours by the life-and-death urgency of it. Held prone in the boat bottom, his head cradled in Hereward's lap, Edwin had fluctuated between the anguished thrashing of consciousness and eerie, death-like insensibility. At Lindcylene, the priests from Stowe came out in the wilderness to tend him, afraid to lift him from the boat, for fear he would bleed to death. They had been forced to remove both his metal hauberk and the leathern one under it, which were beginning to scab into his gross woundings. He bled so profusely after that, the priests tried to cauterize him with hot irons. Failing in it, for his agony was overwhelming, they wrapped him in herbed poultices and bound him tight, then gave him a last unction and resumed their travel.

"He babbled incessantly after that," Daffydd told us, "except when he mercifully lost his consciousness. When he was still and senseless, we made good time; but then, his pains would come with terrible violence so that not even Hereward and I could hold him down. Then the others would wade to us, trying to keep the boat from capsizing, trying to still him. Eventually he would submit and then, finally, grow senseless again—" The man's voice broke and he looked away.

"Those frenzies were brief," added Hwell listlessly, "but they caused blood to come from his mouth and nose so he scarce could breathe. I feared the man bled from his brain."

I trembled, but Daffydd spoke out adamantly. "Nay! The priests say not! Edwin could not have lived so long with a bleeding there, is what they told me."

I buried my face in my hands. "What chance has he?"

Daffydd answered, his dark features drawn in a gaunt smile. "'Tis strange to hear it, but they say he will live if he goes into a fever. When we came here, he was mortal cold."

For a long time, no one spoke. Then I described for them the terrible state of affairs in Eorforwic, and the determination of the people there to bargain for the safety of their shire. The Welshmen were quick to agree that it would be best to preserve the city at any cost; it could always be won back again later, God willing, Hwell said. In my heart, though, I wondered what Harold Godwine's son would think of such a course of action. He would hear of our miserable defeat soon enough and would no doubt march his army there. Would he not think it treasonous if Eorforwic had gone to the invaders unscathed? Or would he be convinced by the sad, fractional remain of the Mercian carls and mine?

I was far too weary to make any conclusions, though, and seeing that these brothers needed time to talk together before sleep overtook them, I left them to each other. In the pitchy darkness I made my way back to my cell, where I slept and dreamt of Ælfgar. In the dream I was but a boy, as I had been when first I came to this hallowed place. We were walking together, my father and I, hand in hand. 'Twas not an unhappy dream. My father seemed bold and handsome, as I remember him, and Edwin was healthy and unhurt.

I slept away an entire day and when I wakened, 'twas only because Siward Bearn and my uncle stood over me, debating in low tones whether or not to rouse me. My mind and body were greatly refreshed, but I felt a tremendous weight of guilt, as if I had wronged my brother by not thinking of him in all that time. I begged my uncle to take me in to him, even before I broke fast. At length he agreed to do it. I prepared myself to look upon what I feared most to see. As we moved down the chill halls, we were enveloped by the sweet, somber sound of the monks singing matins. By now, I thought, Harold Godwine's son will be calling his army north.

Edwin lay stretched on a pallet in the center of a warm, herb-perfumed chamber. Three priests hovered round him, one of them Brother Wulfget. On a small bench at his side sat Hereward the Wake, bleary-eyed and unshaven. The man's angular frame was bent with weariness, and I instinctively knew he had not left my brother's side since carrying him from the field. Why it is that I felt jealousy instead of gratefulness, I cannot say. Could be I resented the man for having been there when I was not.

I thought I had readied myself for the actuality of my brother's plight but my grief at the sight of his mortal anguish cannot be estimated. He was pale, open-eyed but unseeing, his whole body heaving with each labored breath. He both shivered and sweated under blankets of blood-soaked wool. For minutes he was still and seemingly senseless. Then, suddenly bitten with pain, would bolt up with unanticipated frenzy, cursing, praying, shrieking. His broken body could scarce stand the agony of this wild movement, so the monks held him forcibly down, cajoling and pleading, and gradually, trembling and murmuring, he succumbed to them.

They had grown used to this; I soon found out it was continual. Soon as they stilled him, Brother Wulfget pulled back the coverings to ensure there were no misplaced poultices or broken suturing. That is when the full impact of the horror hit me. His shoulders and breast were crossed by dozens of slashes, gross wounds made wherever the edge of a sword or axe had sliced through his mail coat. In the act of removing his armor, the lacerations had been further torn and aggravated, so that great areas of what should have been skin and flesh seemed to be naught but bloody pulp. Elsewhere he was torn, bruised to shining blueness, especially over his ribs and other places where the bones were broken. Worst of all was his waist and lower belly: laid almost entirely open where the Wessexman had landed blow after blow, aiming for his manhood in the cruel Viking fashion of fighting. These cuts, too, had suffered gross disfigurement in the stripping away of the hauberk. Even so, the metal coat had plainly saved his life. Without it, even the least of these wounds would have been mortal; the mail had deflected enough of the force to save his organs from total ruin. The bulk of his hurts were confined to the flesh and muscle. They would leave horrific scars but, if they could be kept clean and wrapped, would probably cause him far less trouble than the internal contusions and battered bones.

Hereward did not want to go, but my uncle firmly forced him to seek a portion of rest. He had been in my brother's constant attendance since they fled the Gate Fulford; the man looked haggard beyond measure. Putting my hands upon his shoulders, I thanked him genuinely and we embraced before he took his reluctant leave. As for me, I was resolved now not to leave this room till Edwin's fate was decided.

It proved to be a long and arduous wait.

*   *   *

What disturbed me most was that Edwin did not seem to know me or anyone else. He did not even seem to see us. "All he knows is his pain," Uncle Leofric told me. It gave me little peace. I wanted more than anything to be of some use to him, but I was helpless in the face of his distress.

I watched the priests, well-versed in these arts, douse him with marsh-tea when he bled from the nose or mouth. They were constantly boiling herbs and soaking windings in them. The thick, yellow soup of calendula Mary-gold was poured into the open wounds, and sickly-sweet smelling poultices of borage and leopard's bane were placed hot on his contusions.

On the second day, my brother called out suddenly for forgiveness. My uncle knelt anext him immediately, thinking he had come enough to his senses to make a confession, but afterwards all he made were senseless babbles. I put a hand on Edwin's brow to soothe him and found he was burning hot. My uncle crossed himself and tossed me a victorious smile.

Within a few hours, Edwin was tossing in the throes of high fever, the thing for which his attendants had prayed. Even so, they gave him last rites again that night; he went into a seizure very much like death throes, so violent that he began to bleed again from several wounds at once. It was the fourth time they had unctioned him.

There was little comfort for his bruised body on that hard pallet, and we sometimes took turns holding him when he was shivering or trembling. The morning after the fever came, I felt his emotionless gaze hard upon me and when I spoke his name, he forced a wan, frightened smile. He had worked his way to consciousness, looking not at all wondrous at seeing me there, as as if he had only just wakened from some brief slumber. Excitedly, I fell to my knees at the side of the pallet, clasping his hand.

"How came I here?" he asked me weakly.

I asked if he knew where he was.

"Peterborough," he answered, gritting his teeth.

"Know you who I am, brother?"

"Morcar, son of Ælfgar, son of Leofric." He knew I was testing him. If Death had a voice, it would be that one: hoarse, listless and rife with suffering. Nevertheless, I cried with gladness to hear him. He squeezed my hand so tightly that my blood stopped and whispered woefully. "Send me a priest, brother. Methinks things are grave with me."

"Things have been grave with you these many days, Edwin," I smiled consolingly, then called and bade a young monk fetch Abbot Leofric. By the time my uncle arrived, Edwin was panting in discomfort, and he shortly lapsed again into his daze and excruciation. Brother Wulfget came and joined our vigil, and a little later I took my leave. After a long walk in the fresh air, I went to give thanks, being filled for the first time with hope.

Short periods of sensibility began to come to Edwin with some regularity, alternating with periods of more peaceful sleep. His breathing became more regular, and the violent twitching waned to harmless, intermittent spasms. There was great joy amongst all of us. It had somehow been decided that he would live, and his life had hung a long time in the balance.

With these improvements, though, came greater agonies in his nursing. Once they realized he would survive, the priests applied themselves firmly to the task of making him heal whole and uncrippled. He cried with anguish as they began to sit him up regularly, twisting and turning his muscles so they would not grow useless. The torture seemed needless to me; sometimes my temper flared at the sound of my brother's howls and moans. Finally, the priests suggested I remove myself from the room when they worked on him this way. He needed to limber up his

scars now, while the tissue was forming, else he would suffer all his life
from cruel lameness. Brother Wulfget would come and put a hand on my
shoulder, and lead me out to walk with him in the sunlight. That was
how I knew the merciless therapy was about to begin. Somehow, no
matter how far the two of us meandered, I could always hear Edwin's
pleading and protests. He did not speak them. The pain was such that
he screamed and cried and shrieked.

It was about this time that news reached us of the fate of the north.
Harold Godwine's son, when he heard of the invasion, had marched his
army to the North Humbria with breathless speed. In fact, he reached the
outskirts of Eorforwic only five days after our defeat at Fulford, an
amazing feat which was sung in story and song for many a long year after.
Harald Hardraada hoped to launch his further raids from Eorforwic and,
afraid his ruthless Vikings would waste the city to the ground, he camped
them some miles away in the aet-Staengfordesbrycg. So swift was the
advance of Harold Godwine's son and the Anglish fyrd that the invaders
were caught unawares. The full day's battle was bloody and hard, but the
Vikings had been more than substantially weakened five days earlier by
our forces. In the end, Harold of Angland had the victory. Tostig fell in
the bloody fracas, as did the famed Nor Wegian king, Harald Hardraada.
Their great host was so wasted that there were survivors enough to man
only twenty-four of those three hundred war-ships.

The very day this news came to us, there was a terrible commotion
in the monastery when it was discovered that Edwin had left his bed of
his own strength during a short time he was left alone and presumably
sleeping. He wrought havoc on himself by this foolishness, reopening
several of the worst wounds and causing a long, drawn-out and feverish
relapse. We found him far down the dim corridor, collapsed near the
stairs to the clerestory, bleeding profusely. A great confusion ensued
about whether to treat him there or carry him back to the sick-room.
Hereward and I finally lifted him ourselves. He was suffering from some
sort of seizure, the result of his pain and anguish. All that night, I
listened to his stifled cries as the priests worked on mending him.
Towards midnight, he received final rites yet again.

A few days later, when Edwin was well enough to talk about it, he
told me he had not been able to stand it any more: the stench of blood
and death which permeated his chamber. 'Twas true, too, that it smelled
like a charnal-house; the combination of sweat, urine, and foul blood
hung heavy even over the scents of the healing herbs, which had grown
noxious themselves, just by association. "I had need to find me clean
and healthy air, brother!" Edwin moaned piteously, tossing in his sick
bed. "By God, it near killed me to realize I carried that malodorous smell

of bleeding on me!"

His hair was grown dark and tangled with the perspiration of sleep and sickness and he wore a shadow of beard on his pale face. His eyes were glazed with pain; even the constant application of sponges gave him no relief. He was always bleeding, or had just bled, or was scabbing in old blood—spitting it or swallowing it or lying in it. The fetid perfume of death is what he wore; it burnt through the nostrils into the heart and soul.

It was not to last much longer, though. He had determined to disassociate himself from it, and he began to wax stronger every day. Iron-eyed in his refusal to bow to pain, he drove himself to recovery with an absolute vengeance. He began to take broth, then ass-milk, and finally even fermented apple brew, vile but curative. Now and again, he relapsed, but he was improving considerably.

I asked him one morning which of all his woundings pained him the most. I was certain he would name either the mean rip from his left shoulder to the breast bone below, which had been contaminated from the start, or the gross mass of indistinguishable slashes at the belly. He surprised me, though, running his hand through his thick hair, and saying it was the savage blow to his head which had first stunned him and thrown him to the ground. "It aches me every day, with the same power as it did when first the side of that sword slammed across my skull," he told me. "It throbs."

The priests looked at it carefully. It was neither a slice nor a crack, and there was naught of any visible suppuration there. In fact, it looked the least of all his miseries. But he never well recovered from that injurious bruise, and it caused him much wild suffering, ever after.

CHAPTER THIRTY-SIX

Leofric, abbot of Peterborough, took part in this
campaign, and there fell ill and returned home: he
died soon afterwards on the eve of All Saints. . . .
In his day the abbey of Peterborough enjoyed
complete happiness and prosperity, and he was
beloved by everybody. So the king gave to him . . .
the abbacy of Coventry, which his uncle, Earl
Leofric had founded, and those of Crugland and
Thornie. More than any man before or since he
enriched the abbey of Peterborough with gold and
silver, with vestments and land.

—Anglo Saxon Chronicle
Book "E" 1066

My brother was not the only wounded man at the monastery. Near a
hundred of the good monks had fallen in battle at Gate Fulford and at
least as many had come home to recuperate, in varying degrees of
injury. Several times a week, requiems were sung; there was a great
heaviness of spirit over the whole place. Then, to complicate matters,
fever broke out so that many who bore no wounds at all became
violently ill and required nursing as well. It was not long before our
little circle became wretchedly indisposed—Ywen Carr's son first, then
his brothers, then the Bearn. Finally, I was put to bed myself, tossing
and turning with all the discomforts of phlegmatic flux. I cursed my lot,
especially as it meant I was confined and could not sit and talk with my
brother or keep him company in his more excessive misery as I was
wont to do for most of my day.

The very morning that the priests began to dose me, devastating
news arrived in the form of an alarm from King Harold. While he was
marching back south from his great victory over Tostig and the Norse

king, Duke William of Normandy had landed at Pefnesea. Once again, tales came of an enormous fleet of ships and men. 'Twas rumored the Normans had even brought thousands of horses with them across the channel! Difficult as it was to give credence to such a tale, I remembered only too well my father describing the foreigners' strange way of fighting while on horseback. From what I remembered of glint-eyed William, I knew he would insist upon his own way of wreaking havoc.

Regardless of this detail or that, though, the situation was critical and everyone knew it. After waiting fruitlessly for months on the southern coast, King Harold had been forced to disband the Anglish fyrd. The wind had prevented the Norman fleet from sailing, and the masses of Anglish soldiers could be fed and quartered no longer. Then had come the northern invasion, and Harold hastily recalled them. After that swift enforced march across the country, and a full day's bloody battle, those men were weary, worn, and wasted.

The Normans, on the other hand, were chomping at the bit. The weather had held them back for months and they were eager for Anglish treasure, as well as battle-glory. Harold Godwine's son sent out a desperate summons for fighting men. What he had seen of the aftermath of Gate Fulford must have filled him with deep despair. The Mercian carls, even the earl's prized household troops, were slaughtered and scattered. The North Humbrians had fared but little better. As far as we knew, the Bernicians were unscathed, but their loyalty was doubtful. King Harold could not have forgotten that Earl Oswulf had never bent a knee to him. Harold's own troops and those of his brothers, already battered by marching and warfare, were all he could truly count upon. He was mobilizing to face one of the greatest warriors of the age and he needed every man who could hold a weapon.

Fevered and sick as well as determined not to leave their master's side, Hereward the Wake did not go nor did the Welshmen. But about thirty men from the monastery answered the call: those survivors from Gate Fulford who had not collapsed in fever. I was aghast when I learnt my uncle meant to lead them. He had looked strained and unwell since our long trek through the marshes, and in his constant attendance upon others he had neglected himself to his own detriment. I prevailed upon him, best as I could in my weak and feverish state, not to expose himself again to battle. Even Edwin, in a relapse of pain and raving, understood the man's intent and pleaded with him to stay. Uncle Leofric would not be moved. Electing the good monk Brand, who was Hereward's uncle, to officiate the abbot's duties in his absence, he rode at the head of a well-armed body of monks who took their leave that brisk autumn morn to meet with Harold on the ridge above Hastings field.

At Peterborough, there was nothing to do but wait. My convalescence had been slow, probably owing to my great lowness of spirits. I dreamt time and again of that strange, long-haired star, seeing its spectacular fire and feeling its whisper of doom and destruction. Brother Wulfget attended me constantly and carried messages between my brother and myself. Edwin seemed to have periods of power and then of collapse, and no one could tell how it would fare with him from one day to the next. The priests stood him up several times a day now; I could hear him sob and gasp and curse and beg for long minutes after they lowered him back to his cot.

After his bout with the terrifying dysentery, Siward Bearn looked like another man. His tall frame could not well carry the stigma of such pronounced thinness; his coppery hair had dulled to brown and his eyes were lusterless. He was mourning his dead brother and kinsmen in the hardest way, and spoke incessantly of his lady Gythrun, wondering about her safety and health. She had been packed off to the manor at Ceaster the day we learnt of the burning of Scarbyrig and the imminent invasion of Eorforwic. He had not heard tell of her in all that time. It worried him most especially as he feared she had been with child when they parted. I had not told him of Briana's condition. Must be he had heard of it from the men who travelled north with me but, if so, he never mentioned it. He never spoke her name with me.

I had been on my feet a day or two and was playing at gammon with him in the near-empty refectory, when we were surprised to see Edwin enter the room. Supported by Hereward on one side and Brother Wulfget on the other, he moved stiffly and carefully, biting back moans at every step. There was agonized victory in his flaming eyes, and when he reached our table, I saw him smile for the first time since he had taken his injuries.

After that, he walked every day. I was the one who helped him more often than not, and it pained me to see what a trial simple movement had become for him. In truth, I felt somewhat of a guilt that I had been largely unscathed in battle, though 'twas surely the workings of Providence that had prevented it. I could never have weathered the horrors of recovery and I knew it. All of his wounds were healing now, but from the time he began his walking he complained more and more of the terrible, inconstant pain in his head. One night, it was so overwhelming that Brother Wulfget came and woke me, hastening me to Edwin's cell where I found him crying in painful distraction. He was frightened, and I knew it. He told me he had lost his consciousness.

"I swear I do not remember falling! I fear me my mind is injured!" He took my arm in a grip of iron and spoke in a low, trembling voice.

I assured him not, and Brother Wulfget explained to him that his wounding had been so great he could not fail but have relapses of strength. We were insistent, praising his rapid recovery and saying how much worse it might have been. 'Twas of little relief to him, though. I stayed there chattering and comforting his anxious spirits till at length he fell asleep, fully dressed, upon his cot. He was not a man easily cowed, and this episode greatly disturbed me.

Even so, it was soon to be forgotten in the wake of more important things. It had been more than a fortnight since my uncle and his men had left to join the fyrd. In all that time, we had heard no word. Then news came so thick and fast that we scarce could comprehend it all.

A party of monks returned to the monastery, outstripping my uncle and the rest of the men, to bring us fateful tidings. King Harold was dead. His brothers Gyrth and Leofwine were also cruelly slain. The great English fyrd was reduced to nothingness.

The Norman duke had been victorious.

Those men told of a battle which each man hearing knew had changed our lives forever. It had not been of the scope of the one at Gate Fulford—the field was but a fraction of the expanse of the northern one, far fewer fought and died. Even so, 'twas a battle the likes of which had never been fought before and none could doubt the graveness of the outcome. Gathered in the refectory, hushed with horror and sadness, we heard tell how the Normans, mounted on their war-steeds, rode against the gruesome Anglish war-axe. There followed a terrifying slaughter of unbelievable proportions which lasted from morning till eve.

Thousands of men fell on each side in the daylong battle. Towards sunset, Harold himself was brutally murdered, then hacked to pieces while his army fell back in despair—a bloody, butchered remnant of Anglish manhood.

CHAPTER THIRTY-SEVEN

On hearing of [harold's] death, the earls Edwin
and Morcar . . . went to London and sent their
sister queen Aldgyth to Ceaster. . . .
                                    — Florence of Worcester

Stunned and distraught, Edwin and the men gathered with us and I tried
desperately to establish a plan of action. There was little any man could
do and a feeling of helplessness engulfed us all. Our first thought was for
Aldgyth; as the fallen king's widow, she would be hunted by the
conquering one. We knew little of the implacable Norman's temperament; not at all reassuring. Her position, we knew, was most precarious.

At length it was decided I should ride to Nottingham where both
she and Grandmother Godiva had removed themselves at Harold's
request. It was in her best interest to be moved even farther. The say of
the manor at distant Ceaster, poised on the Welsh border, had reverted
back to the Bearn upon his brother Ealdread's death, and he proposed
we move her there.

Edwin still kept his bed more often than not, but he had recovered
enough to curse his lot. He had finally learnt the fate of his guard, which
the priests had ordered hid from him for fear of the effect such news
would have upon his weakened spirits. The news that so many of his
closest personal men had been victims of the slaughter plunged him into
a deep well of misery and sorrow. There followed a relapse of fever and
pain, through which he wept unrelentingly. He grieved hard for our
cousin Ælfmaer, closest of his friends since childhood, but as much as he
cried for his lost kith and kin, he cried for himself. He was not fit to
travel to with me to Mercia and he wanted badly to go. He charged me
with delivering a huge sum of gold to Nottingham and he issued a writ
to the families of all his men slain at Fulford, telling them to claim a
gold-gift there.

Brother Wulfget took me aside just before I left and told me how my brother fared in truth. The flesh wounds were finally clean and fast mending now, he said, though there was great soreness where the inner organs had been pierced or bruised. But it was his broken bones that remained his bane, keeping him from free motion and inspiring much agony. "Best pray that these splints and poultices will mend him inside," he added somberly. "Methinks he is not a man who would bear being bent and crooked with pain all his life long."

Discussing this prognosis, Siward Bearn and I took our leave with a party of twenty. We were so intent on skirting away my sister that we did not even wait for Uncle Leofric to return from the battlefield. Truth to tell, I did not realize how depressed I had become inside the stone walls of that monastery until I came away from it. The entire autumn-kissed world was like a sigh of relief to me. I felt pleasure for the first time in many weeks. My mind was free to dwell for once on things other than death and anguish.

It surprised me to see Grandmother Godiva looking old as she did, but when we met with Aldgyth in her chamber the sight of her astonished me even more. She was very great with child. Siward Bearn and I stared open-mouthed at the size of her swollen belly till she blushed red and turned away from us. Her bride-ale had been but seven months ago and a number of strange thoughts had already crossed my mind when I heard her say in a low, mournful voice, "I bear Harold two children, brother. One to be his heir, and one to replace Gruffydd's son who was robbed from my very arms."

Then she shivered and burst into tears. I should have taken her in a comforting embrace, but Siward Bearn was the one who enfolded her, lifting her veil to stroke the soft hair beneath it. For some reason, I felt a sullen chill when I saw the two of them together, and had to turn away. It would have been so much easier, I thought, if she would have bent to having that man when he asked her. When I looked back, she had pulled away and wiped her eyes. They looked like glass. A phrase came to me. *Glass-eyed twice-cwene.* Suddenly weak, I leant against the wall, almost overcome with emotion.

"It would sound a strange thing to you, I suppose," my sister said after a while, pacing back and forth, "if I said I had grown to love him, my Harold."

I shook my head. "We expected it. His message to us was that, having seen you, he thought 'twould be a love match."

"Aye," she nodded numbly. "He loved me well. 'Tis my fate, methinks, to be loved by kings and lose them."

I wanted to remind her of the prophecy of the Filidh, but I could not make myself do it. "We have need to move you further away than this," I said instead, sounding casual. "The Norman will be sure to look for you."

"Where do you think to take me, brother?"

Siward Bearn answered. "Ceaster is the place you would be safest. My brother's widow, Lady Gweneth, could use your comfort now. She is distraught beyond measure at Ealdread's death, methinks. She could be of use to you, too." He rubbed his bearded chin with the palm of his hand, then added absently, "My sister is there now, too. You will be glad to know she is also with child."

Aldgyth tossed me a look which froze my heart. "Indeed, cousin," she answered the Bearn coldly. "She has sent me messages. Our children, it seems, will be of an age."

I tried to stop myself, but I could not. Shooting cold glances at them both, I strode angrily from the room.

I found Grandmother Godiva over-seeing some barming in the steamy kitchen house. She came outside and walked with me a while. We spoke about things long past. I smiled to hear her call me "little Morcar" as she always did. I towered well above her tiny, bent form. She chastised me for not wearing a fillet round my hair; I had to remind her that I was the Earl of the North Humbria now and 'twas not the fashion there. She laughed and said nothing. Looking out over the browning lea, where Cynewulf Cenwulf's son rested, she told me they had lost his brother Cynric a few weeks back. Minor wounds he had taken at the Gate Fulford claimed him. I felt a stab of sorrow. Edwin had asked the man to come to Kirton and tend his birds, but he had refused. The deaths of his brother and of his best friend, Earl Ælfgar, had robbed him of much of his energy and drive. Lady Godiva took that man's sad death as hard as the others; she had tended him since babyhood. After they had lain the man near his brother, under the grass, Grandmother told me she looked out oft-times and pretended Ælfgar was buried there, too. "Sometimes methinks I see them as they played so long ago," she told me wistfully. I decided she had no need to know about the extent of Edwin's wounding now.

Siward Bearn told Aldgyth, though. She came to me later in the hall, after the meal, looking somber. She carried with her a purse of skiver and pressed it in my hand. "Siward Æthelgar's son says Edwin would never consent to let me look upon him," she said dolefully, "so you must carry this back to him. 'Tis leaves and seeds of knit-bone. If it is broken bones which ail him, then this should be the first time of three that I open that pouch they gave me."

She did not have to say more. I knew that the prophecy had occurred to her again, too.

Because of her condition, the journey to Ceaster would be tedious and slow. The Bearn decided that I should return to Edwin while he, himself, would accompany the train that would carry Aldgyth west. It might happen that I could not be spared for any length of time; we knew not how things would go when William came to claim his kingdom and ask fealty of the great men. I agreed to my cousin's plan.

Before I returned to the monastery, I rode with my men into the Lindcylene Shire, giving the gold personally to the families of Edwin's men. I knew my brother would appreciate it, just as those bereaved ladies and sons and mothers did. Afterwards, I was sorry, though. It prolonged our journey near a fortnight, and when we returned, I found out Uncle Leofric had been dead two full days.

*   *   *

Brother Wulfget and the other priests, amazed at having precious knit-bone to work with, began to apply it at once. They made poultices and windings soaked in the tea it made, and forced my brother to eat the dried leaves. It nearly gagged him, or so he said, but he soon enough was feeling less pain and moving with greater ease and dexterity. About a month after my uncle's solemn requiem, I went looking for my brother and found him in the wide stone stabling barn. He was sitting a horse.

"This is madness!" I cried, rushing to him.

He glared, squarely and defiantly, then announced he was riding to Lundun City. I scarce could believe I had heard him, and I answered with astonishment.

"To Lundun? You are near-crazed, I swear it! Lundun City is more than eighty miles yonder and you can scarce hold yourself upright a half day! You are confused, surely!"

I could tell my words meant nothing. There was a look to him I knew well: the iron-eyed, indomitable gaze of my father. He made no answer, only dismounted and stood in silence with his back to me. There was a long, nervous silence and finally I broke it.

"I suppose this is some scheme of your man Hereward's?"

Edwin turned with a vehemence which surprised me. "Little you know, brother!" He pressed his arm close to his side. I knew there was still intense pain in his movement and I looked at him with smug know-ingness as he grimaced. Still, he was undaunted.

"Must be you know the invader William will be in Lundun City soon. We of Angland had best be prepared to meet him, one way or the other. Only a faint few of the highest men of the land still live. Think you not they will miss these two?"

I felt a sickening stab of shame. I had not given much thought to the grave affairs of state lately; so much was awry in my own life and my own earldom. We knew that many of the remaining high-born men had already gathered in the capital. archbishop Aldred was there, and the other archbishop, Stigand, whom the men of Mercia called the Unsaintly. So was young Ædgar the ætheling, grandson of King Edmund Ironside. He was only a child but he had a true blood claim to the throne, and the rumor was that the men of Angland were thinking to name him king. Even now, they were working to raise another army to face the Norman invaders. The very thought of that filled me with dread. William, we had heard, had waited near a week at Hastings for the men of the land to come and swear fealty to him. When none had shown, he began marching his newly reinforced army slowly northwestwards up the coast, towards Lundun. 'Twas easy enough to know he was enraged; he had given his men leave to destroy everything they passed over, and they did.

Lost in dire thoughts, I did not notice Hereward enter and I jumped at the sound of his deep voice. "Earl Morcar! I have been looking everywhere for you. You have decided to come then?"

I stared for a minute at the towering man with his open, honest face, not knowing even then whether I liked him or not. He had no grossly annoying faults, near as I could tell, unless a person counted condescension—and that would scarce keep a man from good grace. Yet, by comparison, he knew sins of mine which would make a priest shiver. He had never said a word about that night, but just knowing that he knew of it was enough to make me suspect his motives. When I looked away, my eyes met my brother's and I read the hopefulness there. Almost against my will, I agreed to go. Hereward's smile was earnest, but he glanced at Edwin in an I-told-you-so way which irked me, giving me to know they had discussed my reactions between them, and Hereward's assurances had proven correct. I tossed my head and sent him to make ready my gear and pack the furs and clothes I had brought from Nottingham. Soon as he had gone, Edwin clasped my shoulder, saying, "I knew you would understand the need of this."

I could not help smiling. "'Tis a madness, brother," I declared. "This journey will be a hazard for you!"

"I know as much!" He remounted, not without difficulty, and called back to me, "We leave at dawn."

I could feel the effort it took him to keep his voice level against his pain.

So the misty, grey morning found us riding through the green and gold Bruneswald, a somber but talkative party of thirty men. We stopped at Grantanbrycg the first night, where we were warmly received and our numbers swelled by fourteen. At dusk of the third day, a larger party yet, we neared the great city.

The journey was exceedingly hard on Edwin, just as I had predicted. He had himself well bound, but the wild-fire of discomfort raged in his eyes, giving him a look of surpassing rebelliousness, almost like teeth-gritting madness. Perhaps I have ever been to quick to see my father in him, but he did have the same bold and undaunted look, a resolve born of anguish and enhanced by strong emotion. Nevertheless, by the time we entered the Lundun gates he was panting with agony. Hereward led him away to quarters in the king's house while the rest of the party sought lodging in the town, crowded now with those men who had survived the mind-numbing trio of awful battles that had marked the past months: Gate Fulford, the aet-Staengfordesbrycg, and Senlac Field, now called Hastings.

With Siward Bearn and the Welshmen, I made my way to the West Minster. A far cry now from the hollow stone shell I had visited once upon a long ago day with my father and Cynewulf, King Edward's hallowed church was the greatest and richest in the land. 'Twas whispered by many that miracles occurred where the old king was buried within. In my innermost heart I prayed, not without skepticism, that the rumors were true. If ever Angland needed a miracle, that time was now.

A silent, unsmiling cleric led us to a chamber where a dozen men, all in arms, sat in a hushed council round a square, stone-legged table. I had not seen Aldred, the famed and scholarly archbishop of Eorforwic, since we took our leave of each other in the confusion following that tragic day at Gate Fulford. I spotted him right away amongst the warrior-priests; he was a brawny man who looked younger than his years, with a strong air of command. My pleasure at seeing him was dimmed by the sight of archbishop Stigand making his way into the room from the doorway opposite where I stood with my men. All knew the man had received his pallium from a false pope but, having made himself a pawn to them, he was honored nonetheless by the House of Godwine; 'twas he who had deigned to crown Harold king without the combined consent of earls or bishops. He now stood in good grace with the men of southern Angland, who followed the example of their earls. Consequently, this arrogant and grasping church-man deemed himself the equal of saintly men like Aldred and blessed Wulfstan, while openly flaunting the riches he had earned from the beneficent house which supported him. As for me, despite my regard for Harold Godwine's son, I despised Stigand. He was a wiry, thin, ascetic looking man with a hard and cold manner, and he had shown my father much unkindness.

Soon as he saw us, archbishop Aldred rose and greeted us with obvious excitement. After we had bent knee and kissed his ring, he

embraced us, first me and then the Bearn, as if we were his long-lost kin.
"You are truly well-come," is what he told us both, smiling a greeting to
the stoic sons of Carr as well. "Must be you know folk had heard tell that
you died on the field of the Gate Fulford, Earl Morcar. Yet my own
prayers and those of many others were answered, and you are whole!"

I explained, very briefly, that it was my brother who had been sore
struck down there; he questioned me worriedly about it and was
reassured to learn Edwin was with us. His wide, pale face creased with a
smile and he nodded complacently. "We had hoped you both would be
here, but we knew not how either of you fared."

Then we sat down, and I told him all that had passed. When I
informed him of my uncle's death, he crossed himself, greatly saddened.
"He was a good and saintly man of Christ," he told me earnestly, and
asked me who had succeeded him.

"He himself chose the good monk Brand," I said, helping myself to
a generous handful of nuts; I was famished. "Of course, he has not yet
been consecrated."

"Then Ædgar will be the one to approve him," he said, scrutinizing
my face for a reaction. I did not disappoint him; I was literally stunned.
He was saying, in effect, that they had agreed to accept young Ædgar
Ætheling as king! True, he was the only living close kinsman of King
Edward—but he was only nine years old! Realizing suddenly that I was
trembling, I cast a worried glance across the table to the ashen face of
Siward Bearn. Before I could say anything, I felt a hand on my shoulder.
Æthelwine, Bishop of Dunholme, chief church-man of the Bernicia,
pierced me with a look of determination.

"We have counciled long and hard on this, Earl Morcar," he said,
trying to make his gruff voice sound reassuring. "We all agree we must
have an anointed king before the Norman reaches Lundun City. 'Tis the
only logical excuse we could offer for refusing him the crown. Surely you
see the wisdom in it, even if it only be stalling for time."

I studied him carefully. He was a warrior-priest who had never taken
to tonsured hair or priestly robes—just the sort of church-man they
venerated in the wild Bernicia. Numbly, I shook my head. "Ædgar!" I
mumbled low, feeling very confused. "By God, he is but a boy! 'Tis a
farce to suppose men will rally to him with any heart."

"Earl Morcar, what would you have us do?"

Glancing nervously from the Bearn to the Welshmen, I shrugged. At
Peterborough, we had listened to the rumors that men were thinking to
fight behind the boy, but I had more or less dismissed them. The state of
Angland was too precarious to admit of a nine-year-old boy-king.
Speechless, I felt a wave of hopeless desperation creeping over me. With-

out even thinking, I stood up suddenly, hands on my hips.

Thinking he read something in that gesture, ice-eyed Stigand spoke aloud, with words like biting weapons. "King Harold and his house were well loved in this part of the country, Earl Morcar, and 'tis well known that neither you nor your brother stood behind his standard in the aet-Staengfordesbrycg or at Hastings field. Methinks the men of Wessex all would sooner die than see you or Earl Edwin crowned king, whether you believe you have king's blood in your veins or not."

Flooded with anger, I slammed my fist on the table and opened my mouth to speak. Aldred stopped me with a commanding stare. "You are fatigued from your hard journey, my lord," he said, as if in reassurance. "You go now, and your men with you. We will all meet together in the morning to decide what is to be done."

Gripping my elbow firmly, he steered me to the door. I could not help shooting Stigand a cold snarl over my shoulder. I could almost smell the man's sinfulness and it amazed me that men like Aldred or Æthelwine could stand the presence of one like him. In return, the sallow Stigand stared back—a staunch, emotionless smirk.

Outside the door, Aldred reached one hand up to my shoulder and one to Siward Bearn's. He reminded us that Abbot Stigand was, after all, a man of the cloth. "He was hard taken by the deaths, one upon the other, of Harold and Gyrth and Leofwine. Those men were as sons to him. Even Tostig—"

He must have felt me tremble with loathing, because he broke off apologetically. "Must be you know he well loved that house," he added low, when I had relaxed.

The archbishop looked at me meaningfully, then traced a cross on my brow with his fingers. Biting my tongue, I took the blessing, and went to find my brother.

*   *   *

Every time I looked at Waltheof Siward's son, I was reminded that he was the son of the man who murdered Oswulf's father. I could not help it, the thought just occurred to me. That is not to say I hated the man for his father's sins, for in truth I never much liked or disliked him. He himself had done naught to offend me or my house, save taking the shires of Huntandun and North Hamtun when King Edward offered them, and he had shown great courage fighting alongside us at Fulford. Even so, there was something ingratiating in his manner which made me keep a distance between us from the very first, and every time I looked at him I recalled what a gross murderer the old warrior-earl Siward the Ursurper had been.

Waltheof was of average height, broad-boned but thin, with a common, fox-eyed look that did not sit well with me. Nor did I appreciate his humor, which was coarse and rude, or his manner, which was extremely pliant and indecisive. Edwin, who made friends faster and firmer than ever I did, seemed not to notice the man's peculiarities, or at least he never remarked openly upon them. I confided my own disapprobation to him, though, and he early on insisted it was all because Waltheof liked to pretend he had a claim to my earldom since his father had once held it. He had never actively exerted that claim, never made a move to defy or challenge me, but he always dressed and combed himself in the North Humbrian fashion, and went about with the air of a man who has been cheated of a great treasure.

Nevertheless, I grew to appreciate him somewhat during those harried days of councilling in Lundun, because, for all his susceptibility, at least the man was thoroughly open and honest about everything he heard or saw. If Stigand told him one thing and then told us another, Waltheof was certain to let us know. If a man said anything against me, I could count on the son of Siward to report it. The man was singularly unable to keep anything secret.

He sat himself between Edwin and me one cold day at the great meal, and told us with a puzzled frown that Stigand had assured him we had opted to offer the crown to the invader. My brother and I exchanged a glance. The wily man had approached us earlier in the day, in an unusually humble way, telling us the same thing about Waltheof and Aldred and others of the high-born men. That was our first suspicion that the conniving politician was pressing for us to recognize the invader's claim. Later, we were to learn that many of the thegns and merchants of Lundun, afraid their city would be reduced to rubble if we attempted to hold out, had offered him bribes of gold and treasure to convince the rest of us to submit. Almost immediately, we went to Archbishop Aldred, and finding he was not of a mind to do it any more than we were, we declared then and there for the Ætheling, along with Siward Bearn, Waltheof, Bishop Æthelwine, and a good many others. We were sick at having to make a choice of such two poor alternatives, but there was no other way.

In a small and unceremonious service, Aldred consecrated wan Ædgar as King of England. He was unable to crown the child, however, because the golden coronet had been lost with Harold at Hastings, and there had been no time or inclination to fashion another. Later, this was to prove fortuitous, but at the time it seemed a foreboding omen indeed, and indicative of things as they were then, dark and ominous. I watched the pale, undemonstrative, white-haired boy fondle the scepter. In his hands, it looked like little more than a toy. I was sick with uncertainty.

His first royal decree was to affirm Hereward's uncle, Monk Brand, as abbot of the monastery at Peterborough. A messenger was dispatched there immediately to inform the monks of this action, and swear them to the new king.

As William made his slow, wicked approach, word came to us that King Edward's widow, Edythe, had surrendered her dower city of Wintan-ceaster to the Norman duke. Those of the House of Godwine had always had an unfailing ability to sense the turn of the tide and swim abreast of it, so this seemed a dire portent. We worked hard at fortifying the walls of Lundun, and sent out summons after summons, full well knowing there were few men left in Angland able to answer the call.

One morning, we learnt that a party of the invader's men had ridden with arms to the bridge at Southwark, attempting to cross to Lundun. The bold Anglishmen there had beaten them back, killing several of the Normans. William, already enraged by the news that our half-hearted Witan had opted for young Ædgar and not himself, announced he would starve us all into submission. He would lay waste a great circle around the city and occupy it so that we could neither flee nor receive provisions. As a prelude, he burned Southwark to the ground.

As he commenced to make good his threat, we were assailed by horrifying tales of his army's doings. One snowy afternoon, looking out from the towers of the minster, we could see the fast approaching glow of harrowing red flame. That was the day Stigand rode out of the city gates with a party of priests to meet with the Norman. We did not know it then, but that very evening he swore fealty unto the duke.

CHAPTER THIRTY-EIGHT

... Earl Edwin, Earl Morcar, and all the best men
from Lundon submitted from force of circumstances,
but only when the depredation was complete.

—Anglo Saxon Chronicle
Book "D" 1066

By now, the entire city of Lundun was in a furor of fear amidst preparations for battle. It soon came clear to us that William would not attack
us and make a confrontation of it. True to his word, he meant to encircle
us with utter devastation while sparing Lundun itself. 'Twas not his aim
to destroy the greatest city of the realm. He meant to have himself
crowned there.

Stigand and his party soon returned with more tales of the terrible
rape and murder being inflicted all around us. But William himself, they
all assured us, was a gracious and not unpleasant man who swore he
would treat us well if we came to him immediately. Stigand even vowed
that the duke had apologized for his rapacity and plunder, adding that
the man had a special word for the earls of the House of Leofric. He
would be a gracious liege lord unto us, he declared, because he knew we
had not raised arms against him at Hastings. He told Stigand to tell us
that chief of the men at his side right now was our avunculus, William
Malet. This was a circumstance in which we had no hand, a natural
outgrowth of my uncle's dedicated service to the late King Edward and
his brother, the haplessly blinded Ælfred Ætheling, when they were
exiled to Normandy and welcomed by Duke William's house.
Nevertheless, it was plain to see that many of the southern Anglish now
held the fact against us.

Early the next morning, a great noise of rioting and unrest filled the
yard outside the minster as we came from the Mass. Frantically, the
people of Lundun, in fear for their lives and property, petitioned us to
ride west and submit to the Norman before the ruination was complete.

I remember shivering under my heavy northern furs and realizing there was no other recourse. Looking from one to another, the entire party of earls, thegns, and high-born men made the decision to submit. Then we went to deck ourselves in all the splendor of state so that we could offer hostages and honor to the victorious Norman. So eager were the city folk for this move, that men volunteered in great numbers to serve as hostages, so many that we had to choose from amongst them.

Silent and lost in thought, I let Siward Bearn array me in the court dress I had carried there, robes that had been Grandfather Leofric's. We did not speak, but there was communication, a crossing of emotions in the static air. I did not know what to expect of this foreigner and tried to conjure memories of that far-away Yuletide in the court of King Edward. Only a vague remembrance of his impressive stature and kingly air came to me, but I recalled that my father, who was not friend to many men, had liked him.

I had not worn my robes of state for months, and leaving that place decked in them, I felt a stranger to myself. Edwin sat regally on his wild grey. Beside him, Waltheof Siward's son stared emotionlessly, his stallion, like mine, richly arrayed in the North Humbrian style.

It was a cold morning; the sky was purple with tumultuous winter clouds. In the chill wind, which permeated even our layers of furs, we rode out west from the city, an incredibly impressive entourage.

We had reached the surroundings of Beorh Hamstede when we caught first sight of the Norman. Eyeing our party, he held his men still and they waited for us in scrutinizing silence. He was in full battle-gear but helmetless, as tall and commanding as I remembered him. Though his wind-ruffled black hair somewhat softened his stern outline against the steely sky, I had never seen so imposing or magnificent a man. His eyes were sullen but his look impassive. One could read that he was both surprised and satisfied at our approach. Drawing near, leaving his men behind him, he eyed us carefully, then spoke in an iron voice.

"Those of you who proffer fealty, I offer my earnest friendship. But those of you who harbor treason or treachery, know that I will smite you as the falcon smites the field-mouse."

I stared at him, not knowing what he read in my look. He inspected us, from one to the other. Ædgar he recognized immediately and he seemed to have no trouble knowing Edwin. But he glanced from Waltheof to me, and then asked, "Which of these two now lords the North Humbria?"

Stigand spoke up, like a bowing page. "He on the left is Waltheof son of Siward, new Earl of Huntandun, my lord, and on the red stallion—" I silenced him by reining my horse forward, cutting him off from the Norman's view. The sound of his ingratiating snivel was abhorrent to me.

"I am Morcar, son of Ælfgar, son of Leofric, Earl of the North Humbria," I announced, trying to keep the defiant edge from my voice. My hands shook.

"You are well-come, Ælfgar's son. I might have known you, but it is many years since last we met."

I made no answer. He motioned me to him, and I drew my horse up, facing him. I could see that his handsome face was worn, ravaged by fatigue and illness as my uncle's had been. He smiled and spoke to me in low tones no one else could hear. Gesturing towards Edwin, who only gazed silently, he said with candor, "Your brother and yourself are honored men to me, Morcar of North Humbria. Never have you defied me. It is fitting that you stood not by the tyrant Harold, breaker of holy oaths. For this, I offer you my hand." He held it out in the Norman way, and I found myself taking it, somewhat stiffly. "These men with you, will they take me as their liege lord?"

I asked them formally and there was a general consent. Then William rode to Edwin and saluted him the same way.

"Edwin of Mercia, much you are like your father when I knew him. I would have you for my ally."

Coolly, Edwin gave him his hand, saying, "Rather I would have you my ally than my bitter foe, Lord Guillaume." He addressed him in formal French, as I had. The Norman did not appear to understand Anglish.

In turn, William greeted Earl Waltheof and archbishop Aldred and the other great men. Lastly, he turned to Ædgar, who trembled under the duke's cold, unnerving stare.

"How do I greet you, child Ædgar? As Ætheling or as King?" There was no mistaking his tone. Ædgar lifted up his eyes to that man and levelly replied he bowed as Ætheling; he had never worn the crown.

"Keep you clean and fair then, Ætheling, and I will see no harm comes your way."

After that, he did not detain us long, but he bade us return to the city and prepare the people for his coming.

"I expect no resistance," he said severely. Directing our gaze to his restless army, he added ominously, "These men have fought hard and well in my service. I have promised them the spoils from Pefnesea to Lundun. So you will not be surprised if we harry our way there after you. I am a man ever of my word, and my word was that they might claim these rewards. It might have been different if you had come to me after Hastings, for I had made no such promise to them then."

Looking beyond him to the blackened desolation of the distant villages, I felt a sickening swell and at the same an overwhelming thankfulness that this had not been the fate of the North or the Mercian sweeps. I could not have borne the sorrow of seeing my homelands in that horrid state of waste.

Wordlessly, we rode back as we had come, leaving our hostages behind. None knew what to expect in the coming days.

It took William nearly till Christ Mass to work his army that short stretch to Lundun. He let them meander in every direction, wasting everything they came upon those two long weeks. We waited in suspense. When at last he came, he did not let his force enter the city, for fear of what they would do to it. He parked them at Berecingas, a pretty, provincial town some miles outside the gates, and brought with him a hand-picked select-guard of honorable, high-born men. Then, on Christ Mass day, my third Christ Mass in Lundun and my second in that man's company, he took the crown, which we had so recently seen placed with such hope on Harold's head.

We learnt that William had almost died from dysentery earlier. At Cantwarabyrig, he had taken the sickness and watched scores of his men die of it, but had been saved after a hard month of the disease. He laughed as he told us, "God willed me to be crowned king, and so He stilled the hand against me."

Unhesitatingly, he chose Aldred over Stigand to solemnize the coronation, to the latter's discomfiture. It was an impressive ceremony, and I knelt in gem-encrusted robes with the new king's brothers and all the men of Angland in the crowded West Minster as the archbishop of Eorforwic performed the rites. That spotless man had the courage to confront William before he would place the crown; in the hearing of all he made him swear he would be as good a king as any were in Angland before him. Holding the scriptures out to the kneeling king-elect, he commanded in a loud, stern powerful voice. "Pledge to me on the gospels, William of Normandy, that you will govern this country according to the best practices of your predecessors."

There was a great hush over all the church. It was obvious that the Norman had not been prepared for this. But at length, he placed both his hands on the holy book and swore to this sacred oath, which seemed somewhat to appease the apprehensive men of Angland.

Then a strange thing happened. Aldred faced us in the old manner, his hand on William's shoulder, and presented the man to us, asking if we assembled would accept him king. A loud affirmative cry went up, but William's men, hearing this from outside where they were stationed and understanding it not, thought we had turned upon their duke. They set fire to buildings all around and rushed in like madmen, arms drawn.

The commotion of the moment was overwhelming: men rushing here and there, some to fight the blazes and some to assist the Norman. In the confusion, I marked that William, alive to the terror and bewilderment, trembled mightily, and he caught my eye as I gazed on him unabashedly. But the coronation continued. Amidst the smoke and noise, Aldred placed the gleaming golden crown, his hands shaking vehemently.

Immediately after, Edwin, Siward Bearn, and I begged the Norman's leave. We had been away from our earldoms near three months now, and in truth, I truly longed for the broad northern reaches. William, however, would not let us go until we had sworn ceremonious public fealty to him. This time, 'twas not to be the vanquished bowing to the victor, but subject men kneeling to their crowned king. He hoped this would work to still the rampant rumors of rebellion and dissension which were already at work throughout the land.

CHAPTER THIRTY-NINE

Edwin and Morcar, the sons of Earl Ælfgar and
the most powerful of the English nobles from their
birth and possessions, now came to the king,
asking his pardon if aught they had offended him,
and submitting themselves and all they had to
his mercy.

—Orderic Vitalis
Book IV, Chapter I

With great state and fanfare, William led us to the manor he had taken
at Berecingas, and in a wide field there received us in formal submission
before a great crowd. He had let it be known that anyone who had not
knelt to him at Beorh Hamstede could take this opportunity of putting
himself right, and there were a great many men from Mercia and the
North Humbria who came to him there for the first time. One whom he
had most expected did not come. William took Oswulf Eadwulf's son's
absence as a personal affront and he did not take it well, by any means.

The new king dictated that the day of homage was to be an occasion of great celebration, peculiarly ironic as there was little left in the
environs of Lundun with which to make a feast. Even so, William
managed to do it, making a marvelous pretension of our vows of
loyalty—laughing and talking casually with us as if it had all come about
naturally and was not enforced at all. If not entirely easy-going, he was
at least a gracious man, and the whole episode might have been bearable
except that his guest of honor through the entire ordeal was Tostig's
purple-eyed man, the towering Copsige Sword-Stinger. The man had
become very dear to William because he had actively fought against the
oath-breaker, Harold, and nothing could have weighed more favorably
with the new king than an Anglishman denying the Wessexman's claim.

Copsige, always an ambitious braggart, made the most of his dazzling
day of acclaim. His hatred for Edwin and me had never quelled since the

days of Tostig's power, and he took vengeful advantage of the earliest opportunity he found to corner us away from the Norman's hearing.

The first thing he did was to ask after our mother, with a cruelly mocking laugh. Then he turned slyly to Edwin, calling him brother and saying he had done well to ignore Harold's summons to Hastings. "No doubt William believes you held back in deference to his claim, eh, Mercian?" He narrowed his glittering eyes and pursed his wind-burned face into an artificial smile. "Could be he does not know how we hacked you near to nothingness!"

As I wondered how many of my brother's gruesome wounds this man had personally delivered, slicing while he was downed and senseless, Edwin turned his head and spat. I thought it took him all his power of self-control not to do more. Copsige pretended not to notice the insult, and leant close, speaking in a low voice. "You cruelly disappointed us, Edwin Ælfgar's son, by escaping the field which should have been your grave. My lord Tostig grew drunken with fury when your bloody corpse was not to be found."

My brother trembled with rage, but his Welshmen and I held him forcibly to stay his attack. The Norman was exceedingly anxious for a show of solidarity, and the confrontation would have put Edwin in no good light. I tried to convince him of this, all the while glaring into the Sword-Stinger's purple eyes with an urge to smash him which I barely could control.

To make matters worse, William announced publicly during the feast which followed the ceremony that Copsige was now one of his earls—Earl of the Bernicia! Oswulf Eadwulf's son had refused to make pledges of loyalty unto the new king and now his earldom was forfeit. I was surprised and a little bit disgruntled when I found out I was the one who would journey north to bring the news.

"You are his kinsman, Earl Morcar," the king said knowingly, "and till now, you have been his over-lord. Best you tell him that I am lenient enough to put no disfavor on him yet. If he travels back here with you to offer fealty, then I will retain him somewhat of his dignity. If not...."

He did not have to finish. Biting the inside of my cheek, I exchanged a glance first with my brother and then with the Bearn, picturing the scene which would ensue when the Sword-Stinger went to claim his domain. William knew little enough of my cousin if he thought the man would hand it over without a fight.

William bade me choose three of my own men to ride with me, saying the rest would come from amongst his Normans. Something told me more was meant than said; the king was wroth to let me out of his presence, it seemed, and by choosing me a Norman guard, he thought to ensure my return. Somewhat hopefully, I picked my brother as one of the men to travel north, but the Norman laughed when I said it. "An earl chooses from amongst his select-guard, sir," he declared in a tone of reproval, "and not from amongst other earls."

Edwin, then, was to be hostage against the possibility of my defection! One look told me my brother was not pleased with the arrangement. Flushed and grim-eyed, he downed a huge horn of ale, staring morosely into my eyes as he did it.

The fact that he had been drinking heavily all the day did not escape my attention. I knew he was not feeling well; the stress and tension of the emotionally arduous day had obviously magnified his complaints. He early in the day had grumbled of a throbbing head-pain brought on by the burst of anger which had almost brought him to arms with the new Earl Copsige. A man who almost infallibly grew merry with drink, Edwin had brooded all the meal through, stiff, somber, and unsmiling. It lent him an air of cool dignity, not entirely unimpressive to the new king, I am sure, for William was a man of such mien and manner himself. Even so, I wondered how long my brother could last without betraying his distress.

Worried, I sent Edwin's man, our cousin Æric, to find Brother Wulfget, whom I had lost sight of in the crowd. Hereward had not come, saying he was a man of no great privilege and so the Norman would neither know nor miss him. The good monk, then, was the only one we could count on to understand and cope with my brother's indisposition.

I was deep in converse with the king about my uncle, William Malet, when Edwin stood to take a formal leave. The sunny richness of his costly garb and the dazzle of his gold and jewels were impressive enough to the court, but those who knew him well—kinsman Æric, the Bearn, the Welshmen, and a handful of others—cast me furtive glances of apprehension vas he left. My brother was pale and tremulous, his eyes glassy above his frozen smile.

The night was not yet old. The minstrels and harpists had not even begun to ply their crafts. Despite a prevalence of heavy Anglish hearts, there was a genial and relaxed atmosphere which was not unpleasant. Most of the men present seemed to be enjoying the moments of ease and comfort which the king now offered. After the emotional and physical trauma of the last months, such peaceful partying was blissful balm, and if the smiles and laughter were somewhat forced, everyone pretended not to notice. William had declared it a night for merry-making, a respite gratefully accepted.

Even so, I was tired enough from the day's events to make an earlier excuse than most, and soon as I left the hall, I sought for Edwin. I found him in the chamber we shared, pacing back and forth in a distracted way, while Brother Wulfget watched glumly from the shadows.

"You should take to your bed, brother," I began, trying to lighten their mood, "and give your body a rest."

Edwin muttered something in reply, but I could not make it out.

"He is talking to himself," Wulfget told me. "He makes as if not to notice us."

"Because I have no need of nurse-maids!" my brother answered curtly, without turning to face us. He leant hard against the wall, pressing his hands to his head. Wulfget shrugged. I rebuked Edwin gently, remarking on our concern for him. He muttered something more about Copsige Sword-Stinger, something dark and low, then resumed his pacing.

As I watched him, a strange thing began to happen. His shoulders heaved suddenly, twice or thrice, and then began a violent twitching which almost immediately took over his entire body. He was thrown to the floor, as if by some invisible force. Instantaneously, Wulfget was at his side and I with him, grasping Edwin's shoulders as if to still the violent shaking. It took all our combined power to hold him. Seeing his face, I gasped with distress. The strange possession was complete. Even his features were in the grip of it: twisted, eerie, unearthly. A strange whiteness had come over his eyes which were half-rolled back into his head. He foamed and bled from the mouth and nose. Nostrils flaring, lips parted, he emitted some strange guttural tones entirely foreign to me. I crossed myself quickly and watched dumb-founded as Wulfget jammed the coarse cloth of his own wide sleeve into Edwin's gaping mouth.

There was a dull thudding noise as my brother's head slammed repeatedly on the hard floor. I thought to cushion it with my hand and winced hard at the force his skull exerted on my knuckles. Suddenly, a tremendous tension took hold of him, lifting his trembling form several inches into the air and dropping him all at once, sodden and seemingly lifeless. Then all was still. He groaned loud and piteously, and began to choke on the heavy wadmal still crammed in his mouth.

Swiftly I lifted him to a sitting position, dabbing at his face with my tunic while Wulfget pulled the sleeve free, pounding him on the back to clear his passages. Momentarily, he came back to life, looking blank and bewildered, then he collapsed senselessly in a deep sleep. Wordlessly, we lifted him to his cot. He slumbered undisturbed a long time, and eventually the both of us fell into sleep, as well, as we sat keeping our terrified, silent watch over him.

Edwin woke confused at finding us at the foot of his bed. Trying to explain away the turmoil of the chamber and the blood on his tunic, I told Edwin a senseless story: that he had fallen from his wine. Brother

Wulfget blushed a little, as if it pained him to lie, but he said nothing. Edwin eyed us both curiously a long while as we straightened things. Nothing more was said about it and I was glad. I resolved to dismiss the happening myself, as if it had been some monstrous nightmare, not rightly remembered.

       *   *   *

One of the men Siward Bearn had left in Ceaster with Aldgyth came that morning with news that my sister had been delivered of two sons, and had named them Harold and Wulf. They were strapping and healthy and had been born near full term, a rare thing for double-babes, the women said, and considered most auspicious. Aldgyth had regained some of her former spirit, we were told, now that she had been safely birthed. She planned to stay on at Ceaster, despite the fact that Oswulf had moved on to Dunholme, his lady and household in tow. Ealdread's widow, Gweneth, was little help in her grief, but Gythrun Olavsdätter, Siward Bearn's wife, remained there for both of them. She was talented in nursing, despite the fact that she had lost a five-months' babe herself, only shortly before the twins' birthing. The Bearn was resolved to visit her, soon as our business with Oswulf was over and done with. He had seemed to cool strangely towards his woman, Gythrun, since last he met with her at Ceaster. I inwardly prayed that it was not because I had sent him journeying with Aldgyth and rekindled old passions within him.

We had some chance to talk of this matter and others as we made our way to the North Humbria on the king's mission. My cousin, as it turned out, had learnt of several indiscretions on the part of his wife, and from her own lips no less. Between his pressing duties as Bearn of the Diera, and chief man of the Earl of North Humbria, not to mention the tremendous confusion of the invasion months, he had not bestowed much pleasure on the woman and she had taken her needs elsewhere. "'Tis something Danish women are wont to do," he said somewhat mournfully to me in conclusion. "Every Anglishman knows as much, so I was foolish to trust her."

I told him the word was "skirt-blind," not "foolish," and we both laughed heartily.

My kinsman's union, in truth, had been ill-favored from the first. Everyone knew that he had married far beneath himself, and his bride was a foreign woman without Anglish blood besides. Grandmother Godiva and many of our other relations had refused to share the bride-ale with the unfortunate couple, and those of us who did were not favorably inclined towards the woman. Despite the rutting heat the Bearn had exhibited all the while he chased her, Siward himself was near emotionless about the entire affair. The only match that would have truly suited him had been lost years ago, when my father had gifted Aldgyth to the Welsh king. Now, I wondered at his urge to visit Ceaster, connecting it somehow with Aldgyth's presence there. I resented his passion for my sister yet felt foolish for it. My indignation was a mockery, circumstances being what they were.

That wintry journey seemed uncomfortably tedious, owing perhaps to our lowness of spirits. It was difficult for us to adjust to the strange position we found ourselves in those months, not really knowing what to expect but understanding perfectly that things as we had known them were now changed forever. Our very freedom was questionable. The Norman men in our party did not seem to play the part of watch-hounds, but we knew there was no question that we would return immediately to William's side when our message had been delivered, and felt instinctively that those remaining behind with him were hostage against the proof of it. William was solicitously diplomatic and entirely in control.

And it was a harsh season. As we wended our way northward, the wind grew meaner and the sky more sullen. Shadowed grey iciness was everywhere: a world in mourning for itself. The daylight dulled too early to allow for swift travel. It took us more than a week to come to Dunholme, and then we found that Oswulf had removed another twenty miles north. It was late the next evening when we finally came to the gates of my cousin's small estate at Hagustaldesea, and our arrival caused a flurry of alarm till it was ascertained just who we were. Though unordered and sloppily run as usual, the house of Oswulf Eadwulf's son was most thoroughly on its guard. My cousin, no doubt, deemed himself a hunted man now.

It was his Bernician guardsman, Beornwald Strong-Leg, who settled us in the rush-strewn hall, directing us to the center hearth where a timid fire smoldered. He threw some small logs on it, and the Normans quickly huddled round. I smiled a little at their plight, these first of William's men to feel the North-breath. I was thoroughly familiar with it, yet waxed frozen myself.

Even standing close to the fire as I could get, the harsh chill had barely begun to flee me when Oswulf's man returned, summoning me to follow him. Siward Bearn rose also, but Beornwald stopped him.

"'Tis Earl Morcar he wishes to see," Beornwald said coldly. "He bids me bring none other."

My cousin shot me a glance of vexation, then shrugged and sat down again. With a reassuring smile to him, I made my way after the broad-shouldered Bernician, who did not speak as we hurried through the dark corridor. When we came to Oswulf's chamber, Beornwald knocked once on the heavy timber door, then shoved it open. I entered alone and he pulled it shut behind me.

"You are well-come, Morcar Ælfgar's son!" Oswulf stood over a silver basin, splashing his face. He flashed me an unreadable smile. In the glow of the newly lighted pitch torches I could see that he had just begun to dress. He wore a fresh tunic over braies, and after he had dried his face with the sleeve of it, he slipped on a heavy dalmatic, belting it with his knife girt.

"There was no need to waken yourself," I told him apologetically. "All my words would wait until the morrow."

He silenced me with a wave of the hand. "Nay, I am anxious to speak with you, cousin! Not much of news has sifted this far north yet. How stand things?"

"You have well maddened him!" I told him, and related why William had sent me. My cousin laughed.

"By God! I would not swear to the Saxon Harold, and the Norman was mad if he thought I would swear to him! Tell him 'tis not a thing that runs in my blood."

"Methinks he will not be as reluctant to make war on you as Harold was," I told him somberly. "He says your earldom is forfeit."

Oswulf's eyes narrowed. "You listen to this drivel?" he asked me accusingly. "You pretend with him that he has the power to enforce those sort of words?"

"He wears the crown now."

"Well, it ill fits him!" Oswulf sat down on the edge of his pallet. I took a chair, studying his look in the gloom. Fair and arrogant as ever, I thought, somehow knowing the Norman was never to have his pledge. As if reading my mind, he threw me a handsome but cold grin, "You may as well tell him I am not a kneeler by nature, but that if he comes here, to my very door, I will give some thought to it before I spit in his face."

I tried to smile but could not. "That message you can send by some other messenger," I said firmly, and he scowled.

"Are you not bold enough to deliver it, then? 'Tis strange, Morcar Ælfgar's son, for of late I have come to think of you as more manly than ever I had before." His voice grew sullen, and I felt a tremor of apprehension. "Mean you not to ask me how my lady fares?" he asked, staring hard into my eyes. My instinct told me irrefutably that he knew.

"Is she well?"

"Aye. Well enough. The suckling she brought forth was a boy-child. Her ladies say he is a comely and well-formed thing but he looks not like much to me." He yawned, then stretched and stood.

My voice remained impassive. "Must be you are a proud man, then."

"Not as proud as some other one, I trow," he whispered, and grasping the table-edge with both hands, he leant towards me. "Not as proud as the one whose name she cried over and over in her frenzy of pain!" Tossing his head, he laughed with an amusement I almost thought genuine. Feeling a sudden pulse of anguish, I found myself on my feet, gazing guardedly into his eyes. Meeting my look with a hard smile, he bit into his lower lip momentarily, as if to force back an evil thought. "Think you not it is a fitting thing," he asked me in a low voice, "that the first sound ever the creature heard in this world was the call of your name, Morcar Ælfgar's son?"

I was so stunned that I could make no answer. 'Twas more than a year now since first I had lain with Briana, and in that time I had often imagined what Oswulf's reaction might be to learning of it. Frenzy, murderous rage, viciousness, violence—those responses I had considered. Laughing and sane-eyed boyish grins I had not. Now I stood speechless and amazed, more helpless and vulnerable than ever I could have been had he drawn arms upon me. My confusion must have been apparent in my look and manner for he laughed again, this time in a cold and angry way.

"Surely you do not suppose you are the first man I have shared her with?" The mockingness of his tone cut. He was daring me, and I knew it, but I stayed myself against him, even with a passionate furor rising fast over me. His whole countenance lit suddenly with a mirthful smile, "By God, you do!" His grin was one of sheer delight. "You think I am the only man ever she measured you against!"

I snarled and leapt suddenly, grasping his ashy locks tight in my fist, forcing his head back till he pulled away from me. "Be sure not to handle me, cousin!" he growled low, hand on his knife. "Hers is not an honor worth dying over!"

"Best you would make clear to me your gross accusations then," I demanded, impaling him with a look of sheer hatred, "and I will decide upon my own."

Relaxing all at once, he turned away, walked a few paces, then slumped into a heavy, bolstered chair, his back to me. Letting go a loud sigh of vexatious resignation, he asked in a dry voice, "Seems it not strange to you, cousin, this whole affair?"

I sat down, too—still wary, still bewildered that he would not fight me. "What mean you?"

"I am wedded to the woman," he said flatly, "and you have abused her. Yet you attack me as if I were the sinner and you the one sworn to defend her!"

"Methinks I am not the one who abuses her, Oswulf Eadwulf's son."

"Then you are a curious man!" Elbow on the high arm of the chair, he rested his chin in his hand casually, turning on me a look of sober scrutiny. "How is it you excuse your own sin so lightly when mine have impressed you with such horror and distaste?"

"Your sins are more, kinsman, and worse!" My voice was iron. His burst of laughter echoed in the hollow chamber.

"So well you fooled me with that bristling righteousness that I swore it was Edwin who had her! Had you coupled with her already when you let him keep her with him those months?"

I nodded numbly.

"Then, you are even more dull-witted than ever I thought! Had you no misgivings, seeing the way she trembles at the very sight of your pretty brother?"

I was on my feet so fast there was not time to think what I was doing. "God choke you on your evil words!" I cried hoarsely, lunging as if to threaten him. He did not flinch.

"Do not be a fool, Morcar. I know the woman and the fashion of man she pants after!" His eyes narrowed to icy cold slits. "Young and high-born—in that you meet her ideal, I trow. Yet she craves a certain audacious roughness, a recklessness you lack, which your brother—"

Trembling as with madness, I gave him no chance to finish, but wrapped my hands tight around his throat, pulling him to his feet, shaking him with murderous frenzy. I walked him backwards to the wall, slamming his head hard against it and holding him there. "You should die for the things you have done to her!" I hissed, in a voice I scarce recognized.

He spit in my face, and I smashed him hard into the timber again, kneeing his groin with all my strength, losing my grip on him as he lunged forward with a groan of pain and fury. Almost instantly I saw the glint of his dagger as he drew it and felt my own in my hand. Instinctively, we backed away from each other, and I realized of a sudden that I was protected by a hauberk and he was not—that because of it there almost was no contest to my taking him. I hesitated just a moment, undecided whether or not to slash at him in his disadvantage. In that very instant he leapt at me, throwing me to the floor and pinning me there, tossing his own blade half-way cross the room. Then, deftly avoiding mine while we struggled, he sank his teeth deep into my wrist, biting down with all his force until the weapon dropped. As it clattered to the stone floor, he put his hand hard over my mouth to force back my cry of anguish. The fire of his eyes near burnt through me as he brought his face close to mine with a savage whisper.

"If you are determined to come to blood over her, cousin, I will make you hear the truth of it first!" He pressed so hard on my face that I gasped for breath, feeling blood in my mouth and trying not to hear him. "I understand the both of you well enough to know you were not the one who chased after her. She came to you, did she not? How long does Lady Briana tease a man now? With me, 'twas near on a fortnight before I found an opportunity of taking her. Seems it did not please her, in the end, that I took what she threw at me. Mayhap she whispered her passion and fondled me just for sport. The lady sad misjudged my fire though, cousin, and she has regretted it ever since. I am a man of instant urge and I do not play those lover's games she thrives on! Must be you do or she could never be so smitten! Still, it would stun me well to find she had never reached for your brother. He is the image of your father, and she swears to me even now that Ælfgar Leofric's son was the only man she ever really loved! Could be he was the only one who could teach her anything, for since then, fair men younger than she are the heart-felt urge, and she does the teaching. One thing is certain, your father and I are the only two who ever bedded her at our own need, for the lady is wont to do her own choosing of time and place, as well you must know by now!"

I was dying. Despite the light of the new, grey dawn which slunk uneasily through the casements, things grew dark. Blackness pressed in from all sides. I had latched onto the glinting light of his eyes but now even that grew dim, and his face was fading and there was no way I could breathe. Then his image grew clear again: there was that absurdly innocent, boyish smile—white-toothed and gleaming.

The man is mad! My last thought in all the mortal world: Oswulf Eadwulf's son is mad!

＊   ＊   ＊

When I wakened, it was to the feel of snow and iced water and to a rushing buzz of voices.

"He is making his way back to awareness," someone said. "Stand back and give him some air."

"You are a lucky man, Oswulf Eadwulf's son," came another. It was Siward Bearn; I recognized his powerful voice. "I would sure have slain you had he come to any harm!"

"Swallow your evil threats, earl's man. If I meant to murder him he would not be blinking his precious eyes at you now! You can see I threw my own blade away and wrested his from him, can you not?"

"Aye, then smothered him unconscious." Siward rubbed my brow.

"The man leapt on me first; I swear it by all your precious saints! 'Twas not a quarrel worth wreaking death over."

"I know well enough what your quarrel was!"

"Do you? Then you show her no honor as a brother if you side with that man against me. Seems 'tis a forgotten thing amongst you that she is my wedded woman, and not his!"

That cold voice brought it all back to me: the vicious lies, the flash of iron and temper, the hatred that had brought me to the very brink of kin-killing. I groaned, then pulled myself shakily to my feet, cold and dizzy. Sitting at the table with a bucket of mead, Oswulf beamed his mendacious smile, holding out a hornful to me. Though faint, I took it, swallowing most before I lowered myself heavily onto the bench anext Siward Bearn, who grabbed the remainder out of my hand, emptying it back into the bucket.

"By the Virgin!" he cried to Oswulf with disgust. "'Tis barely morning and the man has ridden all night. Mean you to spare us a chamber or not?"

Oswulf tossed a wounded glance from one to the other of us. "I was the one who would have settled this with words! Now my skull aches, and more besides. Seems the both of us will have need to numb ourselves before anything like to sleep will come our way."

Siward Bearn stared open-mouthed as I agreed with him by dipping another hornful. "Truly mean you to sit here and drink with this madman before the break-fast?"

"Aye, cousin," I told him firmly, staring into the other's trothless eyes. "We are to make a balance of it now, using naught but words."

"Words boil blood—and tired blood boils fast!" Siward Bearn was adamant, trying to lift me with him as he stood.

"There is no more blood between us," Oswulf declared, never unlocking his gaze from mine. "That is true, is it not, Morcar Ælfgar's son?"

"He speaks true," I answered. "Take all the men and lodge them somewhere, and get you some rest. We will not talk any great length now, and then I can sleep till late."

Dismissing the other men into the great hall, Siward Bearn shook his head. "I think 'twould be best if I stayed beside you, Morcar."

"For the devil! What think you? That I will pierce him through the minute you look away?" Oswulf's voice was a curious mixture of surprise and anger. He gestured to an open door. "Take that chamber then. 'Tis airless, but you can sleep four men there with the door ajar and be upon me the instant I mean to take my revenge. Forget not to sleep with your sword buckled on you, though, kinsman!"

The drink was coming upon me already, and I laughed. Even Siward Bearn smiled a little as he rose, putting his hand on his brother-in-the-law's shoulder. His voice was earnest and low. "You misjudge me, cousin, if you think my words disparage you. 'Tis an evil situation we stand in, that is all. Nothing brews poison better than a shared woman."

His grey eyes grew suddenly dark and brooding. "Ever I have thought you a makebate and a grabber, Oswulf Eadwulf's son, and sorenesses there are between us that never will heal. Any man knows as much, and most of all you do, I trow. Yet you are my kinsman as well as this other one, and maybe more since you stand both as cousin and brother-in-the-law to me."

"Even so, you would like to see me hand the lady and her babe over to him, would you not?" Despite the look of bemused innocence, Oswulf's voice was arrogant and sharp. "'Twould pay me well for all my sins and weaknesses that have heaped pain on her. Is that not your thought?"

"Nay. I see well enough that you are the one wronged in this matter. I suffer no man to steal another's wife. If even the lady were other than my sister, I would see naught but shame and dishonor in what Morcar has done. We have had it out between us already, and he well knows my feeling." A yawn escaped him, and he stretched his angular frame awkwardly before turning to the door. "I pray you settle this finally and fair between you," the Bearn said, unbrooching his mantle. "So we may have an end of it."

He looked out into the hall, but our other men must have already taken their lodging, for he made no word or signal. Turning back to the small chamber Oswulf had pointed to him, he chose to sleep there, closing the door behind him. For a long time after we were alone, Oswulf just stared at me indifferently while the both of us sipped in silence. 'Twas his way of goading me into saying what was on my mind, and at long last I did.

"I want to see the child."

He shook his head. "Nay, she wears it on her bosom. There is no way to see it without seeing the lady, which thing I will not allow you."

"I want to see him!"

"By the Cross, where come you by this awful boldness?" The show of dazzling white teeth came again but whether in smile or sneer, I could not say.

"I ask not much, cousin. 'Tis my right to look on him, I trow." I dipped another hornful, watching him carefully. He looked pensive, gazing distractedly while playing long fingers through the tangle of his abundant tresses. It took him a long time to answer.

"Nay. You have no rights nor claims with this one, cousin. I gave my name to it."

I gaped open-mouthed, amazed that he would do such a thing, knowing as he did that the child could not be his own. "Here is strangeness!" I exclaimed, leaning back far as I could, trying to make myself comfortable in the massive chair. "What brought you to that decision?"

"Want you really to know?" he asked, standing slowly. There was candor in his look and it seemed strange, so accustomed was I to seeing falseness there instead. I nodded. Staring past or through me, he drew in a deep breath. "I thought long and hard on it. I assure you, 'twas an important thing to me to choose that which would hurt most."

Swallowing hard, I shifted uneasily. His eyes narrowed over a slight, weary frown. "Take comfort," he continued, meeting my eyes now. "You were not the one I sought to put the spite upon; my avengement was for her only. I meant at first to disavow the child, call it bastard and let her wear the shame like any man would have done. Yet I mused on it and it seemed to me she might have liked it that way. Surely, she would have found a way to turn it against me—attribute it to my hardness and come out winning sympathy for being so misused. Too, she would have gotten her sufferance worth out of the creature that way: using it to taunt me, console herself, and keep hold on you. By God, she would have worked the child to death!"

He stood suddenly and walked a few paces. Standing at the hearth with his back to me, he poked at the embers with an iron rod, added kindling and then a birch log. With a sudden pang, I spotted the stain of blood on the back of his head where I had battered it. The man had truly not wanted to fight me; I knew him well enough to know that. No man ever drew blood on him without paying for it. Only Siward Bearn and I had ever escaped the fury of his revenge, though looking on him now, 'twas hard to credit him with all his legendary crimes and murders. He was not a large man, though his lean strength was apparent in his lithe and gracile form. Briana was right: it was his look of pretty juvenescence that fooled people. He had been looking particularly innocent tonight. I decided to be on my guard. I was still thinking it when he turned, and I felt almost relieved to see his look had hardened somewhat, and his voice grown closer to its more usual baleful coldness.

"Briana has hated me from the first moment I laid with her. Nothing could have pleased her more than to have had this happen. She planned it! When the lady came to your brother's house, she fought me like a blood-thirsty wench, to make sure I had no chance to be with her. First I thought she did it as a game; she has played that way for me before. I was wrong, though. She was hoping—even then—to grow a child she could prove was not of me." He strode back to the table, dipping more mead and drinking it all at once. His look grew truculent, and he leant towards me, trembling. "That is why I put no blame on you, cousin. The woman would have used any man to accomplish it."

"You have a madness, kinsman!" I whispered, shaking with anger but forcing myself to keep my seat. "You have fooled yourself into believing this evil rather than accept that she could love another while despising your style of passion."

"Think you truly that she loves you, Morcar?" He sat down across from me, drumming his fingers on the heavy wood and laughing. All at once, he stilled himself and shrugged. "Believe it, then! If it eases you, believe it!"

"Ever have you thought," I asked him, "that she turned to me because you disgusted her with your scores of women? Or is that explanation too simple—not involved or complex enough for your liking?"

"Believe it if it pleases you," he said again. "Mayhap it is what you need to make excuse for taking her."

"Nay, cousin. You had made any excuse that either of us needed, the lady or I. Think very well on how you have treated her."

While I spoke a churlish, half-mocking smile spread over his face like an inspiration. "If 'tis true you really want to see the childling, I can strike an easy bargain with you."

I answered with an interested look.

"I will let you see them both, if that is what you crave." There was a sullenness behind his yielding tone.

"Speak!" I commanded.

"Rest yourself well after we talk this out, cousin. Then take yourself up to her chamber and visit there as long as you like. Hold the thing; fondle it. Watch her do her mother's work, suckling and petting it. Spend all the evening with the two of them. I bid that you do only one thing in return."

Stiff with suspicion, I expected the worst; his look was too stoically pleasant. "What mean you to ask of me?"

"While you chatter, question her thrice. Ask her if ever she has lain anext your brother."

With a violent shudder of rage, I rose to my feet. "Would you not delight in making it appear that I suspected and accused her? Near as much as you delight in trying to spur my jealousy with your foul falsehoods, I trow! It will not work for you, this planting of rotten doubts between us."

He only grinned with calm amusement and went on. "Ask her that first: if Edwin has ever enfolded her."

Biting my tongue, I sat back down. "Let me hear all your insolence at once," I told him without perturbation, though I had to choke it down. "Then I will decide whether or not to take advantage of your craven contentiousness!"

Stroking his smooth cheek as if he were musing over words, he latched his brazen gaze into mine. "Ask her also what she did with herself after the Midsummer Night feasting, the year we all kept that time at your father's house in Grantanbrycg. You recall it, I trow?"

I felt a quivering of unwanted fury. "What mean you?"

"I mean ask her, that is all. Ask her where she watched the dawning from. I was too young to care then, so I would not have marked it much against her but that she thrills to speak of it so often to me."

The man had an evil bent. Already, against my will, I was wracking my brain for details of the night. I turned my back on him so he would not get a chance to glimpse my perplexion. He walked around the table till he was facing me again and, taking my shoulders firmly but gently, he made me look at him. There was a look of icy strangeness in his eye colder than anything I had ever seen there before.

"Remember you some years after that, when the lady and I were wedded at your father's house in Kirton?"

Powerless to resist, I nodded.

"Then ask her thirdly where it was she spent the second night of our bride-ale. Make her name the company she kept that night and the sport she played."

I wrenched myself away before he could feel my trembling rancor. "I spit on your stinking bargain, cousin!"

"Only because you do not dare ask for fear of hearing the truth."

"Nay. Only because 'twould serve the two of us ill to take advantage of your insanity."

Oswulf let go a howl of laughter. "You are a fine man with a defensive word, Morcar!" Suddenly he was stern and snarling, "I challenge you to ask her!"

"And I will not stoop to do it!"

"Then there is no manliness in you."

"I see plainly enough your game, Oswulf Eadwulf's son. Ill words and mistruths are weapons of desperation, so I realize easily you know you have lost her to me. I need not see them now—not at that price, leaving her with a misgiving as gross as that. I can well picture you playing on it in my absence, too! Nay, I will bide my time. Providence will bring the child to me—the woman too, I trow."

"Not while I live!" he hissed, his wonted malevolence restored.

"Then I pray I outlive you!" I yawned with casual ease, disguising the hatred I felt for him. Already he was pouting.

"Let me sleep some while," I said. "Then I will give you all the king's words and warnings before I take my leave." Without hesitation, I headed for the door but he stopped me.

"Nay, Morcar, stay here and take your rest in this room. I will remove me to the lady's chamber. Who knows? If I can move the wailing, squalling thing from off her pillow, I may even find me some comfort."

Backing through the archway, he kept his eyes on me, searching intently for the reaction it took me all my strength to stifle. When the door closed behind him, I heard his appallingly wanton laughter. I smashed my fist down hard on the solid table.

*   *   *

"Morcar, the great meal is being put to table. 'Tis well past the noon-time!" Shaking me and talking low, Siward Bearn interrupted my death-like, dreamless sleep. I groaned and bade him wake me for the late meal.

"You have already missed one late meal," he exclaimed, pulling off the furs so the cold would rouse me. "You have slept a day and a night and all another morning! Pull yourself up now."

Gripping my shoulders hard, he turned me over and I answered him with moans. Despite the surplus slumber, my head was pounding. All of me was sore and bruised from the frenzied fighting, and still I felt exhausted: spiritually and physically drained in the worst way. I had drowsed off fully clothed, still wearing my necklaces and armlets. When I finally forced myself to sit, I realized how that ill-suits a man's comfort. Resting my head in my hands, stroking my own scalp to make the blood flow in my weary brain, I let go a number of miserable, whining noises.

"A man always pays when he sleeps on barley-mead," my cousin told me with a smug and satisfied look. "I have been trying to tell you that for years now."

I silenced him with an ominous look and dunked my face in the basin he offered me. The water was like ice and sent a tremor through my entire body. "Find you a man who can comb me," I demanded, teeth chattering. With a snort of long-sufferance, he took a silver comb from out the reticule he wore hanging with his knife-sheath and began the job himself. My locks hung half the way between my shoulder and elbow now, and were nothing but a mass of snarls and tangles. I missed the luxury of home-life where a man could order them brushed. What is more, I needed to be shaven and I felt it sorely. I would not ask Siward Bearn, though. If he shaved with the same gentle touch he used in combing, my throat would be laid wide from ear to ear.

"You will hear no Mass today," he told me matter-of-factly. "Cousin Oswulf keeps no priests."

"None?" I was incredulous. "Not even healers?"

"He has a Danish hag who does mid-wiving and blood-letting, but otherwise he sends to the church up the Tyne for everything, and it is ten miles hence."

"What about clerics? Who writes his letters, keeps his records?"

Siward Bearn shrugged. "He sends for them when he needs them, that is all. You know his way."

"Aye," I mumbled half to myself, and then I thought of something. "Would he let you, as avunculus, go and look upon the child?"

"I have seen your son already, Earl Morcar."

I spun round to face him, alive with questions I could not put into words. "What think you?" I finally blurted.

"Well, 'tis hard to say. The babe is still very small, swaddled and wrapped. He is healthy, they say." He paused for a moment, as if searching for anything else that might be of import to me. "Fair-haired he is; so silky blond his baby-locks that his red skin shows through."

I scowled. "Is there nothing more about him? A look, perhaps? Nothing of a—" I cut myself off.

"Mean you, could I tell at a glance he was yours?"

"Did he have a resemblance?"

"Morcar, when be the last time you looked on a newborn babe?" He looked so amused that I tried to calculate, but could not remember. "They look not like much of anything!" he said with finality, pulling the door open for me.

"Aye. That is what Oswulf told me. Methinks I might see him differently though." I thought about it as we walked through the short, narrow corridor.

The hall was fast filling when we got there. Making our way to the earl's high table, where Heard Ulf's son, Gamel-Beorn, and the Normans already sat with Oswulf and his chief men, I scanned for a glimpse of Briana. She was not to be seen. By now, surely she knew I was here. Her husband had not surprisingly contrived to keep her locked away.

Pages heaped collops of salt beef onto trenchers. Oswulf was talking loud, telling how he would wreak his perfect avengement on Copsige Sword-Stinger. The Normans watched him critically, catching phrases here and there but unaware for the most part of the treason he was spewing forth. "William is the worst sort of ass," he was saying, "if he thinks his mock gifting of the Bernicia will hold any weight up here."

"In these parts, his writ is naught but a death-warrant for the Sword-Stinger!" Beornwald Strong-Leg added, staring menacingly at the king's men as if to dare them to carry the message back. Oswulf laughed whole-heartedly. I took my seat anext him. Curse the man, he smiled in an infectiously care-free way, taking my shoulder in brotherly concern as if never a shadow had passed between us. I was near-famished yet I feared the sensation he wrought on me would keep me from eating. When he addressed me, I could not even force a smile.

"What say you, cousin?" he started in a low tone. "Is it not proper that we drink the health of my new-born heir?" He raised his horn, and his men followed. "To Ædmund Oswulf's son!" he said loud, and every voice answered him the same.

Last of all, I raised mine, and said loudly, "To Ædmund!" It pleased his men, who thought naught of it, but both my cousins glared at me in a way which gave me much satisfaction.

CHAPTER FORTY

King William then set sail in the month of March,
and crossed the sea in safety to his native
dominions. he took with him in honorable
attendance Stigand the archbishop, AEdgar
AEtheling, cousin of King Edward, and the three
powerful earls, Edwin, Morcar and Waltheof . . .
The king adopted a courteous policy in thus
preventing these great lords from plotting a change
during his absence, and the people would be less
able to rebel when deprived of their chiefs. Besides,
it gave him an opportunity of displaying his wealth
and honors in Normandy to the Anglish nobles,
while he detained as a sort of hostages those whose
influence and safety had great weight with their
country-men. Many of the French nobility were also
there, beholding with curiosity the long-haired
natives of Anglish-Britain, and admiring the
garments of gold tissue, enriched with bullion. . . .

—Orderic Vitalis
Book IV, Chapter II

July 1067
The king was talking. He was saying, "Here, on a day when the wind is
hollow and not too strong, a man can sit and listen to the hours sung
from two houses at once. The monks sing from there, Ste. Pierre. The
women's voices come from the nunnery at Ste. Leger—that way."

It was the same summer sky, crystalline blue and cloudless, and the
same steep grassy hill. The air, fragrant with a thousand nameless odors,
was the same, and the mild kiss of the breeze whispered through my hair

just the same way. It had all happened before, ages ago, and yet I knew
it could not be. Although we had been in Normandy four months, we
had only come upon Pont Audemer that very quarter hour.

"Brother!" It was Edwin's voice now. "My lord William speaks to
you, Morcar! Does something ail you?" He had reined his fine Norman
mount close to me and was peering into my face, a look of concern in
his flashing eyes.

It snapped away from me like a fleeting dream. I felt dazed.
Stumbling for words, I tried to make an apology and then the king drew
close to me, too.

"Are you faint, Lord Morcar? Do you need to dismount?" There was
a patronal tone to his normally guttural voice, and he narrowed his
demanding eyes as if to look inside me.

"My lord, no—there was a … I am sorry, sire, I only missed what you
said to me!" I tried to gain my composure; it had been an odd sensation.

"I asked, would you like to view the castle?" He gestured in the
opposite direction, and I followed the wave of his hand to a massy stone
fortress perched atop a pretty, wooded hillock a few miles distant.
Immediately, the feeling was upon me again, and so strong that I shuddered from a point deep in the pit of my stomach and had to close my
eyes against a feeling of remembrance so haunting it was almost
tangible. Now they were dismounting; I knew they were going to take
me off my horse. Then, suddenly, I was sitting in that long, velvety grass
with my arms around my knees—just the way I remembered it—and
Edwin was shaking my shoulders and calling me.

Then it was gone again.

Brushing his hands off me, I cried, "I am well! I swear it!" I was
annoyed with him for having ended it, and yet I was glad it was gone.

"By the cross, you gave me a fright, brother! What dizziness came
over you?" Both he and the king were squatting next to me, staring in a
way which flushed and bothered me.

Not even hoping to explain it, I only shrugged. "It was just a curious
feeling."

"Well, sit here and rest a moment before we go on," William said,
tossing me a water-skin.

Then he led Edwin over to the hill's edge. "This was the first castle
of the Beaumont's," I heard him say, "and the site of many a bloody siege
and murder. The House of Tosny was bitterly hostile to Lord Roger's
house when I was a child. His brother Robert died here, and it was after
he avenged that death with the slaying of the chief of Tosny that he
built Beaumont-on-the-Hill where we are lodging now."

Watching Edwin and William together, except for the obvious differences of complexion, they might have been father and son. William had grown very fond of my brother. He was a man quick to note and reverence what was admirable in another, and Edwin's powerful bearing, grace, and nobility were perfectly suited to William's liking. In fact, most of the Normans seemed to approve of the Earl of Mercia, as much for his striking appearance as his well-tempered, high-born manner. The king's obvious affection for him had not deterred their respect, either; there was no question but that William favored him over any other of the Anglish. When he had come to Beaumont, late last night, I overheard the aged Lord Roger, who was the king's most trusted advisor, remark to him, "In that personable Mercian lies your hope for a true alliance!"

William had seemed to agree. In the last few months he had come to show us honest friendship, and it had surprised us. We had been very unsure of ourselves—and of him—when first we landed in Normandy.

The early weeks there had done little to give us confidence. Always dressed in the utmost of splendor, we had been paraded endlessly from one end of his domain to the other with great pomp and ceremony. Like gilded, captive birds we were, always on display: stared at, admired, and remarked upon. At his capital city of Rouen, where the great cathedral was, William had allowed the courtiers to touch our hair and finger the richness of our embroidered garments. We were hard-pressed to tell whether we were hostages or guests but one thing was certain: we who had been the highest men of Angland were now the spoils of victory—shining, gorgeous treasures. William found endless delight in showing us to his rejoicing, cheering subjects, passing us around as freely as the golden prizes which he distributed in every town we passed through—golden prizes which had once belonged to another world, just as we had.

It may have been all this festivity and celebration which began to inspire in him an appreciation for our private company. I was quick to see that he was a man very much at home in a small, intimate group. The constant attendance of great crowds wearied and bored him. He began to seek us out for reasons of coming to know us and rapidly developed a special kinship with Edwin. Whether out of true regard for me, or because he realized we were inseparable, I was included in his select circle and treated with the highest honor. In fact, Edwin and I were the only Anglishmen he seemed to hold in this respect. Perhaps it was because the House of Leofric was the oldest and most powerful of the noble Anglish families. Even Waltheof, son of a murdering usurper, could claim no such distinction. Or perhaps because of our mother's Norman blood. I tend to think, though, even now after all that has come to pass, that his was a true and genuine personal regard for both of us, and Edwin particularly. He had almost come to love us like sons.

Not that I could blame him after meeting his own. I had not yet met the eldest, Richard, but his second son, Robert, some fourteen or fifteen years old, was a simpering, effeminate, contemptible brat. Young William was still a child but already spoiled and haughty to an unforgivable degree and seemed exceedingly cruel. Except for Cecily and Adela, mere tots, we had not met his daughters but we soon would. They lived here under the protection of old Roger of Beaumont and were taking their education at the nunnery of Ste. Leger. If they were anything like their mother, I would be favorably impressed.

"How like your lovely mother you are!" the duchess Mathilda had said when first we had met at Rouen. She had seen Ælfgiva at Le Havre and, not intimidated at all by her madness, had been struck by her exceptional beauty. Very quiet in the Flemish way, Mathilda's reticence endeared her to me immediately. She was genteel and complimentary and a particularly well-favored lady, though very small. She stood little past my elbow and, despite the blackness of her hair, was very fair-skinned. What struck me most was that she was possessed of the most remarkable eyes: dark, shining, almond-shaped jewels of incredible depth and brilliance, which seemed to see and understand everything.

Another thing about her impressed me: she was very obviously in love with her husband. She was so attuned to his spirit that she was able to tell, even before he did, when the great press of his triumphal return had come to wear on him. That was when she suggested he take a leave from his duties and spend some quiet weeks with her, and with his family, in the domain of old Beaumont, their trusted friend.

"I am committed to make many more appearances and endowments!" he had argued feebly.

"Nonsense!" was her indignant reply. "You have made appearances and ecclesiastical endowments since you disembarked. You are the Duke of Normandy, conqueror of Angland, and the greatest lord of the realm! You have the power both to make commitments and to rearrange them!"

Duchess Mathilda's voice was soothing, and she was not afraid to be affectionate with William in public. From the outset, it was plain to see that the broad-shouldered, robust warrior was no match for this tiny beauty. She managed him as well as she had managed his duchy while he was overseas.

So it was that we had come to Beaumont-on-the-Risle, where the three famous castles of the powerful house of Beaumont stood, and where the king and his family were very much at home. One thing was the Norman's special delight: making a show of the riches and vastness of his holdings and telling us the histories, facts, and legends which made up his well loved world. It was not so much that he wanted to impress us, but I could tell that he craved our respect. So, though we had arrived late at night, William summoned Edwin and me early in the morning to join him, and that was how we had come to be at Pont Audemer, just the three of us.

Standing, stretching, and feeling much relieved, I worked my way over to the grassy ledge where the two of them were still standing, deep in conversation.

"It has passed, eh?" William smiled when I reached them, and I nodded. The feeling of familiarity was far away now as I looked out over the rolling Norman countryside. Along the verge of the vivid green horizon, great chestnut forests pierced the deep blue sky in strong relief. Round, sloping hills tumbled suddenly into low, cultivated lands, various in color and exceedingly beautiful, threaded with white pathways. With some effort, the eye could follow these on through mossy lawns and blooming wildnesses of shrubs and starry flowers until they disappeared into deep dells of wood. I was following the course of one such perplexingly winding road when I spotted a mounted party, some twenty in number, emerging from a pretty copse wood at the lofty summit of a distant hill. When I pointed it out, William exclaimed with obvious excitement, "It will have to be the party from the old castle which fetches my daughters from Ste. Leger!"

I could see it was a rich train, women, priests and well decked men-at-arms. As I watched the king strain his eyes to follow them out of sight, I knew what he was thinking. Apparently Edwin did, too.

"It would be easy game for three men on good mounts to chase and overtake them in an hour's time!" he said, with a knowing smile and a merry twinkle in his eye.

"By St. Peter! Such sport would suit me!" cried William happily, slapping my brother on the back in friendly fashion. "And if it is agreeable to Earl Morcar, I will give you such a race over-hill as you have ever known before!"

Almost as if in answer, his fiery black steed, a few yards away, snorted and threw back his handsome head, making us all laugh. Grasping the silver and jeweled pommel of my fine Neustrian saddle, I lifted myself lithely onto the back of my own spirited mount, calling back, "My lord, for a prize such as a glimpse of two fair maidens, I would race you the length of your proud dukedom!"

Pleased and exhilarated, William told us it had been more than a year since he had seen these daughters, and there was no hiding the tenderness in his voice as he spoke of them. Then with an exaggerated flourish he counted the start of our good-natured contest, and we were off like the wind.

By the time we were near to overtaking them, we were flushed and breathless and in high spirits. Then we grew quieter and slowed to a precise, aristocratic canter. Riding along a fertile ridge, festooned with vines and heavy bunches of well formed, unripe grapes, we could see them below and not too far ahead of us, still ignorant of our approach.

"It surely will not do to come upon them like madmen," William told us. "These are good men who ride with them, soldiers of Lord Roger and his sons. They would be hard men to contend with, even singly. Do you see the two who ride in the very midst of the ladies? They fought behind young Robert de Beaumont at Hastings Field, and I raised them both to king's men there. Both live here, and it is their special task to ride as companions to my children. As king's men, though, they will live with me in Angland, of course, so I bade them sail back to take their leave of this place. What think you of them—will they serve me well?"

Scrutinizing them, Edwin answered promptly, "Surely, you will find them obedient men, my lord. They do an admirable job of taking their leave of the ladies!"

Smiling at that, William asked us, "Who do you think those dark-haired treasures be that they ride abreast of?"

From the pride in his voice, there was no need to guess. Besides, I had already chosen those two for the king's daughters. Even with distance between us, I could see they were much like their mother: tiny figures with long, shining black tresses. Like the other finely arrayed women, they rode on high, side-slung saddles so rich with precious metals that they sparkled in the sun, and they were dressed in colors deeper and richer than we were used to seeing in Angland. As we watched them wordlessly, William told us, as if in answer to an unspoken question, "She who wears her locks in braiding is Agatha; Adeliza is the one with hair unbound."

Without warning, William spurred his horse into a gallop, as if to close the space which kept him from them. We followed, riding hard behind him, until he reined to an abrupt stop at the top of a rise in the straight-of-way behind them. Drawing himself up to the fullness of his impressive stature, he bellowed in a powerful voice which, echoing through the summer stillness of the narrow vale, brought that entire party to a sure halt.

"Soldiers of Beaumont," he cried, "keep your pace! But you who are king's men, trace back to the side of he who lords you!"

A tremendous shout went up as they recognized him, and the two whom he had called turned and rode furiously in our direction, with wild, exultant shouts of salute, the weight of their arms not seeming to slow these fine Norman mounts at all. As they drew close to us, the elder of them, a large, black-haired man, called out in genuine surprise, "What mean you, master, riding unguarded through the countryside in such an over-bold way as this!"

The king laughed heartily. "St. Peter shield me! I am not such an old woman yet that I cannot venture out of a morning into my own fields! Besides, Gilbert Rouquin, I do not travel alone, but I carry two of my best men with me!" He gestured our way and both of them nodded a somewhat uncomfortable greeting. Sure from the rich look of us that we were nobility, they were very unsure what address to give.

Pulling his horse back, as if to get a better view of us, the younger one, after a few seconds of careful scrutiny, addressed William in a very solemn tone, "I pray your pardon, sire, but I do not think that they could very well avail you, wearing no hauberks and carrying no arms."

There was something familiar about his look and I was drawn to study him, feeling almost rude as I stared into his dark, impassive eyes. He was not much older than me, and I could see he was not a broad-shouldered man, for his leathern hauberk did little to disguise his slenderness. Yet he was tall and had a manner of calculated, cunning strength which, coupled with the sternness of his gaze, gave him a formidable appearance, the undeniable look of a warrior fierce in arms. So taken was I with watching him, that I missed what answer the king had made, but I soon enough heard him telling these two men that my brother was Edwin, his Earl of Mercia and then, pointing my way, that I was Morcar, Earl of the Diera. That was what he called me, now that he had taken the Bernicia away.

"Indeed, I knew them at once," said the one I had been puzzling over. Then he turned to me and added in Anglish, "I did not want to think I had been forgotten by the only true friend I ever made on Anglish soil."

"Fulke d'Aubermont!" I cried happily, amazed it had taken me so long to recognize him. Except for transforming him from a boy to a man, nine years had done little to change his look. Smiling, he held his hand out, and I took it. We fell to talking, laughing, and reminiscing, much to the amazement of the king, who was most surprised that we knew each other.

Later that night, we sat to a great feast in the hall of Beaumont-on-the-Hill. It was an immense room, bigger than any I had ever seen in England. In the Norman way, it had a gallery above, which overlooked the lower level on every side. That was where the women sat, because it was not the habit in this country to sit them with the men. After taking board, the men were allowed to go and mix with them. There was no limitation there, but is was considered bold for a woman to enter the hall proper, so they sat up there, all the while looking down, pointing and talking—very discomfiting because a man could not tell what they were saying.

The tables ran along the walls in a great rectangle, and here the men sat on both sides of them facing each other, for which reason they were much broader than the plank tables of Angland. The benches, however, were the same: stark, hard trestles with no back, making maneuvering in and out very difficult. Sitting to meal had never been a comfortable thing for me, and I always remembered with fondness the Welsh way of sitting on soft pillows around low-standing trays.

Taking table was a very important thing in Normandy and they were apt to stretch their supping time out to an almost unbearable degree, two or three hours every twilight. A man was expected to be social the entire time. It may have been made easier for the native countrymen by their constant drinking of bubbling and sour wines, but the taste of these were so vile to me that I could not partake of them happily. I early noticed that William took no wine, either. It was said that he abhorred drunkenness in any man and he set a rigid example by his own abstinence. Nevertheless, he took great delight in this evening ritual, which seemed to be the crown of every Norman's day.

Another thing which lessened my enthusiasm about it was the quality of the food. It turned my stomach. Meats they served half-cooked, bleeding and red, except when it was pig meat, which they served all too often, rubbed with foul garlics and roasted in bread ovens. Any Anglishman will tell you the only way to cook it is to sear it on a spit. They served a nightly variety of unpalatable things: strange roots and toasted grains and watery leaves of endive and kale. A favorite with them was a small, tasteless fruit called olive. They rubbed their bread with the oil of this noxious thing instead of with butter. Fish and eel were soaked in the same, and then so highly salted a man could not tell what they were. Even their eggs were cooked in the stuff. By the time we had been in Normandy four months, I noticed Edwin had grown thinner and I suppose it was the same with me.

We sat at the king's table, which was upon the wooden dais at the end of the hall where the great fireplace was. This was not a free-standing bonfire in the room's center as in our halls, but it was built into the very wall, a thing they could do here since they built these castles all of stone rather than timber. Since it was August, I had not seen this fire lit, but I had seen them in other castles. They were marvelous to look on, all encased within a high, wide mantel, chiseled and inlaid with glossy marble. No cooking was done in the hall; that function was performed in the great kitchens only, and I was glad for it. The smell of all those garlics and stinking herbs would have further disgusted any attempt with me to partake of provender.

At that honored table the king always sat with his sons Richard and Robert beside him on the right, and old Lord Roger on his left, a square-jawed man whose face was wrinkled into a perpetual scowl softened only by wizened, kindly eyes. Chosen king's men and high-born guests, French or Norman, sat with them, and we Anglish faced them from the opposite side. I sat to Edwin's right, Waltheof sat to his left night after night. The Earl of Huntandun was fonder of Edwin than Edwin was of him, but he was not bad company. I grew more tolerant of that man in Normandy than ever I had been before.

Sometimes Ædgar sat with us and sometimes not, but when he did he usually beat an early retreat with the king's son, Robert. The two of them were too boyish to last the whole long time with nothing but men's talk to entertain them. The rest of our countrymen, thegns and churchmen, sat at other tables. The king could not abide Stigand the Uncanonical, and the others did not seem to interest him.

That night, Gilbert Rouquin and Fulke sat at the table with us, and every night after that. It was plain to see they were very highly favored. After we ate, or tried to, and the board was cleared, Fulke asked the king's permission to sit with Lady Mathilda and her daughters in the gallery, and to bring us with him. The king readily assented, bidding Waltheof go as well. I was very shy about it.

When William had introduced us to his well-prized maids, they had stared full upon us, wide-eyed and open-mouthed, as if we looked exceedingly strange. Without a greeting to either of us, they began to remark openly on our long hair, bracelets and armlets, leaning in close to inspect my earrings—even reaching to touch the fillet in my brother's hair. As if we had not been there, they had fired questions about us to their doting father until I was blushing so uncomfortably I wanted to flee. When he told them our names, they giggled.

Sitting now with Lady Mathilda, their cousin Judith, and other high-born ladies, they seemed far more composed and gentle, asking Fulke with obvious intrigue whether it was true he had known us as children.

"True indeed!" he exclaimed with a wink to me. "These children of the north grow up in gold-cloth swaddlings and put rings through their ears while they are yet babes!"

"You are wicked to jest, Fulke d'Aubermont!" cried the one called Adeliza, who seemed the warmer of the two. "I have never seen such fair-haired, pretty men, and you tease me for my interest!" Then I understood what the fascination was. Those sheltered things had never seen Anglish before!

Both of them were pretty and young, so alike they might have been twins. Agatha was a somber sort, withdrawn and quiet with a constant, unreadable smile. The other, Adeliza, was more interesting to me, compact and very fairly made. I had noticed at once that Norman women wore dress more perfectly fitted than Anglish fashions, and the soft shape ladies had where their little waists flowed gently into hip-bone was very pronounced indeed, and teasing to the eye so that a man had to look away to keep composure. The tops of their tunics were square cut, and far more revealing than what we were used to. It was confusing to know exactly where to look, particularly for me, as I was not bold enough to look into their eyes the entire time the way my brother did.

"Does it hurt to put those silver things in your ears?" Agatha asked me suddenly and I shook my head, though that was not the truth of it. She looked at me curiously, but her sister backed my answer by saying, "You well know you can suture a man's thigh by pinching it hard so the nerves will confuse the pain. Why not an ear?"

This embarrassed me so much that I felt hot and flushed. I noticed Lady Mathilda put a finger to her lips with a disapproving grimace. Edwin laughed. "You talk like a priest!" he said. Then Adeliza blushed, too.

The more we talked, the more I liked them. Fulke, who seemed to know both daughters very well, was not afraid to jest with them the way a brother might do, and he knew just how to draw a comely blush. We talked until the duchess excused them all. The next night and the next after we joined them. By then, we were friends and my discomfort had entirely disappeared.

Then Fulke began to invite them to ride with us, for it was our habit to take to the fields every afternoon with Robert and Waltheof and a handful of others—sometimes the king himself. Agatha accepted the offer several times, and Adeliza began to come with us regularly, her host of giggling ladies in tow. Those were happy, unhurried days filled with a variety of entertainments, all pleasant. Sometimes we walked to the wide gardens, all overgrown with blossoming wildness, where the ladies made us circlets of baby's breath to wear on our heads and fancy garlands for our collars. Sometimes we rode, singing country songs and merry tunelets, to the high east ridge where we could all sit in comfort and watch the common folk below picking the grapes which were everywhere in varying degrees of ripeness. They carried them in great baskets on their heads, and once Edwin, with Fulke alongside, was bold enough to ride down and ask them to let him try it. The peasants took great delight in watching him try to balance the heavy hamper. Though he made a sore mess of it, his merriment was genuine and infectious and the folk gathered about him, fingering his golden armlets and marveling at the embroidered richness of his garb.

One day we gathered chestnuts, climbing up to shake the heavy-laden boughs of the giant trees, for the fruits were not yet ripe enough to fall of their own accord. There never was a dearth of things to do.

But though the time passed in merry amusements, my mind was often laden with thoughts of my homeland. It was hard not knowing what was happening there. Edwin alone could share this uneasiness with me. Waltheof Siward's son had not the same connection with his earldom; 'twas not a piece of his heritage. Ædgar had never overseen so much as a shire, and perhaps was not fully formed enough to have loved one if he had. Strangely, it was Fulke d'Aubermont who seemed most to understand our longing for home. His boyhood years in Angland had grown him a fierce love for the countryside, for the embrace of the winds and sea and the woods. Though it was Wessex that he knew best, he could relate to our home-sickness, if not to the fear for the safety of loved ones that we constantly felt.

Adeliza, too, worked hard toward an understanding of the intense feeling we had for our lands. Oft-times she sat with us, her small, perfect frame pensive with interest as she had us relate this detail or that about our life there. Her inquisitiveness sparked in us a delightful urge to talk about our boyhoods, and we reminisced many an hour in her company, Edwin, Fulke, and I.

And so, both slowly and quickly, passed our Norman summer. Never another summer were we to have such ease and pleasure.

*   *   *

My brother greeted his twenty-third year on the first of September in Normandy. All that day, he complained of head-pains, and they seemed to grow worse with the hours. By the time we went to table, he was pale and exhausted-looking as well as quarrelsome. Though he was unable to eat much, I noticed that he drank copiously of those sour French wines, thinking perhaps to dull the ache with them. After a while, his having grown somewhat incoherent as the night wore on, I realized that he was really suffering, for he continually pressed his hand to his brow, sometimes both hands, with a force he could barely steady himself against. Fulke, who had partaken of enough wine to make himself thoroughly agreeable and even convivial, did not seem to note any discomfort, but eventually remarked upon Edwin's extreme distraction and tried to stop him as he reached for yet another beaker of the wine, forcefully laying hand upon his wrist.

"Methinks that the Earl of Mercia has not yet graduated from his Anglish ales," he said with a laugh.

Pulling away from the Norman's grip, a strong shudder went through my brother's body, and it frightened me. Without even realizing it, I had begun watching for signs of what had overcome him at Berecingas. He muttered something senseless, and Fulke answered him sharply, saying he feared he would dishonor himself in front of the Norman court. "In fact," he added, looking directly at me then, "I see that the Lady Adeliza watches down on us with interest. Have you noticed how she eyes your brother, handsome prize that he is?"

There was something icy, almost vindictive, in his off-hand remark, and I started a cold answer. Just then Edwin crossed his arms on the table and laid his head down upon them with a gasping moan of pain.

"Help me with him!" I commanded sharply, and Fulke rose swiftly. Together, we steered my brother to his feet and forcefully headed him out of the hall, trying to attract as little attention as possible. Some heads turned, but if any comments were made, I did not hear them, and no one rose either to help or hinder.

When we had him outside in the coolness of the deserted corridor, he began to resist us. I realized with horror that he was in considerable agony. Cursing, he pulled away from us, staggering aimlessly, and when the bewildered Fulke reached him, he fought violently but was too weak to make much impact. Eventually, we pinned him helpless to the wall with his arms behind him. Not knowing what else to do, we held him there, and he gagged and sobbed in his wild and powerless fury.

"By God, this hot-tempered Mercian has no wine-tolerance! He battles like a madman!" Fulke's strained voice was incredulous. "What do we with him?"

As if in answer, a soft voice behind us ordered, "Bring him in there, in the king's chamber!" It was Adeliza. I felt a sinking sensation at the sight of her. Boldly, she took a pitch torch from off the wall and led us further down the passage to a dark, empty room. Having spent his energy, Edwin was easier to handle now but still he tried instinctively to throw us off him. We wrestled him down onto the hard, unmade pallet. When we relaxed our grip, he fell back trembling and exhausted, his face and hair drenched with sweat.

Without flinching, Adeliza stroked his forehead. Finding nothing else, she wiped his face with the linen of her sleeve. Murmuring incoherently, he tossed from side to side a few times, then quieted. With all the adeptness of a well-schooled priest, she loosened Edwin's beltings, then covered him with a heavy blanket, while I lit a fire with the torch at her command.

"I will need some things from the kitchen," she said firmly, unemotionally, gazing levelly at Fulke as if to let him know he was expected to volunteer. He hesitated, his look momentarily hardening, then shrugged his shoulders in resignation and looked to her for her bidding.

"Bring towels and water. Ask for henbane and nutmeg. Brother Heirome will assist you, so tell him what you've seen here. But tell only him—no other!"

Trying to hide extreme irritation, my dark-haired friend nodded brusquely and turned to withdraw, getting all the way to the door before Adeliza stopped him.

"Fulke d'Aubermont!"

"My lady?"

"Thank you." Earnest and gracious, the tone of her voice forced from him a lean smile, and I realized suddenly that he was smitten with her. When he had gone, she looked at me hard and long, and I squirmed under her silent interrogation.

"Drink agitates him, lady. He has a ferocious temper."

"It was not the wine alone," she said with certainty. "I could see it welling in him from the moment he sat to table."

"Well, 'tis true he has complained all day of headache."

She motioned me closer to the fire, away from Edwin's hearing and with a sternness and concern which caught me off my guard, demanded to know whether he had ever gone into convulsions! My shocked and hushed hesitation must have given her some clue, but I managed finally to deny it.

"Truly I am surprised," she whispered. "Violent fevers and pain-rages of this sort are almost certain to mark a seizure. Do they always end like this?" She gestured to him. Still sweat-soaked and drawing in labored breath, he was nevertheless peaceful now and edging towards sleep, flat on his back with his arms crossed over his head, as if to ward off some base intruder. I shrugged, not wanting her to know.

"Tell me then: does ever he waken and know not where he is or why he slept? Does he complain of dreams too vivid? Has he privation of memory?"

Throwing my hands up in defense, I spun away from her, so I would not need to look her in the eye.

"Has he ever taken a sore wound to the head?"

"No." My lie was defiant and I was surprised at myself. Her voice came ever so gently in response.

"Turn back and look at me, Morcar. I do not accuse you, or your brother! I mean only to offer you what I know, for this is not entirely foreign to me. From what I see tonight, I must tell you that the day will almost certainly come that he will take to fits. Would you know what to do for him?"

My misery and helplessness must have been apparent. She did not wait for me to answer but went on with authority and confidence.

"If he becomes as pain-wracked as he was tonight, loosen his dalmatic and his under-tunic. You will need to bare his chest if he gets in seizures and it will be hard to do it once he starts. In his agony he will let you manage him, but later he will have no control, so you must be swift. Take away his knife and give him a strap to bite upon if he will take it. Keep him to the floor if you can—and away from fire! Do you know what is the 'beautiful lady?'"

Intrigued, I shook my head.

"It is our name for a singular healing herb. We call it after the Italian name, bella donna, but you Anglish call it night-shade."

"The deadly night-shade? I thought it a poison!"

"If you eat it in quantity it is a poison but it can also be a potent medicine. When you see his pain-rages coming, put a drop in boiling water and brew a strong soup for soaking poultices. At the very first sign of paroxysms, you must lay the poultices over his heart and then over his chest. If you can open his mouth without restraining him hard against his will put a spare drop on his tongue or under it. It will be easier to do if he has the strap in his mouth. But remember, a drop only—no more—and wait until he is convulsing, for it cannot draw out the pain or the fit or the fever until then."

Inching closer to her in the near-darkness, I looked directly down into her upturned, earnest face. "I say you are greatly mistaken about this," I protested, trying to convince myself with my own words. "My brother is surely sound of mind. He has not even seen his twenty-third Christ Mass!"

Her look was sheer reproval. "The falling sickness is a sufferance of the head, Morcar, not the mind. My father told me once that your King Harthacnut died of such a seizure when he was but twenty and five years."

"But Edwin is a moderate man," I told her, remembering the story my grandfather had told of cruel, intemperate Harthacnut, falling dead at a well-laden feasting table. I heaved a deep, involuntary, very dejected sigh. She reached up and touched my cheek gently, a pretty gesture of compassion. Her concerned kindness puzzled me somewhat, but I was glad for it. Gazing into the soft, dark loveliness of her intriguing eyes was confusing to me suddenly. In the flickering firelight, she was beautiful.

Fulke chose to return at that very moment. We both jumped at his sudden appearance in the doorway, causing him to eye us with curious misgiving which I immediately supposed to be suspicion. He said not a word, and a few seconds afterwards another figure appeared right behind him, a short, balding, almost comical-looking man in monkish dress.

Over one arm he carried an enormous basket crammed with all manner of strange things: dried plants, herbs, weeds, and leaves. Without a greeting to any of us, he pushed his way past my Norman friend and padded hastily to the foot of the pallet, looking over my brother's inert form top to bottom with the look of a disgruntled pony merchant.

"So this," he said finally, in a rasping, wheezy kind of voice, "is the drunken Anglishman lady Adeliza bids me leave my stew to look in upon!" He turned as she approached him and shot her a look of repugnance. She smiled back sweetly.

"Brother Heirome, this is the man my father has retained as his Earl of Mercia in the new kingdom. He became accidentally drunken on our strong, bubbling wine, and the pain of his stupefaction was so great, I feared he might have broken a vessel. I bade these men bring him here to my father's room, and I sent d'Aubermont to fetch your good opinion. My father, you know, would be very wroth if anything befell his man while he was away!" She added those last words pensively. The stout little monk gave an odd grunt, then lifted first one, then the other, of my brother's eyelids, peering under with unwilling resignation.

After casting a short, knowing look my way, Adeliza rose suddenly with a mild exclamation of surprise, "It is very late and it would not do for my ladies to miss me!" She turned a coquettish gaze on Fulke, who by now looked totally bewildered. Holding her tiny hand out to him, she beseeched him, "Will you escort me back, now, Fulke d'Aubermont? We two have surely done all we need do, have we not?"

She was a sly one, I thought, as she glided to the door with him. When she reached it, she looked back and added, as if it were an afterthought, "Brother Heirome, if you think it wise he should not be wakened, let him and his brother lodge here tonight. I am positive my father would give the room if he were here, do you not think? Good night, Earl Morcar." Then she swept away.

For some minutes after they left, the strange man said nothing, only poked, probed, and prodded. I watched him with considerable interest; he was a most interesting character, and totally unlike anyone I had seen before, both the shape and look of him. He was slight of build, nearly as wide as he was high; not fat, but solidly round, strong, and hearty. I could not begin to guess his age. What little was left of his hair was a non-descript color and texture. His face was pale like an older man's but totally unlined. Something looked old about his eyes, though, wizened and watchful. He was running his plump, white fingers through Edwin's thick hair and when he came to rest them on a spot just above and behind the left ear, my brother's whole body jerked with such violence that I feared he would fall from the cot.

"No more than a year!" the monk announced with finality.

"What?"

"It was certainly no more than a year ago that he took this beating."

I gulped, the battle at Gate Fulford had been eleven months ago, but I did not know whether to say anything.

Brother Heirome turned his strange eyes on me. "What is it you want to know about him?" he asked.

I shrugged my shoulders, and he frowned disdainfully. "What should I know?" I asked finally.

"He intoxicated himself well, that is certain, and he should take care not to do it repeatedly. If the wound in his head is still mending, you may expect this for another year or so. It will not take him often. Pressure, anxiety, fear will bring it on, sometimes to pain or brain-torture, sometimes to fits, even senselessness. It will always pass."

"And—?"

"And if it is healed as much as it will heal, then he will live with it all his life." Saying this, he sat down on a small stool bed-side, lifted his basket onto his lap, and rummaged through it. Then he held up a small earthenware flagon and signaled for me to pull over another stool, which I did. As he worked at removing the swollen cork, he asked, "Do Anglishman drink serat?"

I shook my head. "What is it?"

"The most salubrious of all nectars, a Norman miracle brewed from buttermilk and onions and garlic, all fermented together into a life-sustaining liquore." He was tugging on that cork with such violence that even to my untrained eye apoplexy looked imminent. I took it from his and in a very short time worked it free. The burst of aroma made me reel and my companion laughed heartily.

"It is a concoction for which a man must develop a taste!" he told me, swallowing a great gulp. When he offered it to me, I refused gingerly, and he laughed again but was kind enough not to press it on me. He scrutinized me carefully as he sipped it, taking in every detail of my rich dress and paying particular attention to the fine embroidery of my knee-length tunic. After a few minutes of this silent staring, which made me exceedingly nervous, he licked his lips and asked, "Which one are you?"

"I am Morcar Ælfgar's son, Earl of the North Humbria," I said, because it was the natural thing to say. Then I thought about it a moment, and not knowing where this odd creature stood in relation to the king, I added hastily, "At least, I was the Earl of the North Humbria … Earl of the Diera now."

"One's the same as the other to me!" he said agreeably. Glancing at my hair he wondered aloud, "Why would a man go about with locks all unshorn like that?"

"'Tis the North Humbrian way."

"Well, it is long even for an Anglishman, and they all wear it too wild to suit me. Good color, though: good sun-colored and wheat-streaked tresses. You won't find much of that in Normandy, you know." Abruptly, his eyes narrowed and he changed the subject. "You do not believe Lady Adeliza thought your brother was only drunken, do you?"

"No."

"That is good. She is no fool, I tell you. She has studied from behind me, looking on birthings and dyings and grievous wounds, and she has the eye, hand, and heart of a healer. Such a thing as this would surely not have escaped her." He pointed to the fine embroidery at my hem. "That is what your noble ladies pay to learn in England," he said, "but in our country they pay to learn of arts more useful. Her father has tarried me here going on three years to instruct and guide her, and she a maid of but sixteen years now. She was a child when I started with her. Duke William would gladly build a nunnery all around that girl and give it to her, keys and everything, if she would but dedicate that great talent of hers to the lord."

"He means to make her an abbess?" I mused half to myself, the thought not sitting well with me because I could not picture it.

"Oh, he would like it well, and Lady Mathilda, too. But Adeliza is a fair treasure. Surely you must have seen that! And now, with all this new kingdom business, he will probably have to sign her away in some polit-ical wedding or such. A shame!" He recapped the flagon, and I was glad for it. Each time he breathed on me, I thought I was going to die.

Once he had reburied the treasure safely in his basket, he stood. After making a last observation of Edwin, who still slept soundly, he took his leave of me. "Remember I am called Brother Heirome!" he said, making a sweeping and exaggerated bow which looked quite peculiar. "I can be found about this manor, in one occupation or another, night or day. If I am not in the kitchen when you seek me, wait for me there or leave a message where I might find you." Clutching his basket, he raised his free arm in a half-hearted fare-well and called, "Vale, friend Morcar, vale!" as if we had known each other all our lives. Then he trundled off, leaving me staring after him and thinking what a strange, though not entirely unpleasant, personage he was.

The fire was gone now, which heartened me, for the warmth of the room whilst it had burned had been almost unbearable. I realized with some trepidation that Adeliza had bade me light it against the possibility of having to boil water for poultices, and I was exceedingly relieved that the need had not come to pass. It seemed a good sign to me, as did my brother's tossing yet deep and unperturbed sleep. All the information that had come to me that night was assailing me now, hanging over me like a weight in danger of dropping. Uppermost in my mind was the threat that it might be a permanent condition and though everything in his circumstances seemed to argue against it, I felt myself surrendering to a depression of spirits just on account of the possibility. I realized it was going to be a sleepless night and I was trying to settle myself comfortably on a pile of rugs when a muffled knock came at the door. It was Fulke.

The moment I opened the door I sensed a tenseness in him, an indescribable something which hinted all was not well. At first I thought he was nervous about our being in the king's chamber. I had the feeling it was a place not frequented by many men but William. He slid past me wordlessly; his dark, stern face was its usual mask of impassiveness. There was a smoldering resentment in his glittering eyes, though, which belied the customary indecipherable moodiness which I had become accustomed to in him. He turned on me almost immediately, his voice a hoarse whisper that little disguised his anger.

"I have held you in a good regard for many years, Morcar Ælfgar's son," he said, his gaze piercing through me, "and I have considered you my friend and called you so. Only now you take advantage of that friendship and ply me with deceit."

My mouth must have been hanging open in puzzlement, but I did not get a chance to say a word before he continued. "I am a man who stands high in the king's favor and I am not used to being sent on kitchen errands and mindless tasks."

Now I felt my own ire rising, and my tone was not gentle. "By the relics, d'Aubermont! You come to chastise me because the lady sent you to fetch a priest?"

"I come to chastise you, Anglishman, because the both of you deceived me to steal a secret moment alone together."

"You are mad!" I spat on the floor.

Fulke snorted. "It was not nursing you were about when I returned with the healer. A blind man could tell as much! Adeliza is as cunning as any of her kin, but when next she is pressed with a great urge to whisper endearments, she will find it takes more than a fool's errand to be rid of me!"

"You are sorely mistaken, Norman!" I trembled with anger now, but when Edwin groaned and took to tossing I lowered my voice. "You accuse me and you insult the lady. For that alone I would gladly draw your blood! But what is more, you knew full well my brother's suffering and that Adeliza had reason to suppose a remedy might be wanting."

"No!" he shook his head defiantly. "I only know she had reason to suppose it was safer to whisper her secret things with you when I was not around to hear them!"

"What mean you? For what reason safer?"

"Because she knows full well with what task I have been charged by the king. Do not pretend she has not told you!"

Something made me move closer to him, ominously closer, until I was staring straight into his drawn, determined face. "You be the one to tell me, d'Aubermont!" I demanded.

He started to turn away, but I caught his shoulder roughly and spun him back towards me. "By God, tell it! With what did he charge you?"

"With telling him everything you say."

I was so stunned I could make no answer. Looking at him, I thought for some incongruous reason of how those glittering eyes of his looked like they might have belonged to a wild bird. I stared into them as he went on.

"You know that he has never been able to comprehend your tongue. So he bade me tell him what you say between yourselves in Anglish."

There was a long pause during which our eyes never broke contact. Then Fulke stepped back and added low, "The lady was there when he charged me, and she is not fool enough to suppose I would not also report those things you said to her ... in French."

I was so suddenly full of loathing that my look must have dreaded him; he moved back more and was shaking. Following his apprehensive gaze to my own belt, it surprised and shook me somewhat to realize my hand was on the hilt of my dagger and I was on the very verge of drawing it. So strong was the urge that my knuckles were white and my whole arm quivered with the resistance which I forced upon myself. In that very instant of fury, I heard my own icy words, astonished that they could come from me.

"You have dared to charge me with dealing in deceitfulness when all along you have been steeping yourself in this despicable duty! Well, I tell you this, Norman: not only have you betrayed me but you have accused me falsely, a thing which has never sat well with our house. Now I will have an apology from you or, I swear it, I will be avenged in a way that will do me dishonor."

He just stood there, his complacency having been restored very quickly once he determined that I did not mean to take my weapon. His usual emotionless manner was in ascendancy again, and his tone was much calmer than mine. "If I am wrong, you will have your apology. I have ever trusted you to be a forthright man, and if I can believe you have not pretended with me then I will owe you an apology and more. A debt of honor, perhaps."

"Look for me to claim it, too, d'Aubermont!"

"Indeed! I hope that you will, Anglishman. I would not want to live in fear of your avengement!"

I did not appreciate his mocking tone. "I think if you value your calling as king's man, you would be wise not to tell the lady of your groundless suspicions!" I told him, wondering suddenly if jealousy had caused his outburst. He seemed to consider my advice carefully.

"Of course you are right! I mean to mention them to no one again since you so boldly contest my speculation. There is always the possibility you will prove me wrong. In fact, I hope you will. You will find my temper is not inflexible in matters of these sort. I try to attain to honor, that is all. Besides, ours is a long friendship and I value it. Let us not abuse it, either one."

He held out his hand, the way the Normans do to seal things, and I took it though my provocation had not entirely subsided. As if reading that in me, he added more mildly, "Make sure not to send me away on merry chases, and I will be certain not to conjure up the happenings in my absence."

He meant it with good will, and I managed to flash him a slight smile. I was feeling somewhat sheepish for the burst of temperament that had almost made me draw a dagger on a friend. I considered this was something my father might have done in fury, or Edwin, but it seemed strange to me to have suffered such an excess of vehement emotion myself. It was not like me, and it left me puzzled, though in a queer way I cannot say I regretted it.

"One thing more!" I called to Fulke, just as he opened the door to go. He turned and looked.

"Tell the king that when we talk between ourselves in Anglish, we say he is a two-faced bastard!"

He made no answer.

CHAPTER FORTY-ONE

William gave the area of the North humbria north of the Tyne to Copsige who had served earl Tostig . . . Oswulf, driven by Copsige from the earldom, concealed himself in the woods and mountains in want, till at last having gathered some supporters whom the same motives had brought together, he surprised Copsige while he was feasting at Newburn. Copsige escaped through the midst of the confused crowds; but being discovered while he sought sanctuary in a church, he was compelled by the burning of the church to run out, where at the very door he was beheaded by Oswulf's own hands in the fifth week of his charge of the earldom.

—Simeon of Durham

"Rein her in tight, Lord Morcar! And step her sideways, or the foul beast will scurry right through her legs!"

I tried to do what young Robert commanded, but my mind was not truly on the pig-baiting any more and my reflexes were slow. It was late the next afternoon and we had been gamboling on horseback for near two hours now, the king's son Robert with his closest companions, and Waltheof, Ædgar, Fulke, and I. Edwin had started with us but had not lasted long at the rough play and that in itself was one reason for my distraction. My gaze kept wandering to where he sat, half-heartedly watching us from the shade of a giant, twisted tree. He had dismounted some time ago, as if he did not have the stamina to sit his horse any longer. There was a glazed and bewildered look to his eyes which truly worried me. It had been there since morning and, though he had smiled and jested with Fulke all through break-fast about the evil effects of his wine hanging over, I knew that his head was still hurting and I was nervous for him.

"By God, Anglishman! Close the circle or drop out of it!" Robert's voice was imperious this time, and my horse reared in surprise as the sweating, panicked sow rammed into her front legs, squealing with pain and fright. Galloping at me simultaneously with shouts of irritated dismay, Waltheof and Fulke raised a dusty cloud which hid them momentarily as they tried to block the animal's frenzied flight. By the time the dust settled, they had arrested the desperate creature between them some yards away, and seeing that the center of action had so shifted, the other riders followed them there with noisome and dreadful hollers. 'Twas boy's play, but it was Robert's pleasure and we were bound to appease the little lord.

Once free of their ring, I headed my feisty mare back to the clearing's edge where my brother sat, and dismounted, tethering her to a tree lest she take off again and join the mock hunt on her own. "Fine creatures!" I exclaimed to Edwin, slapping the horse's neck, but if he heard me, he made no reply. Lowering myself to the grass, I sat cross-legged next to him, wiping my neck and brow with the sleeve of my tunic. Until that moment, I had not realized how uncomfortable I was and I could not help but comment on it.

My brother made no answer to that, either. He gestured instead cross-field to where Robert was calling commands and directions to his fellow-players. "I hate that head-strong Norman brat!" he said sullenly.

"Well, you had better get used to him, brother!" I retorted, smiling. "Apparently he is acting sovereign until William returns with his lady and the elder boy."

"Do you know when he might come?"

I shrugged. "Five days … a week, they say. No one seems to know."

"I am sick of this place, Morcar!" Edwin said in the manner of a great confidence, leaning forward and looking at me earnestly. I noticed he was sweating profusely. "I am sick of this air, this food, of the drooling sound of their horrid tongue, and I long for Mercia. Only I pray God that underling Robert does not follow us there. He rubs me like salt in a wounding!" With a weary sigh, he leant himself back against the tree's rough trunk, putting his hands to his forehead as if to shield his eyes from the light. He was very pale, and I did not like the look of him, but I tried to laugh it off.

"Surely, you are in an ill-humor! What ails you today?"

"I think I crave sleep. It is this damnable head-pain! Two days of it and I feel like a dying man!"

"Well, you ought to have said something!" I said reproachfully, pretending not to have noticed his discomfort before. I went to fetch the horses. Returning with them, I watched Edwin pull himself to his feet with a great deal of effort, steadying himself against the tree as if dizziness were going to take him. We both mounted in silence, but when we had ridden a little way, I mentioned meeting Brother Heirome and that I had been impressed by his thorough knowledge of healing. Then, casually, I suggested to my brother that the strange little monk might be able to prescribe a cure.

"In fact," I added carefully, scrutinizing him for his reaction, "he looked in on you last night in your stupefaction!"

Edwin grimaced. "Well, he did not do me much good then! I wakened worse than when I went to sleep. If what Fulke tells me is true about the way he helped you throw me around, it must be the two of you I have to thank."

"Well, you had better mind your drink from now on!" I told him severely. "I can hardly believe you have no memory of the pandemonium you put us through! 'Twas awful to see." In truth, it gladdened me that he could not remember; he probably would have died of shame if he knew Lady Adeliza had seen him flat on his back in a stupor. He was that way.

"I think you know me well enough to realize I am not intemperate!" Those steely eyes were flashing with indignance now. "I drank of their foul and rotten wines for one cause only; I wanted to ease an ache!" Relaxing again, he added mournfully, "It did not work, either!"

"You ought to detail your pain to this monk, and let him work you up a cure. You have nothing to lose, you know."

"What is there to detail? I have a pounding in my head and it drives me to distraction. There is all the detail! And I can tell you I do not appreciate the idea of some Norman priest going over me and accounting all my bruises and scarrings to the king!"

"So you would rather suffer." I was annoyed with him.

"What I would rather do is lay my body down and sleep this pounding away, if you really want to know!" He kneed his horse to hurry her but I held mine back out of exasperation. Watching him, even with the glint of golden sunlight making him shine, I wondered how a man could be so esteemed of his own beauty that he would let himself hurt rather than let another man know he was marked and injured.

Having ridden for about a quarter of an hour, we were a half mile or so from the manor when we met a party of the king's men-at-arms riding out in the direction we had come. Catching sight of Edwin, they hollered a greeting and drew up alongside him, jesting and passing time. Most of the Normans were very fond of my brother. He was almost as popular here as he was at home amongst the Anglish. There were few, men or women, who could resist his openness and golden charm, and he always had a sizable store of friends and companions. I noticed how well he swallowed his discomfort in order to be social with them. Hurrying to catch up, I could hear them tease him for his last night's discomfiture.

"I will tell you," laughed one, "my heart warms to see a good man feast on French wines for the first time! Therein lies a lesson hard learnt but remembered forever!"

"By the Virgin! I mean to let that lesson last me a lifetime!" agreed my brother with good humor. "I still feel its knocking against my brain!"

They laughed, and someone added, "'Tis said here that a marinade on the brain leads often enough to a price on the head!"

Edwin laughed heartily at that, and I with him, until Gilbert Rouquin called out to me. "And what of you, Lord Morcar? Have you no yearning to experience that precious elevation like your pretty brother here?"

"I suppose I would be more suited to sample that than some potent and valuable medication one of your monks showed me and called *serat!*"

My further words were drowned by a burst of laughter, and Gilbert, still chuckling, asked me, "Who was this priest who treated you to such a complete course of medication?"

"Brother Heirome," I told him, and they laughed again.

"The king's physician, and not to be snickered at!" Gilbert declared firmly. "An odd creature, but do not be fooled. He knows all there is in the cosmos to know about healing, and he spares no effort in applying what he knows."

"Yet I doubt you would deny he carries a distinct perfume of serat!" cried one of his companions, and it occasioned more of the same mirth. We made our good-byes on that note and rode on.

After we reached the manor and gave our mounts over for stabling, Edwin wasted little time getting to his rooms, where he could be more comfortable. I helped him undress. Here in Normandy it was almost unheard of for a noble-man to undo his garments himself; that was page's work and there were always dozens of high-born young snivellers lingering about, waiting to be called on to do it. It was not something that ever appealed to me. I did not mind being combed or shaven. Like my father, though, I thought there was something decidedly indecent about relying on another to dress and undress you, unless you were being bothered with some heavy ceremonial outer garb which could not be well managed alone.

Once his linen tunic was unloosed, my brother relaxed and became less flushed. After rolling his wide sleeves and splashing his face and head with water, he looked better than he had all day. I was greatly relieved. "When you return from supping, bring me some bread and a goodly portion of milk," he told me, stretching himself out on his pallet, which he had made comfortable and high at the head's end with a number of bolsters. "I think that I need to take something, but this head aches me so sorely that I cannot even consider mingling with all that crowd and confusion tonight."

"I had thought to take provender here with you," I answered, fingering his gold brooch and the jeweled accouterments which were laid out on the little wooden table.

"Nay!" he declared firmly. "I told you I crave sleep, and what man can rest with another one hovering over him? Surely you have things to attend to. Only, if you would, come back by, and if my pounding is at all eased, you can companion me while I take some fare."

As if the matter were concluded, he exhaled a loud and weary sigh, then settled himself down into a position of repose. Seeing that he was peaceful, I quietly made my way out, and went to dress for table.

*   *   *

Thank God's tender mercy that I returned when I did.

The dinner had been dismal. Robert, blazing in his finery, directed the tide of talk to matters of his own narrow interest, glaring at me and pretending he was not. He was sullen with me for having taken leave of our afternoon's play without his permission. My quietude, even more pronounced than usual, seemed to irritate him the more. Edwin would have smiled and talked with him in such a way as to ease his bother, but me—well, I have not the power to present a merry face when the mood is not upon me.

Waltheof, sitting on my one side, entirely ignored me, engrossed in telling tales of his father's valor to some of the king's men who had gathered round him. Having already heard the stories, and knowing them to be greatly exaggerated—proclaiming old Siward's scant virtue to excess and excusing his gross iniquity—I could hardly feign interest. Sitting at my other side, Fulke was working ambitiously to make me feel things were the same between us as they had always been. Yet I was very aware that they were not. It had become an unconscious habit with me at table to scan the crowded clerestory for a glimpse of Lady Adeliza, to watch her move or sometimes meet her eye for a moment. Now that innocent pleasure was tainted with a furtive sense of guilt. I greatly resented my friend for putting this extra weight on me when my mind was already so heavy.

Despite my withdrawn silence, Fulke tried to stay me when I rose to go. "A ship docked yesterday at Calais, and there are men here who will tell news of England when the board is cleared," he told me, gripping my arm. "'Tis said the kingdom in nowise lies still to await the king's return, and there is particular news of the North Humbria. Sit and hear it with us, lord Morcar!"

The temptation was strong to linger but, weary and depressed, I decided against it, knowing news would reach me soon enough if it were of any consequence. Taking a beaker of ass's milk and a chunk of bread wrapped in a linen cloth, I made my leave, throwing Adeliza a smile as I made my way out.

Having felt lowly the better part of the evening, I meant only to drop these things with my brother and take a portion of time to myself, to sort out the perplexing busyness which crowded my tired mind, to pray and then sleep. The moment I opened the door, though, and saw how things were with Edwin, I knew such respite was not to be.

He sat curled in the corner of his alcoved pallet, drenched with sweat, yet obviously in the grip of an intense and overwhelming chill which caused his teeth to chatter and brought an unsurpassed pallor and whiteness to his skin. Now and again, he bit his own hand as if in pain, murmuring senselessly and staring with a blank-eyed gaze. I called his name; he did not answer. I shook his shoulders. He did not seem to know me and my touch inspired in him a moment of awkward, violent thrashing. Coupled with the uncontrollable tremble of his shivering chill, it was horrible to look upon.

Glancing around the room, I saw this had not come on suddenly. He had stoked a fire to warm himself and pulled down blankets from the garderobe. The window coverings had been dropped against the harmless August night, and now, he clutched his heavy mantle tight around him, despite the warmth of the room which was almost unbearable. Things had been worsening gradually for him, building probably from the moment I left. Crossing myself, I told him I would be back, then ran for all I was worth to fetch Adeliza.

Strangely enough, I recall nothing from the time I left that room until I mounted the second story of the great hall, breathless from the steeply curving, narrow stone stairs. Trying to appear calm and nonchalant in spite of the wild pounding of my heart, I sought and found her almost immediately, drawing her aside with a courteous bow. She smiled warmly but her look changed when she caught the urgency in my eyes.

"Lady, are you disposed to help me another time with my brother?" I gasped, keeping my voice low. Waltheof was near at hand, courting with Judith as was his wont after supping and I did not want him to hear. "I fear he is in a grave way. Is the herb you spoke of available."

"I can have it here in a moment, Morcar! Where is he?"

"In his chamber."

"Make sure there is water both hot and cold, and linen enough for poultices. Let me make my excuses and gather what I need from the kitchen. I will meet you there. Now make your way out—calmly." Stressing the last word, she squeezed my hand reassuringly. "Make some courtesies to my sisters and ladies on your way out—and do not look hard pressed!"

This I did, making my way slowly across the floor and just as slowly down the dark stairway. At the bottom, though, I quickened my pace and retraced my way back through the dimly lit corridors to the wing where Edwin waited, meeting no one and glad of it. Outside the door, I was suddenly clenched with a powerful urge to turn away; it almost seemed better to linger aimlessly in the hallway and wait for her than go back in the room and helplessly watch him. Nevertheless, I forced myself to go in and, thankfully, she was there in very little time.

Opening the door to admit her, I was dismayed to see Fulke, who must have seen me in the gallery, standing behind her and making very clear his intent to come in. He would not bend to my feeble argument.

"D'Aubermont, it would be better perhaps for you not to come in here," is what I said, knowing it would hold no weight with him. His voice was stern and his look unyielding. "We have talked of this already, Anglishman," he told me. Then he pulled the door closed behind him.

If Adeliza was appalled as I had been at the sight of my brother, she hid her feelings well, only eyeing him with consternation as she tore a length of linen into quarters. She tried to make conversation with him, just as I had done, to satisfy herself that he was unreachable. Seeing that he was, she took him firmly by the shoulders and forced him to lie. His twitching increased in momentum and he made small, choking cries.

"His hurt is all he knows now," she said softly and I remembered Uncle Leofric saying the same thing at Peterborough. "His state is truly sorry; mayhap Brother Heirome should be here!"

I looked at Fulke, but his look was resolute and he stood immobile. I knew he would not go, whether out of defiance or shock at the sight of Edwin's tortured form, I did not know. Momentarily, I thought of going myself, but I knew instinctively that there was no time and the swiftness with which Adeliza moved seemed to confirm this. She had added the healing herb to the water pot which hung in the fire, and it filled the room with a strange, indescribable fragrance, dreamlike and delicate.

"You will have to bare his chest for me," she told us. "If you cannot take it off him, then tear it down the front. Only, be swift!"

Fulke jumped to help me, probably feeling the same relief I did at having a function to perform. My brother was tossing so violently now that there was no hope of removing the tunic. Taking his wrists, I held them firmly over his head, while Fulke ripped the soaking shirt open with his knife.

"By God's light!" he exclaimed hoarsely, and I heard Adeliza stifle a scream. Indeed, I had almost forgotten myself how evil looking were the uncountable wide, shining pink and white scars which crossed Edwin's breast and belly. Even after all these months they were glazed and sore. Chest hair had not grown back where they marked him and under his sheen of sweat they looked menacingly alien, almost inhuman.

"The man should not have lived!" Fulke whispered with horror, shaking at the sight.

"But he did!" Adeliza had regained her composure and with it her competence. She dipped compresses, wringing them deftly between two sticks she had carried with her. The first she placed over his heart. He writhed at the touch of it. One after another she placed them, so that within minutes all his chest was covered with the steaming rags. He fought none of them like the first, and by the time she was finished, he was visibly calmer, though still writhing and twitching.

"Now help me get a drop to him, Morcar!" Adeliza took the shredded end of one poultice and dipped it, while I tried to force my brother's jaws apart. He fought and I was suddenly horrified to see blood come from his mouth.

"He has only bitten his lip and tongue!" was the lady's reassuring cry. "Now hold his head still!"

I did this, and she squeezed a drop of the bella donna into his nose, then pinched it closed to ensure he did not lose it. He gagged and she let him go, seeming relieved and satisfied. "It will only be seconds now!" she whispered.

Before our very eyes he began to pacify himself. At length, his head fell back and, though his teeth were tightly grit and his breathing harsh and labored, the terrible trembling ceased in him. When he had grown entirely calm, Adeliza crossed herself and knelt for a few minutes in prayer. When she stood again, she looked at me with eyes full of indignant reprimand, making me flush. "You were not honest with me about him, Lord Morcar! This is a falling sickness!"

Fumbling for words and not finding any, I slumped down dejectedly and sat on the floor at his bedside, exhausted from those nerve-wracking efforts in his behalf. Both of them followed, and we all three sat there for some time, like children, without saying anything.

Finally, Fulke, still white and shaken, broke the silence by asking whether Edwin had taken the woundings at Fulford.

"Aye," I told him miserably. "Under the sword of rotten Tostig Godwine's son, and bold Copsige—now William's Earl of the Bernicia—who dashed and axed him while he lay senseless in his own blood."

"Then surely he took a blow to the head," Adeliza mused, but the reproach was gone from her tone.

"There was not a place where he did not take a blow!" I snapped spitefully. "The priests who carried him from the field say only his hauberk held his body together. They took him to my uncle's seat at Peterborough, unctioning him on the way and five times more before he mended, so sure they were he was dying. I sat with him day and night and I tell you he bore what no man should ever have to in this life. God! How he suffered!" I shivered at the memory; Adeliza put her hand on my shoulder as if to comfort me and erase the thought.

There was a long and gloomy silence before Fulke spoke thoughtfully. "King William said he felt you bore Copsige a hatred more than could be accounted for by his taking the Bernicia. He remarked on your manner at Berecingas."

"Hatred?" I cried. "Do you know what manner of man he is? He and Tostig murdered my father in his bed!"

Adeliza suddenly blanched and leant forward to look into my eyes. "Such men are paid for their misdeeds, Morcar," she whispered confidently. "You know it is true!"

"Oh, indeed!" I hissed, fired by the thought of it. "Copsige Sword-Stinger was well paid! The king gave him my cousin's earldom and whatever he could gather of his goods!" But biting back my temper and considering that she had meant to comfort me, I added with rueful agreement, "Tostig, it is true, was somewhat more justly rewarded."

"You well knew my meaning, sir!" she exclaimed reproachfully. "Or is your faith in God that small?"

"Lady," I replied in earnest. "I do not know what measure my faith is now! I have tried to be His subject. I have bended to His will and I have tried to do all He might expect of me, but when I pray—I do not feel an answer."

"He answers all good men, Morcar!" she declared with certainty.

"Then perhaps I have some grievous sin," I said, thinking of Briana. There was not much answer anyone could make to that.

After a long while, Adeliza stood and began to sponge Edwin's face with cold water, making him stir and murmur. He did not waken, though, so she began to remove the poultices, which had grown cool, and replace them with hotter ones. It was while she was doing this that Fulke gripped my arm and told me he felt a need to make his apology.

"I told you I am a man of my honor, and that I would give you your due," he said, gazing in my eyes with open honesty. "I know I have wronged you, Morcar Ælfgar's son, and I owe you some debt of honor that you would take me in your friendship again."

I gripped his shoulders, just as though he were an earl's man. "Then let this be your debt of honor, d'Aubermont," I told him, "that the king will never know why it was that my brother did not come against him at Hastings field; that he will not know how Edwin fares, or what violence he suffered."

"That is all you ask of me?" he asked, frowningly.

"That is all."

"Then it is sealed!" he said and he smiled a true smile, seemingly a rare thing with him.

When he stood to leave, Adeliza told him she could not think of leaving Edwin's side till he had come to consciousness. He did not say anything, but nodded. I followed him out into the corridor. "You may send a priest to chaperone us if you want," I told him solemnly, "because you must know I cannot leave him either."

Hands on his hips, he eyed me levelly. "Already I have sworn my trust to you, Morcar. Take care not to blame me more for those foolish words of mine!" He motioned me closer. "I can tell you this, knowing all my fears were unfounded, even though it be a hard thing for me to say to any man. 'Twas my own gross vanity that made me suspect a friend."

"I do not understand you."

"I hardly understand myself. I have known Lady Adeliza a long time. Ever since my father died, I have lived at Beaumont, and I have watched her all that time. Mayhap you would not think a man like me would set his hopes so high; but when I left for Angland again, I knew I wanted her. The one thing that marred the glory of being chosen king's man was knowing I would not see her more!" He leant back against the wall, hands behind him, staring morosely to the closed door which hid her. "I could see she was smitten with you."

"With me?" My voice was incredulous, and I laughed. I had seen her oft enough eyeing Edwin, as many maids did. Could be Fulke had misjudged the target of her flirting.

"I am not as fair a man as some," he continued, as if he had not heard me. "I am not high-born, but I have had her father's favor many a year, and I have thought to…." His voice trailed off, as if he had suddenly grown wary about sharing himself with me. I could feel for him, knowing as I did the feeling of wanting a woman who was not to be had. I gripped his arm.

"I know you have duties to be about tonight, my friend," I smiled, "but if you find freedom from them, come join us here and we will talk!"

I watched him for a minute as he walked away, and then I went back into the room, closing the heavy door behind me softly. As soon as she saw me, Adeliza smiled a knowing smile. "I gather you have tossed words with d'Aubermont?"

"They are forgotten now."

Tossing her unbound hair behind her shoulder with a pert gesture, she sat down at the edge of my brother's bed. "I have known Fulke a good long time," she said, "and we have been friends since we were children. One thing I can tell you about him: no matter what he would have you believe, he is a man who does not forget a thing."

"Lady?"

"Oh, he is harmless, really, and he has oft been like a brother to me, but his heart is a cold keeper of accurate records. You can read that in his eyes. He has been like that ever since he came here."

"He was my friend long before he came here, lady."

"D'Aubermont has no friends. Not really."

"'Tis a harsh thing you say of him!"

"And I mean no harm, either! Truly he has been very kind to me, and I have no personal reproach. Indeed, I can love him in a way. He is a very ambitious man, though, and a man who feels he has lost much is always quick to blame. This is what hardens me towards him." She looked away.

"I do not remember—"

"Well, perhaps he has changed since you knew him. You were children then, were you not?" She turned then to look at Edwin who tossed uncomfortably, then grew still. "No matter!" she added, turning back to me. "He is off to Angland to be my father's man and it is a purpose in life that will suit him well. I pray 'twill bring him happiness. Father has a way of picking out men who are very much like him, and they grow even more so in his close service!"

I could not tell how she meant it, but it did not seem to matter much as she suddenly changed the subject. Knitting her brows into a pensive frown, she asked, "Did you say that Edwin's particular enemy was the man Copsige, whom my father named to your earldom?"

I nodded.

"Did you know he had been slain?"

For one tremendous moment every nerve in my body was taut. It was as if I knew her answer before I asked the question. "By whose hand?"

"A fellow who was Earl of the northernmost part before Copsige was given it."

"Oswulf Eadwulf's son?"

"That is the name, indeed. He has made himself earl there again, and to hear people talk, he is a madman and a vengeful one at that."

"He is my kinsman," I told her, bristling and not knowing why.

"I meant no harm, Morcar! Only they say that he is savage."

"Indeed, they say right," I admitted, lowering myself to the edge of my brother's cot also, but afraid to get too close to her. "Always he has been a prideful and angry man. How met he with Copsige?"

"To hear it told, Oswulf rode to Dunholme with a force of men and, knowing he was bent on murder, the man Copsige sought sanctuary in the church there. When Oswulf Eadwulf's son found out where Copsige was, he ordered the timber church put to blaze. His men set fire to it all at once. Then Oswulf waited at the sanctuary door, and he was very, very cruel with his axe when Copsige tried to make his escape. He beheaded him and blood-let him so badly that my father's men debated a long time who it was they found there."

She shuddered, and I said nothing. For a long time the only sound in the darkened room was my brother's labored breathing. Oswulf had done it, making good the vilest of his threats. I thought of Briana and wondered if she was with him, sharing his bed and his victory.

"When did this thing happen?" I finally asked. I was nervous and so I was twisting the ends of my leathern beltings and playing with them ceaselessly. She watched my fingers as I did it.

"Near five months ago now—in March. Some men came just today who brought the news from Angland. They have just come from Rouen and said father was furious when he heard of it."

I brightened. "Will we make our way cross sea now?"

She put her hand on mine to stop the constant toying. "Are you in such a hurry to go?" I noticed how very soft her touch was, and I shook my head.

"Nay, but I have much to see to in Angland," I told her. "My home, my sister and her childlings."

"Father surely thinks your interest is of another nature!" she said. I looked away, blushing, not wanting her to think of me as her father's foe.

"There are a good many men who would fight to have me there," I admitted. "Good men who crave my brother's presence and mine. My land is in a turmoil."

"Is your land like Normandy?"

I thought about it a minute. "Wider, perhaps, and broader," I said. "Kissed more by the wind and less by the sun." Before I knew it, I was telling her all about it: the green and golden sweeps of Mercia, the craggy purple luminescence of the North Humbria, and the eerie wildness of the fen-lands. I told her how I had ridden ponies through the meandering, blossom-kissed leas of the Lindcylene Shire when I was little, and how my father had ventured us into the Scirwudu so we would not grow up afraid of the dense forest. Lundun City I described for her, and ancient Eorforwic and all my heartfelt love for the high passes of the northlands and the infinite beauty of the misty mountains, their green flanks littered with black crags and tumbling grey steeps. I talked the night away, sharing everything that was important to me, gratified that she was so intrigued and interested.

As the hour edged close to dawning, Edwin began to stir, speaking and tossing bitterly as if in the grip of some night-raving. Adeliza gave him droplets of remedy and soaked more rags, but she did not apply them as poultices, only wiped him with them, his face and brow and neck and chest. She touched them to him gently and the heat of them very gradually brought him to consciousness.

You might think that a man who had suffered what he had in the last hours would waken grateful for relief, but from the very first that was not the case of it. Even as he opened his eyes I could see a glitter therein that was very unlike him—so arrogant and mean looking that for a moment I thought the sickness was still hard upon him.

"Do not touch me, woman!" was the first thing he said, whispering it in a hoarse and angered voice. Adeliza smiled and raised a finger to her lips as if to silence him. Then she continued with her nursing, wiping him well, unembarrassed by either his proximity or his condition. He struggled to lift himself but I pinned his shoulders gently. He turned, glaring at me with fury.

"Unhand me, Morcar!" he hissed, and I was puzzled by the overly strange look in his eye. Worried, I glanced to the lady. Very calmly she spoke to me.

"Now I need those dry linens, from the table there."

As soon as I let go of him, he reached up and grabbed Adeliza's wrist, stopping her. I was almost at the table when I heard him dare her in a savage whisper. "Do not touch me more, maiden, unless you mean to satisfy me!"

I spun round to see her pull away from him, serene and undisturbed. "Be not foolish, Edwin!" That was all she said, but the answer fired him.

"Foolish is not the word for what a man feels when pretty hands play all over him, is it, lady?"

An oath escaped me, but before I could stop him, my brother had seized her again, this time forcing her down beside him. I tore into him with rage, trying to pull him away from her. Even after all he had been through he was powerful and my stranglehold did not move him. Adeliza herself reached up and stilled my effort by putting a hand upon my arm. Backing away momentarily, I cringed as he kissed her roughly.

Both my hands went tight around his neck and I used every unanticipated ounce of my power to lift him bodily away from her. Even as he began to give way to my rabid anger, though, I caught the lady's eye.

In a moment of shattering shock, I realized she wanted to be with him!

Despite d'Aubermont's suspicions, it was not me she fancied but my brother! I had known that from the start. He was comely, and she welcomed his bold embrace, mayhap longed for it. Looking into her face, I saw her mouth my name, silently entreating freedom from my defense.

It was as if everything that made me what I am drained out of me at that instant. My arms fell, wasted of strength, and I stood there helplessly as he put himself hard against her and she let him. I was stunned, unable to move until Edwin turned to me and commanded my dismissal with an arrogant glare and a single word. "Brother!"

I backed away like a wounded animal. Whether the trembling which overtook me was anger, shock or sorrow, I cannot say. It might even have been fear. It had suddenly occurred to me how evil the king's wrath would be if he discovered the situation. Once outside the chamber door, I was undecided whether to stand a falsely innocent guard there, or to flee and leave them to their own destruction. Indeed, the latter was strongly my inclination, but looking up, it was Fulke d'Aubermont I saw, striding towards my brother's lodges and obviously intent upon looking in on him. Bracing to meet him, I acknowledged his greeting with little more than a hard stare.

Puzzled, he questioned me. "Did he not come out of it?"

"Indeed. He has entirely overcome it." I winced. I could hear faint noises from behind the door, whispers of desire doled roughly and accepted with passion. I blocked him by putting my arm across the doorway, thankful that these Norman houses had doors of timber and not just heavy hangings. Arms crossed on his chest, Fulke scrutinized me for an indication of my purpose. "I swear you are mad!" he said, and he prepared to move past me anyway. I summoned all my will.

"Do not enter there, d'Aubermont!"

He looked at me strangely.

"I pray you do not enter."

There was a cracking desperation in my voice which stopped him, and it must have given him some intimation. He looked past me to the closed door. "Mon Dieu!" he whispered hoarsely, suddenly aware.

Swallowing, I nodded slightly to confirm what I knew he had realized. Then he was shaking, and it was with rage.

"You are my friend, Morcar Ælfgar's son," he declared, "and you are a fair man. But I tell you this, Anglishman, I spit on your brother!"

Rancid with anger, he turned away. I watched him till he disappeared around the dim corner, then I leant back against the cold stone wall and tried to make sense of my emotions. I heard their voices again, or thought I did, and I took off, driven as blindly as a wild cat in a thunderstorm. Outside, I walked until I came to a garden. I sat down, surrounded by the peaceful comfort of the scented, quiet air. I stayed there until evening.

*   *   *

To be left alone for any length of time, especially in Normandy, was unusual. The Normans were constantly in attendance and the Anglish banded so close around us that they were almost continual company. That day, however, no one sought me out and it was indeed fortuitous as my mood bordered dangerously on distemper. Nevertheless, as it neared twilight, I started back to my lodges to prepare for table, thinking it better to be seen in the hall than not, even in my miserable humor.

I did not mean to confront my brother, but when I passed, his door was open and I caught sight of him, splendidly dressed as was his wont at supping time. Standing over a small glass, he was intently arranging his hair which surely did not need to be arranged, it so naturally fell in perfect profusion. Gliding silently into the room, I watched him for a few seconds, lost in his vanity, and then I spoke his name, harshly and low. The sound of my voice startled him and he spun to face me.

"You had no call to put sin against that maiden!" I said.

He looked at me as if I had lied against him in council, then scowled. "Admonitions from one who bounces with his cousin's wife?"

"You are a heathen!"

"Save your false airs for the priests, brother! All your steaming righteousness did not keep you from tumbling with the woman you craved, did it? And she a wedded one!"

"Whatever woman I lay with, I lay with her gently."

"Perhaps that is your fashion, Morcar."

I truly hated him at that moment. Yet I knew well enough how useless it would be to confront him in his sullen mood. Biting back my resentment, I cast him one long icy stare of umbrage, turned my back on him, and walked away.

I cannot say what it was that led me to the chapel, but that is where I came to be. I had no particular urge to pray, and I had surely had enough of reflection for the day. Still, I found myself in the dank, deserted, comforting darkness there and I situated myself, neither my pose nor my thoughts particularly reverent, in the most obscure and gloomy corner I could find. I tried to make my mind a blank, but such comfort was hard to come by. Too many emotions assailed me.

It was not that I hated my brother for having her; it was his manner I despised. That is what I tried to tell myself. Yet Adeliza had allowed him to be overly bold with her, and her willingness had not quieted me, but had fired me even harder against him. I knew I had no reason to feel the way I did. Some strange, strangling sensation had come upon me unawares: the Norman girl had inspired a passion in me—not the way Briana had, but subtly and unwittingly, without my knowledge or consent.

And the thought of Briana confused me the more! If I loved her, as I thought I did, how could I have felt so wounded by what had passed today? Adeliza had given me no cause to suppose she might feel for me. Fulke may have misread her, but I had inwardly seen her attraction to Edwin all along. Yet now I ached just to think about that. With all my will, I vowed I would not let myself be hurt. There was no reason for my reaction; nothing had passed between us. I had only teased myself with the thought of her, without her knowing it and without even knowing it myself.

"Morcar!"

Curse you, woman, is what I thought, *how dare you seek me out?*

"Morcar! I beg you, do not hide from me! Talk with me, so that we can have this thing out between us."

Unwillingly, I rose to meet her. Even as she approached in the candle-lit gloom, my heart leapt involuntarily, and I hated myself for it.

"Do not think badly of me, Morcar."

I made no answer and she hesitated a moment as if afraid. Then she came very close and her voice was a whisper. "You cannot know how sorely it hurts me to know you think me low and sinful! I would do anything to erase that, Morcar, anything to have your respect again."

"Did he hurt you?"

"Morcar!" She reached to touch my cheek, but I stepped back and away from her.

"Play not your coy maiden's games with me, lady!" The coldness of my own voice stunned me. I repeated my question, trying desperately to sound gentle and knowing I did not. "Did my brother hurt you?"

"No." She was crying.

"Well, assuredly he was not the mild and courteous lover of a gentle woman's dreams!" Hearing her sob, I tried to stop myself, but I could not. "Or are you of that modest breed that prefers a tempestuous man, rough and raging? Surely my brother would have satisfied you then!"

Even as I said it, a cry escaped her and she turned, as if to flee from me. Forcefully, I seized her wrist and pulled her to face me once more. Trembling, pale, she looked at me sadly and whispered, "Morcar! I did not expect this of you!"

Gazing into the pitiful misery of her dark eyes, I buckled, ashamed, and asked her to forgive me.

Then she wept more, and I held her tight, trying to ease the agony that had been my doing. Closing my eyes, even in the darkness, I tried not to think of her there, leaning on me, needing me. I did not want to be touching her, but God knows, I savored it and I stood there with her until she was the one who pulled away.

"Say we are friends again, Morcar!"

"You know we are."

"But I need to hear you say it. Say you trust and love me again."

"I trust you and …" I could not say it.

"Say you can love me as a sister, despite what I am."

"Adeliza!" I was so confused!

"Well, I shall love you as a brother, and someday you will come to forgive me!" Her voice was earnest, quavering but earnest. I was a fool! She did not know how I felt. How could she know? I swallowed hard.

"I have forgiven you already, lady." Suddenly, something Oswulf once said occurred to me—something about being a stranger to everyone who knew him. We did not know each other, this lady and I. We could not perceive a single thing about each other. We were strangers. Wordlessly, I backed away into the shadows, dazed as if by a blow, and sat down on a hard wooden bench, my back to her. I felt I was in a dream. Following, she knelt beside me and took my hand.

"Could you love me again if I wedded with him?"

I groaned.

"Father loves Edwin, Morcar! I think he would allow it."

"For the Christ's sake!" I cried, forgetting I was in a church. "He is ungovernable! He acted meanly to you, and you talk of wedding him!"

"Oh, Morcar! Are you so blind?" Her voice was very soft. "He played a part for us—an act of boldness to cover all his torment! You can understand it, can you not?"

I shook my head.

"Your brother is no fool, you know that. If he wakened to find us nursing him, then he knew we had attended him through it. And he is a prideful man."

"Vain!" I said.

"He is fair to see and proud of it; there is no great sin in that. Only he could not bear to think we had seen him like that—that we supposed him weak and helpless—so he tried to prove himself something more. That is all."

I dropped her hand and stood suddenly, not wanting to think about all this. "You are telling me then that he advantaged himself of you to prove something to himself?"

Her voice came mildly chiding. "No, Morcar. Advantage himself he did not. Can you not guess he has been so sore wounded that he has been afraid—"

She stopped, but I was sure of her meaning. Trembling, I tried to calm myself, walking a few paces away. I had never heard a maiden speak of such personal things and I must have flinched. She grabbed my arm.

"Must be my nearness frustrated him is all! He did not want you to think him weak or unable—and he did not want me to think it, either!"

I said nothing.

"Would it comfort you to know we but talked and toyed and kissed together?"

I faced her, incredulous. Her voice seemed to come from a great distance. "Morcar, I have loved him since the moment first I looked on him! And I will wait until he is able to do more than pretend to me."

I nodded numbly.

"God willing, 'twill be overcome, but must be you know this thing would be worse than death to many men," she added.

"I know it."

"Then, be kind to him, Morcar." She took my hand and I followed, letting her lead me to the one place I did not want to be, that crowded noisome hall. The very moment we appeared in the archway, Edwin stood. He had been scanning nervously, expecting or hoping to see us. The moment he did, he rose and started our way. I was thankful for that. At the opposite end of his table I had spotted the back of Fulke's head, and I did not want that man to see me. He was one person I could not hazard to meet with now, as precariously as my feelings were balanced.

My brother seemed distraught, nervous. When he reached me, we just looked at each other wordlessly, and as if there had been some agreement made between us, we began walking slowly, just the two of us, leaving Adeliza behind without a glance. Through all the dim corridor we walked saying nothing, and we had been outside in the mild night breeze and starlight for a good long time before Edwin spoke.

"That pain comes on my head like a kind of madness, Morcar."

We were leaning on a parapet built alongside the stone roadway where it crossed a flushing, wide stream, and we both stared straight ahead into the fascinating glitter of moonlight reflected on the gurgling waters. I could not speak, and when I had been silent another long while, he continued.

"It takes all my control away. I say and do things I do not mean."

"Let us forget them then," I said, trying to keep my voice level. Suddenly, he grabbed my shoulders.

"For God's sake, brother! Tell me what happened!"

I looked at him curiously. "You went senseless."

"Before that!"

"You had head pains."

"I remember the head pains! Did I fall? Was it the falling sickness?"

I drew in a deep breath. The perfume of the night was all around us. "They tell me this is not an uncommon thing," I told him. "A man takes a wound to the head, and it takes a year or two to heal. While it is healing, whenever there is stress or tension—"

"Fits?" His voice shook.

"For a year or two. Then they are gone."

He put his head down on his arms. "Was that what happened to me at Berecingas?"

"That was a mild one."

"Oh, God! Could be I am ruined, Morcar. I cannot—"

I cut him off before he dared say more. I would not hear those words from him.

We stayed there a while longer, in silence again because I did not know what to say to him. I busied myself with the sound of the soft wind and night-birds and the muffled voices of men that carried from the manor-house. Then, unexpectedly, I found myself questioning him, even against my own will.

"Are you in love with the Norman maiden, Edwin?"

Pulling himself from whatever confusion of depressing thoughts had been his, he straightened to answer me. "I am." From the tone of his voice I knew it was true.

"Do you not think it dangerous sport to linger with the king's daughter?"

"I mean to ask him for her."

"You are mad."

He stepped back from me with a look of fierce indignation. "What makes you think she will not have me?"

"I did not mean—"

"What then?" His eyes narrowed and he looked at me. Suddenly, there was trembling dismay in his voice. "Did she see me, brother? Did she look on those convulsions?"

For a dire moment I fought the urge to tell her she had witnessed that and more. Then, looking away, I lied. "She only saw you senseless."

He sighed with relief. "What made you call her?"

"Fulke reminded me of her healing touch." In answer to his wordless question I added, "He saw your scars and knows you were sore wounded. He watched you tremble."

Edwin groaned.

"You need not fear. It will be a well kept secret."

"I am sorry for having hurt you, brother. I know not what I was thinking, my mind was so bothered."

"Still, you are mad if you think the king will have you for her," I laughed. "You are but one of the conquered."

"You do not trust the Norman, do you?" he whispered.

"Do you?"

He tossed that twisted, disarming and knowing smile.

All of a sudden, we were laughing. I put my arm around his shoulder and we walked back, piercing the night with our relief and our rejoicing.

Brothers again.

CHAPTER FORTY-TWO

The king returned to England on St. Nicholas Day
. . . When he returned he gave away every man's
land [and] imposed a heavy tax upon the people of
the country yet, nothwithstanding, he allowed his
men to harry wherever they came.

—Anglo Saxon Chronicle
Book D, 1067

December, 1067
'Twas chill, and in the black sky of Normandy every star was visible over the Channel with an intensity I had never noticed in Angland. I stood staring at them a long time while I stood on the cold sands, listening to the subdued and sluggish slapping of dark waves. Just down the beach, men worked briskly, complaining about the chill, loading the king's vessels and fast making them ready for sea to take advantage of a fair wind that approached with the midnight.

I had seen her—my mother. William took us to where she lived, in a large, windowless room of the priest's house in Le Havre, on the somber seaside estate of her brother, William Malet. But for two old nurse-women, both Norman, she was alone. They could ring the bell for help, they told us, if she lost her temper, and strong-shouldered priests could be there in an instant. Mosttimes, though, she was quiet enough, lost in an absorbing daze of real and imagined memories. She sewed sometimes. They fed and dressed and combed her, and sat with her all the long hours she prayed and wept. She seemed not to know me, but Edwin wore the fine mantle edged in black fox fur which she had embroidered so meticulously in those months after Burchard died. She fingered it wonderingly a long time and then put her head on his chest, so that he could not help but hold her, and wept.

The Norman watched our meeting with emotion. Because he held his man William Malet in genuine high regard, this woman was a symbol to him, a reminder of the cruelty and guile of the cursed House of Godwine, whom he, William, by the divine grace of God, had been able to justly level. He thought of my mother as a hard-won token of honor, like the papal banner he had carried into battle at Hastings Field. He did not strongly feel pity for her, he told us, till he remembered how lively and beautiful she had been the Christ Mass he had first lain eyes on us in King Edward's house in Lundun. "When your father and I rode and dined together as friends," he afterwards told us gravely, "I thought her fairest of all Anglishwomen and fairest of all Norman women, too, save one."

The air of England was biting when we disembarked, but 'twas like a welcoming kiss to me. We laughed somewhat at the discomfiture of the returning Norman company, who had complained so vigorously in Normandy of the chill. No doubt they would find our cold a great deal fiercer; from the way they shivered and carried on, I was hard put to imagine them tasting of winter in the North Humbria.

Lundun city was crammed with folk from all the shires, rich and poor, young and old. Landowners, thegns, peasants, and freemen, they welcomed us, and William could not help but notice that their affection. Archbishop Aldred had already ordered a litany added to the daily Mass in thanks for the safe return of the Anglish high-born, naming Edwin and me by name and conspicuously omitting the crafty Archbishop Stigand who sweated a little under the king's condonation of such an insult. His days of political power had died with the sons of Godwine, and he knew it. He grew more and more a withered old man under William's disdainful eye. Still, he said a thing to me that cold crystalline morning as we rode through the crowded streets, and it has stayed with me ever since.

"You will never more ride through this kingdom, Morcar Ælfgar's son," he said accusingly, his fox-like features drawn into a gaunt, dour smile, "and see a crowd of Anglishmen your own age."

This was a sad truth, I realized when he said it. In two short months, the battle at Hastings Field, the aet-Staengfordesbrycg, and the slaughter at Fulford had near wholly wasted the flower of Anglish manhood. Nevertheless, in the teeming crowd were monks I knew, and my cousin Æric and some other men of Mercia who had been guardsmen to Edwin. I did not expect to see any of my own men; Lundun has never been home very long to a North Humbrian.

Just as we turned into the Wide Street that led to the West Minster, though, two commanding figures pushed forcefully through the crowd. Heard Ulf's son, in a leathern mantle, and Gamel-Beorn, in a Danish coat of seal, burst at me simultaneously; we all three bumped heads as I bent to embrace them best I could without falling or frighting my horse. They traveled alongside me the short rest of the way, all of us babbling, our breath and the horse's misting the crisp morning air. We had not seen each other since our abrupt parting in Eorforwic and had each of us much to tell.

Soon as we left the minster after receiving our bishop's welcome, Edwin and I met with them at the wharves where they came to help us oversee our unpacking. Then we sat to ale in the king's hall together, flushed and happy, in a corner far from the hearth. William eyed us curiously more than once during the evening. Fulke d'Aubermont and Gilbert Rouquin sat with us and made sober, cautious conversation, but out of grudging deference did not crowd our table all the night.

Both these bold North Humbrians looked fiercer than when last I had seen them. The gashes Gamel-Beorn took at the Gate Fulford had healed into shiny welts, very noticeable on his gaunt, wind-browned face. Heard Ulf's son, though handsome and earnest looking as ever, wore a deep scar over his left eye and across his brow. 'Twas not such a distraction itself, being nearly hidden by his thick chestnut brown hair, but it gave a menacing tilt to the shape of his eye, replacing his former gentle gaze with a more formidable one. He had earned the wounding at the aet-Staengfordesbrycg, fighting alongside King Harold despite the bruising he had taken a few days earlier at Fulford. He prided himself to say the piercing was delivered by Tostig Godwine's son himself, moments before that tyrant's fate was sealed forever. My genial earl's man had a way of embellishing a tale with detail that reminded me much of my father's talent. We listened a long time to his vivid descriptions before we began to question them on the turn things had taken in our absence.

The city was crowded, they told us, because the harsh tax William had levied on men of all classes soon after his coronation was due by the Year's End. Those who could or would not pay their half-tithe earlier hurried now to make good their kings-debt or register to make amends. A panic had arisen among landholders that William meant to retaliate with confiscation any person who failed in the end to pay. Word had spread like wildfire over the kingdom: he had taken away the estates of every man he could identify as having stood against him at Hastings Field. Lundun grew crowded with homeless, penniless men who once had been privileged.

Then Gamel-Beorn described how the southerners had fared during the absence of the king and all the native chiefs of Angland. Odo, the worldly bishop of Bayeux, was one of two marshals whom William had made his rule-by-proxy. In fact, he was the king's half-brother, a strapping, bulky man with all William's bad qualities and none of his good. Before we left, William had styled him the "Earl of Kent," which thing would have made the old Earl Godwine roll in his winding sheet, no doubt, the men of Kent having long ago been his staunchest anti-Norman supporters.

Presumably, William was not unaware of the humorous irony of the situation; his countrymen had never forgotten how unfairly King Edward's Normans had been treated by the House of Godwine, and the men of Kent, during their moment of rebellious glory. 'Twas a grudge they had kept alive some sixteen years. As for the Kentish-folk, the hatred they had felt for the old king's retinue was nothing compared to that which they felt for the stone-faced Odo. They rose against him. Almost every strong, chief man of Wessex and the Anglia having been slain on the warfields that autumn, they amusingly chose as a leader the same Eustace of Boulogne whose argument with the men of Dofras had led to the exile of the House of Godwine, and to the bloodshed and ill will so well remembered from my childhood. The count of Boulogne was known to be at odds with Odo, and the Kentish-men who had once warred with him no doubt saw Eustace as the lesser of two foreign evils, for he was in no wise a foolish or wimpish man. With rigorous cruelty Odo was able to quell the unrest. Eustace hastily self-exiled himself rather than face the wrath of the king, and Odo ground his heels into the men of the east coast, with burdensome reprisals and an unbending iron will.

"And his other marshal of Angland, William Fitz Osbern, his so-called Earl of Hereford, fares not much better with the men of the west," Heard Ulf's son said. "In Escanceaster they are preparing to fight even now." Then with a furtive glance at the king's table, he added low, "All men pray 'twill be a long time before he reaches his hand into Mercia and the North Humbria, but we will see him there soon enough, I trow."

Gamel-Beorn nodded glumly. "He has promised away a great many more estates than he can carve out of Wessex and the East Anglia."

"What lame excuse will he use to take our lands," Edwin asked hotly, "when he cannot claim that Mercians fought behind Harold at Hastings Field?"

Gamel-Beorn eyed him darkly. "Mayhap he will be angry that they stood behind you, my lord." My brother flinched, and I turned the talk to other things. Æric had some news of Aldgyth, for the sons of Carr made a point of visiting her frequently and reporting back to him. We learnt, too, that our kinsman Brihtric was a one-armed man now; the wounding he had taken trying uselessly to save his brother Maldon at Gate Fulford had turned gross and crippled him. Grandmother Godiva was well enough; of Oswulf, Briana, and the boy Ædmund, there was no word. We talked almost to the dawn. Both of them, bone-weary as I was, slept the night on the king's cold floor, but Edwin and I were escorted to a private chamber by a Norman priest who had come to look for us. It did not seem ominous at the time.

CHAPTER FORTY-THREE

Oswulf, rushing headlong against the lance of a
common robber who met him, was thrust through,
and there perished.

—Simeon of Durham

It surprises me that I wept when I heard of the death of my cousin
Oswulf. Siward Bearn broke the news to me himself. A few days after our
return, a messenger whispered in the king's ear at the morning mass, and
the king signaled my brother and me to follow the boy out. My kinsman,
wet from snow, dull-eyed and weary, was waiting in the courtyard, a
band of some twenty men-at-arms still mounted in the roadway beyond
where he stood. We embraced, then walked back to our chambers, arms
on each other's shoulders. The mood was grim.

He was exceptionally tall in the frame, Siward Bearn, but he looked
bent as he shook the snow out of his northern furs, then drew a bench
near the fire. The red dyes had faded in his long hair, and I noticed for
the first time that his locks were ashy brown beneath, much like
Oswulf's had been.

"He is dead since Hallow's Day and buried on the Tyne mouth lea.
We kept it low long as we could. Most of our kinsmen know, and I
carried the news myself to the lady Godiva. In Ceaster, Aldgyth knows
naught of it, I trow, but I have sent for the Welshmen to meet us here."

"What of his lady—and the child?" I did not want to ask it, but I
did. Siward shrugged.

"At his house in Dunholme. My sister held his head in her lap while
he bled of a gross wounding. A robber's spear was put full through him,
but it took him half a night to die."

I shuddered. A sudden memory of him helping me make mischief in
the smokehouse of Grandfather Leofric's manor at King's Braumleigh
brought tears to me. Edwin once more mirrored my thoughts. "He was
fair when we were children, and Grandmother scolded and bribed and

soothed us all," he said in a low voice. "Then his only fault was his orphan's temper. He could not help that it ruled his life."

"'Twas more than an orphan's temper with him," the Bearn answered, looking from one to the other of us, his grey eyes sullen. "When he was a babe and our fathers were murdered together, a madness and revenge came to him in his mother's milk. Your grandmother told me this herself. She nursed Lady Ecfryth to her rapid end and with a kind of horror, she said, she watched the babe grow wild-eyed and troublesome as his mother suckled him in her awful ravings. Yet the ring Thored Gyric's son gave him from her he wore to the grave."

I remembered the one-legged man whom Oswulf had rewarded for his service to the dying Earl Eadwulf, first with a war-horse during his own bride-ale, and later, after he had been restored to the Bernicia, with a house near Wiuraemutha. My cousin did have a sense of goodness, after a fashion, when a man's loyalties matched his own. Could be he would escape the eternal punishment, I was thinking; mayhap there was part of him which no man knew. Even as I thought about it, though, I pictured with awful clarity the searing hatred in his glinting eyes and the feel of his breath in my face, hot with distemper, on the night he tried to strangle me in his house at Hagustaldesea. I shivered, remembering it and wondering again whether or not he would have murdered me, had Siward Bearn not burst in and prevented him.

My face must have taken on a meanness. Edwin cleared his throat. "Best we not over-mourn him now and bring ourselves to any grief," he said somewhat coldly, eyeing me suspiciously. "He was no good man to the king, and William will not hesitate to dispose of the Bernicia now."

I growled absently, knowing he made the remark in part to provoke me, as if I had borne my kinsman no love at all. In truth, though, my mind had long since turned from elegy to thoughts of the babe and the widow. William would do as he willed with my hapless cousin's earldom and it would serve no purpose for me to speculate about it. The woman, however, was another matter. After a brief widowing-time, she would be free to marry, and I grew tense with half-formed plans to claim her. All the while Edwin and Siward mused about the Bernicia, my thoughts were on Briana, and I did not even feel guilt for it.

In spite of my tempered coldness though, there were those who truly mourned my kinsman. When Daffydd and Hwell Carr's son arrived late on the stormy morrow, they were greatly saddened by the news. Daffydd, in particular, had caroused with Oswulf Eadwulf's son many a night gone by; my cousin's excesses had been perfectly acceptable to the Cymrians, who had come somewhat to revere his boldness.

The belated toast we shared in place of a grave-ale did not keep the occasion of our reunion from being joyous. The sons of Carr were oldest and dearest of our friends. Noting the attachment, William himself invited them to spend the Christ Mass with us in Wintanceaster, but said our party had grown so large that our men had need remove themselves to one of the many knight's inns in the city. These hostels were something new to the Anglish and Normans alike. William had ordered them into being to quarter visitors to Lundun. Once they had been the homes of wealthy Wessexmen, manors confiscated when the owners fell at Hastings.

Like true earl's men, our friends were not happy about being forcefully kept from our constant company. There was naught we could do, however, against the king's decision. Once they had been removed, we saw them only on announced visits; the king was sly, and this ploy allowed him to know exactly what each of us was about at all times, what company we kept, and how long we conversed. Siward Bearn only, of all our retainers, he allowed lodges in his house, and this because the Bearn, like ourselves, was one of the chief men of Angland, the small remainder of whom William hoped to gather for his first Christ Mass Gemot.

Nevertheless, not many restraints were put upon us and we were in almost constant contact with our men, except when we took bed. They spent the Year's End with us fasting and praying in a cleric's room in the minster, our party having been swelled that morning by the arrival of Edwin's chief man. Hereward's winter-tanned face had grown more lined and somber, his piercing eyes more defiant.

After the Feast of the Nativity, William held his Gemot. He was trying to assuage the Anglish by continuing the customs they had always known, like letting women mingle in the hall till the board was cleared, and keeping all the standard Gemots. His first order of business was to order advance forces into Mercia and the Humberland to ascertain the allegiance of the north and midlands. My avunculus, William Malet was chosen because of his northern connections to establish the king's rule in Eorforwic, and he in turn chose Fulke d'Aubermont as his chief man.

At the Gemot, too, the question of the Bernicia was settled in a way which William, no doubt, thought would be placating to the Anglish. He sold the earldom for gold and sworn pledges to his service. The man who became the new earl there by king's decree was none other than the most mistrusted of my own kinsmen, Gospatrick Maldred's son, who had turned his back on our house by swearing himself to Tostig Godwine's son when that infidel took the North Humbria. His motive had been more greed than treachery; he had not wanted to give up his holdings the way Siward Bearn had been forced to do, along with Oswulf and many other of our Humbrian kin. His service had been genuine, though;

the allegiance had been real. Whether or not he helped, as rumored, to murder my brother Burchard, none of us would ever know. His denials were wrathful and pledged on holy relics.

Heard Ulf's son and Gamel-Beorn could not stand the man, and their attitude towards him was relentlessly unfriendly. If they saw him coming, they stepped aside, and when he invited himself to table with us one night, they exchanged a meaningful glance, then pushed themselves away from the board. "You may trust him if you want to," Heard Ulf's son had told us, eyes burning with indignation, "but I will not break bread or make small talk with a creature who saw my father hacked to death and did not speak out against his murderer!"

I was inclined to agree, and had already decided that Briana and the child must be removed from Dunholme before Gospatrick went north to claim his new domain. I was actually uneasy for young Ædmund's life.

CHAPTER FORTY-FOUR

he [William] was so stern and relentless a man
that no one dared do aught against his will.
The earls who resisted resisted his will, he held
in bondage.

—Anglo Saxon Chronicle
Book "E"

January 6, 1068
On Twelfth Night, Anglish and Norman came to blood for the first time
in the king's hall. A Norman brawler, whom men called Herbert the
Waster, cornered my man Gamel-Beorn during the amusements after
the Epiphany Feast and goaded him to rage with certain remarks
concerning the conquered race. The fight was fierce and bloody and
drew the attention of all the hall. The Waster was a stocky man, one-
eyed since Hastings. Like a bull, he charged the other over and over
again, butting with his head and slashing forcefully with a French short-
sword which bought Gamel-Beorn's blood twice.

At length the two beat the weapons away from each other and
crashed to the floor in a double stranglehold, growling and roaring with
hatred. That is when Gamel-Beorn finally bested Herbert the Waster by
biting the man's cheek with all his might, ripping the flesh and causing a
split second of shock which gave him the final advantage. As the
Norman pulled himself away, arms crossed in defense, Gamel-Beorn,
thinner and quicker, leapt to his feet and began to kick mercilessly till the
Waster was wedged firmly beneath a table and hoarsely shouting his
surrender. After that, Gamel-Beorn was called "the Biter," and near every
man in the kingdom knew him by that name, Norman and Anglish alike.

William was wroth that his hall had been dishonored, especially on
a holy day. Even before we could tend Gamel-Beorn's wounds, the king
ordered both men escorted out and barred from his house forever. The
Biter let himself be led docilely away, but his gaunt, scarred face was lit

by a victorious smile, infectious to every Anglishman there.

My man's expulsion seemed a fitting cap to a bitter day. Early, I had spoken to the king. Knowing I sought an audience with him, William had beckoned me in comradely fashion to join his party, mostly Norman, as they left the minster. In French fashion, the new king always led a party out to inspect the stables and armory after the high mass on feast days, just as King Edward had done when I was a boy. One would not have expected the wide barn to have changed so much since then, but the Norman long shields and horse-mail made it seem an entirely different place, foreign and strange. Passing the trough where Fulke d'Aubermont had been sitting when first I made his acquaintance, I glanced over my shoulder at him. So much had transpired since we were youngsters, is what I was thinking, but he shot me a quick, impassive smile as if in answer to a greeting.

While the king leisurely pointed out one thing and another to his company and inspected the train being readied for the North Humbria, I busied myself looking for favorite arms of old, displayed here and there in the high rafters. I was studying a raven-crested leathern round-shield almost a century old when William caught my eye. The barn was fast emptying by then; only those with tasks to do lingered.

"Someday, Earl Morcar," William said with a gesture overhead, "you will share the history of these with me. Seems an Anglish man can recognize every one."

"Some mean more to some men than to others." I smiled. Pointing out the raven, I added, "That shield was carried by King Edward, whom some men call the Fair, and others the Martyr."

"One of the six boy kings," William added, looking interested.

"Aye." I looked at him with a new respect. "His half-brother Æthelred was holding it for him when he was murdered in the Passage at Corfesgeat."

"By his step-mother, Ælfrida. She held a cup out to him while one of her retainers stabbed young Edward in the back. Am I correct?"

I smiled, pleased. "'Tis certain you have studied this, my lord!"

Smiling, he went on. "Then when Æthelred himself became king, he ordered those arms hung up there for all to see—the arms of his murdered brother."

I truly was amazed. William laughed at my look. "All you Anglish forget how attached I was to the last King Edward—Æthelred was his father, and I have heard the tales of the boy kings many times." He stood back, drawing his large frame erect and crossing his arms under his heavy mantle. "Well do I understand your distaste for the man Gospatrick," he added soberly, watching for my reaction. "Yet there is a certain wisdom in putting an Anglish man there, one who has a claim, rather than a Norman, think you not?"

"I do not say your decision was unpopular, my lord." I picked my words carefully, still not quite comfortable with the formal French. "In fact, I do not argue your decision—nor my brother does, or Waltheof or Ædgar, I trow."

"Then—?" he eyed me quizzically. I swallowed hard.

"Must be you know there never was any but bad blood between Oswulf Eadwulf's son and Gospatrick, the son of Maldred," I reminded him. "Let me go remove my cousin's wife and babe from the house at Dunholme, before Gospatrick goes there to claim it."

At once, he gave a short laugh. "Send your kinsman, the Bearn. He is the boy's avunculus, is he not? The lady's brother?"

"I fain would take the trip myself—" I began, but he cut me off with a grimace.

"The North Humbria is a vast territory, Earl Morcar," he said low, with an irritating mock deference. "In this bitter season who could guarantee your safe return?"

I bristled. "Surely—" He shook his head.

"I cannot send you anywhere that I do not have the force to ensure your safety."

"My safety?"

He turned to face me with a stern, paternal look. "The high men of Angland, the earls, and the ætheling will remain here so that I may call upon their council."

"Hostages?" My voice was cold.

He smiled easily. "Nay, Earl Morcar. Councilmen." He put his hand on my shoulder for just an instant, a gesture of friendship. Without saying anything else, I strode past him, knowing it was useless to argue and feeling a swift rise of anger. I felt him watch after me, but I did not turn to look back. "Pick any man you choose to ride north with the party," he called earnestly. "Let your man bring the woman and child to Eorforwic, and my best marshals will guarantee their safety there."

He knew I heard, but I did not acknowledge him.

I had carried my anger all the day and went to the king's hall that evening short-tempered and morose. Hereward had laughed glumly at my discomfiture, remarking to the Welshmen that sullenness became me, giving me a sparkle I otherwise lacked. I had scowled and made a hand gesture that no man of Lindcylene could misunderstand. He roared with laughter, and the men at our table joined him, bringing stares from all over the great room.

Later, after Gamel-Beorn had been escorted out, we sat remarking on the incident and discussing this part and that of the action. William Malet had joined us; he was in a better humor than the king and not entirely unappreciative of the pride we felt at our comrade's victory. "'Tis well that my countrymen have seen the grit of a North Humbrian in ire," he said, sipping ale from a Norman glass-horn. "Mayhap they will begin to realize that all this land has not yet been conquered."

Appraising my uncle, I thought how lucky William was to have one like him. He was a man well-respected by the Anglish everywhere, even in the north and the midlands where not many Normans were likely to be revered. His sandy hair had grown streaked with palest grey, but his scarred face had grown stronger, if anything, with the years, and his stern eyes more commanding. He smiled as he caught me looking his way. "Perhaps the day will soon be that you join me in Eorforwic, nephew," he said slowly, "and we will be neighboring king's-men, you and I."

Giving a bleak half-smile, I drowned a gulp of mead. "How long think you the new king will require native councilmen to help him in his decisions?" I asked.

His face grew serious. "I myself asked William to allow you to come north awhile," he said, looking at me levelly. "I advised him there could be little harm in it, as you were his sworn man, and that indeed it might be a good thing. The North Humbria no doubt would adopt your attitude sooner than bow to any other man's."

I shrugged and was about to answer, but Siward Bearn spoke up; his voice was angry. "You know well as we do, uncle, that the king will hold both our kinsmen here at his side till you have built castles enough in our homelands to keep the Anglish folk minded that their earls have no power now."

William Malet cut him off with a wave of the hand. "I know neither the king's plans nor his motives," he said soberly, putting his horn down with enough force to draw the attention of the entire table, "apart from knowing that the only hope we have for peace is to make our allegiances all the same."

Edwin looked amused. "Still you talk as you ever have, uncle," he said with a resigned shake of the head. "As if there never were such a thing as a difference."

"You have less of a difference with the Norman than you had with the sons of Godwine, I trow," my uncle's voice hardened. "William was chosen of Edward and has the rightful claim. Nor does he harbor ill will toward your house, but sees a sort of promise there, because of your Norman connections and your influence with the Anglish people."

My brother snorted and swallowed a great draught. "He fears our influence and you know it," he said, but William Malet shook his head.

"Things will come right," he said simply. "Even now the king's family awaits the sea-wind that will bring them here, and then we may see a true uniting. 'Tis no secret that William would be pleased to see you his son-in-the-law."

My brother blushed.

"'Tis no secret Lady Adeliza would be pleased to see you the king's son-in-the-law as well," my uncle added. Edwin blushed more. The Welshmen, usually stoic, laughed at his embarrassment. Siward Bearn, unconvinced, drummed long, ringed fingers on the table. "He would have us all be handsome figureheads," he said in a low voice, "but he would have us all be powerless as well."

The king's man silenced him. "I am your avunculus, Siward Æthelgar's son," he smiled with finality, "and 'twould be fitting if you gave me the last voice."

We laughed because it was so like him to say it, and he had said it many times when we were boys.

*   *   *

"'Twould please me if you stayed just long enough to glimpse her," Edwin cajoled. Looking out over the channel, he added something about the wind being agreeable enough to bring the king's family any day, but Hereward shook his head.

"I am one who fast wears out a welcome," he apologized, brown eyes twinkling, "and most especially with kings."

It was an exceedingly sunny day in early March, and we were down on the coast, Hereward, my brother, and I. We had ridden the old Roman sea roads all the morning and now we walked the stony shore, having tethered the horses at the Norman guardhouse on the sands. The wind was invigorating, though it lacked the salt-kiss of Ceaster wind and the biting blasts of the North Sea. As I listened to the playful arguments, I actually found myself hoping Hereward would stay. Siward Bearn, with Heard Ulf's son and the Biter, had gone north with the king's train well onto two months earlier. In the same party rode both Fulke d'Aubermont and William Malet, as well as those few northerners who had attended the Christ Mass Gemot. I had grown lonely in the king's court, especially after Daffydd and Hwell had taken leave for Ceaster a fortnight later. The only North Humbrians left, Waltheof and Gospatrick, were not my favorites and I had begun to grow quite fond of the hearty, brown-eyed Mercian. Every day he rode from the inn on the Minster Way to the king's gate to meet us. After a stuffy morning's councilling in formal French with foreigners always bent on changing your mind, he was a welcome relief.

Nevertheless, Hereward the Wake had a bold and unbridled tongue. He was a man who ever said things just as he saw them. He had almost come to words with William on two occasions, and on the evening last had shouted oaths in the king's hearing, having grown so wroth in an argument. The Norman found this most displeasing, and said so.

"So now he has marked me," Hereward winced, "and no doubt he will mark me more if I linger."

I watched him thoughtfully as he scooped a handful of stones and threw them out to sea, shading his eyes to follow them as they splashed. There was more of deep silver than brown in this hair these days, adding power to a look already commanding respect. In his youth, no doubt, he had been stockier but even now he was a powerful man, with arms that might have belonged to a seaman or a thegn who worked the land himself. He was broad of back and long of leg; his face was an even brown all over; his features, though angular and strong, looked somewhat boyish … except for the eyes. The Wake's eyes were the same piercing, see-everything eyes that had drawn my attention at our first meeting. They were an old man's eyes.

Reluctantly, though, I was forced to admit he was right, There were few men who could confess a fondness for Hereward the Wake until time and proximity brought them to know him, and William was not a man likely to be inclined to his outspokenness. Truth was, the king had admired the man at first. The Wake was a wealthy landowner and, while not high born in the strictest sense, he was of good blood and carried himself with the air of an influential townsman, fair and honest. He never feared to let it be known that he despised the claim of Harold Godwine's son, and William had heard from Waltheof and Gospatrick how Hereward had refused to feast at that king's bride-ale. The two might have eventually come to a friendship had the Mercian held his tongue better, but that was not his way. One chilling night, so cold that even the Normans kept late in the hall where the fires roared, the man made some remarks that caused William to be wary of his honesty, and there was a coldness ever after.

William was newly returned from Escanceaster, whither he had ridden to suppress the second serious uprising since our arrival from Normandy. Lady Gytha, old Earl Godwine's widow, had taken up residence in that city. There had been great hatred for the Normans there since the time of King Edward, and it had waxed fiercer under the stupid rule of William's vice-regent, the man Fitz Osbern. When the bastard sons of Harold Godwine's son left the safety of foreign exile to join their grandmother in that place, 'twas expected that violence would soon erupt, and it did. Harried attempts at compromise failed after William learnt that men from all over the south were gathering there, making the stone fortifications of the old city even stronger, and hauling in grain and cattle and wood. Swiftly, forcefully, he moved on them.

William had proven himself on the battlefield already. Now, in addition to his strength he showed a wicked cunning that defeated even those most eager to fight. While messengers lambasted the townspeople with threats of reprisals, the king sent his marshals into the countryside to choose hostages from among those most closely connected to the warriors he knew to be at Escanceaster. To the very foot of the walls he marched them. There was great dissension, but at length the rebels threw down their arms and begged peace of the Norman, as many of the best men had decided to surrender rather than see their loved ones, mostly women and children, maimed or murdered. Soldiers who would have fought to the death on any battlefield were brought low by this nasty ploy, and there was much grumbling about it, for the city had held out eighteen days and might have gone on fighting even longer had not the Norman used their innocent kinfolk as weapons.

In retribution, William ordered his men to waste the land around Dornwaraceaster—all but the ancient battlements of Corfesgeat where Edward the Martyr was murdered, and which some still considered haunted and holy. To those who had surrendered to him, though, he was most merciful. In the final toll only a handful had been killed in the fighting, and all the hostages were freed, save one who was cruelly blinded. Lady Gytha fled with her household to the Flat Holme island, and the bastard sons ran for Dublin, else they might have been dealt with more severely.

The king was proud of himself for having quelled the trouble with a minimum of bloodshed, and proud also that there had been Anglishmen as well as Normans in the army that marched on the rebels. He was looking for our approval that night in his hall when Hereward wounded him with an opinion. Those Wessexmen who had marched with the army were naught but mindless mercenaries, the Wake declared levelly, and the king would be hard put to find any like them in Mercia or the North Humbria. "What is more," he added darkly, staring into William's fast hardening eyes, "you have frighted many Anglishmen away from respecting you with this heathen way of making war."

The face of the king remained impassive. He flinched ever so slightly but made no answer. He might have shown more wrath had he not bidden the Mercian to give his honest view.

"Must be he hears few opinions contrary to his own," Hereward had said later, sadly shaking his head. This was the truth of it. All of his Normans had a gift, it seems, for making their own intentions seem to mirror his. They had a courtly way of talking which often masked half-truth and hypocrisy. Too, a good many of them were unabashed fawners and William never seemed to treat those ones any differently than he did his most loyal and forthright men, like my uncle or Fulke d'Aubermont. It made one wonder how good a reader of men he was; 'twas as if he acted towards each man ever after on the basis of his first reaction to him.

Edwin had climbed now upon a staunch jutting of grey rock, and sat cross-legged upon it, wrapped tight in a fur mantle. He had much complained of limb-stiffness since our return to Angland, and of a pulsing pain where his gut had been pierced through. The old head pains, though, had diminished since Lady Adeliza wrought her medicine on him in Normandy and, though I watched studiously for signs of it, there was little hint of the spasm-madness that had overcome him there. This seemed to bear out Brother Heirome's original prognosis, that it had been a temporary, feverish condition, not likely to plague him all his life through. Daily work with sword and battle-axe in the practice field behind the armory had brought back much of his strength and stamina, and the familiar Anglish air had restored his color. Now, outlined against the green sea, with the sun reflecting off droplets of spray frozen in his golden hair, he looked as he had in easier times. I could tell, though, that despite his happy anticipation of Adeliza's arrival, a depression was looming. He was wroth to let Hereward leave. We had no comfortable friends in the king's court, and it was lonely after the camaraderie we had known in our own houses.

The Wake was not to be moved, however. He argued he was more valuably placed in Mercia than lolling in the king's house, and we knew he was right. Deprived of their beloved earl, and with so many of their chief men fallen in the aet-Staengfordesbrycg and at Fulford, the people of the midlands craved a semblance of the leadership they had always known. The chief man of Edwin Ælfgar's son was in these troubled days overseer not only of the great manor at Kirton, but of the earldom as well, just as Heard Ulf's son, Gamel-Beorn the Biter, and Siward Bearn were the mortar of the north.

Early on the morrow the Wake took his leave. Though he told my brother bluntly he doubted that he would come himself, we consoled ourselves with the thought that our other men would be coming to us soon for the Easter Gemot.

CHAPTER FORTY-FIVE

having everywhere restored order by his sudden
movements, he disbanded his army and returned
to Wintanceaster in time for the vacation at the
feast of Easter.

—Orderic Vitalis
Book IV, Chapter IV

Easter 1068
Robert de Comines was a dark-haired Flemish, a soldier through and
through, who wore his hair cropped like a Norman warrior and scowled
perpetually. A tall, hulking man, he had distinguished himself on the
field at Hastings, and considered himself advisor, companion, and
perhaps even blood-brother to the king. So sure he was of his own
importance that he apparently affected William with his attitude,
worming his way into the man's confidence in an ingratiating, almost
bullish manner.

He was not happy when Edwin bested him three times during the
Easter court-games at Wintanceaster: at axing, at mock-spears, and
again at archery, upon which skill the foreigners prided themselves.
Entirely unaware of the agonies my brother had endured before, during
and after these contests in order to claim his wins, De Comines sulked
and wallowed in ill humor all the rest of the festivities. I would never
have deigned take note of him, but that I heard him make a remark
which chilled me. In a crowd of drunken cronies, unaware that I stood
behind him in a circle of my own men, he complained that Edwin must
have been a party to witchcraft, for 'twas unnatural for a man with a
crushed chest and ruined belly, scarred by healed-over death wounds,
and marred by fits, to be so sure with a battle-axe.

The accusation of magick-dabbling was horrendous enough, but the
fact that my brother's woundings were spoken of openly in the king's

household infuriated me. There was only one man in all the world who could have told of them.

Leaving Heard Ulf's son and the Bearn staring after me in astonishment, I strode off angrily to find Fulke d'Aubermont, but the moment was not propitious. The Norman, resplendent in a French-style court dress of dark forest green, was deep in converse with the king and his lady. Though he turned a sullen gaze periodically to Edwin and Adeliza, who spoke and laughed softly at the far end of the same table, I was unable to catch his eye. At length, biting back the urge to call out his name and make him face my wrath, I picked Siward Bearn's tall frame out of the crowd and signaled him to follow me. In the courtyard, we sat on wide slabs of cold stone. I took the huge cup of warm mead he offered me, and drank from it greedily.

My cousin had suffered an exhausting season since last we met, full of winter-travel and worry. He had gathered Briana and the child from the far north and lodged them in Eorforwic, just as I had bidden him. In the coldest part of the new year he had ridden to Ceaster, where he found Aldgyth's little Nesta ailing. The child's being his great favorite, he stayed to help nurse her and care for young Wulf and Harold. Then, feeling the ravages of the inflammation himself, he had made a slow journey back, stopping in the household of our kinsman Brihtric, one-armed and crippled since Fulford, and at many of his own holdings in the Diera, to ensure their well-being. He had wanted to visit Grandmother Godiva at Couventrie, but she had refused to see him. She was growing old and bitter now, and blamed him in part for the intrigues that caused her beloved son to die an outlaw.

'Twas an argument he thought they had resolved in the autumn, when he carried her the news of Oswulf's murder, but she had brooded on it much in her loneliness and reclosed her heart. This was misery enough for him, but what is worse, he returned to his house to find Lady Gythrun, his wedded wife, accused openly of fornication by the city churchmen, and in his rage he had beaten and choked her, then thrown her bodily out in the snow with but a single leathern bag of belongings, none of them precious. He regretted it now, and was doing a penance, because he knew such a woman could have no sinless means of survival. All her family lived in the Dane Mark and, as he had dolefully admitted, she was totally unfit for a nunnery. I laughed when he said it, but then I was sorry. She was extremely well-formed and fair of face, and he had been much smitten with her in the beginning.

I had just made up my mind not to bother the Bearn with the irksome business of d'Aubermont's indiscretion, when he brought the subject up himself. "The man de Comines is an ass!" he said, half to himself. "How think you he came to know of Edwin's hacking?"

I took another draught of the mead and handed the cup back to him, shrugging.

"Even our avunculus has not seen the scars, so far as I know—" he began, but I cut him off.

"William Malet would not dishonor our house by telling it, even if he knew." I said it adamantly, sure of myself. Then I told him how my brother had needed nursing and the two-faced Norman had seen him in his anguish. "What is worse," I managed to add at last, in a low and morose tone, "d'Aubermont witnessed him in some awful seizure."

My cousin's grey eyes narrowed, and I could see their gleam even in the fast lowering darkness. I had to tell him how it came about. When I finished, he stood abruptly and walked some few steps away. "Fulke d'Aubermont sat to table with me in Eorforwic," he said, as I downed the last of the mead and wiped my mouth. "He asked our avunculus if he thought it not strange that two of his sisters had suffered from fevered minds—your mother and mine, he meant, though he named them not. He asked it loud enough for half the table to hear. Even Lady Briana who was standing near us was surprised by it."

I made a helpless gesture. "People know of it, I trow," I said carelessly, picking up a stone and throwing it. "Seems 'tis our house alone that pretends it differently."

"He asked if such a poison could be passed unto the offspring."

I spat and spoke another cold oath; the mead had helped to fire me.

"I thought 'twas just a tense passing moment," the Bearn said mournfully. "I gave not much heed to it." He scrutinized the empty cup as if looking for one drop more.

Standing, I turned my face into the brisk spring dusk-wind, letting it whip my long hair to frenzy and enjoying the feel of it. 'Twas not so much like the northern wind as I would have liked, but it refreshed me. I would deal with d'Aubermont at my earliest opportunity, I resolved. The man needed a leveling. I motioned my cousin to follow, and we made our way back into the hall, heading immediately in unspoken agreement for the mead barrels lined along the hearth. Heard Ulf's son joined us there, somewhat more untrammeled than usual but not entirely happy looking. He had not enjoyed gatherings in the king's hall since Gamel-Beorn the Biter's ignominious expulsion. The Bearn and I, as noble chiefs, were expected to frequent the king's high table which left him often companionless in a room full of bullying Normans, who knew exactly how far they could prod an Anglishman without bringing William's attention and displeasure upon themselves. In truth, I would have been happy to retire to some far corner with these two closest of my friends, but out of the corner of my eye I saw the king's lady, and his daughters and youngsters, preparing to take their leave. 'Twould have a been a rudeness not to have made gallantries so, promising our comrade a hasty return, the Bearn and I made our way up to the table, balancing cups filled precariously near to overflowing.

Ladies Agatha and Adeliza, twin-like in their dark prettiness, giggled at our approach. Edwin, merry and relaxed, said something about searching the rush-strewn floor for a tress-comb. With some disapprobation, I realized that the wind must have tangled me dreadfully. D'Aubermont, with mocking courtesy, said he fain would braid his hair the way the ladies did, if it hung to his elbows and knotted into his golden earrings.

He was in good humor and seemed somewhat taken aback when Siward Bearn and I both shot him a look of unswerving coldness, which no one else seemed to notice. Lady Mathilda, small and lovely as ever, told us in a mother-like fashion to put down our goblets lest we spoil our court clothes, and the other ladies giggled more. This time I blushed. Grabbing my cup, Edwin took a swallow of it himself. "Best I would help you drain this, brother," he said with admirable smoothness. "I meant to help myself to some, but I have been too much distracted."

Blushing herself, Adeliza raised a finger as if to scold him for his boldness. Her mother and father laughed fondly. I did not look at Fulke, but I instinctively knew he was not smiling. Then Lady Mathilda complimented Siward Bearn's costly dalmatic of gold-sewn linen. "Mayhap you will wear it on the fortnight when I am crowned cwene," she said, with a pert smile, but my cousin shook his own tousled locks.

"I will wear something far the more fair for your special day, my lady," he said in a courtly way, not much like his usual manner of speaking. The princesses delighted in it, and I could tell he thought they were worth impressing. Fulke d'Aubermont cleared his throat.

"Perhaps my lord will allow me to escort his ladies to their destination." He spoke it as a statement, not a question. William nodded his head. We made a short, courteous bow and I saw Lady Adeliza sweep her fingers lightly over Edwin's sleeve, lingering on his wrist till he grasped her hand affectionately for a split second. The king pretended not to notice, and I was glad the other Norman had not seen it. When they were gone, we took seats and talked a small while, mostly about plans for the upcoming coronation. Then William rose, and placing his hand on Edwin's shoulder in fatherly fashion, excused himself and went to another table to converse with some of his countrymen.

My brother drew a deep breath when William was gone, and leant across the table to us. "I am fired and in love!" he said earnestly, in a low voice so that those at the other end of the table would not hear. We burst into laughter.

"Think you 'tis a great secret?" my cousin asked when we had finished. "Most the whole country knows of it, I trow—Anglish and Norman alike!"

My brother gave a half smile and looked away. Edwin was looking very fair. He had won the admiration of even the most prejudiced of the Normans by his strength and comeliness during the season's festivities and, because he was obviously a great favorite of the king's, many of them courted him with attention and flatteries which swiftly rebuilt the confidence that had bled out of him after Gate Fulford. The grip of love became him, too; everyone seemed to delight in the passionate attachment that had sprung genuinely between two such well-favored and noble-blooded creatures.

Almost everyone. I glanced instinctively to the other table where Fulke d'Aubermont had rejoined his foreign friends, Gilbert Rouquin and Robert de Comines amongst them. The king was gone now, and those at the table huddled together as if immersed in important decision making—lost, no doubt, in complicated plotting and planning for their own futures. I scarce could believe the man had been my friend. Worse, the man called himself my friend even yet and boasted to all that he had been our comrade ever since childhood. I took a hard swallow. Edwin interrupted my thoughts.

"Our friend Fulke has become a hopeless fawner, think you not, brother?" he asked, scrutinizing me as if to see whether or not he had read my thought correctly.

Smiling grimly, I raised my cup in the Danish fashion and spoke a salute. "To all the hopeless fawners of the kingdom!" said I stiffly, glad William Malet had retired early and could not chastise me for my sarcasm. Both my kinsmen agreed and raised their mead.

"Drink!" we cried all together, then drained our cups in a single tilt and brought them down. We were laughing and dizzy. I pushed myself away from the table after that and went to find Heard Ulf's son. The two of us drank away the rest of the night well enough that I do not remember it.

CHAPTER FORTY-SIX

In this year, the young noblemen, Edwin and Morcar, sons of Earl Ælfgar, rebelled, and many others joined them, so that the realm was violently disturbed by their fierce insurrection. . . . For King William had promised to give Edwin his daughter in marriage, but afterwards, listening to the dishonest counsel of his envious and greedy Norman retainers, he withheld the maiden from the noble youth who desired her so greatly and had waited so long for her. At length, he grew angry and he and his brother were driven to rebellion, and a great number of the English and Welsh raised arms with them.

—Orderic Vitalis
Book IV, Chapter IV

June 1068
Uncle Leofric once told me that no good would come my way until I had an earnest craving for heaven but that no real harm would come, either, until I had the true desire to see another man in hell. I was boyish when he said it and could not imagine wishing the eternal punishment on anyone. The day came though, in the summer of my twenty-second year, that I did. Even worse, I voiced the thought out loud, and the man I wished to hell was none other than King William. I said it to his very face, and in front of his kinswomen.

'Twas on the Feast of St. Petronella, a few weeks after Whit Sunday and the glittering coronation ceremony that had made pretty, visibly pregnant Mathilda the cwene of Angland. I could not have foreseen that things would come to that, for we had waxed strong in friendship with the king in the days since Easter-tide. He rode with us daily, in part to personally oversee Edwin's courtship of his well-prized daughter, but in larger part to have time to council and confide in us away from the bigotries of his own men. We hunted together and sat daily at his table, and when the sons of Carr arrived in his city just in time for the crowning, he showed Edwin the respect of lodging them in his house there, which thing he had refused to do before.

Most of the men bound for the North Humbria, Siward Bearn and Heard Ulf's son amongst them, had left the very day after the Whitsun Feast, anxious to be about the business of the earldom after their long lingering through Easter and Rogation-tide. The king's party, though, had not taken leave till that very morn, just after the mass. Aside from my avunculus, there were none in the group whose absence would ache me, and I was especially glad to see the last of d'Aubermont. I had managed to tolerate him, but with little warmth and barely any converse. Whether he knew the reason for my coldness or even noted it, I cannot say.

They had been gone but a little while when a priest came to fetch me. The king had need to see me, he said, and my brother also. Edwin, though, had gone field hunting with the Welshmen, who had come back to Wintanceaster with us after the coronation. So, buckling on some ornaments, I made my way to William's chamber while the priest scurried for someone to send into the king's wood after the hunters. From the moment I entered the day-bright chamber, I knew something was amiss, but the king seemed wroth to speak it till my brother came.

The cwene was in there with him, and she smiled and made small talk as she was always wont to do with me. Was I pleased with the meals as she ordered them, she asked, and did the dove-cote look promising for the autumn? Had I been to the sea-coast lately with any party, and did I note the ships being readied for Normandy?

I answered I had not ridden the sea-roads since my men took leave in the Whitsuntide. Pacing, his big, broad shoulders bent, William cleared his throat.

"I am sending my children back to Normandy," he said shortly. Seeing I did not comprehend his meaning, he added, "all of them."

"Lady Adeliza—" I began, but William stopped me with a shake of the head.

"These are troubled times, Earl Morcar," he said gravely. "I have no sense of security when my children wander amongst strangers and break bread with men whose tongue they cannot speak." He turned his back to me and stared out the unshuttered window, seemingly intent on something in the courtyard below. I sat down heavily on a carven bench, staring questioningly at the cwene. She lowered her gaze so as not to meet mine.

"When you are a wedded man, Earl Morcar, and have children of your own, you will feel the urge to bestead them." She placed a hand on her swollen belly. Her voice was mild and earnest, but she looked away. I was confused.

"What think you," the king asked suddenly, spinning to face me, dark eyes glinting, "that God appreciates more a man who bends to His will, or who tries to bribe His providence?"

I shrugged, bewildered, and he continued. "I prayed fervently before I made war on your so-called king, Harold Godwine's son. God granted me the victory, and now I am minded to pay Him as I swore I would."

I stood so that I could face him. "'Tis best you tell me what it is that weighs on you," I told him, with a sudden sinking feeling. For some reason I remembered the night my father struggled to tell us he had sworn us away as hostages to the Welsh king, though I know not why I thought of it.

"I have promised Lady Adeliza to a nunnery," he said in a voice scarce more than a whisper. Shaking, I bade him repeat himself. He did.

"What is it minds you of this promise now, when you have as much as made her hand-fast to my brother in this last year?" My voice quivered with anger, but before the other man could answer a knock came at the door and, knowing it was Edwin, we stilled ourselves.

He was handsome in hunt clothes of polished kidskin, smiling, unsuspecting of the treachery about to be played him. Still, the emotion in the air was heavy enough to make him question it, and a frown darkened his features as he looked from one to the other of us. "All is well, or not?" he asked simply, and I bit my lip, curious as to how William would approach it with him.

In fact, he recapped all the same foolishness he had spoken to me, but when he got to the part about having promised his daughter to a nunnery, my brother leant all at once against the solid door and stared at him accusingly. Then, just as I had asked it, but in a voice even more fired, he demanded to know what had reminded the king so very suddenly of his promise.

William's eyes narrowed. "It came to me during the holy season," he said shortly.

I threw my head back and laughed. "No doubt it came to you from the lips of your good man d'Aubermont," I cried belligerently. The king stiffened. I tried to hold my tongue but I could not. "No doubt it came in the form of a counting of certain bruises and a woeful tale of nursing that a jealous man brought unto your ear!"

The king moved forward menacingly, spurred to furious anger himself. "I would have spared you the dishonor of saying it, Ælfgar's son," he hissed at me, "but it came to my mind in a certain room of a certain estate in Le Havre, where a certain lady—"

Snarling, Edwin moved forward as if to grab him, but Lady Mathilda, spry and defiant, jumped between them. "Still yourselves all!" she commanded imperiously. "We will not make of this a dissension that draws either blood or rancor." The two men drew apart as if the tiny woman had the power to stop them. William paced to the window and turned his back again, and Edwin, as if fast grown weak, sat down suddenly on the bolstered pallet, clenching and unclenching his fists.

"What makes you do this thing?" he asked in a voice plaintive and low. "And what says Lady Adeliza of your bargain with God?"

The king made a growling sound. "It matters not much whatever she thinks," he answered. His voice was cold, but Edwin's was colder.

"I will hear it from her nevertheless," he said with finality. "Else there is no honor in you, and both of us will forever know it."

William's face grew taut and his eyes burned. "Fetch my daughter!" he commanded the lady. When she objected, he slammed his huge fist hard on the carven sash, making all of us jump. Quickly, Mathilda pulled open the heavy door and had disappeared before it groaned shut behind her. We stared at the king in silence all the while she was gone, but he did not flinch under our indignant gazes.

When Mathilda returned, a wan creature followed her. Despite the waxy pallor of her fine complexion, Adeliza looked beautiful indeed in a dress of pearl-grey wool made pretty with black stitching and squared low on the bosom in the Norman style. Her black hair was unbounden, save for a silver fillet, and she trembled, almost imperceptibly, with emotion. My brother, himself quivering with nameless passion, could not pry his eyes from her fair face and form, but she obviously would not let herself look upon him.

His voice shaking, my brother rose and made her a greeting, in stiff, formal French. She looked away. "What wouldst you have of me here, father?" she asked in a hollow whisper. The king put his hands on her tiny shoulders and lifted her face to his. Despite the gruffness of his look, his voice was gentle. "Tell the Anglish what best would suit you," he told her. "Tell them that which your heart of hearts knows to be inspired of God … wisest and—" He fumbled for words and Lady Mathilda coughed uneasily, glancing from one to the other of us nervously.

"—wisest and healthiest," the king finished at last. My brother flinched.

The maiden made no answer, only wrung her hands tight.

His voice grew somewhat more demanding. "Spoke you not to me your desire to take vows? To return to God with gracious service thanks for the gift of healing He has in His wisdom bestowed upon you?" His voice shook when she did not reply. "Said you not you fain would enter a nunnery?"

She pulled away from him angrily, as if strength had just come to her. "Aye, father!" she cried in a voice full of emotion. "I said I fain would commit myself to a nunnery rather than wed any man save Edwin Ælfgar's son!"

Stunned by her boldness, William raised a hand as if to chastise her, but caught himself as she burst into tears and threw herself into my brother's arms. Edwin embraced her protectively, stroking her hair and kissing her brow, but William pulled her roughly away, pushing her down on the bench near the window and holding her forcefully there by the shoulders while she sobbed. As if wrought with remorse, Mathilda sprang to her daughter's side, stooping to hug and comfort her. Unable to calm her, the cwene stood suddenly and approached my brother in a maddened way that made him instinctively back away from her.

"If you loved her, Anglishman, you would not wish to taint her children with the curse of your mother's blood!" she whispered savagely, "nor would you wish upon her wedding with one whose manhood is impaired by battle!"

Choking, but helpless in his rage, my brother let go a tremendous oath, smashing his entire body into the carven door as if he had the strength to ram through it. The lady squealed in terror and in a single motion jumped away, shielding herself behind her husband's towering frame. William, as if amazed that she had said it, raised an arm to further safeguard her, but by then Edwin had spun away and stilled himself. We startled as a raucous knocking broke the sudden silence. Shouting, the king bade his retainers, who had been alerted by my brother's outburst, to disperse themselves, then strode angrily to the door, pulling it open to make sure they had gone. Satisfied, he turned to my brother, who had walked a ways away and collapsed, pale and emotionless, into a huge hide-covered chair.

Looking down on him, William spoke in a cajoling voice. "Best you would know I think you a bold and fair man, Edwin Ælfgar's son, and I will ever love you as a father loves a son, and hold you in great esteem."

My brother grew flushed but said nothing, only gripped tighter yet onto the arms of the chair. The king continued.

"As a nobleman yourself, must be you can see the wisdom of my advisors and councilors."

That is when it escaped me, tumbling out before I could stop it.

"Damn you to hell, Norman," I said low, my voice hoarse and defiant. William gaped open-mouthed. Mathilda gasped, and Adeliza buried her face in her hands. There seemed endless silence as I stood facing him, enveloped by a shaft of bright sunlight which, glittering with dust motes, made the whole scene dream-like. I did not tremble or falter in my gaze.

At length William drew his hardened eyes away from mine and signaled his kinswomen to the door. Adeliza would have reached to touch my brother's hand as she passed him, but her mother prevented it, casting me an icy glare as she came between them. When they had gone, William turned to us once more but looked past us both in an offhand way.

"No other man need know what has passed between us today, I trow," he said, shooting me a cold glance of disapprobation as he said it. He stalked haughtily from the room, letting the door slam with full force after him.

We sat together a long while in the dazzling stillness, but I could not bring myself to look into my brother's face or say anything to interrupt the churning passion of his thoughts.

*   *   *

When we had been children, Hwell had been my favorite of the Welshmen, but now that I was grown it was Ywen, the middle one, whom I admired most. Tallest of the three, and still by far the most bold-mouthed, he had chosen himself Aldgyth's special protector and hardly had left her side since the dark day of Harold's death on Hastings Field. I was particularly happy when he decided to join his brothers for the coronation feasting and, indeed, our gladness at being all five together again after so long a time was a great factor in their staying long as they did. 'Twas waxing onto a month we had been together now. Brooding in the midnight darkness of our chamber on the night of the unfortunate confrontation with the king and his lady, Ywen Carr's son decided it was time for him to leave.

"Lady Aldgyth needs me there to keep her ordered," he said solemnly, wiping his mouth on his sleeve after a huge swallow of ale. "She cannot see to estates and such; her children are her only life." She was living still in Siward Bearn's great sea-side manor in Ceaster with little Nesta, nearing ten now, and the twins Wulf and Harold, strapping toddlers of a year and a half. I had long suspected some bonding attachment between my sister and this handsome Welsh prince, but none of the brothers had ever broached the subject with us, and neither the Bearn, who visited there regularly, nor any of our Ceaster men had seemed to note it. I would not be the one to insinuate it, either, knowing both the man and Aldgyth well enough to feel they would have felt no qualms in telling us if the fact were true.

Nevertheless, the Welshman's devotion to my sister was pronounced, and he obviously adored and doted on her children, standing in the stead of their murdered fathers and loving them almost as his own. I appreciated him most for this, being too far separated by miles and circumstances to fulfill my function as avunculus to them, and knowing full well that the question of their safety would prevent it long as I was bridled to the king as I was now.

I oft-times missed my sister, and I said so that night. Ywen answered that maybe 'twas the carelessness of my childhood that I missed even more, and I was forced to admit I had enjoyed little of peace or contentment since I had come to manhood. He said it was the same with him; though things were not so much changed yet in Mercia and the Humberland as they were here, the threat was ever there that they would be.

Edwin had been numbing himself with drink since the noon-tide. Still in his hunting garb, he sat sullen and silent in a corner of the dark room. From the courtyard came sounds of clatter and commotion; by moon's beam and torch light, men were making ready the fleet that would carry his lady away at dawn. Daffydd Carr's son's poetic meanderings had done little to soothe him, but when Ywen announced his intention of leaving in the morning, my brother stood up, shaky but determined, and announced we would all go.

"It disgusts me that ever I believed he had power to hold me here," he declared hotly, "and I have had enough of his stinking councils to last me a lifetime!"

At first, it was just a tempting thought to us, but the more we drank, the more seriously we considered it. The household, having grown familiar and easy with us, was in no wise as watchful as once they had been, and on the morrow, the king's men and his family would be distracted by the busyness of the leave taking. A furious day and night's ride would take us into the aet-Waeringwicum where Siward Bearn held an ancient, stone-built manor, small but well-fortified. 'Twas the very house he had taken when Tostig Godwine's son confiscated his greater holding at Tathaceaster and so we knew it well, and all the lands around it. In fact, it bordered the fields of our own house in Weogornaceaster, where last I had seen my father alive, separated from that place only by the gloom of the forest Eardene. Even were the king were to narrow all the possibilities and conclude we had headed there, 'twould take him a far longer journey than ours. We knew our way through the vast Hwicca Wood and over the Temes; he would have to skirt them both and travel through much country loyal to us, so that we would surely be aware of his approach.

So, before the crack of dawn, still in the rumpled clothes we had worn all the day and night through, we made as if to go grouse-rousing before the mass. The men in the stables, knowing us as they did and trusting us, thought naught of it, and even jested with us a while, seeing we were highly aled and in very merry spirits. No doubt they would have been more cautious had they known what had happened in the king's chamber the day before, but true to his word, William had kept it strictly between him and us.

Once mounted, we rode off in the direction of the king's wood, then turned and headed out to the long grasses of the Searoburg Way. We had hidden two war pieces there earlier in the darkness: a battle-axe and a broad sword. They would have attracted attention in the king's barn, but we could not bear to leave them. Both had been Father's.

It was not a comfortable ride and took somewhat longer than we had anticipated. After some hours in the saddle, the happiness of the drink wore off, leaving the familiar head-pain. Never had I wished harder for hare-water than that day, and I do not recall much of the desperate flight with clarity, nor want to.

Nevertheless, my discomfort was as nothing compared to my brother's. Such hard movement still caused agony in the bones and inner parts that had been injured, and when he climbed from the saddle he was stiff in the limbs for many days afterwards.

Our welcome was a press of exhilarating confusion, and despite our great fatigue we counciled many hours with the Mercians who received us there, till a plan of sorts could be formulated. Men were dispatched straight-away to those nearest points from which we could expect the most aid: to Weogornaceaster, to Lindcylene, to Liccidfeld, where the priests kept a small armory in the church, and to nearby Couventrie where my grandmother still kept household. The news was sent due west, into the Cymrian reaches beyond the Hereford Shire, where many Welshmen remained loyal to the brotherhood made fast by Gruffydd and my father. Daffydd Carr's son wanted to lead the party there himself, for he had much influence in those parts, as he did all along the borders. He was much too wasted from the intensity of our travel, though, and I talked him out of it. In likewise, we had almost to forcefully restrain his brother Ywen from dashing himself to Ceaster. He feared that William, knowing we had fled with the Welshmen, would assume that was our destination, and go there first to make his warfare. Both Edwin and I argued with him.

"Can be no secret that when he marches, he will be marching in a rage," Ywen said, his dark eyes glazed with exhaustion and his voice somber. "If he put harm on my lady's children, I think she could not bear the pain of it. 'Tis in a woman's blood only to bear so much of it before breaking, and she has seen enough sorrow already!"

It chilled me to hear it said, knowing well as I did how broken my mother had been by sadnesses. My brother looked at me as if sharing the thought. "Best we should make it known where we are, then," he mused thoughtfully, "the king will know of it soon enough!"

So we decreed that it be cried from town to town: the Earl of Mercia and the Earl of the North Humbria were housed in the aet-Waering-wicum, and invited Welshmen and Anglishmen everywhere to arm themselves and join them. Then we knew we had but little time before the facing, and that the king would be all the more fired for our bold-ness in proclaiming against him, so we had much need for haste.

Morning next, my brother and I rode fast to Couventrie with a well-armed party. Grandmother Godiva, looking smaller than ever and faded with age, greeted us well and affectionately, but she was wroth that we had made a quarrel with the king and meant not to grant our petition for arms and foodstuffs. Edwin grew livid with anger, and she scolded him. "You are too like your unfortunate father in that you feel it a shame to bend your knee to another man!"

"'Tis not the argument we have!" my brother cried, exasperated. "You cannot know, grandmother! You have not lived anext the man and watched him strip the most inalienable of powers away from your coun-trymen, making and unmaking them to any degree he chooses!"

"He is your king," she said levelly.

Edwin threw his hands up, perplexed and furious. "How is't you can say that? He has robbed the crown off the very brow of your grand-daughter's murdered husband!"

Lady Godiva laughed and shook her head with tried patience. "You begrudged Harold the crown, too, my grandson," she said softly, as if it proved a point. "My son, your father, died to prevent his wearing it!"

Edwin spat, and I broke in swiftly, before he had time to speak some-thing unforgivable. "Seems you do not understand the essence even of our father's quarrel, Grandmother," I said gently, "much less that of ours. 'Tis not as it was in Grandfather's day, when there were blooded kings with rights, and one house respected another."

"You fool yourself if you think it really ever was that way, little Morcar." I could not help smiling when she called me that. "I have lived under Danish kings and Anglish kings and Anglish kings made Norman by their exiles. Not a one was less or more a king than another, and when one wore the crown, all of Anglish Britain united behind him, the earls especially."

I started to say something, but she went on, ignoring me. "True kingship, as you desire it, died with good King Edward, last of Alfred's blood. God made it our duty, though, to choose another, and support him for the good of the land."

"You talk drivel, lady!" Edwin snapped, but he caught himself and added in a gentler tone, "No one chose Harold; no one chose William."

"Even so, God has a wisdom and He works things so that His will is done," she said with finality. "William is king."

"William is a two-faced foreign bastard!" my brother snarled, and Lady Godiva's small figure jerked backwards with surprise at the sound of his oath.

"Seems you have not yet outgrown the brattiness of your boyhood!" she whispered accusingly. "And not even the deaths of your father and kinsmen have mellowed you towards wanting a portion of peace!"

"Nay," he said firmly, fingering the cover of the hand-tooled psalter that lay on her chamber table. "I will not take peace at the expense it is offered—the dissolving of our very house and the loss of an identity that generations of our kinfolk have lived and died for. You are old, grandmother, and you no longer envisage the future: my sons and Morcar's and Aldgyth's."

The lady turned away. Instinctively, I came behind her and hugged her frail bent shoulders. "We cannot bow to a man who means to destroy us!" I told her earnestly. She moaned.

"How oft I heard your father say words like that!" she whimpered. "Yet, in the end, he was destroyed."

"He died for all of us," I said adamantly.

"My heart tells me that he did," she answered mournfully. "Yet so at odds was he always with other men, that oft I have wondered whether 'twere just a portion of his blood that was tainted in some way, that he could not know peace and pleasure."

"He knew peace and pleasure, lady," Edwin insisted, "and he knew that they were as nothing compared to honor."

After that, she did not say anything for a long while, and Edwin, fast growing impatient, began to pace back and forth the length of her pretty chamber. It smelled all of June roses, which twined the stone casements and crept in at the sill, but we were hardly of a mind to enjoy it, so pressed for time we were.

"Mean you to help us or not?" I asked her finally, and, to our great disappointment, she shook her head.

"I could not condone it," she avowed huskily. "'Twould seem as sin to me."

Moving past her to the window, my brother gazed out to where our men, unmounted now but still in arms, lounged in the shade of the fieldstone fence and oaks. "We have strength to take those things we need, grandmother," he said, hoarse and low. "Do not tempt me to use it."

"I could not condone it," she said again, looking into my eyes, as Edwin still looked away. "I am old and weak, though," she added in a meaningful voice, wringing and unwringing translucent, wrinkled hands. "I have not enough force to stop you."

Edwin spun round and looked at her questioningly. "What mean you?" he demanded. "That you would not put your men to guard things, and so make us wreak havoc on them?" She lived on a peaceful, countryside estate; her retainers were old men who had served Grandfather Leofric in his prime, and were now well past the stage of war-usefulness. Of those younger and better equipped to fight, most had already joined themselves to our cause. The household was in truth defenseless.

The lady made no answer, though, and it was clear she would in no way commit herself. Of a sudden, I understood why. Powerless as she was now, she must at any cost appear blameless to the king, else all she knew of comfort would be robbed from her. Realizing her intent at the same instant I did, Edwin leapt to her side, holding both her shoulders and bending to kiss her, quickly, fondly, on the lips. "When I was a boy, grandmother," he said in a small voice, suddenly tender, "I loved you more than all in the world, and I would weep when they took me from you!"

"I remember," she answered, through a mist of fast-welling tears. Edwin had thrown his famous, frenzied tantrum in this very chamber the morning we left for the East Anglia. No doubt the lady was remembering that, as I was. Edwin squeezed her one time more, then dashed to the casement.

"Rip into the storehouse," he commanded in a gruff, loud voice, "take any grain that is bundled and any cheeses or meats you find hanging!"

The men rose to their feet at once, shocked to silence. They stared up at him disbelievingly.

"Be swift, by God!" he cried louder. "Search out arms in the hold of the stable. Swords are there, cased in wood boxes anext the feed closets. Find lances, axes, and short shields. Move fast!"

The men scattered, shouting amongst themselves, still confounded.

"The monk's-box!" Grandmother whispered, and my brother, casting me a sideways glance of wonder, bit his lip a second, then hollered to the men once more.

"Find a way into the chapel," he shouted hoarsely. "Gather up the gold box in the sacristy! Trample not, and do not touch the altar; elsewise strip it!"

He was silhouetted in the paneless casement, a bold commanding figure. In the way he looked and sounded, not a thing was there that was not alike my father. My grandmother, watching him, trembled. I kissed her hastily on the cheek as I fled from the room to oversee the rape of her homestead, but at the doorway I paused and, looking back, saw her fall to her knees and cross herself. As my brother and I made our way furiously down the narrow stone stairway, the lady was praying for us, and we knew it.

CHAPTER FORTY-SEVEN

Then Edwin and Morcar and their men weighed
carefully the double-natured battle that was
presented to them, and by not agreeing to it, the
scales were turned from war to peace. . . .

—Orderic Vitalis
Book IV, Chapter IV

A fortnight later, we stood on the stone battlements of my cousin's
house, watching the king's army, far, far in the distance as they finally
made their approach. It had seemed an interminably long and worrisome time to us, expecting as we had an immediate confrontation. In
the mean while, our forces had waxed strong as men came from all the
local shires, camping in the leas till they were crowded, then spreading
into the planted fields. Hereward had come to us on the tenth day, with
but five well-armed men; William had confounded us with his unpre-
dictability, and not knowing where or when he meant to strike, the
Wake had not dared to leave the Lindcylene Shire undefended. As for
the Bearn, we could not hope to see him, though we assumed the news
had reached him by now. Along with Heard Ulf's son and the Biter, he
was responsible for the safe-keeping of Eorforwic, a city crucial to any
strategy we might develop. He would be sure not to mellow our strength
there, no matter how sorely he desired to join us. William already had a
small but formidable outpost there, under the auspices of William Malet
and Fulke d'Aubermont, and 'twas not unlikely to suppose he would sail
men up the coast to reinforce it. We had talked of this possibility and
many more, spending harried days and sleepless nights trying to out-
guess the Norman. Even now, bracing for the collision, we did not know
what to expect.

Within a very short time, a messenger had come to us and,
dispatching the Wake and the Welshmen to tend the troops, my brother
and I received him personally, letting him climb to us on the ramparts.

"He says he will be at the foot of the hill in an hour's time, no more," was the message he gave us. We knew him, the son of old Roger de Beaumont who had hosted us in Normandy, but he gave no sign of friendliness or acknowledgment. He was a black-haired string of a man, but we knew he could hunt and game well, and William had boasted of his accomplishments on the battlefield.

"Is that his only word?" Edwin asked skeptically, made wary as I was by the man's too-formal manner, for he had been a friend to us before.

"Nay, surely 'tis not his only word," the man replied. Then, loosening somewhat, he added grimly, "Much of what he has said these past days you would not want to hear, my lords. But this he bids me stress to you most of all: that he desires a conciliation above all things, and he will go to any length to avoid crashing arms with you."

"A strange sentiment, surely!" Edwin mused, staring hard into de Beaumont's eyes. "And one I can scarce put faith in."

"The Duke says he counts upon your loyalty and intends to make right with you a certain vexation. He says you both will know what he means. You are forthright to forgive him a grave misunderstanding, is what he told me."

My brother laughed, gazing to the line of men crested against the distant horizon. "I will forgive him with the edge of my war-axe," he whispered low, in a voice strangely deadened and hard.

"He will not fight you," the other replied firmly.

"He will fight me!"

"He will not fight as you want him to. Depend on it!"

"What is his plan then?" I broke in, anxious to be finished. "How means he to settle this thing?"

"He bids you meet him in an hour's time—down there." He gestured haltingly to the ridge bottom where field met craggy hill. "He says he will bring but two persons with him, unarmed, and he bids you do likewise."

"And if we cannot come to an agreement?" My tone was hard as I asked it.

"If he cannot convince you, he will ride back and ready his men. You can well imagine what will follow, I trow!"

"I can imagine it," I replied levelly, "but no doubt I imagine it differently than you do."

De Beaumont's voice grew hard. "I have no quarrel with you, Anglishman, but that you have affronted the man who is my king. Seems to me 'tis a situation easily enough righted, if you have the strength in you to admit—"

Edwin cut him off with a growl and a wave of the hand. "If we have no argument, as you say, be careful not to make one. Ride back to the man and tell him we will meet with him as he wishes, but we are not in conciliatory mood."

"Perhaps you will be more—" the man began, but my brother stopped him once more.

"I have no desire to be goaded, Norman," he said wearily. "I have been goaded too well already!"

Respecting his wishes, the man said a short fare-well, then descended the steep stone ladder. One of our men led him out, and as we watched down on him, he tossed us a gesture—half salute, half friendly wave. Both of us gazed after him as he galloped through the rippling grasses.

"How is it these foreigners can crave friendship," Edwin asked me wonderingly, "at the very instant they are making war on us?"

"I know not," I shrugged. "They are ever a perplexion. I am hard pressed to think what terms he means to offer us."

"And I am hard pressed to determine whether or not to trust him when he names them." He stooped to pick up a colorless butterfly with a torn wing. "I am taking the Wake," he declared, throwing the creature over the battlement and watching it fly unsteadily away. "And you?"

"Ywen Carr's son," I answered unfalteringly, but later, when we were making ourselves ready to mount, I realized I would sorely miss having a North Humbrian by my side. Much as I loved the Welshmen, and I loved them all like blood kin, I would have chosen one of my earl's men, had there been any there to back me.

My feelings of disappointment were swiftly forgotten, though, as a surge of disquiet tensed through my body. I cannot say exactly when it started, but a sudden fear took hold of me as we sat mounted at the bottom the sloping incline which raised Siward Bearn's manor above the meadow. Two horses and only two, dark and dim in the late noon distance, were picking a tedious way over the blooming lea, seeming to stretch the moment infinitely onward. The longer it took, the more apprehensive I became. The sun seemed swallowed by the wicked Eardene to the west, and the meadows, grown shadowy in shades of purple and iridescent blue, seemed to give off a haze of light all their own, dream-like and despondent despite the clearness of the day. I could not draw my eyes away from the riders. William had specifically told us he would bring two others; there should have been three horses. Even as I puzzled over it the far-away specks came more into focus and I heard Ywen Carr's son's sharp gasp.

He said something unforgivable about the king in Welsh. Then I looked harder, and my heart beat faster as the riders came more clearly into view. One was unmistakably the burly figure of the king. There was a child—a tiny, fair-haired child—outlined against his dark mantle. Anext him, my sister Aldgyth rode. As she drew nearer I could sense her fear and sorrow.

Soon as he knew he could be clearly heard, William made us a formal greeting. Coming closer, his voice took on a harsher tone. "Think you back some ways, sons of Ælfgar," he directed us, staring fast from one to the other. "You made an oath to me at Beorh Hamstede, and another at Berecingas. Now you look upon but two of a hundred and fifty I hold hostage against those oaths, her other childlings among them."

Edwin cursed, but William smiled. "You must needs know I would not raise an arm against you," he said, with an almost indiscernible sneer. "I would not sully our sworn allegiance with unnecessary blood!"

Edwin moved forward to my sister's side, reaching to touch her, and she grasped his hand gratefully, as if she craved the strength he had to offer. As for me, I could not take my eyes off the boy-child. He had the definite look of Harold Godwine's son. It was strange to think that, had that man lived, the tiny boy might have been king someday—a king born of my father's blood. Without even knowing why, I crossed myself. Aldgyth, as if reading my thought, burst into tears. Soon as she did so, the babe cried, too, and Ywen Carr's son, with a cry of consternation, leapt from his saddle and grabbed for the boy as if to comfort him. With a menacing frown of disapproval the king held all the harder, lifting the tiny thing higher, out of the other man's reach. The Welshman swore again, but William, not understanding him, only smiled with satisfaction as my friend moved dejectedly back to his horse. Then the Wake, who had been silent all this time, spoke loud, and his voice was like frosted iron.

"'Tis a mockery," he said boldly, "that one such as you who shrinks in fear from honest confrontation, and who uses women and babes for his weapons, should call himself king in a land where only the boldest have ever worn the crown."

William's eyes narrowed. "You still oppose me, Mercian?"

"I will oppose you all your life through, and you will die feeling the strength of my opposition."

For just a moment, the king shifted uncomfortably. Then he answered in a level tone. "Perhaps this day you will become thankful for what you once called my 'heathen' way of making war," he said, using a Flemish dialect he knew Hereward understood well. "No doubt it has saved these two men you serve from a useless slaughter and restored them to their place of dignity in England."

Hereward spat. "There is no dignity for a man chained to the side of a coward like you!"

William laughed. "Here is an irony!" he cried in mock merriment, looking from my brother to me. "The Mercian pretends concern for you, yet he begrudges that I have found a bloodless way of settling a score that was of little account and despises that I do not intend to punish you or make humbling recriminations!"

"We have not come to terms yet." My brother said coldly. "Do not pretend we have agreed to submit."

"But you will submit!" William barked angrily. "Because I understand enough of your honor to know you will not want the blood of your sister and her innocent babes on your hands!"

"Nor you will, I trow," replied Edwin, staring hard into William's eyes.

"Aye. What you say is the truth, Ælfgar's son," the king said seriously. "I would be wroth to carry it out. You misjudge me, though, if you think I would not do it for the sake of my kingdom. Mayhap you will think me cold-blooded when you hear that, but 'tis no worse, it seems to me, than growing hot-headed in an argument, then staking the life's blood of thousands of men to avenge a wounded pride!"

Edwin raised a hand as if to silence him. "I am not here to take a scolding from you," he cried, impatiently. "Tell me your terms!"

"You know well enough my terms," William answered, glancing to Aldgyth as if to remind us of her presence. "I am not a vindictive man, but I will not risk the unrest of the entire kingdom because you took too seriously some words that were said in a bad temper by a man who has shown you every respect of station in the past. The only condition I name is this: You will make good your quarrel with me before your countrymen, so that they will once again see you ride with me, and dine with me, and council with me in good faith and friendship. In return, all your former privileges will be restored. Things will be as they were before your leave-taking. And these two, and the others my men stand guard over back there, will remain unharmed."

Here he gestured to the distance from whence he had ridden, and we could see the crowd of people standing in the midst of king's men on horseback. Nesta and little Harold, we knew, were among them.

"You may ride back there and restore them to freedom with your own voice," he added, as if it were some fine incentive. "They will thank you heartily, and so will many men within your walls there who know them well, I am sure."

I was grown suddenly cold and weak with the realization we were helpless to fight him. "What of our men?" I asked, my voice shaking against all my will to hold it steady.

He glared a moment at the Wake, but finally said all would be left to return to their homesteads without so much as a counting of them or a word of reprisal.

"And I promise you this too, Earl Edwin," he added, his voice relaxing a bit, "we will discuss again that matter which first drove you to this distemper. Mayhap we shall come to a conclusion somewhat easier for you to bear. God knows I did not think the feelings ran so deep that you would risk all to spite my one bout of fatherly over-caution!"

My brother had stiffened at those words; then he leant far back in the saddle, considering all the king had said and pretending that a decision was still to be made, though our first glimpse of Aldgyth had assured the outcome and we all knew it. After pondering a long time, he spoke, saying he cared not much for the king's way of bargaining, but under the conditions he was forced to submit.

"You will ride back to your line," he told William imperiously, "so that our men can disperse without hindrance from yours." He faltered a fraction. "Then we will do what you would have us do, though God knows why you think you will gain the love of the Anglish people by showing us like prizes at your side!"

Squinting, William gazed west into the fast lowing sun and unconsciously tousled the hair of the little boy he held, an affectionate gesture without a moment's thought. "You read me wrong," he murmured, "and that will ever be a problem between us. I want them to see that I rely on your council and friendship."

"They will not be as easily fooled as that!" I snapped.

The king shrugged and his face grew momentarily sad. "Believe what you want," he said resignedly. "Why is't so hard for you to believe I would rather conciliate than conquer? You misread my motives and dote on the anger it causes you; you imagine I have made all manner of plans for your undoing, when in fact, I would fain count you chief of all my men—great earls by a hereditary right that I would be foolish to deny or despise. Nothing would please me more than your voice and support in the governing of this kingdom. Yet you persist in believing my aim is only to unseat you and make you powerless!" He looked away, biting his lip, as if he feared he had said too much. My brother sighed wearily, then turned to Hereward.

"How long think you it will take to disperse all these men?"

"Half a day," the Wake replied casually. "Else the night, as it has grown so late already."

Edwin nodded and faced the king. "We will meet with you at noontime, then." Gritting his teeth against the discomfort it caused him, he slid from his saddle and walked close to my sister, whispering some things as she bent to him which we could not hear. He grasped her hand tightly a moment as he pulled away.

"The lady will not sleep in the field," he told William staunchly, "nor the babe. Ride them to my grandmother's house at Couventrie and board them there till my men have your leave to see them back to Ceaster."

A dim smile crossed the Norman's frozen face. "Are you sure she is welcome there?" he asked quizzically. "Mayhap Lady Godiva has had enough of visits from her kinfolk."

"She has naught of a quarrel with my sister," I said, drawing my horse closer, glad that the king believed that Grandmother had defied us. I reached for the child, who had grown timorous when his tears stopped and sat stiffly now, chewing absently on his tiny finger. Without an argument, William handed him to me, and I pressed him close before I passed him to Ywen Carr's son. "Ride with them," I said simply, and he nodded, smiling as the boy embraced him lovingly. With a shrug, William signaled his assent.

"He may travel with the guard I have chosen for them," he said placidly, "and on the morrow when you disband your men, he can help you pick the party that will ride to Ceaster. I will send no men of my own that way, in keeping with our agreement."

He reined his black mount around and started slowly cross-field. "I will see you both tomorrow," he called without looking back. "'Tis a pretty season for riding, and we can advantage ourselves of it by touring all the favored cities of your earldoms. Methinks your loyal countryfolk will be pleased to see their earls after so long a time."

He came to a sudden halt, letting Ywen and my sister pass him. Then he turned round and looked at us, with just the barest hint of a smile. "No doubt they will be happy to see you have made a reconciliation with your king," he added, his voice strangely at one with the summer dusk-wind which murmured across the darkening lea, "and no doubt they will lay their arms down when they see you and sue for my peace."

That was the first we knew that Mercia and all the Humberland had risen in our behalf.

CHAPTER FORTY-EIGHT

*. . . And they petitioned the king's kindness and
obtained it, but only in pretense. For thereupon
the king built Nottingham castle. . . .*

—Orderic Vitalis
Book IV, Chapter IV

I held Aldgyth in my arms a long time when she came on the morrow.
Our men had taken to the road during the night and the dawn hours,
leaving us alone with Hereward and the Welshmen till the king came at
high noon. Acting out of the graciousness of victory, he sent my sister
in to us, so that we might have some time for private fare-wells before
we went our ways. The man was trying his hardest to seem friendly and
conciliatory, but he had dealt us an unforgivable blow. Once he knew
our men had disbanded, he decided little Wulf Harold's son must be kept
hostage against any future indiscretion on our part. So she came to us,
forlorn and weeping and little comforted by the king's promises of
protection for her bright-eyed babe.

"What safer place for him than the laps of his avunculuses?" he had
asked her lightly, as he sent the little one off in a party of his heavily
armed men and nurse-maids hired from my grandmother's estate. He
told her the babe would be waiting for us at his house in Wintanceaster,
and so our return there was assured. I could not do much to comfort her,
and though we all had much to say, for a long time the room was gloomy
and silent except for the sound of her sobs.

In a swift, sudden movement, Hereward broke the silence,
unsheathing his sword and pulling a single, sleek war arrow from Hwell
Carr's son's deerskin sling. "Next time, we had better work on more than
an impulsive thought or drunken plan," he said, setting the arrow on a
stone bench near the hearth. Then, raising his sword high, he brought
it down on the hapless item, again and again, with a stunning clamor
that resounded several long seconds after he had stopped. Placing his

sword on the bench with a woeful look, as if he knew he had done a great disservice to its blade, he lifted a splintered portion of the arrow and held it up like a precious thing, forcing us all to look at it.

"You will all recognize this tiny piece of war-head, I trow?" he said questioningly, looking from one to the other of us, and we nodded. "'Twill be our signal then," he stated, with a satisfied look. "You have no power to plan a defense from inside the king's house, and well he knows it. So we will make the plan from the outside, those of us who are chief of your men. And when all is in readiness, one of these pieces will come to you, and it will tell you to be watching. Once it is in your hand, be on the alert, looking everywhere for more signs. Within the space of a fortnight, someone you trust will be there to fetch you, and you must be ready to move fast—else all will be lost."

"Is it truly grown this desperate?" Aldgyth cried softly, clenching her fists till the knuckles showed white. "What of his promise to reconsider the marriage promise?"

Edwin cut her off with an angry wave. "What of his promise to send you home safely with your youngster!" he growled in an anguished tone. "Methinks there is no such thing as a promise with these foreigners!"

Hereward nodded glumly. "A portion of this arrow will go to Siward Bearn," he said with finality, "and a portion to Heard Ulf's son and to Gamel-Beorn the Biter. One will go to Osbeorn Dolfin's son on his homestead and one to Brother Wulfget at Peterborough."

Even as he said the words, a pulsing surge of loneliness overcame me, as I pictured those good men and many others like them whom I dearly loved, but had not seen in so long a while. I realized with a sudden surety that I had been naught more than a prisoner all these long months since Berecingas. Those men whom I would have had at my side had grown strangers to me, and I was surrounded by men I could scarce abide: the Normans, and Anglishmen like Waltheof and Gospatrick, whom I would never have acknowledged in days past. I swallowed hard and bent down to caress my sister, who was gently sobbing. Still on my knees, I looked up at Ywen Carr's son, who stood behind her, kneading her shoulders as if to ease and protect her. "When a portion of that arrow comes to you," I told him severely, "I want you to drop all other matters and gather this lady, and Nesta and little Harold, and move them with all haste into the Cymry."

His dark eyes shining, the Welshman began to nod his assent, but then, as if he had suddenly remembered he was sworn first to Edwin's service, he flashed my brother a questioning look. Edwin smiled. "Aye, Ywen Carr's son," he spoke low. "That is the charge I give you, and your brothers also!"

With a gruff cry of protest, Daffydd was on his feet, drawing his stocky frame erect and shooting my brother a look of pure indignation. "I will fight anext you, my lord!" he said. "I am not a man born to be a nurse-maid!"

Hwell had risen, too, and crossed his arms defiantly, looking from one to the other of us. My brother smiled a little. "Most of us remember how my father argued out this point with his chief man on the night he took his leave of us," he said in a near whisper. "I am a childless man and my sister's babes are all there are on God's earth who can carry Earl Ælfgar's blood into another generation."

He looked my way and flushed a little, thinking no doubt of the childling Ædmund, but he went on as if it had not occurred to him. "When a sliver of that arrow comes to me, I will need to know that Aldgyth is safe with her children. You are the only men whom I can trust to handle them, and it will take all your combined wits and strength to do it, I fear."

They protested more, but at length bold Ywen silenced them, shaking his thick mass of black curls vehemently, and declaring that they ought to be honored by the command. "Methinks I need not remind you, brothers," he said in a grave voice, "that the little maid Nesta is last of the blood of Gruffydd of Llewellyn."

At that, Aldgyth buried her face in her hands, remembering her first son, who had also been held hostage of a king, and had died away from her holding. Aghast for the pain he had caused her, Ywen clasped her in a tight embrace, stroking her hair and kissing her, apologizing and telling her he was ashamed for saying it. She touched his brow lightly and said no matter. "You spoke only truth, my Ywen," she whispered, "she is all that is left of him." They clasped hands tightly, and in that moment, my suspicions of their attachment were confirmed, and I was happy for it.

Lost in deep reflection, I watched Hereward stuff all the arrow pieces in a leathern pouch. Catching my look upon him, he tossed me a quick smile. I smiled back. "You are a good man, Hereward the Wake," I told him, offhandedly.

He widened his eyes in mock surprise, but said nothing.

A little while later, though, after we had made our fare-wells and were walking across the lea, he came anext me. "With your brother, I hold you highest of all men," he said simply, turning away as if it embarrassed him to say it. "I fear me neither of you will taste of the king's leniency if ever you cross him again."

"We are like-minded in that, I trow," I replied, staring hard ahead to where William sat mounted, surrounded by a mass of men and metal, some little ways away.

"Then strive to keep your brother under control till we can devise an escape for you," he whispered, motioning towards Edwin, who was walking with his arm round Aldgyth's waist, just out of earshot. "He is hard hurt by the snatching of that maiden from him, and 'tis likely he will have trouble tending his temperament."

"You are a good reader of men," I admitted and he laughed.

"You did not think so when first we met, Earl Morcar!" he said in a deep voice.

"Then I had no reason to think so," I answered, "Seemed you were forever trying to read me—"

"—and you fancied yourself unreadable!" he put his arm around my shoulder in genial fashion, grinned, and then grew serious. "We have been through much already," he said shortly, "and God knows there is much more to come!"

After that, Edwin joined step with us, and we talked of one thing and another lightly till we were in the king's hearing, and then we spoke no more. In a grim silence we all mounted. The Wake and the Welshmen rode west with my sister, to meet with the party they had chosen for the journey to Ceaster. We rode north with William and his army, but much of the joy we should have felt about seeing our earldoms again had dissolved into hurt and anger, made all the more bitter by the king's amiable chatter and the way he pretended so hard to be our good friend and mentor.

*　　　　　*　　　　　*

"By God, your pretty brother is a well-loved man!" Gilbert Rouquin shouted to me above the dinning noise of the crowd that lined the way as we took our final leave of Nottingham. "Methinks I have seldom seen such adoration!"

Riding anext each other, just behind William and Edwin, we were stopped suddenly at the same time as yet more people, anxious to greet their earl, surged forward, once again forcing the king's entire party to a halt. The red-bearded Norman cast me a look of sheer amazement. It had been like this in every Mercian vill, town, and hamlet. Handsome Edwin, stunningly mounted, had been showered with respect and affections that bordered on worship. His people, so long denied his presence, clamored for him.

Nottingham was an ancient city, literally spanning the great Treante River by means of two huge fortresses, one on either bank, connected by a fortified stone bridge-way. When first we had approached the place, all the men-folk of the shire were gathered there in arms, but the realization that Edwin traveled to them in the company of the king effected the immediate surrender which William had envisioned. The sight of their earl, resplendent in his finely wrought hauberk of silver and gold chain, sealed their decision. Whether he rode as friend or hostage was of no consequence to them. They would neither endanger his life nor risk his approbation by insurrection.

The king had been surprised by the intensity of my brother's welcome in Couventrie, and here the devotion was even more pronounced. Near incredulous, he had watched the countryfolk, highborn and common alike, flock to their lord: reaching for him, crying his name, craving even the slightest acknowledgment. William himself, though eyed with much curiosity and some begrudging deference, might have been no more than a mere attendant of my brother's, for all the attention allotted him by comparison. He grew increasingly awed, but even I could see plainly that the respect was tinged with dread. Some of William's men were made sorely uneasy by the marked loyalty and complained much amongst themselves as they came to realize the vastness of our estates and holdings. Others, though, like the man Rouquin, had come to an honest fondness for my brother and allowed themselves to be more impressed than tainted with envy.

Rouquin was a stolidly built, large-boned man and a thorough individual. While the Norman style was clean-shaven, he sported a pointed beard, merely because his face hair grew in a rich shade of red, a notable contrast to the blackness of his hair and brows. Though he was a friend to d'Aubermont, and to other men I despised like Robert de Comines, I tended to like him. The man was what we Anglish would have called a Stalle—a permanent member of the king's household, but with no clearly defined title or duties. Though ambitious, he was genial, and he had done us a great service on the first day we came to Nottingham. This is how it came about.

When we left the aet-Waeringwicum, the king put Henry de Beaumont in charge, naming him the shire-reeve of Waeringwicum. He commanded that one of the square stone castles so prevalent in Normandy be built there, from which the man might oversee the doings of the shire, and presumably, defend himself if the townsfolk rose against him. No sooner had we come into the pretty shire that had been our boyhood home, than he named another man, a gross Norman adventurer named William Peverel, to be shire-reeve of Nottingham. Late in the day, William bade us ride outside the city with him, to see the site he had chosen for his castle. Gilbert Rouquin was the only other man who rode with us, though a party of a dozen or so followed some ways behind.

A good road led from the town proper to the pleasing lea-lands, and there were a pair of carved road-ends at the point where it turned into a field path. The king remarked on these because they were exceedingly fine, and I told him how my father had ordered them made and erected.

"'Tis a strange custom to mark the beginning of a sheep track!" the king exclaimed. He was in good humor because of the town's speedy surrender, and no doubt meant it jokingly, but my brother told him coldly that he had much to earn about Anglish ways.

"The townspeople bury their dead here at the end of the road," he told the two foreigners, "and they have done so for generations. The building of the road-ends was one of the marks of respect for his people that made my father beloved by countryfolk all through his earldom."

William looked at him curiously and admitted in a sober voice that he did have much to learn. "'Tis a reason I would have the two of you by my side," he added with a rigid smile. "I would be wroth to unintentionally insult my subjects because I know not their customs."

"That you seem already to have done, my lord, and often," Edwin returned darkly, but the king let it pass. He was trying hard to force a friendship, and in a little while my brother's mood lightened. The day was exceedingly fair; the scent of thyme and newly blooming gorse and borage surrounded us. The hum of the bees and the kiss of the fragrant air revived many dormant memories. Till then, I did not realize how homesick I had been. There was a sense of snug security in the green sweeps of Nottingham that I had never known elsewhere. As we wended through the ragged meadowland grasses, my brother and I warmed to the feeling of home, pointing out familiar things here and there and remembering out loud in a way that drew our companions into our conversation until we were almost comfortable again. At length we came to a bosky knoll, overlooking an emerald dale which shimmered in the shadowless sun. Across it, on a grassy promontory, was the rugged stone manor which had been our home, and where my father had spent much of his childhood. William gestured beyond it to the velvety uplands where first we had learnt to hunt and ride, barely out of babe-hood, and where Cynewulf and Cynric Cenwulf's sons rested neath the green sod.

That was where he wanted to build his castle.

Before we could protest, the king started down the sloping hillock, picking his horse's way carefully through the budding hawthorn and stern furze. By the time he looked back to account for us, my brother and I had dismounted. Turning his black steed around, he made his way back uphill, drawing anext the other Norman with a look of puzzlement and annoyance. Anticipating a confrontation, Gilbert Rouquin jumped to the ground and walked our way, leading his horse by the head-stall and assuring the king he would sit with us and keep us company while we rested from the saddle. William might have argued more, but the remainder of the party had caught up with us at last and, sensing it was not worth the effort, he gestured them past us and fell in with their company. A little ways away, he turned just once, shooting us a frown of paternal warning and reprimand.

Soon as he was out of hearing, Edwin gave a short laugh. "Every time he looks at me that way, I am minded to make a gesture that would sorely vex him!"

"Well, 'tis best you do not do it," Rouquin said seriously, seating himself on a broad flat boulder twined over with ivies and mossy ferns. Leaning, he picked some asphodel and sniffed it admiringly before tucking it into the beltings that crossed his leathern hauberk. "The man can be implacable, but he is good at heart and reasonable long as you let him think he is getting his own way."

"God forbid he should have his way in this!" my brother exclaimed, his eyes flashing fire. "'Less he is a dullard, he must know every man in the shire would hate him for it, and we most of all!"

"I think he means not to harm your father's house," the other replied, eyeing us earnestly. "'Twould be foolish to waste strong stone and good timber-work. The upland yonder of it is the spot he has chosen."

"The thought of a cold tower on this pretty homestead sickens me," I answered him. I pulled a fistful of clover by the root, crumpled it, and tossed it far away as I could. "Then you would have roads and gravel pavings all through these meadows, and men camped here and ever trampling."

I meant just to voice some disapprobation, but after a little while I told him how we had chosen these lea-lands for Cynewulf's gravesite, and described how that man had died in our defense. Staring across the dale to the very spot, I could see the king's distant party. They looked small now and unobtrusive, but I felt a rushing stab of sorrow and resented their presence.

Gilbert Rouquin was interested in the story. Chewing on a milky stem, he told me he had once met Tostig Godwine's son himself, when that man came to Normandy after his exile. "He wanted William to back him in an invasion of the North Humbria," he said casually, "but my lord despised him, and sent him to Flanders, telling him never to return to his duchy. One thing that has made William love the both of you is the fact that the Godwine's sons were your enemies."

With a smug look passing between us, Edwin and I broke into strained laughter. It had a strange effect on us, this foreigner telling us we were loved by a man who held us prisoner and taunted us with the blood of our kinfolk. Gilbert Rouquin shrugged off our ill-humor.

"Mayhap he is not an easy man to come to know," he told us, "but when you do, he is always predictable."

"Then predict what he will do when I demand him not to build his fortress there," my brother said boldly, as if he had the power to do it, and the Norman laughed jovially.

"He is a man who will swallow the pod if you tell him to eat the pea. Like enough he would make that decision better if you said naught of your feeling." He yawned, breathing in the balmy scents of the summer grasses, then stood and stretched. Edwin's look grew sulky, and I could appreciate his rising distemper, but we both knew 'twas best to say no more. Every word of dissatisfaction that we uttered made its way back to the king. We could not trust his men to keep close our conversations.

Whether or not Gilbert Rouquin reported our words to William that day, I will never be sure. Late the next evening, while we celebrated the Midsummer's Eve in the close-cropped, park-like grassway that bordered the vast Scirwudu, we were beckoned from a circle where we stood with some of our friends and kinfolk from the Nottingham Shire. William wore the look of a man impatient to be about his business, and he neither smiled nor showed emotion when he spoke to us alone, a little ways off from the party of his closest men. He walked stiffly erect and his face was drawn and hollow, as if the constant travel had already become wearisome to him, when there was so much further to go. Nevertheless, his voice was eager. "Early on the morrow, before we take our leave from here, we will have a Mass said on the promontory," he told us. "Mayhap afterward you will speak to your people, Earl Edwin, and determine them to accept the building of the castle there, and introduce my man Peverel as their new shire-reeve."

My brother raised an eyebrow. "On the promontory," he repeated dumbly, walking closer. The king nodded.

"'Tis the plan of some of my younger men," he explained with a thoughtful look, as if he were still considering it himself. "In a place such as this, with the river well-traveled and a great highway to the north passing through, methinks it makes a certain sense. The manors we should leave intact. Outposts." His face was barely discernible in the darkness, straight-lipped, almost grim.

Edwin took his fillet off, shook his hair loose to cool himself and then replaced it. The night was over-warm, and the heat of the bonfires caused our hair and clothes to cling.

"Whatever you think best," Edwin said with a genuine sounding deference. "The folk will be wroth to lose the market stalls there."

"Move the market-way along the river," William snapped, sounding satisfied with himself. "My man Rouquin suggested that, and you will agree there is wisdom in it, eh?"

Wonderingly, I looked at Edwin and shrugged. "There seems to be," I said slowly, and the king continued.

"This way, we hang the hold directly over the village, with a good view of every way in or out. What better place to put it?" In the darkness, his face turned away from the king, Edwin grinned at me maliciously, and I bit my lip so as not to smile myself.

That is why I felt a surge of friendship towards red-bearded Gilbert, and had him ride beside me near the head of the king's parade as we left the city. All the long, hard, restless ride from Nottingham to Eorforwic, he kept me company with vigorous chatter, and 'twas lucky that I had his distraction. The closer we came to my city, the more a single thought obsessed me: Briana would be there, and the child with her.

You might think that in the consternation and busyness of the days since our parting, I had little thought of her, but 'tis not the truth. Ofttimes I had pictured her and craved her with a hardness that pleaded for relieving. Since Oswulf's death, I had come to imagine our reuniting so clearly that it seemed a thing already settled by Providence: the Bearn's men, maybe even Siward Bearn himself, would bring her to me at Eorforwic and Archbishop Aldred, who had so long favored and furthered our house, would give us the dispensation we needed and make us hand-fast. No need for a bride-ale in these troubled times, and most certainly not in the case of a widow with a child. I would take Ædmund Oswulf's son as my son-in-the-Danelaw; when he was old enough I would tell him the truth. We traveled all one day and most of another, and all that time I felt the waxing discomfort of unbidden desire, and the awesome comfort of knowing I was coming near to her.

At Haeafuddene, a party scouted south from Eorforwic to meet with us. I recognized Heard Ulf's son at their head, in full battle gear, and after a few moments of hard staring I knew Gamel-Beorn and Osbeorn Dolfin's son as well. They knew by now, no doubt, how William had claimed Wulf Harold's son and by the time they grew near to us, they had strapped their arms and pulled off their helmets, realizing that they would be forced to greet us now as king's men. 'Twas a joyous moment for me, seeing my best men once more on my own soil. They rode with us through Rich-Ale in the lowing darkness, where a few of the dalesmen came down to the roadside to watch us pass while the town was sleeping. The population had greatly dwindled since Tostig Godwine's son's mad harrying there near two years since, on the eve of the taking of Eorforwic. It was late when we entered the capital. We came through the Gate Fulford, and even though it was dark beyond seeing, I grew chill with inner horror when we crossed it.

Our party arrived late in the mid-night, but news of our approach had long preceded us through the environs. In the morning, it seemed half the shire had gathered to welcome me; I was totally unprepared for the intensity of it, never having equated my popularity there with what the people of the midlands felt for my brother. The king paraded us ceremoniously, and as we rode through the rock-paved city streets, the earth shook with the resonant chanting and crying of my name.

The Archbishop Aldred had ordered every bell in the city to ring when we came to the minster for the Mass. I could not enter there till I had held my arms high in greeting for a full quarter of an hour. Inside the solid, stone-built church, the drone of the frenzied welcome was still audible, and William looked my way more than once during the long service with bemusement, as if wondering what I had done to garner such loyalty.

Even so, the visit was not at all satisfying. Eager to return south to his own court, the king allowed us fewer than three days there, and in that time I had not a single moment alone with any of my men, save for a hurried conversation with Heard Ulf's son, in the midst of a bustling hall. Siward Bearn had ridden to Ceaster soon as he learnt of the perfidy which had robbed my sister of her son, and to the dashing of my strongest hopes, had taken Briana and her own child with him. There was only one comfort for me in their absence. Fulke d'Aubermont had left with them. Siward Bearn was considered too worthy a personage now to be allowed to travel the country without a staunch Norman guard to "protect" him. Though I mourned my cousin's loss of freedom, I was glad not to have to deal with the Norman who had played us so falsely.

On our first evening there, a hastily assembled feast was put in the great hall, and Edwin and I sat as the honored guests at William's table, along with William Malet. The king had made him reeve of the Eorforwic shire, and though my avunculus was proud of the honor, he knew well as we that it was the king's first step in the stripping away of my power. He greeted us fondly but 'twas plain to see he felt uncomfortable, knowing he had usurped the house and hall that had been mine.

"'Tis but a token position," my uncle apologized, shrugging as if it meant little, but we were not appeased.

"He named one of his Normans the shire-reeve of Nottingham when we were there," Edwin told him coldly. "He pretends to us that the man is naught but our watchdog, but you are blind if you cannot see that it is his way of taking the governing out of my hands without having to depose me." My brother was drinking heavily.

My uncle coughed nervously. "The man's business is to maintain peace and order."

"At the expense of the Anglish," I cried angrily, "and to the benefit of his own men."

William Malet shook his head. "There have ever been Anglish shire-reeves and you found no quarrel in that."

"In those days, we had say in our own earldoms, uncle," my brother answered bitterly. "Now he forces us to keep away so he can elect men to rule in our absence. He builds them castles for defense and gives them the power of confiscation. How say you there can be a comparison?"

My uncle put his elbows on the table and leant forward, resting his forehead in his hands, searching for words. The day was warm and his Norman tunic was short sleeved, revealing arms still powerfully muscled though scarred and leathery. "All I know is that he has elected me to live here, to keep order in a city brimming with rebelliousness and all the crimes tendered by political unrest. You are still the earl here, Morcar. Ask any man! Let him name a hundred shire-reeves; let him place a castle in every village and town. Will it make you less of an earl? Methinks it might make you more of one."

"An earl in name only 'twould make him," my brother hissed. "The lord of an earldom owned and ruled by others else!"

"What matter?" William Malet cried, exasperated. "Ever have you thought how the breaking of these vast lands into smaller and smaller holdings will make for a stronger and more united Angland?"

"What mean you?" Edwin asked accusingly, clenching his fists and half rising from the bench, "that Angland should grow powerful by swallowing away her earldoms into nothingness? By letting Mercia wane into a string of unrelated homesteads and stinking Norman castles?" He was fast growing flushed with drink and anger. My uncle stilled him by pulling him back into his seat, smiling wanly.

"Never a man was more like his father, I trow," our avunculus said, staring hard into Edwin's eyes. "Forever wanting to make an argument out of a converse."

Relaxing a little, Edwin swallowed another mouthful of strong ale. My uncle did the same. His eyes narrowed and his voice grew low. "Your king is a man intent on welding this land together. Whether by force, fury, or popular consent matters not much to him. You can both retain your honor, your titles, and much of your holdings, if you let him unite it under you. Elsewise he will unmake you—in any way he chooses—then do what he set out to do despite you!"

I looked at him, puzzled. "You say I might be earl, but with no North Humbria? And Edwin, too, but with no Mercia?"

"Angland has ever been a troubled land because of her rivalries," he replied with a grimace. "You two of all men should know that!"

Tossing his glossy hair back with an angry tilt of the head, my brother stood suddenly. "I will not keep company with a man who espouses the undoing of the land his kinsmen have lived and died for," he said, forcing the words through clenched teeth. "I am sorry that I part from you in disrespect, avunculus, but I cannot bide your traitorous ambition any longer."

He pushed himself sullenly away against my uncle's surprised protest, then turned and faced the man again. William Malet was on his feet now too. They stood eye to eye.

"Ever when I was a child it seemed to me you were championing the king against my father, belittling him and refusing him your support." Edwin's voice shook with emotion. "Never did Ælfgar demean you, because you were a man of honor, and because he respected your dedication to the crown. I have watched you swear yourself to three crowns in my lifetime, but never did I realize what I have come to know about you this very day, mother's-brother! You are not an Anglishman. What you once claimed of Anglish blood has dried into nothing under the sway of this vile Norman king!"

He staggered a little, then strode angrily from the hall. My uncle stared after him, as did the king, who had heard every word of the argument, along with a great many other men, and was grossly insulted. Had my brother bothered to look back into that man's fast-hardening eyes, he would have known that much sorrow was to follow.

$$* \qquad * \qquad *$$

In the heavy hewn beams of the great hall at Kirton, my father had carved a small picture. Anext it, Cynewulf Cenwulf's son had scribed a date deep with his blade and the words "Ælfgar the earl's son and Cenwulf's son, his man." These were near lost amongst many of such, carven here and there by idle hands on winter nights long past, but I found them in the dim light of a stormy summer morning. 'Twas a simple pair of figures, crude and ill-proportioned like the people in ladies' embroideries, each with a sword in one hand and a cup in the other, both smiling. I was glad for the shadowy greyness, pierced only now and again by the eerie brilliance of lightning-crack. Fingering the rough outline, a strange sense of longing come over me, and a fleeting memory of light-heartedness and happiness and everyday pleasures once taken for granted. I shook with a sudden pulsing of emotion. Even though the room was near empty, and those in it far removed and unconcerned with me, I forced myself to swallow back a rising sob, else I would have wept then and I might not have been able to still my weeping.

Outside in the stableyard a fair number of people were gathered despite the sullen downpour, all hoping for a moment with their beloved Earl Edwin, for there was much grief in the Lindcylene Shire that day. My brother, though, had taken to his bed. Rain-weather was apt to make his bones ache where they had been broken, causing him intense discomfort, and his spirits had been so badly crushed the day before that he scarce could stand to face with any man.

Things had gone from bad to worse between King William and him since that night in my hall at Eorforwic. Edwin was a man who could not well take chastisement; since childhood it had been his way. The king had demanded a public apology for himself and William Malet. My brother, hurt and angered by my uncle's attitude, had refused to give it. It led to violent words before the very men William had hoped to impress with our solidarity. When we came to Lindcylene, where respect for our house was highest of anywhere, the two men had quibbled openly, like children—the king refusing to allow Hereward the Wake to join our party, and Edwin standing cross-armed and mute before the townspeople, when the king ordered him to give the pretty speech of affiliation he had been forced to make in every other town. Enraged, but wise enough not to mishandle a man in front of a huge crowd devoted to him, the king had drawn the two of us aside.

"You have tasted of my proffered friendship and despised it," William whispered roughly, clenching his fist as if it took him power to hold it back. "Now you will taste of the vengefulness I offer men who are my enemies. Mayhap it will help you determine that 'tis better to be at one with me!"

So saying, he announced that a castle would be built, within the confines of the town. With a sweeping gesture, he outlined the area his hold would encompass. Tremendous shouts of disapproval, even horror, rose from the assembled crowd. He had chosen the best area of the town, where the oldest and finest homes stood, which housed almost all of the cityfolk, most of them earl's-men or their families, else merchants and wealthy widows. My brother grew ashy pale and in a tremulous voice whispered he would reconsider, but it was too late and the Norman let him know it. He ordered his men to gather timber and gave the populace the space of an hour to move what they needed from their homes, most of which had been lived in for generations. There was wailing and weeping as the people scattered to the horrendous chore.

'Twas like a madness had seized on them, knowing they could in no way salvage much of their lives in that small time, and that there would be no where to put those things they could manage to save. Edwin screamed above the uproar that they should gather in St. Mary's and the other churches, and in the manors on the outskirts, which would be given over to them till they could be resettled. But when he offered them his own manor, his great estate at Kirton, William cut him off with an icy laugh.

"That house is mine now, Earl Edwin," he said in a voice savage with cruelty, eyes glinting as with fever. "I will quarter my own men there instead. We will have need for a strong army in this city, think you not? The people are already predisposed to hate my rule, and no doubt there will be much pilferage and looting amongst the homeless."

He drew close, peering like a madman straight into my brother's eyes, seeming to find satisfaction in the fact that Edwin trembled violently. "There is not a man in the world whose knees cannot be made to bend! You fancy you are stronger than most, Edwin Ælfgar's son, but to me, you are no more than a noxious babe in need of slapping for a tantrum!"

Driven far beyond his own power of self control, Edwin leapt at the king with a furious snarl, raising a hand as if to smite him. With all my strength, I pushed my brother away, grabbing his wrists and forcing his arms to his side.

"Think what he might do to these people!" I cried, horrified. He tore himself from my grasp and spun around, as if the very sight of the Norman might bring him to murder, and he had need to protect himself from the urge.

The king stood awhile, hands on his hips, watching smugly. Then, all at once, his look of rage was gone, and his thin-lipped sneer melted into a begrudging smile. "Your brother has come to see my point, I trow," he said, looking hard at me. "Mayhap by the time we get to Wintanceaster we will be friends again." Then he walked away, calmly confident, to oversee the setting of the fires.

The rest of the day was like a nightmare. We were forced to stand with him on the slight rise of the Foss-Way and watch the burning. In all, one hundred sixty-six homes were put to torch and leveled. My brother looked stoic and grim through it all, but standing close to him as I was, I could see his tears. Much later, when the rain came, successfully smothering the last of the smoldering flames, we returned to Kirton. When we were alone together in our chamber, he wept. Late in the night I wakened, and he was sobbing still.

I knew he had been broken.

CHAPTER FORTY-NINE

The brothers escaped to regions which were under
their own control and there disturbed William's
peace . . . but sympathy for their youth and good
looks, and respect for their high birth secured their
pardon without penalty.

—William of Malmesbury

We began a weary year of stifled living when we returned to
Wintanceaster. As the king had promised when he forced his restoration
to favor upon us, our privileges, such as they were, were restored, and
things became as they had been before our leave-taking. We kept a fine
chamber, and dressed richly in our usual wont. We dined in the king's
hall, at his very table, and rode and hunted at will, so long as there was
a guard behind. He showed us every respect, accorded us every honor,
and in that strange way of his, proceeded as if naught of unpleasantness
had passed. In truth, the sternest eye would have perceived no difference
in his attitude towards us before and after the tragedy of Lindcylene. He
conversed with us amiably, enlisted my help in learning Anglish, and
pretended not to notice the awesome change in my brother.

Edwin had grown so silent and withdrawn that he seemed to me a
different man. In the past, such trauma waxed him petulant, sullen, or
insolent; now he was naught but quiet. In the king's very presence he
scarce uttered a single word. He never smiled or gave any hint of anima-
tion. With other men, he assumed a mood more lively, but still 'twas not
his usual way. He neither laughed nor gamed, nor spoke except in reply
to others. Despite the fact that he had let himself grow bearded, in
appearance he was, if anything, more comely, spending more time than
ever on the details of his dress, glossing the burnished gold of his hair
daily with herbs and flowers, and decking himself in the gold and jewels
he had carried back with him from his storehouse are Kirton. It seemed
as if he had resigned himself to the thought that he was no more than

an ornament, and had resolved to be the best of all possible ones. This is only my conjecture, though, for he kept as still with me in those days as with any other man, and every feeling he had was secret. What is more, he had taken to over-drinking. The spirits increased his despondency, and he wore a look of never-lessening sorrow.

One thing only seemed a brightness to him: the presence of tiny Wulf Harold's son. Though he was a tot still in the care of nursemaids, he was a brilliant, well-formed creature, full of toddling vigor and gamesomeness and love. Both of us doted on him, and the king, as if in apology for the rudeness that had robbed the babe from the breast of our sister, allowed us every freedom with him. Anytime, day or night, we could claim him. He would sleep in our chamber if we wished it, or eat anext us in the hall. Daily, we took him riding through the royal warren or for travels atop our shoulders through the courtyards. In truth, he became every man's little favorite, but he was most special to Edwin, and near the only thing in life that could cause him laughter.

By the grace of God, William was not much in our company those months. He had returned, jaunty from his near-bloodless conquering of the midlands, to discover that the rest of the Anglish he had forced into guesthood at Wintanceaster had taken advantage of his absence. They had followed our example and fled the court. Fox-eyed Waltheof, Earl of Huntandun, and the young ætheling, Ædgar, had gathered what they could of their possessions and made with haste for Scot Land. Having been frighted by the delivery of Wulf Harold's son to the king's house, they were wise enough to bring their closest kin with them, to avoid the one bit of leverage William might have used to haul them back. With them had fled our own despised kinsman, Gospatrick Maldred's son, who had been elated enough when the king sold him the Bernicia, but had cooled rapidly when he was not allowed leave to go visit it.

William, who had never rightly understood the mistrust and alienation between us, blamed us for our kinsman's defection merely because we shared a portion of his blood. Unable to make his revenge on those who had absconded, he wreaked it on us instead. My brother having already been leveled far as the king dared to do it, I was the one who felt of his wrath now. In a move I had been long expecting, he took much of the North Humbria away from me at his Christ Mass Gemot, mostly lands in the Bernicia. With the calculated coldness we had come to expect from him, he made sure to choose a successor from amongst those I hated most. His choice was the Flemish-man, Robert de Comines. Edwin and I passed each other a smirk of satisfaction when we heard it. With his grating mock deference, William explained I was still his Earl of the North Humbria, just as Edwin was still his Earl of Mercia, but that now de Comines was my under-earl just as Oswulf had been. It proved how little William understood the northerners if he thought a man like that could last long there. They had refused to tolerate a Wessexman, and there was no way they would ever warm to a foreign adventurer with a blatant mean streak—a stupid man, besides.

Stupid he was, too. He chose the coldest part of the season, scant weeks after the new year, to claim his domain, and the seat he chose to sit in was the far northern city of Dunholme, which had been chief of my kinsman Oswulf's holdings. Perhaps he underestimated the severity of wind and snow in the far reaches, never having tasted the like in Normandy, Flanders, or France. Or, perhaps he thought the outpost so primitive that the sight of nine hundred Norman knights would bring an immediate, groveling surrender.

Whatever his sad miscalculation was, it cost him his own life and those of all but one of his soldiers. The victory Anglishmen tasted at his expense inspired one uprising after another in the North Humbria that year. Locked away in the king's house, away from the converse of our own countrymen, we were forced to garner what details we could from the Norman news-mongers, and guess what parts were being played in the madness by our own friends and kinsmen.

Not long after the massacre at Dunholme, William hastened to Eorforwic where he quelled another bloody insurrection, begun when the citizens slew one of the Norman commanders there along with a good number of his men. Gospatrick Maldred's son and Ædgar Ætheling swooped down from Scot Land to join the forces, but beat a fast retreat again when the king recaptured the city and built a second castle. Nothing but praise was spoken of our avunculus. William Malet had made a notable defense and was deemed a bold and unequaled warrior by the Normans. It chilled me somewhat to realize that the men he fought against may have been led by his own nephew, my kinsman Siward Bearn.

The king made a triumphal return in time for Easter, but was called even from the very feasting table to crush more rebellion. Upon his return, he decreed the land was in no wise safe for his pretty cwene, and ordered her return to Normandy. Some men were sad to see her leave, but I was not one of them. She had seemed naught but a shrewish hellion to me since the day in the king's chamber. She had tried to set things right again with gay patter and pretty flatteries aimed chiefly at my brother. The silent meekness with which he accepted her converse may have seemed to her like a degree of acquiescence.

What angered me most was a way she had of intimating that perhaps things might be worked out in such a way that Edwin would gain the hand of her daughter after all. No doubt there was much in Edwin's winning person and address that Mathilda admired. Could be she felt a trifle guilty for the great lowness of spirits which vexed him now, and truly hoped it might be a possibility. Tempting him only raised his hopes where there was hopelessness, though, and I felt it needlessly cruel. All the damage had been done, and though my brother occasionally, when hazed by drink, allowed himself to suppose the betrothal still was possible, I knew in the end his dream would only be crushed.

Soon Mathilda was gone, though, and the jostle of events continued as before. The bastard sons of Harold Godwine's son made warfare in the west, sailing in with a fleet of Viking North Wegians and hired Eirish mercenaries. Theirs was more a pirate venture than an uprising, and they were easily routed. Then, in September, the Danish fleet sailed into the Humber, to offer assistance to the rebels, and a good number of Anglishmen flocked thither to avail themselves of the aid. We recognized many of the men said to be there: Siward Bearn, Heard Ulf's son, Gospatrick, Waltheof, the Ætheling and many more. Still no portion of a war arrow came to us.

The gathered army fought the Normans in Lindcylene, then in Eorforwic, where three thousand Normans were slaughtered in combat of the bloodiest kind, ranging from the broad flat of the Gate Fulford into the very heart of the walled city itself. William Malet and his wife and childlings were taken prisoner and much of the city, we learnt, had been destroyed by fire and fight. By then, the king had not been home to rest in months. He hurried from the site of one rising to another, sometimes waylaid by fresh outbreaks which hindered his way.

'Twas on his way to Eorforwic that he met a great host in the Staethford Shire, and much blood was let in the heart of Mercia. Sore wounded Normans came back from there for succoring. William had wasted the shire so completely in his retaliation that there were not even enough provisions to support his own troops. We spoke to as many as we could, and through them learnt details of the bloody stand, including the fact that Hereward had fought them there, ignoring the greater gathering in the Humberland to stand in defense of the midlands. Behind him, 'twas told, stood an army of men drawn from all of Mercia. Of the fate of the men we knew nothing; of the fate of the shire we were well informed. Little existed now that had been before. The great estate at Staethford, King's Braumleigh, where my grandfather had kept his hall for many years, was a smoldering ruin, and scarce a manor or church stood whole now in the blackened waste.

Just at the time when, in other years, our countrymen might be keeping the midwinter feast, William for the third time marched his army on Eorforwic. The very men who brought us the news of it, carried a command from the king. He bade us join him in the ancient northern city for a Christ Mass Gemot of sorts. He bade us bring court dress and finery, and told his men to bring back suchlike for him, as well as the makings of a good feast, for there was nothing to be had in all the Eorforwic Shire. Fiercely agitated, and saddened to the point of misery, we left that very same day in a huge party of the king's reinforcements.

CHAPTER FIFTY

he leveled their places of shelter to the ground,
wasted their lands and burnt their dwellings with
all they contained. Never did William commit so
much cruelty; to his lasting disgrace he yielded to
his worst impulses and set no bounds to his fury,
condemning the innocent and the guilty to a
common fate. In the fullness of his wrath, he
ordered the corn and cattle, with the implements of
husbandry and every sort of provisions, to be
collected in heaps and set on fire till the whole was
consumed, and thus destroyed at once all that could
serve for support of life in the whole country lying
beyond the Humber. There followed, consequently,
so great a scarcity in England in the ensuing years,
and severe famine involved the innocent and
unarmed population in so much misery that, in a
Christian nation, more than a hundred thousand
souls, of both sexes and all ages, perished of want.

—Orderic Vitalis
Book IV, Chapter V, 1069

Never was a land more suited to the splendor of winter than the North
Humbria. The rugged grey steeps and purple promontories wore the
jewel-like glistening of snow with an awesome grandeur, and there was
incomparable beauty in the silvered moorlands and the mountain-
bordered leas iced to glowing, pale perfection. Wrapped in mantles of
thick fur, I was happy despite the bitter rumblings of the shivering
Normans who surrounded me. I rode with elation through the white

wilderness world of molten crystal. The ferocious wind whipped the foreigners into frigid pain, and they wondered openly how I could tolerate the intensity of the northern bite with such seeming ease. The truth of it was, though, that the blasting winter-breath carried with it the kiss of freedom strong enough to cause me intense physical joy. I felt so at home in the dim, frozen hills, that every nerve strained with gladness.

Until we crossed the frozen Humber near the Haethfeld land....

We had come west around the ghostly starkness of the Scirwudu, and passed near the landed estate of my man, Heard Ulf's son, outside Tiouulfingacaestir, and saw that it was waste, the scorched blackness of it already half-swallowed by encroaching banks of snow. Thank Jesus, the season had been too cold to allow a meandering through the Staethford Shire; we had heard enough of the destruction there to know it would have hurt us hard to see it. Here and there, across the Mercian reaches, we saw signs of the king's harrying, but no great concentration of ruin. I was sad struck by the sight of my man's pleasant valley manor when we passed it, and we were soon to realize that 'twas only the slightest intimation of the horror to come.

From Haeafuddene on, we passed not a single house or hamlet that was untouched; from the greatest manor to the simplest hut, all was waste. Where we knew villages once had been, there were naught but great, ashy circles of black pilings, ghastly in the howling wind—desolate, eerie, lifeless. Bodies littered the snow, singly or in great bunches, grotesquely molded into the throes of frozen death where the desperate had lain themselves down to die. Women, children, babes.... Worse yet, men who had died in resisting stained the ice scarlet with their mangled remnants, and wild beasts, made the more savage by the burning of their woodland haunts, grew frenzied on the proffered gore.

Destruction, death, agony were everywhere in proportions beyond imagining; no word can tell the whole horror of it. The closer we came to Eorforwic, the thicker was the carnage. Sickened and aghast, even the king's men crossed themselves and exclaimed vehemently at the outrage, but after miles and miles of it, they grew indifferent. Some of them, their hearts having hardened like the tears on my face, grew bold enough to pilfer now and again.

What was plain from the outset was that the fearful harrying was not the rape and plunder of a conquering army, intent on gathering treasure and loot. 'Twas merciless murder by the hand of a madman; death dealt for the sake of punishment, burning wrought for the sake of systematic, total destruction. Houses and stables and storehouses were razed with all they had in them; corpses still guarded in death their earthly treasure. The Norman had wrought all this devastation as a chastening. The North Humbria had resisted him; this was his retribution on them. For hundreds of miles there was naught but unpeopled, inhospitable emptiness.

But at last the man could claim he was king there now, and could call that slice of doomed wilderness his domain.

CRAPTER FIFTY-ONE

So great a famine prevailed that men, compelled by hunger, devoured human flesh, that of horses, dogs and cats, and whatever custom abhors. Others sold themselves into perpetual slavery so that they might in any way preserve their wretched existence. It was horrific to behold human corpses decaying in the houses, the streets and the roads, swarming with worms while they were consuming in corruption with an abominable stench. For no one was left to bury them in the earth, all being cut off either by sword or famine. There was no village inhabited between Eorforwic and Dunholme; they became lurking places to wild beasts and robbers, and were a great dread to travellers.

—Simeon of Durham

December 1069
God only knows how the king, in all seriousness, could expect us to sit to a Christ Mass feast with him after all that had happened, but he did. His men had carried mead and dried meats with them from Wintanceaster, as well as salted birds, nuts, berries and apples. They set a somber table in one of his grim castles, and so it happened that we drank in the new year with a man we despised, in the absolute ruins of a city once held dear by us. Such is the inconstancy of Providence.

William Malet sat with us, and Gilbert Rouquin, and a handful of other high-ranking king's men, some whom we knew and some not. The very fact that they could dine and make merry in the midst of such death and destruction showed they were a harder, more ruthless breed of enemy than ever we had met before—though the sickening sight of the immense scorched circle of earth that had once been the proud

Humbrian capital was in itself proof enough of the fact. Edwin drank himself to senselessness, and I, unable to eat or drink, sat frozen-hearted and close-mouthed through the whole ordeal, thankful that God, in His infinite mercy, had called to himself the spirit of Archbishop Aldred some months before, and so spared that good man from the sight of this hell on earth.

Nothing of timber stood in Eorforwic anymore. My great stone hall was black inside and out, robbed of every useful thing, roofless and wasted beyond any dream of repair. The stables, courtyard, buttery, and many outer-houses were gone, not a speck remaining but the ashes and cinders. 'Twould have taken a trained eye to trace the outlines of that once beautiful city in the huge heap of smoldering rubble and tumbled rock. After the board was cleared, I went alone atop the battlements of the square castle and looked out in every direction, searching vainly for one recognizable landmark other than the ruined stone minster.

I had not been there long when I heard a deep voice behind me, speaking a muffled greeting. My avunculus, with a thick fur mantle thrown carelessly over his leathern battle-dress, came anext me, following my gaze outward into the fields of death. His arm shook a little as he pointed out a leveled, grey stretch where once shops had lined the street leading to the market square. "I led twenty men into a skirmish there," he told me morosely, "and when I looked up through my sweat, I saw that the man I was fighting was Siward Bearn."

I felt my heart thudding. "Where is he, uncle?"

William Malet shrugged, a look of care and sorrow fleeting across his rugged features. "Like as not he is fled to Dunholme, where most of the rebels are gone. Must be you have heard by now that William ordered murder on every man of arms-bearing age to be found in this shire."

"You did not slay him, then?" My voice was cold, and I felt a little sorry for it. He shook his head.

"Nay. He shouted that he would not fight me, and so further dishonor his mother's grave. I pulled my sword down then and backed myself out of the fracas. I am growing too old to fight."

"You are a great warrior, William Malet," I whispered. "All the country knows as much, and it is openly spoken in William's court."

He smiled for just a second. "God willing, I will not have need to prove me more. I am sick of it." He straightened, then brushed the greying hair off his brow in a swift motion. "The Bearn is amongst the men King William has named outlaw; Heard Ulf's son and your man the Biter, as well. 'Twould be best if they were not found when William goes to Dunholme to seek them."

"Then I pray they are not there," I said icily.

He nodded in agreement. "I do also," he said simply. He rubbed his hands together and blew on them to warm them, his breath misting the air. "Your brother has taken too much to drunkenness," he said in another, harder tone. "'Tis not becoming for a man of station."

"What station?" I cried with a short laugh, but he hushed me with an angry wave of the hand.

"The Norman men will find fault with him for it," he said decidedly. "The king abhors looseness and will not allow it in any other man; you saw how he meted drink to all his own in small measure. I heard much remarking and jealousy because the king would not reprimand Edwin Ælfgar's son—"

"I care not!" I replied crossly. "Nor my brother does, I trow. There is not much more in the way of punishment that William can do to him, less he orders his very death."

My uncle bit back a reply, then thought the better of it. The king of late had strongly championed marriages between Norman and Anglish, offering land and gold grants to any of his unmarried men who would choose a bride from amongst the many widowed Anglish women.

"Must be you can see how the king wants to unite this land, urging his Normans to marry Anglishwomen and rewarding them for learning to speak the tongue. I know you scarce can believe this, Morcar, but he still wishes you to be his earls, and highest of his men. 'Tis the best way he sees of unifying a land that is now both Anglish and Norman."

Leaning over the ramparts, I spat, but made no answer.

"He has ambitious men amongst his own who resent this high regard, and will resent it the more if it is paid to one who over-drinks and carouses in a way they themselves are not allowed to do."

Turning suddenly, I faced him with narrowed eyes. "I have much of a love for you, mother's-brother," I told him, keeping my voice level despite a welling of emotion, "but I think it best that whenever more we speak, you and I, we speak as kinsmen, because I am not minded to listen to lectures from the Shire-reeve of Eorforwic, or from the king's-man, or anyone else, save my avunculus."

As if I had said something amusing, William Malet gave a genuine laugh. Then his voice grew soft. "Well said, Morcar Ælfgar's son!" he exclaimed. "I will mind myself of your words. We will speak as blood-kin, though what we will have to talk about in these times, I scarce can say."

I hesitated a moment, a thought occurring to me. Noticing my consternation he asked what troubled me. My voice turned serious, and I picked my words well.

"One thing weights me, uncle," I told him guardedly. It was beginning to snow and I drew my mantle tighter. I must know where Lady

Briana is, and her babe. I heard they were in Eorforwic, but I pray God they had made a fleeing before all this!" Looking out at the waste again inspired more dejection which must have told in my look. My uncle eyed me curiously.

"She does not share in the schemes of her brother, if that is what you want to know," he said tonelessly. "She is moved away to Dunholme, and the child with her, but they are safe-guarded by a garrison of the king's men."

My relief must have been obvious. "Why ask you?" he queried, and I replied that I wanted to see them both. "'Tis a thing of great importance to me, uncle, and I know you are the only man who can help me."

"Methinks you bear the lady greater respect than her own brother does," he returned, shaking heavy flakes of snow out of his hair. "He would neither visit her nor receive her at Tathaceaster, though she sorely pleaded him. He took the boy and her to Ceaster to visit Aldgyth, but they returned in separate trains, and he never spoke to her more, that I know of."

"I am in part to blame for what is gone awry between them," I told him bluntly. I meant not to say more but he tossed me a dark look.

"How so?"

"'Tis something that will not bear converse," I replied sharply. "I need to see them both, though, and mayhap you can convince the king to let me."

"He will want to know what business—"

"Tell him anything! She is my kinswoman, and I have a right to see her, do I not?"

"Mayhap you do, but she may not wish to see you, Morcar. Her circumstances are greatly changed now, as well you can imagine."

"As mine are, uncle, and all our kinfolk's, I trow. I have waited through much, though, for an opportunity to speak with her."

He came close to me, staring deep into my eyes. "Does it have to do with the boy?" he asked. It sounded to me like an accusation. I bristled a moment, then admitted it did.

"Ædmund Oswulf's son is a fair youngster," he told me in a strained voice, "but there have been rumors—"

I grew suddenly stiff. "Ædmund is my son."

I scarce could believe it had finally been said openly. He paled.

"Your son?" he repeated, as if he had not heard me aright. "*Your* son?" He grew limp all at once, and leant himself against the cold stone wall. "Never would I have thought this, Morcar! Who knows of it?"

"Siward Bearn knows it, and Edwin and you. Elsewise the only other is dead—Oswulf Eadwulf's son."

His brows shot up in disbelief. "Oswulf knew this!" he exclaimed, and he shrugged in perplexion when I nodded. "We must make certain that not another man learns of it—ever."

His voice had the ring of finality. He put an arm around my shoulder, but there was a pained look in his eye when he spoke again. "I will see that you are allowed your visit, Morcar," he said gently as we headed back indoors, "but do not let your attitude or your words betray this secret to anyone, elsewise you will bring misery to many more people than you can imagine, and not the least of all yourself."

His tone was grave, but I was not to know the full import of his words for a while. He left the next morning with the king and his army to make battle on the forces gathered near Dunholme, and it was near a fortnight later before William had his victory and sent for us to join him there.

*   *   *

Pretty Dunholme, which I had so admired when my cousin had lived there, was near unrecognizable when our weary train came upon it in the howling winter dawnlight. Though a much smaller city than Eorforwic, it had been just as thoroughly razed. The gates had been downed and burned earlier by the mob that massacred Robert de Comines and his men, and what was not destroyed then had been wasted in the intense warfare that preceded the hardest-won of all the king's victories. We did not even dismount to inspect the charred remains. William Malet, at the head of a small, well-armed party, met with us in the out-fields and directed us northwards, up the frozen, rolling sweeps to the once-forested High Ridge, now a blackened waste of burned timber. At the top, looking across the snowy fells and glossy iced fields, we were surprised to see the stone manor that had been Oswulf's standing intact and bustling with life. The house stood at the rocky edge of the craggy table-lands which loomed above the wild moorish flats and commanded a view of the dales in every direction. Being perfectly situated for defense and shelter, the king's men had decided from the very outset to make it their headquarters. The main of the battle having been fought within the town proper, it had escaped the bloody fray which finally routed the Anglish rebels, and now housed the victorious king.

Stepping our horses carefully through the heavy, deeply banked snow, we began our slow approach, separating ourselves from the party a little way, so we could converse in private. Edwin had not softened towards our uncle in the slightest, and would not greet or speak to him, but he rode near enough to hear every word of the man's woeful tidings.

The tale was hard to tell, being one of glorious victory for the teller, and of hapless, miserable defeat for us, but William Malet was good enough to say first that which we had wanted to know. Siward Bearn had not been found amongst the Anglish dead, nor Heard Ulf's son, Osbeorn Dolfin's son, Gamel-Beorn the Biter, or any of a half-dozen favorites we inquired about by name. Anxious despite himself for news of his own kinsmen, my uncle had taken it upon himself to inspect the battered corpses as they were hauled in for a mass burning. We crossed ourselves when we heard that our murdered countrymen had been dealt with in such a pagan manner, but the frozen ground was too hard to allow for burial, and the extent of death was so great that the men feared disease and pestilence when the thaws came.

"'Tis said the Anglish remnant is scattered and disbanded now," my uncle said, looking older and sadder than ever he had before. "There can be no hope for anyone who cannot fend for himself. Must be they are fled to Mercia, to the towns or monasteries. There is nowhere in these north-lands they can go for aid or shelter."

"If you can condone this, you are a hell-bound man, mother's-brother!" Edwin growled suddenly, looking grimly at the utter desolation of the burned woodlands surrounding us. My uncle pretended not to hear him but stared stoically ahead, squinting his eyes against a swirling flurry of snow.

"Earl Waltheof made his surrender here," he went on, "and so did Gospatrick Maldred's son. The king waxes generous; he has spared them and even restored them to favor as he did the two of you when you made your peace. His price is on the head of Siward Bearn, though, and on the other high-ranking men who fled without bending to him."

Engulfed in gloom, I made no answer, and we rode in silence for a time, listening to the Normans as they bickered and complained about the hardships of the weather. In a little while, we were at the stone gates of the manor and William Malet leant close. "This is where the lady is, Morcar," he told me, and I felt a sudden surge of heat flush through me.

Once we had dismounted, my uncle led us to the chamber he shared with Gilbert Rouquin and a handful of other men, and we warmed ourselves awhile by the fire. "'Tis an exceeding small house," he apologized, "and there is a certain lack of comfort none of us are used to, but which must be borne."

Rouquin, walking behind us, gave a short laugh when he heard it. "There is discomfort enough in this frozen wasteland to kill a man," he added with an ill-humored scowl. "Patrolling this wilderness and keeping peace amongst the homeless barbarians is the duty most despised, yet the king chooses all of his best men to do it!"

Turning a cold eye on the red-bearded man, William Malet chastised him. "How think you a lesser man could handle the responsibility when chosen warriors like yourself and d'Aubermont shrink from it, shivering and whining like babes because the snow is too cold for you?"

Shrugging, the other bit back a reply, respecting my uncle's station. Then he brightened. "At least the king has made some concessions to lighten our load here. He allows drink and women—else he could not keep a single soldier in this god-forsaken place!"

"Drink and women?" Edwin repeated with obvious interest, glancing at our avunculus just to make sure it bothered him. Gilbert Rouquin slapped him on the back and gave a hearty laugh.

"You are a good man, Earl Edwin!" he cried, and putting an arm over his shoulder, turned and led him off in the direction of the hall. My uncle stared after them with icy contempt.

"Think you Earl Ælfgar would allow this misbehavior if he were alive?" he asked me grimly, and I shook my head.

"Edwin would scarce feel the need to numb himself if things stayed as they were before," was my retort, "and 'twould not have done him harm to have had the woman he loved to keep him in line."

"Pah! He lacks the courage to face his responsibilities to country and king—"

My look must have hardened as he said it; he cut himself off, and throwing up his hands in a gesture of hopelessness, sat down heavily on the table edge. In silence he watched me strip off my heavy woolen garments which had grown soaked soon as I thawed them. When I had splashed with his proffered attars and combed out my hair, he handed me a crumpled but clean dalmatic from the pack I had carried with me.

"I want to see her first," I said, slipping it over my head. "I will be in no mood to make courtesies to the king till I have seen her and the boy."

Rubbing his hands together nervously, William Malet stood and stretched, then moved towards the fire, turning his back as if it ached him to look on me. "I know not whether you mean to further this attachment or not, Morcar, but best you should know something before you meet with her—" he began, and I stopped dead at the tone of his voice. "Best you should know she is a married woman now."

I was so stunned that I could hear the rushing of my own blood.

"She is newly wed. I knew it not when I spoke to you at Eorforwic." Still, I could not answer.

"'Tis not such a strange thing for a lady in her position," he continued, as if my quiet had given him strength to go on. "Must be you know how the king encourages his men to make such matches—rewards them even."

I sat down, trembling a little and trying not to betray it.

"She had many suitors. Except for a handful of guarded, high-born ladies there are naught but camp followers here now. She refused a good many, I will tell you, and even seemed reluctant to accept d'Aubermont but that I urged it, his prospects being fair."

At the sound of that man's name I sprang to my feet, aware of a gnawing in the pit of my stomach strong as the feelings of vengefulness at the start of a battle. My head was spinning. My uncle came behind me, only now sensing the depth of my distress.

"Both the lady and the boy needed the protection, Morcar. Oswulf was not a favorite of the king, and well you know it!"

Grabbing my knife girth off the table and strapping it on in a single, swift motion, I spun round and faced him. "Tell me where she is, avunculus. I fain would speak with her."

He looked confused a moment, unsure of himself. Then, with a signal, he bade me follow, and led me into the hallway, and up a steep, wooden spiral stair to the loft-room. At the far end, in the stacked hay and muslin, some children were playing, and smallest of them, a gold-haired, healthy toddler, cried a greeting soon as he caught sight of us. Trundling our way, he wrapped his arms tight around William Malet's knees in a fond embrace.

"Know you who this man is, little Ædmund?" my uncle asked, kneeling to hug him. The boy scrutinized me with a puzzled frown. "He has hair like my avunculus, Siward!" he exclaimed. "Is he a Bearn?"

We both laughed. "Nay, he is not a Bearn—he is an earl. This is Earl Morcar, your—your uncle." His voice faltered a little and he glanced up at me as if to ensure he had said the right thing.

"Has he plums, I wonder?" the child asked seriously, looking hopefully from one to the other of us. I smiled, trying to hide my amusement, and shook my head.

"Nay, Ædmund," I said, reaching to touch his tousled locks. "I did not think to bring you plums." His face fell, so I quickly added that I would bring him a present on the morrow. William Malet stood, and digging in a small kidskin pouch, produced some dried plums which the tot grabbed greedily.

"Mayhap you would like to stay and talk to the boy awhile," he suggested, moving toward the stair. "I will find the lady and bring her to my chambers when you are ready."

I was grateful for his consideration, and after he had made his leave I sat down on the straw-covered planks, studying the boy in detail as he gobbled his sticky fruits. I wanted very much to make a lasting impression on him, but I did not know what to say. We spoke of a few, childish things, and he told me how the flames had raged in the city three nights and two days.

"Was't too scared to watch on it, uncle!" he said somberly, tiny brows knit in a pensive frown. "But we be'd safe here in my father's house!" Then he added that his father had been "kilt" and his father's father, too. I scarce could believe the intelligent converse from the mouth of such a babe. He was naught but a three-year's child, but he spoke of this thing and that with insightful precision, and seemed very interested when I told him my own father had been killed also. He held my hand a while in his little one, but I could not contain him long. The other children were merry in their play, and he longed to rejoin them so I let him go. Watching him jump and tumble, I realized with a pang that, if times were better, he would be playing now with little Wulf Harold's son and his twin, just as Edwin and Oswulf and I had gamed together as youngsters.

The chamber was empty when I returned to it, and there was a temptation to make my way to the hall and claim a hornful of mead to still the shakiness I felt inside. I had no time, though. Soon as I stood to do it, I heard footsteps in the corridor, and two voices—a stern, manly one that was my uncle's, and another, softer and sweeter, that made my heart leap.

My uncle stood in the archway and looked at me just a moment; then he let her in and left, closing the heavy wooden door behind him.

*   *   *

She was with child. That was the first thing I noticed of her. Before noting the gold of her hair or the green-sea fairness of her sad eyes, I saw that she was heavy with child. A crushing pain came to me unlike anything ever I knew, before or since. Trying desperately to speak, I found I could only stare. I stared and stared till I almost thought I could hear her soul cry out in torment at the sharpness of my stabbing gaze. Then I turned my back on her.

"Nothing ever was sure with you, Morcar!" is what she said, low and mournfully.

A wave of hurt and anger came so strong it made me tremble. "Methinks it could not have been that way—but perhaps naught was ever sure with you."

"You know it was; I was the one who risked all to be with you."

"Were you? I scarce can believe you thought nothing of mine was at stake." Walking a little ways away, still not looking at her, I heard her sigh and sit down.

"Think you truly we could have lived like that, you and I?" Something in her voice was sweet despite the bitterness. "Think you we could have loved that way?"

I shrugged but made no answer.

"One moment you were elated with my love; then afterwards you used me to scourge yourself with remorse! Never have you thought of that? How you waxed hot one day and cold as a priest the next? 'Twas not a thing I could reconcile myself to, Morcar; that you should crave me and then deny me for your penance."

Turning slowly, I forced myself to look at her. She was grown much older, I thought, and there were lines of hardness in her face. I watched her slender white hands as she toyed with a silver cup, thinking how much I had loved the touch of them and hating myself for remembering. My eyes wandered again to the swell of her belly, and I felt the deep hurt once more.

"'Twould not have been that way, once I was wed with you, woman!" I looked at her accusingly and she tried to avoid my eyes.

"When Oswulf died with his head in my lap, I realized some things, Morcar." First she stared pitifully, searching my face for a sign of understanding. Then she closed her eyes. "I realized how little fit I am to love a hunted man."

Of a sudden, rage came on me so tumultuously forceful that I could barely stand against the strength of it. "Never have I heard before that you felt much of a love for Oswulf Eadwulf's son!" I managed to blurt out, grasping hard on the back of a chair, as if that hold alone kept me on my feet. "Never did I suspect the affection."

"Methinks I did not, either!" she said softly. "I gave him little cause to want to keep me, yet with his dying breath 'twas me he sent for—the only touch he craved, is what he told me—" She broke off with something like a sob, and everything in me bristled.

"The man would pile that one last torture on you," I declared knowingly, flushed with anger, "to make you hold and nurse his bloody, broken body. Seems a sort of revenge to me, that he would milk you for guilt and pity with his last gasps!"

She laughed a little. "Six years he bent me to him before ever you came into my life," she said. "Oswulf knew me well as any person ever did, I trow."

"Is it so?" My voice turned cold, and I asked it with a mock wonder. "He told me the same thing himself. Fool that I am, I drew his blood over things he said he knew about you!" I brought myself closer till I was staring down at her. My look must have been exceedingly harsh; I saw her tremble. "Once he bade me ask if ever you had lain with my father."

For just a moment, I imagined she was going to scream. Her eyes grew wide like a wounded fawn's, and her mouth opened just enough to cry some voiceless, silent thing. Then she sprang to her feet and grabbed hold of my dalmatic, pulling me to her with an insistent strength I did not expect. It was almost as if she waxed in the heat of fever, so violently she shook, and her voice was so strained and low that it seemed to come from somewhere else—some great, unfathomable distance away.

"'Twas long before I loved you, Morcar!" she sobbed. She let go of me, clenched her fists and began to pound furiously on my chest. For a moment I was so stunned I let her do it, then I grabbed her shoulders roughly and pushed her back down, feeling no pity. Shuddering like a babe in sickness, I walked all the way across the room, crossed my arms in front of my face, and leant against the wall that way. It seemed an eternity passed before her voice cut into the silence.

"I never pretended there was goodness in me, Morcar—not even when first we came together. Neither did I lie to you. I would have answered this question truly whenever you asked it, then as now. Such has always been my way: to say that what is done is done and cannot be hid, right or wrong."

"Did my father entice you, or came you to him of your own want?" Feeling giddy, I spun to face her. There was naught but sheer rudeness in my tone, and she must not have wanted to answer, but after a little pause she did.

"Earl Ælfgar was a man hot and amorous by nature; must be you knew he was unhappy in his marriage bed."

"Aye. Everyone knew of it, I trow." I spoke casually now, as if we were discussing rye prices or thunderstorms. I sat down easily, looking full upon her, twisting and untwisting my fingers. I smiled coldly and asked when first it occurred to her to relieve his distress. She grew flushed.

"He danced with me once. 'Twas upon the Mid-summer's Eve we spent with you when Aldgyth turned of age."

"I remember it."

"He begged Lady Ælfgiva over and over to dance with him that night, and it grew unpleasant. I know not how it happened, but we found ourselves together dancing." She swallowed hard and lowered her eyes. "I pitied him so. He wanted naught but tenderness, and I was hard smitten with his comeliness, being very young."

I stiffened. "No younger than I was when first you laid me by your side in the grass, lady!"

Her gaze lifted and she spoke boldly, icily. "Aye. We both were old enough to love, I trow." I looked away, running fingers through my hair and biting my lip to keep back harsh words. She went on.

"He told me bitterly that she would not kiss him, and I answered I would gladly kiss so fair a man. Methinks we might have been jesting—it seemed so a while—but then he asked if I would sit and talk with him in the darkness when all had grown still and I said I would, though it must be I knew what he wanted of me. We toyed with each other then, and many another night, but I was too affrighted to give myself to him, being an unmarried woman, and he did not force me. So we went near a three year's time pressing and touching and longing for each other before I finally let him claim me."

"On your bride-ale night!" I whispered disdainfully, piercing her with a mean look. She seemed surprised that I knew of it, but nodded sedately.

"Oswulf had already twice sinned against me by then—before the wedding and on the first night of the bride-ale. I had no need to fear any consequences." Her voice grew suddenly low and earnest. "'Twas a love we had, Morcar, not a passion."

Though I felt more like spitting, I threw my head back and laughed. "What think you we had, lady? A love or a passion?"

Her cheeks burned scarlet. "I could not have known then that ever I would come to love you!"

"'Twas love then? Surely?" I laughed more. My indignance far outweighed my amusement, but I felt strongly compelled to seem unconcerned with it, else it might have overwhelmed me. So I laughed until I caught my breath with a short, sharp cry and turned a look of burning fury on her, ignoring the tears which welled in the sea-green eyes. "How many others have you so loved, Briana?"

She covered her mouth with her hand, looking miserable, inconsolably so. I repeated it. "How many?"

"Oswulf." she voiced it carefully, as if it still had the power to hurt me after all I had just heard. "I suppose I have loved Oswulf in a fashion."

"My brother?" Never had my voice been colder. She gasped my name as if she scarce could believe I had accused her. Simultaneously, we came to our feet, eyes locked together in trembling, momentary hatred. "Ever have you been with him?" I hissed in a burning whisper. I knew she would have run away from me then, but I held her by the arms, forcing her to face me. She writhed like unwilling prey as I voiced the question again, and then another time, my eyes never leaving hers. Then, abruptly, she grew limp and calm; I let her go quickly after that because the touch reminded me too well of an embrace. She did not say anything for a few seconds but a strange, dim smile began to play over her features.

"Surely you are a changed man, my gentle Morcar!" she exclaimed half-mockingly when she had walked a little way from me. "Now you are grown so cruel that I am minded to repay you by being just as cold and heartless!" Her eyes glittered strangely, catching the last rays of dusty sunlight which filtered through the high windows. Heaving a sigh, she sat suddenly as if dizziness had robbed her of all strength. I felt a swift-descending pang of concern for her, considering her condition, but it fled when she turned a frozen stare on me. "Is this what it has all come to—stabbing and agonizing each other? If 'tis so that you care so little for what we once were to each other, then I pray you will find tossing and turning torment in your own vile question. I will not answer it. You may think what you like, Morcar Ælfgar's son, and God grant that you think the worst and suffer on it a good long time."

"There is always another I can ask, lady."

"Ask him then—if you dare."

I pounded my fist on the table. She jumped at the sound, then laughed.

"I loved you, Morcar, and so I never bothered to lie to you. 'Tis what makes me think perhaps I had a love for Oswulf Eadwulf's son as well. Whatever passed between that man and me—and God knows most of it was unfortunate—at least there was always honesty. We knew each other right well, Oswulf and I!" She stopped with a little crying sound and then she was weeping. I was glad to find it did not disturb me and I made my answer in a tone of smothered anger.

"'Tis sweet you thought so highly of him, Briana. You did not favor me so well, I trow, else I would have learnt of all these happenings!"

"These were things which came to pass when I was with him. With you, they were naught but things which went before and you had no need to know of them. Still, I would have told you had you asked."

I could not help laughing again. "Ask?" I cried. "By the saints! Ne'er would it have occurred to me even to suspect!" Then I grew grave, plagued by my own feelings of pain. "How is it then that I knew naught of d'Aubermont? Is he not something which came to pass, as you say. while you were in my claim? Nearer to being mine than ever before since your man was dead? How is it I knew naught of this affair till today, when my uncle schooled me of it?"

Trembling, she flew to her feet. "How say you this? More than a year is gone since I sent my brother to tell you how it fared with me! I bade him make you come to me at Eorforwic. Heard you not his message?"

"What message?" I stood stiff, watching her press hard at that part of her where the unborn child rested. I felt a surge of fear.

"You know that Siward Bearn came north with Fulke d'Aubermont and our uncle, William Malet. My brother told me you wanted me to come to you but he added that he feared it would bode me ill to do it. King William had well hated Oswulf, and believing as every other man did that Ædmund was Oswulf's son, Siward feared the king would take my little one hostage. What is more, he swore William would never let you leave his court. You were almost like a prisoner to him, he said, and it would be your death if you tried to come north to me. Things were rumored all over the country, and by then the king had kept you next to him over a full year.

"Fulke d'Aubermont, who knew naught of what was between us, spoke freely and bitterly that you were courting with the king's daughter, a thing which caused me much pain. He even said you were arguing with Edwin for her hand because you craved her so greatly. At first, I wanted not to believe it, but later I heard our uncle tell some other men that he feared the only way your brother or you could ever live in freedom would be to marry into the king's family and bend yourselves to his will. An emptiness came on me to hear it, but I well suspected 'twas the truth they spoke.

"Then d'Aubermont began to press me to wed with him. I was Anglish and high-born, and these sort of marriages were well favored by the king. I knew not that I loved him then, but I felt certainly you were beyond me and I saw him as a sort of security for Ædmund. The king never would put harm on the step-son of one he favored as well as d'Aubermont.

"Yet I had to be sure you were done with me! I bade Siward Bearn tell you I would meet with you anywhere save a place where the king could get my child. I fully expected that our uncle would bring you back in the springtime after he made his long visit to Lundun; surely I thought King William would entrust you to his care, William Malet being a true king's man. Instead the man returned with no message from you at all—only the news that Mathilda had come from Normandy with her pretty daughters and that you could not leave the court."

She grew quiet all at once and stood with her head bent a little, eyes downcast. There was no bloom of health upon her with this carried child, as there had been before. She seemed slight and thin and pale. Watching her impassively, I could still see somewhat of the beauty that had ensnared me and could not well decide whether it was faded in truth or only in my heart's eye. I realized with a twinge of bitterness, though, that I could not remember her ever looking maidenish. That had been for others before me. Thinking on it, I pounded one hand into the palm of the other. It broke the stillness which had become intolerable to me.

"Siward Bearn brought me no message from you when he came back from Eorforwic," I began when I found my voice. She interrupted me.

"I bade him tell you that if I heard naught of encouragement from your lips, I would be forced to make a match. When I heard nothing, I thought the worst."

"The worst?"

"Aye." Her voice was a miserable, mournful whisper now. "I thought your sense of sin and shame had won you away from me."

I spat and muttered an oath low.

"'Twould not have been so much unlike you, Morcar. I could image your coming to me all calm of a night and saying you had determined not to wed with me now, to punish us for what we had both done."

"I will have you know, lady, you cannot put the blame for any of this unhappiness on me! I never wronged you!" My voice was iron and I was surprised to find I had drawn my silver dagger and now played with it absently, passing it from hand to hand.

"Your conscience was a torment to me," she said, watching it.

"Never your own was, I trow!" I tossed my head, then took a deep breath and said in a hard whisper, "'Tis true I was artless, woman—innocent even! I tasted well of remorse for much we did, and with reason, methinks. If you found that to be a fault in me, though, best you would have said it long ago, instead of coming unto me again and again and robbing me of my resistance."

She laughed recklessly. "You had no resistance to rob, Morcar! You know as much! Do not pretend to me you were unwilling!"

Furious, I sheathed the knife and spun away from her. "Might be I would have been had I seen you for what you were!" Everything in me was trembling now and I was hard-pressed to suppress it. "You blinded me, woman, and you dealt with me harshly, all the while pretending that you loved me."

"I pretended not with you." Her voice was firm. "I loved you and pretended not; I have said so before."

"Aye, and in the same breath you told me you have loved and dealt honestly with half the men of my house!"

Goaded to rage, she grabbed the nearest thing, the silver cup she had been fingering earlier, and threw it with all her might, crashing it against the stone wall. It clattered to the floor with a ringing noise, rolled a little, then grew still at my feet. She came very close to me, her face a mask of unreadable passion. When I least expected it, she reached up and caressed my cheek. Her touch was soft, but it sent unwanted fire through me like the pierce of burning metal. I jerked away from her roughly, putting my own hand to my face where hers had been, stiffening in defense.

"Worry not!" she cried bitterly, "'Tis the last touch ever you will be forced to feel from me."

I stood unmoving as she swept from the room. When she was gone, I bent and picked up the silver cup. 'Twas one from the set my father had

given to Oswulf for his bride-ale. I looked at it a moment, then tossed it
hard away, just as she had done.

                    *   *   *

In one way, I felt that everything inside me had been broken; in another,
I felt a strength I had never known before. In the noon-time, I walked
in the stables with tiny Ædmund, and showed him my own fine horse
and trappings, and my brother's. He was much impressed when I told
him mine was a gift from his avunculus, Siward Bearn. Afterwards, I
gifted him with a silver bracelet, much too big, and the heavy gold
chain, hung with a gold sun and a silver moon, that had been my
favorite when I was a boy. Both were engraved with my name and I
hoped they would one day make him think of me, and remember me
with some sort of fondness. His eyes grew wide with wonder when he
took them, and I was rewarded with an affectionate kiss.

Not long after the austere board had been set, Fulke d'Aubermont
returned from Beoforlic, whither he had gone to quell unrest. He looked
hale and handsome; despite its harshness, the northern air was wont to
bring out the best in a man. He spoke me a stiff greeting in the hall, but
I pretended not to hear him. Across the table from me, Edwin, looking
fair in wool and ermine, and a thoroughly disheveled Gilbert Rouquin
were making themselves silly with drink. Fulke sat anext them for
awhile until the king caught his eye and signaled him away to council
at another board.

So far I had been lucky enough to escape the converse of the king.
He was bone-weary, a glance could tell it, and sick with distaste for the
crudeness of this soldiers' camp. What is worse, his men were rumbling
against him and he knew it. Unmindful of the horrendous cold, he had
decreed a large contingent would leave on the morrow for Ceaster—a
long and painful trek in this chill season. Even against the advice of men
like myself, who knew the north-lands and the perils of winter in a way
these foreigners could not begin to understand, he was determined to
make the journey. The west-lands were the only part of Angland that
had not personally bowed to him; once he had their submission, he
could say he had conquered all the land.

Gilbert Rouquin was in a merry mood; he was certain to be spared
the dangers and discomforts of the trip. William had gifted him for services rendered with a huge stretch of land that included Siward Bearn's
great estate at Tathaceaster. The area was all waste now, but he knew he
could remove himself to the more comfortable quarters of the king's
castles at Eorforwic and wait out the winter there, unbothered but for
occasional scouting parties into the desolate environs. He drank with a

relish and might have grown entirely rowdy but that King William, when he had finished his private talking with d'Aubermont, came to our table, and Gilbert had need to show respect. William was in better spirits than might be expected; the submission of Waltheof Siward's son and our kinsman Gospatrick had done much to lighten his mood.

He made two mistakes when he came to speak with us, though, and they led to much dissension. First he remarked, innocently enough I suppose, how pleased he was that his man d'Aubermont had been wedded with my kinswoman. Then, before I could even make him an answer, he told Edwin how well he prized a good match between high-born Anglish and Norman. 'Twas not the thing to say to that man when he was heavy with ale. My brother grew sullen and called him a liar.

"One way or the other, you speak mistruths, Norman!" he declared loud and boldly. An immediate hush fell over the room for not another man there would have dared speak so rudely to the king. William gripped the table edge with both hands and grew pale with rage as Edwin continued. "Either you lie to these men when you say that you favor it, or you lied to me on a certain day in closed chambers—and that would be the worse sin against your honor, would it not?"

Like an incensed father, William called him a drunken brat, and my brother laughed. Then the king in a strangled voice said his earl had best behave himself, else he would shake what was left of manhood out of him in front of the assembled hall. Still laughing, Edwin stood suddenly, and to the astonishment of all, strode purposefully to the shadows neath the loft and grabbed one of the hired women there, leading her by the wrist back to the table, and sitting her there anext him in the king's presence. Everyone gasped at his arrogance, but he was too far gone in anger and drunkenness to care. In the king's hearing, he began to bargain for her, and told her he would give her a half-penny to relieve him, and another if she let him call her Adeliza.

Then the king was on his feet, eyes so hot with rage they would have melted any other man. His booming voice shook with emotion. "By God, I will chastise the sinfulness out of you, Edwin Ælfgar's son!"

But soon as the king turned mad with fury, my brother grew suddenly calm, and his voice came low and level.

"There is not so much sin in this for me, my lord," he said with genuine-sounding respect, looking suddenly sad and earnest. "'Tis a commodity allowed an unmarried man in time of war, and you of all men must know I am an unmarried man."

So saying, he took the woman by the arm, more gently this time, and led her out of the hall, all eyes upon him in stunned silence. Something in his tone had softened the king, though. An angry, expec-

tant buzz filled the entire room once he had gone, but the king said only
that the man needed prayers, and 'twas hard to believe he could be
blood kin to someone like William Malet, who was both virtuous and
sober. He stressed the last word in a meaningful way, but after that he
did not mention it more, and to the amazement of all, spent the
remainder of the night in easy humor.

As for me, though, I was in no festive mood, and there was little in
the noisy hall that could comfort me. D'Aubermont retired early, and
watching him take his leave and knowing his destination, produced in
me a feeling of dread loneliness, strong enough to make me want to
drink. I tried to retire, but Edwin had the woman in our chamber and I
could not bear to enter there, so I sat in the darkness of the hallway,
weary and depressed. Not long after, my uncle came, and seeing in a
glance my predicament, entered the chamber with a menacing look of
firm resolve. I could not hear what was said, but in a very few minutes a
rumpled figure tumbled out and fled and then my brother, half-dressed
and shaky, dragging his beltings and mantle and sword behind him,
made his way into the shadows and sat anext me on the cold floor.
Never a man looked more dejected, and I suppose we made a pretty pair,
sitting silent in the grim chill. I longed for the comfort of a well-stuffed
pallet and told Edwin so, but he claimed he could not sleep, so I left him
there staring emotionlessly into the blanketing darkness.

I took the cot nearest to my avunculus. Though I could tell by his
breathing that he was awake, we did not speak. Slumber waited long to
claim me, so wrapped I was in feverish thought, but at length I slept.

Harsh voices wakened me, jarring me from a tense and uneasy
dream. In the hallway, my brother was fighting someone. Thick with the
sweat of sleep, I leapt into the frigid night air, feeling in the dark for my
weapons. I was aware that William Malet was on his feet already and
heading out the door. Snatches of the heated converse reached me.

"—you have claimed your prize already," a heavy, angered voice was
shouting, "and I will smite you if you try to wrest this one from me!"

Edwin's voice was choking, furious. "I will murder you before I see
you touch her!" I heard him say, and then my uncle's voice bellowed in
the blackness.

"By God, I will lay you both low that spill drunken blood over the
body of a worthless slutte—"

His admonition was too late. Even as I burst frenzied into the
corridor there was the shattering sound of clashing iron and the clatter
of combat, broken by a woman's scream and the horrifying growl of men
come to arms in earnest. It lasted but a few seconds, then we were
blasted by the jolt of swords thrown hard on the stone floor while they

wrestled and one man howled with pain as the other took the advantage. Suddenly, the scene was lit; king's men rushed in, seemingly from everywhere, with pitch torches. In the eerie light, their shadows magnified and distorted, my brother struggled with Gilbert Rouquin. He was about to pound the man's head mercilessly into the rough stone wall when the king, wrapped carelessly in a heavy mantle, stepped between them and ripped them forcefully apart.

Heaving, gasping for breath, the two stared at each other with sheer hatred, then little by little, relaxed. "I will not hear your arguments now," the king hissed in a low, mean voice, "but on the morrow we will have this out, the three of us, and there will be chastisement of the worst sort if you cannot make me see a reason for this deadly folly!"

"The Anglishman waxes so arrogant he thought to bed the whore I had chosen!" Gilbert Rouquin's voice was a nasal whine; my brother leapt at him again, but William held him firm.

"I have no heart to bed her," he spat, pushing the king's hand away from himself roughly.

Glowering, William grabbed a torch from one of his men. Holding it high, he turned towards the woman, who had fallen to her knees, face hidden in shame. Soon as she lifted her gaze to his, I felt a rush of emotion and realized the nature of my brother's argument. It was Gythrun Olavsdatter, Siward Bearn's wedded woman. It was out of deference to our kinsman that Edwin had tried to keep the Norman from further dishonoring her.

Beautiful as she was, she had the look of a harlot and she shook as the king scrutinized her. It was not fear of his wrath that caused her trembling, though. She feared arrest. My cousin was the most hunted man in the kingdom now. His parents were dead and he had no children; his only sister was married to a Norman high in the king's favor. This was the only person that William might use to taunt him, and it would surely have worked. The Bearn still loved her after a fashion, and was hard weighted with guilt for having left her to her own despoliation, which was now obviously complete.

My brother's performance of late had not given the king much reason to suspect an honorable intent in his curious defense of the woman, and now William stared at him with raw, undisguised disgust. Before he could lambast him, though, my uncle, who realized our situation and the lady's, stepped in to soothe his master's ire. "Do not chastise him, my lord," he said gently, "he had reason to take offense at Rouquin's misuse of her. He knew her before, in other circumstances, and it surprised him to see her so … different."

"How is it that you knew her?" The king's voice was still angry and he looked directly at Edwin, who licked his lips and swallowed hard. He had just begun to explain when William Malet cut in.

"'Tis hard to believe this pitiful creature was a married woman," he said earnestly, "but she once was wedded to one of Morcar's best men."

Looking at my brother, I knew he was as surprised as I was by the half-truth. We had not expected it. The man said it in a way that led William to believe she was a widow, though without actually telling a lie. At that moment, I held my uncle in a higher esteem than I had for a long time. I realized suddenly how hard it was on him to live in forced opposition to his own nephew, hunting him and making war on him because of his own belief in the right and might of kingship. Siward and Burchard had been his great favorites in babyhood, and he had never found aught to quarrel with the Bearn before.

Despite his harshness as a soldier, in some ways the king was generous to a fault, and though he had decided not to take action now, it was obvious my uncle's words had swayed him. He looked at Gythrun Olavsdatter with an expression of mixed sympathy and guilt, as if he felt he might have played some major part in her humiliating downfall. My brother, though heady with drink, wore a proud, defiant gaze which spoke his firm conviction of self-right, and William seemed to appreciate it. He spoke him a civil parting, but to Rouquin, his voice was cold. He was predisposed to punish him, he said, for his breach of trust. "No man in the land is higher than my earls, save me," he said darkly, "and a soldier such as yourself has no right to draw arms on this earl or any other unless I am the man who demands it."

Even in the dim torchlight, I could see Gilbert Rouquin burn scarlet, but whether he flushed from shame or indignation, I could not say.

The morrow brought swirling snow and bone-cutting cold. William ordered a Mass said for the safety of the journey. My brother, still sodden with the after effects of heavy drinking, did not attend it. He had already sparked the first unpleasantness of the day by demanding a private meeting with Briana and young Ædmund, whom he had not seen since our arrival. The king allowed it, saying he did not sense much harm in letting blood kinfolk talk behind closed doors with a sprightly boy in the room. D'Aubermont was angered beyond measure and protested that his rights as husband had been abused because he could neither trust the Anglishman to be honorable nor to refrain from poisoning his wife's mind against him. I was glad I had taken my own opportunity while Fulke was yet away; the man was as rancid with jealousy as he had been when he courted Adeliza. I wondered if he even suspected that the treasure he guarded so closely was grossly tarnished and spoiled.

Later, while men of lesser rank scurried to prepare horses and provisions, the king held a small council in his chamber. At his bidding, I looked on with Fulke d'Aubermont and William Malet while he sorted the facts of the last night's confrontation, but it was plain he had already come to his conclusion. "I know how trying Edwin Æfgar's son can be in his ill-humors," he said wearily, "and if you had come fairly to blows with him without weapons, I might have dismissed it. You drew iron on him, though, in drunkenness, over an opinion of his which you might have seen as honorable had you been right-minded."

Gilbert Rouquin was not a bad man, and he was fiercely loyal to the king, else he might have protested when William took back the lands he had gifted him and ordered the man to make ready for the journey. "I have not fallen you back in rank, Red-Beard," he told him seriously, "because I still count you as one of the best of my men. Methinks I could not ask more of you, unless it be that you force yourself to respect any noble blood that I favor, whether it be Norman or Anglish, no difference."

Rouquin drew his tall frame tense and erect and gave the king a short, silent nod of acquiescence. When he turned to make his leave, though, his gaze caught d'Aubermont's and the look that passed between those two was chilling.

CHAPTER FIFTY-TWO

The troops who had just gone through so much
suffering . . . dreaded the ruggedness of the country,
the severity of the winter, the dearth of provisions
and the terrible fierceness of the enemy. . . . They
were often distressed by torrents of rain, sometimes
mingled with hail. At times they were reduced to
feed on the flesh of horses which perished. . . .

—Orderic Vitalis
Book IV, Chapter V

From Dunholme back to Eorforwic, the winter road was so treacherous
that William Malet offered thanks to God on his knees when he had
safely reached the king's castle there. I was glad that his duties as shire-
reeve kept him put, because the onward march was to prove even worse.
Were it not that the sacred Authority said it was a burning place, I
might have thought the frozen expanse from Eorforwic to Ceaster was
Hell, and many a man more would have agreed with me.

Even in the best of seasons, the wilds of the southwestern Eorforwic
Shire, rugged, mountainous, and dense, made for a hard journey. Now
we traversed the rough terrain in the coldest winter any could
remember. The king's brutal ravagers had already stripped the environs
of any standing shelter or accumulated foodstuffs that might have made
our way easier, and there was naught to hunt. All wildlife had fled from
the scorching. Across high frozen hills, through rain and sleet and
sopping snow, over angry, winter-swollen rivers and marshes of bottomless slush, we marched.

Horses died for lack of forage and were swallowed by the icy swamps
or left to their frosty graves. Men grew feverish and mad with hunger,
hardship, and despair. Though the king himself and his closest men
remained stoic, there was much complaining, cursing, and crying in the
miserable ranks.

Fulke d'Aubermont, Gilbert Rouquin, and the other king's men worked doggedly, day and night, trying to keep the troops in order, but at length the unthinkable happened. The foreigners, who had already endured so much for the sake of their master's endless ambition, and for so little personal gain in plunder or riches, openly rebelled, drawing swords and demanding their own dismissal.

William wasted none of the dwindling strength of his loyal men in trying to rally their affections. Any man who wished leave to fend for himself in the vast frozen wasteland, was free to go. He cared little enough whether cowards swelled his ranks or not, he said—better they should lose themselves than bother him with their moanings. Those who were brave and endured would be well-rewarded; those who were not could make their own way. In the end, the mutineers reconsidered, but only because the king's confessor gave in to their demands to issue a dispensation from the eating of horse flesh. Some two dozen men feasted that night on a once-proud battle mount which had slipped screaming into an icy crevass. The rest of us, refusing the abomination, suffered the more for the smell of it, though we'd forced them to build a separate fire a half a furlong yonder. In the morning, our bedraggled, weary, tortured party labored on, half of us in anguish from not eating, the other half in more pain yet from partaking of it.

Edwin and I were all the king had by way of guidance. His men accused us of purposefully leading them into gruesome wildernesses, but William defended us. It was his will, he declared, to reach Ceaster, the last unsubdued portion of the realm, and his men were bounden to follow him in his necessary course. He never went so far as to take blame for the foolhardy venture, but he declared staunchly that my brother and I had urged and pleaded with him not to attempt it. That was the truth of it, too. We stressed to him how oft-times an earl's entire house-hold would camp in a strange house, if need be, to escape the curse of northern travel in the snow season. 'Twas yet one more thing the Anglish inherently understood that the Normans could not fathom.

After near a fortnight, we came at last out of the barrenness caused by the king's razing. Trees became more plentiful but, sodden and frozen in turn, the wood refused to burn even if the screeching wind abated long enough to allow the striking of a tinder. During a blizzarding wind-storm of nightmarish proportions, the last of the tents was mangled beyond repair. After that Edwin, Fulke, and even King William himself were forced to camp in the icy elements, to my suffering brother's even greater detriment. I myself had been taking bed in the frozen open for a while already, ever since the other canopies were leveled. I had decided then that I fain would rather suffer the force of the driving sleet than the wagging tongues of disgruntled Normans naming me weakling and king's favorite.

We had struggled our way north of the Peaclond, in the realm of narrow, mountainous passes and craggy hills when the hail started. Here we abandoned the last of our horses. Till then I had remained strong and impressed many of the others with my indifference to the weather and misery, and I was inwardly proud of the fact.

Though none knew it, when I loosed that bold, red stallion, I wept. Siward Bearn had made a gift of him to me on the eve of my taking the North Humbria. Decked in proud silver he had carried me through my duties as earl. In armored strappings he had ridden to Gate Fulford. For five years we had hunted and gamed and paraded together, faced danger and fled from it, sought solitude in quiet spots and merriment in boisterous ones. He was best of any animal I ever had, and turning him out to his certain death that day hurt me more than I can tell.

There was little time to think about it, though. All on foot now, we marched for our lives. A full six days we fought onward in rain and hail, drenched and frozen to agony. On the seventh day, we saw a party of six men on a high ridge, taking account of us from a distance. Many of the Normans crossed themselves at the sight; it had been so long since we had seen another living creature that no man gave thought to whether they might be friend or enemy.

On the twenty-eighth day of our wandering, we came to the gates of Ceaster. Seeing that the king had us hostage in his company, the men there did not even draw arms.

CHAPTER FIFTY-THREE

At last he brought his forces to Ceaster, having suppressed the hostile uprisings throughout Mercia with tyrannical power.

—Orderic Vitalis
Book IV, Chapter V

March 1070

"What matters it if you are king, if there is naught but soot and hollow buildings for you to rule over here?" Aldgyth's pretty voice echoed severely in the near-empty hall. The king laughed low.

"I will be king. That is what matters!" he said gravely, pinching off a corner of hard cheese and rolling it between his thumb and forefinger thoughtfully. "I promised those men who attained this place with me that they would be rewarded for their loyalty, and now I am committed to granting them reward. Rest assured, though, Lady Aldgyth. I have pledged God that no harm would fall on this house or any of its lands, and no man or woman in your service will be insulted."

Five days we had been at my sister's house in Ceaster, gifted to her by Siward Bearn before his outlawry. The bulk of the army was camped in the city. William had hand-chosen the men who would relax in luxury with him on the great estate. We had bathed, eaten, shaved, and slept, and now we more closely resembled human beings than the gaunt, empty-eyed creatures who had come here out of the cold.

Both Fulke d'Aubermont and Gilbert Rouquin were on duty in the town, trying to rebuild order amongst the waste and ravaging, and would not be back till nightfall. A few of the Normans lingered in the back of the hall, gaming and making talk, but for all intents, we were alone with William, my sister and I. Edwin had left our company in a surge of anger near an hour before. The king had called us hither with a strange petition: Gilbert Rouquin had asked him for my sister's hand, without a word to us, and the king had said he felt it best to ask our permission to grant it. No doubt our shock, dismay, and outright refusal surprised him. He had not thought it outlandish that the man should ask, he told us amiably, after my brother had stomped away.

"The woman is unattached and very beautiful, and Red-Beard is haughty enough not to see she is too high a match."

If he had been a man of any sensitivity, he would have felt the heat of Ywen Carr's son's smoldering gaze as he asked us. The man sat stiffly, back against the wall and arms folded across his massive chest, on a bench below the dais, guarded and watchful. He pretended it was his usual place to sit, but truth was, all three of the Welshmen refused to take table with the king after his deceitfulness in the stealing of Wulf Harold's son, and even the presence of the sons of Ælfgar could not move their resolve.

William had taken Edwin's distemper with good enough grace, reminded perhaps that marriage was most ill of all subjects with him. We were lucky to have one there who could bring him rapidly back to gentleness. Brother Wulfget had come in the autumn to tend Ealdread's widow, Lady Gweneth, as she lay in fever. When the poor creature died despite his efforts, he stayed on at Aldgyth's request, to give what he could of comfort. 'Twas not an easy time for my sister, for Gweneth had many years been her friend and companion, though she had never been truly well since her husband died at the Gate Fulford. 'Twas surely the hand of God that had planted the good monk there at that particular time, though. My brother had never been in such sore need of guidance and admonishment, and there was not a better one to give it.

So, soon as Edwin made his heated retreat, Brother Wulfget rose from his bench near the hearth and followed him. Watching them go with somewhat of a wry wonder, William shook his head and remarked how Edwin waxed more and more imperious. He said it mattered not much to him, because he was equipped to ignore it, but other men might grow infuriated and make a quarrel he would be hard-pressed to quell. Then, seeing both Aldgyth and I bristle in our brother's defense, he turned the talk to other things. The time did not pass unpleasantly, even though we came at length to discussing the horrible harrying of the Ceaster Shire which William had condoned.

The next day dawned snow-free and slightly sun-kissed. Except for the acrid grey mist that hovered above the ruined town, the sky was slate blue and cloudless, and the booming wind carried somewhat of the smell of the churning ocean. There was still a pronounced coldness, but after the mass, we begged the king to let us ride awhile and enjoy the daylight. After some consideration, he let us do it, with a Norman guard behind and on the condition the Welshmen did not go. He had not punished them for the part they played in our flight from Wintanceaster, but he made it plain that he did not trust them and held them in little regard. The priest could go with us, he said admonishingly, but the black-haired Anglish, which is what he called the Carr's sons, had best take a party of the king's men out to the weald to hunt winter birds. He was trying to gather food enough to make a feast for St. Gregory's day before we took our leave, and he was hard-pressed to do it because he had allowed such an excess of harrying.

Inwardly, I wished he had not chosen d'Aubermont and Rouquin to ride with us, but for most of the way we rode far ahead of them, Edwin and Brother Wulfget and I, deep in converse. The priest had a lot of news for us, and as we wended our way slowly along the crystalline banks of the Big Stream, which perked and sparkled in the sunlight till it near blinded us, the man told much as he could in a low tone.

Hereward had come with Heard Ulf's son to Peterborough shortly after the rout at Dunholme. His uncle, the good Abbot Brand, was on his death-bed there, and Hereward had petitioned him to let the outlaws make camp in the place and plan a defense. "The abbot said he could not in conscience allow it, though," Wulfget said, shaking his rusty-colored head sadly. "He gave them food and gold stuff, but said God had put foremost upon him the charge of keeping safe the holy place, and to invite slaughter and desecration into its walls would be a sin. I am sad to say those kinsmen parted as unfriends and the abbot died a few days after. The Wake and the others have chosen to hide themselves."

Edwin and I were saddened to hear this. We knew full well that if Uncle Leofric had been alive, he would have welcomed the rebels and aided them in this time of sore need. Still, we were glad to hear that two, at least, of our best men were live and whole, and Brother Wulfget noted they had brought favorable tidings of Siward Bearn. "He is strong and fit and well-hid since the king's pronouncement against him," he told us, "and he bids us all remember Hereward's war-arrow."

My brother and I exchanged a glance at that. So much time had passed since the cleaving of the arrow that we near had forgotten it, but Wulfget assured us 'twas still the sign by which our men hoped to gather us. "There are many men scattered across the face of Angland who are waiting to have that bit piece handed to them," he smirked with grim satisfaction, shading his eyes against the sun and snow as the road bent east away from the forest, "and every one will know the part he is to play when he receives it."

Another quarter-hour of furtive chatting brought us to the split in the stream and we dismounted, leading our horses one at a time over the solid stone bridge-span, slippery now with patches of frozen spray and slush. The Normans caught up with us then, grumbling a little about the extent of our wanderings, having already grown wroth with the chill.

"Best we stay unmounted till we have warmed ourselves!" Gilbert Rouquin cried adamantly, pulling a stout leathern flask from beneath his mantle. He held it high as if to offer it all around but when his eyes met Brother Wulfget's, he flushed uncomfortably and quickly withdrew it. The monk had been working hard to make my brother sober-minded and he flinched, then cast me a bitter smile, when Edwin grabbed it, uncapped it, and swallowed a lusty draught. Soon as Edwin took the drink, d'Aubermont walked a ways away and turned his back, pretending to be interested in the glistening tangle of iced willow boughs which near enclosed us in the tiny clearing. He and my brother had grown so hardened to each other that they spoke not at all now, except to exchange rudenesses.

I thought it ironic that the final bitterness between them had sprung from the Norman's possessiveness of his well-prized wife. Thinking of it, I realized suddenly that though it looked different in its winter coat of hoary frost and snow, we stood in the same small dell I used to visit to claim solitude. 'Twas the first place I had lain with Briana, and it seemed ill-fitting that d'Aubermont should be here. Feeling myself grow hard inside and cold, I undid my horse from the tree where he was tethered and led it silently back over the bridge, wanting to fast put a distance between myself and the memory of my weakness.

I managed to keep myself clear of the turmoil that brewed in the hall later, and well my brother might have, too, had he not returned to his wanton drinking that day. The king had promised Rouquin his answer this night, and if he had been allowed his own way, might have placated his man by pretending the decision to deny the match was his own. Poor Gilbert, totally love-struck and entirely unaware that William had approached us on the subject of our sister, no doubt believed the betrothal was imminent. He had been working hard to unbuild the coldness that had waxed between him and Edwin since their unpleasantness in Dunholme and had nearly succeeded, largely by being generous with drink and geniality. His shock was genuine when the king refused his permission; his large frame buckled as if he had received an untoward blow.

Just as he raised his voice in protest, my brother spoke out, standing shakily at the table he was sharing with the Welshmen, themselves all sullen with mead, in the center of the room. "My sister has more worth and honor than certain other of our noble kinswomen," he said loud and belligerently, "in that she would not be lowered to wedding with a common soldier."

Soon as he said it, Fulke d'Aubermont jumped up from his seat flushed and angry, cursing him, and the Red-Beard rushed towards him defiantly, as if to strike. In an instant, all three of the sons of Carr were on their feet, weapons drawn, as if daring the foreigners to lay hand on their earl. Stopped dead in his tracks by the formidable sight of them, Gilbert Rouquin sputtered in helpless rage, shaking and waving his fist, and many of the king's men leapt forward, caught up in the commotion. Then William's iron voice boomed through the hall, commanding every man to sit and take hold of himself. There was a deafening silence, finally broken by my brother's insolent laughter.

As he did every man who drew arms in his hall, the king banished the sons of Carr from the house for the duration of his stay. They made us a hasty but meaningful fare-well on the spot, then went to Aldgyth's chamber to take leave of her before removing northwest to the Welsh encampment at the Dee mouth. William reprimanded Gilbert Rouquin, but not too sharply, saying he understood how a man's temper could wax ferocious when his desire for a woman was thwarted. He looked at Edwin, too, when he said it, as if the words were half meant for him. Then, with exaggerated movement, he took the full cup of mead from off the table in front of my brother and held it upside down, draining it to the last drop.

*   *   *

For a few nights after, Edwin was more moderate in his drinking, but on St. Gregory's night, while I sat talking late with Aldgyth in her chamber, he came there so drunken that we were entirely perplexed as to what to do with him. Unlike some, the man had always been able to keep some-what of a mind about him; that had been the only saving grace in his periods of wildness and debauchery. This night, though, he was so mind-less he seemed unable to speak or to comprehend. At length, we gave up trying to make conversation and had a hurried conference between us. Deciding it would be best to make him sleep, we led him to the pallet and attempted to lay him down. He fought us till we gave up, then tensed himself on the edge of it, pulling his mantle tight around him, refusing to be handled more.

So we tried to make light of it, offering him this thing or that for his comfort, but there was no hint that he understood us. We returned to the small table near the hearth-fire and tried to talk of other things while he sat stony, silent, and stiff as a carven statue. After a while, real-izing he was entirely beyond reach, we began to speak freely about his condition right in front of him, and I explained how it had been with him the last year or more.

The tallow candles were burning low when he began to curse dully, in a slurred and senseless voice. I berated him for letting Aldgyth see him suchwise, but his tone of helpless desperation made me draw closer. Despite the drafty coldness of the room, the man was in a profusion of sweat. He stared blankly for a few minutes. Then, seeming to recognize me, he whispered hoarsely that he had taken a wounding.

If it pained him, he did not show it, and for some reason he was wroth to let us help him. Pensive and anxious, Aldgyth wiped his brow, then moved around the cot behind him, kneading his rigid shoulders to relax him, all the while cajoling him softly to accept our help. Suddenly he screamed out at her touch. This jarred us so entirely that, smitten with a kind of fear, we showered him with questions and cries till he bade us imperiously to be still.

"Fetch me Brother Wulfget," he demanded. I answered I would bring whatever priest first I found, but he said no, Wulfget alone would do, for he had a great need to confess. Then he grew stiff and still again, but his teeth chattered loudly in the disarming silence.

Wasting no time, I ran to the hall, long since grown quiet, and found a man whom I sent to fetch the priest. When I returned, Aldgyth was trying hard to make sense with Edwin, but 'twas to no avail. He had grown icy still as before.

It seemed an eternity passed. I was sinking with weariness when Brother Wulfget arrived, bewildered and apprehensive, vehemently rubbing the sleep from his eyes. With my sister looking on, the two of us took forcible hold of my brother, trying to strip away his mantle and outer garments. He did not really resist us, but being totally unwilling or unable to move, it was a formidable task to disrobe him, made the worse by our not knowing the nature or extent of his injury. He made not a gasp, cry, sound, or shudder of any kind, so I thought there could not be much that grieved him till we had him down to his tunic and saw that the side of it was stained crimson with blood.

Our touch grew gentle then, but after inspecting the stab hole, Wulfget declared 'twas naught but a flesh wounding in the muscle of the waist, mean but not dangerous. We meant to lay him down then, and took his shoulders to do so, but soon as we touched him, he let go another piercing cry. Wulfget bade Aldgyth bring a lantern near, and inspecting him in the light of it, pronounced that Edwin had taken a beating so severe it had broken his bones in the shoulder, collar, and ribs. Wulfget crossed himself and said it was a marvel the man had sat so still through that undressing, and all the time before it, for the pain must have been overwhelming, despite the ale in him and the numbness of shock.

When Aldgyth ran from the room, I knew she was ill. 'Twas not from the sight of blood; she had seen her share of that in the Cymry and was no stranger to it. It was the sight of Edwin's scars from Fulford that frightened her. She had known naught of them till then, and they still looked evil as ever.

While she was gone, we tried to ease him. He found it too painful to put himself prone, so we propped him with pillows and buntings into a half-sitting position, trying to make it as hurtless as possible. He uttered not a sound throughout, and in a little while slipped into senselessness. Barely had we finished with him when Aldgyth reappeared, calm and collected again, clutching something tight to her breast.

"Methinks 'tis time to open this once more," she whispered, holding it up. I sat down heavily when I saw what it was: the small, leathern pouch she had been gifted with in Eireland. Siward Bearn had carried it back to her some time ago. Brother Wulfget stared curiously, then took and sniffed it.

"How came you by Alpine knit-bone?" he asked with wonder, looking from one to the other of us. We made no answer. Taking the pouch back, Aldgyth emptied a pile of the fragrant contents onto a loose woven cloth, and bade him go about preparing it. He hesitated just a moment, staring at us curiously, then jumped to his feet, enjoining us to do one task and another to make my brother ready.

Brother Wulfget applied the poultices and bound him tight in linen. Edwin came to consciousness for this, smiling a little groggily, letting Aldgyth stroke his hair and hug him comfortingly. We heard no moan or complaint from him, but there was excruciation in his eyes. Then Wulfget deftly tied wooden splints around his chest to keep him from moving his cracked bones, and made him drink a ladleful of the healing liquid. He lapsed again into sleep not long afterwards. Our priest friend had heard his confession while my sister and I waited outside, but Edwin had purposefully refused to tell us anything of what had occurred.

Leaving the two of them there with Edwin, I went back to my own chamber. It seemed I had barely drifted into dream when Wulfget came to rouse me. It took a splash of icy water to bring me anywhere near wakefulness. I was so tired, I even let him dress and comb me for the Mass, which was not my fashion at all. Making my way with him to the chapel, I hoped this might be one of those rare mornings when the king heard daily office in his own chamber. I was loath to face him, not knowing any of the circumstances of Edwin's plight, and not knowing whether or what William had heard of it.

A scanning of the chancel relieved me; he had not come after all. I caught sight of Fulke d'Aubermont though, and even as my eyes came to rest on him, he turned my way with a look of cold contempt. Down his left cheek, near to the hairline, was a vivid, angry cut, and his left arm was wrapped in a binding. I swallowed involuntarily and broke my gaze away from his.

Sure in my heart of what had happened, I pondered all through the service. It did not surprise me that those two had come to arms; they had panted for each other's blood a good long while now, though only those who knew them best would have known it. D'Aubermont clearly had claimed the victory in their confrontation, yet there was no sneer of triumph in his look—no hint of it even. In fact, he looked as if he felt his woundings far more than he had need to do. In every glance he sent me I read frustrated outrage and half-suppressed vindictiveness, as if he had not tasted sweet avengement at all, and longed for it more than ever.

God knows I had no reason to love the man, yet I cannot say I felt hatred for him. Rather, it seemed he had always excited in me a certain groundless pity, a feeling that he was a man who drew misery like eggs drew foxes, ill-fated through no fault of his own, and deeply resentful of it. Even his well-prized woman.... I swallowed the pain it cost me just to think of her. That torture, too, would be upon him in time, I had no doubt of it.

He wasted no time coming to me after the benediction, his cold eyes masking any emotion he might have felt. "How came you by such an injury, Fulke?" I asked levelly, trying not to stare at the mean gash.

Stiffening, he eyed me resentfully. "Surely your brother has relayed the tale to you, Anglish?"

"Nay. He has not." It irritated me greatly to be addressed that way, as if the word itself were a vile insult. I tossed my head and threw my shoulders back. "Why think you he would prattle to me of your ills and misfortune?"

His eyes narrowed. "Because 'tis unlike him not to brag of his jaunty conquests!"

It was a strange remark, and I eyed him curiously. I thought he would add more, but instead he jabbed his elbow at Gilbert Rouquin, who had been beside him listening all the while. "Lord Morcar please will understand that the king is expecting us now," he said, in a voice rather too loud and too courteous. Then they moved past me without another word.

I had long ago given up trying to understand these Normans. Their manners seemed to be at once both fastidious and trifling; a man could never tell from converse with them what was of importance and what was not. Either they spoke with winning persuasiveness of cold and unfeeling things, or their voices waxed hard and tonelessly on subjects of worth and beauty. Yet, one aspect of their character had manifested itself most clearly, I thought. When they were open and willing to talk, all was well; but when they grew close-mouthed and secretive, a man would do well to suspect trouble or festering ill-feeling. That is why I stood still and silent, staring after them till they disappeared through the doorway into the wind. The Norman had refused to speak to me; it meant he had something to say.

Brother Wulfget told me it would be best if I did not trouble myself too deeply over d'Aubermont's whims. "Better you would pry the details from your brother, or wonder on the king's reaction to what has passed." He rubbed the palms of his hands absently on the coarse wadmal of his robe as he walked, smiling a wooden smile. "'Tis a misfortune that Lord William will hear all Fulke's melancholy accusations first, but his regard for Edwin is such that methinks he will not wait long to summon out the other side of the tale."

In that, the grave-eyed brother was entirely correct. Even as we settled ourselves to break-fast in Aldgyth's chamber, where my brother still slept in his awkward position, a house-boy came with a message. King William sought to have Earl Edwin join him in the king's private lodges as near to immediately as possible. I shrugged away my sister's worrisome gaze and went myself instead.

At the king's door, I hammered sharply with the bracelets of my right arm. One of William's men answered. He looked at me impassively for a brief moment, then stood back to let me enter. After, he took his own leave, slamming the door into place with a hollow thud. The king was alone except for Fulke d'Aubermont and Gilbert Rouquin. All three stood, more or less involuntarily, when they saw me. William muttered an incomprehensible greeting before he settled back into his high-backed, gilt chair, but Fulke came forward suddenly and placed his hand on my shoulder with some forcefulness.

"We do not mean to involve you in this quarrel, Morcar Ælfgar's son," he said in a low, firm voice. "'Twas your brother that we sent for."

"Aye." I nodded knowingly, forcing a smile as I took a stool and dragged it near to the king, seating myself at the square table. "I have come in his stead, d'Aubermont."

"In his stead?" Fulke tossed the other two men a thin-lipped look of exasperation. "Mayhap someone should be sent to his chamber, sire," he said coldly, looking straight at the king, "to slap the wine-weakness out of him and put him to his feet."

I pointed an accusing finger. "You of all men must know that it is not drunkenness that forces him to keep to his bed this day, Fulke d'Aubermont!"

Gilbert Rouquin cut me off, his eyes flecked with anger. Hands on the table, he leant forward and declared staunchly it was no secret that Edwin was wanton with spiced wines and mead. "He is grown an obstinate man, my Lord William, arrogant and difficult. "

The king stroked his chin roughly, then looked from one to the other of us with stinging slowness. For just a moment, I was reminded of his face the night Edwin bargained for the hired woman in his presence. Swallowing hard, I lowered my gaze, but when he cleared his throat and began drumming his strong fingers on the arms of his chair, all three of us turned and watched him expectantly.

"Never have I felt aught but kinship for Earl Edwin," he began in a muted voice, looking past us. "Yet it is true he has forced me to tolerate much this year past, trying my patience with boldnesses I would ne'er allow in any other man. I have acted towards him—and you, Earl Morcar—as a father to a son, staying my chastisement out of tenderness. Not always has this sat well with my men." He tossed a cool glance towards d'Aubermont as he said this last, and that man flushed uncomfortably a moment, shifting his weight on the table where he sat.

"Well you know I would gladly have had the man for my son-in-the-law, but that it could not be reconciled. Mayhap I have felt a certain guilt towards him—as towards my own prized daughter also—because this attachment could not be furthered in the end." His voice trailed off morosely. I turned a glare of accusation on the uneasy Fulke.

Rouquin drew a sharp breath. "Not a one of us doubts the wisdom of your leniency, sire. I am first to admit a fondness for the Mercian. He is worthy of a particular admiration as noble men come and go. When he deems himself well-ordered, there is naught to dislike in such a comely man. Yet of late, he has entirely given himself over to tides of wantonness and distemper. Surely you knew as much, even back in Wintanceaster. Last night, in a state of total mindlessness, the fool breathed insults of the grossest sort and then drew the blood of a king's-man. Methinks the earl has advantaged himself of your mercy long enough!"

So saying, the wide-shouldered man brushed his hair back with a gesture of contempt, then sat himself down heavily. Fulke tossed him a comradely glance of appreciation.

I was flooded with sudden ire at the memory of Edwin's senselessness the night before. "Think you it was fair to make a life-and-death fight with a man who scarce could hold his feet?" I asked Fulke, impaling him with a mean stare. He bristled.

"I made no fight, Morcar Ælfgar's son! 'Twas your brother's doing."

"From the look of him, you made fight enough!"

"What mean you? He drew his own blade when we carried none and in his drunkenness delivered himself a flesh-wound." He scowled, eyes glittering. I gave a short and bitter laugh.

"'Tis true that the knife did him but little harm, d'Aubermont. The cracks and breaks in his bones and ribs are what ache him!"

At once they were on their feet, all three. "Say you this man wounded him?" William asked in a stringent voice.

I nodded, and Fulke paled. "'Tis an impossibility!" he cried, glancing from me to the king. "The man walked away—laughing!"

"Aye," I said bitingly. "So his vanity always has been stronger than his sense of pain!" I flinched at the thought of him walking any distance in such agony.

The king was moving towards the door. "Tell me where to find him!" he demanded gruffly, hand on the heavy latch.

I hesitated just a moment, knowing Edwin would not be pleased to see him. "He lies now in splints and poultices within my sister's chamber—" Before I could finish, William was gone. I sat wordlessly, staring after him till Fulke broke the silence, walking round to face me.

"If what you say is true, then it is best you know we did not mean to put any permanent harm on him—neither knew we that we did!"

"I can believe it," I said, as graciously as I could. "Else you would not have brought it before the king, I trow." Then I thought about what he had said and came to my feet with swelling rage. "We, d'Aubermont? Mean you to say that both of you fought him?"

Grimacing, Rouquin swallowed hard and raised his palms helplessly. "He came upon us like a madman; in truth, 'twas all the two of us could do to stop him. A demon was inside him, I am sure of it, to make him say things so obscene and work him into such an evil passion."

I focused a harsh stare on the other, who flushed with shame. "We were the both of us warm with drink," he said, not meeting my eyes, "and, by the relics, the man said unforgivable things about my wife."

Letting go a long, labored breath, I turned my back on the two of them. "Must be you were mindless, too, to do what you did unto him without even knowing it," I said quietly. "Mayhap you were as drunk with jealous hate as he was with wine." Neither spoke, but I knew they had exchanged a look.

I walked to the door slowly, without looking back. Over my shoulder, I told d'Aubermont I was glad the bad blood between him and my brother had at last been let, and said it pleased me that neither of them had come to death in the process. "Now may be you two can meet with honor, and talk together in friendly fashion again, as in other days."

Could be d'Aubermont read sarcasm where none was intended. Perhaps my brother had cut too deep with whatever words he had used to wound him. Maybe he regretted a weakness which had kept him from killing a man he despised with a hatred too strong to control. I know not. But in the wake of my words, another sound came: a jarring, steely thunder which spun me round to face him. He had drawn his broadsword, and with both hands on the hilt, crashed it into the stone wall. His face, distorted with rage, seemed drained rather than flushed with his ire. Tense, low, and icy, his voice cut through the echo which still resounded hauntingly.

"This I swear to you," he hissed, sheathing the silver weapon. "If ever I look upon Edwin Ælfgar's son again, it will be the day he dies!"

I stared at him long and hard. His face was a mask of sullenness. I was not to see Fulke again for nearly two years, and in all that time, whenever I pictured him, his thin, haughty face was wearing that same evil look.

CHAPTER FIFTY-FOUR

King William ordered the monasteries of the whole
of England to be searched, and the money which
the richer English had there deposited, on account
of his harshness and rapacity, to be carried off and
stored up within his treasury.

—Simeon of Durham

May 1070

Assuredly, there is never a man more silent and sober than one who has resigned himself to the fact that Providence has irrevocably settled against him. So my brother was all the springtime of that year: distant, remote, and untalkative. He had weathered the laborious journey from Ceaster, his ribs sternly bound in tight-sheets, with no mead or medication of any kind, and without a single visible hint of his misery.

Our party arrived in Wintanceaster on the twenty-eighth day of March, in the very midst of the Palm Sunday parades and gaming. Edwin drank of no spirits at the king's table that night, nor at the great Easter feasting a week later, when even the most conservative of the king's men grew merry and free. It was nearing the middle of mild May, and in over three fortnights he had not partaken even once of drink enough to speak of. Brother Wulfget, whom the king had allowed to return with us, said it was a miracle that he should come so cleanly away from it and well it might have been. When we had been back in the city but a few days, the king had brought Edwin to St. Swithun's grave and doused him with the rainwater they collected there. The hope had been to relieve him of the excruciation he felt in his bones when the weather changed, but as our priestly friend was quick to point out, mayhap God had seen fit to wreak a miracle more sorely needed.

In fact, William had been more than solicitous of my brother's welfare since his hurting, attending him himself, forever looking in on him and suggesting this cure or that for his limb-stiffness. So fatherly was he in his attentions that at times I feared I did injustice to the man, and wished I could have liked him more. He did not seem to comprehend that his concern for us was entirely at odds with the vindictive havoc which he wrought over all our land. He genuinely craved our support and admiration and thought it some odd personal quirk of ours that we could not embrace his proffered wealth and friendship at the expense of our countrymen.

He had made it a grim season for the Anglish. Before we left Ceaster, he decided lawlessness was rampant enough now to demand a larger, more fiercely armed protectorate. In the north, those fortunate enough to have survived the intensity of the winter without food or shelter now faced a worse threat: pestilence. The diseases that accompanied starvation and over-exposure were rampant. The masses of unburied dead were decaying with the thaws, further putrefying the burnt, infertile fields. As if it would somehow relieve the distress, William had prayers for the sick and homeless incorporated into the daily Mass, but word was that thousands died weekly in the North Humbria, in the barren wildernesses that had once held great cities.

With absolutely no means of livelihood, men fought, robbed, and murdered for the most essential of foodstuffs, and the king saw fit to increase his army in order to stop them. To gain the money he needed to support more mercenaries, he demanded that all the Anglish monasteries hand over their riches. When they would not, he issued a writ allowing his forces to enter any holy place at will, and collect what "offerings" they could. The proclamation having been made, almost every monastery had been plundered to poverty, many burnt or leveled according to the intensity of their resistance. A handful of the holy places, like Ely, were yet untouched because they were inaccessible during the springtime flooding of the fen-lands. William pretended he had spared Peterborough out of deference to our house, but we knew it was because he could not hope to reach it till summer.

This is what we were talking about, Brother Wulfget and I, on a particular May morning, luminescent and cloudless. We were alone in a counting-room high in the clerestory, watching my brother in the courtyard below. It was only the third or fourth time Edwin had attempted to sit a horse since our return from the west. Little Wulf Harold's son sat in front of him on the wide leathern saddle, and though they plodded gingerly and gently over the muddy cobbles in a wide circle, the boy cried with as much delight and enthusiasm as a sprightly canter down a pretty path might have inspired. We could not help smiling.

"Soon he will feel well enough to take to the fields again," Wulfget mused hopefully, after remarking how much stronger Edwin seemed this day then last. "Good air, sunshine, and activity will prove a boon for you. Must be you are waning in this gloomy place. Both of you are as pale as death!"

I nodded absently but turned the talk back to the monasteries. "Think you, now that Abbot Brand is dead, that the monks might have allowed Siward Bearn and Hereward and the rest of their men to make a hiding in Peterborough?" I asked him seriously. He shrugged.

"When you live in seclusion as those men do, 'tis near impossible to imagine how greatly changed circumstances can become on the outside. Look at what has befallen in the last years! You scarce can believe the reality of all this yourself, I trow, and you have witnessed it with your own eyes. I know that when the Wake came to Peterborough, most of us thought his tales were gross exaggerations. I surely never expected to see what I did when I left that place—" Stopping with a hard swallow, he crossed himself.

"So you think they would still deny them access?"

"I think they cannot hope to understand the fierceness of the struggle, that is all. Methinks they picture all this like the simple quarrels we were wont to know of old." He wiped both his hands suddenly on his robe, as if willing away an unpleasant thought. His rust-colored hair was fast out-growing its new tonsure, and I was glad to see he still wore my father's knife; it hung from his waist with handsome strappings of unadorned skiver, knotted and twisted into a thick belt. "In a way," he continued in a whisper, "'twould be fitting if those men could indeed be hid at Peterborough. Then the king might be harder pressed to collect his offering when he sends his soldiers there."

He stopped abruptly, as if biting back a sinful thought, and looked at me sheepishly. I tossed him a grim smile. Thanks to my grandfather's piety and the generosity of our house, Peterborough was richer in treasure than all the holy houses in Angland combined. Though the king hesitated now, possibly out of some hard-measured, begrudging respect for us, 'twould not be long before his councilors helped him find an honorable-looking way of raping the place. Most of them had little enough regard for us, though they pretended to it for the king's sake. Many resented the fact that Fulke d'Aubermont had been banished from the court for the space of a year, and Gilbert Rouquin from the king's hall forever for offending my brother as they had. Edwin hid his pain so well that perhaps they did not realize the extent of his wounding, and to them, the Anglish were naught but the conquered—high-born or low, all the unworthy same.

I continued thinking of these things late into the night, long after Brother Wulfget had retired to the priest-house. The next day, when

Edwin decided to try a slow ride down the sea-roads, they still jostled me.

William was glad that Edwin, sober now, was pushing himself towards complete recovery, and offered him every encouragement. He invited himself to join Brother Wulfget and myself and ride with him down the riverside, but my brother said nay, he would rather have the king see him when he was easy in the saddle, and that might be another few days. Laughingly, William agreed. Notwithstanding the pain it caused him to mount, Edwin sat handsomely. The stiffness of his posture gave him a regal, almost haughty look; it characterized his every movement with a bold, solemn gracefulness. There was no doubting that William took pleasure in it, after the many months of my brother's loose-minded carelessness.

"Be sure not to hesitate to call if you are in distress," he said, gesturing to three of his men who were prepared to ride some ways behind us, as was the king's manner of precaution. "And do not over-tax yourself. There are many other fair days in store for riding." With a great deal of exertion, William was speaking formal, stylized Anglish now, haltingly and not always with coherence. He had enlisted both my help and Brother Wulfget's on a near daily basis in order to learn it. With his men, he still spoke his own dialect of French.

Though I had not liked it much when first we came there, a fondness had developed in me for the wealds of Wintanceaster—the pretty threads of road curving along the right bank of the river, the many bridged rivulets and streams, and the ancient stonework marking the causeways all the way down to the sea. This time of year, too, there was a profusion of blossoms and flowering trees, lending a sweetness to the southern air that lingered in the soul. I had not ridden out of the noisy cobbled courtyard since we came and it felt good to taste of the gentle, open wind and to feel it in my face. I managed to lose myself in these sensations a while, as we all rode silently, enjoying them. Then, unbidden, I thought of Peterborough and of my kith and kinsmen being hunted by the king.

Soon as my brother drew anext me and looked into my eyes, I knew he was sharing my thoughts again. He signaled Brother Wulfget, and as the road had grown wider, we rode three abreast a while. Edwin looked behind to ensure that the king's men were without the hearing distance and then he asked me seriously if I remembered how we had robbed the chapel at Grandmother's in Couventrie. I replied that, of course, I did.

"Well, of late, I have wished we had done more," Edwin returned darkly, glancing from one to the other of us in a furtive way. "I have wished we had ridden that last half-mile to the monastery and stripped it all to nothingness."

Shocked, Brother Wulfget crossed himself and darted me a look of perplexion. "Grandfather Leofric lies there!" I began, bothered myself, but he cut me off.

"Aye, Grandfather lies there, but so also was there great treasure—the golden boxes and crucifix all fixed with gems, and the altar frontal."

"Have you no wariness of sin?" the priest asked him, brows knit pensively, but my brother shook his head.

"Methinks God would rather have willed it to us than to the Norman invaders," he answered ruefully. "In the end, they have stolen it all away, anyway." He paused a minute, then forcefully added, "and if the treasures of Peterborough are meant to build an army, best they would build an Anglish army, and not one of church-robbing infidels."

Exchanging a mute glance, Brother Wulfget and I caught his meaning at the same time. Edwin scrutinized us for a reaction. "We do not even know that the king means to pillage there," I began, but this time it was the monk who interrupted me.

"He has chosen the Norman Turold to be Abbot of the place, soon as arrangements can be made for him to go there," he said in a marked tone, "and oft I have tended to think that that will be his sneaking way of robbing it."

"Aye," Edwin's voice was glum. "Turold is a tyrant, more a soldier than a priest. Best we remember that Father and Grandfather and Uncle Leofric bequested those riches to God, and if God is not to have them, they should revert to us. Not to our enemies."

There was a stretch of silence filled with birdsong and the gentle gurgling of the river, and we all mused awhile. Then Wulfget said he did not think it would be much of a sin under the circumstances. "Mayhap some of the monks there will be our firmest allies in this," he added solemnly, "though some, no doubt, will not see the prudence of it."

"God willing, you will be able to convince them all," Edwin said with a dim smile, "but in the meantime you must seek out Hereward and the Bearn. No doubt they are watching for you anyway, since the Wake still holds the portion of that arrow he means to pass to you." He stopped suddenly and his look grew somber. "Mind you not that we draw you into this web of intrigue, brother? Must be you know we count heavily on your involvement."

Wulfget laughed and reached out, touching Edwin's arm in brotherly fashion. "This may be the very reason God has planted us here, Edwin Ælfgar's son," he whispered knowingly. "In His wisdom He has put us each one into the place where we are best able to further His plan."

"If His plan is to make monks into outlaws!" my brother answered. We laughed, and it felt exceedingly pleasant.

Edwin was with the king in his chambers, helping him draw up some deeds, when Brother Wulfget came there the next noontime to beg his leave. In the last months, he had been frequently wont to act as peace-maker between the two, and William had come to appreciate the monk's honesty and simple wisdom. He was wroth to let him go and said so, but knew he could not make the man stay against his will, for Wulfget's first allegiance was to God and to Peterborough and all men knew it. Edwin and I acted surprised at his decision, but we did not have to pretend to the sorrow we felt at his going; it was genuine. We loved his gentleness and learning and admired his faultless philosophy of life. Now we would be friendless again in the king's cold court.

We busied ourselves with what occupations we could, riding and hawking, working with swords to keep our strength up, and sitting in on oppressive, argumentative councils in which we had little say. In addition to the constant stiffness, my brother's recent beating had revived and aggravated some of the conditions he earned at Fulford, including the constant headache and the pain in his side which left him powerless. He spent a great deal of time locked alone in his chamber, tortured and morose. On those days, I was hard-pressed to keep myself out of misery. Better days, though, both of us would ride up High Street to the Castle Hill where there was always sure to be news, carried in by soldiers newly returned from other parts of Angland.

The warrior-bishop Æthelwine of Dunholme, who had become our friend during the harried days of counciling in Lundun City before William took the crown, had joined with Hereward and the Bearn. Their outlaw army grew stronger, well hid in the forests and fen-lands. Earl Osbeorn of the Dane Mark had come to Angland once again to sell them arms, and Waltheof Siward's son, resettled in his spurious earldom of North Hamtun, was preparing to marry the king's niece. This report and many others we received with varying degrees of interest, but it was not until the end of the first week in June that we heard some news that more directly pertained to us and that we had been hoping to hear for a good many days.

                    *   *   *

"Is't true my father was a king, avunculus?" little Wulf Harold's son asked me seriously, brows knit in a tight frown. It was our habit to ride out with him every day, weather willing, into the deeps of the king's New Forest or through the hard-trodden lime-mud streets of the city. Now we were in the stabling barn, watching the hands ready our horses. My brother had been showing him the Welsh cart ponies.

"My father, who was your grandfather, brought them from Wales and after he died they became mine," he had told the wondering little one. "When your father, King Harold, married our sister, we gave them to him as a bride-ale gift. When the new king, William, took this house, they were still here."

"Mayhap they should be *my* ponies then!" little Wulf had exclaimed. We both fell to laughing and Edwin assured him he would talk to William about it. Thus assuaged, the boy had hungered for more information and asked us, as he had a hundred times before, to tell us more about the father he had never known, and we obliged him.

Oft-times we spoke with him about these things as we rode, describing for him not only the bravery of Harold Godwine's son in the aet-Staengfordesbrycg and at Hastings Field, but stories of our father and grandfather, as well. And we reminded him often of his mother, twice cwene and beautiful, and of his twin brother, Harold, whom he could in no wise remember. We had brought a lock of that little one's golden hair back from Ceaster and compared it with Wulf's. 'Twas darker and more of a yellow, very fine and long. Tiny Wulf treasured the piece, especially as we told him it was precisely the color his father's hair had been. It helped him to picture the man.

Sitting proudly in the saddle he shared with my brother, the tot looked like a prince. They were a striking picture, the two of them, in their summer linen finery, decked in gold armlets and neck chains. The day was exceedingly brilliant; coming out of the darkness of the stable, Wulf lifted a hand to shield his eyes from the brightness, and Edwin wrapped an arm about him protectively to better his balance. All three of us enjoyed these outings immensely. It may be hard to imagine we would have felt such a sense of kinship with a toddling nephew of but three-and-a-half years, but we did, and robbed as we were of family and attachments, we savored it.

Any time we left the grounds, the king had instructed a party to follow behind us. We had grown so used to this that it no longer seemed an imposition. The guards were courteous and kept well to the background so as to allow us every freedom of movement and converse. Most of them knew us well after more than three years of our residency in the king's house and offered us every respect. Though our position from the very outset had been undefined, William's household considered us royal guests, favored of the king, and might have been surprised to know we thought of ourselves as prisoners, or hostages at the very least.

The duty of tailing us, too, was a pleasant one, and a happy distraction from the boredom of guard duty. We tried to choose a different gate each day so as to give various soldiers the chance of accompanying us through the cool, shady woodlands. Generally, the king's men were happy at our approach. They called out friendly greetings and small talk as two or three of them mounted; sometimes they offered the boy a sweetmeat or a small carven toy or fur figure.

This particular June day, though, there were no hollered friendlinesses or proffered gifts. Several men mounted soon as they saw us coming. We could see they had councilled together hastily and looked not at all comfortable. Nevertheless, still unaware that anything was amiss, we rode to the gate as was our usual wont and had barely started through it when the mounted riders, four in all, drew abreast of each other, determined to block our way.

"What bothers you?" Edwin asked them, looking from one to the other with a quizzical smile. One of the attendants cleared his throat.

"We are told that you may not ride out through the gates this day, Earl Edwin," he said in an apologetic tone, scarce daring to meet my brother's gaze. He shifted uncomfortably and added in a low tone, "Such is the king's decree."

"What mean you?" I asked, incredulous. The man shrugged.

"You are to ride out no more, my lord," another rejoined, "save in the courtyard or within the bounds."

Wearing a defiant look, Edwin stepped his horse forward, as if to ignore them, but they drew tighter together and one drew his sword.

"I fain would not fight with you, Earl Edwin," he said, holding it high enough to make an impression. He was a burly Flemish man whom both Edwin and I had tutored when the king offered a gold gift to any of his men who learnt Anglish. He looked exceedingly uneasy now, as if he had not expected us to question the command. Edwin, though, was fast growing angry and he told the man to put down his weapon.

"Think you I will wane away all the rest of my life behind these stone walls?" he asked all of them heatedly. "Move now, and let us pass!"

"We cannot do it, sire."

"Must be you will have to hack me, then!" My brother's voice was cold, and he eyed them daringly as he undid his leathern sash, then retied it, lashing tiny Wulf Harold's son firmly to himself, preparing to outrun them. Confused, they hesitated, and he reined his horse to a pert trot, forcing his way around them. Two more drew swords and prodded their mounts into motion but they were obviously bewildered and unsure how far to carry the king's order against a man they admired and knew William favored. Taking advantage of their confusion, my brother threw me one swift belligerent glance, then kicked his horse into a furious gallop. Just as I moved to follow him, though, two of the soldiers crossed their swords roughly in front of me, successfully halting my progress. As if obeying some unspoken command, the others spurred into action at the same instant, apprehensive and angry, shouting and cursing as they lunged after Edwin in awkward chase.

I sat stone still on my horse a long time, watching a pair of dogs romping in the long grass dotted with purple hearts-ease, expecting the breathless, high-strung little party to return any minute. After a while, though, I turned my horse around dejectedly and headed back to the stabling barn, half-hearing and not acknowledging the apologies and explanations of the embarrassed, disgruntled guards.

CHAPTER FIFTY-FIVE

Then the monks of Peterborough heard it said that
their own men, namely hereward and his band,
wished to plunder the monastery themselves
because . . . the king had given the abbacy a French
abbott called Turold . . . a very ferocious man.

—Anglo Saxon Chronicle
Book "E" 1070

I stayed alone in my chamber more than an hour before my gloomy
thoughts were interrupted by the commotion that occasioned my
brother's return: pounding of feet in the hallway, loud slamming of
doors, muffled strains of his converse, and agitated argument. With my
door ajar, I heard William's voice, grown loud and harsh with the willful,
presumptuous tone he used whenever his authority was questioned. I
sensed more than heard his order to fetch me. Brushing my hair quickly,
I was out in the corridor before the messenger arrived. On a whim, I
unlaced the neck of my undertunic, opening the top and pulling my
dalmatic just low enough to let my burnings show. I cannot say what
made me do it; I knew the pagan designs were abhorrent to the king.

Edwin sat, frozen and stiff in an attitude of intense coldness, on the
very edge of one of William's huge, carven chairs. His anger had been
spent in the first moments of confrontation; now he looked drained and
weary. I took a deep breath before lowering myself into a chair beside
him. Half-hidden behind his massive table, the king scrawled furiously
on a length of parchment. Absorbed in what he was doing, he ignored
us both several long minutes, and we sat in silence till he finally threw
down the quill, splayed and useless from the force of his aggravation.
Then he stood slowly, wiping the ink off his fingertips and rubbing it
into the grain of the tabletop before he deigned to speak.

"If you are wondering," he announced imperiously, "that is a writ I
am writing—a writ of excommunication."

When we showed no reaction, his voice grew louder. "'Tis a writ that will no doubt affect many of your friends and certain of your kinsmen."

I stiffened, but neither of us said anything, so he went on. "I mean to have it signed by a bishop. As your countrymen show little regard for my prelates, I am thinking of having your Bishop Æthelric be the one to put it into effect."

Here we exchanged a glance. Æthelric was another warrior-bishop, one well-respected by the Anglish. He was brother to Bishop Æthelwine who had joined with the rebels and he had long been a prisoner of King William's, unjustly convicted and held for no reason. Seeing the look that passed between us, William bit his underlip, then smiled grimly, asking us whether we thought Anglishmen would pay greater heed to a proclamation signed by that man then one signed, for example, by the Norman Bishop Lanfranc. Edwin sat stoically silent, feigning disinterest, but I answered earnestly, saying not many men would be easily disposed to ignore a writ of excommunication, no matter who did the signing. William seemed to mull this over.

"Nevertheless, you Anglish seem to somehow think our Norman church-men inferior, do you not? As if they were not chosen by God at all, but came to their calling politically or by arms or some such."

With an exasperated sigh, Edwin cut him off, pulling himself to his feet and eyeing the king squarely. I expected one of his characteristic flashes of temper, but his voice came evenly, soft and level. "Best you hurry and say what you want to about this writ of yours, my lord," he said in a tone devoid of any emotion, "and tell us how it relates to the matter we discussed in such bad grace a short time ago—the matter of your making prisoners of two men who have done you no wrong."

Surprised at his attitude, William sat down heavily on the table's edge, his broad, meaty shoulders quivering as with the weight of some burden. He crossed his arms on his chest and looked past us as he spoke.

"Must be you know that I sent a monk named Turold, who till now has served as my Abbot of Malmesbury, to the monastery at Peterborough last week, so that he might be abbot there."

I felt a rising in my stomach and, not daring to look at my brother, I replied in a matter-of-fact way. "We knew that you were going to, but we knew not it had been done."

The king's look grew harder, his tone more serious. "What think you he found when he arrived at that place?"

We made no answer; I attempted a noncommittal shrug but felt frozen in my place. William looked me in the eyes.

"He found a blackened and deserted ruin," he retorted, voice echoing ominously in the huge room. "He found the place deserted save one ailing monk in the infirmary, and found no riches at all in a place famous for its wealth and bounty."

My brother sat back down, stunned. "Mayhap your armies reached it first," he said half under his breath, gripping the chair arm with great force. "They are known to have stripped many another holy place."

William growled, springing to his feet with a look of rage. "'Tis no secret who it was that forced the intrusion," he replied savagely. "'Twas a certain man of yours, Earl Edwin, named Hereward, at the head of a gang of outlaws. They did not bother to disguise their doings, and we are told they claimed they wrought all their havoc for the good of the monastery. Some of the monks, it seems, believed him and joined with him rather than serve under a Norman abbot. Others, more devoted, fled and came back to tell the story later, when Abbot Turold arrived the next day with his—"

Here, he unceremoniously cut himself off. Knowing what he had been about to say, I could not let it lie. "With what, my lord?" I asked him in all seriousness. "With his army?"

"Aye," returned the king, eyes flashing. "He rode at the head of a large force. Well he should have. We knew what to expect. 'Tis as I said before. Your countrymen do not trust a man of God if he is not Anglish."

"When my Uncle Leofric went to Peterborough, he took with him four priests, that is all." I tried to compose my thoughts as I spoke, not wanting to goad him too far. "Nevertheless, what you say is in keeping with what I have heard of Abbot Turold—he is a tyrant and warrior."

William snorted a mean laugh. "Your Bishops Æthelwine and Æthelric pride themselves on being warriors. You find no fault with that!"

"Our bishops would never think to take the bounty of God from out of holy places and use it to buy armies." Soon as I said it, I was sorry. William walked close and stared at me venomously.

"Think you your Anglish churchmen are so sinless?" he breathed harshly. "Must be you know it was a monk who led the outlaws there, and argued on their behalf. A monk you know quite well—a recent visitor—a priest with a price on his head now."

The king's anger was so overwhelming that he could scarce speak a complete sentence. I found myself standing, my gaze locked in his, forced to bite back all the things I wanted to say. The man had to be mad! He had excused the wasting of an entire earldom, leaving hundreds of thousands to die of misery, starvation, and disease. No wonder that he could see no wrong in the robbing of riches from monasteries, long as the plunder was to the benefit of his precious kingship! He honestly believed he was in the right—that his own church-robbing was acceptable to God, but the trespassing of the Anglish rebels should by right be punished with Eternal Death. Helpless in my fury, I strode right past him, and grabbing the half-worded writ from his table, I purposefully ripped it in half, then in half again, then tore and tore till it was naught but shreds.

'Twas as if my own mindless fury brought him back to another reality. He stared at me, shocked, a moment, then broke into a bemused smile. Turning to my brother, he spoke lightly in that tone of gentle, fatherly reprimand which we had grown to hate.

"There is your answer, Earl Edwin," he said, hands on his hips and with a condescending, ungracious smile. "There is how this matter relates to the one we spoke of earlier, you and I. You will be certain to keep to the grounds from now on, will you not? Elsewise, I may be forced to raise my arm against you."

I was out in the hall, and the door had slammed loud behind me, before he finished. Shuddering with boundless emotion, I leant weakly against the wall and crossed myself, as much for forgiveness as for strength. I was swollen with the sin of vengeance and there was no way I would allow myself to confess to a Norman priest.

*   *   *

My outburst did little to forestall the execution of the king's writ. Within three weeks it had been issued: William's words written in the hand of Bishop Æthelric. Whether he bribed the man or punished him into doing it, I cannot say. Bishop Æthelwine has told me since that the man would have needed no coercing, He was much older and had a great love for Peterborough, having lived twelve years as a monk there. Even though his confinement by the king was unwarranted, he had no great sympathy for the outlaws, so would never have deigned to join them had he been a free man. Nevertheless, I am hard-pressed to imagine any Anglishman leveling such untoward misery on his patriotic countrymen lest it were he was forced in some way. He died in his prison cell at West Minster soon after, though, so no man will ever know.

*   *   *

Day by day, the gloomy summer passed. William forced us to keep court and council as we had before, even made us break-fast with him every morning after the Mass. He chatted amiably and indulged us with meaningless flatteries. He studied his Anglish with me several times a week and took us privately into his chambers to inform us of affairs of state, now grown so utterly foreign and indecipherable that they were disdainful to us.

We played our games with little Wulf in the cobbled courtyard. He could not quite understand why we no longer rode in the New Forest unless it was in a huge parade of soldiers or with the king right alongside us. William, in a moment of mirthful generosity, had agreed to give him the cart ponies. Edwin had the carter fashion a tiny wagon for him, in the shape of a war-ship on wheels, complete with a gilded bow made like a dragon's head. There was still a small expanse of lawning-field we could ride; sometimes he sat in the saddle with one or the other of us, but by Midsummer, Wulf rode proudly as a man on his own tiny russet mount, saddled in Neustrian leather. He named the pony Eorforwic, same thing I had called the fine red mount Siward Bearn gave to me. I had to bite back a smile when he explained to William that the name had been inspired by the fact that his father, the king of all Angland, had married his mother in that famous city, before it had been "ruin't."

Soon after Midsummer, the rains came, dealing my brother soreness so severe that he hobbled and limped by day and shivered with pain at night, crying and praying for relief. The king put his finest healers to the task, monks and mid-wives who practiced a French art called massage, kneading deep into his wounded muscles in an attempt to heal them. On one day he would be doused with ledum marsh tea, the next with chelidonium or wild hops. William even brought a priest from Cantwarabrycg who knew how to administer powder of aranea diadema, the precious papal-cross spider, most potent of all remedies for bone-pain in dampness. The burning applications gave some initial relief, but caused a violent pain in Edwin's head and a strange flickering in his eyes. This made the priest say the remedy was not indicated in his case, and that, in all likelihood, there was no earthly cure that could help him, so great was the extent of his internal, invisible injuring.

Then William called in a witch.

She was a pretty, dark-haired thing, but wanton-looking and very dirty. The king brought her in during the midnight while Edwin was sleeping, and put her in his bed. Soon as she began to touch and rub him with her potions, he wakened, horrified of her strangeness and her forward caresses. He thrashed mightily and struggled with her, begging us to pull her from him, else he would be forced to smite her, a thing he was terrified to do. At length, she drew herself away, letting go a strange, lowing howl as she did it, saying she could not make magick on a man who had no love of life and no fear of death.

The king paid her anyway, and she made her way out, singing some soft, eerie Eirish song and laughing to herself, as if proud she had worked so noble a man into a frenzy with such little effort. Edwin sat the rest of the night in a cold sweat, wroth to be comforted by my words or William's. There had been no mistaking the woman's power. She had an unearthly gleam in her dark eyes and an aura of bewitching all about her.

Next day, when he had calmed a little, my brother was furious with the king for what he had done, despite the good intentions. Notwithstanding his recent stoicness and quietude, he might have been irate enough to make a screaming issue of it, as he had been wont to do of old, but he had no chance. Even before the mass, the king sent for us to council with him. We found the man not in his chamber, but in the hall, where a great many men were massed, talking low in serious tones, waiting for the king to speak. Haggard and drawn, William's sleeplessness of the night before was very apparent, but his voice rang harsh and resolute as ever as he announced loudly that the outlaws had taken over the island of Ely.

"Hundreds of fighting men from all over Angland have joined with them," he announced seriously, "and now they hold seven square miles of the most inaccessible, highly fortified land in the country. 'Tis time we are done with them!"

A murmur rang through the hall. One man shouted loud that he did not see how they could remove the rebels from a place like Ely. "We have never found an access to it yet through the marshlands," he called glumly, "nor are we likely to now that the fen is swollen like a lake with all this unseasonable rain!"

"Find a way to sail it!" the king commanded. "The outlaws made their way there in the torrents, riding in war-ships which the man Siward Bearn bought from the Danes with the treasure they plundered from Peterborough." He turned and looked directly at me as he said this last. His cold, dark eyes were like daggers.

"But the Anglish know the fen-ways!" another of his men cried out. "A man must needs know the swamp uncommon well before he attempts to cross it, else the strangling weeds and whirlpools will eat a ship as if 'twere nothing."

"Then we will watch them! Day and night we will watch them and we will learn their ways in and out of the fen!" William's voice shook with anger, and he pounded his fist hard on the board before him, making a loud hollow thud. "By the Cross! They have grown a huge and fiercesome army under our very noses, and we did not even know it till they began to kill and plunder us!"

Edwin and I exchanged a silent glance. We were sitting directly anext the king and did not dare a play of emotion, but my heart suddenly beat faster, and I felt an exhilaration I had not tasted in many months. William went on to describe how the rebels had come out of the marshes at Grantanbrycg and again at Huntandun, wreaking havoc on his strongholds there, plundering arms and horses and gold, then disappearing without a trace.

"These are not awesome warriors or legendary heroes who deserve to defeat us!" he chid his men meanly. "Apart from Siward Bearn and Bishop Æthelwine there is scarce a man of note there—just thegns and freemen of little substance, long on the run!" As he spoke, he walked around the table. When he had come directly in front of us he turned, looking at us both in a hardened, hateful way. "Thegns and freemen," he repeated meaningfully, "and a handful of monks and men in the service of the House of Leofric."

I stared back at him coldly as I could, but I found little satisfaction in it. The king's eyes were not on me; they were latched harshly on my brother. Edwin was smiling—a gleaming, arrogant smile that instantly brought back some of Ælfgar's bold look to him. Grinning, he raised himself from his seat, drawing his tall, perfectly built form erect till he stood at a level with the king. He showed as much evidence of strength as the other, more of grace and less of bulk. William flinched ever so slightly as Edwin turned his back to him and, managing to move easily in spite of his pain, strode away. The king's men, acting oblivious of the wordless insult my brother had made, continued their questions and comments, but for a moment at least, the king stared after Edwin Ælfgar's son in stunned disbelief. Then his dark, haughty features grew pensive again and he turned back to his worried assembly.

Soon as William looked away, I followed my brother out of the room. I do not suppose the king even realized I had left his harried council. Nevertheless, something told me the king would seek some biting revenge. He scarcely ever begrudged my brother's obstinacy when it was performed in private; many such a moment had passed unremarked upon when they were alone or with me. That Edwin had crossed him front of other men was a different matter, though. It was the one thing William could not abide.

We stayed late in our chamber the next day, foregoing both the mass and the break-fast. We knew it was a disrespect, and that we would have to explain it later, but we craved the time alone to talk of all we had heard the day before. The rain had abated during the night. The flat, low-lying silver morning clouds were pierced here and there by shafts of pink sunlight. I thought we might ride in the fields, though they would be drenched and muddy, or at least in the cobbled courtyard. The last three days little Wulf had done naught but drive his cart under the roof of the stabling-barn because of the downpour.

The witch's applications having been as unsuccessful as all the other attempts to relieve his distress, Edwin was far too stiff and uncomfortable to ride. As I made my way through the courtyard, I said a silent prayer that this might be the end of the rain and dampness. Then, feeling guilty, I stopped myself. Best the fen should stay glutted and deep. It was our only hope.

Two of the stable boys eyed me curiously as I made my way back to the gated long-stall where the ponies were kept. It was empty. Nervously, I spun round and looked at the side-wall closet; the little saddle was not on its customary fitting, and the pretty ship-cart was nowhere to be seen. Fighting a sudden panic that gripped me, I clenched my fists and thought awhile. There was no way the boy could be out with the saddle and cart at the same time. If the hands had taken the ponies out for airing, the toys would be in their places. I grew flushed with anger. If the king meant to take his revenge on us by robbing the little one of his fondest pleasure—but I stopped myself as another thought, infinitely more disgusting, assailed me.

In a very few minutes I was at the king's chamber door, breathless and brash. I rapped twice with my bracelets, but pushed the door open before I was invited, letting myself in and leaning my full weight back to close it. William was alone, in soldier's clothes now instead of court dress. He did not look surprised to see me. At a sudden loss for words, I just stared at him. Finally he spoke.

"The boy is sea-board, Earl Morcar," he said courteously and quietly. "A ship was sent to Normandy this morning for reinforcements. I put him on it."

"Smite you!" I whispered, glaring. He pretended not to hear.

"The air is better there … the climate is safer." He could not keep the sarcasm from tinting his mock gallantry. I spit on the floor, right at his feet.

"Mayhap they will teach him better manners there than noblemen are wont to learn in England," he murmured condescendingly, then he smiled. "He will live in the castle at Beaumont-on-the-Hill. You know the place and will approve of it, I trow?"

He waited a moment for me to answer, but seeing I would not do it, he went on. "No doubt you can see my wisdom in doing this. Things are so unsettled in this land! Who knows but that outlaws might not clamber out of the woodlands and steal him away."

Still, I made no answer, knowing he meant to goad me.

"Mayhap you and your fair, coaxing, self-willed brother have thought to spirit him away yourselves."

I lunged at him, close enough to feel his breath. "Oft-times it has crossed my mind, Lord William, that your bold front is all falsehood and trickery. This day you have proven yourself a trembling, fear-ridden, groveling coward!"

Eyes burning, he took a step backwards, then dealt me a stinging slap across the face. I laughed as I wiped a trickle of blood from my mouth with my sleeve. "Your fawners call you 'Conqueror,'" I added, still laughing, "but better men—men of honor—see a daunted usurper, who cannot fight unless he has women and children to trade!"

With a violent growl, William reached his huge hand around my throat, tightening just an instant. Then, thinking better of it, he let go all at once. Heaving, he spun away from me, pounding one fist on the other and cursing vilely. Then, suddenly, he relaxed; his broad shoulders bent a little and he cleared his throat, pausing to regain his composure and pick his words.

"Every care will be exerted in your nephew's behalf," he intoned levelly. "I bid you tell your brother that. I will be gone about a fortnight in the field and will not have the opportunity to see him."

"Coward!" I hissed, biting the inside of my cheek. He glanced my way, grim face drawn by haughtiness and his habit of domination. He pulled a glove on with a hard tug.

"I pray you will forgive me the necessity of extra precautions, occasioned by the civil unrest which is rampant." He shook his thick, dark hair into place and scrutinized me for a reaction as he continued. "Neither of you will be allowed horses in my absence. To relieve your unwarranted scruples, I assure you 'tis only temporary."

I felt a pounding in my chest as all my muscles constricted. Whenever his language grew formal, he was on the verge of leveling some cold-blooded chastisement. He took a draught of water from a leathern beaker, swished it in his mouth, then spit it into the wooden basin.

"Must be you know I mean to allow you every possible freedom, Earl Morcar," he said earnestly, "so the two of you may indulge in unlimited converse and privacy during the day as you have been wont to do till now. My councilors, though, have cautioned me about letting you keep chambers together. 'Tis not in the best interests of your safety. Henceforth, you will keep to separate hallways when you retire, and I have named you each a Norman attendant."

Wordlessly, I made my way to the door, knowing full well how useless it was to argue. He stopped me with a grunt, as if he had just remembered something important.

"And, Morcar—let me give you some advice!" He spoke in that despised tone of gentle paternal reproof. "Do not keep yourself from the Mass anymore, either of you. I trust you admit you are not sinless enough to do without it."

I did not even bother to look at him, much less answer.

CHAPTER FIFTY-SIX

Earls Edwin and Morcar secretly fled from the
king's court, because King William wanted to keep
them in confinement, and were for some time in
rebellion against him.

—Simeon of Durham, 1071

Easter 1071

My brother was rabid when he learnt Wulf Harold's son was gone. He
drank himself to senselessness that night and many a night after. There
was no boisterous bawdiness to his drinking now—just melancholy and
a calculated desire to ale himself out of all the hurt, physical, mental,
and spiritual, that had become his world. William found it easier to cope
with despondency, illness, and pain than with rowdiness and
debauchery, and so he was not harsh with him. Untrue to his word,
though, he did not relax his grip on us after he returned from his camp
at Grantanbrycg. Rather, he tightened it, bit by bit, into a stranglehold,
still needing our help and council in order to run the country, and still
pretending to amiability.

The weather cleared, bringing summer's momentary respite to my
brother, but the swamps stayed deep. As autumn departed, so did the
king's chance to gain access to Ely that year. The island was totally inaccessible to strangers in the winter, and would remain so till long after the
thaws. The rebels had outlasted the first siege. William, furious, was
more determined than ever to crush them. He had half a year to establish his plan of action.

Winter brought new, unbearable sorenesses to my brother, but he
pushed himself, when he was lucid, to acquire more strength. He could
no longer manage an axe, but he worked hard with the sword and pike
and developed a talent with the French-bow. Nevertheless, there was a
slackness in his grip and a halting in his gait, mayhap unnoticeable to
any but me, that would forever work against him. He was fine-featured

and golden as ever, but had a wan-eyed, empty look now, and his drinking did not help it much.

At long last, I took my father's sword to the king's armorer and had my name engraved on one side of it. I had wanted to change "Ælfgar" to "Ælfgar's son" but in the end, decided against it. I still aspired to that man's courage and daring; the blade might be lucky for me left as it was.

The Christ Mass Gemot passed with little news of note; the only Anglish who attended were former small landholders made wealthy by turning their backs on their countrymen in order to kiss the feet of the foreign king. The Easter Gemot I looked forward to with more enthusiasm. Waltheof Siward's son would be attending, and though he was surely no great favorite of ours, he had been at Dunholme with the rebels before re-bowing to the king. 'Twas possible he would be willing to tell us something of our men who had been there. Abbot Turold was bringing a contingent of monks from Peterborough, mostly Normans, but undoubtedly a few men we had known from before—priests who had taught us and known our father and grandfather and uncle. That such simple pleasures had become so precious was indicative of our misery.

The king, too, anticipated the Easter-tide with enthusiasm. Apart from the problem of the outlaws at Ely, it had been a peaceful year. He had been able to relax into his role, without having to swing a sword and lay waste the countryside as he had the year before. This one would be without the sinful blemish of the last Easter, when he and all his armies had penanced for the ruining of the north. It was the first of his councils not entirely given over to pressing emergencies. He could have pleasantries and feasting and entertainment. The country, at long last, was his, and he expected he could resume the routine of the Anglish kings before him, secure in his position and assured of his future. Most of the major churchmen had been replaced by Normans. Aldred was dead, Æthelwine was outlawed, Stigand and Æthelric were his prisoners. Edwin and I were under his thumb, and there was no other Anglishman in the land powerful enough to worry him.

Waltheof Siward's son was surely not a threat. The hereditary claim he thought he had to the North Humbria had been shown for its true worth when the northerners chose me to be their earl. In truth, they would have picked Siward Bearn, even Oswulf, before they would have embraced Waltheof, the son of False Earl Siward the Murderer. The mock-earldom which King Edward had carved for him out of Mercia was tiny enough to be laughable: two cities and a small expanse of field and forest. William had honored and upheld Waltheof's claim to Huntandon and the North Hamtun, because he always pretended to a great respect for the late old king, his mentor. The truth was, though, that

Waltheof was totally powerless and that was why William allowed him freedom and favor.

One thing that pleased me when that man came to the king's house on Holy Thursday was seeing that he no longer dressed and wore his hair like a North Humbrian, as he had for so many years to protest my election. He was busy worming his way into the king's close confidence now, and William had never made a secret of the fact that the northern look was an abomination to him. He might not have betrothed his sister's daughter to a man who wore dyed hair to his elbows and burnt pictures on his body. So now the sharp-eyed Earl of Huntandun had a totally ambiguous look to him, as if he were trying to retain the Anglishness that the king admired and look like a Norman at the same time. He had no mustache or beard, and his hair was cropped shorter. He wore dyed moreen court clothes, cut in French fashion, and simple, elegant flat-gold neck-chains and rings, similar to the king's. He looked taller than when last I saw him, and despite a noticeable scar from his chin to his throat, more handsome and somewhat stronger. The freedom to ride and hunt and do as he pleased no doubt gave him a look of healthiness which we had come to lack.

We had never favored his friendship when he was captive in the king's court with us, largely because he kept close company with our despised kinsman Gospatrick Maldred's son, but now we watched assiduously for any opportunity of speaking to him out of Norman earshot. We knew he had sided with the king now and was not the type to risk disfavor, but he would never be rude-blooded enough to refuse us what news he had of our kith and kinsmen.

Good Friday we kept in meditation and Saturday we councilled. Waltheof was ever anext us, but so was the king, so we spoke of things like Waltheof's upcoming wedding with Lady Judith, and the new fortifications in the North Hamtun. Easter Sunday we all dressed in finery, and the king led a gorgeous procession ten miles up the High Street, with half the southlands, Norman and Anglish alike, gathered to see us. Then we sat to a sumptuous feast, richer than any in many years, and listened to various men tell tales of their adventures in the last year or more. Many of these were exceedingly interesting, though we could not always sympathize with the viewpoint of the teller. Ale flowed freely, and most were in a light and friendly mood. William paid particular attention to us. We spoke to him as little as possible these days; a coldness had built between us which both sides had to work hard to ignore. There was no unpleasantness that night, though. I felt he genuinely craved our friendship again. Even after my brother grew sullenly silent with drink, the king jested in his behalf, saying mead was Earl Edwin's meat, he scarce could function without it, and it was an allowable characteristic in a man of such high grace and honor.

I sat for awhile with the monks of Peterborough, all gathered at a single huge table. Even the priests of Norman blood seemed generous and likable, and I noticed they drank as much as any one else in the hall.

Late in the night, Waltheof made mention of the siege at Dunholme, and the king allowed it, thinking mayhap there was no harm in the man's talking to us as long as he was there himself to hear what was said. The Earl of North Hamtun could not tell much; he was rumored to have fought very bravely and murdered many a Norman with his Danish axe, but he was in the king's service now and the talk of it was a grave embarrassment to them both. He did manage to inform us that Heard Ulf's son had taken a wounding there, and Gamel-Beorn the Biter also, but supposed neither wound harsh enough to be crippling. Then he surprised us by saying one of the boldest fighters amongst the gang was Sihtric Ælfric's son. He was the eldest son of Ælfric White-Hair, who had been my father's man, and he was only a child when we last saw him.

William took note of the name with interest; he was forever seeking information about the outlaws—who they were and where they had come from. I could almost visibly see the thought cross his mind that here was yet another rebel in the service of the House of Leofric, a thing he held greatly against us. After that, Waltheof spoke disdainfully of Hereward and the rest of the men, and though we both knew he had to do it for the sake of his standing with the king, Edwin and I made cold excuses and left to take air and appease nature in the well guarded courtyard.

Returning, we met Waltheof again on his way out, empty cup in hand. There was an urgent look in his fox-like eyes; they seemed to glisten in the light of the torches and fire.

"Best you listen to me and know I serve you no dishonor," he said low as we approached, "but all the rest of the while I am here, I will not speak to you more."

Puzzled, my look hardened, and Edwin, somewhat slow in his speech, asked what ailed the man. As if in answer, Waltheof deliberately raised the empty goblet, then dropped something into it. Handing it to me, he swept his gaze meaningfully from one to the other of us, then wordlessly made his way out. Unobtrusively, I fished the thing out.

'Twas a small but unmistakable fragment of a war arrow.

"By God!" Edwin whispered in an awed voice. The sight of it had brought him immediately to his senses. "Of all the men in the world—"

This was my thought exactly, but as we made our way back to the table, I was wracking my brain for the words Hereward had said that grim day in the aet-Waeringwicum. "Be on the lookout everywhere for more signs," he had told us, "and within a fortnight someone you trust will be there to fetch you."

I sincerely hoped it would be someone I trusted more than Waltheof Siward's son, else I might be hard-pressed to recognize who it was.

A while more we sat at the high table. I made halting converse, while Edwin doused himself with copious amounts of honey-water to clear his head. Now and again my gaze drifted appraisingly towards the Earl of North Hamtun, who studiously avoided me. Could be I had misjudged the man. He had always seemed to crave our respect and we had always denied it, forever counting it one of his faults that he was the son of the man who killed Oswulf's father. Waltheof had been no older than Oswulf at the time—a babe in arms. Mayhap he truly did believe he had a claim to the Humbria; who knows what drivel mad Earl Siward taught him. What is more, we hated him for taking Huntandon and the North Hamtun, when in truth it had been none of his doing. He'd only been an unwitting pawn of the Godwine's sons, who had foisted it on him as a means of making revenge on our house. Anglishmen were not wont to choose their heroes carelessly, and in the days before he re-swore himself to William, tales of his valor against the king's forces had traveled all the way from the Bernicia to the king's house in Wintanceaster. Of a sudden, I saw his defection in a totally new light. Hereward could not have chosen wrongly. That was why they called him "the Wake." He was ever watchful of men, and knew them instinctively. I smiled inwardly at the thought of one of the outlaws marrying the king's niece and living in his house.

Next day I was so preoccupied with watching for signals that I must have seemed a scatter-brain to other men around me. But nothing out of the usual happened that day or the next or the next. By that time, the work of the Gemot was finished, and folk began to take their leave. A few at a time, the monks of Peterborough left in small parties, some to return to the monastery, and others with commitments elsewhere, for there was much blessing of crops to be done during the Rogation-tide; the fields in Wessex and the East Anglia needed to be fertile this year for those in the north were barren and useless.

On the fourth day, the king made fare-wells to Waltheof and his party, agreeing to send for him soon as the ship bearing Lady Judith appeared in the harbor. Apart from the usual formalities, the earl had said little or nothing else to us, just as he had promised. At one opportune moment, though, he had caught my eye and shrugged his shoulders, as if to tell me there was nothing more he knew.

The spring rains, which had held off till now, were coming; Edwin could feel it. William, generous in his current good humor had applied to Brother Heirome in Normandy for more clues to a cure. We expected the herbs and medications would arrive in the same fleet that carried the king's niece, so we were greatly relieved when William told us one afternoon that the ships had been spotted. There was much merriment in the king's house that night as he welcomed his kinswoman and many others of noble Norman blood. We ate and drank awhile, but 'twas a hard thing for Edwin, as they spoke incessantly of Lady Adeliza, who was about to take her vows at Ste. Leger. William seemed to understand my brother's discomfort; he agreed to let us take leave of the festivities and did not even bristle when Edwin drew a huge pitcher of barley-ale to take back to his chamber. He had been much more moderate in his drinking since our talk with Waltheof Siward's son, but truth was, his frame was so well adjusted to spirits now that he often drank more than another man could and it did not even make him drunken.

As we made our way out, William signaled the man he had chosen to be Edwin's attendant. He was Hugh Curt-Sword, a jovial, good-natured man of Normandy, too old now for other service but never adverse to sharing a cup or flask. He did not look entirely happy about leaving the hall; no doubt he resented being made to play nursemaid to a fully grown man. Nevertheless, the king's house was still crowded, and there was a good chance the chamber would be full of men who had wandered from the main activity to drink and game and make converse away from the noise and bustle. Hugh was apt to have as merry a time there as elsewhere, so rather than grumble, he jested as he took a swig from the tall, earthen pitcher.

In fact, the room was so crowded that my brother could not even put down a pallet, which thing he had wanted to do. There were near a dozen men in there: two at a gammon board and the rest gathered around two monks of Peterborough, both older and Anglish, who were graphically describing how the hated outlaws had plundered their beloved monastery.

"No matter that we had petitioned for peace and protection," one was saying a doleful tone. "Some of our brothers they killed, others they wounded grossly when they burst in—a motley, horrifying band of outlaws and Danes. Vestments, coins, shrines, books … whatever they could lift, they took."

"One climbed up the steeple and took the precious treasures that were hidden there," added the other. "He was a one who knew the place well—the nephew of our late good Abbot Brand, God rest his soul."

"I have heard of the man," one of the king's men grunted. "The rogue named Hereward, called 'the Wake.'"

"I scarce think I can bear to hear this," my brother whispered mournfully, half to me and half to his attendant. "Think we should go to your chamber, Morcar?"

Old Hugh had found one of his cronies amongst the lingerers, however, and was wroth to leave, so Edwin took a long, mean swallow, then ordered a Frenchman from off the casement sill so that he might sit down. As he lowered himself stiffly into a more comfortable position, both the monks stood suddenly, and one of them, looking directly into my eyes, asked whether 'twould not be better to send all the men from the chamber and let Earl Edwin rest.

The monk was Osbeorn Dolfin's son, clean-shaven and tonsured!

A lump rose in my throat which nearly choked me. The other monk was leaning close to my brother, scrutinizing him carefully, staring into his eyes. Then he signaled Hugh Curt-Sword and, drawing him close to me, made as if to council quietly with the two of us.

It was Æthelstan the Fen-man! I scarce could believe it. I had not seen the man in more than seven years, but even in the shadow of his monk's hood, I recognized those glistening, hawk-like eyes.

"Earl Edwin needs relaxing," he announced in a low and serious tone. "Best you two move these men from here and help me prepare him." Curt-Sword tossed my brother a glance and saw that he was visibly, genuinely trembling.

"Nay," the other monk said gently. "No need to discomfit him that way, in front of strangers. Let us walk him to the priest-house."

Old Hugh looked relieved. He was used to the constant, furtive ministrations on my brother's behalf, but in no way wanted the responsibility of overseeing them or explaining the situation to other men when the king had explicitly commanded it be kept quiet.

"Mayhap you should walk him through the storerooms and out the doors that lead to the kitchen-house," he whispered, nervous and concerned. Edwin had paled all at once and slumped weakly in his place. "That way, men will not see and question you."

Osbeorn Dolfin's son patted the old man on the shoulder in a priestly, comforting way. "May we send for you, good man, if we need your aid in the priest-house?" he asked in a gentle tone. When the Norman nodded, he added low, "God bless you," making a sign of the cross in the air before him.

Curt-Sword, relaxed, went back to his conversation. In a very few minutes we were outside in the darkness. Brother Wulfget was waiting near the priest-house, with as many of our belongings as he had been able to carry out unnoticed. We donned monk's robes ourselves and walked a small way down the river. There was a boat from Peterborough there; the watch-men standing in small groups along the banks either did not notice or did not care when we boarded.

By the time we came to the sea-mouth, it had begun to drizzle. We made our way west along the wooded coastline, past the Isle of Wight and, where the shore grew rocky between Corfesgeat and Swanawic, a ship met us. Under cover of rain and dark we climbed up on it, pulling the smaller vessel aboard with ropes and pulleys. Deck-side, we were surrounded by more monks, faces invisible in the darkness, some with voices we knew. Then the men parted away from us as a tall figure made his way across the boards with a lantern, which he handed to Osbeorn Dolfin's son. Soon as he came near, he threw his hood off and embraced us, both at the same time.

It was Hereward the Wake.

CHAPTER FIFTY-SEVEN

Morcar, and the very valiant man hereward, went
by ship with many others to the Isle of Ely . . .
Æthelwine also, bishop of Durham, and Siward,
surnamed Bearn.

—Simeon of Durham, 1071

"For a king who genuinely believes he is all-knowing, this one is easy enough to deceive." Hereward's muscular frame was silhouetted against the roseate gold of sunrise on the sea. Even in his monkish robes there was no mistaking his strength. "You might think he would pay particular attention to priests," he added, his hard-set, firm mouth twitching into a momentary smile as he looked at me. "He knows we inhabit one monastery and grossly plundered another, yet it has not occurred to him we might have stolen wadmal along with gold and silver."

There were fifteen men on board, and every one was dressed like a hooded monk. We were in a short Danish ship, the carven bows sawed off, and the sails painted to look Eirish. The plan was to sail around the western foot of Wessex and up into the channel that kissed the mouth of the river Afene. We would disembark on the Welsh side and wait for Siward Bearn; to any who bothered to look, we would appear as another of the many groups of bold priests, sailed across from Eireland to make Christians in the heathen Cymry. Then the Bearn would take the ship up the Welsh coast and on to the wilderness inlet of Hefresham, where horses and men were waiting to travel a hundred miles across the northernmost area of the Humbria to Bebbanburg. There, near the Scottish border, in lands still outside William's grasp, Gamel-Beorn the Biter and the warrior-bishop Æthelwine were camped at the head of an ever-growing fleet of men and ships, waiting for him.

As for the rest of the party, they would sail the small boat up the Afene far as they could without arousing suspicion, hopefully as far as the aet-Waeringwicum, all the while pretending to be monks on their way home to Peterborough. At some point, they would take to the fields, forests, and fens, and so make their way to Ely. 'Twas a marvelously complex and precise plan. I could see now why it took such a long time for the portion of arrow to come to us, so intense was the strategy involved in the laying of it.

Some things still puzzled me. "Why did you let Brother Wulfget go back to the king's house?" I asked quizzically, looking across to where that man sat with my brother and Æthelstan the Fen-man. "Surely you knew his face would be well remembered by the king!"

"Aye," the Wake grinned, "but he was the only man who could show us where to find you in that big house, and the only one who could find your belongings and sneak them out, a few at a time."

As he said it, I fingered the hilt of my father's sword which hung from my waist. We had not even given a thought to the sword and the battle-axe as we took that hurried leave, but we would have sore missed them both all the rest of our lives.

"What is more," Hereward added, watching me appraisingly, "we needed a reason to spirit you away, and Brother Wulfget was the only one who knew that Earl Edwin required consistent medications."

I followed his worried gaze to my brother's nearly inert form. Edwin sat cross-legged on the deck, elbows on his knees, face in his hands, while Brother Wulfget kneaded his shoulders, trying to chase away the pains that had come with last night's rain. "Waltheof Siward's son told us something was amiss with him; he said the man looked undone."

Wanting to change the subject, I made a grimace. "Waltheof Siward's son!" I shook my head slightly. "There was a surprise!"

"The man is not as bad as you think, Earl Morcar, and he has been one of the most valuable to us. Methinks he would lay his life down for our cause. When he begged the king's pardon after Dunholme, we thought that William would force him back to court and keep him there with you as he had done before. 'Twould have been a way we could reach you with our plans. The king decided to trust him and let him wander, though. Now he has set up his household in Huntandon again, a stone's throw from Ely!" Hereward gave a genuine laugh, appreciating the unusual way fate had played into his hands.

"He might have found an opportunity to tell us some of this," I scowled petulantly, "instead of leaving us in such a whorl of suspense!"

"He knew nothing more than to give you the arrow-piece." Hereward toyed with a length of thick-woven rope as he talked. His voice was serious. "Not a single man knew more than he had to know. Besides myself, only the Bearn and Heard Ulf's son saw the entire plan. Elsewise, each one had a certain set of things to do immediately, soon as he received the fragment, and all those seemingly unrelated efforts put together are what freed you."

There was a silence as I pondered, broken when the Wake spoke in a loud, gruff voice. "Best you put that hood on, Earl Edwin! It grows light now, and if the waves wander us closer to shore men will wonder at the sight of a priest with flowing golden hair!"

"He is ill—" Brother Wulfget began, but Hereward made a forceful gesture and the monk hurriedly complied.

"Would that we had some chelidonium," I mused miserably, "or some arnica daisy."

"All the arnica in the world will not help that man, Earl Morcar," Hereward whispered coldly, "and you know it. The man is sodden. His head is pounding because his brain craves mead. Must be you cannot imagine how rigorous life is in our camp if you think your brother can weather it in that condition."

So saying, he walked away, leaving me staring after him in astonishment and displeasure. Nothing more was said. By the time we came ashore in the Cymry, across the shore from Wessex at the widest point of the mouth, I am sure he more honestly knew the truth of the matter. The dampness, the exertions of the escape, and the sea-motion had all combined to bring on the stiffness and excruciation, and though Edwin neither moaned nor complained, the agony that twitched across his wan face now and again was enough to tell the story.

Noon of our fourth day of freedom found us building a camp in the spring mud of a vast, stony lea-land, bordered by craggy rises and the ghost-like remains of a forest destroyed long ago by the madman, Tostig Godwine's son. We had banked late the night before, in the twilight before dawning, and slept in the open boat in a drizzle made ominous by silent, flickering lightenings that lit the sky and the sea to a dream-like bluish haze. We watched anxiously for signs of the Bearn and his men, but Hereward had allowed him six days against the possibility of our finding bad winds on the ocean, or having to hide in the New Forest while soldiers searched the river. We had made good time; now there was naught to do but watch and be ready to move when we saw him.

We had chosen a sheltered spot next to a tumbling stream, within easy reach of our vessel, but invisible from the shore. After hauling rocks to sit upon and carrying what we needed from the ship, I sat with Osbeorn Dolfin's son while he roasted four hares and a scrawny wild kid that Brother Wulfget and two of the men had obtained with traps. His hair a thick ashy grey now, and his visage worn with care and the grimness of hard living, my man looked older and sadder than I remembered him. He had lost his wife and children in the razing of the North

Humbria; his rich homestead had been laid waste, and as none had seen or heard word of his family since, he assumed they had perished like so many others, of want and disease—or worse.

First thing he did when we found a moment together was ask to see my burnt-on necklaces and bracelets, so that he could admire his own handiwork. My pictures were the finest he had ever done, the man told me. "I never thought that I would be the one to decorate the Earl of the North Humbria!" he exclaimed merrily. Then he added more seriously, "Of late, I thought mayhap I would never see the earl again—" He broke off suddenly, and I clasped both his shoulders. Like Heard Ulf's son and the Biter, he was dearest of all my sworn men to me, except Siward Bearn, who was also my kinsman. We laughed and went back to the cooking.

Now and then my eye wandered to a nearby ledge where the Wake sat in serious converse with my brother, who was pacing back and forth in front of him, trying to keep himself limber. Hereward was gesticulating forcefully, trying to make Edwin see a point. A shadow crossed the man's brow when my brother lifted a flask of honey-mead, then wiped his mouth after taking a long swallow. After a few minutes Hereward stood, and the two of them embraced in the comradely manner of an earl and his man. If the Wake begrudged him the solace, I thought bitterly, 'twas his own blindness. Every other man could see that even simple movement was an effort for Edwin.

Late that night, though, when everyone but the watch was sleeping, Hereward made his way over, and putting his own pile of furs down on the ground anext mine, asked quietly if I was sleeping. It had begun to drizzle, and the ground was so hard and cold that my body would not allow sleep, and I told him so. He laughed.

"Three years of stuffed mattresses in the king's house have softened you, Earl Morcar! Pray God we can bend you to our outlaws' way of life!"

Then he described how sore they had struggled for survival. "Must be you know there is little comfort in a place like Ely under the best conditions," he explained casually, stretching and yawning as he spoke. "Most of our days there are spent scavenging for food. There are only a few amongst us adept at fishing and eeling, those who are priests, and much of the wildlife fled because we had to set fire to the island to make the monks submit to us."

"By the Cross!" I exclaimed, astonished. "Mean that you fought the priests to get the monastery?"

"What think you? That they would welcome us with open arms and let us make a war-camp of their peaceful home?"

"I had not thought on it.… "

"Well, we fought them, I can tell you. We frightened them finally with flame and they decided mayhap 'twas better to let us claim the place than level it. The boldest stayed and joined us; Abbot Thurstan led the rest into the fen. Now we hold the whole island—but for how long? The king will make an access sooner or later, and only God knows what the outcome will be." He took a deep breath and turned on his side, facing me; I could feel more than see him in the dim, damp blackness.

"For now," he continued, "we move in and out of the place secretly to gather arms and men. Sometimes we travel the roads in disguises, but most oft we creep through the marshes and woodlands, day after day in all sorts of weather. Every journey we make is a hard one and fraught with peril. Unless we come to the door of some Anglish we can trust to feed or shelter us without reporting it, we sleep on cold ground and pick what we can find to eat. If there are men in the forests, we hide in trees by day; at night we build no fires. Then, when we have accomplished our purpose, it is back to the camp. There is somewhat more comfort in that place, in the fact that we know we are safe for the time being, and there is a roof over the cold stone floor we sleep on. We spend hours mapping and traveling the secret passageways of the place, knowing that when the time arrives, we will be forced to live in the walls—like rats in the burned out north, Heard Ulf's son says—and make our battle from the inside, silently hid."

He sighed and, pulling himself up, sat with his arms around his knees, staring at me in the darkness. "This has been the chief of our ambitions for many months, Earl Morcar," he pronounced slowly and thoughtfully, "to reclaim the two of you from the king's grasp. Long I have waited for the day that I could be earl's man to Edwin Ælfgar's son again. Oft I have imaged how his golden presence there would stir those men to bolder action and draw others to our cause. Well you know how the very sight of him has wrought a fire in the hearts of Mercian men. Too, Siward Bearn has anticipated this time with a fever, when he might ride north behind you, and let the sight of you build us a great army."

Breaking off suddenly, he swallowed hard and his tone hardened. Somehow, instinctively, I knew what he was going to say next. "Your brother is an unfit man now, Morcar; must be you realize he can be of no use to us at Ely."

I stiffened. He went on. "Methinks I knew as much when I carried his broken form that long way from Fulford. Few men fight again after taking grief like that. Yet it almost seemed he might have overcome it, his spirit was that strong. Before he broke it."

"Blame d'Aubermont—" I mumbled, feeling empty, "and William the Bastard for forcing him to make that winter-trek, and moving him from Ceaster before his bones were healed."

"Know you something, Morcar?" Hereward quizzed, lowering his voice and drawing nearer to me. "You have been your brother's shelter ever since your father died."

"How so?" I felt myself bristling just as I used to when the Wake tried to read me of old.

"If you cannot see it now, could be you will some day. For tonight, the thing is to make a decision. Well you must know, we need a one of you in the camp, else our standing there is meaningless."

I did not answer. He chose his words with caution, no doubt sensing my touchiness. "I would that you would allow me to be your man now," he said tonelessly. "Let me fight behind you for the good of England."

I felt like spitting. "Curse you, Mercian," I hissed, gritting my teeth. "You would abandon him!"

"Think you this is an easy thing I do?" Hereward snarled. "Never a darker hour was for me than when I realized that man was ruined. Would that the times allowed me to ride away with him somewhere and guard and nurse and shelter him! My love for him is such that I would gladly do it, and you know as much. I am needed elsewhere, though, and you are, too, Morcar Ælfgar's son. 'Tis as if the fate of everything we have loved and held dear in this life hangs on our willingness to fight for it!"

He turned his back to me in the darkness, and I could feel the depth of his emotion. In the distance, thunder lowed and rumbled. I could hear that the sea had grown fierce; my heart pounded. I felt dizzy. Thoughts spun away from me so fast that I could not catch on to them. Then the Wake's voice came again. I could tell he fought to keep it level.

"You must come with me, Morcar. It is our last hope for Angland. Let Edwin ride north with Siward Bearn. He can hide in the Scot Land while we build the climate for him here. A few months or a year to let his bones mend and his mead-curse fall away, without the stress of being hunted—"

He stopped and rolled over, as if to assure himself I was listening.

"I will ask him on the morrow," I answered miserably.

"Nay. You will not ask him. You will tell him."

"If he needs me to go with him, I will do it."

"With both of you fled across the border there will be no reason for Anglishmen to fight any more for the land," his voice, a hollow whisper, sounded thick with frustration and despair. "Think you that your responsibility to him is greater than your duty to the country? To the Humbria or to Mercia? Mercia is the essence of the blood of your house—and your blood is the very substance of Mercia."

I started, thankful for the concealing darkness that hid my discomposure. "How is't you would come to say that, Hereward the Wake?"

I asked accusingly.

"Earl Edwin told me how oft your father said those words to the two of you. Think you he said them for naught? He was willing to part himself from the sons he loved for the sake of Mercia. Methinks, if he had a brother, he would have pulled himself away, no matter."

Shifting uncomfortably, I crossed my arms over my face, suddenly assailed by unbidden memories that did little to relax me. "When the dawn comes, I will speak to him," was my numb reply, but even as I said it, I was picturing how it would hurt and disturb Edwin, maybe even fire him to rage.

"He will not be pained or angry, Morcar," the Wake said gently, emphatically, as if he had read my mind. "It should not surprise you to learn he prizes Mercia above his own self. No doubt he has already in his heart demanded him to do what is best."

I made a half-hearted, sleepy reply and turned myself face down in the damp furs, hoping he would say no more. He did not, but even so, it seemed hours before I slept, and then my dreams were restless.

*   *   *

Never was a dawn more suited to my melancholy mood than the one that broke the morrow: miserable, dismal, and grey. Thunderclouds of threatening mien had gathered from one horizon to the other; there was no break of blue sky between them, and they hovered low, breathing a cold clammy breath of depression over everything. I had no stomach for food. While the other men gathered around the fire eating a strange pottage Æthelstan had concocted from wild winter grains, I sat a ways off with my brother, on a high stony bank overlooking the boundless, mean-looking sea.

Below us the boat bobbed and squirmed on the angry waves that lashed the tiny inlet where it was moored; it minded me of a ram fighting the rope while being led to slaughter. We shared a kyll of potent mead and talked about the mysterious game of life. Climbing the rock-strewn slope, Edwin had stopped and exclaimed that everything about the moment seemed familiar—the smell of the dank sea, the look of the place and the feel of the air.

"Even it seemed I knew what next you would say!" he said wonderingly. "'Twas as if I had lived that brief awareness once before."

I told him how the same thing had happened to me, on the grassy ledge in Normandy, and I had been frightened by the intensity of it. "What think you it means, that instant of remembering?" I asked him, taking a deep swallow and shuddering from the impact. He mused a minute. Unshaven and unkempt as we all were, he looked decidedly heathen as the wild wind whipped his long hair and flapped through his heavy mantle. I was reminded of my father for the first time in a long while; Ælfgar had worn much of the same look that other time we had been on the run when we were children, hiding in the Cymry as now. I had to forcefully shake the images away. I could not afford to be burdened with memories. My heart could scarce stand the weight of the present.

"Mayhap those moments are meant to mark something special," Edwin said softly, as if to himself. "Could be they are signals we have given ourselves in some long ago dream."

I looked at him, puzzled.

"Uncle Leofric told us there was no time in dreams—remember it? So could be our selves creep out in sleep and look about, and if they chance to see a moment they think is interesting and they watch it, mayhap they will remember it when it really happens."

I stared at him open-mouthed, then took a deep draught. He laughed, shrugging his shoulders and looking away, as if embarrassed. After a while, he put his face in his hands. He was shivering with discomfort. I asked if he wanted to go back, but he said nay, that he could not stand men staring at him all the time, as if to measure his resistance.

He finished the kyll off, squeezed it flat, then tucked it into the beltings at his waist. Taking a deep breath, I told him that I thought things might go better with him if he made his way to Scot Land with the Bearn, and languished there in safety till his strength was back. I spoke fast as I could, so it would all be out before I faltered, or he interrupted. He turned his head and looked at me silently a while; his deep blue eyes emotionless and unreadable. Finally, he nodded his head in silent agreement, breaking his gaze from mine and looking out to sea.

Instinctively, I gripped his shoulder, wanting to communicate a portion of my own distress and alleviate some of his at the same time. He stiffened when I touched him, and said low that he had wondered if I would gain the heart to tell him this. "God knows I will be wroth to part with you, brother," he added, breaking a chunk off the over-hanging sod and tossing it over the edge into the churning water. "It is true, though; we must needs make a parting. Ely needs an Ælfgar's son, and, just as Hereward told you, I am a ruined man."

I flinched, realizing now that he had overheard our furtive conversation. I sore regretted it. Edwin lifted a hand as if to wave it off. "Makes no matter," he said, reading me. "There is naught either of you said that had not occurred to me before."

The salt spit of the wind suddenly became intolerable to me. I pulled myself to my feet. Lost in miserable thoughts, I had walked a ways down the slope back towards the camp before Edwin hollered. He was picking his way more carefully after me, and as I looked back, he made a funny face and gesture as if to indicate he had drunk too much mead to keep his balance. I could not help laughing. When he caught up with me, he put his arm around my shoulder and we walked thusly the rest of the way, trying to lighten our moods with talk of one subject and another.

The rain held off till near noon. Just as the torrent started, a cry arose from the north ridge. "Four riders! Four riders!"

In an instant, the camp was a flurry of activity as men rushed here and there, making their arms ready and adjusting their monkish costume as Hereward directed them. Alarmed, my brother and I hurriedly pulled wadmal robes over our leathern hauberks. I crammed my long hair back into the cowl and raised my hood. The party we were expecting was a much larger one than that approaching, and there was no telling who these men were. The air was so swollen with mist and dampness and the daylight so grim that we scarce could make them out, but in a very short time they had come close enough that we could see mud flying and water sloshing as furious hooves pounded the boggy lea. Then we recognized Siward Bearn.

In one lithe motion he pulled to a halt, slid from the saddle, and embraced me; how he knew my figure in that shapeless wadmal I do not know. His powerful voice shook a little as he made a greeting. I held him back at arm's length and scrutinized his tall, finely muscled frame. He was bearded again and his long hair, grown totally back to its natural ash brown hue, was soaked and matted, but he had never looked bolder or more handsome than he did at that very minute, grinning in the downpour as he squeezed my shoulders. Appraising each other wordlessly a scant time longer, we embraced again. Then he called my brother's name, and as Edwin moved forward, the other riders dismounted: the three sons of Carr, drenched and muddy and talking all at once.

After making his greetings, Hereward led us a little way off from the main party, all scurrying now to break the camp and load the ship. Osbeorn Dolfin's son passed around a chunk of white cheese with some hard barley bread, and the riders ate while they spoke, all in exuberant spirits, though visibly fatigued and famished.

"Hast been a treacherous fortnight for me, cousins!" Siward Bearn said seriously, wiping his face and hair with a cloth Brother Wulfget handed him. He said he had delivered more than a dozen portions of the war-arrow in that time, to men at various points in the north and the midlands, informing them that the army was being built and urging them to join him in Bebbanburg. A hunted man with the king's highest price on his head, he had found it difficult journeying. Somewhere just north of the Peaclond, he had been recognized, but someone gave him warning that a pack of Norman horsemen was approaching in arms. To mislead them, he sent his entire party straight east into the Scirwudu, a place they were known to frequent, while he galloped furiously west for Ceaster, alone and unguarded. By the grace of God, the ploy had worked. He made it to my sister's house unmolested, and found the three sons of Carr making ready to spirit Aldgyth and her children into the Cymry—their responsibility upon receiving the arrow fragment. He rode with them to the new camp they had built for the purpose, south of Rhuddlan. Once they had secured the woman and children in warranted safety, the brothers had joined themselves to the Bearn, and the four traversed the entire length of Wales in but four days, with no change of horses and in the most prohibiting weather.

"The worst is yet to come, though," he told us ruefully, though with a certain gleam in his eye that gave me to know he somehow appreciated the adventure. "We must mark more than a hundred miles across the North Humbria on horseback. You scarce can imagine it now, Morcar! 'Tis a wilderness, interrupted here and there with black, burnt reminders of homes and cities. The dogs have all gone back to wild, forage is scant, and the desolation uncanny. A man can go ninety miles without seeing a living soul, save an occasional beggar or man on the run. Then suddenly, there will be a king's patrol, when you least expect it. They ride out from their hives at Eorforwic and Dunholme, and visit about at random, looking for any distresses they can sink their teeth into."

He paused for a moment to chew and swallow, then leant towards me with a knowing grin. "You and I will have the advantage over them though, cousin! The foreigners are only just beginning to know their way around, but we have the war-grounds indelibly mapped."

My brother and I exchanged a mute glance, and Hereward took the opportunity to tell of the change in plan, which Edwin and I had discussed with him earlier. My cousin was disappointed I would not be with him, but he glossed over it, saying he would be at Ely in a few weeks anyway, so we would not be long parted. Still, there was a certain dejection in it for me. I would have liked three or four weeks of freedom to ride the countryside with my kinsman before locking myself up in the grim coldness of that monastery.

Edwin interrupted that thought in a way that made me smile. "Best you just tell yourself this way is for the best, brother," he said with a knowing look, "else God would not have inspired it."

He was in better spirits now that he realized the Welshmen would be alongside him, and I was glad for it.

Siward Bearn wanted to leave immediately; men were waiting for him at Ceaster and at Hefresham, and he was afraid they would disband if they did not see his ship when they expected it. Brother Wulfget told him it would be foolish to risk his own life as well as my brother's and the other men's by sailing when the sea was so foul. Finally, Hereward cajoled him and the Welshmen into grabbing some much-needed sleep while we waited for the rain to abate. All was in readiness except nature, he said, so they might as well rest themselves for now, and be ready to fly when the sky grew calm. My cousin replied he was too worked up in spirit to take a portion of rest, but soon as he put himself down on the furs under Osbeorn Dolfin's son's wolf-skin awning, he was out.

A little ways away, under no cover at all, Daffydd, Ywen, and Hwell slept face down in their coverlets, oblivious of the elements. All the other men were busy with ordering the two boats, so my brother and I talked alone awhile, sitting cross-legged on the ground in the pouring rain. Neither of us could remember a storm so fierce and lashing. It would have seemed ominous but that Brother Wulfget reminded us that all the prayers of Angland were directed towards keeping the fen-land deep and unreachable, so the torrents were a portent in our favor.

Nevertheless, I was over-awed by the sight of the giant lightenings crashing into the sea, and the jolt of the thunderings did not sit well with me at all. Edwin laughed at my discomfort and told me with a mirthless smile that 'twould take his bones and marrow a fortnight to dry out from the cold and chill of it. "Does not hearten me to know I will be in a saddle all that time," he said mournfully. Suddenly he gripped my wrist, and leaning forward, brought our hands, by then intertwined, between our faces, the way earl's-men signaled unity and bond. "Ours has been a special brotherhood," he said softly, looking directly into my eyes. "Best I should tell you now you are the boldest and best man ever I have known, Morcar Ælfgar's son."

It made me tremble. "Seems it would be better we did not speak thusly on parting, brother," I replied, forcing my voice level and squeezing his hand hard. "You, though, know I have always loved and honored you as the finest of men."

In the mistiness, my eye caught the gleam of the ring he wore, the one that had been our father's and grandfather's before him. "Carry Mercia with you," I whispered on an impulse. He smiled. We stood and embraced, then separated and busied ourselves. Unable to say more, we avoided each other.

Later, when the downpour stopped and the fast-lowing Cymrian wind had scattered the titan clouds enough for us to leave the place, I stopped in the middle of packing the monk's-boat and turned to look for Edwin. He was standing on a rocky knoll at the sea's edge, watching Daffydd and Ywen fight the horses up a gang-plank onto the ship. At the same moment I spotted him, he turned, as if the urge had come on him to seek for me as well. We smiled at the synchronicity, and in exactly the same moment raised our right arms in fare-well. 'Twas not so much a fond parting wave that we gave each other, but a heart-felt salute.

CHAPTER FIFTY-EIGHT

... Then came bishop Æthelwine and Siward
Bearn with many hundreds of men with them.
But when King William learnt of this, he ordered
out naval and land levies, and entirely surrounded
the district, built a causeway, and made naval
patrols to seaward.

—Anglo Saxon Chronicle
Book "D" 1071

May 1071
"Well-come to our humble hearth!"

Brother Wulfget was speaking in a mirthful tone, but his voice
sounded very far away. We had come out of the deep moat of the fen
onto the raised island where the monastery stood, and now in the
shadow of its looming stone greyness, a strange thing was happening. I
was remembering everything about it—the sounds and the smells and
the voices—and drowning in the feeling that it had happened before,
this moment, and that I was only recalling it. It seemed odd that it
would happen to me again so soon after Edwin and I had talked of the
sensation. Then a strange thought struck me: in all the many years since
first I had come here as a boy, I had suffered nightmares of the place.
Mayhap what my brother said was true; some part of me had traveled
here in those dreams and watched on this minute.

"Earl Morcar!" someone shouted my name and grabbed my shoulders in greeting, jostling me from the idea before I could finish it. "By
the Virgin, 'tis good to see your face. You look well!"

"And you, Heard Ulf's son!" I crushed him in a genuine embrace
and drew back, scrutinizing him. "Must be this outlaw's life agrees with
one such as you!" I pulled jokingly at the growth of beard he wore,
precisely the same color as his long chestnut locks.

"Aye," he mumbled, grinning. "I am not one who goes out and tries to pass myself off as a priest, so I allow me the face hair." He stopped to embrace his uncle, and Osbeorn Dolfin's son batted him playfully.

"Other men sneak from this camp with every precaution, on important missions to find men and arms," he told me, eyes twinkling. "My pretty nephew here makes his way through the fen in blackness just to bed maidens!"

"Only once!" Heard Ulf's son started to defend himself, but the other men broke into amused laughter. Apparently it was a well-known story, and I would assuredly hear it from someone later. In good spirits, we laughed and talked as Hereward led the way into the huge, stone-built hall.

Hereward's war-arrow had brought men from many parts of England. More than a hundred and a half were gathered in the refectory to greet us, and Æthelstan told me there were at least that many more camped elsewhere on the island, in tents or other shelters placed strategically at spots where a crossing might be made. "We expect twice this number or more to come from Bebbanburg," he added solemnly. "By God's grace they will get here before the king's men work their way through the fen."

"Our hope is to draw the king himself right onto our island," Heard Ulf's son told me, dipping ale for us from a bucket in the middle of the table before he took his place. "We will no doubt have to withstand the best of his men before we can get to him, though. So for now we must needs hold them off until the Bearn arrives with more strength. Once they are here and settled, we will invite the Normans to dine with us!"

A cheer arose amongst the men immediately anext him, and it was soon picked up by the entire hall. Then Hereward stood and gave a short account of his adventures to and from Wintanceaster, helpfully embellished by many asides from Osbeorn Dolfin's son. He introduced me, and there was more cheering. Some the men were known to me, like Ælfric White-Hair's son Sihtric, grown now into an able-bodied warrior, and Beornwald Strong-Leg, who had been chief of my cousin Oswulf's men. Others I knew by sight. Escgar the Chamberlain, who had long ago brought me the news of King Edward's death and Harold's accession, was there. So were a number of monks I remembered from Peterborough, and landholders and kinsmen of ours from Mercia.

Nobles, thegns, earl's-men, and priests all mixed easily in that company. Amongst them I recognized Wessexmen and Mercians, North Humbrians, East Anglians and Welsh; there seemed not so great a difference between Anglish men now as there was before the Normans came.

Exhausted and famished from a fortnight of hard flight, I had difficulty focusing my attention. It seemed I was ever on the verge of falling fast asleep. Men came to me singly and in groups to give greetings and discuss different matters, some lightly, and some in depth. How I managed to make converse, I do not know, but at length I felt myself nodding, then jerking hard awake.

"'Tis a pity the king's men believe this place is crammed full of the treasures stolen from Peterborough," I heard Osbeorn Dolfin's son say ruefully. "You know how the Normans will risk anything for booty. Even now they are drooling to take this place and divide up the goods."

"Let them think it," came Hereward's level answer. "It is best that they do not come to realize we bartered it all away to the Danes to secure the fleet that is building in Bebbanburg."

That was all I heard. Next thing I knew, it was morning, and Brother Wulfget was coaxing me awake. I was laid out fully dressed on a pile of furs and covers in a corner of a dim chamber, having arrived there by what means I know not. After the Mass and a simple break-fast of cold fowl and boiled eggs, Hereward and Heard Ulf's son began my education in earnest, taking me the length and breadth of the camp and explaining as much as they could of its workings.

They were particularly anxious to show me the network of secret hallways and passages that were concealed with great care and ingenuity throughout the place. I surprised them when we came to the alm's-house, though, by pulling back the heavy, dust-permeated tapestry that hid the entrance-way to the grim, dark maze. I remembered it so well from the visit I had made there with my father and Uncle Leofric that I was able to point the way to the sanctuary and, once inside the close, stifling passage, to lead them to the wide, dim-lit inner corridor where water ran in the troughs and sunlight filtered through. I was only slightly less amazed than they were that I remembered the complexities of it; truth was, I had to work at fighting off that strange sensation of famil-iarity. I could feel its rising and I did not want to be overcome in the tomb-like stillness, for fear of panicking.

In the same room where, in ancient times, monks had hidden precious relics from the heathens, the outlaws made their treasure store. I was astounded by the wealth contained there, and recognized much of it as riches salvaged from my brother's houses and mine in Mercia and the North Humbria. Alert to coming disaster, Hereward and Siward Bearn had moved quickly ahead of the Conqueror to empty our estates and manors of the best things before they were confiscated. Other high-ranking men had brought their goods to the camp and stored them there, too. Even without the treasures of Peterborough, there was easily enough loot to whet the appetites of the greedy foreigners.

"Best you spend some time in these passages and learn the feel of them," Hereward said severely, perhaps sensing my discomfort. "When we finally let the Normans come, we will live in here—wreak our havoc in the open, then hide in these confines."

"Like rats in the burnt-out north!" Heard Ulf's son interrupted with a mischievous grin and well-rehearesd manner, as if he knew the saying irked his friend. Hereward mock-punched his shoulder, then went on.

"We know the king's way of fighting well enough to suppose he will make his headquarters right here in the monastery. We will have the advantage of knowing where they are at all times, and of being able to get to them and away from them without being seen. If we are cunning enough, we can pick them off one by one and make our escape. When they are baffled and confused to the point of hopelessness, William himself will take over the campaign, as he always does when his councilors and soldiers fail him. Then he will be the one we stalk unseen."

We made our way further through the darkness, without benefit of lantern. If any light were to shine through the chink of the stone, Heard Ulf's son explained, the king's men would be alerted and the plan would fail. "Of all the men we have gathered here, only a few know of the passageways," he added gravely. "Those chosen to live and fight in here will know the map of it inside and out; otherwise, the fewer with privy, the lower the risk."

I managed to keep myself calm, but after we climbed the narrow, rock-cut steps and pushed open the wellhidden door that opened into the sick-room, I breathed a heavy, audible sigh of relief. I instinctively knew it would take a great deal of effort and concentration for me to feel any degree of comfort in there, and resolved immediately to force myself to the task.

*   *   *

'Twas a sunny morning near a fortnight later when we stood in the turreted spire of the monastery and watched as King William moved himself into his newly built castle. It adjoined the manor at Grantanbrycg that had once belonged to my father. The king had a giant force with him, many hundreds of men and horses, arms and armor glinting in the spring brightness. Downwind, their voices carried to us now and again when they cheered or hollered an answer all at once. They were less than a half-mile away, but as any fen-man knew, it was the most dangerous half-mile on the face of the earth, and the lengthy continuation of the rain-season had increased its hazards the more.

"Think you they know we are watching?" Heard Ulf's son asked, brows knit in a tight frown. Brother Wulfget said he thought not.

"But when he stands on the ramparts and discovers that he can see this spire, he will know we can see their every move down there," the priest laughed.

I smiled at the picture which occurred to me then: the Conqueror's grim features pinched with fury when he realized they could not make a secret approach.

To our intense amusement, the Normans had decided they could reach us by building a bridge over the marshes. Day after day we watched them scurrying like ants below, cutting and hauling lumber, fashioning and driving piles. While William was so intent on his hopeless task, we managed to send party after party out in other directions, tripling our supplies of arms, food, and necessities.

I was down in the walls with Osbeorn Dolfin's son and Brother Wulfget one afternoon, when Æthelstan came to fetch us to the tower at Hereward's insistence. Heard Ulf's son and the White-Hair's son, Sihtric, had taken some men out in silent long-nosed eel boats and, well hidden and unreachable in the reeds, they pelted the hapless workers with rocks, arrows, and other missiles of all sorts. We roared with laughter as the king's men swatted and batted the air helplessly, some losing their balance and toppling into the mire, others unabashedly turning tail and running like mangy hares from a pack of dogs. After that, men took turns harassing them on a regular basis, and found a certain amount of relief in it. As the forces grew closer, the camp was itching for warfare, but we had long ago decided not to confront them till they had worked their way so deep into the fen that there would be no escape for them when we hit.

In a very short while, I became adept at making my way through the dim, dank passages of the walls and floors. We had decided we could comfortably house about two dozen of the best fighters in there and though we all instinctively felt the Norman's bridge would in no wise carry them to our doorstep, we hurried to stock the place just in case. Osbeorn Dolfin's son had returned from one foray with several barrels of fine Norman spiced wine, which many of the Anglish had never yet tasted. That night, we feasted to the point of silliness in the huge hall, to celebrate the collapsing of more than half of the king's bridge. The piles had refused to hold in the slimy marsh bottom; from the spire we had seen the structure's sagging long before the workers did. We cheered as the thing was sucked under, then watched in silence as they pulled twelve heavily laden bodies out of the mud and made a grim retreat. "Methinks this calls for a celebration," Hereward said as they disappeared from our view. Though somber, all of us had heartily agreed with him.

Those who quartered within the monastery feasted as usual in the hall, but before we joined them, Hereward and I, with the closest of my men, visited all three of the outside camps on the island, drinking and visiting with those bold men of lesser rank who had been elected to guard what we jokingly referred to as the "front tier." They were good men all, and we tried to keep close contact with them; their duty, in the end would prove just as important and every bit as perilous as that of the noblemen, earl's men, and priests inside. Nevertheless, I was already so dizzy by the time we made our way back into the hall that I was forced to refuse all the proffered cups and beakers men tried to pass me.

"Mayhap he is not entirely as bold as the real North Humbrians," I heard one man remark. He was a wide built, ferocious looking Bernician named Oslac Osmud's son, whom I knew but slightly and had never much admired. In his youth, he had been earl's man to the usurper Earl Siward, and had held vast estates in Dunholme and Hagustaldesea before Oswulf Eadwulf's son reclaimed them. Later, he had sworn himself to Copsige Sword-Stinger after William named that man Earl of the Bernicia in my cousin's stead. Could be he thought he would take again the properties he once owned, but, like Copsige himself, he had far underestimated Oswulf's fury and strength. In the same fracas that had seen the Sword-Stinger hacked to death, mangled, and burned, Oslac Osmud's son had lost his left eye and a portion of his ear and cheekbone to my kinsman's own sword. That is what gave him his intimidating look.

In other times, he would have been a man slavering for revenge. Though he had never said aught to me one way or the other since I came, I knew it must have irked him to be forced to keep company with the over-lord and blood-kin of the dead man who had been his bitterest enemy. This night, the wine had made him over-hot and bellicose. Nevertheless, tales had reached me of his daring and courage against the Normans, and I was minded to let the remark pass, but that he followed it immediately with another, meaner taunt, not exactly to my liking.

"Could be there is a particular reason King William kept this one by his side three years," he spoke aloud in a cold voice. "Mayhap he likes pretty men with long hair and beardless faces. Even God knows that against all odds neither of the Ælfgar's sons ever took them either wife or mistress!"

He rose to his feet as I sprang at him, backing away as if to protect himself from an unexpected predator. My hands were wrapped tight in his mouse brown hair, and I was hissing something, I know not what, while I jerked his head back with all my strength. He was growling in return, but his deformed face was pale with a mixture of shock and fear which he was totally unable to suppress. I let go of him all at once as I became aware of the commotion surrounding us: Hereward shouting madly, Heard Ulf's son and Osbeorn Dolfin's son livid with anger, cursing the man and waving knives. Other men were pulling and prodding me to end the encounter.

"Best you mete your words more carefully next time you speak," I breathed low as I turned away from him, pushing Hereward and Brother Wulfget out of my path as I strode away. There was an uncomfortable silence as I made my way back to my own seat, but Sihtric Ælfric's son broke it meaningfully by lifting high a cup and calling a salute.

"To unmarried men everywhere!" he cried, and the hall erupted with laughter as the toast was taken up with lusty cheers. I had to smile. I liked that man immensely. He was well-formed and amiable, robust and jaunty, and had inherited not only his father's wavy white hair, but the same instinctive understanding and regard for other men that had made bold Ælfric such a favorite of my father's. What is more, he was a true Mercian in spirit and in look, and did not use the adverse conditions as an excuse to grow mangy, as many of the North Humbrians did. Like me, he insisted on being shaven, and no one would dare to call him priest-like or womanly because of it. He had a hard-earned reputation as a ladies' man and, along with Heard Ulf's son, had oft-times risked much to relieve himself of the tedium of abstinence which characterized the rigorous camp life. There was near five year's difference in our ages, which had kept us from being close friends as children, but it was not noticeable now. That night we drank together, man to man, for the first time, in circumstances neither of us could have imagined those many years ago before our fathers were murdered together.

Next day, heavy-headed, I made my way up to the spire. Hereward was alone there, watching the king's army in the distance, puzzling over their new plan of action. They were still building portions of bridge-work and carrying them into the fen. After some time we determined they were hauling barrels and inflated hides with them, to float the sections where the piles would not hold. Their activity was so intense; their numbers so multiplied, it would only be a matter of a day or so before they had worked themselves to the deep section of bog, a throwing distance from our ramparts, where we planned to ambush them.

"Like so many foxes," Hereward mused, shading his eyes to better his view, "thinking they are sly while they slip themselves right into our trap." He turned, hands on hips, and asked half-jokingly how it was he had managed to keep peace in his camp without a single disturbance, until I came.

"I have no quarrel with that man," I answered hotly, "and I know not what quarrel he thinks he has with me."

Hereward laughed. "The One-Eye is the sort of man who thrives on discontent. He thinks all Anglish men are equal, now that there is no real king and all the earls are dead save the ones he never liked to begin with. No doubt you have heard him complaining how you keep a private chamber when all else sleep where they fall, and grumbling that men call you earl and show you deference, saying every person here works as hard and risks as much."

"Nay. I have not," I answered sharply. "Nor do I care what he babbles behind my back."

"His quarrel is the same as the one you had with Waltheof Siward's son. He sees you as no more than kinsman to someone who murdered a man he appreciated."

"Well, mark him for me—else I will be forced to burst him!" I cried fiercely, and Hereward threw his head back, laughing for all he was worth.

"Glad that I amuse you, Mercian!" I growled half under my breath, but smiling.

"Never you cease to amaze me, that is all," he replied, wiping his eyes with the corner of his faded sleeve. "Just when I think I have you read, you wax unpredictable!"

"Good." It gave me some satisfaction to know it.

I spent the rest of the day piling rocks, stones, and arrows along the ramparts, preparing for the attack. That night, exhausted and bone-weary, I carried my pile of furs into the hall, laid them out in the very center of the room, and slept there. The cold floor felt precisely as hard and uncomfortable in that place as it did in the tiny monk's cubicle where Brother Wulfget had originally planted me and, truth to tell, I did not feel half as trapped and lonely. No one said a thing about it until the next morning, when Heard Ulf's son declared he would rather eliminate the One-Eye altogether than see my dignity insulted because of him. He vowed he would continue to address me as earl and to make certain that others did, too. He was chief of my men in the Bearn's absence, and took the duty seriously.

"What else are we fighting for if not to preserve the Anglish ways?" he grumbled as he helped me into my heavy coat of iron mail. "And it has always been the way of folk to respect their earls. That man is a North Humbrian and would never have dared insult you like that if times were right."

"He thinks I am not a man of the Humberland, that is all," I answered, fumbling my arms into the rigid sleeves and trying not to get them pinched. "You know he is not the first northerner to hold my Mercian blood against me."

"Pah! You are a scion of Morcar of the Seven Boroughs, esteemed by all of the Humbria, and you have proven yourself well as any man in the earldom. What more does the dog want?"

"Face-hair!" I whispered through my teeth, sounding serious. "For some ungodly reason, the Humbrians crave a beard and think part of the man is missing if they do not see one."

I wrapped my hair around my fist and held it to my head while he adjusted the helmet, then slipped my hand out, leaving the locks caught in place. Heard Ulf's son laughed. He had shaven himself that morning to protest Osmud's son's unseemly remark, as had a good number of other men, even Mercians like Hereward who had grown bearded for the first time in this camp. Those men who knew me best had always appreciated my clean chin; it reminded them of how Mercia and the North Humbria had been so closely joined for awhile, and of the power we had known in that brief time.

After I was dressed, I tried to be what help I could to my man. When we were ready, we joined the others in the church and Brother Wulfget said a hurried Mass while we stood, near two hundred of us, in the nave, fully armed. It was fast nearing daylight and, though we had heard no alarm yet from the watch, we knew the king's men would soon be where we wanted them. Anxious and silent, we mounted the ramparts and prepared to wait.

Even in the dimness of dawn, we could see action in the Norman camp. As the sun rose, the glitter of armor was blinding; hundreds upon hundreds of men were massed at the mouth of the marsh. In the fore-front, a dark figure on a black horse, the king no doubt, was urging them to some conformation, while figures darted here and there, hauling huge wooden frames, stretched over with hides, several dozen in all. "A sow, by the Cross!" Hereward exclaimed when he saw them. "They are building a sow to ward off our arrows!"

"Must be they are men of great faith if they think they can balance that thing above them and walk their frail bridge at the same time," Brother Wulfget said cheerlessly. They must have known all along that we planned to pelt them from above and had only dragged the strong coverings out now, at the last moment, so that we would not have time to change our strategy. Balefully, we watched them latch the portions together into an exceedingly long, lightweight shelter. If it held, they could practically walk right to the island, and our piles of rocks and arrows and javelins would be useless till they were firm on Ely's ground, fighting hand to hand with the men who held our front tier.

They chanted as they took to their bridge, single and double file, moving slowly and rhythmically, invisible inside their barn-sized shield. They wove themselves deep into the swamps, now exposed and now hidden from view by the murky overgrowth. 'Twas impossible to make out the meaning of their strange battle call till they came closer. "Le roy le veult!" they cried in one deep voice. "Le roy le veult!" *The king wills it....*

Some men mounted their arrows, others armed themselves with hefty rocks, but Hereward raised his hands high to stop them from action. "I will blow a single blast," he said in a gruff, somber voice, just loud enough for us to hear. "Then everything must hit them at once, at the very front of their line, when they have grown vulnerable from waiting for it!"

So we held ourselves, and over long, drawn out minutes they approached us. Every one of us had an eye on Hereward's silver Flemish trumpet. Directly below us, wedged between the walls of the monastery and high turf barricades and lumber pales, the rest of our men were poised and braced for the attack. They could not see into the fen as we could from our vantage point, and no doubt they wondered why we had not commenced our hurling, as the plan had been laid. By now, the enemy was scarce a furlong away from the hard ground of the island, moving warily ever closer, confused by our stillness and passivity, and still chanting. Across the fen-way in Grantanbrycg, we saw the tail of the army disappear into the swamp. The king and his advisors, still mounted, watched and waited. As the front of the line slowed in caution, more men crowded forward, seeking the coverage when they came aground. We could make out the voices of rank-men, urging them on to plunder and victory, haranguing them with promises of treasure and glory. The sow took on an awkward tilt.

A sound rent the air—shrill, high, discordant. Rocks, stones, tree limbs, and sawed rounds of oak trunk flew, a single, wild mass of weighty missiles, well-aimed. The floating passageway faltered as men shifted into positions of defense. A dozen arrows whizzed through a single rip in the battered hide; we heard screams of pain as they caught their mark. The sudden surging and falling back of men cost them their precarious balance and the wooden floor slid forward under the weight, then up-ended. The sow splintered apart at the first seam as fully armed men, weighted by armor, slid helplessly into the bottomless bog, screaming with horror and despair. Behind them, the army crammed backwards, upsetting the balance of the rest, and the horrific spectacle was repeated. Those determined to press on with the attack, and lucky enough to find footing, moved forward, to be met by the swords and axes of the Anglishmen below, who hacked them back before they could clamber out of the mire. The noise was deafening as section after section of the sorry bridge collapsed, spilling men, ladders, shields, and Norman gonfalons into the depths. Across the fen, men struggled their way back, soaked, filthy, and terrified.

The screams of agony and fear diminished as the army retreated. There was not even a semblance of an attack now, only men fighting for their lives against the suffocating marsh. Our cheers of victory had long subsided ere the last of the woebegone Normans crawled out of the mud at Grantanbrycg. Familiar, eerie stillness settled over everything as we disarmed and made our way into the hall for a full night's feasting.

CHAPTER FIFTY-NINE

heart must be keener,
Courage the hardier,
Bolder our mood
As our band diminishes.

—Anglo Saxon Poet

September 1071

"There is no other recourse," Hereward said firmly, tugging a rope belt firmly round his waist to fasten a rough-made jerkin of undyed burr-lap. "Someone must make a way into the king's camp and determine what he means to do next. The men here wax too uneasy and I, for one, have no desire to see the final result of tension on hot-blooded warriors imprisoned all together in a grim place like this. Mayhap we will have more of what was seen last night."

Oslac Osmud's son and Beornwald Strong-Leg had drawn each other's blood the evening before in a brawl over—of all things—the question of Oswulf Eadwulf's son's manhood. Hereward had been rabid, threatening chastisement of the grossest sort on anyone else who dared to raise any old and useless quarrels to disturb the brotherhood of the camp. For near three months, the Norman had continued with his useless attempts at attack, and every would-be approach, whether by boat or bridge or raft, had been repulsed savagely.

Then, suddenly, all activity stopped. In near a month there had been no sign of movement on his part. He had withdrawn to formulate another plan and by now, no doubt, was in the last stages of launching it. No one knew when or where to watch for him, and the suspense was taking a toll on the Anglish. Even the women which Heard Ulf's son and Sihtric Ælfric's son had carried back to the monastery with them, well met and appreciated, had done little to relieve the aggravation men were beginning to feel towards one another.

I knew William well enough to know he was hoping to goad us to laxness with the wait. Meat and mead were plentiful on the island, and he wanted us to grow so comfortable we would not make a good defense. Hereward was right. We needed an inkling of their purpose so we could put ourselves to building our strength instead of waiting helplessly for the king's cunning strike. Nevertheless, I was troubled.

"I see not why you should be the one to take the chance of going—" I began, but he cut me off, his eyes glinting.

"Who else can go? You? You would be recognized immediately! Heard Ulf's son and the White-Hair's son would distract themselves with trifles; they take far too many chances now! Æthelstan and Osbeorn Dolfin's son have not the strength or swiftness any more to make a clean escape. Wulfget is too well needed here, and there is none other I can trust to do it right!" He paused, taking a handful of white ashes out of the long-dead hearth and rubbing them into his hair, successfully dulling the sheen, making him look older and more faded. "Besides," he added when he had finished, "I have never been caught yet, nor am likely to be. They would never believe me bold enough to take such risks!"

We laughed because that was the truth of it. On two other occasions, the Wake had moved right into the midst of the Norman encampments, both times in singular disguise. One visit had been fruitless, but the information he had gleaned while posing as a deaf potter in the camp at Brandune had won us a great cargo of arms, remedies, mead, and clothing. Still, the adventure he proposed now had more of a danger to it. Before, he had entered the camps when he knew certainly that William was elsewhere. This time, he sought the very presence of the king; he was making his way into the headquarters at Grantanbrycg, and I knew he would dare anything to discover their well hid plan of attack.

We were still talking about it when Osbeorn Dolfin's son made his appearance, lugging a great sack full of strange odds and ends which Hereward had requested him to gather from different parts of the monastery. Throwing the bag over his shoulder, the Wake assumed a lumbering attitude and hunched forward, folding his shoulders at an unseemly angle and distorting his face into a twisted, dull-looking smile.

"Now I am Leofwine Hulda," he said in a thick Hereford Shire accent, "and I served the Norman earl, Ralph the Timid, back in the days of good King Edward."

"How does he do it?" I asked Osbeorn Dolfin's son with a genuine wonder. The man laughed.

"Strangest of all," he said merrily, "by the time he leaves that camp, every Norman who ever visited Ralph's manor will swear he remembers him, and any who did not will claim to have heard tales of old Hulda's service there. Without question, 'tis a special talent!"

After Hereward took his leave with Beornwald Strong-Leg, who was going to row him to the fen-edge and wait for him there, I made my way up to the turreted spire to visit with Heard Ulf's son who was watching there this day. I am sorry to say I caught him in the most compromising of circumstances, but it did not disturb him. He laughed about it, saying in a situation such as ours, a man sought solitude where he could find it—though solitude, I am sure, is not exactly what he had in mind. The object of his affections was a strong-looking, gold-haired thing, surely not noble, but a merchant's wife or daughter, perhaps, made wretched by the times and hungry for both the adventure and the tokens of payment men such as ours could offer. It bothered me greatly that she did not even try to hide her nakedness, and I am ashamed to say it bothered me in the way such things wreak havoc on a man who has been without a woman of his own for a long time. Even my leather dalmatic could not hide the fact. After she had gone, Heard Ulf's son slapped me on the back, teasing me for it and urging me to take advantage of the pretty prizes while they lingered here for the purpose. "Take that very one," he said lightly, pulling a tunic over his head and girting it with a knife belt. "She is my particular favorite, but I do not have any jealous care of her."

I broke him off with a cold stare and answered, not in direct reply, that I would need his help to keep peace in the hall during the Wake's absence. He shook his head, grinning, knowing the subject was a hopeless one with me. I have never been one who could warm to a loose woman. All my upbringing had been against it, and my temperament was such that it needed much stirring from another direction to bring me to action where a lady was concerned. For some reason, I felt a great need to love her. Whatever other faults may be mine, I do not reckon wantonness as one of them, and mayhap that is why I took Lady Briana's deception so harshly.

Knowing that Hereward had taken action to remedy the morass of depression and inertia which engulfed the camp inspired the men to better humor. There was no trouble that day or the next, and on the third we were positively exhilarated. Our network of messengers had brought us the news that Siward Bearn had set sail, with scores of ships and many hundreds of men. Two days later, they entered the swollen Ouse and sailed far as they could maneuver their large ships into the fenways, then abandoned them, to be dismantled later for the building of more fortifications.

I felt a surge of unfettered gladness when Siward Bearn stepped through the iron draw-gates of the monastery, thrown wide now in welcome. He put his hands on my shoulders after his own fashion to greet me; there was cheering when we embraced. A thousand questions came to me at once, but I knew I would have to hold them till later. The camp was in a fury of commotion that would hinder any attempt at private converse.

The Bearn had brought with him thrice the number we expected—near six hundred strong men from all corners of the country-land, many of whom I knew by sight and name. At the head of the second mass that came ashore was my man Gamel-Beorn, browned and hale from the rigors of outdoor life. Heard Ulf's son let out a holler of delight when he spotted him; the two had been best friends since childhood. The three of us tussled like children and embraced over and over again, laughing and talking. I had not seen the Biter in years. Eorforwic had stood whole and the North Humbria was untouched when last we met, and that seemed a lifetime ago.

As the three of us stood thusly, the exuberant talk going back and forth, Siward Bearn led an impressive figure over—a gaunt, leathered, bold-looking warrior, fiercesome despite his years, with drooping mustaches and wild-looking, long grey-streaked hair, thin tresses in the North Humbrian style growing out of a once tonsured head. Bishop Æthelwine had spoken no word and made no signal since he disembarked, but soon as I addressed him directly, his grim features relaxed into an easy smile. We walked together, exchanging pleasant rejoinders, confident in the urgent sense of kinship and purpose that had drawn us together in this place.

That night, the entire island sat to a great feast, within the monastery and without. Æthelstan the Fen-man had overseen the setting of it: great quantities of venison parboiled and steam-roasted in the East Anglian way; wild swine, aged, salted, and marinated in foaming ales; a great quantity of ducks and other fowl, boiled off the bone and seasoned with herbs and wines from our vast, well stocked storehouse. Ale and mead flowed freely.

We were taking our last respite before the battle that would determine everything; 'twas as if every man savored the feeling of it in a special way. Halfway through the night, Brother Wulfget raised high an ale-horn, overflowing, and saluted the fact that we sat all together, Anglishmen from every shire and every persuasion, united in a single effort. He bade Bishop Æthelwine to pray over the company and bless it. Not a one of the outlaws had taken the king's writ of excommunication seriously, least of all the bishop, condemned by his own brother's unwilling hand. We all paused silently for the benediction, then resumed our merry-making with as much or more fervor than before.

I grew heady as the night wore on, and when Siward Bearn whispered to me of a need for fresh air, I immediately offered to accompany him, grasping happily at the opportunity to speak with him away from others' hearing. The night was warm, dank, and clinging in the way summer sits on the fen-land. Once outside, I unlaced the top of my kidskin tunic and lifted my long, damp hair off the back of my neck for a spell. We walked a little way in silence to further remove ourselves from the noise and smell of the massive hall. At length, the eerie gurgling and babble of the marshes and the frog and toad song drowned some of the clamor of merriment. Siward Bearn drew a deep breath, then turned suddenly and laid his arm across my shoulder. Instinctively, I knew his mood was heavy and I tensed.

"Think you not, Morcar, that Fate is a strange mistress?" he asked slowly, as if it were difficult to speak what bothered him. When I nodded a silent assent, he went on. "Scarce can I believe I have come to be a brother-in-the-law to a Norman dog like d'Aubermont. Edwin told me you were not so broken by the news of it as he thought you would be."

"Things had already come apart between us." I said, half truthfully, not comfortable with the subject. He cleared his throat.

"Mayhap you should know this, mayhap not," he whispered glumly. "I have wrestled me whether to tell you or let it pass." He paused and, uncorking a large flask that he had carried from the hall, took a deep swig, then passed it to me. I took one, too, feeling a rush of heat as the Bearn continued.

"Oft-times my sister gave me messages for you, and I carried them not. Likewise I did not work hard to make her think you loved her over-much." His voice was shaking. I told him morosely that I knew as much and he seemed surprised.

"These things came out between the lady and me when last we met," I said, sounding shaky myself. "I had no reason to distrust you, nor she did, but you had your reasons, I trow."

He seemed dashed by this, but took another swallow and said coldly that 'twas true, he had reasons. "Not what you suppose them to be, though—pride or anger. 'Tis just that I knew things about her that would wound you in the end."

"Methinks I know of them now," I returned darkly. "Best we not waste time counting faults long past, though. 'Tis an adventure in my life that is over. Done with. There is naught but uselessness in looking back on it."

In a slow, strangled voice he mumbled an apology, but I laughed it away. "You are closest of my kinsmen, Siward Æthelgar's son," I said firmly, trying to smooth the talk a bit, "and best of my friends. There is naught you have done that I hold against you."

"Could be Edwin would resent me if he knew, though," my cousin added weakly. "He blames d'Aubermont that he lost the hand of his own woman, and says he hates him for coming between you and yours.

Mayhap it is the root of the fury that broke him so badly at Ceaster."

"They wounded each other well that night," I agreed, "and no one knows the full cause of it, beyond Fulke's jealousy and Edwin's bitterness. I have heard them swear each against the other to the death, so 'tis no passing quarrel."

"You should know that Edwin is resolved to murder him!"

"Aye. It can be believed," I said lightly, not understanding his import. The Bearn shook his long locks vehemently.

"I mean he has gone to seek him out."

Suddenly chilled, I stopped dead. "How mean you this?"

"When we parted, he was not on his way to Scot Land. He said he knew all the parts of the Humbria that d'Aubermont frequented, and he was going to make the man face him."

I shivered. "How was his—" I fumbled for words. "How was his strength?"

"God knows, Morcar!" My cousin's voice was heavy with exasperation. "He was forever crazed with pain and strong drink that I could see. Half the time, Daffydd Carr's son was holding him upright, elsewise he stumbled or could not sit a horse. One morning, in the north of the forest, we hid in over-growths of a gorse ridge while king's men passed so close that we could smell them. I had to stuff a sleeve in his mouth to still his moaning. The man is a walking mass of death-wounds and the mindlessness he puts himself to does little to relieve his distresses!"

"Then why would he attempt this—" my voice broke off suddenly. Siward shrugged, looking grim in the darkness.

"Mayhap his pain has driven him to madness," he suggested, "or could be he is just too strong a man to let agonies keep him from doing that which he would do."

I was miserably silent a while. My cousin tried to comfort me. "We had a skirmish with a king's patrol south of the aet-Eamotum. Edwin fought better than any, though his bones paid for it later. Towards our parting, he had forced himself to ease up on spirits, and that, too, will be in his favor. What is more, and we both know it, never was a man bolder or more determined. There is little that can withstand the drive of such a one as that."

"Better he had just gone to Scot Land," I whispered belligerently, but Siward shook his head.

"Nay, 'tis better he has set himself to some purpose, no matter how dangerous in our eyes. The man would wane away in hiding, and you know it. He told me his greatest fear was that he had grown useless."

I heaved a deep sigh, remembering how he had overheard Hereward use the word.

"Besides," the Bearn added in a lighter tone, "he may yet go to Scot Land. He told me that when he is done with d'Aubermont, he plans to gather those Anglish who linger in exile there, and force them to come back with him and fight."

I smiled. It had the ring of something Edwin was wont to say. I scarce could condone his making his whereabouts known to the king by forcing the issue with d'Aubermont, but a part of me respected him for doing it. Either the quarrel was that important to him, so weighty a question of honor that he could not let it lie or, as Adeliza once said, he needed to prove something—not only to other men, but to himself.

"He has taken the Welshmen with him," my cousin broke into my thoughts, as if in answer to an unspoken question, "and twenty of the best Mercians. Must be you know they fought each other for the privilege of riding with him."

I took the flask when he offered it, somehow knowing from the heat of the swallow that the world would seem garbled by the time I got to the hall. We drank more as we made our slow way back, and it was.

*   *   *

Just as we had begun to fear for their safety, Beornwald Strong-Leg and Hereward the Wake returned to the camp, flushed, dirty, exchausted, and grim. It had been a narrow escape this time. After two days in the headquarters, Hereward had been goaded into a fight with one of William's men and they had come to arms, a thing which never sat well with the Norman. Hereward was dragged into the king's very presence. By the grace of God, William had not recognized him. Nevertheless, he meant to deal with him harshly, as he did all men who drew blood in his camp or his hall.

"He ordered him put in chains and marched to the nearby castle," reported Beorwald Strong-Leg, who told me most of the story while the Wake caught up on much needed sleep. "Your man fooled him, though. He begged the guard to let him stop and gather all his gold and precious trinkets, which he claimed to have hidden in the reeds of the river bank. The greedy fool let himself be led to the very spot where I was waiting, and between the two of us we managed to overpower him and—" He stopped as if searching for the right word to use, then triumphantly finished. "We disposed of him!"

Always in the past I had appreciated the Strong-Leg. A bold, intelligent Bernician, Beornwald was not tall, but strongly muscled and powerful. He had single-handedly held Oswulf's household together for many years, performing most of the earl's duties when my cousin's dissipation prevented him from doing them himself, which was often enough. Of late, I had come to genuinely like and admire the man. I counted him among the boldest in the camp and instinctively knew I could trust my life in his hands. Along with Hereward, the Biter, Heard Ulf's son, Osbeorn Dolfin's son, Bishop Æthelwine, Brother Wulfget, Siward Bearn, and myself, he became one of the chief planners of the defense—one of the nine whom the rest of the men only half-jokingly referred to as "the war-council."

He was with me in the large room called the alms-house, which we had claimed as a private council chamber, late on the same day the two had returned from their misadventures. We were waiting for the rest of them to join us, so we could base some plans on the information that Hereward had gleaned in the king's hall—information that, he assured us in his bleary-eyed stupor of fatigue, was momentous. We spoke of one thing and another as we waited, but after a while the talk turned to times past, and came to rest most naturally on the subject of my dead kinsman, Oswulf Eadwulf's son. Beornwald, who had been there, told me how Oswulf had grown sober and noble with approaching death. He said 'twas as if Oswulf had become, at the very end, the man God had meant him to be.

"He did not lose his senses when that long-spear entered him," Beornwald said in a somber tone, as if he regretted remembering it. "The man knew not it was a death-wound and bade us pull it out of his flesh, bearing it with neither sob nor groan. We could see it had come two hand-lengths through his back, though, and was bound to kill when we removed it. He bade his woman come and cradle him, and she soothed him all the while we worked it from him. God knows for all his faults, he was a strong man! It took his body some six or more hours to stop shivering and shaking. No blissful slide from consciousness for him, either; he suffered all of it."

"And she with him?" I asked nonchalantly, trying not to sound over interested. He nodded.

"She never left till it was over. So it was they came to a peace between them. He asked forgiveness for all he had done unto her and in return, he forgave her in the matter of—" Here he broke off suddenly, flushing with discomfort, and pulled his eyes away from mine.

"In the matter of the childling?" I asked levelly. He gave a grim nod.

"Then she asked him, would he have a priest? And he said nay, but that if it pleased her, he would let one give him comfort and he would make a confession if he did not have to beg God's mercy. Nevertheless, by the time one could be found, he was so mad with pain and writhing that 'twas little help to him. He died unshriven, though they managed to hold him down long enough for an anointing."

I swallowed hard, but said nothing. Truth was, in spite of all that had happened between us, a part of me had come of late to mourn and miss my kinsman. Burchard had taught me long years ago that things might have been different with Oswulf had Providence not played so mean with him. Both his parents died when he was a babe, and he was handed round from relation to relation. Earl Eadwulf's base murder had made the man somewhat of a saint with the Bernicians; Oswulf had never known his father but had been expected all his life to be his image. What is more, he had early been impressed with a cruel dread of being betrayed like his father had been, by noblemen and friends, and he never really trusted any man because of it. Uncle Leofric once said he lived his entire life trying to avenge Earl Eadwulf's death. This he did by fighting fiercely to have and keep the Bernicia. His father had been slain and the earldom wrested from him; Oswulf had regained it, standing successively against Earl Siward, Tostig Godwine's son, and King Edward till it came his. Then he held it with a vengeance, murdering any, like Copsige Sword-Stinger, who dared try to take it. 'Twas his finest hour when he became earl there; by recognizing him, King Edward and all the Godwine's sons admitted a guilt and complicity in Eadwulf's murder; they had accepted the murdering usurper Siward and made no attempt to punish his gross misdeeds.

Mayhap his whole life might have changed then, but the constant warfare which followed kept him hardened, and it winced me to look back and see how it had hurt him, Lady Briana's deception and mine. I realized with a pang that he had handled the affair more decently than many another man would have done. Whatever he claimed his motives were, he had seen that no dishonor came to the lady, nor to me. He took all the responsibilities and for once stayed his revenge. Only now it came to me that he had done it out of love for her. Desperate to keep her, he had played the only way he could, and in the end, he had died with his head in her lap, having made her love him in spite of everything. In truth, she had deceived him over and over again; from the second night of their bride-ale he had known it. Mine had been the betrayal that wounded him, not hers, and after all was said and done, he won her back by proving I was a self-righteous liar. He had known her for what she was and loved her anyway; I had rejected her soon as I found out. He was willing to share her if he had to in order to keep her; I most assuredly was not. Despite all his coaxing, selfish obstinacy, he had needed and wanted her. Whatever else they had been to each other, Lady Briana once told me, at least they had been honest. Could be nothing else mattered in love but that.

"Earl Morcar?" The Strong-Leg was peering into my eyes with a worried look as the others filed into the room. I had been so deep in thought I scarce heard him finish. Must be he sensed my emotion. Grasping my arm, he leant close and whispered low. "He bade her promise to teach the boy tales of Earl Eadwulf—likewise of Earl Ælfgar and his sons."

Swallowing hard, I thanked him with a look. I wondered why it had been so important for the man to speak these things to me. Could be he felt it some kind of duty to his dead earl. I had not much time to muse on it then, for Hereward was etching a crude map on the stone wall, using the charred end of a piece of kindling. A rectangle surrounded by a misshapen circle was meant, no doubt, to represent the monastery seated on the island. One large cross meant Grantanbrycg, and another meant Brandune, but the rest of the squiggles were indecipherable. There was a sturdy knock, and Æthelstan the Fen-man came in at the doorway, wrapped in the unmistakable scent of cooking-fire, wiping greasy hands on a rag he wore threaded through his belt. Hereward beckoned him forward courteously, then handed him the drawing-stick. We rested ourselves in chairs, on tables and casements, curious and enthusiastic. Hereward cleared his throat.

"'Tis an amazing thing," he said seriously, "but the Normans seem to have realized they cannot bridge the fen." A few of the men snickered, and Osbeorn Dolfin's son said something insulting about the king's intelligence; then Hereward went on.

"They have not been idle, though. I heard two men tell how the king had bribed some wandering monks into showing him one of the old Roman causeways. There was a crew of men at Grantanbrycg who had come from a strange duty—sailing boat-loads of stone and rock from Cottenham to some point at the marsh-ends where the king's men unloaded them onto rafts. Also, along the banks of the Ouse, cutters are felling trees."

"Trees by the hundreds!" Beornwald Strong-Leg added emphatically. "Could be they mean to build a castle."

"Nay!" Hereward shook his head firmly. "If they could not foot a bridge, they ne'er would be able to stand the foundation of one of their cursed keeps. The clue is in the finding of the causeway."

"Rocks and trees to raise the level of the causeway!" Heard Ulf's son exclaimed with a wonder, and Hereward nodded.

"By the Cross, they will have their work cut out for them," Siward Bearn mused thoughtfully, shaking his long locks. "In some places those old roads are thirty or more hands under the water."

The Wake gestured helplessly to Æthelstan, who was already lost in deep consideration. "Mayhap you will be able to help us, Fen-man!" he said brightly. "'Tis said you know where every causeway is. Is't true?"

"'Tis indeed!" There was no hesitation in Æthelstan's gravely voice. "By now, even you Mercians and Humbermen know that the fastest way through the fen is to glide your boat directly above the old stone roads. No trees or weeds grow through the pavement, and there are no drop-offs or whirlpools anywhere near them."

As he spoke, he was criss-crossing the diagram; having snapped off the blackened end of the stick, he drew with the flat side of it to make a thicker line. "Some are well-known," he continued, pointing to one such line. "Here, near Grantanbrycg, the old Devana way goes right into the waters. When you see an ancient road lead into the slime, you can assume it continues. The weald was not all flooded in the olden times when the ways were built."

"Is there any near to Ely, scarce known and shallow enough that the king might believe he could fill it and move his army over it?" Brother Wulfget's tone was low. His years at Peterborough had familiarized him with the fens to a great degree, and you could see he was wracking his brain trying to recognize the spot.

"Near Haddingham—" the Fen-man began, but Wulfget said nay. "We could see them from the spire," he returned, knitting his brows, "and there has been no action there that I know of."

"The road at Alrehethe, then," said the other, and he drew it in its approximate place.

"Even so, would they not fell their lumber in the Bruneswald then," Heard Ulf's son asked, "and not bother to carry trees up-river when so many abound there?"

Hereward opened his eyes wide in mock surprise. "By God!" he said jestingly, "I had forgotten the man could think so well!" Heard blushed, knowing he had made a good point.

Suddenly, Brother Wulfget was on his feet. Lunging forward excitedly, he grabbed the stick from Æthelstan's hand and slashed a wide, bold mark on the map at a point just south and east of the island.

"He is building up the road that leads from the Stunt-Knee!" he cried fervently, naming one of the causeways Uncle Leofric had used in times past to journey from his own seat to Ely, and sometimes beyond to my father's house in Grantanbrycg. The Stunt-Knee, or Foolish-Bridge, was an ancient stone bridge-work, joining three causeways at a strategic point, and it was so called because the entire complex stood under the water for nine months out of the year. Even fen-folk seldom used the way; it dipped into the slimiest, most inaccessible area of the fen where it grew deepest, and met the River Ouse between the two great streams, Grant and Reche-lode.

"Could be he is right!" Æthelstan's normally cautious voice bore a note of excitement. "'Twould certainly be invisible to us here!"

"He knows we are well fortified on the west side," Siward Bearn broke in, "because his men have met with us there. But no doubt he thinks the east side, backed against the bottomless river-swamp, is unguarded."

"It is unguarded!" added Gamel-Beorn, who had been silent till now, knowing little of the fens other than what he had learnt in the last few days.

"Not for long, though!" Hereward said decisively. "We will put a long-boat out tomorrow in that direction, and if we find the Normans raising themselves a road, we will undo all the ships we have aground in the marshes, and build some wood and turf walls all along the east side."

It seemed it was settled for now, and we came to our feet, making our way out as we discussed all we had just discovered. We had just come to the door, when Hereward stopped us all with a clap of his hands.

"Best I should tell you one thing more," he said soberly, as we turned to face him. "I heard other talk in the king's camp—talk of a strange new weapon which the king means to use against us."

"What weapon can the Normans have that they have not already tried?" Heard Ulf's son asked crossly.

"'Tis called a 'pythoness.' That much I gathered from the talk."

"A pythoness?" I repeated after him, looking from one to the other of the gathered men. I had never heard of such, nor had any of the others. "What heard you said of this weapon, Hereward the Wake?"

"That it would bring heathens to their knees. That men who shook not at writs of excommunication would nonetheless grovel at the very sight of it!"

Siward Bearn threw his head back and gave a hearty laugh. I was minded to tell him how hard we had joked long ago when old Earl Ralf brought his Normans to battle on horseback. In the end, the mounted soldiers on Hastings Field had been the undoing of Angland. I did not see much use in mentioning it, though, so I put my arm round his shoulder and laughed with him instead. Outside, it was bright and sunny, but there were clouds overhead, bearing the promise of rain.

*   *   *

We were living in our arms: sleeping in leathern hauberks with swords at hand, working all the warm day through in battle gear, our iron coats unrolled and ready. Any hour they would be upon us. When Æthelstan, Heard Ulf's son, and Beornwald made their expedition by eel-boat, they discovered that the Normans had already come about three furlongs into the fen, on a high, dry road of solid planking atop sunken rocks, trees, and sand. They saw scores of small boats, wagonloads of arms and armor, and a half-dozen catapults, waiting and ready. There was no sign of the dreaded pythoness.

Feverishly we erected high turf ramparts, backed and made strong by the lumber salvaged from the ships Siward Bearn had brought us. The east end of the island, wild and overgrown, had never been fortified; it had always been inaccessible. Moving the main of our fight there posed us another discomfort. 'Twould be near a half-hour's hard run for a man in arms to reach the safety and shelter of the monastery. Hereward was minded to make us two lines of defense, one at the edge of the island, and another inside the monastery, ready to pick off the king's men who made it through the first struggle. Brother Wulfget and many of the other men argued against it, saying the best fighters, then, would not be at the front to ward off the initial attack, and mayhap would see no action at all. Siward Bearn told him grimly 'twas wishful thinking.

"Best we just hold ourselves still in the beginning and wait for them as originally we planned," he said darkly, using a Wessex-stone to sharpen his Danish axe. "In the end, we will see enough battle from these walls to make us wish we had never thought of it."

I tended to think he was right. Other parties had gone out to assess the situation, and brought back ominous news. The size of the king's army was overwhelming. William had called soldiers from every part of Angland, and sent a bid to the continent for mercenaries. What is worse, our spies discovered Norman ships in every river, stream, and tributary. Not realizing we had wrecked most of our own ships to build fortifications, he had called out his naval levies to cut off any escape by sea. Siward Bearn's great fleet had not passed unnoticed.

Scarce a fortnight after the Wake had made his return from Grantanbrycg, someone roused the entire hall in the twilight well before dawn. The watch had heard the king's men, working under cover of darkness. So close they were to the island, the splash of their rocks and the sound of their voices and wagons could be clearly heard in spite of their attempts to muffle them. With five other men, Bishop Æthelwine went down to the east edge, where the hundreds of men were already making their battle formations. He gave then a hasty blessing, and when he returned bade us arm swiftly and make ready. The silence of the fen had been broken by the sound of oars and ripples. William was launching an attack by boat to distract us from the building of the causeway. In the pink glow of a warm and muggy daybreak, the battle began with an awful shower of Norman arrows and the rending of the air by a single, booming roar: "Dieu aide!"

From the turret, we could see it all happening. Boats of all sizes and shapes were everywhere, coming not only from the southeast where the builders worked feverishly, dropping load after load of rock and lumber into the mud, but from many directions. Soon as the first one touched shore, and eight well armed Normans tumbled out behind the line of turf walls we had erected to stop them, I lost my composure. Instinctively, I grabbed my helmet and headed for the door, breathing a low oath. I was fully ready to clamber down the stone stairway and make my way cross-field to the action, but Hereward put his hand roughly on my shoulder to stop me, signaling his disapproval.

"Think you those are babes down there, helpless without you? Methinks we had decided on two lines of defense."

I hesitated, the truth being that the idea had entirely passed from my mind.

"Could be there are men here who think themselves too noble to take orders and follow directions," Oslac Osmud's son returned coldly, and the glance that went with his sour words was not toward Hereward, but me. I shot him a mean look. The Wake's eyes glowed with humor when he caught it and he loosened his grip on me.

"The temptation is on all of us to run down there and spend our strength, Earl Morcar," he said simply, stressing my title for the other man's benefit. "Nothing would please the Norman more than for us to do it, too. That is his ploy, no doubt. These few who come from here and there in boats are only a nuisance. If we grow rowdy chasing them, our defense will fall apart, and we will not be ready to face the real menace—the army that will be marching over that causeway in some little time from now."

He gestured past the island's edge, and I could see that he was right. There were naught but a hand's breadth of yards to fill, and the wide, planked road would be butted up against the firm ground. Just behind the workers, who were scurrying to finish amidst a hail of arrows, javelins, and rocks, a gigantic catapult was being positioned and readied by a half-dozen men. The hastily built wall of turf and timber would not hold long against it. Directly below us, the hapless soldiers who had come aground had already met their fates by sword and war-axe. Another boat drew near, but capsized when the occupants stood all at once to protect themselves from a downpour of Anglish missiles. They were swallowed all at once into the oozing mire.

A few minutes of acute observation convinced me the Wake was right. Those in the boats were but decoys. If they came close, it seemed only by accident. For the most part they hovered just out of range, rowing this way and that, making a pretense of attack only to lessen the force of the blows on the road-builders. Where the causeway reached now, the water was no more than waist deep. Two or three loads more of their land-fill, and the king's men would have a solid, complete passageway.

At the edge of the island, our men grew rabid with their close approach. The Normans pulled a large hewn beam forward and balanced it on two stacks of timber. Archers climbed atop it. Once positioned, they fired a steady stream of arrows into the Anglish line, above the heads of their workers. In a very short time, the last stretch of causeway rose through the grey water. The road was complete.

Three blasts of trumpets cut the air. All at once, the king's men retreated. The boats turned and rowed furiously away; the archers, builders, and soldiers marched back out of sight along their newly built way. The silence was deafening. Most of the Anglish returned to their lines; a few ran to plunder the murdered Normans, ripping away their arms and armor and helmets and boots. I was amazed at how quickly and easily they did it, throwing the bodies one by one into the fen when they had finished.

After a little while of quiet, Bishop Æthelwine and Brother Wulfget said perhaps they should gather all the priests and look through the lines, to see if any men there needed succoring or unctions. We all agreed there could be no harm in letting them go. The Normans were entirely out of our sight by now, and could not possibly make an attack in anything less than a third-hour, and even then not without being seen well in advance. Hereward was reluctant to leave the turret, though. The king's way of fighting unnerved him somewhat. He said he had never before come against an enemy who used suspense as a weapon the way that man did. "Any other would drop the last stone and then rush his army over it," he grumbled. "This one disappears a space of time till we are all grown frenzied with wondering what he is about!"

"He is only gone to line his soldiers up," Heard Ulf's son broke in helpfully, "and to haul out the pythoness."

I drew a deep breath, suddenly uncomfortable for the weight of my arms. "Cannot be you expect us to stay in this damnable, hot tower till William decides to pay us a visit!" I exclaimed crossly, pulling my helmet off to loose my matted, damp hair.

"I do not like it," Hereward replied seriously. "Everyone knows how strong the Norman steeps himself in trickery."

At length, Siward Bearn suggested sending a spy or two out to appraise the situation, and everyone readily agreed it made sense. Beornwald and Æthelstan were the two chosen to go, with a strict injunction to stay well hidden and return with all possible haste. Then, leaving Heard Ulf's son, the Wake, and a handful of other men to their careful watch in the tower, we made our way out to talk with the men below and assess the damage that had been done.

We scarce had made it to the island's edge—Siward Bearn, the Biter, and I—when the small eel-boat made a sudden reappearance, flying through the water swift as a river snake. Spotting us, they gestured frantically, signaling us to meet them at the monastery, then whizzed past. Sweaty and uncomfortable from the exertion of walking a quarter-mile in the heat, weighted with iron coats, we cursed and complained as we turned back. Brother Wulfget and the bishop joined step with us; the Anglish casualties were fairly light, they told us: a score and a half dead and twice that number being carried somewhere so priests could rip the arrows out of their flesh and mend their lacerations. I crossed myself, wondering how much worse was to follow. By the time we made our way into the crowded refectory, everyone else had heard the harried report.

"Hereward wants the council in the turret!" one man shouted as we came in at the giant doors. "Must be they have seen something fiercesome there!"

Others called us worried greetings, and Sihtric Ælfric's son, looking bold and large in his war-gear, bade me hurry back down with news of what was being said there.

"Most of us already wax in agitation from holding ourselves back from the fight!" he said vehemently, his purple eyes flecked with passion. "'Tis a hardship to fidget time away here, not knowing what it is we are up against!"

I clasped his arm warmly and pushed him ahead of me, up the winding stairs. "Hear it now!" I said decisively. "Mayhap you can help me draw some conclusions."

He turned, throwing me a wordless glance of thanks; his face was flushed with pleasure.

The air inside the little room was thick with tension. Hereward paced, lost in thought, a habit he had acquired in my brother's service. Beornwald stood stiffly, back against the wall, his face a somber mask. "There will be no fighting this army, Earl Morcar!" he muttered low, letting go a deep vexatious sigh. "They are stretched twenty abreast from the Stunt-Knee half the way to Huntandon!"

Shocked, I looked at Æthelstan for confirmation, and he nodded glumly. "Thousands, my lord!" he whispered low. "An army of thousands! And ready right now to march!"

I sat down heavily on the edge of the battlements. We had seven, maybe eight hundred men. We might outlast the first leg of their siege. We had no way of reinforcing ourselves, though, and the king had endless numbers of men waiting to refill his ranks. No doubt the manor at Huntandon, once Earl Waltheof's, was crammed with them even now.

"So much for our two lines of defense," I heard Siward Bearn exclaim grimly. "Our only hope is to be strong enough at the very front tier to keep them from accessing this island."

"Little hope of that, though," Beornwald mumbled by way of reply. "Soon as we knock ten men off the roadway, twenty more will move up to take their places. Once they have broken our line and marched onto firm ground, they will move right over us."

"Best they do not come to firm ground, then!" Hereward growled viciously.

Morosely, I stared past him, out the open turrets to the east edge. The abandoned catapult looked eerie outlined against the high trees, like an evil, wooden animal. "No reason to let them use that thing against us," I muttered heatedly, "we ought to go burn it while they are forming their precious lines!"

Both following my gaze outward, Siward Bearn and Hereward rose at once. "By God, kinsman!" the Bearn cried excitedly, sitting upright on the ledge. "That is what we ought to do!"

"Aye" Hereward rejoined dryly, "We ought to put him in the hell where he belongs!"

"And all his thousands of soldiers with him!" the Biter broke in with a grin, coming up behind me and putting both his hands on my shoulders in a comradely way. Suddenly the room erupted in excited babbling. In scant seconds a plan was formulated, and we thundered down to the refectory, bidding half the men there to follow us across the grassy lea to the front tier. There, Hereward and I climbed atop the turf walls and spoke loud to all the men at once, telling them an action had been decided on that would be passed around in whisper, lest the king had spies in hearing range. We stood and watched the delight on their faces as the idea sank in. When it had entirely made the rounds, I lifted my right fist high in the air, and every man there did the same, signaling acquiescence with a lusty, loud cheer that was surely heard by the Normans massed at the other end of the causeway.

Then Æthelstan and a dozen men came from the refectory with torches, and here and there they lit small campfires, well-contained in circles of rock and sand and well out of the area where fierce combat might occur. Satisfied, we loosed our helmets and sought coolness in the shade of trees and walls, making ourselves comfortable for the wait.

After a while we hushed our low conversation; the air shuddered briefly with distant movement. Seconds later, a single trumpet blast from the turret told us the king's army was on the move. Bishop Æthelwine recited a brief litany, answered by the harmonious voice of many priests in unison. We adjusted our battle-gear. Briefly there were sounds of whispered prayers and words of encouragement; then we grew still, straining our ears for the noise of their battle-cry.

For a long time we heard nothing. Then, as they came closer, an indistinct sound of wailing, like the crying of a female cat in longing, rode to us on the motionless dank breath of the wind. As it grew louder, it grew stranger. All along the back of my neck and shoulders, I felt my hair stand on end, despite the heavy press of iron and the sweat of the sweltering day. A few men crossed themselves, others looked around inquisitively, eyes anxious, hoping someone else might explain the sensation. At length, Hereward pushed himself through the sea of tense men, climbing the turf wall at the very foot of the raised road. Shading his eyes, he stared far down the way as he could, but the indistinct specks in the distance gave him no clue. Resigned, he worked his way back to us, shrugging. "We will know what the ban-shee is soon enough, I trow," he said with a grim smile, using an Eirish word that had meant the worst to me ever since my long-ago childhood days in exile. I shuddered and he laughed.

I grew dizzy after a time with heat and expectation. We stood on a low, natural rise in the boggy sod, between the first line at the turf ramparts, and the archers, perched behind us on a higher, artificial height built of stone and mud. Try as I might, I could not pry my eyes away from the advancing force. Something did not look right about their approach. At first, I thought it was the distance playing tricks on me; then I reminded myself 'twas strange to see Normans moving into battle unmounted. There was something more, though, and as they came closer, I realized they were pushing something before them— something cumbersome and heavy, a huge wooden tower. Apparently, the thing was on wheels, and so ungainly that it took the combined efforts of many men to lug it over the rough lumber slats that topped the newly constructed way.

The abominable wailing had grown so noxious that it gave me shivers, and as the thing drew nearer, I suddenly became aware of two things at the self-same moment: the howling was coming from the portable tower, and 'twas in no way meaningless. The weird sounds were words—hideous, devilish words, blasphemous curses and threats, cried and hollered and screamed in swift succession. Almost simultaneously, I caught sight of an odd creature perched atop the moving room, and heard Hereward's awe-struck voice.

"By the Virgin, men!" he cried aloud. "Here is the king's pythoness!"

Every eye was on the witch. She was naked to the waist, then wrapped in deep black skirting that billowed behind her. Round her

brow was tied a thick black band; the long tails of it, separated into
many strands, near indistinguishable from her wild black locks, hung all
the way to the wheels of her strange vehicle. She held something black
in either hand; a pouch or bag in one and an ebony goblet, oversized and
gleaming in the other. Some of the men crossed themselves at the sound
of her filthsome words, hoping to ward off the gross curses. Others, more
vulnerable, visibly shook with fear, never having seen such an apparition as this, nor even imagined it. As for me, my gaze was hard upon her,
too. I had recognized her as the same one William had put in my
brother's bed, and I scarce had the power to avert my stare. Suddenly,
though, Bishop Aethelwine was shaking my shoulders hard, and yelling,
not only to me but to all the men.

"Pull your looks away from her, for Christ's sake!" he cried hoarsely.
"Can you not see this is his ploy? To paralyze us with the sight of her so
he can trample us!"

His words brought life and emotion back to our ranks. There was a
dinning thunder as men shouted battle cries and oaths of all kinds.
Above it came the voice of the Wake.

"Fire the reeds and timber!" he boomed, and men dashed to lay hold
of the torches. There was a flash and a roar as all the dried grasses and
kindling we had placed so carefully erupted into flame all at once. Over
our heads, our archers fired a volley of burning arrows well into the
Norman line. Oslac Osmud's son and one of his kinsmen had sneaked out
earlier, waist deep in the bog, and scattered straw as far down the
causeway as they could. Now tongues of fire leapt ominously wherever
the arrows had met with it. The Norman line buckled in fear and panic.
The witch's awesome spells turned to terrified screams as the tower,
abandoned and motionless, began to burn. The air was thick with smoke.
The entire front of the island crackled and blazed; columns of orange
flame leapt high, scorching everything with the intensity of their heat.

The turf and timber ramparts were an impassable hell. Those who
broke through were cut down and slaughtered, but not without vicious
combat. Further down the causeway, men lowered themselves into the
shallow and slimy mire and waded to the firmer ground, outskirting the
inferno, climbing onto the island wherever they could find footing. We
spread our line thinner, rushing to meet them. They were suicidal in
their frenzy. The clamor of metal, the stench of smoke, sweat, and
searing flesh numbed all senses. Mad from the sweltering heat and the
fury of the fight, men murdered and were murdered with a vengeance
that defied imagining.

Hereward was everywhere, it seemed, hollering commands and
directions, urging men forward or back as the situation demanded,

forcing his sword to meet the enemy as they descended on him, singly and in droves. As for me, I stood firm. I was used to fighting within the confines of a shield wall, my guard gathered tight around me. I had never learnt to make battle on the move, following the action from one point to another as the other men seemed to do instinctively. Nevertheless, my training did not fail me. The heavy weapon was sure and swift in my hands. Æthelstan the Fen-man had long ago told me to aim for the face: it moved the least and was least protected. The first Norman who lunged at me nearly took me to the ground. He was blind with fear and panic. My father's sword kissed him well, through the mouth and jawbones. A hideous specter, he shuddered fast into lifelessness. I stepped myself over him to meet the next, and that, for the most part, was all the footwork I had to do.

For awhile, they came one after another. Only once I faltered. I had grown blind with sweat, and taking advantage of my momentary hesitation, two came at me at once. Scarce had I time to consider the situation before Heard Ulf's son crashed forward, knocking me behind him with a shoulder butt that sent me spinning. I know not how he realized my distress or thought he could help me by attempting to handle them both. He was dazed-looking, covered with gore, and moving with less ease than he was wont to do otherwise. Somehow, I managed to regain myself, squinting away the sweat-blindness, and rushing headlong into the hopeless fight he had taken on to save me. Both of them were rushing at him simultaneously with hideous oaths; one had his gleaming sword poised high over my guardsman's head. Lifting my own weapon even higher, I crashed it down with all my force. With a sickening sound, it crunched through the man's iron coat, severing the arm at the shoulder; the lifeless limb flew several feet forward, sword and all, quivering and gushing. Heard Ulf's son kicked it away as he fast finished the other man, who had grown frozen at the sight of it. Then, for just an instant, my man and I eyed each other, steeped as we were in the heat of battle. He was wet and grim, his face ashen with the fear of his own savagery. We exchanged a harried, helpless smile, then turned back into the fray. I have never forgotten the mask of pain and horror Heard Ulf's son wore at that moment.

The fire was raging out of control now. It had traveled down the wooden planks that topped the causeway, devouring the portable tower, the catapult, and all else that served to feed it. Far beyond the confines of the island it spread, burning anything not sodden enough to resist it. Clothed as they were in iron, the enemy found it increasingly difficult to break through the ever-widening pillars of flame. They came less and less; those who finally lunged through were oft-times helmetless, making them easy prey. The entire rim of the island was ablaze. Fatigued from the onslaught, the Normans could no longer wade or swim far enough to find an opening through the fiery columns. Gradually, the din died away, till all at once I realized the thunderous roar of burning timber was all I heard.

A trumpet blast sounded, followed by two agonized screams in quick succession. From far away, I heard the voice of the Wake, urging us back to the monastery. Cautiously, I lowered my sword. Soon as I relaxed, I was confused. Trembling, I looked all around me for a landmark, and finding none, began to walk blindly into the billowing smoke. Then I saw Siward Bearn, helmetless and flushed, his entire body shuddering from the strength of his exertions. He signaled me with a move of the hand. Not far away, Sihtric Ælfric's son raised his axe and brought peace to one of William's men, writhing on the lea in death throes. Carnage was everywhere. We walked back, with scarce the power to hold ourselves upright, stepping heedlessly on the mangled, sopping bodies of the fallen.

Brother Wulfget, grimed with blood and sweat, waited for us at the doors. He had proven himself a bold warrior that day, but now looked harrowed and grim. There had been a crew under the command of Æthelstan the Fen-man that had labored to carry the wounded back for succoring; one look at my friend's face told me there were men we loved amongst them.

"Mayhap you will wait here with me for Heard Ulf's son," Wulfget said low when we were near enough to hear him. From his tone, I knew immediately what had happened. A long while passed, though, and my man did not come. The Bearn and I, right there on the wide stone steps, removed each other's hauberks, groaning with the effort and sighing with relief when they were lifted. Then Beornwald Strong-Leg and Osbeorn Dolfin's son came, half-carrying, half-dragging a scarce conscious Heard between them. At the very tail of the battle, he had taken a barbed Norman arrow, swift enough to tear his mail and lodge deep in his side. Aground from it, he had been trampled in the fury of the retreat and, somehow, by accident or intent, his left hand had been pierced through by some weapon, whether sword, knife, or lance, we knew not. We brought him to the sick-room; the bad news would wait.

That night, though, Heard Ulf's son, who had pulled his own metal hauberk out of the grossly contused wound, and sat soundless and tight-lipped for over an hour while Brother Wulfget used burning hot pliers to fish inside him for a metal arrow-head, cried like a babe over the lifeless body of Gamel-Beorn the Biter. And I cried with him.

CHAPTER SIXTY

Never had huger
slaughter of heroes
Slain by the sword-edge
such as old writers
have writ of in histories
hap't in this isle . . .

—Anglo Saxon Poet

September 1071

The end of summer was more pronounced in that blackened, desolated fen-land than ever I have known it to be, before or since. So strong was the emotion which it produced in me, that I found myself saying the phrase over and over—"the end of summer"—as if it explained things. The charred and strangled foliage gave no clue, but in the dulling sky, birds crossed noisily on their way to the Channel. That, our overwhelming sadness and anxiety, and the sudden, cold bite of the wind bespoke the season's closing more emphatically than the signals we were wont to note of old: changing leaves, falling nuts, and the sounds of woods alive with kindlingers and tree fellers. We grew very scarce of food, scarce of energy, scarce of hope.

Twice more the king moved his war machine across the causeway, and twice more we met them, turning them back with a vengeance. He was spending his men to wear us down, and we knew it. The number on the island was so greatly reduced now that every man we had could fit within the confines of the monastery. The naval levies still kept us surrounded. Our spies brought word that William had sent for the best of his councilors to join him in an all-out attack, hoping to crush us before the inaccessibility of winter came to our defense.

'Twas not long after Michael Mass that the Normans gained their long-awaited, hard-won foothold. They came just after dawn, in droves, fully armed. For once, we did not meet them at the east edge; mayhap they knew by then there were not enough of us left to fight two fronts. They spent all of the first day making a camp and tortured us that night with the smell of roasting beef and lamb. The wildlife had fled with the setting of the fires, and had not bothered to return to the blackened, treeless waste. We had tasted naught but eels and scrawny fish, garnished with what wild fruits we could gather, in all that time.

At first, we thought they meant to wait us out, conquer us with starvation and the madness of captivity. On the third day, though, reinforcements arrived: many hundreds of men with catapults, rams, and scaling ladders. From the spire, a handful of us watched as the moment we had most dreaded arrived. William the Conqueror, in gleaming silver arms, rode his proud black horse over the causeway behind them. At his right side was my avunculus, William Malet, the shire-reeve of Eorforwic. Siward Bearn let go a low whistle and cursed when he saw him. "Mayhap he thinks he can talk us out of here," he said in a troubled whisper, "but he is wrong if he thinks we will not fight him!"

That night, dressed for battle, we went over and over the plan we had formulated. For myself, I listened with a languid interest. The grim inevitability of defeat loomed larger and nearer than ever before. My spirits were so weighted with the thought of what was to happen shortly that I scarce could muster confidence or strength. Brother Wulfget came and sat anext me after awhile, reading in my look the frustration I felt. Later, when most of the men had gone, he drew me far aside.

"Mayhap you and the Bearn feel a special fear of kin-killing," he said staunchly, staring into my eyes with an intensity unusual even for him. His features were ascetic, boldly modeled, and remarkably fine; his rusty hair, untonsured now, was wild and untamed. But for the wadmal beneath his hauberk and a heavy reliquary and cross strung round his neck, he might have been any other warrior. My eye caught the gleam of my father's knife at his waist, worn proudly, shined to perfection. He moistened his lips nervously and turned his eyes from mine.

"Methinks mayhap this will be the telling battle, Morcar Ælfgar's son," he said with pretended indifference, "and I had vowed me long ago to share some things with you that never till now have I had the opportunity to tell."

"What is it ails you, brother?" I asked worriedly. He had paled and grown tremulous, as with fever. Giving a short laugh, he looked away.

"'Tis apt you have asked me just that way!" he exclaimed, and when I looked at him curiously, he went on, drumming his fingers on the table. He stopped suddenly, and reached down to touch the knife, lifting it just enough to draw my attention to it. "Remember how you gave this knife to me, Morcar, and told me that in his death-murmurs Earl Ælfgar told

Gruffydd 'twas for his son who was a priest?"

"Aye. I remember it," I said, raising a brow. He cleared his throat.

"He was not mistaken in his frenzy."

I did not understand him. "What mean you?" I asked slowly. He flinched and looked away.

"That I am brother to you, Morcar Ælfgar's son!"

I stared at him in troubled amazement.

"I am brother to you, and if I raise a sword to William Malet, then I, too, am guilty of kin-killing."

My mouth fell open in wonder. "Mean you to say you are my mother's son?" I asked, totally incredulous, but he shook his head.

"Nay," the reply came softly. "I am your father's son!"

"Then how say you William Malet is your kinsman," I asked, puzzled, "less it is you mean by marriage?" He shook his head again.

"I am your brother," he said slowly, looking past me, "and I am brother to Siward Bearn, as well."

I sat down heavily. "Must be you are mistaken," I began, but he cut me off, saying how both Grandfather and Uncle Leofric had sworn as much, and even my father had admitted it to him, the day he paid the gold-gift for the ordination.

My father! Siward Bearn's mother—my own mother's sister! A great confusion of thoughts came upon me all at once, and I worked to recall all the things I had ever heard said of Lady Æthelfryth, Ælfgiva's unfortunate sister, who had bladed her own throat. Of a sudden, I understood the dark shadow that had always stood between my father and my avunculus. I even fathomed my mother better than ever I had done before and, with a pang, I realized the intensity of a burden my father had carried all his life.

Wulfget's voice came from far away. "Oft-times I have wanted to tell you this, and now I hope 'tis not like a wound to you, knowing it. 'Twas a thing that happened unforeseen, he told me. Lady Æthelfryth was dead by the time Edwin was born. Folk said her sorrows had weighed enough to kill her."

Touching his arm, I cast a dim smile. "When Edwin comes, he will be glad to know this," I said, wondering why it did not disturb me in the least. "Oft-times he has said how much he feels a kinship to you." Still, I wondered if it would rub my brother to know he was not Ælfgar's true first-born son.

Wulfget swallowed a sob; I heard it rising in his throat. "Best you would tell the Bearn about this," I added, embracing him. "Methinks he will not be disappointed to know of it. Ever since Ealdread passed, he has sore felt the want of a brother."

That night, between mulling over all I had learnt of this shadowy secret, and worrying about the morrow's outcome, I could not sleep. I grew so tired of tossing and turning that I pulled myself up and walked out to breathe the night air and clear my head. It irked me that when I most sorely needed relaxation, it would not come to me, and I prayed I would not be wilted for the battle. Siward Bearn must have seen or heard my leaving; he came out after a while, dressed in a loose and unlaced shift like mine. The only good thing about having the Normans right on the island is that they could not surprise us with attack. I had grown weary of sleeping in heavy leather with my hand on a sword hilt.

In the moonlight, I scrutinized my cousin's tall, proud frame. He shivered a little. I thought it might have been the chill of the night air, but then, out of the corner of my eye, I saw something which greatly displeased me. He was clutching a rounded, good-sized kyll. Soon as I saw it, I became aware of the distinct perfume of hazel-nut wine. For the most part, the Bearn was a sober man, I scarce could believe he would choose this, of all nights, to undo himself. When I reprimanded him, asking whether he would be fit enough to carry out his part in the morrow's plan, he laughed.

"Could be you did not listen well in that council, Morcar Ælfgar's son," he said tonelessly, running fingers through his long, tangled hair. "Our part in the plan is to fight till they have a foot inside the monastery, then hide in the walls till they have moved all their high-ranking men inside. Methinks I will be equipped enough to handle— what? A quarter-hour of battle, think you?" He took a long swallow, coughing at the richness of it. "Must be you know we cannot hold much longer against the weaponry we have seen today!"

He handed me the kyll, and I took a drink without even thinking. For all its sweetness, it burned going down and felt hot inside me. I had taken no food for hours and I noticed the effect, even of a single swig, immediately. I cleared my throat.

"Mayhap we will be able to do the job from within those walls, Siward Bearn," I told him firmly, handing it back to him. "The hardest part will be sitting still while our comrades fight the battle."

"While they are slaughtered or captured, I think you mean!" he exclaimed with uncharacteristic coldness. I put a hand on his shoulder.

"Never have I seen you shirk before, kinsman!" I said seriously, looking hard into his grey eyes. "Surely 'tis a passing moment. You are boldest of any man I know, and one we counted most on when this plan was laid."

He hung his head morosely, then shrugged. "Seems it not hopeless?" he asked in a grim whisper. "Seems it not we will be in those walls till we are killed or taken?"

"My only care is this," I answered with a short laugh. "That we are in there when the king himself comes to find us, so we can pick him off and be done with the bastard."

He laughed a little, but his tone was mirthless. Then we both grew silent a spell, listening to the music of the fen, noises which no longer seemed strange to me.

"What think you of Brother Wulfget's tale?" he asked me solemnly when a little time had passed. I answered that I believed it wholly, and took another drink.

"Oh, aye. And do I," he replied curtly. "She who was my mother was never spoken of as having the best of honor. In that, my sister resembles her, it seems. Both of them are ladies oft remarked upon."

We talked about it a while, my cousin stressing that Brother Wulfget had proven a tangible link between us.

"In a way, seems we are almost brothers because of this, does it not?" he questioned, his tone lightening. With a quizzical smile, he leant closer. "Think you we should make a blood brotherhood, Morcar Ælfgar's son?" he asked. "Mayhap 'twould serve us well to strengthen our kinship now."

I thought about it a moment. That was the strictest of pledges, more binding even than the oath between an earl and his man. 'Twas an honor between equals, and a promise to stay each by the other through the greatest peril and worst of circumstances, much in the way my cousin and I had done already, even without the formal tie. I did not hesitate long.

"I would be proud to make a brotherhood with you, Siward Æthelgar's son," I said firmly, rolling up the loose sleeve of my tunic. I was a little heady with the wine, and the sight of his gleaming dagger when he drew it, sent a rush of blood through my body. Suddenly, I was wroth to make a mean slice through the burnt-on bracelet of stars and flowers I wore round my wrist, and I told him so.

"Seems it would heal without scarring your designs," he pronounced slowly, looking at his own decorated wrists in the moon light, "but I see no reason we cannot make the incision elsewhere, as long as there is a good flow of blood."

We both swallowed another draught of wine. Then I took his knife and cut a cross in the palm of my hand, deep enough to bleed freely, and he did the same. Clasping those hands tight together, we sat there wordlessly, letting the essence pass between us till we were certain our spirits had joined. Then we embraced. 'Twas a long embrace, but manly, and I am not ashamed to say it soothed me.

*   *   *

Atop the ramparts next morning, standing beside Siward Bearn, I wondered at the complete transformation in him. There was nothing of the panic and indecision he had shown the night before; he was a warrior: cold, hard, and eager. Then I looked at Heard Ulf's son on my other side. Anxious to fight despite his woundings, he wore the same intense look, a look almost of hunger. I decided perhaps that was the nature of man—to quake at the thought of battle but wax strong in the face of it. When the Normans let go the trumpet blast that announced their rush upon us, I saw the same gleam in every eye around me.

We fought boldly that morning, and though we lost over half of our men, by the grace of God we were able to repel the attack. Dejected and bedraggled, the Normans withdrew to their camp, where the king waited, furious. His booming voice carried to us as he reviled his men; at twilight, another two hundred came over the causeway and set up camp.

There were less than four score of us left. Gathered in the refectory that night, Hereward offered each man the choice of fighting more or fleeing into the fen. Every man chose to stay. At daybreak, the next attack commenced; by noon, we had driven them away once more, but our walls had been broken and breached. The next onslaught would carry them into our very midst.

Bishop Æthelwine led us in a short, solemn Mass; men embraced and made fare-wells. Some climbed back to the battlements, and others scattered here and there throughout the monastery in the manner we had earlier prescribed. Now our war would take on a new and harsher strategy—fighting with no front, no line of defense, and no massive, straight-forward attack. Every man for his own, it would be, on our side and theirs. Each small contingent concerned itself with safe-guarding a specific area of the huge stone hall. The war council, with the other men we had chosen, moved into the alms-house, long our private domain. From there, we disappeared into the walls, building stones back up behind the tapestry as we did so. Not a single man besides ourselves, Anglish or Norman, suspected we were there. In the darkness we waited. A few hours later, they attacked again.

Mercifully, the depth of the walls muffled most of the sounds of the fight, though we heard enough to know when the Normans had made their way in. The clanging of iron drew our attention here and there; skirmishes were being waged in the various wings. A series of horn blasts announced the victory to the king. Things grew still; there was a trampling and barrage of voices as prisoners were led away. If our plan had not failed us, there were still other men hidden in various places.

Eventually the Normans would meet with them or be pounced upon unawares. When things had been quiet a long time, a small party came. They rode mounted into the refectory, then unhorsed. Siward Bearn and I heard one voice we recognized there, that of William Malet. Sliding noiselessly closer to the area, we forced our ears to the slits carved deep in the rock near floor level.

"Must be they have disappeared into the fen," we heard one voice say. "There was not one man of note among the outlaws."

Another man cursed low, saying that the king would be rabid to hear it, but my uncle replied there was no changing it, so best they send a messenger now, while there was still daylight enough for the army to chase them.

"Take a party of five, and go all through this place!" he added sharply. "If any of our men lay wounded, we will want to claim them now, not by torch light. 'Tis too eerie a place to stumble around in darkness."

Squirming, I managed myself further into the narrow passage, till I could see a narrow stretch of the room through the small openings. When his men had gone, William Malet sat down heavily on the edge of one of the tables, and put his face in his hands, an abject posture of fatigue and sorrow. My cousin and I made our way back to the others.

"'Twould be well if he sent the bulk of his forces out on a merry goose chase," Hereward mused thoughtfully when we told him what we had heard, "long as the king himself stays here and comes in to meet them."

Osbeorn Dolfin's son coughed, and one of the men reached over, covering his mouth to stifle the sound. Heard Ulf's son shifted uncomfortably; he was still feverish from his woundings. Sihtric Ælfric's son and I made him a pillow of folded wadmal and put it under his head. Though we were all exhausted and had made provisions for rotating a guard, only Æthelstan and Bishop Æthelwine were able to sleep. One by one, the hours crept by in silence, till a stirring in the hall, where a dozen of the king's men had spent the night, gave us to know it was dawn.

Siward Bearn, Hereward, and I crammed ourselves into the narrow passage that backed the refectory walls, where the voices of the Normans could be clearly heard. We smiled with amusement as they argued amongst themselves. The one who had carried my uncle's message to the king the night before was a bull-necked man of Ghent named Udo, one of William's well-respected councilors. I recognized him from my days at Wintanceaster. He was regaling the other man loudly and adamantly with vivid tales of the marvelous riches stolen from Peterborough, and describing in detail the gold and gems Edwin and I had supposedly taken with us when we fled. All this and more was here, in this very place, he was saying, and it could be theirs for a simple look around. As if disgusted with the man's greed, William Malet twice told him to hold his tongue, saying another dozen king's men would be riding through the gates soon, and once reinforced in number they would make a thorough search. Udo had convinced half the men, though, and now they whined and complained about being forced to divide the booty with lackards who had no hand in the capturing of the camp.

"Must be you have lived in Angland long enough to know that the people here always hide their goods in the sanctuary, sir shire-reeve," Udo told my uncle accusingly, "a quarter-hour's visit there could make us all rich men!"

"Go, then!" William Malet exclaimed finally, gesturing toward the door. "If you can find your way through this mass of grim corridors to anything like a church or chapel, then look there—but do not tarry!"

Seven men headed out the door at once, and my uncle laughed when they had gone. "Do not be fool enough to think the Anglish left their riches behind them," he told the other men severely. "Gold buys passage and arms for men in exile. No doubt they long ago bought themselves foriegn land in which to hide!"

We scarce heard him finish, though. Silently, swiftly, we pushed ourselves back through the darkness to the others. With a silent gesture, Hereward urged the men to follow him, and leaving Heard Ulf's son, Æthelstan, and the bishop to keep an eye on the hall, we made our way through the twisted, stone-cut labyrinth to the dimly lit, ventilated center of the hidden tunnels. From there, we entered a close, cramped passage which led into the sanctuary through a hidden door in the hollow altar.

Weapons in hand, we hid ourselves and waited as the Normans, unfamiliar with the place, picked a slow way through the dark, winding hallways. We would have the advantage of surprise, and we needed it. In the interest of silence, we had discarded our metal hauberks when first we entered our hideaway; the king's men were helmetless, but fully clad in armor. I crossed myself quickly when I heard the distant babble of their foreign voices. Then, well secreted in the spot I had chosen, just behind the heavy, carven vestry door, I raised my sword and held my breath. Across the room, Siward Bearn stood behind the other door, features drawn with concentration. He cast me a swift, hopeful smile. Rowdy and unrestrained, the men entered in the church, but I could scarce hear them for the pounding of my heart.

They wasted no time, but made straight for the front, not even bothering to genuflect in their haste of greed. "Look in the sacristy!" I heard Udo of Ghent command. "Search the closets and vestry!"

Every one of my muscles stiffened as two men came in the door, squinting in the darkness, no more than an arm's length away from me. Suddenly, there was a thick, thudding sound in the sanctuary, and the clang of metal on stone. Both men spun round to look, and soon as they did I leapt forward, bringing my weapon down hard as I could on one man's shoulder. It felled him instantly, but his friend jumped forward, slashing his sword fiercely at my throat. I jerked my head back swift enough that it missed me. Before he could swing again, Siward Bearn had laid him open, crown to chest, with his powerful Danish axe.

By now, I had grown numb to gore. I stepped over the quivering body without even a thought to it. On the altar steps, two Normans were dead already, and Hereward was fighting hard to be rid of another. Siward Bearn rushed to aid Brother Wulfget, who was at the distinct disadvantage, having been knocked weaponless into a dark corner of the sanctuary. For a moment, I hesitated, unsure where the last of the seven men was to be found. Then, a flash of movement drew my attention to the shadowy dimness at the back of the church. Osbeorn Dolfin's son was locked in vicious combat with a bear of a man who was trying desperately to reach the hallway and signal for aid. It was Udo of Ghent, and he had suddenly thrown down his sword and drawn a knife, moving at brave Osbeorn with a powerful thrust.

A rush of hot blood through my veins moved me forward instinctively, but before I could reach my guardsman's side, he was down, and the other man was stabbing at him mercilessly. As I threw myself into the panic of the situation, the Norman spun around, grabbing me in a stranglehold of immense power, near paralyzing me with his strength. His face was a mask of vengeful madness, distorted with the furious intensity of his rage. He threw me from him with a violence that sent me sprawling; my sword clattered from my hand. Lunging, I retrieved it and was half on my feet when he came at me again, forcing my body backwards with a mean kick and raising his own weapon above my head, ready to slam it down with force enough to kill me.

Suddenly, though, Beornwald Strong-Leg crashed out of nowhere, axe in hand. The Norman turned to meet him, piercing him through with a single, strong thrust. In the split second it took the man to pull his sword from the limp and lifeless body of the bold Bernician, I was up. Violent with fury and fear, I slashed him again and again till his quivering form folded to the floor, an indistinct mass of blood, iron, and mangled flesh. I would have continued hacking, so mindless was my blood lust, but Brother Wulfget was suddenly there, urging me to flee. Siward Bearn and Hereward lifted Osbeorn Dolfin's son and ran with him. Coming suddenly to my senses, I followed Wulfget as he led me ahead of them to the altar. We forced open the hidden entrance.

Osbeorn groaned with agony as they maneuvered his body through the small opening. I pushed Sihtric Ælfric's son through, then moved in after him. Looking over my shoulder, I marveled at Brother Wulfget's presence of mind. He had run back, and tearing a length of wadmal from his own robe, wiped away the trail of blood that led to the secret opening. Soon as he was inside, we pulled the door shut, locking it. Drawing a deep breath, I relaxed all at once, then realized my whole body was shaking and my teeth chattering as with cold.

Stealthily, we made our way to the central passage, where there was water to cleanse our friend's woundings. As Brother Wulfget began to work on him, I ran ahead to find Heard Ulf's son, still on guard at the refectory. The news of his uncle's condition hit him hard, as I knew it would, and he berated himself for paying so much heed to his own discomfort that it kept him from fighting at his kinsman's side. I scarce could comfort him. His pain near kept him powerless, and his spirits had been sore weighted by the Biter's death. I put an arm around his shoulder as we walked and told him how Beornwald Strong-Leg had been murdered in my defense. In the telling, I came to realize how a noble and heroic death well befitted that man, who had always lived in honor despite the debauchery of Oswulf's household. I did not let myself mourn him, though; grief would have been devastating, and the grimness of our situation would not allow it.

A single glance told us how it fared with Osbeorn Dolfin's son. "The best we can do is try to keep him quiet," Brother Wulfget told us glumly, his voice cracking with strain and sadness. "If his moanings grow loud we will need to gag him, else we are all lost."

Heard Ulf's son dropped to his knees at his uncle's side. The man was lucid, and smiled and jested best he could, which granted us a portion of hope. As they whispered low, I caught Hereward's outline in the shadows of one of the approaches. He signaled, and I followed him quietly back to the area of the church. Standing on a thin ledge, I was able to look through a small crack, high on the wall of the sanctuary, behind the rood. My uncle and the four other Normans stood talking low on the altar steps, aghast at the carnage there.

"Mayhap that dead one in the back there murdered these, and met with Udo as he tried to make an escape," one man suggested hopefully. William Malet eyed him with disdain.

"Men are dead here of axe, sword, and dagger!" he exclaimed coldly. "Methinks there is more than a single madman at the cause of it." One of his men began to look around fearfully. My uncle snapped him back to attention by pounding a fist hard on the altar. "When you met with the king on the road last night, whither was he riding?"

"To Grantanbrycg, sire, to inspect any prisoners his men pulled from the fen."

"Then ride to him at Grantanbrycg. Tell him we were wrong. The Anglish have not fled. They are still here, hid somewhere in the marshes. Tell him to send me men to help flush them out. He paused a moment, as if a thought had just occurred to him. "When you pass the encampment at the island's edge," he added darkly, "pick out seven of the best men there and send them back to help me hold this place till you return."

The other looked surprised. "Only seven?" he questioned, wagging his head like a nervous dog. William Malet scowled.

"This could well be an Anglish trick," he replied severely. "Mayhap they planted a few men in the closets awhile as bait to draw us into this place. Could be there are many more in the fens and forests waiting for us to relax our lines so they can follow us here and slaughter us. Best we do not weaken the front we have already established."

They spoke low a little while longer. When the solitary messenger took his leave, I was minded to follow him to the refectory and meet with him, before he could carry out his mission. Hereward stopped me.

"If we sit tight a scant time, we shall have seven more for the same amount of effort," he whispered knowingly, "and we will draw haughty William here all the sooner."

I climbed down, heavy in spirit, and looked at him accusingly. "We scarce could deal with those in there!" I began, staring in the darkness at the stone wall as if I could see through it into the church. My uncle and others were dragging the bodies out now; we could hear the scraping of their hauberks on the stone floor. Involuntarily, I crossed myself. The memory of the horror was still fresh and pulsing. Hereward reached in the dark and gripped my shoulder.

"We will fight till we can fight no more, Earl Morcar," he said in a gentle yet insistent tone. "If God is merciful, the king will come to us here and we will be done with it. Elsewise, we will wreak havoc till it is useless to do more, then we will escape into the fen and bide our time till we have another chance."

The dim voices died away in the church anext us. The Normans had moved back to the refectory, where they felt safer, to spend the night. For some reason, I kept picturing the Strong-Leg's corpse, mutilated and abandoned, fast growing stiff where it had fallen.

"We dare not move him now," the Wake whispered furtively, almost as if he had read my mind. I nodded numbly, but resolved to claim him at the first opportunity. I owed the man a portion of honor; he had saved my life.

A little while later, we all met in the central passageway. Those with an appetite ate and drank a bit, but I had no stomach for food. We decided to break into smaller groups and scatter ourselves throughout the network of hidden halls and corridors. Siward Bearn and Sihtric Ælfric's son went back to the church wall; Hereward and a small party kept watch on the Normans as they slept. Bishop Æthelwine and Brother Wulfget moved from place to place, encouraging the men and talking to soothe their spirits.

I stayed with Heard Ulf's son. We both knew Osbeorn Dolfin's son would not live through the night. There was no mistaking the rasping of death as it seeped through his body. We took turns holding him in the darkness, but it was hard to give him comfort, he writhed and panted so. Near to dawn, he grew rabid with the pain; we put our fingers and sleeves in his mouth to keep him quiet, just as Siward Bearn said he had done with Edwin when they needed to be hid. For awhile, I made my man calmer by recounting how he had burned the pictures on my chest when first I was Earl of the Humberland. He said nothing throughout, but when I finished, he reached out suddenly, grasping my hand and reaching for his brother's son. When he had us both close, he whispered three names.

"Ægytha!" he cried, not unhappily. "Margyth, Gyrda!" These were the names of his lady and two of his daughters, unheard of these last years so that no one knew whether they were alive or dead. Heard whispered wonderingly that it seemed as if his uncle could actually see them, for he grew peaceful after he addressed them, then smiled and relaxed. An hour of rest and comfort came to him, during which he grew stiller and stiller, colder and colder. When we were sure of it, Heard Ulf's son and I embraced each other in the dim morning greyness and wept silently.

*   *   *

The news of the passing spread quickly through our dark and dismal camp. There was not a man amongst us who did not honor Osbeorn Dolfin's son in a special way. He was a warrior and a guardsman of the first order, honest, bold, and true. What is more, he was a friend to every man who knew him, and seldom had had an evil word for any.

As if in retaliation, Heard Ulf's son led seven men in a daring, defiant raid before daybreak. They snuck through the darkness to eel-boats hidden in the fen, and rowed silently to the island's edge. There, they loosed all the horses in the Norman encampment, covering the deed with a great barrage of flaming arrows. They killed and maimed many men and set all the canvas tents ablaze. By the time they returned, making their secret entrance through the abbot's lodges, the king's well disciplined force was in chaos, more convinced than ever that the forest and fen were full of blood-thirsty outlaws. When my uncle was joined by the seven men he had sent for, we heard them discussing it. They truly believed they were facing an army of hundreds, and it had in no way occurred to them yet that we shared the same roof.

"Pray God we can flush the bastards out of the brush and undergrowth by the morning after next," we heard one of them say as he snacked on bread and cheeses. "I would like to see the way made safe for King William's coming."

There was a gleam of hardened eyes in the darkness as we exchanged glances of satisfaction. This was precisely the news we longed to hear. The king was rushing against the threat of the autumn rains, brewing even now and certain to save us for another season once they began in earnest. He meant to take possession of the island and make the monastery his headquarters, so he could continue to war against us after the water made the island inaccessible. The sooner he came, the better, I thought; we did not have the strength to spend in waiting.

Realizing the final confrontation was imminent, Hereward ordered us all to don metal coat and helm. The feisty little band of reinforcements was comprised of some of the king's best men, and they were armed befitting their station. Without mail, we were as vulnerable as Osbeorn and Beornwald had been; we decided that the risk of being heard was the lesser of the two threats. In the central passage, we helped each other arm, moving only one and two at a time, to avoid drawing any attention. There was a general uplifting of spirits when we saw each other boldly decked again. Siward Bearn, Heard Ulf's son, and I made our way slowly in the darkness to a cramped recess, where slits in the wall at floor level allowed us to keep watch on the church. Apart from the refectory, which the Normans used as their headquarters, only the alms-house and the church had doors to the outside. Like the abbot's lodges, with its underground tunnel to the bake-house past the garden-yard, we never left them unguarded.

We stayed still most of the day, while the Normans paced the entire length and breadth of the monastery, looking for men or treasure and finding neither. They lingered a long time near the altar, describing for the newcomers the slaughter that had been discovered there the day before. They had finished removing the corpses of their own comrades, but had no respect for Beornwald's body, congealed now in its awkward position. One of the soldiers kicked meanly at it as he passed; I vowed I would kill the man.

Late in the noon, it began to drizzle. William Malet ordered a couple of his men to ride out to the encampment and bring back a dozen men to help ready the place for King William. When the hapless two went alone out to the buttery, Hereward surprised them there. Oslac One-Eye and Sihtric Ælfric's son were gleaming in arms beside him. The fight was vicious, but it ended soon enough. Heard Ulf's son slapped the two saddled horses, sending them unmounted into the fen, so the other Normans would assume the mission was being accomplished. Afterwards, using an axe and two silver lances, they murdered the rest of the horses, swiftly and cleanly, then dashed back through the green rain, running low as they could to the lea. When they reached the heavy, arched door to the alms-house, I pushed it open from the inside and admitted them, both soaking and breathless. From across the room came a sharp, half-suppressed cry of consternation. Siward Bearn and Brother Wulfget, guarding the door to the corridor with axes raised, signaled an approach. Not far away, we could hear the heedless stomping of iron on stone as the king's men marched with no thought for the silence that had become second nature to us.

Panicked, we glanced one to the other. There was nowhere near enough time for all of us to disappear behind the heavy tapestry and into the walls. The movement along with wet footprints and the stirring of dust would betray the secret of the passageways and endanger all the men. Finger on his lips, Hereward motioned us toward the outside. We moved slowly and quietly till we were out in the cold rain. Closing the door silently, we ran fast as we could for the weight of our armor, across the slippery lawning. As was our agreed-upon precaution, we parted ways. Hereward, Sihtric, and Wulfget headed to the east door of the church, while Siward and Heard ran for the west one. Oslac Osmud's son and I made straight for the refectory. We were almost at the steps when a half-dozen Normans burst out of the building behind us, barking curses and threats as they followed in hot pursuit. Suddenly, they let go a shrieking barrage of arrows. One whistled past my ear, then another. There was a sudden, burning sting in my left shoulder, a rush of pain which spun me around. I stumbled. Almost immediately, a second arrow caught me in the breast, tearing through the mail and slamming me to the ground with a gust of agony. There was a grating of wood on stone as the heavy door opened and closed again. I struggled to reach it. Suddenly, I felt a tight grip under my arms and a surge of energy as strong arms pulled me to my feet.

"God speed, Earl Morcar!" Oslac Osmud's son grunted, pushing me ahead of him. Never had he addressed me with that title of respect before. Looking over my shoulder, I caught his eye for just a second. He gave a twisted, grim smile. "Bar it from the inside and be hid quick!" he whispered, pulling the door open just wide enough to admit me, and pushing me roughly through the opening. Inside, I heard the slam and his cry of mortal anguish at the same instant. Blinded by the sudden darkness, I hesitated momentarily, then lowered the weighty bar with a resounding thud. Almost immediately came a thunderous pounding as a half-dozen frustrated men-at-arms tried to force their way in.

Trembling and dizzy on my feet, I made my way through seemingly endless darkened halls to the church, where I knew the others would be gathered. Heard Ulf's son was waiting for me in the shadowed entry to the nave. To my rapidly fading senses he seemed at one with the ornate stone carvings of angels and saints which surrounded the giant arched doors. Knowing from my look that it was hopeless to wait for the One-Eye, he pulled me in silently. Once I heard the great latch drop, I began to tremble with a violent frenzy.

Hereward rushed at me, turning me around and pinning me to the wall. I let go a single cry of anguish as he ripped the arrow out of my breast with his bare hands, tossing it hard against the floor. That was the cry that drew the king's men—my uncle, William Malet, among them. That was the cry that tainted my memory with nightmarish sights, sensings, and sounds, indelibly etched: the look on my uncle's face as he raised his axe to smite me ... the agony of its smashing into my shoulder, my side, my leg ... the hollow echo of weapons crashing on stone ... and my uncle's overwhelming love for me, easily read in his fast-fading eyes as he twitched at my feet in a river of his own blood and gore.

Still air spews grave tempests. Once, when all dismissed the notion, my avunculus said I would make a fearsome warrior.

And I had proven him right.

CHAPTER SIXTY-ONE

All the outlaws surrendered to him, namely bishop
Æthelwine and Earl Morcar and all their followers,
except Hereward alone and all who wished to
follow him; and he courageously led their escape.

—Anglo Saxon Chronicle
Book "E" 1071

So it was I wakened from the nightmare of my uncle's killing, locked in the dark vestry with Siward Bearn and Heard Ulf's son, writhing in an agony I scarce could imagine surviving. The others were safe in the walls, Heard kept reassuring me, and would come for us soon as the Normans were preoccupied elsewhere.

"Mayhap it will be soon," he whispered. "Could be the Normans are camped for the night now. They have not come back to the church for a while—" He broke off, gasping as with pain. I asked if he had taken a wounding, and he laughed dismally. "Not a one amongst us who is not sliced and bruised," he replied. "By God's grace we have all our limbs, though, that I could see."

"Scarce telling whether there were other skirmishes since, or how many of us are left—" Siward Bearn began, but he stopped himself when I grew tense and a tremor ran through me. Then we lapsed again into a silence, broken only by my panting and an occasional groan that I could not suppress.

After a time, the dim light that showed through the crack beneath the door disappeared, and the damp chill of night began to settle. My teeth chattered, and I shivered so violently that my hauberk rattled against the floor. My cousin asked if they could remove it, and I murmured a dazed consent, knowing that by now the lacerations were congealing to the metal, a thing which oft-times caused the greater part of suffering and scarring. Siward Bearn sliced a length of leather off the hemming of my tunic, then crammed it in my mouth. They worked swiftly but gently to undo me. I began to shudder uncontrollably, and the pain magnified itself, till at last I could feel no more. I drifted in and out of awareness till a tap and a whisper came, and Hereward the Wake let himself into our small narrow room.

"Best hurry!" he rasped, reeling a little against the smell of sweat and blood that filled the chamber. "The king is on his way. They expect him at the first crack of daylight. We could not come sooner. The Normans are camped at both the church doors and have only now drifted into sleep. Be swift!" So saying, he tried to lift my limp frame, and a cry of agony escaped me that brought two hands down on my mouth at once.

"Must be they still think we are out in the fen, then!" Heard Ulf's son exclaimed as he tried to make me more comfortable for the move.

"Aye, they think we have found a way in and out through the sanctuary. They are moving the headquarters into the church on the morrow. Methinks we had best plan on fading into the fen by then. He is bringing two hundred men with him and has put out a summons for hundreds more to join them."

Siward Bearn whispered something I did not understand. He and Hereward lifted me suddenly, taking me out gently as they could, while Heard Ulf's son held the door open. There was a rush of motion, followed by blinding pain as they folded my body into the tiny opening of the altar. Then voices, more movement … and nothingness.

∗   ∗   ∗

When next I knew anything, I was in the abbot's lodges. Narrow slants of sunlight filtered through the high casements. They were holding me on the floor now, my arms crossed tightly behind me, their full weight against me as Wulfget tore the second arrow-head out of my shoulder with his burning pliers. The agony blinded and stunned me, but it did not deafen me to the nightmarish sound of my enemy's voice, distant but discernible.

"I challenge you, Morcar Ælfgar's son, upon the life of your brother, my hostage, Edwin the Mercian, to submit to me my due. I promise you I will smite him elsewise!"

The cruelty in his voice caused me shivers. "They saw our blood trail, and hacked the altar to pieces to find a way into the walls," Wulfget whispered morosely, holding my hand to comfort me as if I were a babe. "They will not find the way to this room, but when they realize we are not down there, they will be here looking."

Gaunt and hardened, Bishop Æthelwine moved towards the barred door. "I will stall them in the sanctuary," he pronounced firmly. "I will assure them of our surrender and lead them all another way, so you have time to escape."

Nodding in reluctant agreement, Hereward bent forward, as if to lift me again. Gagging and retching on blood and tears, I pulled myself upright, out of Siward Bearn's stranglehold. The strangely painless gash in my side gushed hot blood, but I worked my way to my feet as the voice came again.

"I will smite him before your very eyes and make you kneel to me in his blood!"

Silence. My knees buckled. Grabbing out into nothingness for support, I felt the blackness closing swiftly in on me again. Arms reached and caught me. I was helpless, but somehow still aware as they lowered me to the floor. Gasping for breath, determined to make my words come, I tried to still my shaking by holding tight onto the Wake. I dug deeply into his shoulder and he winced, but held my weight.

"You are the truest of men," I whispered. There was no tone to my voice. I looked him in the eye as best I could for my maddening weakness and trembling.

"Take every man who is able through the bake-house—"

"Not without you, my lord!"

"Leave anyone who cannot swim the fen."

He shook me. "If you would trade yourself for Edwin now, he will kill you both, Morcar! He will not spare you now."

"Man of Lindcylene! Leave anyone who cannot swim the fen!" As if to emphasize my point with him, I glanced meaningfully to the blood-sopped mess of my torn and filthy under-tunic. From the axe-slashes and the arrow wounds, I still bled profusely. He stared at the woundings, then searched my face as if to determine my true meaning.

When I was certain he understood, I eased my grip on his shoulder. As I fell back, our gazes met, and the wealth of emotion which passed between us cannot be described. It was more than knowing we would never see each other more; it was the realizing of a bond, almost as strong as kinship. Still staring at each other, we embraced just once. Then I bade him pull me to my feet, which he did. I wanted to stand eye to eye when I made fare-wells to those good men.

Sihtric Ælfric's son said he would stay, on account of his crushed and useless arm, but we all knew he was stronger than that. I embraced him best I could for both our woundings, and I gestured him to Hereward's side. Smiling dolefully, he went. Heard Ulf's son and I came to tears and so said not a single word of parting, but I told him he was boldest of any man I knew. Æthelstan the Fen-man ... I hugged him like a boy might hug his uncle or his father. He wept unashamedly, and I joined him.

Then I urged Siward Bearn to make his parting, but he would not do it. "I am sworn to stay anext you, kinsman," he whispered low as I leant on him for support. "Methinks 'twould be a useless blood brotherhood if I took a leave right now."

Brother Wulfget also refused to leave me, shaking his head to my arguments and declaring he would not even listen. Hurriedly, Hereward and the Wessexman Escgar lifted the heavy flat cobblestone that hid the tunnel to the bake-house. Within minutes, they were gone. Siward Bearn slid the flooring back into place. Then he and Brother Wulfget did what they could to bind me in windings torn from linen vestments. I tried to choke down the furious pain, but when it came time to strip my under-tunic from me and put me in a clean woolen one, I would have shrieked uncontrollably had the Bearn not made me bite upon a leathern belting to check the agony.

Whatever the pain—and it was fierce—it was nothing compared to the agony in my heart and spirit as I prepared myself for the final, humiliating surrender. The marauding tramp of the Normans echoed through the hollow halls; the sound seemed to come from everywhere at once. There was no way to judge where they were in relation to us. Supported on either side, I lowered myself from the table where I sat, and steadied myself on my feet. At that very moment, the door crashed open and he was there: the black-haired warrior-king, surrounded by his sullen men.

He stared at me, long and hard, and I trembled under that vicious gaze, but kept my balance and looked back at him levelly as he approached. Whether from fear, respect, or knowing his intent, those men around me stepped back, and I faced the man's awesome rage alone. The glittering furor in his eyes was like a madness. Almost before I realized what he meant to do, he struck me a powerful blow to the ribs. Wheeling, spinning, falling into darkness, I was on my knees when I heard the room explode into frenzy as bold Brother Wulfget flew into the king with uncalculated fury.

"How dare you strike Lord Morcar, Earl of the North Humbria!" he screamed with a vengeance. "In the name of God!"

He stopped. Staggered. Fell forward. There was a splintering noise as the weight of his body shattered the Norman arrow protruding from his breast. Then there was shouting and agony and the frustrating weakness of knowing my wounds had opened again and my strength was gushing out of me with my blood. And then, darkness.

CHAPTER SIXTY-TWO

*During that time, he basely made an end of the
well-favored Earl Morcar. . . . Afraid lest Morcar
seek vengeance on him for his fearful injuries to him
and his compatriots, and in order to prevail as king
of Britain in some way, like a person clearly
worthless, he became implacable. . . .*

—Liber Eliensis

From somewhere far away, a voice said, "Be gentle with him; I knew not
he was wounded."

It was my enemy's voice. I knew I was being carried, but whence I
could not tell. I only know that when I awakened, I was in my father's
lodges in the manor that had been his in Grantanbrycg. Gazing on these
unexpected yet hauntingly familiar surroundings caused in me a dazed
and confused senselessness; I felt myself totally at the mercy of time and
space, and knew not what was happening to me. Then, to confound me
more in my delirious state, I felt a strange, infringing presence beside me.
Unable to speak, I tortured myself to turn over and gaze on the person I
knew would be there. I looked up with bewildered amazement into the
stern, sulky gaze of my once-friend, the Norman, d'Aubermont.

I knew him right away. He did not speak to me, only gazed at me
with a sort of detached sympathy. Too weak to bear up my own weight,
I fell back as my strength gave out all at once, feeling for the first time
the full import of my wounding. I remember gasping, then drowning in
my own painful confusion. I was slipping into nightmare, and I knew it,
but I had not the power to keep my consciousness. Slowly, my father's
rooms at Grantanbrycg merged mistily with the cavernous, chill corridors of Ely. I was calling for Ælfgar, but he could not be found. I could
not tell whether I was at the monastery or in my father's East Anglian
house. As I became more confused it seemed that I was a small boy, at
Gruffydd's quarter in the Cymry.... I heard Welshmen fighting and
cursing in the distance and their voices were familiar.

Suddenly a voice said to me, "It is not your father you seek, but your house, and it is gone." I turned, and it was Fulke d'Aubermont, but he faded away and the room began to look more and more like Ely to me, blackened and desolate. I wandered through the cloister aimlessly, but with a dreadful sense of urgency; in the church, the monks were singing the requiem and the sound grew louder and louder until it enveloped me and I began to panic. I ran in horror through the halls trying to find a way out and at last I found my way through the sick-house and into the fen. I was filled with thrilling terror as the marshes closed in about me. But the fen was glutted with bodies, as it had been at Fulford. I ran dry-shod over the quivering corpses and it seemed like that ghastly, bloody day at the Gate Fulford.

Only now, the corpses were people I knew: Ælfgar and Burchard, Cynewulf and Brother Wulfget, Harold Godwine's son and Uncle Leofric, Gamel-Beorn and Osbeorn Dolphin's son, and Gruffydd and Oswulf and Beornwald and Oslac and William Malet....

*   *   *

Coming to consciousness was unlike any agony I had ever known. My arms, bound with cords above my head, ached with a killing coldness and, try as I might, I could force no movement from by body. It was dark of night. The room was torch-lit and eerie, flickering shadows betraying the presence of strangers, and the low murmur of foreign voices teasing me with their strangeness. I was in my father's rooms and I called for him, but the one who came in answer to my voice was Fulke, again, looking more worn and hard-pressed, but with inquisitive hope in his dark eyes.

"This time you are truly awake, are you not?" he whispered.

"Truly." I choked out the word with effort.

"Then you should know your father and your brother are not here."

"Untie me," I begged him, and he hesitated before he finally reached for the cords and undid them with trembling fingers.

"You have been senseless. We had need to keep your hands from your woundings." Apologizing, he lowered my arms gently to the cot, and I tried to recollect something, anything, to give me a reason for my being there. A priest came over and lifted my head while another tried to give me water. I must have screamed; they lowered me quickly and Fulke bent and held my shoulders while everything wracked with pain and the room spun with frenzy. I vaguely remembered holding tight onto the priests, knowing they were anointing me, knowing I was dying. But I must have dreamt it.

"You may confess if you want to—but in Latin. These priests speak not your Anglish. You have already had your unction." I felt that he scrutinized me for signs of life. Strange. It had seemed as if I hovered above myself, and watched them do it, and I wanted to tell d'Aubermont about it—but surely he would think it madness.

"God knows I am clean enough to meet my maker," I murmured, but then I thought of my sins of vengeance, and suddenly, I remembered. I had been taken at Ely! I forced that memory away, for it was too much to bear now.

"I have need to know this, Fulke d'Aubermont," I whispered with as much strength as I could gather. "Are you my friend or my enemy?"

"Both, Mercian."

I had to be satisfied with that, but I looked away from him, because my spirit was as close to being crushed as it had ever been. Nevertheless, I instinctively knew I was back in the grip of life. Whether for better or worse, Death had fled from me.

The very next day, the priests began to sit me up regularly, to limber the scar tissue and keep it from laming me. The one comfort in that torture was knowing that nothing could hurt me more.

Fulke was always there, a constant companion. I knew he felt a special sense of duty in it, whether out of sympathy or some kind of obligation to the feelings of former days, I could not tell. The hours turned into days and nights, which I could barely distinguish one from the other, and a wary, guarded closeness sprang up between us. A semblance of our old friendship built on a cautious avoidance of facts and feelings we knew we never could agree upon. It had early occurred to me that he was my jailer, but I did not think of him as such, though I knew I was William's prisoner, and I knew he was William's man. Over the years I had come to hate him, and yet there had always been honesty in him and a solemn purposefulness, both of which I was forced to appreciate.

I could not blame him for the distance that had grown between us. Even those actions I had considered betrayals were only natural consequences of who and what he was, whom he was bounden to and what was required of him. I should not have expected it to be different. In the days since our close camaraderie, it was not he but I who had changed—and it had been a bitter, unwilling transformation wrought by sorrow and death, despair, and hatred.

And Providence. Fate had settled against us, leaving us nothing but the spiteful, poisonous taste of the injustice. Ironically, in all of my world, there was one thing only that had not changed: d'Aubermont had been born a Norman, and I was an Anglishman. That was a solid, unalterable fact, and it was our accountabilities, each to that for which he was bound to fight, that had alienated us.

CHAPTER SIXTY-THREE

That fair youth, Earl Edwin . . . was determined to prefer death to life unless he could free his brother Morcar from unjust captivity, or avenge him fully in Norman blood. So for six months he sought support amongst the Scots, Welsh and Anglish. During this period, three brothers who were his closest followers betrayed him to the Normans, who struck him down along with the twenty horsemen who defended him to the last.

—Orderic Vitalis,
Book IV, Chapter VII

In those early, torturous days of my recovery, even though I tried to deny feeling friendship for d'Aubermont again, he became something very vital to me. More than just a tangible link to an elusive past, he was my only link now to a frighteningly unreachable present, which I could perceive only as the vague bustle of endless Norman attendants and a motionless blaze of autumnal colors through a high, small chamber window. As my periods of consciousness grew longer and more frequent, we talked at length—at night usually, when my body cried for sleep, but my mind resisted it. I found myself telling him much about Ely, harmless episodes, without the power to pain me. He was much interested, for all the country, Normans and Anglishmen alike, had spoken and rumored of us constantly, so that already our opposition was embroidered with legend. One night, I told him how I had battled William Malet and murdered him.

On the fourth or fifth night after I regained my senses—I still did not know how long I had been a captive—he told me that on the afternoon of the morrow the king was due to arrive there. This communication stabbed me; I did not know where the strength came from to hate William as I did.

"What means your king to do with me?" I asked Fulke. It was not his habit to nurse me, but at night he would apply compresses and do other small things for my comfort in order to avoid calling on the priests. We spoke more at ease when we were alone.

"He means to keep you his prisoner."

I tried to spit. "I tell you there is not a castle in all Angland that can hold me!"

"He means to keep you his prisoner in Normandy."

His words traveled through me like ice. "Will I be his gilded hostage as I was when you knew me there, or will he keep me in chains? What will be his delight with me?"

"I do not know."

I grimaced at the heat of the poultice on my ribs, where the bones were broken. "And what of my brother?"

Fulke made no answer.

"What of Edwin? Will he suffer him also to be a guest in his handsome Norman court? Will we see each other—or does the bastard king fear we will plot intrigues?" My sarcasm moved him not; he made no answer and backed away from me. I felt a frightening insistence in my own voice.

"Tell me, Norman—what of my brother, Edwin?"

When Fulke answered it was with a tone of resignation. He moved closer to me in the torch-lit dimness and his eyes avoided mine. "I had hoped you would regain somewhat of your strength before you asked me," he stated softly, "for, truly, this is not something which it lies easy on me to tell." He stared past me into the shadowy corners of the room. I was clenched with a fear worse than any physical pain.

"King William has deceived you. Edwin is not his hostage."

Whether my outrage numbed me or magnified my miseries I cannot say.

"Edwin was never his hostage." He worked loose a small, black pocket pouch from around his neck and opened it. Taking something out, he looked at it momentarily and then pressed it into my hand. With enormous effort, I raised it to the dim light, and gazed upon it.

Father's ring! The ring of the earls of Mercia. Edwin's ring. Edwin was dead! The realization ripped through me. My brother, dead! My hand opened and the golden prize slipped to the floor. Forcing, heaving, carrying myself with what power I knew not, I rose from my pallet and stood, facing him for a moment, wordlessly. Then I made my way, oblivious of everything, to the chamber window, dragging my useless leg and stumbling to support myself at the wall. I stood trembling in the cold breeze and stared out into the starry, uncomprehending night.

"Tell me."

"Not until you sit. You will kill yourself!"

"What matters it? Tell me!" The faintness swelled, even above the pain and the fear and the horror. He slid a great heavy chair behind me, and I fell into it with a tortured moan.

"His own men killed him!"

"Liar!"

"Listen to me! By the holy relics, I swear that I tell you truly! Do you think I would lie to you?"

Though sore tempted, I made no answer to this, drowning in hurt and sorrow as I was. Still staring into the midnight sky, I heard him pacing behind me as he went on.

"The sons of Carr came to us at Tiouulfingacaestir, saying that in exchange for the king's peace they would tell us where to find your brother. They were tired, they said, of serving an outlaw with the king's price on him—one who was so oft distempered that they feared he was mad. It would be an easy capture because Edwin was camped against the river north of there and could not cross; 'twas dangerously tide-swollen. They swore he had but a half-dozen horsemen behind him, all unruly, drunken Scots and North Humbrians. From the first, I wanted not to trust them, but Gilbert Rouquin read this as his chance to win back King William's favor."

I muttered an oath, but if he heard me he gave no sign.

"We chose two dozen soldiers, and sent for reinforcements to meet us there. Then the brothers led us to to the camp. 'Twas a grim day and drizzly; mayhap my men were not as sharp as is their wont. We came around a knoll and the Welshmen disappeared of a sudden into the forest. I knew then that it was a trick."

Here I smiled smugly, but I do not know that Fulke saw me; he continued in the same tone. "Moments later, eight of my men were felled by arrows and we could see a well-armed score or more above us on a wooded ridge. The one at their head was Edwin Ælfgar's son."

"A score of men, say you?" I breathed haltingly, wondering who they might be.

"And women, too! The warrior anext him lifted a helmet as we spoke, and I could see it was the gold-haired Danish wench he had come to blows over with Gilbert Rouquin."

"Gythrun Olavsdätter!" I marveled, wincing with pain as I worked to picture Siward Bearn's wedded woman.

"Aye, that very woman. She pointed to Red-Beard, crying she was wont to kill that man. Edwin laughed and declared she would be given the privilege. Then he called loud that 'twas Fulke d'Aubermont whom he himself had need to kill, swearing he would fell me that very day, or die in the trying."

"He could have saved himself," I whispered fiercely, "but he risked all to avenge your mean lies against him."

"Nay. He risked all to save you, Morcar."

"What mean you?"

"Methinks you would have supposed already how the king tricked your brother, same as he did you! He sent word that you were his prisoner—that you were in fetters and that he would smite you should Edwin himself fail to submit."

I trembled but said naught, so he went on.

"Edwin thought that I was the one who betrayed you to the king. I swore I was blameless; he did not believe me."

"With reason! You have proven trothless before, d'Aubermont." Shaking, I fought to keep my voice level.

"'Tis true," he admitted woefully; his misery seemed genuine. "He had a mad scheme. He would slay me and then ride to your side disguised—helmeted and dressed in my arms. My lady would fain ride with him, he said, and help further the deception. Together, they would find a way to free you, for all and any would trust Fulke d'Aubermont, favored of the king, and his wedded wife, and so would allow them ease of commerce with the imprisoned Earl Morcar."

"Not impossible!" I exclaimed stiffly.

"Nay. With Lady Briana's help he might have succeeded. He had visited her in secret, he told me, and she had agreed to his plan. There was naught she would ever refuse to do, he told me, to help you. And I believed him."

I raised an eyebrow; my tone was cold. "Truly?"

"Aye, Morcar, truly. In the past long months I have come to know with surety that my lady loved you once, and now I realize must be she loves you still."

"'Tis not likely.... " I mumbled, panged with sudden, overwhelming emotion.

"Else would she consider a plan that depended upon my being murdered to save you?"

The silence that followed was fraught with his misery. I am not ashamed to say that I found no joy in it, though it was the moment of leveling I had for so long envisioned.

After a long while I cleared my throat. "Seems all this is naught but speculation," I told him. "Better you would continue your tale of the day you made battle on him."

"Truer would be to say that he was the one who made the battle,

Morcar! We had no urge to fight them. The sons of Carr, with others, had made their way back by then, and we were surrounded. When Edwin announced his aim to slay me, I reined forward and told him 'twere better we talk this out between us. He answered aye, and that 'twere better I had bitten back the falsehoods I had cried to the king about him, too, but I had not stayed myself then, and he would not stay himself now. Thunder crashed, and then they were hard upon us, just as the sky gave way to pounding rain."

He paused for a long time. I said nothing, but waited, faint and light of head.

"Best you should know that Edwin fought hale and fierce; we hacked at each other grimly while others battled and fell. When our horses folded, we fought on foot. At length he had me on the ground, well-gored and trembling 'neath the fury of his sword. I braced for my death blow, eyes clenched shut."

Here he paused again, and for so long that I grew anxious. "What more, Norman? 'Tis plain he did not squelch you!" I hissed at last. He laughed with a low wonder.

"Nay! When I dared a last look, he was smiling. 'Twas a bold and winning smile, as of old. For some reason, he could not kill me."

I tried to spit but my mouth was too dry.

"I told him then the report of your capture was false and bade him flee. Must be your brother believed me; he pulled himself away and hollered loud to call what was left of his company back," d'Aubermont continued. "Rouquin rushed him, though, and Edwin had already spent much of his strength and swiftness in fighting me. The Red-Beard lunged at him, and they plunged fast into a deadly combat. Those of Edwin's followers who were able rushed to defend them, but the Red-Beard hacked them back. When Edwin fell and Rouquin raised his sword, I tried to put myself between them but was too weak for loss of blood. I commanded the man to stop, crying that for certain the king would demand this prisoner alive. Rouquin was rabid, though. He forced Edwin a death blow, then another and another in his madness, laying him open then doling more yet, without mercy."

After this, seems it took Fulke d'Aubermont much effort to go on. Mayhap it took me as much to listen, too; I grew flushed and hot and could scarce hear him over the pounding of my heart.

"I crawled to the Red-Beard. He was not expecting it and so I was able to latch my grip onto his leg and drag him to the ground. I fumbled for my knife, then stabbed him. I would have gutted him methinks, but that one of the Welshmen crashed down upon him mightily with a battle-axe then, and it dispatched him!"

'Twas a fitting end for Rouquin, I thought sullenly, but even so it sickened me. As if grown worried of a sudden, Fulke hurriedly dipped water
into a copper cup and held it out to me. I took it, and once he saw that I
was sipping, he resumed the tale, his voice gravelly now with emotion.

"I turned back to your brother then. His wounds were mortal, and
we all knew it. The woman Olavsdätter ran to him, and they kissed with
a passion; she was mad with weeping and drenched in his gore. Edwin
Ælfgar's son begged someone, anyone, to hoist her away and tend to her.
One of their fighters, your kinsman Æric I think, galloped close, lifted
her, and rode hard into the forest. We could hear her screaming your
brother's name over and over until the sound of her wailing was lost in
the rain and thunder."

I was picturing this, and the anguish could not have been stronger
had I watched on it all. Fulke's voice sounded far away now as he
described how he and the Welshmen tried to comfort my dying brother
and quell somewhat his agonies. "We labored to bind his wounds, all the
while knowing they were far too grave." Here Fulke paused, trembling.
"He kept crying, 'God's mercy, murder me!' Over and over. By Christ's
Cross! I can hear it still!"

Shaking visibly, he swallowed a sob, sat down heavily, then looked
fast away. I knew he was weeping. Something in me wanted to try to
console him, but I could not say a word. My mind, my heart, my tongue:
all were paralyzed.

"He begged to die again, begged us to kill him, and finally Hwell,
the youngest son of Carr, jumped forth. He was frenzied by compassion,
I could tell it. He raised his axe and—well, God only knows what I
thought I could do. I jumped up and fought that man for your brother's
life. I sore wounded him, too! But Edwin Ælfgar's son was in his death
throes and they were horrible to look upon. When the elder brother
lifted a sword to finish him, I let him have his way. Edwin had spent all
his life's blood by then, and not a one of us could bear to hear his
pleading longer. I let the man have his way. He swiped the head off in
one blow, weeping loud with agony whilst he did it."

It is exceeding strange how one feels totally emotionless at the very
height of emotion. I did then, though a thousand thoughts and feelings
assailed me. My brother was dead—and a part of myself as well. Now I
was the last of the line of Leofric. Fighting the overwhelming agony it
cost me, I rose to my feet and hobbled to the narrow window, looking
up. Whatever there was of vastness in the great celestial ceiling was
nothing compared to the emptiness inside me. And despite it all, my
eyes were tearless. Even as I remembered all the golden, gleaming fairness and the fiery, iron-eyed vehemence of Edwin Ælfgar's son, Earl of

All Mercia, I was wondering if I would ever weep again.

At length, I tore my gaze from the cold, unfeeling night sky and turned round to face Fulke d'Aubermont. Shuddering with pain, I steadied myself against the wall, but my voice, totally impassive, admitted nothing of my torture.

"And even before he came to Ely, William knew my brother was dead, did he not?"

"He knew it."

"Bastard!"

"Twelve men-at-arms, the ordered reinforcements, arrived just as Daffyd Carr's son dealt the blow that finally finished Earl Edwin. As they tried to tend me, I lapsed fast into unconsciousness, so all I know of the rest is what others told me later. They put the three brothers into fetters, and made them carry the head to King William. There was no deceit in what they did; they had no way to know the deed had been done out of mercy. All dozen had been present when we received the Welshmen earlier, and had heard them plan their earl's betrayal. Later, when I was lucent, I was able to tell King William the truth of it, that the slaying was put upon your brother when he waxed already in his death rattle. The king gave all three the mercy of exile then, but the legend had already spread that Edwin had been basely done by his own men, and the king was wroth to correct it. It served his own purpose well enough, and all in the kingdom had heard it."

"Save for those holed low in Ely," I mumbled, biting my lip with a vengeance to keep back an oath of rage. Suddenly, I could no longer hold myself up against the welling tide of sickness and excruciation. Before I hit the floor, d'Aubermont had somehow seized and pulled me, against my anguished resistance, to the pallet, forcing me onto it and heaping hot furs and blankets over me, as if they would hold me there.

"God smite!" I whispered hoarsely, again and again, fighting against the torture, clinging miserably to a wisp of consciousness though I knew only insensibility could bring me any measure of relief. After a moment, I heard d'Aubermont cry for the priests. The roar of his voice was unexpected; it stunned me. Then I realized he was holding my shoulders and, over my own agonized gasps of breath, I heard him whisper insistently.

"He wept, Morcar! The king cried for Earl Edwin, bitterly hard, and in our very presence. Not a one of us had ever seen that man weep before, but by God, he shed tears over your brother's head!"

That was the picture I carried with me into unconsciousness.

CHAPTER SIXTY-FOUR

When the news of Edwin's death spread through
England, it was the cause of deep sorrow, not only
to the English but also to the Normans and French,
who lamented his loss like that of a close friend or
kinsman. He was, as has been said before, born of
pious parents, and he had devoted himself to as
many good works as possible for one so burdened by
problems of state. He was so handsome that few
could compare with him; the graces of his person
were so striking that he might be distinguished
among thousands; he was generous to and loved by
the clergy, the monks and the poor. Moreover, King
William, learning of the treachery which had
destroyed the Mercian earl, was moved to tears,
and when those betrayers carried the head of their
earl as if hoping for his favor, he sternly ordered
them into exile.

—Orderic Vitalis,
Book IV, Chapter VII

"Tell me the extent of it."

"Arrow woundings, in the back shoulder and the left breast. He
took a sword thrice—in the side, near to the lung there, but not through
it, then again at the shoulder and at the hip where the bone is mangled.
There is bruising of the worst sort at the collar, but it seems not to be
cracked, and at the ribs, where some breaks are."

"Priest's penance taken for that last injury! God knows I have
regretted my own temper, and many a time, too! Sometimes I think
myself a madman. What chance has he to heal whole?"

"A good chance, I think. But he will never walk gracefully again."

"Well, for saint's mercy, wash and shave his face before she sees him! And soon as he is strong enough, shear off that pagan North Humbrian hair. By the relics, it is despicable to me!"

"Your will, my lord."

"Let us leave him sleep now."

I thought it strange that they should think me sleeping. I was so perfectly aware. Neither the king's imperious entrance nor his tones of pretended pity had escaped me. And my own hatred! It had come over me like a wave of sickness at sea, churning through the emptiness that had once been my soul and conscience. God forgive me my sin of vengeance, and let it not sour my death as it has my life.

Pretty Adeliza—could she truly be the issue of such a monster? Once she had told me I moved like the wind. "You are a proud figure when you move, Morcar Ælfgar's son—proud as your howling Anglish air!"

He never will walk gracefully again.

Strange they should think me sleeping. And yet, it is true I am not moving. Not a thing of me moves—not even my eyes. I have not the strength to open them and look upon this bitter world.

Thank you, my Savior, for crippling me now, for in my poisonous hatred surely I would have killed him, liar and bastard and breaker of oaths! If I am to be stilled like this, though, let me sleep indeed, for no more can I bear to listen to it. Everything I hear is injury to me.

The Norman monks handle me gently, wiping my face of dried sweat and tears, scraping it with their well-honed blades. They are good men, these men of God, and the smell of my blood does not offend them. One fingers the blue-and-purple star that is burned upon my chest. Curious.

"These North Humbrians are a wild and heathen lot, are they not?" he asks.

"This one is a Christian," says the other. "They say his house built and supported many churches and monastaries."

Sleep, take me!

*   *   *

Fulke was beside me when I woke, as usual. "Day or night?" I asked him.

"Morning," he told me. Then I could hear the wind. They had covered the windows with skins to keep out the cutting coldness. It was November, nearing winter now. I remembered a few things, then reached up to touch my face which still tingled from the shaving.

"You are clean-shaven like a Mercian," Fulke smiled.

"Like a Norman," I said, not smiling, recalling by whose command

I had been shaven. Then I felt to see if my hair was still there; it was.

"We have made you presentable. The king is here."

"Indeed, I know it. I heard all about his priest's penance and vile temper. I heard you count to him all my pains and bruises."

He looked at me strangely. "You should have spoken."

"I could not." I was not lying and I suppose he knew it. I touched my face again. "When I went to the North Humbria," I recounted slowly, "I grew my hair like theirs and put tallow and quick-lime on to redden it, the way they did. I even let them burn pictures on my chest and arms. But do you know? I would not grow face hair. I could not do it. Now, of Anglishmen, Mercians alone keep their faces clean of hair; even the East Anglians wear mustaches down their cheeks! So, despite my earrings and my pagan hair, still I was a Mercian. I carried Mercia with me. Some of those North Humbrian men, when first I came to Ely, were very bold to me. They called me 'priest face' and thought it a very curious thing. And almost till the end, I shaved myself—till things had begun to move so fast there was no time for it. Then I let a beard come."

I stopped there, musing. I might not have gone on, but that when I caught a look of my friend, I realized he thought me delirious.

"Morcar," he started, "lean back and rest—"

I stopped him with a wave of my hand. "I have made a grave mistake these many years, Norman," I told him somberly.

Brow furrowed, he looked at me questioningly.

My voice was solemn. "I realize something now."

"What is it, friend?"

"Scraping the face is an uncomfortable thing—it hurts!" I said it without a hint of a smile, imparting that thought as though it were the key to all the great universe. For a moment he looked at me, his face a mixture of shock and bewilderment and fear for me. Then, suddenly, we were both laughing.

Laughing! I had not laughed in a good long while, and in truth, I had no call to laugh even then; it hurt me immensely. But I did. We both laughed hard until the pain began to flare ominously and I fell back with a heavy groan, tasting tears and realizing I had cried with laughter. "I swear you are mad!" Fulke exclaimed, trying to make me comfortable. "But I tell you, it rejoices me to see life in you again. I did not know if ever I would."

"After his wounding at Fulford, when he lay like this between life and death, Edwin grew bearded." I was surprised at how easily I had said his name, as if he were just a pleasant memory now. Already. "Later, he left side hair down his cheeks but he shaved his chin—like you saw him in Normandy."

Fulke nodded.

"After William denied him his woman, he let his chin be bearded, because he did not want to look anything like a Norman."

"Morcar, do not go on about him. You will only pain yourself."

"'Twas because he did not want to be anything like a Norman—not even clean-shaven. I only realized that now."

"I will not listen longer. This talk bodes only ill."

He dipped a cloth in water, and wrung it, and gave it to me for comfort. I let it drop.

"He did not look uncomely in a beard."

"Stop it!" He grabbed my shoulders, as if to shake something out of me, but caught himself as I winced. His face was grave. His voice graver.

"Listen to me, Mercian. I must beg this of you."

I looked directly at him, wordlessly, and he continued. "It was William's decree that you were not to know about your brother."

"Why did you tell me then, king's man?"

I was sorry I had asked it so coldly. His hurt was obvious as he answered. "Because I could not bear to think that he might deceive you again. Because I thought it would hurt you somewhat less to hear it from a friend—" Here he paused, then added low, "From one whom once you thought your friend."

"You fought for my brother's life, did you not, d'Aubermont?"

He nodded. "Would I could have saved him, Morcar!"

My tone was earnest. "You were his friend then; you are still my friend now." I was surprised to realize I meant it.

He smiled uneasily. "Then I ask this of you. Tell him not that I have disclosed this thing to you. He will mark it hard against me, I swear it!"

"He has me in his grasp now. What purpose can there be in hiding it?" I wondered aloud.

"You will not accept this from me, Morcar Ælfgar's son," he said hesitatingly, "but I only tell you what is true. He has great regard for you. I have heard him confess it. And he feels a need to let you know about this thing in his own way. It lies heavy on him truly; he means to make it gentle for you."

"Was it gentle to betray me with my brother's death?"

"He did what he felt he had to do."

"He wronged me. He wronged my brother! Let me hear you say that you know it is so!" I demanded this fiercely; 'twas important to me. Fulke paused a long time before he answered. Finally, I heard it.

"I know it is so." His voice was a hollow whisper. I lnew it had been hard for him to admit something that hurt his heart and honor.

There was a long silence, and after a while I realized my head was pounding and pulsing. I fell back suddenly, drained of strength, feeling faint and very aware of the wet, feverish heat of my body.

"Do you need the priests?"

"No. Only help me sit—else uncover me."

"I will uncover you!" he said firmly. "Sitting would be too much now. You have almost proved to me today the adage that a good man dies laughing!"

He should not have said it; it made me want to laugh again, and I could not afford it for my weakness. It helped to have those heavy woolen weights off me. My tunic, stained with oozings where the wounds refused to close, clung uncomfortably to my sweating chest and belly, and I tore it open to the waist. Starving for the kiss of cool air, I begged Fulke to remove the skins from the window, but he would not for fear of chill. Then we heard the approach of heavy footsteps and he flashed me a grim look.

"Is this thing to be between us, then, Mercian?" he asked in a whisper, but before I could make an answer, they were at the door: the king and beside him, looking paler and more frightened than ever I remembered seeing her, my sister.

"God's mercy!" is what she cried. "What is done to him? I ask what you have wrought upon him!"

Rushing to me, she knelt to touch my cheek, sobbing and trying not to. I realized how appalling I must have looked. My eyes traveled past her to the ashen-faced king. Staring with impassive hardness into his eyes, I whispered, loud enough for him to hear. "Do you not know they have prettied me up for you to look upon?"

William flinched. "Cover the man!" he commanded. When Fulke hesitated, he himself snatched the blankets from the floor and approached me with them.

It fired me to think he could not bear to look upon my woundings. "Do not touch me, Norman!" I hissed, finding myself sitting up to defy him. It was Aldgyth who calmed me, pushing my shoulders back gently, her fingers carefully avoiding the sore and swollen parts.

"Morcar, he is right!" she said mildly. "You are drenched and soaking, even to your hair! Now, let me cover you before you go into shivers. Look! Already you tremble!"

After putting the blanket on me, she stood confidently and faced the king. "Lord William, mayhap he is not yet ready to bear your company. Indeed, I do not think he is able!"

There was no contempt in her voice, only a cool courteousness that begged to be obeyed; it was the voice Harold Godwine's son had said no man could bear to resist. William did not resist it now but, before he turned away, he shot me a look I could not quite read and spoke in a surprisingly earnest tone. "You are in my prayers, Morcar Ælfgar's son." Then to Aldgyth he added in his more usual voice, "I bid you firm him up to receive me. I will speak to him before this day is out."

But I had long ago resolved I would never speak to that man more, and when he was gone, I relaxed visibly. Aldgyth, at my side again, squeezed my hand with tender understanding. "I never dreamt I would see you this way, brother—ever!"

"Well, do not let it ruin you," I answered tonelessly. "I have seen many men the worse."

"Bring me cloths and water, Fulke d'Aubermont!" Aldgyth ordered. As he handed them to her, I gestured him near.

"Did you know she was coming?" I asked him.

"I bade King William send for her."

"And what meant you keeping the news secret from me these many days?" I asked, thinking how long it would have taken to call for her at Ceaster. "I will have your word now that there will be no more secrets between us."

Aldgyth protested in his defense. "I enjoined him not to tell you I would come. I was afraid you would refuse to let me see you the way … the way Edwin did when he was harmed so cruelly."

Did she know? I scrutinized her for a sign. She went on hurriedly. "Edwin thought it would hurt me to see him injured and you, good brother, I thought you might reason the same way he—"

She looked at Fulke as if for help, and he whispered softly, "He knows, my lady. I have told him."

When she looked back at me, there were tears in her eyes, and I reached instinctively, wanting to cradle her and cry with her. I could not hold her without harsh pain, though. Worse, I could not cry.

I had known from the very beginning that I would never be able to weep for my brother. It was not coldness that ordered it, but emptiness. Still, I was very glad that Aldgyth could weep. Seeing her today, I had been forcefully reminded of our mother. Indeed, except for the hair, Aldgyth very greatly resembled her, and I could not help but consider how Ælfgiva had been so ruined by death and sadness. Then it was brought to bear on me that Aldgyth—pretty, harmless Aldgyth—had already seen as much death or more. Twice widowed, fatherless, a tender son in the grave and another locked away in a foreign land, and all her brothers dead but the one lain out beside her now in the undecided balance between life and eternity.

Why was it I could not grieve? I prayed in my heart that I would not become cold as my mother, and I prayed I would cry, but I was dry-eyed when Aldgyth lifted her head and tried to force a smile.

"I carry a gift with me, brother, that it will lighten your heart to see." She took something from her girdle and held it up—a small kidskin bag. At first, I did not understand.

"Leaves and seeds of knit-bone," she pronounced slowly, in a strange and quiet voice. "Reaped in the high mountains of Italy. I have brought it to soothe the wounds of one I love—victim of robbers! It is the third time we open this pouch."

The prophecy of the Filidh! Unexpectedly, a tumble of memories was on me so heavy that I groaned with the weight.

"God's blessed mercy, dearest Morcar! This is the last time ever I need open it!"

CHAPTER SIXTY-FIVE

Some of them were blinded, some of them were
banished, some of them were brought to shame.
So all traitors to William were brought low.

—Anglo Saxon Chronicle
Book "D"

By the time Aldgyth took her leave a fortnight later, I had grown much stronger. The priests had been forcing me to walk for over a week, against my vehement protests. I brought myself out into the sunshine for the first time to see her off. We had stayed awake most of the night talking, and I had bade her commend herself to Ywen Carr's son's care. He was in the Cymry now; William had banished him from Angland forever, and his brothers with him, for the part they played in my brother's demise—though we all knew this was a mercy more than a reprimand. I knew Ywen would be waiting for her, so when she rode off in that heavily guarded train, I suffered a long, tense moment of welling sorrow, knowing I would never see her more. I kept my feet till she was out of my sight, but grew faint after that and sat a long time on the cold stone steps, miserable. After a while, the priests grew worried and forced me to return to my chamber, half dragging me between them as if I were a naughty brat. I kept my bed all the next day, and whenever they left me alone, I wept.

The day after, I demanded to see Siward Bearn. They had kept me from him since we came, and given me no hint of his condition. A part of me had begun to fear he was in truth dead. After my side, shoulder, and leg had been rebound, a daily, agonizing ritual, I made my way to the hall where Fulke d'Aubermont presided over a harried council. The men were mulling the news that Hereward and his band had murdered four Normans on the outskirts of the Scirwudu Forest, whence they had removed themselves when they fled. To me, 'twas a joyous disclosure, knowing they were fit enough to fight, but the king was rabid, and had left that morning for Nottingham to try and force a confrontation.

D'Aubermont seemed surprised I had come and cut himself off in the middle of a sentence to greet me. I neither smiled nor showed emotion of any kind, but insisted then and there that I be admitted to the Bearn's presence. Elsewise, I told him, I would wreak havoc—though of what sort I did not know, being crumpled and crippled and weak. He excused himself and walked with me into the shadowy corridor.

"I scarce can condone your meeting with him now, Morcar Ælfgar's son," he said somberly, as if I were not to be trusted. I glared at him meanly. Then he shrugged and said mayhap he could bypass the king's order this one time, seeing it was so important to me. "The man was offered the opportunity of visiting your sickbed," he added darkly, "but he would not go."

He led me through the halls to a door that opened out to the courtyard, walking extremely slow so that I could keep his pace. Once out, he gestured to the storehouse, a small, two-roomed building with wide casements, where my father's men had been wont to winter the meat when we were children. There was a hesitation in his manner and a haltingness to his words when he spoke again. "For your own health, I would stay with him but a short time, Morcar," he said in a low whisper as we approached the door. "He is grown sullen and morose and is likely to take no heed of your condition."

So saying, he pushed the narrow door open, and closed it behind me when I had entered.

I came a little way into the damp coolness. A figure was outlined at the window—a straight figure, tall and erect, sitting motionlessly on a backless bench. 'Twas Siward Bearn, dressed in a simple wadmal shift, belted at the waist. His wild abundance of hair and a single, heavy earring of gleaming silver were all I needed to identify him. There was a still intensity to his presence. He played absently with a short length of white bunting which he passed from hand to hand, clenching and unclenching it.

I dragged myself nearer, unsteady on my feet and hampered by the heaviness of the wounded leg. When I was but a breath away, he turned slowly, putting his back to me completely and staring out the open casement into the autumnal greyness beyond.

"By God, 'tis good to see you, kinsman!" I cried hoarsely, rejoicing to see he was alive and well.

"Morcar Ælfgar's son!" he cried with a wonder. "Are you whole?"

"In a fashion," I answered, flashing a grim smile as I started around him. "I knew not whether we would ever look upon each other again!"

His voice caught in his throat as he rose. "Never we will, cousin!"

Feeling a surge of sickness as we came face to face, I stared only an instant at him before he spun away. The look of him I will never forget. His handsome face was gaunt and bruised, almost unrecognizable. As I backed away in horror, he took the white linen he had been toying with and tied it like a band around his eyes.

But no—not his eyes! Where his fine, impassioned grey eyes once had been, there was naught but dried blood and tissue.

I swallowed an oath, then embraced him and wept

CHAPTER SIXTY-SIX

[William] threw [Morcar] into prison without any
distinct charge, committing him to the custody of
Roger de Beaumont, and confining him in that
man's castle all the rest of his life.

—Orderic Vitalis,
Book IV, Chapter VII

1072-1087

It was the same summer sky, crystalline blue and cloudless, and the same
steep grassy hill. The air, fragrant with a thousand mingled scents, was
the same, and the mild kiss of the breeze whispered through my hair just
the same way. 'Twas the summer of my twenty-seventh year when I
returned to Pont Audemer. I was overwhelmed once more with feelings
of the familiar. I knew then, with a certainty, that my brother had been
right. I had come to that place in a long-ago dream, mayhap a nightmare,
and looking on it had known it would be my prison. Edwin's heavy gold
ring hung on a chain round my neck, and I fingered it, remembering.

There is a square stone tower in the castle called Beaumont-on-the-
Hill, and it has a casement, tall and narrow, looking over the fields and
forests. Oft-times I have stood there these many years and imagined I
was free to roam them. In my heart, a perfect picture is: I see the green
sweeps of Nottingham stretching forever into the vastness of a world no
child or innocent man can ever imagine. There is a sweetly flowered
hill, and just beyond it I have a household where my father is young and
handsome and fire-eyed. He keeps a hall full of boisterous and merry
men. My mother has grown gentle and she helps Aldgyth, still a child
herself, to tend her happy, healthy babes.

I ride the leas and lawnings with my brothers. Weaponless, we wear
wreaths of asphodel and corn-flower and sing together as we wander
where we want. Our many kinsmen call us greetings. We stop and talk

of this thing and that for a while. It is never growing late so there is no need to hurry.

A path leads to the forest, which is endless. Somewhere, there is the ring of laughter and familiar, well-loved voices carry on the hollow wind. Gruffydd gives me courage; Uncle Leofric soothes my spirit; Cynewulf Cenwulf's son tells me tales. I remember a word that man sometimes used to describe my mother. He said she was one of the *friorig-ferth*—those who are mind-frozen by sorrow. Must be I have come to be like her. There is no thought or memory or dream that wounds me now, no longing of remembrance or sadness for days long past.

I shut my eyes sometimes and walk with my father through the pleasant greenness of the midlands. My hand is in his; I am running to match his manly stride. The wind and daylight are in his wheaten hair. His finely muscled arms are bare, tanned and freckled by the gentle sun. His voice is strong.

"Listen well, Morcar," he tells me. "Wherever it is that you go in this life, carry Mercia with you. For Mercia is the essence of the blood of our house, and our house is the very substance of Mercia."

We walk a long time. At length the sky grows cool and dim with purple twilight, but we go on forever because there is always something waiting for us, far away.

EPILOGUE

The heroes have fallen,
The hall—joys have vanished.
Weaker men linger,
possessing the world
in days that are troubled.
All glory is dead.

— Early Northumbrian Poet

Morcar Ælfgar's son lived in the castle of the Beaumonts until the death of William the Conqueror in 1087. He was not alone. Ever true to their oath of brotherhood, Siward Bearn, also exiled at William's command, stayed by his side. Wulfnoth Godwine's son, Harold's brother, who had been a hostage since boyhood, resided there also. In time, he and Morcar formed a firm friendship, strengthened, no doubt, by the presence of their common kinsman, young Wulf Harold's son. The son of Harold and Aldgyth grew to manhood in the grey stone tower.

Morcar's captivity ultimately helped ensure the immortality of the House of Leofric, against all odds. When, at King William's request, the monk Orderic Vitalis wrote his official history of the Conquest, he was able to hear portions of the story from Morcar himself and preserve them. When the famous Bayeux Tapestry was commissioned, Morcar prevailed on William the Conqueror to include the most vivid symbol of the Norman's justification in wresting the crown away from the House of Godwine—his mother, descended of the noble Edmund Ironside and step-sister of the Norman duke's chief man, William Malet. Lady Ælfgiva, whose first husband, Burchard's father, was cruelly slain during the massacre of Ælfred Ætheling's retainers ordered by Earl Godwine, is consequently the only woman to be identified by name in that magnificent work. In a scene that takes place in Normandy, under Latin words that translate "Where a priest and Ælfgyva … " she is shown confined in her chamber at Le Havre, receiving from a member of the Norman clergy the exorcism mercifully ordered by King William. Beneath her image, small embroidered vignettes vivdly illustrate the rape, murder, and violence that occurred during the horrendous event that helped tumble her into madness.

Adeliza, a nun in the nearby convent of Ste. Leger, was a frequent visitor in the household of her guardian, Roger de Beaumont. Joined by their common love of Edwin's golden and vibrant memory, she and Morcar remained close as a brother and sister in spirit, and if ever their attachment managed to come to more in those days, no one was wont to tell. They spoke oft of Edwin, and all found solace in the fact that the Earl of Mercia had loved and been loved in the end. Siward Bearn did not even regret that it was his own discarded wife who had been Edwin's support then and, to Morcar, the fact was just another proof of how alike they had truly been, those brothers, that their secrets mirrored one the other same as their outward lives.

Hereward and his band, housed in the great forests of Bruneswald and Scirwudu, which in time came to be called Sherwood, continued their exploits against the tyrannical Norman rule. At length, England lapsed into a state of wary peace. The Conqueror began to divide his time between his Anglish kingdom and his duchy in Normandy. In 1086, he was ruptured internally when thrown against the horn of his saddle. His agony and suffering were extreme and prolonged. For three weeks he lingered between life and eternity. Knowing he was on his deathbed, he repented of the great injustices he had done. The chronicler Orderic Vitalis reports William's dying words thusly:

> *I have long kept in captivity Morcar, the noble English*
> *earl; in this I have been unjust, but my fear has been*
> *that if he were liberated, he would raise disturbances in*
> *the kingdom of England…. In like manner I confined*
> *many persons to punish them for their own offenses*
> *and others to prevent their causing future rebellions….*
> *Being now, however, at the point of death, I order that*
> *the prison doors shall forthwith be thrown open and*
> *these prisoners released and ordered to go free.*

Within hours of the king's death, a party of his men came to claim Morcar, Siward Bearn, and the others. As the freed men traveled to the channel, where a small fleet was waiting to carry them back to their homeland, they were overtaken and massacred at the order of William's son, William Rufus. Having been named as his father's successor, he still dreaded Morcar's great popularity with the English people, who had never ceased to love him and pray for his welfare.

Author's Afterword and historical Notes

When Earl Morcar of North Humbria first approached me about writing this history, I couldn't help but wonder whether events that happened so long ago would be of any value or interest to modern readers. Both of us were twelve when we first met; he had just lost his beloved grandfather, and I had recently realized the existence of a vast realm of ancient wisdom and tradition which beckoned from beyond the omnipotent reach of the Roman Catholic church, in which I had been strictly, yet happily, raised. We were both equally traumatized.

From then on, each and every memory he shared was etched indelibly in my heart; some almost seemed vague reminiscences of my own. As time went on and I realized the more universal appeal of his story, I began writing down episodes as he described them. Later, bypassing modern histories and returning to ancient chroniclers, I was able to verify much of what he told me, and I have never found anything in original source materials that served to negate his treasured memories.

Therefore, I use this opportunity to ensure readers that the incredible tale which follows is a true one. I encourage all who wish to test its veracity to focus on sources contemporary (or nearly so) with the events described in these pages; the quotes used as chapter epigraphs will provide some direction in this. These were years crucial in the forming of England's national folklore—from Lady Godiva to Robin Hood—and no less in the defining of the national self-perception as one of a united kingdom of folk valiant, righteous, dedicated to the common good and, in short, unconquerable.

Yet most of what we know of the era is based on the colorations, not to mention bias and propoganda, of later apologists as well as by England's truly timeless tradition of preserving a rich, romantic history based on rudimentary facts and loosely remembered local legends. It is not to be forgotten, either, that the commonly known accounts of the events of the Norman Conquest—as all are—were written from the perspective of the "conquerors" and those who most need to morally legitimize their ascendency: the subsequent generations who prospered in effect of their forbears' victory.

Much later, episodes of history are usually colored yet again by the affections of the age which first researches and chronicles the importance of the personages and events involved in them. This was strongly the case in this particular tale. I early noted that their contemporaries seemed to revere Edwin and Morcar and their family, presenting them as main players in the history of the Conquest and noting with respect the vastness of their holdings, their power, the antiquity of their house, and their great popularity with the English people. Yet, in modern texts, the entire House of Leofric (with the possible exception of Lady Godiva) is largely dismissed as inconsequential; their actions, when noted at all, are usually regarded as traitorous, indolent, self-serving, or a combination of the three. Intrigued, I sought the source of the discrepancy, and found it in the person of E. L. Freeman, a dedicated, overwhelmingly credible historian of the highest caliber.

Freeman wrote his four-volume "definitive" history of the Norman Conquest at the height of the Victorian age, an era in which English history was being systematically romanticized, glorified, and idealized as in the writings and paintings of Dante Gabriel Rossetti, John Ruskin, William Morris, and Howard Pyle among many others. No notion seemed more tragic, romantic, or revered than that of Harold Godwineson, the last Anglo-Saxon king, standing valiantly alone and unaided against the treacherous Norman military machine of William the Conqueror. (Likewise, and quite ironically, there was no ancestral claim more desirable than that of being descended from one of the companions of the Conqueror.) It is in the shadow of these popular ideals that Freeman's otherwise magnificent and important work palls. Like a novelist burdened with two heroes and no villain, he backtracks from the failure of Edwin and Morcar to fight behind Harold Godwineson at the Battle of Hastings and presents the family as one rife with jealousy and steeped in generational treason, a natural consequence of their somehow being morally and socially inferior to the last great warrior king. Creating a traitorous past for them by emphasizing the repeated exiles of their father, Earl Ælfgar, at the hands of the Godwines, he virtually ignores contemporary evidence that vindicates Ælfgar and his sons, as if fearful of insulting the memory of Harold by presenting the family of the hero-king in an uncomplimentary light.

Freeman's are errors more of omission than intention; it is as if he purposely trivializes the roles of Edwin and Morcar in hopes that his readers will think them and their family too inconsequential to merit further research. He mentions the reverence of the North Humbrians for the Ealdorman Morcar murdered at Oxford in 1015 along with his son-in-law Siferth, but fails to mention that the one Morcar was the great-grandfather of the other. The relation between the two Morcars is crucial; it at once establishes for the House of Leofric a respectable connection to the earldom of North Humbria, and hints of a relationship between Aelfgar's sons and the great English hero, King Edmund

Ironside. In 1015, the Ironside fell in love with Aldgyth, the daughter of his murdered friend Morcar, and wed her. After his death, she fled for safety to Normandy, raising her two daughters there. Both dressed, spoke, and lived a lifestyle thoroughly Norman; though surely aware of their aristocratic English heritage, neither was to see England again for years, until returning there as young adults.

The elder, Æthelthryth, lived to become the mother of Siward Bearn and his siblings Ealdred and Briana—but not much longer, committing suicide soon after the vicious murder of her husband. (Twenty-one-year old Æthelgar Bearn, along with his nineteen-year-old cousin Eadwulf—father of Oswulf—was hacked to pieces while ostensibly under a truce issued by King Harthacnut, who had become King of England with the strong support of the House of Godwin.)

The younger daughter, Ælfgiva, in time, became the mother of Burchard (by her murdered Norman husband), then of Edwin, Morcar, and Aldgyth, the last two of whom bore the names of her grandfather and mother, respectively. Morcar remembers as a young child over-hearing snatches of whispered arguments between his father's men and house-folk. Some claimed Ælfgiva was the daughter of Aldgyth's first husband, Siferth, who was hacked to death defending his father-in-law in the ambush where both were murdered. If so, in her sons' veins would be mixed the blood of Ealdorman Morcar, her grandfather, and Earl Siferth, her father, two North Humbrian noblemen of great reverence and reputation; men whose valorous lives and deaths lingered still in living memory at the time. If she was Ælfgiva Siferthsdätter, her sons would have had a legitimate claim to the earldom of North Humbria, stronger than any boasted by their contenders. Why then, did King Edward and the other earls of England proceed as if Morcar had no claim?

The answer lies in the fact that King Edward, like Lady Ælfgiva, had also been raised in Normandy and was thoroughly Norman in habit and outlook. In Normandy, whence Lady Aldgyth fled after that suspicious death of young King Edmund, legend held she had fled thither, pregnant with the Ironside's third child—the girl who would be named Ælfgiva in honor of Edmund's mother.

This is an intriguing scenario. If Lady Aldgyth had been pregnant when she fled to Normandy, Morcar's brother Edwin, through his mother's blood, would have had a stronger claim to the throne of England than did Harold Godwineson (who, in fact, had no blood claim at all).

With the advent of the internet, more information is available to us than Freeman might have hoped to garner. Still, one cannot help but be amazed at his seemingly conscious effort to dismiss the family of Leofric as unimportant. Rather than inspiring speculation on the above subjects, he effectively quells it by consistently presenting, then questioning, any information that does not support his carefully crafted portrait of the House of Godwine and the earldom of Wessex as superior to all others. By what authority, he wonders, is Ælfgiva supposed to have been related to the Norman William Malet, a main player in the reigns of Edward and Harold and one of the chief men of William the Conqueror? Malet's relationship to Edwin and Morcar would, in and of itself, have proven the family's importance to the events of 1066, but Freeman drops the subject, as if distasteful to him, after scarce more than a footnote.

Later, still avoiding the Norman connection which would have rendered Edwin and Morcar of particular interest to the Conqueror, Freeman questions the "validity" of a monument (still existent) raised in the cathedral at Rheims by Earl Ælfgar to the memory of his son, Burchard, who died there while on pilgrimage. Why, Freeman muses, would an English earl have a son with such a Norman-sounding name? Rather than encourage investigation into Ælfgiva's parentage, he wonders why this family had been made "the particular sport of pedigree makers." (It mattered not to him whether Morcar or Edmund Ironside was the lady's father, for both possibilities worked against his popularly accepted theory that the brothers were unimportant players in the drama of the Conquest.)

By dismissing such questions, Freeman effectively discouraged speculation for more than a century on their possible impact. Because of the comprehensiveness of his scholarship, there seemed little reason for modern authors to go beyond it.

Now, internet access to worldwide genealogies, meticulously kept in various European countries since the Middle Ages, suggests that many long-standing "legends" have proven popular and prolific, albeit beyond the realm now of conclusive proof. These include the "kinship" between William Malet and the House of Leofric, and that between King Edmund Ironside and the same house, as evidenced in chronicles, local legend, genealogies, and the passing along of the family names Aldgyth, the Ironside's widow, and Morcar, that lady's father, to two of the children of Lady Ælfgiva and Earl Ælfgar.

While the former is a common Englishwoman's name of the period, the latter, Morcar (sometimes spelled Morkere) is so unusual as to ensure a family association between the two men who bore it. Occasionally mistaken to be Danish, it is in fact of older native English origin and may date back to ancient times when the Angles (Anglians) existed as a separate ethnic people along with Saxons, Jutes, and other early societies derived of traveling Germanic tribal groups. (The Angles were forerunners of the Mercians, North Humbrians, and East Anglians. The Saxons were the ancestors of the Wessex (West Saxon) men, Sussex (South Saxon) men, and Essex (East Saxon) men.)

Lady Ælfgiva, scarcely regarded by Freeman, in fact figured prominently in the history of the Conquest. She was raised from babyhood in Normandy, where her mother, the beautiful Lady Aldgyth, as described earlier, had fled after the mysterious death of King Edmund Ironside, and married into the prestigious Malet family, special favorites of William of Normandy. As described in this book, her first husband was murdered during the horrible massacre of Prince Ælfred the Ætheling, an incident which created great enmity between Normandy (where Ælfred and his brother, later King Edward the Confessor, were raised in exile) and the House of Godwine (whom the Normans correctly suspected of masterminding Ælfred's murder.) This alone would have made Ælfgiva a veritable "poster child" for William's life-and-death crusade against King Harold Godwineson: a beautiful noblewoman of good Norman connections driven to madness by the cruelty of the House of Godwine; a woman, no less, in whose sons' veins was united the blood of leading families of both Normandy and England—William's great hope for a peaceful uniting of the two lands and cultures.

William, a cunning politician, would certainly have made tremendous use of her distress as a tool to justify his invasion of England. By then, she had been returned to Normandy where her madness required her incarceration in the tower of one of the Malet family estates, as described by Morcar in his memoir.

Historians have long argued the identity of the only female figure to be labeled by name on the Bayeux tapestry, where she appears to be taking a blessing from a priest under a caption so cryptic that it surely indicates an event that was well-known at the time and needed no further description: "where a cleric (priest) and Alfgyva...." Exorcism was the prescribed cure for madness in that day, and that is almost certainly what the carefully embroidered scene represents. Further, there is a border that runs the length of the tapestry top and bottom, in whose margins are illustrations of motifs that seem to further identify and describe the actions being depicted in the main body of the cloth. Surrounding Alfgyva are bloody vignettes accurately illustrating details of the horrible massacre of the Ætheling as described by chroniclers of the day.

Lady Ælfgiva's brother, William Malet, was a chief man first of King Edward, then of King Harold, whose lifeless body he carried from the carnage of Hastings Field, then of William the Conqueror. Ælfgiva's daughter had been the Queen of Wales, and was Queen of England at the time of the Norman invasion. Her two surviving sons were great earls ruling more than half of England between them. To one of them, William had promised the hand of his own daughter, noting with pleasure the genuine love and attachment between the two.

Lady Ælfgiva's first husband had been murdered by the Godwines. So, almost certainly, had her eldest child, the stepson and heir of Earl Ælfgar, Burchard, whose death (while traveling on a pilgrimage to Rome with a large party of which Tostig Godwineson was a member) has been remarked upon. The daughter she had named in memory of her own mother, Aldgyth, had been queen first of Wales and then of England. Ælfgiva was well known, then, to King Edward, King Harold, and King William, each in turn. Surely, this was a woman of extreme prominence and importance at the time of the Conquest.

Yet, implying her unimportance, Freeman dismisses her from amongst the candidates thusly: "Ælfgiva was the name of the widow of Ælfgar, the mother of Harold's wife Aldgyth. According to some accounts, she was of Norman birth. Could she have been living or visiting in Normandy at this time?"

In the end, Freeman seems to have put most faith in the far-fetched suggestion that the woman called "Ælfgyva" represented Queen Emma (the mother of King Edward) and supposing (though there is no evidence for it) that the English people may have called the Norman-born queen by that name (Ælfgiva) instead of her own because, coming from another land, she seemed as a "gift from the elves" to them!

But it is not our intention to criticize another's work, especially one of such panoramic importance, but to encourage exploration of earlier sources. I therefore urge the curious reader to explore open-mindedly and without the prejudices that have become popular in the last century and a half. And should the printed page hold no answers for one, it occurs to me one might do well to lie in the grass on a warm summer's night and allow the self to be lost in the vastness of the infinite stars, as I have often done. These are the same stars that shone down upon the long-ago lives described in this memoir, and perhaps they hold, within their deep, distant and mysterious light, a glimmer of the truth that connects us to our ancient kinsmen, players in the infinite drama of life then, as we are now.

Mead Hall Press

www.meadhallpress.com

Now available
Dorflin's Daughter
Book One in the *Vana Avkomling Saga* by S. Leigh Jenner

The portents of the Ragnarok are revealing themselves one by one. The final fate of the gods, and the universe, looms larger with each epic battle. In arrogance, some sequester themselves in the protected haven at Æsgard. There are two, however, who have a plan for survival … but it will mean defying Odin himself.

Set in the pre-Christian Viking era, *Dorflin's Daughter* details the epic quests of Iseobel, a young Anglo-Saxon holy woman, and Vanaash, the fierce Viking warrior who abducts her for mysterious purposes. They find their future being dictated by rebellious Norse deities who are deeply involved—perhaps unwisely—in the fate of this unlikely pair. While this novel stands alone, it is actually the first book in the Nine World adventure entitled *The Vana Avkomling Saga*.

Coming soon from Mead Hall Press

Understanding Runes
By Eric Wilmoth
An illustrated manual exploring the archetypal principles of the runes and their practical use.

The Stranger's Son
Book Two in the *Vana Avkomling Saga* by S. Leigh Jenner

Mead Hall Press